# Laura Gilmour Bennett

# Distant Echoes

VIKING

VIKING

Published by the Penguin Group
Penguin Books Ltd, 27 Wrights Lane, London W8 5TZ, England
Penguin Books USA Inc., 375 Hudson Street, New York, New York 10014, USA
Penguin Books Australia Ltd, Ringwood, Victoria, Australia
Penguin Books Canada Ltd, 10 Alcorn Avenue, Toronto, Ontario, Canada M4V 3B2
Penguin Books (NZ) Ltd, 182–190 Wairau Road, Auckland 10, New Zealand

Penguin Books Ltd, Registered Offices: Harmondsworth, Middlesex, England

First published 1992
1 3 5 7 9 10 8 6 4 2

Set in 12/14 pt Monophoto Ehrhardt and Garamond
Printed in Great Britain by Clays Ltd, St Ives plc

A CIP catalogue record for this book is available from the British Library

ISBN 0–670–83750–4

# Chapter 1

Rachel picked up her matron-of-honour's bouquet of white freesias and roses, lying among the collection of plates and glasses on the round table where the Meddlar clan had congregated. Throughout the wedding in the church and now at the height of the reception in the ballroom of a country club overlooking the sun-baked hills to the south-east of San Francisco, she found she could not concentrate.

The bride and groom waltzed into view, and as Rachel focused on her sister's radiantly happy face, she thought how lucky Natalie was to have met the tall, distinguished stockbroker who had just become her husband at a time when she had almost given up the idea of marrying at all. Rachel watched her disappear in a swirl of white lace and pearl-encrusted embroidery, thinking how different in every way this stylish extravaganza was from her own quiet wedding, held in her parents' garden ten years ago.

The waltz died away and the orchestra broke into a lively jitterbug, bringing many of the five hundred guests on to the dance floor. When she saw no one was going to ask her to dance, Rachel kicked off the grey satin pumps that were pinching her feet and tried to gather her flying thoughts. Seconds later a chorus of catcalls followed by a wave of applause made her look up. She was amazed to see her elegant, self-possessed sister clutching her voluminous skirt above her knees and doing a little cancan to show off her blue satin garter.

Aunt Grace, sitting next to her, was still chuckling in amusement. 'I hope they got a picture of Natalie kicking up her heels for posterity, because it may never happen again. And will you look at Dinah and Ken? Those two can still dance the pants off anybody.'

Rachel spotted her mother swooping gracefully beneath her

1

father's arm again and again. People stepped back to give them room to execute a beautifully timed manoeuvre.

'The jitterbug was always Dad's speciality.'

'He's just as light on his feet as he was twenty years ago, and Dinah hasn't gained a pound. How does she do it?' Grace wondered.

Rachel suppressed a comment as her aunt reached for another sugared almond and popped it into her mouth. Her mother's plump, blonde sister was glittering with diamonds, and a flamboyant corsage of orchids was pinned to the lapel of her mauve dress. Her eyes glistering with nostalgia, she patted Rachel's hand.

'You look so pretty in blue. That shade brings out the depths of your eyes. Do you know, when you were standing at the altar next to Natalie I thought to myself, you'd never know those two were sisters, they're so different. To think that Natalie's thirty-five and you – can you really be thirty-two? My little Rachel . . .'

'It doesn't seem possible, does it? I wish you could have seen Natalie when Chris lifted her veil. She looked no more than seventeen. Seventeen . . .' Rachel repeated as a host of images came flooding back. 'In those days I envied her looks to distraction. If anything, she's more beautiful now than she was then,' she added, feeling nothing but pride in her sister.

'You're *just* as pretty in your own way as Natalie. I always told you that, though I know you didn't believe me.'

Rachel slipped her arm round her aunt's shoulder and hugged her. 'I think you should have more champagne.' She reached for the bottle.

Grace gave a hearty laugh. 'I mean what I say. And I suspect Natalie has envied you too, in her time. Think about it: all these years you've been happily married to a dynamic and attractive man while Natalie has been searching for Mr Right. You have a beautiful son and you've helped Alain build a business that has brought the two of you all sorts of acclaim. Your life was complete, while hers was missing that vital element.'

'Do you really think so? Well, she has it all now. Chris adores her, and she's had the wedding she always dreamed of.' As she spoke, Rachel was conscious that for her, her sister's great day had been overshadowed by something unexpected, something she seemed unable to put aside.

When her aunt turned to talk to someone else, her words about the completeness of Rachel's life lingered in Rachel's mind as if it required an answer. Rachel turned her head and met her own still blue eyes in the mirrored wall. The self-possessed woman with sun-streaked brown hair swept back from her forehead was undeniably a different person from the shy, rather serious girl on the brink of her twenties which was still how Rachel thought of herself. She found herself remembering how her husband used to praise her fine skin and good bones, how he had extolled her distinctive nose – dubbed aristocratic by the family – and her generous laughing mouth, saying this was what had first attracted him to her that day in the bookshop. Rachel had heard it said she had a captivating smile and a contagious laugh. But that afternoon she felt herself responding less rapidly than usual to the frenetic gaiety all around her. She watched the couples dancing, anxious now for time to move forward so she could solve the riddle her husband had unknowingly left behind him that morning when he departed. She was about to reach for her grey satin clutch bag to examine the contents once more when her aunt broke into her thoughts.

'Thinking about Oliver?'

Rachel nodded. 'You've read my mind.'

'You're not worrying about him, I hope.'

'If I'm honest, I suppose I am fussing a bit. I don't like admitting it, but all my cherished theories about wanting him to be independent went out the window when the limousine drove away. I had the most awful feeling – I almost hate saying it out loud – that I might never see him again.' Voicing her fears, Rachel realized how foolish she must sound to her aunt, who was the soul of levelheadedness. 'Were you ever like that with your children, Aunt Grace?'

'You may not think so, but I was. All mothers are like that and you're no different.' Grace took Rachel's hand and gave it a comforting pat. 'Now you shouldn't get worked up about it. It's perfectly normal for you to feel anxious. Oliver's only just eight, after all, and that's still quite young to be a globetrotter. I think it's wonderful Alain wanted to take him along on a business trip. How many men would do that?'

'Not many,' Rachel agreed.

From the day Oliver was born Alain had unreservedly adored the child who looked so much like him. This closeness between her husband and her son had been a source of deep contentment to Rachel in the past. Throughout the day she had kept remembering Alain's surprise announcement the week before that he was going to France and wanted to take Oliver with him.

When a small boy popped his head out from beneath the tablecloth, Grace laughed, 'Why it's Greg Junior. What are you doing under there?'

'Hiding from Tom. Is it true Oliver went on a plane today with Alain, Aunt Rachel?'

'That's right. They should be nearly halfway there by now.'

He gave a whistle of admiration, then scampered away.

Grace said, 'Oliver's a very lucky boy. Now I want to hear more about this cookbook Alain is writing. Why did he have to go off suddenly? Couldn't he have put it off for just a few days until after the wedding?'

'You don't know what publishers are like. They called last week asking him to join a photographer to scout for locations in the region where he was born. Naturally he couldn't say no.'

'Well, it's lucky for him he's got you to mind the fort. You must be getting quite used to it.'

'Yes, Alain has had to go away several times to France and New York. We have a great team working with us now, but it makes me feel good to know I can handle the business on my own if I have to.'

When another guest stopped at the table to talk to her aunt, Rachel picked up her handbag and discreetly took out an envelope stamped with the name of a well-known travel agent in the city. A workman had discovered it behind a filing cabinet in the office, and when Rachel had dropped in at the restaurant that morning, her assistant had given it to her.

Rachel took out the paper inside the envelope, thinking it was uncanny how it had turned up, and wishing that it hadn't. The slip

4

of paper from the travel agent confirming two seats, one adult, one for a child, on that morning's flight was dated three months ago, revealing not only that Alain had been planning his trip for much longer than he had said but that it had always been his intention to take Oliver with him. All day Rachel had been trying to find a satisfactory reason why her husband would have lied to her.

She stuffed the paper back into the envelope, but not before she had glanced once more at the charming old postcard of a ruined château called Brissac she had found with it. It was postmarked forty years ago and the spidery handwriting was all but illegible. A fresh message, scribbled on the photograph above one blurred window had been running through her mind since she'd first read it, turning curiosity into something resembling uneasiness.

Rachel whispered the words to herself as she tucked the troubling envelope out of sight: *ta cuisine, à bientôt*. It occurred to her that the writer of the postcard, who addressed Alain familiarly as *tu*, might be waiting for him to arrive in Paris at that very moment. She tried to contradict the idea the minute it entered her head, but Alain's handsome bearded face at the window of the limousine as it drove away had imprinted an image as clear as a snapshot in her mind's eye: his dark-fringed blue eyes, normally full of such probing directness, had been hidden behind dark glasses.

Rachel put on a smile when she saw her parents approaching the table. Her mother was furiously fanning the ruffles on her bright print dress with one hand and tucking hairpins into her chignon with the other while Rachel's father followed in her wake. He had unbuttoned his morning coat and was mopping his brow with a handkerchief as he passed the tables of guests, exuding his own unique brand of *bonhomie*. Rachel felt a rush of pride in the knowledge that her parents were such vital, happy people. It had come home to her that day how rare it was for a couple to survive nearly forty years of marriage with their sense of humour and their love for each other intact. The glitter and the pomp of Natalie's wedding day seemed to have summoned a number of such important truths Rachel knew she would mull over later.

Dinah flopped into a chair next to Grace and fanned herself vigorously. 'My dears, the years are finally starting to tell.'

'All I can say is that when Greg got married I must have been a hell of a lot younger,' exclaimed Ken with a laugh, waving to his eldest son and daughter-in-law as they danced by the table.

'This is just about the best party I can ever remember at the club. It's been perfect in every way. Don't you think so, Rachel?' said her mother with a sigh.

'Absolutely fabulous,' Rachel agreed. 'You and Dad were the stars of the show a minute ago. Dad, you were doing some very fancy footwork out there.'

As laughter and conversation travelled round the table Rachel retreated into herself, calculating how soon Alain and Oliver would arrive in Paris, and already rehearsing what she would say to Alain when he phoned. Across the room at the buffet table the towering ice sculptures were starting to melt. A few guests were still heaping their plates with lobster salad and Pacific salmon, and the battery of waiters were making the rounds with champagne.

Rachel's mother began to reminisce about her elder son's wedding seven years before, comparing it point for point with Natalie's extravaganza.

'How about it, sweetheart? Want to dance?' said a voice behind Rachel.

Her younger brother, Todd, was smiling down at her, his hands on the back of her chair.

When they were whirling round the dance floor, he asked. 'Am I that bad a dancer?'

'Why do you say that?' she inquired, then realized he was joking.

'This is a wedding, not a funeral,' Todd said, making Rachel laugh.

'Was I looking that glum? I started the day at dawn to get Oliver and Alain off before I drove down here and I suppose it must show.'

'You should have gone to France with them. Why didn't you?

'Someone had to mind the store. But it's a godsend, in fact, because it gives me a chance to catch up on all sorts of things.'

'I still don't understand why the three of you have never been to France together – you, the arch Francophile. Since you married a Frenchman you've never even been back. It's crazy.'

'We'll do it some day,' she assured him. 'We've been so tied down until now at Chez Alain.'

'I was just talking to somebody who's been to the restaurant and was singing Alain's praises. I told him Alain speaks English almost like a native now. Did it ever occur to you he must feel like a foreigner in his own country when he goes back?'

'I think there's some truth in that,' replied Rachel. A powerful longing to be in France came over her unexpectedly, something she hadn't experienced for years. Alain had spoken little about his recent trips back home, and she hadn't questioned him on this complex sensitive issue. It touched on a past he preferred to forget.

When they saw Natalie dancing with the groom's father, Todd remarked, 'You were smart not to have a big wedding. In an hour this party will be nothing but a memory and a big hole in Ma and Pa's bank account. As great as it is, does it really matter? Look at you and Alain: after ten years of marriage you're still passionately in love. That's all that counts.'

Her brother's eyes were shining with an idolatry Rachel felt she didn't deserve. She wondered what Todd would say if he knew what was troubling her, or how rarely she and Alain had made love in the last year or so. All day she had been avoiding the thought that Alain's neglect and his carefully planned absence were connected.

Todd said, 'That bridesmaid, what's her name – Susan? She's a knockout.'

'Isn't she, though? It's funny, I was thinking a minute ago she was just your type. Lots of couples meet each other at somebody else's wedding, you know.'

'Do you suppose this is my rendezvous with destiny?'

'Stranger things have happened.'

'They have; look at you – if you hadn't gone to the Sorbonne, you might have been a maid of honour today, not the matron.'

'I hadn't thought of it that way, but I suppose you're right. If I hadn't learned to speak French as well as I did, I doubt whether Alain and I would have got together. He's still the only man I've ever wanted to marry.'

The music stopped and Rachel returned to the table where her father was telling an anecdote about his first law case that she had

7

heard countless times. Looking at the happy faces around her, Rachel had a sense of being a stranger among her own friends and family, but it was a feeling that she had become used to. Much as she loved them, Rachel had always set her sights beyond this tight-knit, prosperous group of people with predictable opinions and occupations. Just then her mother changed places with Aunt Grace and took Rachel's hand.

'Hasn't it all been out of this world?' she said, her blue eyes full of contentment. 'They're going to be leaving in a few minutes. I think Natalie wants Susan to get the bouquet, but she's so petite compared to the other bridesmaids that I don't know how she'll ever catch it.' She whispered in Rachel's ear, 'I wish you had had a wedding like this.'

'Mother, it was different for us.'

'You've never regretted it?'

'You can't have everything,' Rachel replied with a philosophical shrug, not wanting to say how little such things meant to her. But she considered the idea that this great tribal ritual, one she had disparaged at the time, served the purpose of making the newcomer feel part of the family.

'I'm sure the money a wedding costs was better spent setting you and Alain up in that first little place you had in the city, but at a time like this, I can't help wishing . . .'

Rachel was distracted by her brother Greg's two children playing tug of war with a ribbon from the flowers on the table. Her mother saw her watching them and knew what she was thinking.

'It's too bad Alain and Oliver aren't here. Especially Oliver. He hardly ever gets to see his cousins. I've had so little chance to talk to you. Tell me more about Alain's trip.'

Rachel's vague replies seemed to satisfy her mother, who remarked, 'I sent photocopies of that last article about Chez Alain in the *Examiner* to so many people. A lot of them are here today and they've all been asking about Alain. Well, I guess we just have to accept that Alain is famous now, and that the demands of his work come first.'

'I'm so glad that you understand, Mother.' A surge of the fierce loyalty that had always been Rachel's reaction to anything resembling criticism of her husband welled up in her. Sensing the wedding had put her mother in a sentimental mood, Rachel felt vulnerable to the declaration she knew was coming.

'I know you used to think we disapproved of Alain, but we only wanted what was best for you. If we were doubtful about Alain, it was because he seemed like a scruffy, bearded vagabond with no money or education. Looking back, I know we didn't make him feel as welcome as we should have. Perhaps we were narrow-minded at the time. But now Alain Ribard is a name to be reckoned with. He's proved all of us wrong, and we don't mind admitting that. I think what really impressed your father was when Alain paid back all the money he had borrowed from you to start out. That shows character, and if he was here today, I'd tell him so.'

Seeing her mother's eyes misted over with emotion, Rachel grasped her hands. On the heels of such praise there was no way she could say what was on her mind.

'It's a shame you couldn't go on this trip too. You must be so curious to see the place Alain comes from. Now he's so successful it must mean such a lot to him to go back. Let's get together as soon as Alain and Oliver get back. I want to hear all about their trip.'

Her mother's offhand remark sent a jolt through Rachel. The room emptied of movement and sound as an idea crystallized in her head. It was clear what she must do.

'Say, are you the little lady who runs that fantastic restaurant in Sonoma with her French husband?' boomed a voice behind her.

Their conversation was interrupted for a few moments by a blustering friend of the groom's father. When he had gone, Dinah rose from the table.

'I'd better go and see how Natalie is doing. I've got some Kleenex stuffed up my sleeve. I just know I'm going to cry buckets when they drive away.'

'Mother, listen to me. I need your help.'

'My help? What's the matter?'

'What you said just now about me going along on this trip. I know this sounds wildly impulsive, but I could join Alain and Oliver on Monday if I can get on a flight to France tomorrow.'

Her mother stared at her in astonishment. 'But Rachel, surely you can't leave the restaurant.'

9

'Never mind the restaurant. René can take over. I'm expecting Alain to call me here tonight or tomorrow morning to say he's arrived safely. When he does, I want you to tell him . . .' Searching for explanation, she saw the remains of a lobster on a plate. 'Tell him that I've got shellfish poisoning, that I'm perfectly fine, but I'm in bed because the doctor gave me a sedative.'

'Rachel! And make the poor man worry all because you want to surprise him? No dear, think again. It would be far better if he were expecting you. It would still be a wonderful surprise.'

'Please bear with me, Mother, because I'd rather he didn't know I was coming.' As she said it Rachel knew it might sound odd, but her mother was too distracted to notice.

'All right, but there's no time to talk about it now.'

The music had stopped and people were beginning to assemble at the entrance for the departure of the bride and groom. Rachel looked at her watch and realized she would just have time to call the airport.

\*

A ground attendant in an Air France uniform stepped forward as the passengers disembarking from a 747 came through the gate.

'Monsieur Ribard,' she called, holding up a sign with the name printed on it. 'Monsieur Ribard, *s'il vous plait.*'

A dark-haired, broad-shouldered man with a clipped beard stopped when he heard the name.

'*Je suis Monsieur Ribard.*' He took off his sunglasses and stepped away from the crowd. A young boy who looked remarkably like him, with shiny dark hair and identical deep-blue eyes fringed in black, followed in his wake.

'What is it, Dad?' the boy asked impatiently as his father read a message the attendant had given him.

'*Merci, madame,*' Alain said to the woman, folding the paper and stuffing it into the pocket of his jacket. He motioned to Oliver to follow.

'Where are we going?' the child asked as they approached the moving walkway that would take them to the central terminal of Charles de Gaulle Airport.

'What does that sign say?' Alain said to distract the boy while he considered the message.

'It says . . . let's see, *bagages* . . . that's baggage, and *sortie* . . . exit, right?'

'Right. Oliver, listen, there's been a sudden change of plan. It's something to do with my business and we'll be stopping here in Paris instead of going to Bordeaux today.'

'Paris? Wow!' Oliver exclaimed, whirling around with a smile. 'Can we see the Eiffel Tower?'

'I'm sure we can.'

'Neat!'

Alain placed a hand on Oliver's shoulder to steady him while he stood there wondering what could possibly have happened to cause this break in their journey. Moments later he saw Isabelle de Montjoi waving to him at the exit. He felt acutely conscious of his son at his side as they approached her.

'*Bonjour*, Isabelle,' he said politely, transmitting the message, already agreed upon, that their meeting be restrained.

'*Bonjour*, Alain.' Drawing away, she looked at him for a second, her golden eyes sparkling with amusement at the falseness of their greeting. But the fleeting intensity on her face conveyed the reality behind the masquerade.

'Isabelle, I would like to present my son, Oliver. Oliver, this is Isabelle de Montjoi, who is a very good friend of mine. She came to Sonoma last summer.'

'*Bonjour*. I'm so happy to know you, Oliver,' she added in English.

Oliver dutifully presented both cheeks for her to kiss, looking up at the beautifully groomed woman who looked like a movie star and exuded waves of strong perfume. Her bright red lips kissed the air and he felt her smooth powdered face brush his.

'What do you say, Oliver?'

'*Je suis heureux de faire votre connaissance*,' he said softly but without hesitation.

'And he speaks French so well already. How marvellous!' A laugh bubbled in her throat. 'Come this way to pick up your bags. It might take a bit longer than usual because they were directed to

11

Bordeaux, but I've already arranged everything. You can have your tickets changed after we've got the luggage.'

Alain dispatched Oliver with the trolley to look for the bags, then turned to Isabelle impatiently.

'Now, would you tell me what's going on?'

'Aren't you going to say first how glad you are to see me?'

'Of course. I'm delighted, you know that. It's just that it's so unexpected. Nothing's wrong, I hope.'

'Yes, something is wrong, but not as bad as it first seemed to me. We've had a setback, that's all.' Isabelle smiled reassuringly. 'I've known since the will was read, and that's two weeks ago, but I hoped to sort it out before you got here. We have a few legal things to tie up, anyway, about the hotel and our partnership, and it occurred to me that, as our time is precious, we ought to investigate our options right away, in case . . .'

'Options? What are you talking about?' Alain's mind jumped back to the day when, her voice expressing relief, Isabelle had called him to say that at last all of their plans could go forward. Now he realized that there had been a mishap and that she was trying to break the news gently.

She took a deep breath. '*Chéri*, I'm afraid that Armand Bataille has left Brissac to someone else, not to me.' She gave a helpless shrug.

'Oh my God,' he whispered in English. 'My God . . . I can't believe it.' When he had recovered himself, he said, 'How did this happen?'

'I'll tell you on the way into town. I've opened up the apartment and I thought we could stay until Monday or Tuesday to see what the legal loopholes are, in case we have to use them.'

'Jesus – I hadn't planned on this.'

'Imagine how I feel after all these years of loyalty, of planning and dreaming. I was sick about it, then I was furious. I felt he betrayed me. Tell me,' Isabelle said, glancing towards Oliver who was standing by the luggage carousel, 'have you told your wife?'

'No, I thought it was better this way, to cut out without saying anything and go back in two or three weeks on my own to finalize the sale of the business and get the divorce started. Oliver doesn't

12

know anything, and I don't want him to know for the time being, especially now.'

'What do you mean, "especially now"?'

'Now that Brissac has fallen through. We may have to rethink the whole thing.'

'Alain, you mustn't say that. I know you're shocked, but I haven't any doubt that we'll find a way around this problem.'

'Why didn't you tell me right away?'

'I told you why – because I thought I could work things out before you got here. You see, I made an offer to the heir, but it was refused.'

Alain shook his head, feeling his hopes sink further into the ground. 'All of this sounds pretty ominous,' he murmured.

Isabelle gripped his hand tightly in hers. 'Alain, we're going to get Brissac back one way or the other, though I'm not sure exactly how. You look doubtful, *chéri*. Aren't we in this together?'

'Of course we are,' he said with a defeated sigh.

Oliver trotted up to them. 'It wasn't our bag, Dad, but one that looked exactly like it. When are we going to get to see the Eiffel Tower?'

'Oliver, you'll see the Eiffel Tower today, in a few moments from now on the taxi ride into Paris. And not only that, but you can see if from the window of your bedroom because you'll be staying nearby in the Champ de Mars, in my apartment.'

Oliver looked at her incredulously, and then at Alain, who nodded. 'Wait till Mom hears this, Dad. She'll be amazed.'

'That's absolutely right,' said Alain with a bitter smile. When Oliver had gone off again, he turned to Isabelle. 'You haven't told me yet who the heir is.'

'No, I haven't. And you're not going to believe it when I do.'

# *Chapter 2*

By early Monday evening Rachel was driving a rented car towards the village of Roquelaire in Gascony. Despite some difficulty, she had managed to locate it on the map spread out on the seat next to her. Nothing could have been more different from what she had expected than this landscape of dream-like beauty bearing little relation to Alain's description of the dull, featureless countryside of his childhood. The road twisted through avenues of mottled plane trees, past fields ablaze with sunflowers. Their vibrant yellow stretched for miles, interrupted by acres of ripening corn watered by great irrigation jets that trailed rainbows across the sky. Every now and then she passed an enormous expanse of golden stubble where the straw had been rolled into giant discs that supported the megaliths of some vanished tribe. The hot air coming through the open windows carried the rich smell of France in summer and the ceaseless calls of crickets. As she covered the miles, Rachel's mind journeyed back, recalling forgotten details about the young Frenchman she had met at the university bookshop, whose English was so inadequate.

Over a cup of coffee she had listened to Alain Ribard recount his experiences in the restaurant trade from Paris to London to New York, then San Francisco. She had sensed that Alain's ceaseless movement didn't spring from restlessness, but centred on a search for something. He had declared that in ten years he would be one of California's most famous chefs and somehow she had believed him, though she had been wary at first of his good looks and facile charm.

She had given him her address, never expecting to hear from him again, but a year later he had written to her from San Francisco, where he had become a sous-chef in a prestigious restaurant. Soon he came back to claim her, the girl he hadn't forgotten, the girl who spoke his language. He laid siege until she agreed to marry him, and soon afterwards they set up in business together.

Thinking it over, it seemed remarkable to Rachel that she should find herself again doubting him as deeply as she had done that first day in the bookshop. Now they had ten solid years behind them, a thriving business and a son they both adored. In the middle of such beautiful country, so far from home, all she really wanted was to keep things the way they were. The word 'deception', which she had consciously avoided, had already receded in her mind. She didn't want a confrontation; what she wanted was the idyllic family holiday that they should probably have taken years ago. She wanted Oliver to get to know France; she wanted Alain to see his own country afresh through her eyes.

A glimpse of a walled town on a distant hilltop made Rachel think how self-absorbed she and Alain had been all these years, depriving themselves and their son of such richness. This was the France she remembered; it hadn't changed and Rachel embraced it like an old friend. It seemed to her that Alain's birthplace was a gift of good fortune, not the curse he had always made it out to be. Seeing for herself the land that he purported to despise, Rachel began to wonder how well she really knew the man she loved.

She drove on, her thoughts turning to Oliver. She could picture him throwing his arms around her, talking in a rush in his high-pitched, excited little voice about everything he had done and seen since leaving Sonoma. She had missed him so. In her newfound forgiving mood, Rachel was far more doubtful about confronting Alain than when she left home, and she felt a nervous little pulse beat at her throat at the prospect of an argument when he saw her. After he had recovered from the shock and expressed his annoyance that she had left the restaurant without telling him, she supposed they would explore the village and find a charming little bistro. They would tuck Oliver in bed in the little hotel where Alain was staying. Then they would sink into bed themselves, and negate all those loveless months in a burst of passion. Thinking about it, Rachel felt a craving for her husband's lovemaking, which had lost none of its power over the years.

'I did this mad, crazy thing because I love you,' she whispered. Those would be her opening words when she saw the familiar flash of anger in Alain's dark-fringed eyes. She wouldn't mention the postcard or the travel agent's letter.

Arriving at the top of a hill, Rachel caught her first sight of Alain's birthplace: a harmonious cluster of cream stone houses roofed with rose-coloured tiles, set in the shallow valley. The fortified town was much larger than she had imagined and far lovelier than Alain had described. As she rounded the curve of the road, she saw a fortress some distance ahead, which she recognized with a start as the château on the old postcard. She slowed down to make sure, staring at the forbidding twin-towered building silhouetted against the darkening sky. Coming to a halt, she reached for the card in her bag to confirm she was right. She could see that what had been a ruin when the picture was taken had been greatly restored. Somewhere there was the window that had been marked *ta cuisine* on the postcard, but she didn't bother to look for it. Her mind still swimming with the prospect of a happy reunion, she didn't want to think about it.

In her haste to get to the village she drove too fast down the stretch of empty road. A figure darted out from nowhere, and Rachel swerved, then slammed on the brakes to avoid a ditch. The impact threw her forward against the seat belt, which cut painfully into her chest. Fighting to free herself, her hands shaking, Rachel looked back in the rear-view mirror and was indescribably relieved to see that there was no body lying in the road. She got out of the car as a woman in a straw hat popped up from the overgrown ditch, clutching her skirt with one hand and holding an enormous rabbit with the other. In rapid French, which Rachel found difficult to follow, the woman was clearly furiously scolding the rabbit, which she held suspended by his ears.

'*Méchant, tu es méchant,*' she muttered. '*Bonsoir, madame,*' she called to Rachel, seemingly unperturbed by what had happened.

'I'm so sorry, *madame,*' Rachel called in English, hurrying forwards to her. She was so shaken that her French seemed to have deserted her.

'It's not your fault,' the woman said. 'It's this one – he managed

16

to get out of his cage when I was feeding him. Naughty, you are naughty,' she repeated.

Rachel looked in surprise at the woman, dressed as she had seen only French peasants on postcards, in a navy cotton dress and apron and a broad-brimmed straw hat trimmed with a black band. The rabbit's bemused expression and the woman's flow of chatter, as if she were speaking to a badly behaved child, made Rachel want to laugh. No cosmetics or creams had ever soothed the woman's weathered skin, and no colouring had ever been applied to the greying brown hair escaping from her bun. Her wrinkled upper lip was shadowed by a faint moustache and her chin sprouted a few whiskers, although Rachel thought she might easily be no older than her own mother. The woman peered up at Rachel from beneath her straw hat, her black eyes full of a lively curiosity that contradicted the impression of age. She was slightly stooped, yet she moved and gestured with surprising energy as she spoke with the rolling accent of the region.

'Are you sure you're all right, *madame?*'

'Thank you. I'm fine,' Rachel replied, though she was still shaking. 'Please excuse me . . .' she began, but the woman brushed this aside.

'You look a bit pale. Won't you come and sit down and have something to drink?' she said, gesturing to the other side of the road.

Rachel turned to look at the faded blue house set back from the road among the chestnut trees, brightened by pots of nasturtiums and geraniums. Beneath the rampant vine that shaded the doorway she saw a hand pump that was still in use. A rusting green metal table and wicker chairs stood under a fig tree, and beyond the vegetable patch she saw a tiny shed that looked like an outside privy. In another mood, Rachel would have longed to linger in this island of tranquillity that seemed straight out of an Impressionist painting.

'That's very kind, but I must get to the village. I just wanted to make sure you were all right.'

'It must have been such a shock when I jumped out of nowhere. I didn't hear your car, I was so intent on chasing this one,' she said, glaring at the rabbit.

17

'No, it was my fault. I was looking at the château in the distance, not at the road.'

'Ah, Brissac, you mean?'

'It *is* the Château Brissac, then?'

'Yes, it is.'

Rachel sensed a pride in the declaration.

'How did you know its name?' asked the woman.

'Oh, I saw a picture of it before I came – an old postcard. Does anyone live there now?'

'No, not at the moment.' Caution crept into the older woman's voice and her manner changed.

Sensing this, Rachel didn't pursue the subject.

'You speak such good French, *madame*. You are English?'

'I'm American. I studied in Paris years ago. But my husband is French. In fact, he was born on a farm near Roquelaire, but he left here when he was seventeen. Perhaps you know him. His name is Ribard, Alain Ribard.'

The woman's dark eyes registered nothing. 'Ribard, yes, I know the name. I seem to remember a family called Ribard, but they all moved away a long time ago.'

Was it Rachel's imagination or was this subject closed too? The look on her face told Rachel the woman knew exactly who the Ribards were, but that she preferred not to speak of them.

'My husband should be in Roquelaire now. He arrived with our son on Saturday. The view is so beautiful from this side of the village, maybe they walked by?'

'No, I haven't seen anyone of that description, but then it's been very hot the last few days. Today's much cooler.'

Meeting the woman's steady black eyes, which held no trace of unfriendliness, Rachel wondered how many times she had left Roquelaire in the course of a lifetime, and guessed that she had probably never been to Paris, or even as far as Bordeaux.

'Well, goodbye, *madame*,' Rachel said reluctantly. 'It was a pleasure meeting you.' She added. 'Is the Hôtel de la Poste in the middle of the village?'

'Hôtel de la Poste? There's no such hotel in Roquelaire.'

Rachel stared at her. 'No Hôtel de la Poste? Are you sure?'

18

'Of course, *madame*. The only hotel in the village is the Hôtel de France.' Seeing Rachel's confusion, she said. 'There is a hotel of that name in Labarderns, a village about fifteen kilometres away.'

'That can't be,' Rachel murmured.

'Just a moment – here comes Père Auguste. He might be able to help.'

Rachel saw a stocky man with cropped white hair coming down the road carrying a fishing rod, a spaniel at his side.

'*Bonsoir*, Agnès,' he called. '*Bonsoir, madame,*' he nodded to Rachel.

'Father, this woman is Madame Ribard. She is supposed to meet her husband and son at the Hôtel de la Poste in the village, but I told her there's no such hotel.'

'He's not actually expecting me,' Rachel offered. 'My husband was born here; his family name is Ribard.'

'The name is familiar to me,' said the priest, 'but as far as I know he's not staying in the village. You could try the Hôtel de France. There might be some confusion.'

'That's what I told her,' said Agnès.

'Thank you very much. Well, I'll be on my way,' said Rachel distractedly. Recalling the formalities of French leave-taking, she extended her hand to both of them. '*Au revoir, monsieur, madame.*'

She returned to the car and drove up a slope past the communal *lavoir*, a dark square pool sheltered by a low tiled roof. The jagged line of rooftops disappeared as Rachel passed under a fine stone archway and up a street lined with narrow houses, opening into a large impressive square dominated by an ancient covered market that had been carefully restored. Distracted as she was, Rachel took in the magnificence of the medieval brick-and-timber buildings wedged between later dwellings of cream-coloured stone. Roquelaire seemed to have survived the centuries from the Crusades to the Revolution and on to the present almost untouched by time, and it was breathtaking.

Driving slowly around the square as she looked for the hotel, Rachel suddenly felt lost and strange. For a moment she was like any other tourist staring at the group of old men in berets sitting in the shade against the backdrop of the red brick church that stood at one end of the square. At a small bistro a family was already reading the menu, and the café was packed with tourists in shorts and T-shirts sitting under the umbrellas, but she could see no sign of Alain or Oliver.

She got out of the car and stood for a moment to get her bearings. Her eyes followed a swarm of swifts screaming overhead, as she scanned the shopfronts. She saw the Hôtel de France, and walked across the square.

'*Bonsoir, monsieur,*' she said to the man behind the counter. 'I believe my husband and son might be staying here. The name is Ribard.' She glanced at the keys hung in rows behind the counter, feeling both anxious and expectant.

The man thought for a moment. 'Ribard? I'm sure there's no one here by that name at the moment,' he said, glancing at the register. 'No, *madame*, and all the rooms are occupied until the end of the week.'

'Are you sure there's no booking for a Monsieur Ribard?' Rachel asked, trying not to appear as confused as she felt at this news. Suddenly she was very tired. All the hours lost in the time-change caught up with her, leaving her vulnerable.

She mentioned the Hôtel de la Poste in the neighbouring village. 'Do you think you could telephone and ask if they're there? It's just that I must find them and I don't know what to do. I'll be happy to pay for the call.'

As he dialled the other hotel, Rachel tried to keep calm. She thought about what she would do if there were no sign of them. Even so, when the man said that they were not there either, she felt a crushing disappointment, verging on dread. None of the reasons that had brought her there seemed important now.

'Do you have a room? Oh no – you said you were fully booked, didn't you?'

'Unfortunately, yes.'

'Are there any other hotels in the village?'

'I'm afraid not, *madame*. Here's a list of all the hotels and restaurants within a few kilometres, but you may find the others are booked too. It's our busiest season. You can phone from the call-box next to the post office across the square if you want.'

Rachel left the hotel feeling utterly defeated. Her eyes were burning and her limbs were heavy. The sky, now a pale mother-of-pearl at the edges of the rooftops, reminded her that night would fall very soon. She walked towards the café, holding the brochure and intending to have a cup of coffee to revive herself while she looked at her map and the list of hotels. She tried to reassure herself that Alain had simply had a change of plan and hadn't had time to communicate. Seeing the call-box, she wondered how difficult it would be to telephone the United States to see if he had left a message at home. A man who looked familiar crossed the road ahead of her and Rachel realized it was the priest.

'Ah, *madame*, have you located your husband yet?' he asked as she approached.

'No, I'm afraid he's not here. There has obviously been some misunderstanding. The hotel is full, so I have to find some other place to stay. I don't really want to leave Roquelaire in case he arrives. You see, he was supposed to be doing research for a cookbook he's writing – he's a chef by profession. He might be travelling with a photographer . . .' She stopped, aware that she was going into unnecessary detail, but the priest was looking at her with a concerned expression. He thought for a moment, considering her predicament.

'*Madame*, if you'll permit me, I think I know of a place where you might stay. It will only take me a moment to inquire. Why don't you wait at the café?'

'It's so kind of you, really. I wouldn't want you to go to any trouble.'

'No trouble at all. Please, just wait and I'll be back soon.'

Rachel did as he suggested, with a relief at having the burden of finding a room lifted from her. Presently, she saw Père Auguste coming across the square. The cup of coffee had cleared her head and she realized that what she needed was a good night's sleep before considering her next move. All at once the absurdity of her impetuous journey bore down on her, and she felt foolish when she thought of Alain calling home and being told she was ill with food poisoning.

Rachel smiled as Père Auguste approached. She could tell by the cheerful expression on his face that he had been successful.

'Everything is arranged. You have a place to stay not far from the square. It's only a minute's walk from here.'

Rachel had a vision of a gloomy convent.

'There's a compatriot of yours, a Monsieur Cooper, who teaches a painting course in Roquelaire in the summer. He has a big house, where his students stay. If you'd like to drive, I'll give you directions.'

Rachel gathered up her bag. 'I can't thank you enough, Father.'

'I'm pleased to help. It was fortuitous that we met, because only this morning Monsieur Cooper mentioned to me that one of the students had dropped out at the last moment. It took me longer than I intended, because he didn't hear me knocking. The house is full of the art students having a welcoming drink before supper. He said he would be delighted for you to join them.'

'*C'est gentil*,' Rachel said with a smile, although she didn't welcome the idea of a party. All she wanted was to go to bed.

Bob Cooper lived in a big shuttered house on a street signposted Rue Cazat. It was almost dark, and a few weak lights illuminated the empty street, so narrow that Rachel had to park on the kerb.

When Père Auguste offered to take her suitcase, she said, 'I'll just take this small overnight bag. Can I leave everything else in the car?'

'Of course,' said the priest. 'You'll probably want to lock it, but no one has ever stolen anything from a car in Roquelaire, as far as I know.'

'How amazing.'

The priest was looking at her with a veiled curiosity that Rachel couldn't help noticing, but she told herself that he was observing her with the detached friendliness of someone helping a stranger in need.

Père Auguste knocked at the door, which was answered by a thin, smiling man in his late forties, with cropped dark hair and a goatee beard sprinkled with grey. He wore a Russian peasant shirt and baggy trousers, corresponded perfectly with Rachel's idea of an American expatriate artist.

'*Soyez la bienvenue!*' he exclaimed. 'Come in.' Taking her bag, he held out his other hand. 'I'm Bob Cooper – and you're Mrs Ribard.' His blue eyes twinkled behind his tortoiseshell glasses.

'It's so nice of you to put me up at such short notice,' Rachel said, looking into the huge beamed sitting-room, lined with bold, splashy canvasses. She could hear the babble of voices drifting through the open doors from the terrace.

'I'm delighted to be able to help a fellow American in the lurch. It must have been awful for you to arrive in search of your family and not find any room at the inn. Wasn't it marvellous that Père Auguste thought to bring you here? You were obviously fated to use the room that just happens to be empty. Normally, you know, we're full to bursting at this time of year.'

The sound of Bob Cooper's familiar American accent and his exaggerated, uninhibited mannerisms dissolved Rachel's reserve. His rush of genuine hospitality made the idea of passing a night in Roquelaire suddenly bearable and made her realize she wasn't as exhausted as she had thought. She was standing in front of a vivid, busy landscape illuminated by a spotlight.

Bob Cooper's paintings, like the man, were larger than life.

'You'll probably want to freshen up in your room, and then I'd be very pleased if you'd join us for drinks and a buffet supper. Père Auguste, won't you join us as well?'

'No, no,' he said, throwing up his hands. 'It's very kind of you, but Odette will be cross if I don't come right home. *Bonsoir, madame,*' he said to Rachel, shaking her hand.

'Thank you for your kindness, Father.'

'You're most welcome,' he called with a wave.

Bob Cooper led the way up a narrow winding staircase. 'Père Auguste might as well be an old married man. He's henpecked by that housekeeper of his.'

Rachel had a fleeting image of Odette as a dark, bad-tempered woman with a bun. She thought too, of the old woman with the rabbit, of the priest: all three belonged in the same gallery of French characters she had met as a student, filling her with a sense of homecoming.

Bob turned on the light in a charming bedroom with whitewashed beams, decorated in blue toile de Jouy.

'A Miss Knight, one of my students, dropped out at the last minute. She does rather delicate little watercolours. Poor thing had a stroke just days before she was due to leave England, so here it is. I hope you'll be comfortable. You share a bathroom with Rosamund Morton, who is English. I'll introduce you when you come downstairs.'

A short while later Rachel emerged from the room, feeling revived by the healing power of hot water and fresh clothes. Bob Cooper came over to her as she entered the sitting-room.

'What's your first name, Mrs Ribard? I can't possibly call another American by anything but her first name.'

'Rachel,' she said, looking at the disparate group of people gathered on the terrace.

'Rachel, I'd like you to meet my friend and right-hand man, Ted Bridges.'

'Hi, Rachel,' said a balding, wiry man as he passed bearing a casserole that smelled pungently of garlic. He wedged it on a long table already covered with bright pottery dishes of appetizing food, and Rachel realized how hungry she was after all. She could see at once that Bob and Ted were an established couple. Bob beckoned her to the terrace and handed her a glass of bubbling liquid tasting of oranges.

'*Pousse rapière,*' said Bob. 'The local cocktail. We always kick off with a few of these on the first night.'

Rachel beheld the breathtaking, shrub-filled garden bordered by a low wall that looked out on the hills beyond Roquelaire. Spotlights placed in dark corners illuminated huge urns spilling with geraniums, statues in verdant niches and a pergola overgrown with wisteria, which pressed like black lace against the fading sky. Cocooned in a sense of unreality, she could scarcely believe how she had come to be here.

'It's indescribably beautiful,' she said to Bob.

'You can't imagine what a state it was in when we saw it for the first time. Ted is the one who transformed it. He used to be a landscape architect.'

'How long have you had this house?' She glanced up at it, the walls shrouded in creepers that seemed ready to envelop the green shuttered windows.

'Ted and I have been coming here every summer for fifteen

years, and do you know, buying this house was the smartest thing we ever did.'

As Bob talked enthusiastically about Roquelaire, Rachel glanced through an open window into a room with a big desk that was obviously the study. Seeing a telephone under the lamp, she wondered if she could ask to call home.

'Have you always lived in France?' she asked Bob.

'Almost from the day I left art school. That was my sole ambition, to come to France and paint. As the years went by, I became a teacher. We live in Paris during the winter, and in the summer I teach three courses, each lasting a fortnight. I keep it very small and select, but we try to maintain a casual and intimate atmosphere so we can get to know each other. Ted creates the ambience and the food. We pride ourselves on the quality of the accommodation and the instruction. We like to think it's something rather special.'

The description sounded as if Bob were quoting from a brochure and for a moment Rachel wondered if he thought she might like to replace Miss Knight.

'I've always wanted to paint, but I can't even hold a brush.'

'It may surprise you, but I've had several very successful students who had never painted a thing in their lives before they came here.'

She laughed. 'Some other time I'd love to.'

'I didn't quite gather from Père Auguste what you were doing here.' Bob was staring at her with a frank curiosity that made Rachel suddenly reticent.

'I'm just passing through. I was supposed to meet my husband here.' Seeing that Bob was waiting for her to elaborate, she added, 'There's obviously been some confusion about the hotel where we were supposed to meet. I'll straighten it out tomorrow. It was too late to do anything tonight.'

'What a nuisance for you,' said Bob politely, but Rachel had the distinct impression that he didn't quite believe her.

He mentioned the price of the room without board, adding 'If you need to stay here a bit longer, it's no problem at all.'

'That's very kind of you,' she replied, unnerved by the suggestion that she might be marooned in Roquelaire alone for more than one night. Turning her head, Rachel saw that Ted had been listening to their conversation. Catching her eye, he smiled and hastily moved forward to replenish their glasses.

'More *pousse rapière*?'

'No, thank you. I really shouldn't.' The drink had made her light-headed, exhaustion and nerves had altered her perspective, and she saw the floodlit garden now as if through gauze.

'I've monopolized you long enough, Rachel. Come and meet the group,' said Bob, leading her towards the others. 'This is Colonel Stroud, and his wife, Mary, old friends who have been coming here for several years whenever they can tear themselves away from Sussex.'

Rachel held out her hand to the tall, trim man with steel-grey hair and bristling moustache, who looked every inch a colonel, although his gaudy shirt and red neck scarf suggested he was trying to play the part of a painter in France. His wife was a big hearty woman with a braying laugh, who sported gold chains and ropes of imitation pearls. A few moments later Rachel met a shy young bank clerk with big, soulful eyes, talking to two schoolteachers from London, who laughed hysterically at his jokes. Observing the two dowdy woman in their mid-thirties, their shoulders sunburnt, their faces flushed with wine, Rachel could almost feel them peeling off their inhibitions in the company of the bland young banker, who had now launched into a monologue about colour fields. There were two other students – a lively Cockney youth called Barry, who had a plumbing business, and a young girl with fawn-like eyes and wispy blond hair named Melissa, who didn't utter a word. Watching the last light fade on the horizon, Rachel had the sensation that she had stepped on board an ocean liner where the ordinary lives of the passengers were in limbo for the duration of a journey. Time seemed to be unravelling with magical slowness, making her forget why she had come. She was brought back to reality by an Englishwoman's voice.

'Hello, I'm Rosamund Morton. I'm in the room across the hall from you.'

Rachel turned to see a tall, fortyish blonde woman, wearing a vivid print dress. She had delicate skin and china-blue eyes, and something in her manner appealed to Rachel at once.

'I was hoping you'd be one of us when I saw you come in,' she said to Rachel. 'They're all completely different from the group we had last year, except for the Strouds, of course.'

'I'm only staying the night, unfortunately,' Rachel replied with a regretful smile. 'Do you come here every summer?'

'This is my second time. It's my big treat every year to get away from everything and everybody in London, including my husband and two teenage boys. They're all mad keen on sports. This house, this village, Bob and Ted – everything is perfect bliss for me. We work very hard all day, but they really cosset us in the evening.' They sat down by a little oval water basin fed by a cupid. 'What are you doing here if you're not on the course?'

'I flew to Paris from San Francisco yesterday and then to Bordeaux.' Until now she had pretended to take the upset of not finding Alain and Oliver in the village in her stride, but something in Rosamund's open manner invited confidence and Rachel was suddenly tired of the burden she had been carrying. Explaining how she came in pursuit of Alain on the spur of the moment, she said, 'When I got here, he wasn't registered at the Hotel de France. They had no knowledge of him or my son. You're the first person I've mentioned this to. I'm trying not to panic.' She gave a self-deprecating little laugh.

'Oh, how dreadful for you. And you've come all this way.'

'The thing is, I don't know whether to feel alarmed that they're not here or like a fool because I didn't let him know I was coming.'

'And have you no idea where they are?'

'No. Of course, they can't be very far from here. They must have had a last-minute change of plan, and I can only assume that when Alain calls home, he'll leave a message to tell me where he is. I know it's silly to worry.'

'I'd feel exactly the same in your place. Why don't you ask Bob to use his phone? He wouldn't mind a bit; he's as nice as can be.'

'Of course, you're right. It's only to put my mind at ease. I was going to do it later, after dinner.'

They looked at each other, and Rachel realized that perhaps she had been putting off the call, not wanting to face the prospect that Alain might not have phoned. 'I'll do it this very minute.'

She asked Bob if she could use the phone and he led her to the door of the study. A moment later she was listening to the distant drone of a phone ringing in California.

'Hello, René, it's Rachel,' she said, intending to tell him she was calling from a phone booth. He had seemed unperturbed when she called the restaurant before her departure to say that she was taking a few days impromptu vacation with her parents at Lake Tahoe. 'René, has Alain called to say where he is?'

There was a pause. 'No, I'm afraid not.'

'He hasn't called?' she said incredulously.

'No, not that I know of. Listen, this is a terrible connection. It sounds like you're calling from Bangkok.'

Rachel felt at a complete loss. 'Are you sure?'

'Rachel, listen, I don't know what's happening, really I don't. The restaurant's packed and I have to go. Alain probably called your home and left a message on your answering machine. Have you thought of that?'

'But why didn't he call the restaurant? Surely he ought to have done that.' Suddenly she wondered if René was telling the truth.

'I'm sorry, but I really don't know.'

The dismissive tone of his voice made Rachel conscious of the lies she had told to keep her journey secret. Her desperation was falling on deaf ears. She said nervously, 'All right. If he does call today or tomorrow, would you take down his whereabouts and number? I don't know when I'm coming up to Sonoma.'

'Fine, no problem. Listen, I have to hang up. I don't want to tie up the phone. See you soon.'

When she had put the receiver down, Rachel stood in Bob's office for a moment, wondering if she should return to California as precipitately as she had left; but she knew she couldn't go back until she had found her husband and son.

Feeling numb, she returned to the terrace, intending to slip up to bed unnoticed if she could. She paused at the door that led to the garden, and saw that someone else had joined the group. A tall, glamorous looking Englishman was talking to Bob. She could only see him in outline, but got a quick impression of his sharp, attractive profile and the fact that his hair was drawn back in a ponytail.

28

Stylishly and expensively dressed, he seemed out of place among the rather ordinary people who made up the painting group. She couldn't help overhearing what he was saying.

'. . . and so she went to Paris on Saturday to meet him and his kid. The poor bastard, I wonder what he said when she broke the news. I hope to hell her lawyer can come up with something. I tell you Isabelle is going to shit her pants when she hears his wife is here; they'll be coming back on Tuesday or Wednesday. Are you sure she's his wife?'

'Ribard – she must be. How many Ribards can there be married to Americans? If you ask me, I think he told her he was staying at a fictitious hotel in the village. I offered to put her up. I recognized the name right away and I thought Jesus . . . – talk about *in flagrante delicto*.'

'What's she like? Would I fancy her? She might be in need of some consolation.'

'You're a real pain in the ass, Julian, do you know that? Yes, she's attractive and charming, as a matter of fact,' Bob said, stroking his beard.

'What about that well-preserved blonde in the corner? She's a bit long in the tooth, but you can't be fussy in the provinces. It looks as if I'm going to be stuck here until I have to be back in London for a meeting in the second week of September.'

When Bob turned suddenly and saw Rachel, his face dropped.

'Oh, Rachel . . .' There was an awkward pause as he weighed up what she had overhead.

Rachel's only thought was to make a quick exit. 'If you'll excuse me, Bob, I'm going up to bed. I'm feeling very tired.' Her eyes swept over Julian and she turned abruptly and walked back through the sitting-room. As she left, she heard Julian say, 'Do you think she heard?' A strangled laugh escaped his throat. 'Christ, how awkward.'

'Rachel, Rachel, please wait a minute,' Bob called after her, but she didn't stop.

Rachel hurried upstairs and closed the bedroom door behind her. Her breath coming in gasps, she peeled off her clothes so that they fell in a heap, and crawled between the sheets. Turning off the light, she found she was trembling uncontrollably. She fought the tears as she lay rigidly in the dark, the impact of the Englishman's words penetrating her defences like knife points. At last, when the church bell tolled midnight, she sank into an exhausted, miserable sleep.

*

Père Auguste leaned back in his chair and studied the chessboard. His partner had just moved his knight, radically altering the game. While the priest was pondering his next move, Michael Lowry got up to fetch the Armagnac bottle from the sideboard and held it up.

'Would you care for a drop? It's 1976.'

'A good age. But no, thank you. I need all my wits for my next move.'

When Michael sat down, the priest said, 'I nearly didn't come this evening, as it was so late. When I came back from fishing, I helped an American woman find a room because the hotel was fully booked. Luckily, Bob Cooper had a last-minute cancellation.'

Michael stared at the chessboard and sighed. 'I remember a time in this village when the hotel always had a room, even in high season. Roquelaire is no longer the sleepy little town it was when I first saw it.'

'Of course it has changed, but for the better, I hope.'

'I recall when Virginia and I bought this house, the Rue St Jacques was slightly run down, pleasantly so. Now, of course, all the houses have been tarted up, including mine. But I must admit I miss the atmosphere it used to have.'

'That's only because you come here as a visitor. Those of us who've lived here all our lives feel differently,' the priest said as he made his move.

'Of course, and I'm not complaining. But the Duchamps have put their house up for sale, and I found myself bristling this morning when I saw a Dutch couple looking at it in the agent's window. I thought of next summer, when the sound of pneumatic drills and shouting workmen will fill the air. If foreigners buy that

30

house, they'll spend a whole summer and umpteen thousands to put it back into the same state it was in in the Middle Ages, with olde worlde beams and quaint niches.'

'You've done wonders with *this* house. It was so dark and unfriendly before.'

'It was mostly Virginia who did it.'

'Yes, she was a lovely girl. Do you miss her?' It was the first time he had ever asked.

'It's been nearly three years, so I don't think about it much any more.' He moved a pawn and waited for the priest's reaction.

'Well, I'm very glad you didn't sell this place.'

'Where would I be now? In my flat in London. The truth is I realized just in time that I'd be losing the best chess partner I ever had.'

As if to illustrate the point, the priest cunningly moved his queen, taking Michael by surprise.

'Now that's a crafty move, very crafty,' Michael said, leaning forward to consider how he could avoid checkmate. 'What news of the hotel project?'

'None. It seems to be at a standstill; at least that's what the members of the council are saying. Some of them are glad, others sorry. I'm sorry, because we need more employment here. But I gather you won't mind, after what you said.'

'We need another hotel to accommodate tourists and pilgrims going to Compostela, it's true, but a luxury spa hotel complex of the kind they're planning would draw the wrong sort of people here. It sounds like inverted snobbery, but who needs designer boutiques in the square and that sort of thing? Before you know it, they'll be having jazz festivals in the market.'

'I like American jazz,' said the priest thoughtfully.

'Speaking of American, what was that woman you met doing here?'

'She's looking for her husband. Ribard is his name.'

'Ribard? Any relation to the Ribard involved in the hotel venture?'

'I have a hunch she is. She spoke French and she said she was looking for her husband and son, who were supposed to be

31

registered at the hotel. The husband is a chef apparently, so I suppose it's the same person.'

'Do you know this Ribard fellow?'

'I remember him when he was young. He left here in his late teens. Now he's made such a success of himself in America, I was happy to hear that he came back with the idea of developing a hotel. It was very enterprising.'

'Well, he's certainly come a long way in life if appearances are anything to go by,' said Michael, remembering the fit, prosperous-looking man he had seen in the square in the spring with Isabelle de Montjoi. 'Do you think Isabelle is going to buy the château from Agnès; or rather, will Agnès sell?'

'Everybody is saying so, but she's taking her time.'

'Who – Isabelle or Agnès?'

'Agnès.'

'Shrewd lady, Agnès. She's playing cat and mouse. It's amazing,' he muttered to himself, 'how she was left the château out of the blue.'

'That's where I met Mrs Ribard. She was with Agnès.' He told Michael about the incident.

Michael had a vivid picture of Agnès in a blue smock and straw hat bent over her vegetable patch the last time he walked by her cottage. 'Wasn't there something disreputable about the Ribards?'

The priest shrugged. 'It was during the war. The grandfather of the present Ribard was thought to be a collaborator with the Germans, but it was never proved. They were a tragic family. The mother died when the boys were young, and the father was an alcoholic.' He added reflectively, 'Some terrible things happened during the war, but that's in the past now and I hope people in Roquelaire who still bear a grudge won't make Ribard feel unwelcome.'

'I guess it's not surprising when you think about it.'

'There are things in Roquelaire that are deeply hidden, Michael. Make no mistake. Feuds, hates, rivalries that are handed down from one generation to the next. They go back centuries. So you can imagine that the war is still fresh in some people's minds.'

'In a way, I prefer to think of the village as a charming place full of nice people, not a sort of French provincial soap opera.' As he said it, Michael knew he would give a great deal to know half the secrets that the priest held in confidence, which he suspected had all the riveting elements of a popular novel.

'Those people I'm referring to are in the minority. It's time to forgive and forget.'

'Tell me, Père Auguste, have *you* forgotten?' He had long been haunted by the knowledge that as a boy Père Auguste had helped cut down the bodies of eleven men hanged by the Germans in a neighbouring village, though they had never spoken of it.

'I have forgiven, yes, but sometimes it's hard to forget.'

They fell silent for a while, concentrating on the chessboard until Michael said, 'It delighted me no end to see that Agnès is still selling rabbits in the market as if nothing has changed. Where else in the western world would a woman like her be left a fortune and continue about her business as if nothing had happened? In America or England she would probably be on a junket to Disneyland or Monte Carlo in a Rolls Royce, wearing a tiara.'

The Armagnac had mellowed him, conjuring up a loving image of Agnès. 'I often think of her living in that primitive little cottage, taking care of her rabbits and chickens. She still pumps water from the ground, has an outdoor privy and lives off her garden. To someone like me, fed up with living in the city, it seems like a halcyon way of life.'

The priest looked at him sceptically. 'But hard, my friend, very hard. In winter, for example. Her hands, her face, they tell the story. Agnès looks much older than she should for her age.' Michael looked abashed.

'Of course my view is absurdly facile, the bucolic fantasy of a city slicker.' Yet he still clung to his sentimental view of Agnès. She, and the handful of people like her, was one of the reasons he cared so deeply about the village he had adopted.

When the priest said, 'Agnès has had her share of tragedy,' Michael wondered what he meant but thought he would probably never know. In the village you became accustomed to secrets.

The priest leaned back, savouring the cool little breeze that reached them through the open terrace doors at the end of the long

33

sitting-room. The room, with its stone walls, old tiled floor and beamed ceiling, was sparsely furnished with the sideboard, sofa, bookshelves, a few chairs and the table before the fireplace where they were sitting. By the window stood a large table that served as a desk, now completely covered by writer's paraphernalia.

'How's the chronicle coming along?' asked the priest, nodding towards a faded blue folder on the desk.

'I read it in one sitting on Sunday. I couldn't put it down. Let me know if you want it back.'

'Keep it as long as you want. I don't need it.'

'I've already started a rough translation of it.'

'Oh? What about your own book?'

'The one on the Middle East is already outdated. As for the thriller, it's over there,' Michael nodded to the rubbish bin. 'I'm toying with the idea of doing something with the chronicle now, even though I haven't much time left. How long have you had it?'

'Oh, years. It was in a box of books that belonged to my predecessor, whose hobby was local history. I haven't read it for a long time, but it's obviously a translation from much older French. I seem to recall somebody telling me a copy of it was in the Bibliothèque Nationale in Paris. It's a well-known source for studies of the plague.'

'It's the only first-hand account of the plague I've ever read, except Boccaccio's *Decameron*, of course. I read Froissart's *Chronicle* at school, but he doesn't even mention the plague, which has always puzzled historians. This is the best-known chronicler of the time.'

'He was more interested in the war between the English and French, I recall. It's interesting, isn't it, Michael? Here you are, an Englishman in France, studying John Stratton's chronicle. The two of you have a lot in common, when you think about it. You've retreated to Roquelaire after being wounded in combat in a way, just as he did.'

'Maybe that's why I'm so taken with it. That, and because it's about the plague years, which are now a blank history. It's a period that has always fascinated me. I don't know if you noticed it, but there are a striking number of parallels between 1348 and the present in Roquelaire.'

'I hope that doesn't mean we're going to be visited by another plague,' the priest joked.

'Not that so much, but there are people living in this village who had real counterparts then, more than six hundred years ago. Reading the chronicle, I had the uncanny feeling that the wheel of time had turned full circle and that they had all reassembled here.'

'Now that's interesting,' the priest said, suppressing a yawn. 'I'll have to reread it to find out if I resemble anybody.'

'You can take your pick. Roquelaire was crawling with priests and abbots.' Observing him, Michael transposed the rugged strength of the priest's face to a far-off century.

'Well, if you're going to assign me a counterpart, please choose the best one to represent me, will you? Not one who embodies all the rampant licentiousness of the age, but one who liked fishing. That's how I see myself,' he said, making Michael laugh. 'And, of course, you're John Stratton.'

'As you said, he and I have something in common, though I'm not a soldier. But I am a writer of sorts.' Michael saw Père Auguste was amused.

'You're a journalist, and a very fine one, judging by what I've heard.'

Michael glanced again at the blue folder on his desk, wondering if it had the power to awaken him from a long summer of self-indulgent days that had slowly melted one into another.

'Well,' said Père Auguste, 'I ought to be going before the wheel of time turns full circle on me and it's tomorrow.'

'The wheel of history always turns full circle, but not usually before our eyes.'

Rising from his chair, the priest said, 'It sounds as if you're going to make a fortune by turning this spare little chronicle into a blockbuster. You won't forget your friends, will you, when the royalties arrive, and the church still needs a new roof?'

Michael laughed. 'No, I won't forget. A new roof it is. I'm sorry I'm too late to help much with the other restoration work.'

'That's all right. The Society for Historic Monuments took care of that, but we can't ask a second time.'

Michael walked the priest to the door. 'Come back during the week to finish the game.'

'I'll try. I'll be a real bachelor soon: Odette is taking her annual holiday and that means I have to fend for myself a bit.'

'You're not taking your usual retreat to Assisi?'

'How can I, with all these tourists wanting to see the church?'

As Michael watched him walk down the dimly lit street, the church bell struck eleven, with the same hollow cadence that had disturbed the peace for centuries.

# Chapter 3

The next morning Rachel came downstairs at nine o'clock. She had awoken in the night to hear the church bell tolling the hours, and had then drifted in and out of an uneasy doze. Feeling fragile and lost, she went to the terrace. The students had gravitated with their easels to the other end of the garden, where they were preparing to begin the first composition of the day. The dappled shadows on the blue and white china, and the bowl of summer fruit looked like a composition for a still life on the table set for one.

'Hi there,' said a voice behind her. 'We thought you'd sleep until noon.'

Rachel looked up at Ted, his scrubbed, cheerful face, his brusque but kind manner reminded her of a male orderly in a hospital.

'I'll bring some fresh coffee. There's orange juice, and croissants are in the basket. I'll bring the butter out too. If I leave it here, it melts within minutes. *Café au lait?*'

'Yes, thank you,' said Rachel. Her mouth moved in a smile that seemed unnatural, even to herself.

Ted had just set down the coffee when Rosamund came through the house.

'Good morning,' said Rachel.

'Good morning,' Rosamund replied with a smile. She looked down at Rachel through big dark glasses. She was wearing jeans, a baggy white shirt and a straw hat, and her paints were stuffed into a canvas bag slung over her arm. As she took off her glasses and their eyes met, Rachel could tell that she knew everything. It occurred to her that there were few secrets in the little painting group, that they soon knew all there was to know about each other. Remembering yesterday, she wondered if even the priest had known

37

her predicament before she had, and the old lady with the rabbit outside the town; perhaps even the concierge in the hotel.

'Ted, I'd love another cup of coffee, if I may,' said Rosamund, sitting across from Rachel.

'Sure thing.' He disappeared tactfully.

'How are you this morning?' Rosamund asked.

'If you want to know the truth, I feel awful.'

'You overheard what that friend of Ted and Bob's said, didn't you?'

'Yes, I overheard,' she said, sipping the hot, strong coffee, which helped quell the churning in her stomach.

'Bob thought you did. When I asked him where you'd gone so suddenly, he told me what had happened. He was very upset you'd found out like that. I'm so sorry. We've only just met, but I can imagine what you must be going through.'

'I feel like such an idiot. It's obvious that everyone but me knew what's been going on from the minute I arrived in the village. Twenty-four hours ago I thought I knew who I was and where my life was going. And now it's as if I've been cut in two. I'm breathing, I'm alive, but everything else has gone dead. Here I am with a group of people I've just met who probably know more about my life than I do.'

'It only seems that way. I gathered your husband has become involved in a situation that is very public in the village.' Rosamund thought for a moment. 'Look, maybe it's not as bad as it sounds. When I talked to Bob last night I couldn't help feeling that a large element of all this was just gossip. You know how people talk in a small town like this.'

'Yes, but will you tell me what you've heard, even if it is just gossip?'

'Of course, but it's not much. Your husband knows a woman called Isabelle de Montjoi, who lives on a big domaine outside Roquelaire. He's been seen in the village with her several times.'

'But I know her!' Last night Rachel had been so confused that the name hadn't registered, but now she remembered Isabelle clearly. 'She came to our restaurant last summer with a French party touring the vineyards of Sonoma.' The adrenalin shot through

Rachel. Suddenly she was alert. 'Excuse me, but it's falling into place. My husband mentioned to me a few months ago that she had introduced him to people who could help with the locations in his book, but that was the last I heard. Do you mean he's been visiting her here?'

'It seems so. Do you know the Château Brissac at the entrance to the village?' Rachel nodded. 'Bob told me last night that the owner died recently and Isabelle was expecting him to leave the château to her. Apparently the whole village is talking because he left it to some old woman who raises rabbits. Imagine! As I understand it, Isabelle was planning to turn the place into a very grand complex centred on a spa. I hate to think of what it would do to this little place, although the village itself seems to be divided on the issue. But then the will was read, and the bombshell dropped and I don't know what's happening now.'

'Would you have any idea where my husband and son are? That's what's really upsetting me – to find they've vanished into thin air.'

'Bob might know something. I dropped out of the conversation at that point. I only arrived here yesterday.'

'Of course,' said Rachel. 'Do you know how the man I overheard talking last night fits in?'

'Julian Paine is his name. I talked to him for a while when you'd gone. He's a property developer who represents English interests, people who are going to invest capital in developing the project. Something on that scale is going to cost a lot of money and I'm sure it needs important backers. I can kiss goodbye to my quiet painting holidays for the next few years if it all goes through.'

'Where does Alain fit in all this?' Rachel asked. 'I don't understand.'

'Apparently people in the village have been saying that he will be the chef and Isabelle de Montjoi's partner in the hotel enterprise.'

Rachel fell silent. The idea that Alain would do such a thing without consulting her was incomprehensible. The sunny terrace seemed to go dark as she remembered Isabelle de Montjoi's visit to Sonoma the summer before. Strikingly attractive, she exuded an aura of what Rachel had always regarded as French sophistication.

One by one she remembered the details: her clothes, which were dramatic and original; her not-so-slim but voluptuous figure; her inquisitive, interested expression as she spoke in rapid French and fluent English; and now, more important in retrospect, her unconcealed interest in the restaurant and every detail about it. The jealousy that Rachel was always careful to hide when Alain preened in front of an attractive woman had dissolved when she sensed how much he enjoyed speaking his own language. For the first time she could remember, he had become almost nostalgic about France. It had seemed such an important meeting for him that she had failed to notice if there were sparks of attraction between him and Isabelle de Montjoi. Rachel supposed that this affair must have begun almost immediately, which explained all the trips Alain had made to New York and abroad after meeting Isabelle. She understood the significance of the postcard and the airline reservation.

Now that she faced the probable truth, Rachel's mind had cleared somewhat and a new calm descended on her.

Rosamund was looking at her in sympathetic silence. Rachel realized she must voice the question to which she already suspected the answer.

'Tell me the truth. Have you heard that my husband is having an affair with this woman?'

Rosamund hesitated. 'I can only tell you that Bob told me people have been talking. But then they would, wouldn't they? That doesn't necessarily mean it's true.'

'I wish I could believe that.'

'If you want my advice, don't believe anything until you've talked to your husband.'

'If I can find him.' Articulating these words, Rachel thought of Oliver. She had a sudden intense longing to be with him that made her ache inside. 'From what I overheard last night, he and Oliver will be here by Wednesday.'

'Rachel, we hardly know each other, but I can't help thinking if you want to keep your marriage together, you have to ignore any gossip you hear until your husband has had a chance to explain himself. Only then should you decide whether you believe him, or whether you want to believe him. It amounts to the same thing.'

Looking at Rosamund, Rachel realized she must be speaking from experience. She deferred the question of whether she was capable of ignoring deception or forgiving it.

'At this moment, really, the only thing that concerns me is finding my son. I'm acutely aware that I'm in a foreign country. Alain is French and he has Oliver's passport.'

'That's something you'll have to tackle when the time comes. Are you worried your husband might be trying to take your son away?'

'It has crossed my mind, but quite honestly I can't even take it in. It's too unreal to contemplate.'

Just then Bob Cooper walked on to the terrace. He stopped when he saw Rachel. 'Good morning. How are you?' he said to her with an embarrassed smile.

Rachel looked up at him, glad to see embarrassment, not pity, on his face. 'I'm all right,' she replied, not knowing what to say.

Rosamund said solemnly, 'Rachel knows, Bob. She put two and two together from what your friend said last night.'

'Oh God,' Bob muttered, pressing his hand to his head. 'I was afraid of that. Believe me, Rachel, I'm deeply sorry that you should come to my house and this should happen. That damn Julian. He's got such a big mouth.'

'You're very kind, but it's much better to know about it if something is going on.' Rachel didn't want to elaborate on the compulsion that had driven her to Roquelaire in the first place. Looking Bob in the eye, she said, 'Do you remember exactly what your friend said last night about my husband and son staying in Paris *en route* to Roquelaire? I want to make sure I heard correctly.'

Bob looked at her with a pained expression. 'Yes, he mentioned that they'd be back by Wednesday. Julian's a business associate of Isabelle and he's waiting to see her. I gather your husband and son are supposed to be staying at her house outside the village.'

'Well,' said Rachel, putting down her coffee cup. 'I suppose I'd better get moving and try to find out exactly what's going on.'

'Why don't you just relax today and have lunch with us here?'

'I really have to do something with myself or I'll go crazy. If you don't mind, I think I'd be better off alone.'

Rosamund patted her hand sympathetically. 'That's right. Go have a good think. We're here if you want company.'

It occurred to Rachel that she was lucky to be so warmly received in the painting school. Stumbling on the truth in a gloomy hotel room would have made the situation unbearable. Seeing the students working at their easels against the backdrop of the sunfilled garden, she said, 'Well, I guess the next question that remains to be asked is, may I stay here until my husband comes back?'

'Ted and I would be very upset if you didn't. If there's anything we can do to help, we'd be only too happy. If you'd like to read, there are several shady nooks in the garden and there are lots of books and magazines in the library. Just consider yourself our guest.'

'I really don't know how I can thank you,' said Rachel. It was on the tip of her tongue to remark how much it would please her to repay his hospitality if ever they were in California when she realized that Chez Alain and the life that went with it might be in the process of disintegrating as she spoke. She stood resolutely. 'I think what I really want to do is explore the village and to a bit of thinking. I hope I haven't kept you from your work.'

Rosamund said drily, 'I think the world will keep turning if I don't do another watercolour.'

'Oh, come on now, Rosamund. Why so gloomy? You're on the verge of really discovering yourself this summer. I feel it,' Bob exclaimed.

Rosamund rose reluctantly and looked at her watch. 'Yes, perhaps if I could spend the whole summer here in this lovely green cocoon with everything laid on for me, I might unlock the genius buried deep in my soul.'

Hearing her laugh, Rachel thought how true it was. Bob and Ted had created a paradise in this remote corner of France; but she was not fated to enjoy a moment of it.

Rachel left Bob Cooper's and walked up the Rue Cazat through the cool shadows, then turned at random down another street. The aroma of fresh coffee drifted through an open window where a woman was watering geraniums on a ledge. She saw a young mother pushing a pram across a threshold. Another ordinary day was beginning in Roquelaire, making Rachel conscious of the precarious state of her own existence. For the first few moments she felt utterly lost at being so far from familiar surroundings in a crisis, but soon the sights and sounds of a French village in summer brought on a painful sense of nostalgia, as she recalled her past love for everything French. She heard dogs barking, women scolding their children, and a radio playing a romantic ballad by Jacques Brel that summoned up a time when she was so much younger and a carefree student.

At the end of an hour's walk Rachel's energy had come back and her gloom had begun to lift, but when she passed two women huddled in whispers on a door-step, she relived in a painful instant the full shock of the night before. She walked on, conscious that her moment of escape was over and that she would have to start planning what she was going to do. A sudden break between two houses revealed a field of sunflowers shimmering in the morning sun, reminding her of Alain. She had always imagined that her first walk through a Gascon village would be with him and Oliver.

Trying to imagine where they were and what they were doing was more than she could bear. The thought of Alain with another woman while Oliver tagged along upset Rachel so deeply that she began to shake. Hugging her arms to her chest, she stood in a patch of sun on a street corner and regained control of herself. She was a fighter by nature, she argued with herself, imagining a confrontation with Alain.

She ended up back at the church in the square, where she glanced at the intricate sculptures over the door. The Romanesque façade had a primitive beauty that seemed far closer to nature and to God than the cold granite symmetry of northern churches. She pushed open the heavy door and went in. She heard her own footsteps resound against the startling interior, frescoed in bright jewel-like colours. The vaulted ceiling was a deep blue, painted with misshapen stars that had the naïve charm of a child's drawing. Looking around, Rachel couldn't detect a single reminder of death or damnation, and she found a sense of refuge and peace in the coolness and silence.

The roses on the altar, the snowy white altar cloth and the scent of beeswax told her that the church of Roquelaire was lovingly tended. She walked a few steps to a side chapel, attracted by an extraordinary statue of St Anne, the patron saint of mothers, set above the altar. It was made of wood and was remarkably lifelike. Dressed in a light-blue gown stamped with silver stars, the little saint had a pale, smooth face as pretty as an antique doll, and had obviously been groomed, repainted and cared for by generations of worshippers. The votive candles were reflected in her black eyes and her lips were parted in a reassuring smile. Rachel reached in her bag for some coins and put them in the candle box: then lit a candle and placed it on the highest spindle. As it blazed, she let its flickering light take the place of thoughts.

When Michael Lowry entered the church he was surprised to see a woman, whom he could tell at a distance was foreign, in the chapel, her head bowed. Tourists often came to the church to study its remarkable interior, but they seldom came to pray. He walked down the nave noiselessly in his rubber-soled shoes, feeling he was intruding, when she turned to stare curiously at him. Her direct, challenging eyes caused him to register all the details about her, from her sun-streaked hair swept to one side with a comb to the suggestion of her lithe figure beneath a loose-fitting jacket and trousers.

Michael stopped to study a column, which was why he had come. That morning he had had a sudden urge to look more closely at the sculptures, which were vivid images of medieval life, suggesting that seven centuries ago the sculptor had used the citizens of Roquelaire as his models.

He glanced over his shoulder and saw that the woman was still in the chapel. Continuing to browse, he found his attention wandering back to her profile, haloed by the votive candles. He was suddenly curious about who she was and what she was doing there. From the corner of his eye, he saw her begin to move down the nave, accompanied by the sound of quickening footsteps. Impulsively, he strode after her out into the brilliant sunshine, where he expected to see her crossing the busy market-place, but

44

she had vanished. He was surprised that she had gone, then distinctly disappointed, which made him wonder whether a summer of solitude had driven him to follow strange women in churches. He walked away, considering what he could possibly have said to her had they met, and why it should matter to him.

When Rachel left the church, she was in a hurry not to waste another moment, and she dashed across the square to the newsagent, where she bought a detailed map of the area around Roquelaire. She tapped her foot impatiently as a Dutchman emptied his pocket of coins to pay for a newspaper. Leaving the newsagent, she walked quickly back to Bob Cooper's.

Ted was making preparations for lunch in the big, sunny kitchen lined with saucepans, colourful pottery and baskets hanging from the ceiling stuffed with dried herbs and flowers. It was the kitchen of a devoted cook, where every surface was crammed with paraphernalia. A cauldron simmering on the back of the old-fashioned black stove filled the kitchen with an aroma redolent of the harvest of summer.

'Hi there. Have a good walk?' he asked with a grin.

'Yes, thank you. It was exactly what I needed to clear my head.'

'Glad to hear it. I always say the air here is as good as champagne. Want some coffee or a cup of tea? Or even a glass of *rouge* or *blanc* if you're so inclined.'

'No, thanks.' Rachel watched him dump a pile of onions into a huge frying pan generously awash with olive oil. 'I'm wondering if you could tell me how to get to Isabelle de Montjoi's house?'

Ted shot her a look, the wooden spoon suspended in mid-air.

Rachel smiled. 'Look, don't worry. I'm not intending to storm out there and make a scene, if that's what you're thinking. All I want to do is see if I can confirm when she'll be back and whether my husband will be with her. More important, I'm terribly anxious to see my son.'

'Of course,' he exclaimed with evident relief. 'I'd feel exactly the same in your position. Here,' he said, wiping his hands on his apron, 'come in the study and I'll draw you a map. I should warn you, the front gates might be locked if she's away. It's a very impressive house, though Bob and I have never been invited there. Just between you and me, it's not really my taste. Too fussy. It's called Terre Blanche.'

Driving from Roquelaire, Rachel found the road marked on the map, which turned out to be a shady country lane lined with scrub oak. Passing a rundown farm with geese penned outside, she wondered if she was anywhere near the spot where Alain had grown up. He had said the place was in ruins, but she decided to go in search of it later, almost believing it would reveal the workings of his mind.

The woods became thicker and she came upon a high stone wall that obviously protected an important estate. A pair of wrought-iron gates standing ajar told her she had arrived at Isabelle de Montjoi's property, confirmed by the sign: Domaine Terre Blanche. Peering through the gates overhung by towering cedar trees, Rachel's eyes followed the white gravel drive to a stone mansion of the type built by country gentry during the previous century. Impulsively, she swung the car through the gates, half expecting to be pursued by a pack of baying mastiffs. She slowed down, taking in the full view of the cream stone house. Built on a raised foundation, the façade seemed composed of innumerable tall, grey-shuttered windows. The wide balcony terrace spanning the front was reached by a staircase flanked with an ornate metal railing. The wheels of the car crunched on the gravel as she rounded an oval pool banked with bright red and yellow cannas. She got out of the car and looked round at the tree-filled park singing with cicadas, noting the arcaded *pigeonnier* in the distance, which looked as if it were a guesthouse, and the hint of a swimming pool beneath a sloping bank of grass at the back. A suffocating sense of hurt came over her at the thought that Alain had been here long before she had.

She slammed the car door to announce her arrival and, when there was no sign of movement, walked up the steps towards a heavy door set with glass protected by a wrought-iron grille. Her stomach fluttered nervously as she rang the doorbell, but there was no reply. Ringing it more insistently a second time, she glanced around, wondering whether Alain had ever walked along the terrace, where pots dripped with jasmine, and orange trees grew in white

46

tubs. She pictured him sitting at the white table in an intimate tête-à-tête with Isabelle de Montjoi, in the shade of the overhanging eaves. The glamorous chatelaine of Terre Blanche, whose kingdom this was, had a taste for old-world luxury that seemed a far cry from Alain's love of sleek modernity.

Abruptly, the glass door behind the grille flew open and Rachel found herself looking into the wary dark eyes of a prim little housekeeper. Her sharp face and pointed nose recalled a bird keeping watch over a clutch of eggs.

Up to now Rachel had spoken French well enough, but she stumbled before she got the phrase out correctly. '*Est-ce que* Madame de Montjoi *est chez elle?*'

'*Non,*' the reply shot out. '*Madame n'est pas là.*'

The housekeeper was looking at her suspiciously. Now that she had discovered the intruder wasn't French, she peered over her shoulder at the parked car in the drive, as if she had been ordered to memorize the number, a thought that amused Rachel, reminding her of the fierce breed of female concierges she had known in her time.

'*Quand est ce qu'elle sera de retour?*' This time she managed to reel off the words in the proper order.

'*Dans la soirée, Mercredi.*'

'*Elle est à Paris?*'

'*Oui, je pense,*' she said after a pause, as if she disapproved of Rachel's questions.

'*Est-ce q'il y a un garçon Américain ici?*'

'*Non, il vient demain avec son père.*'

The relief Rachel felt at this confirmation that Oliver would soon be there was instantaneous.

'*Votre nom, je vous prie?*'

'*Ça n'a pas d'importance.*' Rachel reached in her purse and took out a note she had written. '*C'est pour* Monsieur Ribard.'

'*Ah,* Monsieur Ribard. *Je vais faire la commission.*'

Rachel felt herself go cold, for she realized without a doubt that the woman knew Alain.

She sensed the housekeeper's beady eyes watching her through the glass as she drove away. She was shaking all over, as if she had done something dangerous, but she had made the all-important discovery that Oliver was due to arrive on Wednesday. She would have to wait another day to find out the truth.

*

Just before noon Michael returned to the square and walked through the crowded aisles, where the market vendors were starting to pack up their wares. He savoured the warm air spiced with the aroma of ripe melons, cheese and garlic, and stopped to greet some farmers he knew, distinguished by their strong sun-tanned arms and ruddy faces beneath black berets. They spoke French with a rolling Gascon accent, but when he walked on, they resumed speaking the patois that owed more to Spanish than French. Michael passed a number of tall, fair Europeans, incongruous among the stocky, black-eyed local people, who had the blood of Romans, Visigoths, and Moors in their veins. He was about to leave the market, when he saw Agnès Grimal loading cages of unsold rabbits on a cart hitched to an ancient bicycle.

'*Bonjour*, Madame Grimal,' he said. '*Vous allez bien?*'

'*Ah, bonjour,*' she said with a smile. '*Ça va, merci. Et vous? Vous allez mieux, maintenant?*'

He assured her that he had completely recovered his health as a result of the food and excellent climate of Roquelaire.

'*C'était bon, le marché?*' he asked.

'*Pas mal, pas mal. J'ai vendu quelques petits, sauf lui.*' She pointed to an enormous buck rabbit that had failed to find a buyer, making him laugh.

Michael looked into Agnès's bright dark eyes set in a weathered face, remembering what Père Auguste had said. He realized how much older than her years she seemed, something in the sweet innocence of her expression seemed to have passed unscathed from childhood. It was the first time he had spoken to her since Armand Bataille's legacy had become known, but he didn't intend to embarrass her by mentioning it. It had made her the richest woman in the village, with the exception of Isabelle de Montjoi.

He bought a newspaper, walked to the café and sat down under

48

an umbrella in the sun. When he unfurled the paper, the headlines about the Middle East gave him a momentary yearning to be back in the centre of events, but his nostalgia quickly passed. He looked up at the blue sky overhead, preferring to forget that in less than a month he would be back in London. Putting down the paper, he looked round the square, which was fast emptying. The image of the woman standing, head bowed, in the chapel of St Anne had stayed in his mind, but he saw no sign of her.

'*Ça va*, Monsieur Lowry?'

The owner of the café was standing beside him, tray in hand, a harassed expression on his face.

'*Ça va, merci*, Claude. *Et toi?*'

'*Ça va*, but I can't take the heat,' he said, wiping his brow. 'I wish I could close in August,' he added with a shrug, nodding to the tables crowded with sunburnt tourists. '*Un pression?*'

When Claude had gone, Michael watched a bus stop in front of the church to deliver a group of tourists, causing chaos in the square. The party of Belgians jostled past a group of foot pilgrims in sturdy shoes, who leaned on their staffs as they consulted their guidebooks in front of the renowned Romanesque church. Michael could find no resemblance whatsoever between these enthusiastic walkers and the medieval pilgrims in Père Auguste's chronicle, who had passed through Roquelaire on the way to the shrine of Santiago de Compostela. He imagined them, centuries ago, exhausted from the journey but steeped in piety, as they strode through the square in their heavy cloaks and distinctive wide-brimmed hats sewn with the emblem of St James, the cockleshell. Michael studied the brick-and-timber houses, that had survived intact since the Middle Ages, trying to reconstruct what Roquelaire had been like in the plague year. His train of thought was shattered by the squeaking of the postcard rack behind his chair.

'Henrietta . . .' an Englishwoman shouted to her companion, 'you must come and have a look at these. Let's sit in the sun and write a few cards while we have a kir . . .'

Michael nodded to the waiter delivering his beer and let the Middle Ages slip from his grasp.

\*

Returning to Roquelaire, Rachel parked her car off the market square, where the shops were now closing. She wandered past a *brocante* shop, a dress shop, a pharmacy, feeling utterly aimless but determined not to spend the next day and a half in a state of nervous anxiety.

It was just past noon and time had begun to crawl already. She walked through the sunny square to the café with the red and white umbrellas, where she had sat the night before.

When she sat down and ordered a Coke, a man reading an English paper at the next table looked up. Their eyes met for a moment, and she sensed he was observing her with more than casual interest. She found herself looking back, registering all the details about him. He had strong, regular features, an expressive mouth and intelligent light-blue eyes set in a tanned face. The shock of brown hair that brushed his sunglasses was peppered with grey, and she guessed he was in his early forties. Something about him seemed to invite conversation. She surprised herself by saying, 'Do we know each other?'

'No, but I think I saw you this morning in the church.'

'Oh, the church. It's incredible, isn't it? The interior took me by surprise when I walked through the doors. I've never seen anything like it.'

'The interior is something very special,' he agreed. 'Even better than Moissac.'

'I've never been to Moissac. Is it very beautiful?'

'Yes, but there are plenty of lesser-known churches, like Roquelaire, that are just as interesting in their way.'

Her first few words had told him she was American and as he removed his sunglasses he took a good look at her. Michael liked her face and the brown hair that had a sort of fire in it, and something in him responded to the expression in her deep-blue eyes. Her preoccupied air had vanished in the bright sunlight. Automatically, his eyes dipped to her left hand and he saw she was wearing a wedding ring.

'You're not part of the art class run by Bob Cooper, are you? Of course you're not, or you wouldn't be here now – you'd be painting.'

The waiter brought her drink.

'You're not far off,' she said, pleased to have someone to talk to. 'I'm staying at Bob Cooper's. When I couldn't get a room in the hotel yesterday, he was kind enough to take me in.'

Michael shook his head. 'There was a time when you could get a room in the hotel without booking, but not any more.'

'Really? Are you staying here?'

'I have a house in a street off the square. What about you? Are you on holiday?'

'Not exactly.' She paused a moment, wondering what to tell him. 'I'm supposed to be meeting my husband and son here,' she said, offering no more. The Englishman seemed charming and her evasiveness made her feel awkward. It crossed her mind that perhaps he, like everyone else, might know who she was.

'Did a priest put you in touch with Bob, by any chance?' Michael asked, remembering what Père Auguste had said last night.

'Yes, as a matter of fact he did. How did you know?'

'Now it all fits. I saw him yesterday evening and he mentioned it to me.' He looked at her more closely now he knew she was the wife of Alain Ribard.

'What a small world,' she answered, thinking how fast news travelled in Roquelaire. 'You know the priest, then?'

'If you live here long enough, you know just about everyone.'

'Yes I suppose you do. Does that mean you've been coming here long?'

'For about seven or eight years, it must be.'

'Then you know Bob Cooper?'

'Good Lord, yes. Bob's a local institution. He was here long before I was.'

'Are you about to become an institution too?' asked Rachel.

Michael laughed. 'I certainly hope not. Normally, I'm just here for a few weeks, but this year I've been here since Easter, recovering from an accident. I'm a journalist.'

She raised her eyebrows. From where she sat, Michael looked

51

perfectly fit. But observing him more closely, she noticed a hollow-ness about his eyes, a somewhat haunted look that was not unattrac-tive. She wondered if perhaps it was boredom.

'I'm almost back to normal now. The doctors ordered me to rest for six months, and that will be up in September.'

'What happened exactly?'

'I was on a story and got myself into a pickle in Beirut. There was some shooting and a car accident and I was invalided out to London eventually, where I spent a month in hospital.'

'But you're all right now?'

'More or less. I broke a leg, some ribs. Had a lung punctured. I've had to learn to live life in a lower gear. This is certainly the place to live quietly: it's ideal for all the books I haven't managed to write.'

Rachel laughed. She leaned back and looked at the sun-drenched square. It was beautiful, but it was quiet. 'You must be going stir crazy here.'

Michael smiled indulgently. 'It might seem so, and it's true that when I started feeling better I wondered what I was going to do with myself. I took the classic journalist's route and decided to write a thriller.'

'A good way to fill the time, I imagine.'

'As it turned out, it wasn't. I've given it up.'

'So soon?' He didn't look the sort of man to give up on anything easily.

'It was something I always wanted to do, but regarding it in the cold light of day, I had to admit to myself that it was rubbish.'

Rachel was amused by his frankness. 'So now you're back to reading thrillers instead of writing them, I presume?'

'By chance, last week, when I was casting about wondering what to do, Père Auguste – that's the priest you met – gave me a chronicle of Roquelaire in the fourteenth century. I've only just read it, but I've been seriously considering trying to shape it into some kind of book.' Michael waited for her reaction, surprised at himself for chatting so easily about the subject with a perfect stranger.

'Have you decided what form it will take?' She leaned forward with interest, glad to get her mind off herself.

52

'I don't really know yet. Probably a novel loosely based on the truth. Of course, it's only in the idea stage, really something to occupy what's left of my time here.'

'I'm ashamed to say I'm not quite sure what a chronicle is exactly.'

'It's simply a narrative of historical events, written without any interpretation. This particular one was written by an Englishman by the name of John Stratton.'

'An Englishman? Something to do with the Hundred Years War between the English and the French, I imagine.'

Michael looked pleased. 'I see you know your history.'

'It's only because I happened to read a very good account of it a few years ago and it stayed in my mind,' she said, remembering how she had wanted to know more about Gascony because of Alain, in the days when she had harboured romantic notions about his roots. 'What is the chronicle about? Tell me; I'm very interested.'

'It was written in the plague year. Six hundred and forty-three years ago, probably almost to the very day, the plague was making its way from Marseille to this village, decimating everyone in its wake.'

'How terrible. Did everyone in Roquelaire die?'

'Many did, yes, but no one knows how many. The account stops abruptly and there is no record of what happened to the writer. He, along with all the inhabitants, sealed themselves off from the world, hoping to escape the plague within the walls of the château just outside the village.'

When he told her something of Brissac's history, she said, 'The Château Brissac? How incredible.'

'The man who owned it died a few weeks ago and it's empty now. He left it quite unexpectedly to an old woman named Agnès Grimal, who lives in a cottage as you approach the village by the road that passes the château.'

Rachel nodded.

'Do you know her?' he asked, surprised.

'Not exactly. I nearly drove into her when I arrived yesterday. She darted right in front of the car, chasing a rabbit.'

'That's Agnès all right. Now you say it, I think Père Auguste mentioned it to me.'

She said casually, 'I heard at Bob Cooper's that they're thinking of turning the château into an hotel.'

Michael was surprised that she seemed to have been totally in the dark about her husband's plans. 'It seems to have run into problems. But I'm not the person to ask; I'm only here temporarily.'

'Who should I ask, then?'

She was looking at him anxiously, which made Michael aware that beneath her composed exterior Mrs Ribard was in turmoil.

The church bell struck one and Rachel realized that nearly an hour had gone by. Reluctantly, she stood up to go.

'It's been great talking to you, but I've just remembered there's something I must do. I didn't realize it was so late.'

'What a shame. I was just going to offer you another drink. I'm afraid you got me on one of my favourite subjects – local history. I hope I didn't bore you.'

'No, you didn't bore me at all. On the contrary,' she said.

Michael rose from his chair. 'I haven't even introduced myself. I'm Michael Lowry.'

'And I'm Rachel Ribard,' she said, offering him her hand. He showed no sign of knowing the significance of her name.

An impulse overtook Michael not to let Rachel disappear a second time. 'When did you say you were meeting your husband?'

She hesitated, thinking that if he were to meet Bob Cooper he was bound to hear the truth about her, if he didn't already know.

'Oh, I'm not sure exactly. There's been some mix-up. Perhaps tomorrow.'

'I realize we hardly know each other, but if you're on your own, maybe you'd like to have dinner at my house this evening.'

'Dinner?' The unexpected invitation took Rachel by surprise. Her first thought was that it wasn't the right time to be having dinner with a man she had just met; but, thinking about the time she had to kill and how knowledgeable Michael Lowry was, she said, 'Yes, I'd like that very much. I'd like to hear more about the village.'

'Splendid. I live up the street on the corner, by the church, the Rue St Jacques. It's at the end, the last house on the right – the one with shutters and a handbell outside. Come any time after seven. My terrace is the perfect spot for viewing a spectacular sunset.' He grinned at her, absurdly pleased that she had accepted his invitation.

'I'll look forward to it. Goodbye until then,' she said.

Rachel walked away with a hunch she had met someone she could trust. Debating whether she should be open with him, she decided that Michael Lowry had been in the village long enough to know everything that was going on and he might be able to shed some light on the situation. She went back to the car feeling as if the cloud she had been living under had begun to disperse. She resolved to use the time wisely so that when at last she and Alain were face to face, she would be armed with the truth.

She drove through the hot, shuttered streets, out of the village to the faded blue cottage in the shade of chestnut trees. Opening the little metal gate, she walked up the path bright with flowers hearing the sound of two women chattering coming from the open door.

'I'll pick a kilo of green beans for Sunday. Pascale is so fond of them, and there's nothing better with roast beef.'

'And we'll finish with a gâteau Basques.'

'You're right. This is her day and everything should be just as she likes it.'

Hesitant to interrupt what seemed a family conversation, Rachel called, *'Est ce qu'il y a quelqu'un?'*

At the sound of her voice Agnès came out, wiping her hands on her apron. She looked entirely different without her hat, her wispy greying hair pinned into a bun at the nape of her neck.

*'Mais, c'est l'Américaine! Bonjour, madame. Entrez, entrez.'*

*'Bonjour Mesdames,'* Rachel replied, warmed by the older women's friendliness. She stepped across the threshold of the kitchen and into the past. A blackened pot bubbling over an open fire emitted the sweet aroma of apricot jam. A scrubbed table surrounded by straw-bottomed chairs was covered with jam jars. Herbs hung from the blackened beams and the floor was laid with uneven tiles polished over time to a glossy burgundy. A fresh baguette stood on a chair next to a sleeping cat.

'May I present my sister, Madame Gachpour. This is Madame Ribard.'

Rachel introduced herself and they shook hands. If the name Ribard meant anything to Madame Gachpour, she gave no sign. 'I'm sorry to disturb you.'

'Not at all,' said Agnès.

'I drop by every day to deliver bread from the bakery,' Madame Gachpour added.

'My sister and her husband keep the bakery on the corner near the market,' explained Agnès. 'We're discussing my niece's homecoming this weekend. She's just taken a diploma in accountancy in Bordeaux. She speaks English very well.' The pride in her voice was unmistakable and her black eyes sparkled with enthusiasm. 'She passed with the highest marks, but I wasn't surprised at all.'

Madame Gachpour laughed and blushed, obviously embarrassed by Agnès's uninhibited praise of her daughter.

'There's a picture of her,' she said, nodding towards the mantelpiece.

Leaning towards it, Rachel couldn't believe that the striking girl with a mane of platinum hair was Madame Gachpour's daughter. 'Isn't she beautiful – *très, très belle*,' she commented.

'*Oui, c'est vrai, elle est belle,*' affirmed Agnès.

Madame Gachpour said goodbye and left. After Rachel had tactfully declined the offer of a cold drink, she said hesitantly, '*Madame*, I was told in the village that you are the chatelaine of the Château Brissac.' The word chatelaine came automatically to her lips, for her it had romantic medieval connotations, but it didn't seem to suit the wiry, greying Agnès Grimal.

Agnès looked wary, and for a moment Rachel wondered if she had offended her.

'*Oui, c'est vrai.*'

'I hope I am not imposing, but could I please have your permission to walk round it?' As their eyes met, Rachel felt for a moment as if Agnès Grimal understood exactly why she wanted to go there.

'By all means. Feel free to go inside the courtyard and look around if you like. The only person living there is an old man, the caretaker, Monsieur David. If you see him, tell him I sent you.'

'I'm very grateful to you. It means a lot to me.' No explanation was necessary, but Rachel wished she could tell Agnès the reason for her visit. She had to conquer a strong urge to ask whether the old woman knew if it was true that Alain and Isabelle were partners in a hotel venture and what she intended to do now she was the new owner, but Rachel was not ready to take another stranger into her confidence.

As Rachel walked out the door Agnès said, 'You are the first person to ask to see the château. You see, I haven't been the proprietress very long.' Her eyes softened and Rachel realized that Madame Grimal didn't mind her request at all. In fact, it seemed to please her. Agnès continued, 'If you would like to see the inside sometime, I would be happy to show it to you. It has an interesting history.'

'I wouldn't want to trouble you. For the moment I'd be very happy just to look around the outside.'

They said goodbye, and in a few minutes Rachel was driving slowly down a gravelled road with the château in sight. She parked the car near the entrance and got out. In the village she had bought a little guidebook, which she now removed from her bag. She found a paragraph about the château and read it as she studied the façade. Built in the early fourteenth century for the reputed bastard of a French pope, it was rumoured to harbour a buried papal treasure. There was a brief mention of the plague year and the terrible calamity that had occurred behind its walls, echoing what Michael Lowry had told her. The stone rectangle, pierced with transom windows and set with towers at opposite ends, commanded the entire valley. The western face was cut by an arched portico, where Rachel supposed the drawbridge had once passed across the moat, which was now dry. Behind the château, high walls enclosed a small hamlet, where empty windows overgrown with ivy suggested where houses had once stood.

A hot wind ruffled the parched grass as she rounded the east-facing side of the château and came to an abrupt halt when she recognized the window that had been marked *ta cuisine* on the postcard. She stared unblinking for a few moments, feeling betrayed. Gazing up at the soaring stone façade, she realized that if the rumour were true, then Alain was on the brink of a venture that made their restaurant in California look insignificant by comparison. She knew in her heart that he had the talent to accomplish anything he set his mind to. She confronted his dream, unable to comprehend that it excluded her.

Turning, Rachel searched the hills divided by farms, wondering which green copse of trees, which stubbled field marked the place where Alain had been born. Looking up at the edifice that had endured so many centuries she put herself in the place of the lean and hungry young man for whom Brissac must have seemed an unconquerable summit, as remote as the Himalayas. The château stood out boldly on the horizon as a reminder of the power, money and glory that lay tantalizingly beyond the gulf of poverty, a gulf he must have been desperate to bridge.

Returning to the entrance, she passed under the stone arch and entered the cobbled courtyard. In the centre was an oval pool fed by water that trickled through moss-covered rocks. The water reflected the blue sky and a wavering image of the château. In the hush, pierced only by the cry of swifts, Rachel became aware of a powerful atmosphere pervading this stone cloister. She thought of what Michael Lowry had said about the residents of Roquelaire sequestrating themselves here against the plague and imagined the courtyard full of doomed people waiting by the oval pool, not knowing whether they would live or die. Looking down into the water, she had a fleeting impression of their blurred faces hovering beyond the reflection of her own head and shoulders outlined against the sky. The magnificent courtyard seemed to hold ancient secrets, which would reveal themselves if only she waited, watched and listened, so terrible was the tragedy that had happened there.

Without warning, the painful thought of losing Alain brought tears to her eyes. This fortress was her rival as much as the flesh-and-blood woman who had taken away her husband. She left the courtyard feeling glad to get away. Passing under the arch, Rachel took a backward look at the château. She was as acutely aware of its future as she was of its past.

Rachel arrived at Michael Lowry's door just after seven, when the sun was still streaming down the narrow street. She lifted the bronze knocker in the shape of a hand and let it fall against the door, which was opened immediately. She felt an immediate positive sensation at the sight of Michael waiting on the threshold. He was wearing a faded denim shirt and white jeans, and his ankles above his espadrilles were deeply tanned. The sound of baroque music came from the depths of the house.

'I saw your shadow through the window. Come in,' he said ushering her into the hallway.

'I love your doorknocker.'

'The hand of Fatima. It's from North Africa and is supposed to bring good luck. You see it on a lot of houses here. It hasn't brought me much luck yet so far as I know.'

'Maybe it's the long-term variety,' she said, making him laugh.

Rachel looked round. The ground floor of the house consisted of one large room and a kitchen. 'I didn't tell Bob I was coming here. He probably thinks I want to be alone and intend to go to the café for dinner.'

'The crowd staying at Bob's can be a bit overwhelming, I imagine.'

'Yes, but they've been so kind and helpful to me. This may sound odd, but could we keep this evening just between us?' Their eyes met and she saw there was no need of explanation; he understood perfectly.

'I rarely see Bob, because he's occupied with his students, but I won't mention your coming here to him, or anyone else,' he said.

'Now I've said it, it sounds ridiculous.'

'Roquelaire is like all small towns in that respect. I'm glad you decided to come, anyway.'

He crossed to turn down the stereo and she took in the details of the long, narrow room with plain white walls that opened to a garden in the back. Michael's simple, almost austere way of arranging the converted village house was in complete contrast to Bob Cooper's flamboyant decor. There were a few paintings, and no bric-à-brac apart from an olive jar filled with cats'-tails. She could see this was the comfortable lair of a single man, who spent his time working at the trestle table, crowded with papers and books,

59

that obviously served as a desk. The chessboard and the innumerable cassettes and discs told her how he passed the time. She imagined him napping or reading on the big sagging sofa or in the chair by the fireplace. The variety of books, papers and magazines on the bookshelves indicated his insatiable appetite for the written word. He ducked his head out of the kitchen as she was scanning his interesting collection of books.

'What would you like to drink? I've got some *rosé*, which I can recommend. I'm having pastis, but there's gin or rum.'

'A glass of wine would be great.'

'I'll join you in a minute.'

She walked through the double doors leading to a small gravelled space bordered by a low stone wall. Like Bob Cooper's house, the garden was on the ramparts, but it was a fraction of the size. There was no overgrown shrubbery, pretty furniture or statues here. Under a small trellis overgrown with a vine was a table set for dinner. She sat down in one of the canvas-backed chairs, her eyes roaming over the roses and hollyhocks, the untended flowerbeds, the spindly geraniums that grew in cracked pots. The garden had gone to seed, but it had an unselfconscious charm that told her something about the character of Michael Lowry.

Michael came back with a bottle of wine, a pastis for himself and some dishes of olives and nuts. Sitting across from her, he raised his glass. 'Cheers – welcome to Roquelaire.'

She took a sip of the cold wine. 'It's delicious.'

'What adjectives would they use in the wine trade?' he said offering her an olive. 'Let's see, flinty, earthy, gutsy?'

She laughed. 'Were you ever a wine critic by any chance?'

'Never,' he protested. 'Now and then I toy with the idea of throwing over journalism and going into the import business in England.'

'Why don't you?'

'That's a good question.'

Michael was smiling at her affably. Evaluating her impressions of him, she decided overwhelmingly in his favour. She liked his ironic but self-assured manner, the reflective depths in his eyes that told her he was no stranger to heartache himself and would be a sympathetic listener.

'What have you been doing all afternoon? Exploring the village?' he asked.

'Not exactly the village, but not far away,' she replied, unsure how to open the subject of Alain and Isabelle de Montjoi. 'I went up to the Château Brissac.'

'Did you? I sometimes take a walk near there. It's a shame it's not open to the public.'

She waited for some comment on the rumoured hotel, but when he said nothing more, she replied, 'When I left you this afternoon, I went to ask Madame Grimal if I could walk around in the courtyard.'

'Now she's the owner I hadn't thought of asking to see it. I've never even been beyond the moat. Did you go there for any particular reason?'

She thought for a moment. 'It's a rather complicated story. I'll get round to it in a minute.'

'Take your time,' said Michael politely. 'But in view of what's happened lately about the château, I was just wondering.'

'That's just it. Could you tell me a bit more about what *is* going on? I've picked up bits of information from a number of people, and then you mentioned it today too.'

'The owner died, let's see, about three weeks ago, maybe a bit more. I'm sorry I never met him. He was an interesting chap, apparently, a Resistance hero and a self-made man who came from a modest background, but he had some very influential friends. He bought the château as a ruin in the Fifties and spent a fortune restoring it. There was some tragedy in his family and he ended up living there alone when he retired. He was somewhat of a traveller and a collector, and though he was respected greatly in the village, he was a remote figure, I think.'

'It seems amazing to me that he should leave such a property to a woman like Madame Grimal. Was she a relative?'

'No, not that I know. Nobody understands why he left it to her, but, as you can imagine, it has caused an awful lot of gossip.'

Rachel hesitated. 'I heard somebody else expected to inherit the château – a woman called Isabelle de Montjoi.'

'Yes, that's true. Do you know her?' asked Michael.

61

'No. I've met her, though. She came to Sonoma in California, where my husband and I run a restaurant. I paid a call on her today, but she wasn't at home.'

The formal way she said it had opened up the subject. Sensing that Michael was waiting for her to continue, Rachel wondered how to begin. 'We've only just met, but I think I'd better be perfectly frank with you. I'm anxious to talk to somebody, somebody like you, who knows the village and what's going on because at Bob Cooper's I heard some disturbing rumours about the château, involving Isabelle de Montjoi and my husband.'

Michael was surprised but relieved that she had brought up the subject first. 'Is that why you came to Roquelaire? To find out what was going on?'

'I didn't tell you the whole story this afternoon.'

She glossed over the anxieties that had provoked her into the sudden trip, still feeling that it would appear odd for her to speak to a stranger before she had even seen her husband.

'I'll be glad to tell you anything I can.' Recounting everything he had heard, he said, 'Isabelle's plans for a hotel and spa have been the talk of the village during the last year while Armand Bataille's health was declining. Everyone thought Isabelle was going to take over Brissac with his blessing, but it didn't turn out that way.'

'That's what I heard from Rosamund – she's a member of the painting class.'

'Rosamund – yes, I remember her from last year. And you had no idea your husband was involved?'

'None at all.' Rachel explained Alain's trips to France and his visits to New York were supposedly in connection with the book he said he was writing. 'Now I'm beginning to wonder if that wasn't all some sort of smokescreen.'

'Don't you think it would be wise to withhold judgement until you've talked to your husband?'

'It's not just the business part of it – there's more.' She told him about Bob's conversation with Julian Paine. 'This Englishman left no doubts about the nature of their relationship.'

'What did the Englishman look like?'

When she told him, Michael exclaimed, 'Oh, him. I've seen him around.'

'Rosamund talked to him after I went to bed. He's some kind of property developer, and represents backers from England.'

'You have to hand it to Isabelle. Here she is, cut out of the will and she's still making plans.' He looked at Rachel ruefully. 'Forgive me. That sounded rather insensitive.'

Rachel shook her head. 'You don't have to spare my feelings. I must face reality, whatever it is. Alain's going to be horrified when he finds out I'm here.' She watched him tip more *rosé* into her glass.

'Nature's tranquillizer,' he remarked.

'I'm feeling better already. The *rosé* – and talking to you.'

'What sort of man is your husband?'

'Alain? He's a very dynamic sort of person, absolutely driven by his ambition to create a first-class restaurant. I suppose you could say he has the classic chef's temperament: he's very intelligent, a perfectionist, and talented. He has a gift for motivating people, which you have to do in the restaurant business, and he also has boundless energy. The truth is, he's a great guy,' she said with a shrug. 'At least I always thought so.'

'Are you involved in his business?'

'I'm up front and I help run the administration, among other things. But Chez Alain is really my husband's thing, which has always suited me fine. We're complete opposites in many ways, and that's always seemed an asset.'

'Different backgrounds?'

'Very, very different. My parents are conventional middle-class people: my father's a lawyer. I spent my junior year of university at the Sorbonne studying French literature. I suppose I've had a privileged background compared to my husband. Alain came from a poor, rather unhappy background, although he never talked about it much. My family tried to persuade me not to marry him, but now they realize what a dynamo he is. He's made it, and they're terribly proud of him.'

'Maybe the praise came too late.'

'You have no idea how right you are.'

63

'He's come a long way from a man who started with nothing. You have to live here in this region a while to understand what I mean. It's full of stubborn, tenacious farmers, who live very close to the soil, who aren't interested in change. Some of them are millionaires, but you'd never know it. It's as though they were still living in the Middle Ages.'

'I'm beginning to understand that.' Rachel thought of Agnès's kitchen, and the narrow, cobbled streets of Roquelaire, where time seemed to have stood still. 'Of course, I realized from the beginning that Alain's difficult background had formed his character. That's why he fits in so well in America: he has the attitude that with hard work he can achieve anything. He never seemed interested in coming back here – until now.'

'I can imagine what developing a place like Brissac would mean to him. It's the classic story of the prodigal son, isn't it?'

'Yes,' she murmured. 'And to think I never really understood that. When I looked around Brissac today, I realized what it might mean to him.'

'I was thinking, maybe your husband didn't tell you about his plans because the whole thing was so precarious. Have you thought of that?'

'I wish I could believe that. Do you think Madame Grimal will sell the château?'

'It stands to reason. What's she going to do with a property like that? But people are saying she can extract a good price from Isabelle.'

'Presumably that's not a problem for a woman like Madame de Montjoi,' Rachel said bitterly, thinking of the substantial house she had visited that afternoon. 'But if Alain is really a partner in this venture, as they say, then to get the money, he'd have to sell out in Sonoma. It would mean . . .' She could go no further. 'Frankly, I can't quite take it in.'

Seeing the anguish on her face Michael said, 'You look as if you could do with some dinner. You've probably still got jet lag.'

Moments later, when he lifted the lid off a chicken casserole fragrant with garlic, she breathed in the aroma appreciatively.

'You've gone to such trouble.'

As he handed her a plate, he replied, 'I was thinking, it's a bit presumptuous to invite a woman who runs a restaurant to dinner.'

'That's what people always think, but it's not like that at all. Quite the opposite, in fact. I love nothing better than simple home-cooked food.'

As they ate, they talked about how Michael had discovered Roquelaire.

'. . . and so Virginia and I fell in love with this house and with the village. We were both writers and we thought it would make the perfect retreat, though Roquelaire has changed more in seven years, I sometimes think, than in seven hundred. The local people are philosophical about it: they say it's the second English invasion. The last one was in the fourteenth century and a lot of them did rather well out of it. England provided wool, France had the wine – and it still does.'

'May I ask what happened to Virginia, the woman you mentioned?'

'We split up. She works on a magazine in London. We lived together for years. Finally, she was ready to get married and she wanted to have children. That was three years ago, but the time wasn't right for me. I was at the height of my career and travelling constantly. We broke up and she met another man and had a baby. She's divorced now. She came to see me in hospital and for a moment I thought maybe we could start again, but I realized it would be a mistake.

'I didn't come here at all, one year. In fact, a couple of years ago I was thinking of selling this house because it had been something we did together and I didn't know what to do here on my own. Luckily I didn't sell or I wouldn't have had a place to come when I was convalescing. My flat in London is much smaller and even more cluttered than this house.'

When Rachel had refused a second helping, Michael asked, 'Feel better now?'

'Much, thank you. Which Frenchman was it who said "Nothing can harm me, I have dined well tonight"? That's how I feel.'

'Sounds like Montaigne, or perhaps Voltaire.'

When Michael had cleared the plates away, Rachel brought up the subject that had remained on her mind all evening.

65

'I've been thinking about Isabelle – I wish I could remember more about her. That's not true: I remember quite a lot. She was rather –' she searched for just the right word, 'overpowering.'

'She must have been a real beauty when she was young,' he speculated.

'How old is she? Do you know?'

'She'll never see forty-five again.'

'Are you serious? That would make her nearly ten years older than Alain; well, eight, anyway.'

'You look surprised.'

'I am,' she admitted, feeling her vanity bruised.

'I find her a bit of an enigma. I'm not French, and no judge, perhaps, but I'd say she wasn't to the manor born.'

'Clawed her way to the top,' said Rachel, making Michael smile.

'Isabelle is the kind of woman who cultivates people she can tap for favours. She used to spend most of her time in Paris, where she did all sorts of things after her husband died. She never seems to be idle. This desire to come back to live in the country is something new; in fact, I seem to remember she once told me she found life here a bit quiet.'

'The Scarlett O'Hara syndrome. She never wants to be poor again, and she has her feet in the soil.'

Michael roared with laughter and Rachel joined him. 'I didn't imagine for a moment I'd be laughing tonight. But please go on.'

'Well, there were family tussles over the will, I believe, and some unpleasantness. She never got along with her husband's family. She must have been a child bride when he married her; that's about the extent of what I know.'

'Would you say she's a hard woman?'

'Some people might call her that, but then maybe they're simply full of envy.'

'And what about the men in her life since the husband died?'

'I don't know of anyone. Aren't you rushing your fences a bit?'

'Am I? What do *you* think?'

'I think you're a woman who has stumbled on something that looks suspicious. I hardly know you, but my advice is, don't burn any bridges unless you're sure you want to.'

Near midnight Rachel looked at her watch, surprised at the hour. The chirping of a lone cricket in the garden filled the night.

'Talking to you has been such a help, Michael. I don't usually unburden myself like this to complete strangers.'

He nodded affably. 'I've been very pleased to have your company. I have friends in the region, and a few visitors, but it's always a pleasure to meet someone new.'

'I've taken up the whole evening talking about myself, but I don't know that much about you. We didn't even get a chance to talk about the book you're working on. What you were saying about Roquelaire really intrigued me.'

'Come back again. Tomorrow if you like, and we'll pick up where we left off.'

'I wish I knew what tomorrow will bring . . .'

'Will you be staying at Bob's?'

'I suppose so. The hotel is full and I don't want to leave Roquelaire. Bob is kindness itself, but I feel the odd one out in a group of people on a painting holiday.'

'I was just thinking, if you need to stay longer, friends of mine, Nora and Jack Peterson, have a little house just up the street. They usually spend September here, but I'm sure if you were staying for a week or so, they'd be happy to let it.'

'Thank you. But if Alain and I run into problems, I'll just take my son and go straight back home. I doubt I'll stick around. While I was driving here I had a picture of surprising Alain, and I imagined somehow we'd be off on a family holiday,' Rachel smiled ruefully.

'Maybe that will still happen. How old is your son?'

'Eight. He's just a baby. I only hope . . .' She stopped herself from making vain wishes and rose to go.

'You were saying you hoped something,' Michael said as they walked towards the door.

Wanting to end the evening on a positive note, she replied, 'Yes, I hope very much that we have a chance to meet again.' She extended her hand, reminding him that they were still little more than strangers.

'I'll walk you home.'

'No, please don't bother. I'll be fine; it's better this way.'

'I understand, but don't go away without letting me know what happens, will you? I'll be wondering how you got on.'

'I promise,' she said with a wave.

Michael closed the front door and went back to the terrace, where the candle was flickering in the breeze. The smell of hot wax took him back to the church and his first glimpse of Rachel Ribard on the same consecrated ground where, according to the chronicle, the Englishman John Stratton had met a woman called Margaret Prior six and a half centuries earlier. Looking into the blackness filled with stars overhead, he thought of his conversation with Père Auguste and found it pleasing to suppose that the rich complexity of Roquelaire's past was not lost or wasted for ever, but waiting to re-emerge centuries later. The weight of the thoughts accumulated through all his months of solitude suddenly lifted, bringing a heightened sense of awareness that something new and startling might have entered his life. The pilgrim stranger in the church – Rachel Ribard – had existed in his mind before he had ever met her, and now she was real. He pressed the burning candlewick between his fingertips, letting the flame bite his flesh for just a moment before extinquishing it. The acrid smell lingering on the air once again reminded him of the evocative fragrance that inhabited churches.

# Chapter 4

Margaret Prior pushed back her thick wool cloak and took off her hat to enjoy the cool of evening now the sun was sinking towards the horizon. It was early August and she and her companion had emerged from a thicket to a plateau that gave them a sweeping view of the wooded hills of Gascony, broken by stubbled fields of wheat and barley. The green valley cradling the fortified village beckoned the tired travellers from a distance. Keeping watch on a knoll above was a fortress with towers and battlements.

'If you look just over the trees there, you can see the rooftops of Roquelaire,' remarked Margaret to the old hunchbacked pilgrim walking at her side.

'It seems a fair prosperous village from a distance, but it's not for me to say, my lady. I've never come this way before. And once is all there will be for me. I shall be lucky if God wills I make it to Spain and Compostela,' he wheezed, mopping his brow.

Margaret gave him a kind smile, touched by his faith that God would straighten his back with a miracle at the end of his long pilgrimage from England. The old man had told her he had discarded his sandals a week out of Paris, and had gone barefoot ever since. Now, after following the pilgrim's route for two months, his feet resembled the cracked clay they were walking on. His heavy woollen cloak and wide-brimmed felt hat with the cockleshell sewn on it, the mark of the pilgrim, were even more soiled and battered than her own.

Margaret wondered if the atmosphere of peace that Roquelaire radiated from afar might be an illusion. Peace was not what she was seeking – not yet, not there. Not until she had accomplished what she had come to do.

The hunchback sighed wearily and, screwing his craggy face, uncannily echoed her thoughts. 'There are few havens for us travellers, my lady. It seems to me that God is visiting his wrath everywhere of late. All people talk of nowadays is floods, earthquakes, drought and famine, not to mention sickness, but there seems none of that here from what I can tell.'

By sickness he meant pestilence. The further south she went, the more she heard talk of the mysterious deadly scourge that had been raging to the east for the last year. Sages said it had begun in China where the earth ripped open and a foul deadly vapour escaped into the air. But it was far enough away not to concern them.

Watching the old man sink piously to his knees, Margaret gripped the knob of her pilgrim's staff, feeling impatient now to reach their destination, but she owed him a kindness. They had met the previous day on the road. She had been tending to her stricken lady-in-waiting, and the old pilgrim had come to her rescue by going ahead to the hospice to fetch a litter for her. Ellen Woodruff, her nurse and companion since childhood, had died of an apparent seizure in the night. They had buried her that morning in the churchyard of the hospice, and Margaret and the old man had set out together long after the other pilgrims had left at daybreak.

Larks sang from the thickets, and the shadows veined the fields bordering the road, which was deserted except for a merchant with a train of pack mules hastening to the village, trailing white dust in its wake. Beyond the woodlands she could see groups of peasants toiling in the distance, bent double as they gathered the straw and tied it into sheaves, which they stacked in two-wheeled carts hitched to oxen. Their labours were interrupted when the wail of a horn sounded across the valley.

'My friend, curfew has sounded and the gates will soon be closing,' she reminded the old man. As they continued on their way, Margaret ignored the burning of her blistered feet and fell into the dogged stride that characterized this long, monotonous journey. She pegged her tall staff forward with one hand while with the other she balanced the satchel that hung on her shoulder; it contained the sum total of her worldly goods. What money she

70

had was tucked about her person, and so far she had avoided being robbed and beaten.

'Milady, permit me to ask, what is that mighty fortress on that hill.'

Margaret had been staring at its high battlements flanked by towers. 'It's called Brissac, and was built by the Holy Father Clement V. Would that we could get a drink of water there, for I believe that a pure cold source has flowed within since pagan times, but the gate has already closed and, anyway, we must be on our way.'

The mention of water gave her a sudden terrible thirst. Her throat was parched and the gourd suspended from her staff had been empty for miles. She had mistrusted the rank wells they had passed, full of stagnant water now the summer was coming to its end. The mortifying thirst of the journey, and the hunger too, was part of the pilgrim's way.

'Permit me to say what a marvel it is that you seem to know every landmark on this road.'

'When I began this journey I had a book of my father's. It told about the perils and hardships as well as the wonders on the road of St James from France to Spain.' Until now she had talked little of herself, feeling it unwise that anyone know too much about her, but at the sight of Roquelaire in the valley, her caution broke and she felt almost cheerful.

The old man gaped at her in awe at the suggestion she could read, and she supposed it likely that he had never met a woman who knew letters, or even many men for that matter, other than priests or wandering scholars. The guide, which she had read avidly when she was young, was meant to assist pilgrims to complete the second holiest pilgrimage in Christendom, and was already a relic when her father acquired it for his library. She had delighted in its pungent observations, which were more practical than pious. From it she had learned that Gascons were lascivious, deceitful and greedy, and yet, she thought ironically, it hadn't kept her from marrying one. She had no idea all those years ago when she read from the pilgrim's way by firelight one winter in England that the book would prompt her to disguise herself as a pilgrim

71

and retrace the footsteps of its author on a journey that promised to give her back her life, or else destroy it.

On their way down the hill Margaret and her companion were saluted respectfully by the peasants returning from the fields, stocky men and women with bronzed arms and faces, who followed behind the ox-drawn carts piled high with sheaves. Their friendliness seemed to contradict Margaret's prejudice against the Gascon people, learned not so much from the old guidebook as from bitter experience. She could not help wondering whether they were all as treacherous and cruel as her husband, Roch Arnaud, whom she half-expected to encounter at any moment, though Roquelaire was several days' journey from his domaines to the west.

When a tall, dark-haired shepherd stared at her with penetrating eyes, Margaret felt herself retracting, like a crab in its shell. The handsome shepherd reminded her strongly of Roch and she watched him disappear down the road with his bleating sheep, wondering what she would do were she to stumble upon her husband without warning.

Rising above the brambles that lined the road was a landmark Margaret had been expecting to see for the last league. At the sight of it she opened her satchel and took out a wreath of box that she had made that morning, aware that the Pilgrim's Stone was but a short distance from the village of Roquelaire. The once-pagan shrine, a stout column of weathered cream stone, had long been a Christian holy place, and its towering cross was a well-known landmark. Coming nearer, Margaret saw box wreaths, many of them pale with age, piled at its base proving she was not the only pilgrim to believe in the power of wishes as well as prayers.

'My good man, I bid you continue on your way. I can walk faster than you and I plan to rest here for a moment,' she called.

He went on his way with a polite salutation, and passed the shrine as if unaware of its significance. As she watched his bent figure, she felt a twinge of sadness at the realization they would never meet again. All her life Margaret had hated partings of any kind, which held for her the latent fear of death; so often she had parted with those she loved, never to see them again.

Swifts wheeled overhead in the violet twilight as Margaret stood before the rough-hewn pillars of stone, reputedly as old as time. The elements had scoured away the Latin inscription at its base, but the scrolled cockleshell, chiselled to commemorate the cult of Venus but associated with St James for the past three centuries, was clearly visible. Margaret had read that the Romans had erected the monument when Gascony was part of Gaul, and she supposed that it would continue to draw pilgrims down the ages until the world came to an end. Margaret added her clumsy wreath to the pile, renewing the vow that had brought her there, as was the custom. She closed her eyes and made a wish to see her son, Thomas, if God willed. At the very least she asked to know that he was alive. This was her real journey's end. Opening her eyes, she stared at the engraving of the shell. She couldn't doubt the power of old stones to grant wishes, nor did she really dare hope it was true.

'Please,' she whispered, 'please grant me this one wish before I die.'

She had stayed much too long, and hurried down the road on tortured feet towards the village, thinking wistfully of food, water and a place to lay her head. The road was deserted, and Margaret felt apprehensive about spending the night in the open if the village gates had already closed, but she resolved she had come too far, enduring too much, to be killed by wolves, devils or brigands.

She was surprised when she came within sight of the village ramparts to see the lone figure of a nun coming towards her with a basket slung over her arm. Seeing a kind face beneath a coarse wimple, and the nun's impressive coral rosary with an olivewood crucifix, Margaret genuflected.

The nun, who introduced herself as Mother Clothilde, radiated a welcome kindness and the clear-eyed serenity earned through a life of good works and piety, although, looking at her, Margaret was sure that she was no more than ten years her elder.

'If you're hurrying towards the village, you'll find the gates still open for a little while yet. The gatekeeper is waiting to admit someone.'

73

Margaret's first thought had been that they could take refuge for the night together.

'But what about you, Reverend Mother? Will you spend the night in the open?'

The nun seemed surprised at the question. 'Oh no, I'm returning to Brissac.'

'Brissac? The château I just passed?'

'Yes. There are seven of us sisters living there under the rule of St Benedict.'

Margaret had seen the drawbridge at Brissac was closed tight, but supposed that it would open for Mother Clothilde. 'I've come from St Antoine today,' she remarked, adding that she had lost her mount and her companion.

'You'll find the town a welcoming place, bursting with pilgrims at this season. We have no shelter to give you at the convent, because our quarters are small, but our well is full of pure water even in the driest season, and we are happy to offer it to poor thirsty souls. But you are tired and hungry, and must be on your way. My blessing to you.'

'Thank you, Reverend Mother.' Margaret genuflected again, wondering what the nun would say if she knew the pilgrim she had just blessed was an impostor. People had been heaping blessings on her since she left England in June, and Margaret was fully convinced she would be condemned to hell for posing as a pilgrim. The nun cheerfully bunched her long habit beneath her girdle, preparing to climb the hill, reminding Margaret of the tireless vigour of saints who had founded refuges, convents and hospitals throughout the ages. On her long march south over hard stones Margaret had begun to envy these pure-hearted visionaries, whose precious self-containment set them apart from other people.

'May God speed you to the end, child, and bring you near your heart's desire,' called Mother Clothilde with a wave.

Her parting words touched a chord in Margaret, and she watched the other woman toil up the hill, haunted by the notion that it must be wrong to love anything or anyone but God as much as she loved Thomas.

Margaret ran towards the arched gate in the stone ramparts with a sudden burst of energy. Passing the *lavoir*, a low rectangle of stone shaded by a roof, she swallowed in renewed thirst at the sound of the running water. She didn't dare stop to drink, but hurried on to the arch, where she could see the burly gatekeeper through the portcullis. With one hand holding her hat, and balancing her staff and bag with the other, she ran awkwardly across the wooden bridge that spanned the dry moat. Hearing footsteps behind her, she glanced over her shoulder to see a tonsured Dominican monk in brown wool habit, his breviary swinging from his waist as he, too, hurried towards the gate. He had a rugged, rather austere face, and stared coldly at her, as if the sight of her femininity buried in a dusty cloak offended him. The two of them stooped to pass under the portcullis that had been raised a few feet off the ground.

When it came down behind them, the gateman closed and bolted the heavy gates with a thud. Margaret walked silently alongside the priest up a narrow street smelling strongly of ordure rotting in the heat, a pungent reminder of civilization after travelling for weeks through open country.

Braving the priest's solemnity, she said, 'It was fortunate for me that he was waiting for you, because I know he wouldn't have opened it on my account.'

'I was with a dying shepherd in the hills.'

Margaret then saw that his unfriendliness was merely an intense preoccupation with some weighty spiritual problem. The monk's thoughts seemed to return to the present and he smiled thinly. 'When darkness falls, gatemen aren't known for kind hearts, even to pilgrims. How does it come that you're alone and without fellow travellers?'

'My feet were blistered and I lagged behind.'

He glanced at her dust-caked boots. 'To my ear you seem to be English.'

'Yes, I am.'

'We have many of your countrymen here, many.'

He gave her a penetrating glance that said he was a keen judge of people and could easily assess her status in life, as well as the state of her soul. Margaret had the uncomfortable feeling that the stern-faced priest was not fooled by her disguise.

'We are staunch supporters of your good king in this town. These last years have been prosperous since King Edward has claimed back his rights, and we have begun to rebuild what war destroyed. The people here prefer to forget that Philip of France ever existed.'

Margaret pretended to be pleased at this, but Gascon fickleness was legendary in England, and she had often heard her father say that they would just as soon swear fealty to France if they were better rewarded, and that it was England's insatiable thirst for Gascon wines that inspired their loyalty.

'You'll find your countrymen here are of every description, from knights to pilgrims, merchants and adventurers. The town is full to overflowing and perhaps the only lodging you'll find will be a doorstep somewhere. But there are plenty of good people who will sell you bread, or even give it to you.'

They entered an impressive square of brick-and-timber buildings. In the centre a vast red tiled roof held up by a network of cross-beams sheltered a thriving market. The arcades beneath the houses, now bathed in a roseate light, were swarming with vendors, testifying to the prosperity of the people of Roquelaire. Pack animals were being watered and fed, and people were praying, chanting, cooking their supper over little braziers. Pardoners were selling pardons, barbers were bleeding patients, beggars were begging, and a *jongleur* was strumming his lute.

'Roquelaire seems a thriving place, unlike some of the places I've been.'

'We are blessed in this little valley, which has escaped the worse retribution of man and God these last years. The people here have come to believe they are favoured.'

Again Margaret was conscious of a solemnity in the priest's voice that contradicted his optimistic words. She said, 'Perhaps you know of a hostel that might have a room. I long for a quiet place to lay my head other than a doorstep.'

'There is one place I know that might take you in, but it is for paying guests.'

'Can you take me to it?' she said, for once feeling the need for a better class of refuge than she had been used to.

She followed through the market, where lamps and flares were being lit. The appetizing aroma of roasting meat and bread baking in ashes mingled with far less pleasant smells. She took in the careworn faces of pilgrims, slumbering, praying, curling up to sleep for the night wherever they could. She knew it was likely that by morning one or more would be found stiffly clutching their rosaries, dead from disease or exhaustion. The odour of their unwashed bodies, the confusion of their varied accents, from north and south, their pious murmurings recalled her journey south.

They left the crowded square and went down a narrow little street, where the priest stopped before a spacious timbered house on the ramparts, a hostel for pilgrims. As they stood in the dim foyer Margaret noted that the tile floors were spread with clean rushes and the walls had been newly limed. The mouthwatering aroma of soup wafted in from the kitchen.

A rubicund Dominican named Brother Cazat welcomed them heartily. 'There's always a place for a person such as yourself,' he remarked graciously, regarding the dusty, tired lady pilgrim with a smile.

Brother Cazat seemed to Margaret more like a jolly innkeeper than a man of God and she sensed he was summing her up as a customer who could afford to pay extra for the conveniences of heated water and a fresh loaf of bread.

'Thank you for your help, Father,' she said to the priest.

'May God speed you on the way of St Jacques, my lady. And may your pious journey be rewarded.'

Following Brother Cazat, Margaret entered a large courtyard where pilgrims were talking and praying or already asleep, though it was just dusk. Their only light that night would be the stars and they would be up before sunrise to continue their journey. Seeing the well, Margaret drew a gourd of water and drank deeply, not minding the drops that trickled down her neck. She washed her face and hands in full view of two dozen or more travellers, mostly old men, who showed some surprise at so young a woman in their midst. For a moment she felt uncomfortable, not from modesty, but from the apprehension that had dogged her throughout the journey that someone would discover who she was. She pulled up her hood, though the air was heavy, and sat inconspicuously on a window ledge, pretending to read her breviary while looking around. She was satisfied that the lodgers in the hostel were the usual rag-bag of pilgrims from England, Germany and the Low Countries, with a few Frenchmen among them.

Another monk, Brother Theodore, entered the courtyard and moved among the pilgrims, passing out loaves of bread still warm from the oven, and cups of fragrant spiced wine. Margaret took the food and drink with gratitude. Slipping her satchel from her shoulders, she took a bite of the crisp, snowy bread and a sip of the dark, spiced wine. It was longer than she could remember since her pilgrim's diet of prayer and mortification had been broken by anything so delicious. She watched the other pilgrims eating, praying, reading their breviaries and using the last hour of daylight to attend to wounds, blisters, and vermin. The peace and order that reigned in the house was in such contrast to the chaos and filth found in most hostels that she felt the burden of the day being lifted from her shoulders.

After she had eaten, Margaret was directed upstairs to a small cupboard of a room, furnished only with two straw pallets. By the dim light of a small window Margaret saw she would be sharing the room with a woman easily thirty-five or more, with a broad, handsome face and the fair hair of a northerner. She was busily polishing something and nodded a greeting as Margaret dumped her satchel and hat in the corner, then removed her cloak. The garment, which she detested by day in the heat, came into its own in the evening as a blanket. Margaret let her chestnut braid fall down her back, shuddering at the movement of vermin at the roots of her hair. She longed for a bath, but knew that it was useless to ask for more than a basin of water in such a crowded lodging run by priests. Her companion seemed to read her mind.

'There's a bathing house outside the ramparts, just near the *lavoir*, where you can wash for a sou in water that is passably hot and steeped with herbs.' Seeing the doubtful look on Margaret's face, she added, 'You needn't worry. It's perfectly respectable. It has a private curtained place only for women. An abbess who is fond of cleanliness and order established it.'

She spoke Anglo-Norman, but incorrectly, and hearing her accent, Margaret asked, 'You're not French, are you?'

The woman shook her head and continued polishing what Margaret could now see was a psalter with a tooled leather cover embellished with a miniature of the Virgin painted on bone.

'No, I'm English.'

This set Margaret thinking, but she was reluctant to start asking questions of a stranger. Loosening her bodice, she sat down and propped herself up against the wall. It was the best moment of the day, the moment when she sank into a kind of stupor at the prospect of rest in a clean, safe place. She slipped off her boots and rested her feet on the cool floorboards. Seeing no sign of a cloak, staff or hat, Margaret asked, 'Are you on your way to Compostela?'

The other woman shook her head. 'I was, once, some time ago, but I got no further than Roquelaire. I was sent from Canterbury to do penance but I fell ill and since I obviously cannot go home without first doing penance, it seemed that I may as well stay here. The brothers turn a blind eye to my waywardness, as this hostel is only for true pilgrims.' She announced these details with nonchalance, as if her lapse didn't concern her.

Seeing that Margaret was not offended by her frankness, the woman shrugged. 'I can obtain a paper absolving me easily enough for my sin, which is nothing grave – vanity and sensual indulgence that let me into lechery. I was always easy prey for a soft voice and a handsome smile. Yet strange to say, both my husbands were ugly and surly.' She gave a great sigh and settled back. 'A pardon doesn't cost much to buy, you know. I advise you to do the same if you feel too tired to go further. There's a fellow in Roquelaire who does nothing but travel between France and Spain getting certificates from the friars in Compostela, and they're worth what he asks. As for me, I'm happy here for the moment. I live by making psalters like this one. Sometimes I journey to Moissac when business here is bad. Anyway, they say the end of the world is coming, so what's the use of worrying?'

'Are you referring to the ... pestilence?' Margaret said the word reluctantly, as if it might taint her tongue.

'That, or whatever comes first – fire, earthquake, famine. They say we haven't long to wait for the end.'

Margaret had no desire to dwell on the rumours she had heard. For the night, at least, she was safe, and the world beyond the village seemed remote. Leaning forward, she asked, 'May I see your handiwork more closely. It interests me.' When she opened the prayer book, she saw the margins were filled with colourful birds and flowers, with crude but vivid portraits of long-necked ladies in wimples and gowns with trains, enacting the ritual delights of the four seasons, designed to provide distraction during long-winded sermons. The psalms were printed in clear, bold letters, suggesting that her companion had been convent-trained.

'Your work is very fine,' said Margaret. 'I once had a splendid Book of Hours,' she added fondly, remembering its ivory cover. Her father had bought it from a merchant returning from the Holy Land, but it had been stolen at the beginning of her present journey.

'I find that these sell well to rich churchmen and to ladies. Whenever a lady arrives in town on a horse with her retinue, which is not all that often, I importune her to buy one, and they can't resist. The trouble is, they seem so few these days – ladies, I mean. Did you come on a horse, by any chance?'

The hopeful look on her face amused Margaret so that she laughed out loud as she shook her head.

'Now, if you'd arrived on a horse this evening, I might have sold this psalter to you. But if you haven't a horse, I dare not hope you can pay me much,' she said mischievously.

'I could pay you very little for all your trouble, but something as beautiful as this will find a buyer. Do you not think you might continue your journey to Compostela?'

'I try not to think of journeys, forward or back. I'll tell you why: it's because I had a dream when I left England that my journey would end in death. That is why I've stopped here. I find that I prefer living to dying. That's the truth.'

Margaret was struck by the woman's blunt forbearance. The prospect of death, which had always stood between her and her son, seemed somehow greater now than when she left England. She couldn't bear to think of leaving the world before she had done what she had set out to do.

'What is your name?' asked Margaret as she spread out her cloak for a blanket.

'Susan Wyndgate.'

'I am Margaret Prior.'

Their conversation continued softly as the darkness grew, and Margaret discovered that before her current troubles Susan had waited on a lady whose husband was seneschal to the king, the same post that Margaret's father had once held. This discovery prompted Margaret to consider whether she could trust her companion with the truth about herself. Her voice dropped to a whisper as she decided to tell Susan her story.

'So you see, I am a false pilgrim, a pretender. I have come thus far supposing my husband, who repudiated me, is on his domaines in Gascony.'

'You must love your child very much to have come all this way for him, and not for the love of God.'

'I love my boy more than life, though it may sound blasphemous. Love was planted in my heart from the moment he opened his eyes and looked at me. He was a lovely babe, healthy and happy. I haven't seen him for a year. I don't know who to ask, who to turn to now I'm here. Roch – that's my husband, Roch Arnaud – is about to wed a twice-widowed noblewoman from the house of Montferrand, if the rumours are true, and I don't know what he has done with Thomas.'

Susan was sympathetic, but she couldn't offer any advice. When Margaret asked her about herself, she said, 'I'm once widowed and now parted from my second husband. I have four sons, grown up. My three daughters all died. The death of the first two broke my heart, so afterwards I could never feel again. But that is the way of the world.'

They both retreated into their own thoughts, but as Margaret was drifting to sleep Susan said, 'There's an English knight in the village by the name of John Stratton who might help you. He was wounded at Crécy and has since been in the service of the King in

81

Guyenne, but has retired here to nurse his ill health and, they say, to devote himself to scholarly pursuits. You're a lady without a champion, which might rouse his sympathy. At the very least he might apply himself to making inquiries on your behalf.'

'Do you think he is trustworthy?'

'I don't know about that, but he's a fine figure of a man and well placed. He's spent his life in the King's service, and now he wields a pen instead of a sword. People find it strange that he lives alone. It's a pity, I think.'

Susan's voluptuous sigh as she sank into sleep reminded Margaret of a cat as it made itself comfortable. Her frank sensuality was a change from Margaret's usual dry companions, who prayed themselves to sleep with arms piously folded across their chests. The shouts, coughs and prayers resounding through the thin walls of the house gradually quietened until the only disturbance was the church bell in the square sounding the hour. Margaret curled up and studied the stars pulsating in the black heavens until Susan rose and closed the shutter with a whisper that they surely ought to keep out the poisonous night gases. When darkness had enveloped her, Margaret resisted sleep as her mind turned round the events of the day: the death-hardened face of the beloved friend she had buried that morning, the old hunchback who had walked with her from St Antoine, the Mother Superior of the convent she had met on the road, the priest who had guided her to shelter. As Margaret touched the silver cross at her throat and drifted into sleep, she was thinking of her son's face.

John Stratton stood at the back of the church, noticing that not a single seat was empty and that even the aisles couldn't contain another kneeling pilgrim. He had come in late, and discreetly dipped his finger in the font and made the sign of the cross in a sweep across his chest. Even the pleasant coolness of the brightly frescoed interior and the rich chasubles of the priests swinging their gold censers could not distract him from the strong odour of the unwashed congregation. He looked down at the sea of souls in hats and cloaks, bearing tall staffs that rose like the masts of ships in a harbour. The church seemed like a brightly decked vessel full of grumbling drab cattle as they repeated their paternosters. It was impossible to tell the sex of most of the pilgrims from their androgynous uniform, but the one thing he was certain of was their shared ill health; the coughs and wheezes that wracked their chests suggested that many were so feeble they wouldn't survive the rigorous journey over the Pyrenees, which would take a strong man with good legs the best part of a week. John watched them trail to the altar to take communion, thinking most of them would surely leave their bones along the road to Spain – all but one, whose face he glimpsed beneath her wide-brimmed hat. He stared at the woman as she came down the aisle, her eyes downcast, surprised to see such a youthful, pretty pilgrim. On reflection, he wondered if the young woman wasn't, in fact, a boy.

When mass was over, John idled near the back of the church, studying the faces of the pilgrims as they passed, speculating who each one was and why he or she had embarked on this arduous journey. They loomed before his eyes in a perpetual march of hope and grim-jawed determination, which he admired but could never emulate, due to the strong passions that had always ruled him. When the last of them had left the church, John sat in an empty pew and looked down the nave towards the crucifix above the altar. The figure of Christ was stained with light pouring through the coloured windows, an image that he found beautiful, but disturbing when it seemed that the stigmata were pouring blood.

He was distracted by a movement at the corner of his eye: a pilgrim had stayed behind to pray in the flower-filled chapel dedicated to Anne, the Virgin's mother. Getting up to go, John glanced at the figure kneeling before the statue of the patron saint of mothers. As she raised her head, her hat fell back revealing braided hair and he realized she was the pilgrim he had supposed to be a boy. The woman turned and their eyes met. The dignified annoyance that creased her brow and the regal gesture with which she swooped up the hat told him she was a lady. He traced the line of her slim, boyish figure under the cloak, sensing the grace of that lithe body, affirming to himself that she was like no other pilgrim he had seen in Roquelaire. The cumbersome gear disguised

83

a spirited, beautiful creature, who called unholy thoughts to his mind. Reluctantly he left the church, feeling irreverently disturbed and subject to an unwholesome curiosity.

Wondering who the woman was and what her journey meant, he walked to the covered market to buy some fish. He was oblivious to the din of voices and the rank odours around him as he turned to stare at the church doors for some sign of the mysterious pilgrim.

'"Her hair was golden, her eyes blue and laughing, her face dainty to see with lips more vermeil than ever was rose or cherry in the time of summer heat . . ."'

'What's that you say, seigneur?' interrupted a vendor whom he knew well. 'Something about the summer heat? You won't find lamprey any fresher than these. They came by barge from Bordeaux this morning.'

'Get on with you, you old liar,' John said with a laugh. 'They're a week old if they're a day, and sluggish too. I saw you stir the water with a stick before I walked by.'

The vendor slapped his thigh and hooted with pretended indignation.

John stared at the lampreys circling in the trough, wondering if he should buy them. He loved lampreys stewed in wine, but had recently heard it said by an itinerant scholar that, among other foods, such creatures were thought to be the cause of the mysterious pestilence. While the vendor was talking to another customer John remembered the beloved words from the tale of Aucassin and Nicolette that he thought he had forgotten, and repeated them softly to himself now: '". . . and the daisies that she broke with her feet in passing showed altogether black against her instep, and her flesh so white . . ."'

'They're white inside, as white as the driven snow, as white . . .'

'Never you mind. I'm not talking about lampreys. Give me the two fat ones in the middle there. I'll send my servant down with a bucket.'

They argued about the price, and the vendor was securing the choice lampreys in a net when John's eyes returned to the church just in time to see the pilgrim stranger come out and slip into the crowd. Even if he had wanted to, he couldn't have followed her. She was too far away and they were separated by the chaos of the market. He stood and stared a moment, then distributed a few small coins to a gaggle of deformed beggars who hovered near the church, alms that he hoped would make up for his lack of attention at mass, and perhaps also his failure to confess for a week. But as he walked home his thoughts kept returning to the provocative face of the woman in the chapel. He imagined her setting out on the road to Santiago de Compostela to expunge a sin, to seek a cure or perhaps obtain a secret wish, thinking to himself that she was as courageous as she was beautiful.

That evening at dusk John was hunched over a blank sheet of vellum, his pen poised over his inkpot. Although the small open window still admitted a blast of hot, fetid air as well as swarms of flies, there was a redeeming suggestion of lampreys simmering in the lees of a keg of wine, which his servant was preparing in the courtyard for his supper. He stood and stretched and scratched his bare chest – he worked wearing chamois trousers and sandals when it was hot – and then looked down in disgust at the pitiful jottings he could hardly call sentences that had taken him all afternoon to compose. He compared himself to a poor swordsman taking sharp jabs at his unruly subject, without getting to grips with it. Try as he would, his account of the battle of Crécy, when the flower of French chivalry fell to England, seemed disorganized and lacking in the proper emphasis. He sighed heavily, thinking how the memory had faded since he witnessed the battle two years ago. What he had composed in no way resembled the eloquent document that he wanted to present in homage to his king. Realizing it was useless now the light was going, he slipped on a tunic over a loose linen shirt and carelessly bound it with a leather girdle before escaping from the house.

Though it was evening, the heat hung in the narrow cobbled street like a pall. He walked past the church, where pilgrims were streaming through the open doors for vespers. The chant of the monks echoed in the candlelit depths, beckoning him, but he resisted. The market was still full of people, vendors and pilgrims who had begun to settle for the night. The smell of roasting meat being cooked over charcoal braziers filled the air, drowning out more pungent odours. The breadsellers were doling out their last loaves slashed with crosses. The barber was letting the blood of an ashen customer as a crowd watched, and his rivals were crying out the merits of holy water and potions. A pardoner was the centre of a crowd of kneeling penitents eager to kiss a document spattered with a bishop's seals in exchange for money and jewellery. The letter writer, with a long straggling beard and yellowed face, was bent over a tablet as he wrote a missive for a pilgrim, who watched his scribblings with mixed suspicion and awe. A *jongleur*, perspiring from the heat in his heavy, rainbow-coloured tunic, was lazily strumming his lute. Two streetwalkers past their prime were discreetly importuning the merchants – the pilgrims were too old and decrepit – pointing to the red knot tied at their wrists, the sign of their caste. In one corner of the market a wandering scholar, from Toledo by his swarthy appearance, was holding court among a group of adolescents, who had put down their slates. Having dispensed with a cursory lesson in letters, he held the youths in his thrall with a lesson in geography, explaining the perils that travellers encountered on the way to the Garden of Eden to the east: men with dogs' heads and six toes, horned pygmies, and forests so high they touched the clouds; stories John had heard a hundred times before.

John exchanged a few words with a fruit vendor whose baskets were nearly empty, and when the man offered him a handful of sweet plums, John ate them at arm's length, to keep the purple juice from staining his clothes. He stopped eating when he saw a woman in a pilgrim's cloak approaching him, realizing it was the woman he had seen in the chapel. To his surprise, she walked up to him as if she had been seeking him out. He wiped his mouth with his hand and as they looked at each other a whole world came back to John Stratton – the world as it was when he was young and the look in a pair of blue eyes had the power to chase away all thoughts of war, words or wine. This pure, delicate face, set with clear questing eyes and framed with braided auburn hair, was full of a pure intensity such as he had never met before. The face that gave him so much pleasure to behold seemed to be expecting something of him, even before she spoke.

'You are John Stratton?' Her words were like an accusation.

'You're English,' he retorted with a smile, delighted by this discovery as much as by her comeliness.

'I am English, yes,' she said in a soft voice, as if she didn't want anyone to hear. 'I approach you, sir, for an important reason that I would rather not speak of here.'

Margaret made a quick judgement of the man, liking the frank openness and intelligent, forceful aspect of his stubbled face. He had a noble forehead, with receding hair peppered with grey, a prominent nose and deep-set blue eyes. He had folded his arms across his chest and was studying her thoughtfully.

'We could walk further on. Or perhaps you could come to my house, though it might be unwise.' He shook his head. 'Are you a maiden?'

'No – that is – no.'

'Not quite a maiden?' He was about to make a joke of it, but a sorrow in her eyes stopped him. Whatever the reason for her riddle, it was troubling, not humorous. 'Maiden or married, it's all the same. I live alone, and it would be awkward if you were seen at my home. You could come after nightfall, when my servant had gone to bed and you wouldn't be observed.'

She thought for a minute, wondering if she could escape her lodging and return again unnoticed. 'Tell me where you live.'

He explained, and she bid him goodbye abruptly and immediately disappeared again. Her voice and beauty contradicted her mantle of poverty, and it intrigued him that she was alone. A lady of such standing as he guessed she was usually travelled in state, with horses and attendants and every comfort that could be had. John walked back home enjoying the prospect of her visit. In the barren months since he had been in Roquelaire he had had little to do with women except for brief visits to prostitutes, shortly followed by a trip to the confessor. He had lived at the fringes of the court in England and Bordeaux, and had learned to value the company of women of intelligence and breeding who could converse well and make him laugh. His health and the question of whether the world was ending, in addition to his writing, had preoccupied John all that long summer and now the prospect of hearing a feminine voice, of enjoying a woman's caprices, her gestures, her charms beneath his roof lifted his spirits. There was no compelling mystery in solitude or celibacy, he thought, entering his house to find his servant laying the table before the cold hearth, which seemed to symbolize the condition of his heart.

Later, when he was trying to write again by the glow of the stars, somewhat assisted by a smoking oil lamp, he heard a knock at the door.

'Come in,' he shouted, thinking it was his servant, who usually brought him some ale after supper. The door opened and Père Xavier, still wearing the white wool surplice in which he had just said mass, crossed the threshold. He was followed by the servant who did indeed carry a pot of ale.

'Bring another for the Father, Cassius,' said John. 'Or would you prefer some wine?'

'No, I think not wine. Ale is better for thirst in this heat. I can't stay long. There is never a night when someone doesn't require the last rites, but if you are inclined, I'd welcome a few minutes' diversion at chess.'

By the light of an oil lamp John opened the leather chest in the corner and brought out the bone chessmen and board, placing them on the table between himself and the priest. They settled down to play in silence for a while, but the priest sensed that John's heart wasn't in it.

'Are you writing well?'

'As well as can be expected. Or to be more honest, not well at all. I fear on my return to England I won't have much to show for all these months of living like a captive. I find I can no longer wield a pen any better than I can wield a sword.'

'Your strength will come back when the wounds of mind and body heal, and not before. You're too impatient.' Père Xavier studied him with concern, as he would a son whose troubles pained him.

The priest's fine, penetrating eyes had none of the inquisitioner's zeal, but radiated a humanity that reassured John whenever he looked at him. Unlike many pompous and corrupt churchmen

John had known in his time, Père Xavier had passed his life building an interior glory that withstood close scrutiny. Not for him the shallow piety speared by ambition, the gold cope and mitre. He helped everyone he met, and his thoughts were pure, his motives unimpeachable. When John's faith burned low, Père Xavier led him from darkness back into the light, but gently and not with threats of the punishment that John supposed awaited him on the Day of Judgement.

'A messenger for the abbot of Fontfroide passed this way today,' said Père Xavier.

The look on his face told John his companion would broach the subject that was in all their hearts and that they were reluctant to speak of.

'And what news did he bring?' he asked anxiously.

'What he told me confirms our worst fears. The sickness has left Marseille apparently, but is still raging in Avignon. The Pope himself has gone into hiding. News travels more slowly than the sickness, it seems. It rages ever westwards, and creeps north.'

John shook his head solemnly. 'But surely, surely . . .' Fear began to gnaw inside him.

'This morning I went to give the last rites to Guirard de Montferrand at Brissac.'

'I supposed that the bell had already tolled for him.'

'He lives, but only just. He seems to be clinging dearly to life, though he is in agony.'

'I hear that vultures have encamped on his doorstep, anticipating his demise.'

'Yes. His niece by marriage, Roxonde, and her retinue are all there.'

'Including her betrothed. Or rather, her lover. I hear she hopes to claim what is hers before the week is out.'

'Hers?' The priest scowled, his usual tolerance dissolving. 'It was her poisoned husband who was Brissac's heir, not the lady herself.'

'This explains better than anything why old Montferrand clings to life,' said John with grim humour. 'But pray continue what you were saying about his condition.'

'His appearance seemed strange to me, but I believe he is only suffering from some kind of poison in his body. I was startled when I saw his lips were blue and his body had erupted with sores. His servants are burning aloes and juniper on the fire all day, and they sprinkle vinegar and rosewater all around him, but to no avail.'

'Do you think he has this sickness, this pestilence that we've heard about?' John's voice was barely audible.

The priest shook his head and his voice dropped to a whisper, as if he feared being overheard. 'No, I think not. But the thought was in my head yesterday when I watched old Fulke, the shepherd, die. Every time I'm called I expect to see signs of this pestilence – black buboes, vomit of blood . . . We won't long be able to ignore that God wills our destruction. It seems to me inevitable. We can only prepare our souls for death, not our bodies,' said the priest.

'Your faith is a greater shield than I ever carried into battle.'

The long shadows on the priest's face made him look as though he had already entered the mysterious world of death. Although John thought of it incessantly, death always seemed far enough away from Roquelaire itself. It had been possible till now to pretend that the plague sweeping the east was no more than an ill wind that would blow itself out. The village had appeared to be safely tucked away to the west, beyond the reach of deadly humours. But the priest's words had the impact of a bell tolling in his mind, making John realize that they might not be spared this terrible contagion. Confronting the possibility that his years might be cut brutally short, John found the idea of perishing on foreign soil with his life's work uncompleted too painful to bear.

When at last Père Xavier rose to go, John was relieved to be rid of his doom-laden countenance, much as he loved him.

'Farewell, my friend,' the priest said at the door. 'It would be wise to say our goodbyes nowadays as if they were the last on earth.'

'If we don't meet again here, then you and I shall never meet, because after this life, you'll be sent up above, and I shall be below,' replied John with a wry smile.

'Your faith is stronger than you think, and your desire to do God's will.'

90

'My faith . . .' John repeated with a helpless shrug, watching the priest disappear down the narrow cobbled street into the night.

The visitor John was expecting came not long after the priest had left. A discreet knock signalled the arrival of a lady just when John had almost given up hope, thinking the beautiful pilgrim hadn't the courage to slip through the dark, empty streets. He opened the door to see a figure completely concealed in a cloak and hood, though the night was hot and still. He gestured for her to enter the house and closed the door behind her before any prying eyes could detect her arrival.

Margaret had been swept through the streets by a maelstrom that overcame her conscience and good sense, but it was too late to turn back now. The closing of the door reminded her what a rash move she had made in coming to a strange man's house in the night. Dropping her hood, she turned to face the one man in Roquelaire who it seemed might help her, reassured by the perspicacity of his gaze, which suggested he would wrest the truth from the devil himself if he were inclined. She summed up his soldier's erect bearing and the watchful depths in his eyes and concluded the former knight had not been broken by war, but was still a force to be reckoned with. Now he was taking his ease, he was dressed more like a peasant than an illustrious soldier who had served the king, and she hoped that a chivalrous heart still beat beneath his battle-scarred exterior.

'My lady, pray be seated,' he said, gesturing to the straw-bottomed chair on which the priest had been sitting. As she sat down he saw that though she seemed no more than twenty years old or so, there were worry lines etched around her eyes and mouth that suggested her honour or fortune had been threatened and that she wasn't at peace.

'Sir,' she began, 'I come on a difficult errand, which will seem strange to you.'

'How did you come to seek me out?'

She had prepared a little speech to get round this problem, not wanting to be too precise, but now she faced him, she doubted that John Stratton was susceptible to flattery or deception.

'A pilgrim in the hostel told me there was an English knight in Roquelaire, once attached to the King's service in Guyenne, whose knowledge of France and England combined was rare. Rarer still in my eyes, it is said that you are a man as much at home with a pen and books as with a sword, a temperate man, a wise man. They say you have come to heal your wounds and write a chronicle of the King that will make your name immortal.' When she had delivered these words, Margaret stopped breathlessly, noting he looked amused.

'These are rich compliments indeed. I had no idea I was so famous, and it would please me if only part were true. But how can I be of service to you?'

'I dare not ask service. Your knowledge and advice would be enough. I fear I have come late, too late . . .'

'I am at your service, my lady.'

Margaret tried to smile, not knowing what to make of his tone of voice, which seemed intended to dilute her seriousness. 'I must begin with my name, which is Margaret Prior. My father, Sir Geoffrey Prior, was seneschal to the King in Dorset, and I am, or was, the wife of Roch Arnaud.'

'Roch Arnaud?' John repeated in surprise. 'And you say that you were married but are no longer?'

'My marriage was dissolved by papal decree some months ago on the basis of consanguinity.' She said it with the simple dignity that had taken twelve months to learn; twelve months of wounded pride, hurt, rage and despair, which had now largely seeped away.

'This dissolution was grave news for you, no doubt.'

'That I could bear. But my husband, who is a Gascon, has refused to return my dowry, with the excuse that my father never honoured his original intent. There were lands due to me that my husband coveted and never saw.'

'Why did this happen?'

'Sadly, my father died three years ago, and before his promise could be fulfilled, the lands in question were sold to pay the ransom of my two brothers to the French king. At the time my husband rejoiced as much as I did at my brothers' release, or pretended to. You see, time changes things, and fortune changes men. A hand that can give can also take away. Roch is no longer the man I married. I have little hope of getting my dowry back, but I cannot rest until I see my son, my only child, whom he has taken away.'

'You have one son?'

'Yes. Two others, a boy and a girl, both died at birth. That is why my boy is doubly precious to me. My husband sent him as page to a family of Gascon nobles, the Durforts, long before the annulment was sought, so he could begin his education. Slowly, I began to realize that it was my husband's plan to divest me of everything that is dear to me.'

'You're not a pilgrim, then?'

She shook her head. 'When news of the annulment reached me, I left England disguised as one, believing it the best way for a lady to travel discreetly.' After telling him how she had lost her companion and their horses, she continued, 'My brothers hate Roch and have sworn revenge, but they are too busy waging war in Scotland to help me. I am a burden to them and I think they would prefer me to retire to some convent and accept my lot.'

John Stratton shook his head. 'That is the way of the world, I'm afraid, poor lady. So you have no champion, neither father, brother nor husband. And your son?'

'I do not know where he is, for I received word that the Gascon nobles in whose care he was supposed to be claim no knowledge of him. That much I knew before I left England. My husband has hidden him. He values our son, Thomas, above anything, except perhaps riches.'

'Your son is a bastard now, with his mother's name and no paternity.'

'Sir, bastardy is no obstacle to rising to the heights, if you think of it, but it grieves me none the less.'

'Yes, it's true,' John admitted. Numerous royal and papal bastards who had ended their days wallowing in titles and riches came to his mind.

'What kind of man is Roch Arnaud, and why this annulment? It puzzles me, particularly as you say he was not nobly born, which suggests to me that you are higher born than he. Was this not enough for him?'

'Ah, you will hear the tale. He is a product of pure ambition, an adventurer. He rejected the Church as a ladder to success, and chose war instead, aiding and abetting the English cause in Gascony. He was shrewd enough to see the English would regain Aquitaine, and was knighted by King Edward and given lands near Bordeaux as his fief. This happened seven years after our marriage. By then I must have seemed a poor catch to him, the more so since my father's promise could no longer be honoured and because after Thomas I bore him no more sons who lived. Now the man who is still my husband in my own eyes is betrothed to Roxonde de Montferrand, a twice-widowed adventuress, who repudiated her first husband and is said to have poisoned her second.'

'You seem to know a great deal about these circumstances.'

'All this is known to me because I was determined to find out the truth.'

The hot night, heavy with smoke from the lamp, had fallen silent. There was no gentle way to break the news that he must give her.

'My good lady, prepare yourself for what I am about to say. I wonder if you are aware that your husband is here, in Roquelaire, with his mistress, unless I am mistaken.'

Instead of swooning or crying out as he might have expected, Margaret gave an incredulous little laugh, as if she didn't believe him. 'Here, in Roquelaire? My husband and his bride-to-be?'

John told her that they had arrived recently and were encamped with their retinue less than a league from Brissac. 'Your husband intends to marry her near Bordeaux, from what I hear, as soon as she is mistress of Brissac.'

Margaret's eyes seemed to grow larger. 'I had thought as much, from all I heard, but I never expected to find him here. I was told he was travelling. At most, I hoped to uncover some clue, some trail that would lead me to him, so I could discover the whereabouts of my son. I was hoping against hope that you could tell me, and now you have.'

'It would seem to be written in your stars that you and he should cojoin in this place. I should think he would be even more startled than you if he were to hear of your presence.'

'That is certain. But he must not.'

94

John sensed her mind working, and though she had had the courage of a man, she aroused a protective instinct in him, an urge to shield her from her own impetuosity.

'Now what will you do?'

'I will confront him, and demand to see my son, wherever he is.' She stood abruptly, as if she couldn't wait until morning.

'No!' He took her by the wrist to restrain her, then let go again. 'Forgive me. First of all, remember that the gates are closed.'

'Of course. How foolish of me. You see what a turmoil my mind is in; I can't reflect as I should.' She sank back into the chair.

'Second, it would be dangerous and foolhardy to go to your husband without first taking the measure of what you're up against. You are about to do battle, my lady. And in any battle a scouting party is sent ahead to determine the strength and position of the enemy before an attack is attempted.'

She weighed his words. For a year she had been struggling with shadows and invisible powers without once confronting her enemy first hand. At the thought of Roch and his future bride so near to Roquelaire, she felt vengeful and impatient, but also fully come to life again, as if years and cares had peeled away. She was suddenly younger and fired with the recklessness that fed her youth.

John said, 'And now it remains to decide what to do. I have my sources and will make inquiries.'

'I must see him face to face; I must.'

'If he's keeping secrets from you, he won't tell you anything. Better remain silent and unseen for your son's sake.'

'You have my deepest thanks for your counsel, sir.'

'It would be an honour to aid a lady in distress, but I have done nothing yet.'

'You have done more than you know by what you told me.'

Margaret looked at the stark room, with its smoke-blackened beams, the quill and inkpot on the writing desk, a few books on a shelf and a chess set on the table, trying to probe the character of the man who had already proved himself honest and frank, a man ready to befriend her.

'May I ask to know the thoughts that take you so far, my lady?' John asked.

95

She returned his curious gaze with a disarming smile, inwardly comparing the man and the place to the many quiet evenings she had spent with her father in the study of his manor in Chepstow.

'Your desk, your quill, the chessmen and books take me home to England and my father, who raised me as a son more than as a daughter when my brothers were gone from home.'

'He must have been a wise man.'

'Yes, he was wise, very wise. It saddens me now, because he is dead and my own life has continued so ignominiously. And yet it began so well. I was taught devotion to God as my first duty, a love of beauty and a respect for knowledge, as well as physical courage and a resourcefulness in trouble. Things that counted as much as a dowry in his eyes.'

'They have stood you in good stead, my lady. You would never have made it thus far without your father's legacy.'

'A legacy I misused. He never liked my husband and tried to persuade me against marrying him.'

'And you defied him?'

'Never that. I failed to see reason and, being wise, he realized he had to let me follow my heart.' Margaret shrugged off her thoughtful mood, hearing the clock strike eleven. 'It is late and I must leave you.'

She got up to go, but John was determined to persuade her to stay. 'I cannot let a lady wander through the streets alone. The doors of the hostel will surely be closed now.'

'I'll find a doorway somewhere. There aren't many hours left until dawn.'

'No, wait. There is a good unused room near the stables in the courtyard where you could be comfortable if you wish.'

She debated it, sensing his keenness that she should accept his hospitality. She was as much impressed by his courtesy as by his good sense, but beneath the sweet refrain of one Christian helping another lay the power of John Stratton's maleness, which insinuated itself into her feminine conscience. Though she and he could count a number of grey hairs on their heads, though the wheel of life was slowly breaking their bodies and hearts, she was aware that some dangerous and wonderful attraction was flickering between them.

Speaking frankly about herself after so many months of living in the shadows had exhilarated Margaret, and she felt she could as safely cast off her reticence as she had her pilgrim's cloak.

'If I seem to hesitate it's not because I'm ungrateful, or fear for my life or virtue.'

'I understand,' he said as she paused.

'I'll stay,' she said simply.

'Are you hungry?' John asked abruptly, masking his delight at her impulsiveness, which was without a trace of coquetry.

'But surely your servant has gone to bed and you do not want to wake him . . .'

'Never mind, that doesn't matter. If you like lampreys, there are some in the pot beside the fire, and they could be washed down with as fine a wine as you've ever tasted. When sleep beckons you, I'll show you to a pile of fresh hay in the stable.'

John started moving round the room, galvanized by the happy prospect of her company. He had hardly touched his dinner earlier and felt his appetite return at the prospect of an impromptu supper in her company. As he was clearing the chess set away, she said, 'Leave it, if you like, and if it's not too late, I'll play against you.'

At the discovery that Margaret played chess, his face broke into a broad smile and he shook his head. 'If anyone had told me this morning that tonight I would meet a comely chess-playing pilgrim, I would have called him a liar.'

Later, when they were seated across the table from each other and he had heaped a portion of succulent lampreys swimming in black sauce on Margaret's plate, he saw her stare at it silently.

'Let me point out to you that I'm still alive, and yet I tasted this dish earlier in the evening.' When she looked puzzled by this remark, he explained. 'I refer to the rumour you may have heard that lampreys are a cause of this pestilence we hear so much about.'

'Forgive me. I was only staring because they are such a welcome sight to one used only to bread and water.'

'Should you change your mind, there is bread . . .'

Lifting the spoon he had given her, an unexpected luxury she hadn't seen since she had left England, Margaret said, 'Sir, because

97

of your kindness, I no longer feel afraid of anything, so I could certainly not fear lampreys in wine sauce.'

The room where John had dwelled alone with only his thoughts to keep him company was enhanced by Margaret's presence. He raised his goblet to her in silent acknowledgement of her courage and beauty.

# *Chapter 5*

Rachel stared absently towards a spotlit statue of Pan, half listening to Bob talking to Rosamund, as she waited for the telephone to ring. She had kept herself busy all day, willing the hours to pass and dreading it at the same time, trying to keep her mind off the questions surrounding her husband's behaviour. She was sure Alain had arrived at Terre Blanche by now and had received the note she left with the housekeeper.

'I'm serious,' Bob was saying. 'Your compositions have taken on a new clarity. That is, well, simply dazzling. If you improve as much as this next year, I won't be able to teach you anything more.'

Rosamund laughed. 'Where would I escape to in the summer, in that case?'

Dressed in a fuschia pink sundress and radiating scent, she was even more vivacious than the night before and Rachel suspected the reason. Earlier in the evening, Rachel had filled her in on all that had happened and Rosamund had let it drop that the following night she was having dinner in a country restaurant with Julian Paine.

'I know I shouldn't have said yes,' she had murmured, trying to be blasé, but her eyes were luminous with excitement. 'He's the sort of man that any woman should have the good sense to stay away from. But he's very charming, and within five minutes he suggested we get together when we're back in London. Can you imagine?' she had added with an amused laugh. Rachel had said nothing. She had seen Julian Paine only once, in the shadows, and even at a distance he exuded danger. Now she noticed a new lilt in Rosamund's voice as she spoke.

'Those vast vistas daunted me at first — all those endless

undulating hills packed with trees and patterns of colour in the light, well, I found it quite overwhelming when I started.'

'Never forget that you must be in command, like a lion tamer. Imagine yourself with the brush in your hand like a whip. It's up to you to crack it confidently when the field tries to get the better of you.' Bob flicked his wrist to illustrate the point.

'Beautifully expressed, Bob,' said Ted, his soft voice full of admiration.

The bank clerk, Kevin, poured himself another glass of *rosé* and Rachel saw him cast a longing look in Rosamund's direction, but she was completely oblivious to his existence. The two schoolteachers on either side of him were trying to engage his attention with flattering remarks about the powerful impact of his landscapes. Barry and Melissa were laughing together. The colonel and his wife were in a reverie of their own, gazing up at the plump, unripened grapes suspended from the trellis as if trying to memorize them for a composition. Rachel suspected they would transfer their impressions into pools of colour on paper some grey winter day back in England.

When she heard the telephone begin to ring, Rachel's stomach leapt. Ted returned and whispered in her ear, 'It's for you, Rachel. A local call, a man.'

Feeling her knees buckle, Rachel left the table as unobtrusively as she could, and though the conversation didn't skip a beat, she knew all eyes were following her.

She took a deep breath and picked up the receiver in the study. 'Hello?' she said, with a beating heart.

'What the hell are you doing here? What on earth's happening to the business?' came Alain's voice, full of rage.

'You have no right to be angry with me,' she retorted, taken aback none the less.

'No *right*? Anything could be happening and neither one of us is there to take care of it.'

'René is perfectly capable of handling any crisis that comes up. Anyway, none of that matters now, Alain. I arrived to find you're not where you're supposed to be. Why did you lie to me? You weren't staying in the hotel in Roquelaire; they don't even know

100

who you are.' She swallowed the lump in her throat. 'And what were you doing in Paris all this time? That's what I want to know.'

'There was a change of plans. I don't have to call home every time I change my plans.'

'How could you go off and not call to tell me you had arrived safely? What do you think was going through my mind about you, about Oliver?'

'Rachel, I have called home, several times. You obviously didn't get the message because you were here, in France, without telling me. What's all the secrecy, anyway? I just talked to René, who was shocked to hear where you were.'

'I want to talk to Oliver.'

'You can't. He's asleep. I just carried him to bed. It's nearly ten o'clock, for Christ's sake.'

'You have no right to drag him around like this.'

'You've gone crazy. Oliver is having a wonderful time. Look, I don't know what you mean by arriving here unannounced. We'll go into this tomorrow when you've calmed down.'

'Calmed down. You're the one who's shouting.'

'You're hysterical.'

Rachel paused for a moment, then she said in a low voice, 'Alain, I'm not hysterical. I came here for a reason, because I felt uneasy after you left . . . and because you left something behind, something that . . . that upset me.'

When he demanded to know what she meant, she said, 'Never mind. I don't want to go into it over the phone. And now I come here to find you're not where you're supposed to be and that you are staying in the house of a woman I didn't know you knew so well. What's more, I've been here long enough to hear some very upsetting rumours.' She hadn't intended to be so blunt on the phone, but it came out in a rush.

There was a long pause during which she could almost hear his mind ticking over.

Finally, he said, 'This is absurd, this shouting on the telephone.'

For a instant she thought he was going to hang up. She thought quickly. 'Alain, I'll meet you in the Café des Sports in Roquelaire tomorrow at nine o'clock.'

There was a pause. 'Nine is too early. I have some phone calls to make.'

It took all her self-control to reply calmly, 'All right, then, ten o'clock. Is that still too early or is it too late?'

'I'll be there,' was his curt reply; he hung up before she could make sure he would bring Oliver.

Rachel stood for a moment to compose herself, then slipped upstairs to her room without returning to the terrace. As she climbed the stairs her feet seemed to weigh her down, her conversation with Alain pulsating in her mind. She could no longer delude herself. She knew a nightmare was about to enfold her. She was climbing a precipitous staircase in the dark, groping every step of the way.

When Alain had finished talking to Rachel, he closed the door of Isabelle's study behind him and walked down the long black-and-white-tiled corridor. The light coming from under the double doors of the sitting-room told him that Isabelle hadn't yet gone upstairs and was waiting for him to tell her how the telephone call had gone. He touched the doorknob, then dropped his hand and slipped noiselessly up the curving wooden staircase lit by a cut-glass lamp suspended from the ceiling by a chain. The shards of light it cast on the carpet reminded him of a shattered mirror. He paused a moment on the stairs, thinking of his conversation with Rachel. His life, like the light from the lamp, seemed to be spread at his feet in a thousand pieces. The accusation in Rachel's voice followed him as he walked down the carpeted hallway, illuminated by shaded sconces, towards Oliver's bedroom. He opened the door carefully, expecting to see his son sound asleep in the little blue room lit by a nightlight. Alain displaced his sombre, distracted expression with a smile when he saw his son was propped up in bed reading a French comic book.

'Hey, are you still awake? When you fell asleep over your sandwich a while ago I thought you'd sleep until tomorrow.' He bent to stroke Oliver's forehead.

'I wanted to know what was happening to Tintin – I couldn't wait until tomorrow. I'm just looking at the pictures, trying to figure out it they're going to find the treasure.'

'So that's it,' said Alain, taking the book from him. Sitting on the bed, he read a few phrases aloud. 'Do you understand that?'

'Sort of. Keep going.'

Alain read from the book for a few moments, stopping to answer Oliver's questions. Seeing the boy's eyelids grow heavier and that he was no longer listening, Alain quietly closed the book.

'And that's all until tomorrow, when Captain Haddock and Tintin depart to find the treasure of *Rackham le Rouge*,' he whispered in French. Oliver was fast asleep. When his son stirred, Alain paused before extinguishing the bedside light, waiting until his breathing was even. He bent and kissed his cheek and drew up the covers. But his contentment in the rare pleasure of putting his son to bed was incomplete. Rachel's voice was still echoing in his mind, bringing with it the thought of tomorrow.

Alain went downstairs and pushed open the door to the sitting-room. The big, high-ceilinged room opened on to a terrace that overlooked the park. The soft night air brought the sound of crickets and the smell of the country through the tall windows, draped in pale blue silk. Pools of light from the lamps fell on the Persian carpets, and cast shadows on walls and moulded ceiling. The room was furnished with painted antique commodes, tables and chairs, and a mixture of old and modern pictures in heavy frames, family mementoes culled from Isabelle's years of marriage. As he walked across the room Alain felt a sense of unreality that this was to be his home from now on. Nothing in it seemed familiar yet, and it almost felt as if nothing ever could be.

Isabelle was curled up on the leather sofa, her feet tucked beneath her, pretending to read a magazine, but Alain could see that she had been waiting impatiently for him. She had changed into a pink track suit, but her relaxed posture didn't conceal a latent tension, which translated itself as a readiness to act in a crisis.

He sat on the sofa beside her and began to stroke her foot.

'You were on the phone a long time.'

'I went up to check on Oliver afterwards. He was still awake and I read to him for a while.'

When he didn't say anything for a moment, she said, 'Well, what did she say? Tell me, I'm anxious to know.'

'The conversation was brief and not very cordial. I still don't know what made her come, but I didn't want to go into it on the phone.'

'But didn't you protest?'

'Of course I did. I told her I was furious that she had left the business. She made some vague accusations that suggest she must suspect something is going on between us.'

'Why did this have to happen now?' Isabelle let out an exasperated groan. 'You said you were sure she had no suspicions whatever. Then why, suddenly, only twenty-four hours after you left, did she up and follow you?'

'I wonder.'

Isabelle's face hardened. 'Well, if for some reason she has found out about us, then you may as well get it over with now. Tell her you want a divorce. There's no point in waiting, is there?'

'I don't need her to start making trouble on top of . . .' he hesitated, 'on top of everything else.' Resentment that he hadn't expressed was fermenting inside him, as it had been since she had given him the catastrophic news that Armand Bataille had changed his will at the last minute.

Isabelle ignored the accusation in his eyes. 'You and I have both had a setback, but it doesn't mean the end of the world.'

Until she told him about the loss of the château, they had never had a misunderstanding. Isabelle's offhand way of delivering the shattering news, as if it were only one more hurdle to surmount, had shocked him. He would have understood better if she had seemed as upset and confused as he was. He felt an unnerving disappointment, as if he had put all his money on a sure winner that had failed to come through.

'What are you going to do tomorrow?'

'Wait.'

'Wait?' he said, surprised. 'You'll need to do more than that.'

'We're not ready to move yet, Alain. It's only been three weeks since the offer was made to her. We must wait a few days now you're here, otherwise Madame Grimal will think we're desperate, don't you see?'

'I don't trust Julian Paine. He might advise the backers to pull out right away.'

104

'That's not true, Alain. He understands that it's only a matter of time before we have the château in our possession. These things happen and it takes time to iron them out, that's all. We've been through all this a hundred times.'

'We don't *have* time. The trip to Paris – that was pointless as far as I'm concerned. The lawyer couldn't come up with anything concrete, and he never will.'

'Perhaps your wife's coming here will turn out to be for the best. It will push things along and you can get your divorce right away. When you told me you intended to keep Oliver here and enter him in school I knew that your wife would be on the next plane to France the minute she found out. She's just come a little bit sooner. At least now we know where we stand.'

Alain looked uneasy. 'I don't know how Oliver is going to react when I tell him he won't be going home. He's not going to like it.'

'*Chéri*, he's a child. He'll do what he's told.'

'You know nothing about children.'

'Obviously,' she said coldly. They were perilously close to an argument.

'I want to offload Chez Alain first, before proceeding with the divorce. With the laws about community property the way they are in California, Rachel might end up getting far too much of the proceeds if she becomes vindictive, even though the restaurant is all in my name. René and I should be able to wrap things up when I get back, before Rachel has even had time to file. I need to get the money out right away.'

'And supposing something goes wrong with René and he doesn't come up with the financing?'

'I have no reason to believe that he won't. You can be assured that I will keep to *my* end of the bargain.'

Isabelle brushed aside this veiled accusation. 'You'll never have a better chance to cut clean from your ties in America – your business, your marriage – and to bring Oliver to France without any fuss.'

'Without any fuss?' he repeated ironically. 'It's too late for that. What I intend to do is try to persuade Rachel to go back home, tomorrow if possible.'

'Oh, come on. She came here because she suspected something. She's not going to give up just like that and leave you alone.'

'It's too late. I can't even think straight. Let's not talk about it any further.'

'When Fernande said she had come to the house, I simply couldn't believe it. She must be a very determined woman, not at all like the quiet person she seemed when I met her last year.'

'I really don't know what's got into her head.'

Suddenly Isabelle's expression softened. The tension slackened from her body and she slid her feet under Alain's legs. 'I think I can guess. She knows you no longer love her. Did you make love to her before you left home?'

He hesitated, not really wanting to answer. After a moment, he said reluctantly, 'No, of course not.'

'That's why. That's what made her cross oceans and continents to get here. She knows she's losing you.'

'Nonsense – just because of that . . .'

'You're a baby, Alain, a baby,' she said with an indulgent laugh. She moved to kiss his cheek, cradling his chin in her hands.

'This baby is tired.'

'Not too tired, I hope? This is the first night I'll have you in my own bed.'

He stroked her thigh and smiled gently. 'No, never that tired. I'll have to go back to my own room before it gets light, though.'

'All right,' she said with a sigh. 'If you insist, but I really do think that in America people make too many concessions to children. Adults have to get on with their lives, you know, and children must accept that.'

'Isabelle, let us understand each other. I raise Oliver the way I see fit. It's always going to be like that.'

'I've already told you I accept that. But what if your wife wants to take him home? What would you do?'

'It's simple. She can't have him.'

She snuggled closer to him. 'Let's not think about it tonight, or the hotel, or anything.'

'You're remarkable the way you can lock everything out,' said

Alain, shaking his head. Isabelle was arousing him with her cat-like posture on the sofa, the sensuous purring of her voice.

'It's the way to survive in life. One must love, even among the ruins.' She rose and began turning off the lamps. He watched her, then got to his feet.

'*Chéri*, you go upstairs and have a shower. I had Fernande put your bags in the dressing room for now. I'll join you in a minute.'

He kissed her. 'All right, but don't be long.'

When Alain had gone, Isabelle went to the window and looked out into the park. The new moon cast a faint white light under the dark trees that shielded the house. Half hearing the cadence of crickets, she toyed with the heavy gold chain set with a heart of diamonds that Alain had given her on his arrival. She stood for a moment, then closed the windows. Passing the mirror above the fireplace, she caught her own reflection, feeling disturbed by what she saw. The last few days had taken their toll, and she needed more than a smile to disguise the lines around her mouth and more than make-up to erase the blue shadows under her eyes. She ran her fingers through her hair with an exasperated grimace, then went to the office adjacent to the sitting-room.

The sight of stacks of files on the big marble coffee table reminded Isabelle how much work lay ahead, a challenge she usually relished. Normally, she would have been filled with the desire to get to work even though it was late and Alain was waiting upstairs. Instead, she went to a wall safe hidden behind a gilt console. Opening it, she sorted through envelopes containing cash and documents until she found one containing old photographs. She noticed the corner of a frayed velvet box tucked away at the back, and took it out along with the envelope. She lifted the lid and looked at the garnet necklace and pendant earrings set in heavy gold that rested on the faded satin. The garnets were large and lustrous, and of the best quality, and the ornate, outdated settings contained a good deal of gold, which had greatly increased in value since they had been made by a jeweller in Tunis so long ago. Perhaps, Isabelle thought, she ought to sell them, even if she didn't actually need the money. She rejected the idea and snapped the box shut. The garnets were her only connection with her past, a past that might never have been.

Isabelle turned her attention to the photographs. Sifting through them, she stopped when she found one of a young man with a sharp, handsome face, taken over thirty years ago. It was hard for her to believe that he would be in his fifties by now, if he were still alive. The photograph was too faded, too out of focus to confirm what she was anxious to know. She couldn't help hoping that he was dead. Her mind flashed back to a scene earlier that evening, and she found herself reliving it moment for moment.

Driving back from Bordeaux airport on the motorway towards Roquelaire, they stopped at a layby crowded with a convoy of brightly painted lorries belonging to a travelling carnival. Isabelle waited in the car while Alain took Oliver to the men's room, pondering how she would have to spoil the boy when they got home, lavish him with presents, win him over by giving him free run of her property, even though it went totally against her inclination. Spending the weekend with Alain and his son, she had become acutely aware of her own childlessness as never before.

On their way back to the car Oliver ran excitedly to look at the pictures of the carousel painted on the sides of the lorries. Isabelle watched him impatiently as Alain stopped and exchanged a few words with the swarthy men talking and smoking near the lorries, probably gypsies who owned the carnival. Then, glancing in the wing mirror, she had a glimpse of a man with a moustache coming up behind the car. He sloped along morosely, his shoulders hunched, smoking a cigarette. Then a familiar gesture gave Isabelle a jolt. She peered into the rear-view mirror to get a better look at the man's face, her memory casting up a likeness from the past that could not possibly have anything to do with the stranger a few feet away, who was obviously part of the carnival. And yet . . .

The man passed the car and walked on for a few feet, then turned and stared. Isabelle was shocked by the malevolence in his face. Even from a distance he seemed to exude menace and his very look sent a second wave of fear through her. She clutched the steering wheel, unable to turn away, paralysed with terror – terror in case she missed some vital detail that would confirm or deny his identity, terror that he would mistake her interest for acknowledgement. The sound of Alain's voice as he and Oliver approached the car broke the spell.

'What were you saying to those men?' she asked Alain, acutely conscious that the man was still loitering only a few feet from the car, and that he continued to stare through the windscreen.

'Oliver wondered how they could get such a big thing inside such a small truck,' he said with amusement.

'They've got forty-eight horses on it!' All Oliver's stubborn shyness vanished as he smiled eagerly at her. 'And do you know what? The man said it takes five hours to put it all together, with five men working, because it's in hundreds and thousands of pieces.'

'Is that so?' Isabelle fumbled for the key. Suddenly she was in a terrible hurry. 'Did they say where they are going?' Putting the car in gear, she pressed the accelerator as hard as she dared, averting her eyes as they passed the man.

'Dad, maybe they're coming to Roquelaire!'

'Don't be absurd,' said Isabelle. She directed the car on to the motorway.

'What's so absurd about that?' Alain replied. 'You said there was a fête in the village next week. But don't worry, Oliver, there will be one just as nice I'm sure.'

Isabelle looked in the rear-view mirror at the brilliant sunset behind them. A dark shape that could have been the carnival caravan was looming up on the horizon. She could feel it coming closer.

*

Rachel entered the stifling little room under the eaves knowing she would never be able to sleep. A moment later she slipped from the house unnoticed and walked up the dimly lit, deserted street, grateful that cool air had displaced the heat still imprisoned in the stone houses. As she passed them, she caught snatches of conversations, the rattling of dishes, the blare of television sets; but an image of Alain's face flushed with anger wouldn't leave her mind. Somewhere, not far from where she was standing, Oliver was asleep in a strange bed in a house belonging to her husband's mistress.

On impulse she walked up the Rue St Jacques, where Michael lived. All the houses were shuttered except his, where light poured through the open window. She hovered indecisively near the door for a moment, not wanting to bother him again so soon, when the door opened unexpectedly and Père Auguste emerged. Surprise lit up Michael's face when he saw her in the shadows.

'Rachel! I didn't hear you knock.'

'I was just about to, but I thought you had company,' she said, feeling her cheeks burn with embarrassment. 'I was just out for a walk. Good evening, Père Auguste.'

'*Bonsoir, madame,*' he said, extending his hand. 'Don't think you've interrupted anything. We've just finished a game of chess and I beat him too easily. His mind was not on the game, so it's time to call it a night.' He was looking at her with almost unbearable kindness.

'It's awfully late, I know,' she said, feeling awkward, 'but I'm still not on French time.'

'I can imagine. Even when I've been to Rome, though it's only an hour away, it's enough to upset my rhythms,' said the priest. 'Well, I'll be getting on . . .'

'Listen, I won't take no for an answer,' Michael said when he saw Rachel looking doubtful. 'You've got to console me for my losses by having a drink.'

'Goodnight to you both,' said Père Auguste, disappearing down the street.

'How nice to see you,' said Michael, sweeping her across the threshold before she could protest. 'You look as if you could do with a glass of something.'

She nodded, and swallowed as tears welled up unexpectedly. 'My husband called tonight. We had a pretty unfriendly conversation and I couldn't sleep.'

She went out to the terrace and he followed with a bottle of wine and two glasses.

She smiled up at him, determined to make an effort. 'Let's make one thing clear. I'm not going to talk about myself, and that's a promise.'

'Whatever you say. We'll talk about any and everything but that.' He filled the glasses, lit the candle and pulled up a chair.

110

They talked about politics and history for a time, until the subject eventually got round to Michael's background. By now Rachel was curious to know more about the stranger who had befriended her so unexpectedly. She discovered that he had grown up in a small country town, the only son of a struggling working-class family, and had been awarded a scholarship to a public school, where he did well enough to go on to Oxford. After university, he began work as a journalist, eventually landing a job on *The Times*. He had travelled the trouble spots of the world for most of his career, and his witty, frank way of talking revealed layers of achievement and experience. Rachel had began to relish his wry, understated humour, which, to her, was characteristically English. She detected in him a strength that came from going forward with determination no matter what obstacles lay in his path. As he talked about the demanding and erratic occupation that had consumed his life, she imagined him struggling with the temptation of cigarettes and alcohol during his period of isolation in Roquelaire, trying to break strong habits bred over years of living on his nerves. She could picture him spending long broken nights tossing in bed that summer, his shallow sleep interrupted by the chiming of the church bell in the square.

'The risks you've taken make me feel as though I've been in a cocoon all my life.'

Michael laughed. 'I hope I haven't over-dramatized myself to that extent.'

'Will you pick up where you left off?'

'That's what I've been asking myself. It's natural, isn't it, when you've had a crisis, to rethink your life. I've wasted time here in a way, but I was too tired to do anything but lie in the sun and read the newspaper when I arrived. Life was suddenly flat, like a map without contours. The thriller, as I told you, didn't get very far and a book on the Middle East I thought about doing is already outdated. The thing about the Middle Ages is still hypothetical. Gradually, I've decided that I'm through with the kind of journalism I've done in the past. I don't want to die in a helicopter crash or perish by a sniper's bullet. I want to live the kind of life that has always eluded me, the kind that includes contemplation,

111

introspection, tranquillity, domesticity, maybe even boredom – all those dull desires that descend on you in mid-life.'

'You seem a bit young to call yourself middle aged.'

'I'm forty-three.'

'That's supposed to be the prime of life.'

'Not unless you do something about it.'

She smiled. 'You're right; it's only a platitude. Well, what *about* this book you were thinking of writing about the Middle Ages? That sounded wonderful to me.'

'The chronicles . . .'

'I didn't see any dusty tomes lying on your desk.'

'I'll show it to you.'

Michael went into the house and returned with a dog-eared faded, blue folder, which he set before her. It was smaller than she imagined, only forty pages of fine print on yellowed paper.

'It's hell to read. It's probably been transcribed a number of times in the last six hundred years. This version was made by a priest over a hundred and fifty years ago. It's a unique document about life during the plague. There are very few direct accounts as specific as this one.'

Rachel opened the folder to the first yellow page of the monograph. 'I can just about make sense of it. My French isn't anything like it was in my student days at the Sorbonne.' She read a few lines. 'This is absolutely fascinating.'

'It was probably a best-seller of its day – or deserved to be. Of course, novels didn't exist then, but between the lines the chronicle is as full of sex and violence as any blockbuster.'

'Nothing changes, does it?' she said in a resigned tone.

'That's just it,' he responded excitedly. 'In John Stratton's little masterpiece there are people just like you and me, so like us, in fact, that it's uncanny.'

'What do you suppose a fourteenth-century woman would do in my place? No, wait – I promised not to talk about myself, didn't I?' She had said it jokingly, but suddenly she wondered.

'She would have prayed, because that would have been her only hope in an unjust world.'

'I did pray – yesterday morning in the chapel.'

112

'Were you really praying?'

'I'm not sure. I think I've forgotten how.' She looked at the blue folder lying on the table, intrigued by what Michael had said.

Following her eyes, he said, 'You're welcome to borrow it if you like.'

'I'd love to read it, but I doubt that I've got the concentration it requires just now.' She looked at it regretfully: it was like a path disappearing invitingly into the distance, a path she knew she would never take. 'If I ever hear that you've made a book out of it, I'll certainly read it. What a thrill it would be: I could say I'd met you and encouraged you to do it.'

'It might not come to anything, but the material is there. The pathos of the dry prose is as poignant as when it was written. It just needs transposing into a modern idiom by someone who's fired by the idea.'

'You seem to be that person.'

He responded to the challenge he detected in her tone and saw in her eyes. 'You make it sound easy,' he said, 'but it would be a mammoth project and there are some real technical difficulties to surmount. The book would have to encompass the history of the fourteenth century and the Hundred Years War, and I'm no historian.'

'There must be a way to get round that. And what do you mean by technical difficulties?'

'This could be very boring for you . . .'

'Not in the least.' She leaned back with her arms folded, provoking him with her interest.

'All right, but don't say I didn't warn you.'

When he started to articulate his thoughts in detail, it came home to Michael that what he had lacked all these months was a whetstone for his intellect. After an hour of intense discussion, there was a pause and Rachel glanced at her watch.

'I can't believe how late it is. I'm afraid time is finally catching up with me.'

'I've exhausted you.'

'No, you've taken me out of myself. Just as you did last night. I'm sane again, and can face tomorrow.'

Michael felt a sharp sense of disappointment that she had to leave. Their conversation had inspired that familiar surge of creative energy he hadn't enjoyed for a long time. He was moved to start working in earnest.

As she prepared to leave, Rachel said, 'Your idea that life in Roquelaire is a replica of its past is wonderfully romantic. It intrigues me to think that all our days are repetitions of other days, all our thoughts and hopes.'

'All our hates and loves and fears,' murmured Michael.

Once again Rachel declined Michael's offer to walk her back to Bob Cooper's house. They shook hands and she turned to wave goodbye when she was halfway down the darkened street. The sight of him framed in the illuminated doorway filled her with mixed emotions. It was as if she hadn't the right to enjoy his company with all that was weighing on her mind. But she had enjoyed this evening, she realized, more than she would have thought possible. She had hardly thought about her own problems.

Walking back through the empty, dark square, where the only lights came from the café, Rachel glanced at the church tower jutting into the midnight-blue sky. As conversation in thickly accented patois seeped through the shutters of the house she was passing her thoughts shifted to the vanished world of the fourteenth century. The miaow of a cat, the creak of a shutter being closed seemed to hark back centuries. Looking up at the stars, she found comfort in the fact that they had been there, then as now, shining down on ancient streets that had absorbed centuries of prayers and tears.

# Chapter 6

Rachel arrived at the café early and sat down at a table shaded by an umbrella. Retreating behind her sunglasses, she unfolded the newspaper she had just bought, but after reading it for a few minutes she realized she hadn't taken in a word. She couldn't ignore the glaring presence of the clock near the church, which seemed to be advancing with disconcerting speed.

A few moments later she was surprised to see Alain arrive at the wheel of a white Golf convertible with the top down. As he sped round the square, slammed on the brakes, and swung into a parking place, she realized Oliver wasn't with him. Alain leapt from the car and slammed the door, and Rachel felt a bracing anger well up inside her, counteracting her nervousness. He strode towards the café and spotted her at once. She knew that stride: it was usually the confident swagger of a man in charge, but today it suggested aggression. He was wearing sunglasses, a crisp white shirt rolled up at the sleeves, and bleached jeans; the gold chain she had given him glinted at his neck. Reassessing every familiar detail about Alain as he approached, Rachel sensed there was something different about him now he was back in France. She stayed in her seat and refrained from making any friendly or welcoming gesture. He stared down at her; his mouth, partly concealed by his beard and moustache, was a grim line.

'I had hoped that in spite of our conversation last night you might have brought Oliver with you,' she said as evenly as she could.

'This is no place for him. He's enjoying himself having a riding lesson this morning.'

'Fine. I'd like to see him for lunch then.'

'Let's leave Oliver out of this. This is between you and me, and we have some things to discuss.'

115

She stared at him, but before she could reply they were interrupted by a waiter, who took their order. When he had gone, Alain took off his sunglasses, folded his arms across his chest and looked at her with accusing blue eyes of startling intensity.

'Now, would you like to tell me what you're doing here?'

She looked at him incredulously. 'On the contrary, I think it's you who needs to do the explaining. I found these in the office after you left.' She reached in her handbag and brought out the booking slip and the postcard. 'These two things, on top of your behaviour in the last few weeks, gave me no alternative but to come.'

Staring at what seemed damning evidence, she was too proud to mention that his lovemaking had been perfunctory and infrequent lately, that for longer than she could remember he had been cool and distant, and that now he had made no move to kiss her or even to touch her. She fought the sinking, helpless sensation that might trigger off a flood of emotion.

Alain glanced at the booking slip and the postcard, then shrugged as if he couldn't be bothered to explain.

'It's obvious to me that you've been planning this trip for some time.'

'Hold on,' he interrupted her irritably.

'No,' she said firmly, 'let me finish. When I found this postcard, wild horses wouldn't have kept me away.'

'Don't be stupid. The photographer sent it. He wants to use it as a location in the book.'

She had built up a momentum now. Her heart was pounding, her face flushed, and she was no longer afraid. 'That's bullshit, and you know it. What does it mean, "*à bientôt*"?'

'I don't know what you're getting at,' he said coldly.

'Getting at? If I hadn't come here I wouldn't even have known where you were. Alain, there is no Hôtel de la Poste in Roquelaire.'

'Well, so what? Memory plays tricks after so many years. It's the Hôtel de France now.'

'But they had no booking for you. I checked. And you still haven't explained why you booked your ticket, and Oliver's, months ago.'

116

'Look, I don't appreciate your tone of voice. It's like an inquisition. But, as you're here, I'll explain what happened. The photographer, Dick Murray, was stuck in London. He had Isabelle de Montjoi meet us in Paris. Isabelle is a friend of his, and she insisted we come and stay with her, which is great for Oliver because she has a pool and horses. It's paradise for a small boy. I don't know if you remember her – she came to Sonoma,' he added casually.

'Yes, I remember.' She held his gaze unwaveringly and it was he who looked away first.

'What were you doing in Paris?'

'Oh – Isabelle met us at the airport and had arranged a meeting with some French publisher who wants to bring the book out here. The guy was going on vacation right away, so naturally I jumped at the chance. How could I refuse? We've nearly tied up the deal.'

'Is that so?' she said, not believing a word of his explanation.

'Yes, it is so.' Alain leaned back and stared belligerently at her. 'So when did you come here and what have you been doing?'

'I've been talking to people, listening and thinking.'

For the first time Alain seemed unsure of himself. 'What's that supposed to mean?'

'Whatever you think it might mean,' she countered.

'I don't want to guess, I really don't,' he sighed irritably. 'All I can say is that you've let me down, you've disappointed me. I never would have gone on this trip if I'd known you were going to do this. If you want to repair the damage, I suggest you leave Roquelaire today and return home.'

'I'm not going anywhere. And I'm certainly not leaving without Oliver. I'm not just an inconvenience to be disposed of . . .' She broke off, feeling hurt and outraged by his dismissal.

At that moment Rachel caught sight of Michael crossing the square, a baguette under his arm. He looked directly at her, then at Alain. He walked by without saying a word, and when he came out of the newspaper shop, he walked away instead of sitting down at the café as she knew was his habit. When she looked back at Alain, she saw his face had hardened in an expression that made her suddenly apprehensive. 'In that case, you leave me no choice but to

117

tell you now, instead of when I come back.' His thick-lashed eyes were coldly serious.

Rachel felt as if a trapdoor had opened and she were staring into a bottomless pit. She couldn't move, but waited for what was coming.

'I haven't been happy for a long time; that must be obvious. Putting it simply, I want a divorce. I have a lot of respect for you, and we had some good years, but as far as I'm concerned it's over. It's been over for some time. I don't believe in looking back; I want to move forward. I've decided to sell Chez Alain. I'll be truthful with you: René and I have discussed it and he wants to buy me out. The final details are almost in place. I'm here to start a new venture, and that's what I've been doing this year. Isabelle de Montjoi is my partner. She's had a fantastic opportunity to develop a property here in Roquelaire into a hotel and spa. Our plan is to turn it into one of the finest establishments of its kind in France. There has been a hitch, it's true, but we will overcome it. I'd rather you kept this to yourself, Rachel . . .'

All through his monologue she had been struggling to keep up with him, fitting the words to the movement of his lips. She heard herself speak in a whisper.

'But you can't. The château belongs to Madame Grimal now.' Her inadequate reply came out in a whisper. She was shaking all over.

Alain narrowed his eyes. 'I don't know what sort of rumours you've heard, but you don't know what's really going on.'

The château had already faded from her mind. Swallowing the tears she still refused to let fall, her chest heaved with emotion. Alain stared at her in stony silence, waiting for her to speak.

'This isn't as much of a surprise to me as you might think, but it's still a terrible shock.'

'I'm sorry, Rachel, but there was no way to break it gently.'

'Just tell me this: are you in love with Isabelle de Montjoi?'

Alain frowned, but as well as she knew him, she couldn't read his thoughts. Running his fingers through his hair in exasperation, he said. 'This is so terrible, all these rumours in the village. If you had stayed at home, this would not have happened. We could have talked in a calm, civilized way. You've always hated fights and dramas, so why are you making things difficult?'

She shook her head. 'Alain, it's you who are making things difficult. If I hadn't been half prepared for what you have told me this morning, how do you think I could have coped with it? You've just destroyed my whole life. I deserve an answer to my question: are you in love with her?'

'I don't expect you to believe me now, but Isabelle and I are business partners, pure and simple, and if people here choose to put another interpretation on it, it's not my fault.' The gentle Alain, sorry after an outburst of temper, broke through for a moment. 'I'm truly sorry that you had to hear it like this, in a public place so far away from home. I had planned to talk to you when I came back to Sonoma, where you have your family and friends around you. I know how difficult this is going to be for you.'

He sounded tired and distraught, and for a moment Rachel could almost forget he had said he was leaving her. She wanted to reach out for his hand to bring him back.

Gaining control of himself, Alain said, 'I think the best thing you could do, and this is nothing to do with the business, is to go home as soon as you can. You'll probably want to see a lawyer. Believe me, I'm not going to be unreasonable or anything. We'll work this out in a civilized manner, like two grown-up people.'

She tried to gather her flying thoughts. Only one thing seemed important. 'Does Oliver know? That's the main thing. And when do you expect to tell him?' Suddenly she wanted her son there, in her arms. She wanted to crush him to her for comfort.

'Of course he doesn't know. Look, he's having a wonderful time. I didn't tell him you're here. It would only upset him, Rachel, because he wouldn't understand why we weren't together. He's not a baby any more. He's old enough to sense what's happening if he sees you. Why spoil his holiday? Let him enjoy himself. He's even starting to speak French.'

Absently she snatched the postcard and booking slip and tucked them in her bag. Suddenly the sight of them was unendurable. 'I don't know; I can't think straight at the moment,' she whispered, slipping on her sunglasses. She saw long summers stretching emptily ahead, while Oliver was here in Roquelaire with Alain. As the reality of what divorce was going to mean dawned on her, the world actually seemed to stop.

Alain was looking at her steadily. His self-control seemed inhuman.

'You always said you hated the way parents made their children pawns in a break-up. It has happened to lots of people we know.'

'I never thought it would happen to us.'

He stood up and put on his glasses. 'We've said enough for one day. Believe me, I'm sorry it had to happen this way. In the end you'll realize it's the best for all of us, even for Oliver.'

'You have to follow your dream at any cost, don't you?' A sudden picture came to her mind of all those years when she had worked in the background while he took the glory.

'Don't be bitter, whatever you do, Rachel. It's not like you.'

'How do you know what I'm like?' She looked up at him, the naked hurt distorting her face. He shrugged and looked away.

'I'll call you tomorrow. There's really no alternative but for you to fly home this weekend, back where you belong. I'll follow with Oliver as I planned before.'

'Is this where *you* belong, Alain?' Rachel asked, angered at this repeated dismissal. He walked away as if he hadn't heard her.

She watched him go to the car and drive away. It was nearing ten-thirty and the town was filling up. The people around her melted into meaningless swirls of colour, and the sounds of their comings and goings became a roar in her ears. She felt someone touch her hand.

'Rachel? Rachel?'

Looking up, she focused on a familiar face.

'Rachel, are you all right?' It was Michael Lowry, looking down at her with concern.

She nodded, and moved her lips to speak, but only a whisper came out.

'Just stay here and don't move. I'll be right back.' He returned with an Armagnac, which he set in front of her.

'Here, drink this. You'll feel a lot better.'

She did as she was told. The shock of the burning liquid in her throat brought tears to her eyes. A powerful shiver went through her as the warmth came back into her body.

'You came back,' she said, remembering she had seen him a quarter of an hour ago.

'I never left. I was across the square in the *épicerie*, waiting for your husband to leave. I thought you might like to talk to somebody. I realized some kind of confrontation was going on.'

'It's so sweet of you, Michael.' Her own voice sounded as though it came from a distance. 'He wants a divorce.'

Michael reached across and squeezed her hand. 'Rachel, you're going to be all right. You've had a terrible shock, I can see that, but you're a strong woman. Here, take another sip of Armagnac.'

She took a deep breath and then another sip from the glass. She looked at him with an air of grim determination. 'Just give me a second to get my thoughts together.'

'Take all the time you need. I won't leave you until I know you're all right.'

'Michael, that house you mentioned the other night – can you arrange it for me?'

'Are you sure you want to decide this minute? You haven't even had time to think yet. I mean, you might want to get out of here right away.'

'No, I have to have a base right now. I have to stay here in Roquelaire, and I need a place where I can be alone to think, and where I can have my son with me. Do you think I could move in today?'

'I'm sure it can be arranged.' Suddenly the strong, independent woman sounded as vulnerable as a child. It would pass, but Michael knew he would remember this side of Rachel Ribard. 'Do you feel like telling me what happened?'

She nodded. 'It was all over in minutes. He's leaving California, selling Chez Alain. He wants to move back here to develop the château with Isabelle de Montjoi. I asked him if he was in love with her but he denied it.' She stared at the square where life, other lives, were going on as if nothing had happened. 'I think he was lying.'

121

'Did you think to ask him about the little detail of getting possession of the château?'

'He seems to think it's not a problem. He seems so sure of himself, Michael. He's like a complete stranger. It frightens me. Oh, my God!' she gasped, her hands flying to her face.

'What's the matter?'

'Why didn't I think to bring it up while he was here? He's got Oliver's passport.'

'Has he threatened to keep your son from you?'

'No, not exactly. He said he didn't want me to see him at the moment, that it would be too upsetting for Oliver. He doesn't even know I'm in Roquelaire.' She told him that Alain had urged her to go back to California, saying he would follow with Oliver.

'Don't you think you might be jumping to conclusions? Sit tight and wait and see for a day or two.'

'I'll go crazy if I have to do that.'

'No you won't. The time will pass, believe me. I'm an expert on passing time.'

She gave a twisted smile. 'Maybe I could take up painting.'

'No, don't do that.'

The way he said it made her laugh suddenly, relaxing the knot in her stomach. 'I must be mad – only a few minutes ago my life fell apart and here I am laughing.'

'Is that so strange? If you lose your sense of humour you're done for, believe me.'

Rachel nodded. There was a sea of tears inside her, waiting to be shed when she was alone. Now it seemed almost a miracle that she was living, that she had survived, for a few moments at least, the worst thing she thought could ever happen to her.

They left the café and walked up the Rue St Jacques to the house belonging to Michael's friends. It was simple but comfortable, and Michael opened all the shutters to admit the hard morning light and let in the fresh air. Rachel went back to Bob Cooper's to fetch her bags. When she returned, Michael was putting some groceries in the refrigerator.

'Just a few basics. The shops are closed until three. If you need anything, I'm always there. You're welcome to come by anytime for lunch, dinner, even breakfast, or just to talk.'

'You're very kind, but when you're in limbo, you don't need to eat or sleep or think. You just exist.'

'You feel that way now, which is only natural. Just remember that if you need me, I'm down the street.'

'I can't thank you enough for everything you've done.' She paused. 'I hadn't thought of it until now, but it might be better if you and I still weren't seen together. You can imagine how Alain would interpret it, and I don't want to give him any ammunition. I'm feeling so unsure of myself at the moment, and I wouldn't want to do anything, however innocent, that he might use against me.'

'Of course. I hadn't even thought of it. Well, I'll be going. Don't forget, if you need anything . . .'

'I won't forget.'

She saw him out the door. Watching him disappear through his own doorway, Rachel felt suddenly very alone and wished she had asked him to stay. She braced herself to face an empty house filled with cobwebs and sunbeams, for she must face the crisis alone. But for the moment in the hot, dark hallway her composure broke, and she began to cry.

At a table laid for lunch under the lime trees in the park at Terre Blanche, Isabelle and Alain watched Oliver poised to dive into the pool. His angular brown shoulders sparkled with droplets of water as he positioned his hands over his head. When he hesitated, Alain called, *'Vas-y vite! N'hésites pas!'*

His encouragement caused Oliver to spring from the board and crash into the blue rectangle of water. When he surfaced, Alain burst into applause. 'Bravo! You've almost got it! Now try it again.'

But Oliver climbed out of the pool and began to run across the grass to the elegantly set table. The pale pink cloth was laid with brightly coloured faience and a jar of summer roses nodded in the centre.

As Oliver started to slide on to the cushion of the wicker chair, Isabelle exclaimed, 'Not on the chair with wet trunks!'

123

'Go get the towel, Olivier,' Alain ordered.

Oliver did as he was told and raced back to the table, where he bolted the food on his plate.

'Would you like another slice of ham, Oliver?' asked Isabelle.

The boy shook his head.

'"*Non, merci*" is what you say,' said Alain.

'*Non, merci,*' repeated Oliver, not looking up from his plate.

'Don't forget that Fernande's grandson will be coming later, so you'll have a playmate while you're here. Jean-Marie said he'd bring him over after lunch,' said Isabelle.

Alain broke off a piece of bread and chewed it irritably, waiting for his son to reply. 'What's got into you today, Olivier? Isabelle is talking to you.'

Isabelle shook her head and sighed. Her bracelets rattled as she reached for a bowl. She was coolly dressed in pale blue linen and her hair was swept away from her face.

'Would you like some salad?'

'Yes, please,' Oliver replied, studying Isabelle as she heaped lettuce and tomatoes on to his plate. As she smiled down at him, he stared at his reflection in her enormous sunglasses. He reached for a glass of Coca Cola next to a glass of water into which Alain had poured a few drops of red wine to colour it.

Isabelle tried another tack. 'You should have seen Oliver this morning at his riding lesson, Alain. The master was very impressed. He couldn't believe that Oliver wasn't an accomplished rider already. When I told him this was almost Oliver's first time on a horse, he didn't believe it.'

'That's fantastic,' said Alain.

Oliver looked down and said nothing.

'Olivier is good at everything he does. He always comes first, don't you?'

'I try to. Sometimes I don't.' He shrugged as if he didn't really care one way or another.

'I think we should start calling you Olivier, don't you?' said Isabelle in French.

Comprehending what she said, Oliver looked at her suspiciously. 'Only Daddy can call me that. But nobody else,' he said defiantly.

'His comprehension is remarkable after a few days. It's because you read to him so much in French,' Isabelle said to Alain.

'Why do you want to call me Olivier?' Oliver persisted.

'Because it's French and you're a French boy, or at least half of you is.'

'No I'm not,' said Oliver flatly. 'I'm American. My passport says so.'

'But you're still half French,' insisted Alain. 'Isabelle can call you Olivier if she wants to.'

'No she can't,' he retorted, stuffing some salad into his mouth.

Alain was about to comment on his son's rudeness when Isabelle said tactfully, 'Let's not make an issue of it. I can just imagine what you were like at his age: stubborn and independent.'

'I don't remember,' said Alain.

Pushing away his plate, Oliver said, 'I'm finished for now. Can I go back into the pool?' He looked at Alain.

'No, no, you shouldn't so soon after eating,' interjected Isabelle. 'Anyway, there's gâteau for dessert. I'll cut it in a minute, when we have finished.'

When Oliver grimaced, Alain said, 'Never mind. We're here to watch him. Go ahead, Olivier,' he said with a wink.

After Oliver had gone, Isabelle said in a low voice, 'I wish you wouldn't contradict me in front of him, Alain. He'll begin to ignore me if you always do that.'

A look of annoyance crossed Alain's face, but he didn't reply.

'Tell me again what happened this morning. I want to hear exactly what she said.'

'I told her we were partners, but that's all.'

'What do you think really made her come over here?' A frown furrowed Isabelle's brow.

'Who knows? Female intuition. She claims it was a paper she found, proving that I'd booked the flight a long time ago. It's true, but I wanted her to think I'd done it at the last minute in case she objected. I knew she wanted me to go to the wedding and the only way I could bring Olivier with me was to appear to make the arrangements at the last moment. If it had only been one ticket she might have believed me, but I bought two the minute you called to tell me Armand's condition was worse because it was high season and I was worried I wouldn't get a second one. And another thing, she found that old postcard you sent me, the one with a picture of Brissac on the front. I just said it was something to do with the book, but I don't think she believed me and I don't know if she believes we're just friends. If she thinks we're lovers, then it will make things even more difficult. That's why we still have to be careful.'

Isabelle put down her fork and sighed. 'She's not going to believe anything now you've said you're leaving her.'

'Maybe it's better this way. But I have to convince her to go back home soon. I could tell she's dead set on taking Olivier with her, and I don't want to appear too insistent, otherwise she might suspect that I plan to keep him here.'

'How will we know when she's gone? I won't breathe easily until she has.'

'All I can do is to call her at Bob Cooper's tomorrow. She needs a while to get over the shock, I guess.'

'Do you really think she's going to simply vanish?'

'I know Rachel. She'll see reason after she's had a chance to think about it. She won't oppose me.'

Watching Oliver's brown body as he cavorted in the pool, Isabelle said, 'I'm worried that she might try to cause trouble here and stir up feeling against us. I've gone out of my way not to antagonize anybody. Think of the number of people I've cultivated all these years, even Armand Bataille's housekeeper, Hélène, for example, a tedious busybody, who gets on my nerves.'

Alain wasn't listening, and he interrupted her. 'One thing you really must understand, Isabelle, is that Oliver stays here with me, no matter what.'

She looked at him. 'You don't know how women think. But I'm a woman. I know how your wife will feel in this situation.'

'How could you?' he said, without thinking.

Disbelief crossed her face and she blinked in shock.

'Isabelle, I didn't mean it the way it sounded. Please forgive me. It was a stupid thing to say.'

'Of course you didn't,' she said quickly, holding back her anger.

'Though I've never had children, I understand a woman's motivations. She has no choice but to accept the divorce, but custody of Olivier is another matter entirely.'

Alain changed the subject abruptly. 'Are you going to call Madame Grimal this afternoon?'

'No, not yet. I was thinking, the best way to approach the matter might be to see the priest.' After a pause, she continued, 'About the loan to pay off Madame Grimal – I was thinking, *chéri*, I don't want you to be burdened by financial worry now, especially since you haven't sold Chez Alain yet and might have financial entanglements with your divorce. I'll finance your share on my Paris flat or even this house.'

Alain looked at her in surprise. 'That's very generous of you; but would that affect my percentage of the shares when we float the company?'

'No, not at all. We'll make sure it doesn't.' She smiled and touched his hand. 'Don't be so suspicious. I love you. I want to share everything I have with you, don't you understand?'

Alain looked somewhat embarrassed by her generosity. 'I don't know what to say.'

'Say you love me too.'

'*Je t'adore,*' he whispered, grazing her hand with his lips as his eyes caressed her face, radiant with happiness. 'You're a marvellous, courageous, clever woman. I've never met anyone else like you.'

'And I hope you never will. I only wish I could give you a child as fine and beautiful as Oliver. He's so like you. I can give you myself, and everything I possess, but not that.' She couldn't keep the regret from her voice.

'You know that doesn't matter to me. Oliver is enough. I don't think I could ever love another child as much as him. I've given everything of myself to him.'

Isabelle leaned back and looked at the sun-dappled lawn shaded by trees that bordered a field of brilliant yellow sunflowers. The feverish whirr of cicadas made her eyelids heavy and the scent of Alain's skin, like earth and leather, stirred her senses. She allowed herself to imagine that the problems besieging their dream could not scale the high wall protecting the house.

'Just think,' she said with a sigh. 'A year ago I hadn't even met you. I was thinking about turning the château into a hotel, yes, but it was still in the dreaming stage. I didn't realize the vital spark was missing – someone to share it with.'

'I still can't get over Armand Bataille doing this to you. It wasn't as if you were plotting behind his back.'

'No,' Isabelle said almost wearily. 'I thought it was agreed: I would purchase the lease and the money would go into a family trust fund. But now, of course, all the gossips in the village have forgotten about that.'

'Whose idea was it, yours or his?'

'Mine, to be honest. I didn't want any trouble with his family when he was dead, even though he hardly saw them. After what happened to me with my husband, I know how savage people can be about what they regard as their rights.'

'Well, it was very clever of you, Isabelle, but it didn't avert what happened.'

'Who could have predicted it? I wonder what connection there is between him and that old woman. I simply can't believe they ever had an affair or anything like that. She's nothing but a peasant and he was a cultured, sophisticated man, who counted some very influential people in France as his friends.'

'*Madame*,' called a voice. '*Madame est demandée au téléphone!*'

They turned to see the housekeeper at the top of the stairs to the house.

When Isabelle had gone, Oliver came back to the table, panting from exertion and smiling.

'Come here, I want to talk to you.' Alain slipped his arm around the child's cool, wet shoulders. Oliver squinted up at him against the sun.

'Olivier, I want you to make sure you are polite to Isabelle and that you thank her for everything she's done for you. I don't like you answering questions with just "yes" or "no". At home you don't do that with people. Why do you do it here?'

Oliver shrugged his shoulders and tried to squirm away, but Alain held him fast. 'I want you to be on your best behaviour, do you understand? I hope you know what a lucky boy you are to have been taken to France at your age, to be in this beautiful place.'

'Yes, Dad.'

'Now, finish your lunch.'

Oliver sat down reluctantly and took up his fork. 'Where did Isabelle go?'

'She was called to the telephone.'

'When are we going to call Mom?'

'It's too early to call. Anyway, I don't want to make long-distance calls when we're staying with somebody.'

'We can reverse the charges, can't we?'

'I didn't tell you because I thought you'd be disappointed, but I called her last night when you were asleep and found out that she left yesterday for Lake Tahoe with Grandpa and Grandma.'

'Lake Tahoe? Why?'

'She was tired after the wedding and needed a rest. I left a message telling her to call us when she got back.'

'I thought she had to stay home and take care of everything.'

'Well, this is just for a few days.'

As Isabelle came down the steps leading to the garden Oliver fixed his deep blue eyes on Alain. 'It's a shame that Mom isn't here for a rest. She'd love it, wouldn't she?'

Alain didn't meet Oliver's eyes as they searched his face. Hearing Isabelle's footsteps on the gravel, he turned.

'That was Julian,' she said, seating herself at the table. 'He's just about to leave St Tropez. He'll be back tonight.'

'What are we going to do now?' asked Oliver.

'I'm going to have a rest, but you can stay here. Your new friend will be arriving any minute. Later on we'll go for a drive.'

'Where?'

'You'll see.'

Late in the afternoon Rachel left the house and drove through the village. All the shutters were closed against the heat. Shops in the square were just beginning to reopen and a few old men were playing *boules*. She took the road that had brought her to Roquelaire and stopped in front of Agnès Grimal's cottage. At first the only sign of movement was from the shimmering butterflies fluttering among the flowers. She spotted Agnès, dressed in blue, a hat shielding her eyes, watering a row of lettuces.

129

'*Bonjour, madame,*' Rachel called.

Agnès put down the watering can and hurried towards the gate.

After they had exchanged greetings, there was a pause. Using carefully rehearsed phrases, Rachel said, '*Madame*, when I first met you the other day I mentioned my husband's family, the Ribards. You said you remembered them and I was wondering if you recall where they used to live?'

Her question took Agnès completely by surprise. She looked at Rachel, trying to decipher her motives for asking about the Ribards. She saw a torment in Rachel's eyes that the young woman could not conceal, suggesting that all the rumours about Alain Ribard and Isabelle de Montjoi were true.

'The Ribard farm is only a ruin, *madame*. And the road to it is no more than a track.'

'Even so, I would still like to go there.'

'Well, if you're sure – you take this road for about a kilometre . . .' she began. When she had explained, and Rachel had repeated the instructions to show she had understood, they said goodbye.

Seeing Agnès waiting at the gate as she drove off, Rachel wished she had had the courage to ask her whether she hoped to sell the château.

She found the bleached dirt track, which cleaved wide fields of stubble dotted with the giant wheels of straw she had grown used to seeing on her journey to Roquelaire. She brought the car to a halt at the end of the lane, which dissolved into hardened ridges of white clay. A thicket of dead elm trees surrounded a heap of rubble that had once been a cottage and barn, keeping it prisoner on the little rise from where the towers of Brissac could just be seen in the distance. All that was left of the house was a pile of crude earth bricks. The roof had collapsed and decaying beams protruded through a heap of shattered red tiles. The one wall that remained standing was pierced by two small windows with glassless frames hanging on their hinges.

Rachel stood in the silence that enveloped the ruin, stricken with disbelief at what she saw. She realized as never before how humble Alain's origins were and how far he had come in life. From the serene and prosperous vantage point of northern California, it had been impossible for her to imagine; the contrast was too great. He had talked about it so seldom, and when he did, his allusions were bitter and dark. The years compacted into a seething mass of impressions. She wondered if she had ever understood Alain. She stood beneath the blazing sun listening to the deep silence as regret and sorrow coursed through her: regret for failing to understand; sorrow that she couldn't remake the past.

Looking at Brissac across the valley, she was amazed that Alain had wanted to come back to Roquelaire at all. When he was growing up where she now stood, she realized, Armand Bataille must have been restoring the château to its former glory. Its towers had cast long shadows on the sons of a broken, alcoholic widower who were baling hay and tending cattle. She couldn't imagine a harsher, more brutal life. That Alain had forged his own destiny seemed almost miraculous.

Driving away, Rachel couldn't put what she had seen out of her mind. Her incredulity at Alain's past revealed the poignant truth that he deserved some measure of forgiveness. After so many years, she understood his veiled reproaches about her privileged existence, reproaches she had borne though they had made her angry. Now she had visited the barren, tumbledown farm Rachel could see that Alain's ambitions were conceived on a grand scale in order to dwarf the past, and she felt ashamed at her own simplistic notion that her husband's creative spirit was nourished by some mystical tie to his peasant past.

By the time Rachel returned to Roquelaire, outlined against the deepening blue of the sky, her mood had reversed and she was determined to turn the situation around. She began to believe that their marriage wasn't over. She could not offer Alain a château, but she could persuade him to see reason. She was convinced that, ultimately, staying in Roquelaire would not make him happy; the shadow that hung over the Ribard farm would always be visible to him from Brissac.

She entered the gate of the village determined to swallow her pride and hurt – for Alain, but most of all for Oliver. However wounded she might be, she had to try. She let herself into the empty little house, deciding that when tomorrow came she would fight to get back what she had lost.

# Chapter 7

Alain and Isabelle were in her large, airy bedroom. The shutters had been closed against the midday heat, casting a premature twilight on the high, moulded ceiling. Isabelle pulled back the embroidered white coverlet and smoothed the white linen sheets that bore the monogram of the Montjoi family.

'What are you thinking?' she asked Alain, who was thoughtfully studying the provincial bedhead, painted with garlands of roses.

'I was just wondering how many people have been born and died in that bed.'

'Or made passionate love. Isn't that much more pleasant?'

Alain cast a glance around the sumptuous room. He was suddenly aware of how profoundly it contrasted with the bedroom he shared with Rachel. In his mind he saw their light, sparsely furnished room, its walls covered with paintings by artists they knew, the king-size bed facing the redwood terrace and commanding a view of the tree-clad hills around Sonoma. For a moment it seemed more real than Isabelle's feminine and unreservedly French surroundings, full of antiques and muted colours. In one corner stood a curved dressing table, fussily draped in lace and cluttered with crystal perfume bottles and monogrammed silver-backed brushes. It began to sink in that he was destined to spend the rest of his life here, that he would never return 'home'. The thought gave him a jolt, as if he had touched a live wire. He looked up as Isabelle brushed past him and disappeared into the dressing room that led to the white marble bathroom.

Isabelle was removing her clothes and laying them across a tapestried prie-dieu in front of a long mirror. Reaching to unhook her brassière, she saw Alain's reflection behind her as he entered the dressing room.

'Can you help me? The hook is caught.'

When Alain had freed the hook, Isabelle clasped him firmly and held him to her. 'It's so good to be alone for an afternoon.' She tilted her head and closed her eyes in anticipation. His hands cradling her hips, he kissed her indifferently.

Looking up at him, she whispered, 'Come on, *chéri*. I know we have a lot to do, but let's slip into bed for half an hour.'

When she began to undo his trousers he pulled away. 'Isabelle, I'm going to go outside by the pool with Olivier.'

'But why? Jean-Marie is there. I told him to work around the pool and keep an eye on the boys just so you could relax.'

'No, it's not that,' he murmured. 'Quite frankly, my mind isn't on making love. It was that meeting with Rachel this morning . . .'

Isabelle tried to smile. 'I understand, really I do. But you and I have to live a moment at a time, in the present, not in the past. To postpone pleasure means to lose it for ever. This morning cannot be changed by denying what we feel for each other. We are only half alive if we don't live here and now,' she nodded towards the bedroom, 'in each other's arms. I need you more than anyone else needs you, Alain, and I need you now.'

She began to kiss him and his resistance ebbed away. When he had slipped from his clothes, he pulled her violently to him and they embraced in front of the mirror, their two sun-bronzed bodies forged together in a white heat. Alain admired her broad shoulders, her strong hips and shapely legs crushed against him. Seeing himself about to possess her, he was reminded he had seen her once years ago swathed in mink, standing by her husband's silver Jaguar in the village, though he had never told her. Poor and without hope, he had passed her by, sensing her condescension at a distance. Seeing her face now transfixed with desire, he wondered what she would say if she were able to recall the young man in a shabby coat. In a ferment of desire, he moved her towards the prie-dieu, where she bent forward with a little cry of anticipation.

Half an hour later Isabelle was back in her office, dressed in black culottes and a T-shirt, her pale blonde hair sleekly combed into place, her make-up freshly applied, all the dreaminess gone from her eyes. Through the open window of her wood-panelled study she could hear Alain playing with Oliver and Lucien by the pool. Picking up the telephone, she dialled Père Auguste's number. While she waited for it to connect she glanced at the room she had redecorated after her husband had died. It had long since ceased to be the private retreat of a gentleman who enjoyed a good cigar and an Armagnac by the fire; who read the *Figaro* and *Le Monde* until he nodded off to sleep. She had swept away every trace of old-world masculinity: the racing sheets, the auction catalogues, the tarnished golf trophies. She had reduced the collection of framed photographs that occupied a marble-topped table, assigning to the attic the pictures of people and relatives who had failed to call when she was widowed, people she had never liked, and a few whom she had come to hate, members of her late husband's immediate family who had tried to take her inheritance away from her.

The sophisticated feminine touches she had added to the room disguised the fact that this was now a place of business. The focal point was an old leather-topped chart desk between the windows, where her husband had once pored over wine catalogues and stock-market reports and which was now dominated by a computer. The only detail of her husband's office that Isabelle had not been tempted to alter was his large collection of books, shelved along one wall behind fine, gold-meshed doors. These were dusted, but never read. Her husband's younger brother had tried to wrest them from her through a lawyer, but she had insisted on keeping them as a symbol of the kind of life she had grown into after all these years.

Someone had picked up the phone at the other end.

'*Bonjour*. May I speak to Père Auguste?' she said when she heard the voice of his housekeeper on the line.

'*Oui, j'écoute,*' came the priest's voice, thick with sleep, conveying that she had woken him from his afternoon nap.

'Father, this is Isabelle de Montjoi,' she began, acutely aware that she had never entered the church in Roquelaire.

'*Bonjour, madame,*' came the reply.

'I was wondering if I might see you about an important matter. It's not something I wish to discuss on the telephone.'

'I am rather busy in the parish at this time in the week. Is it urgent, *madame*?'

'No, no,' Isabelle assured him, not wanting to seem too eager. 'No, I was thinking about Monday. Could I come to see you in the morning?' She had been on the verge of asking him to come to her house, but something in his manner changed her mind.

'You can come at ten o'clock if you wish.'

'Thank you. Thank you very much, Père Auguste.'

When Isabelle had hung up, she felt dissatisfied with the call. She valued her ability to pick up the slightest nuance or hesitation in a person's voice, and she sensed that Père Auguste was not especially pleased to hear from her; nor did he seem surprised.

Isabelle slipped into the chair in front of her desk and tried to concentrate. The sensuality that always enveloped her after making love with Alain was spoiled by an old anxiety, which had taken her unawares that afternoon. It seemed a lifetime since she had been afraid of anything or anyone, but now a pack of little demons that represented all her crimes, sins and omissions seemed to dance around her head. The clock on the mantel chimed three, yet time seemed to be going backwards, taking her far away from the well-ordered present into a much harsher world. Faces of people she hated, some she had loved, though none she ever wanted to see again, came back to her in a slow procession, like weathered milestones that had long since passed out of sight.

Dust and heat were what she always thought of when she remembered the Villa Claudia, twenty-five kilometres outside Tunis on the road to Bizerte. Dust left a fine film on the heavy French furniture in the bedroom and on the red tile floors that cooled her bare feet. There was even dust at the bottom of the glass of sweet mint tea, or so it seemed when she swallowed the sugared dregs.

The Moresque servant had placed it on the ivory and sandalwood table by her side, near a stack of detective novels and French magazines.

Isabelle was just sixteen, but her pregnancy had been a troubled one from the beginning and now, nearing the fifth month, she passed most of the day slumped in a chair by the doors opening into the central courtyard of her husband's house. From its gravelled walks sprang palms; orange and lemon trees hung with cages of singing birds; and in the centre there was a tiled fountain

136

that whispered through the long hot days and nights. The old gardener sweeping the path, in a long djellaba and a turban, was one of a dozen people employed in the house, many of whom had lived for generations in one-roomed whitewashed *gourbis* at the edge of the property. Villa Claudia had once been famous for its hospitality to passing dignitaries, including the French governor-general himself and any number of prominent Frenchmen. The patriarch of the Loval clan, who had settled there at the turn of the century, had built the low, rambling house on a hilltop overlooking olive groves and vineyards, which produced a potent red wine reputed to have fortified some of the better vintages of France in years when the harvest there had been bad.

Isabelle had arrived too late to enjoy the halcyon years of the domaine. Her husband's father, who had become famous more for good living than for managing his estate, had died not long after her marriage, leaving his affairs in a tangle and Raoul, his only son, in charge. For the last few weeks Isabelle had been conscious of intense whispers behind closed doors, the voices of her mother-in-law and two sisters-in-law arguing, and sometimes sobbing. They excluded her entirely from the family's affairs, ostensibly because of her condition, but she knew it was because they had never accepted her. Raoul's mother had opposed his marriage to the daughter of a shopkeeper, because she had practically no dowry. Though Isabelle was acknowledged to be one of the most beautiful girls in Tunis, her widowed mother had never had the time to spoil her or her sister, and they had been strictly educated in the arts of household management at the local convent. Isabelle's sister, who was less than a year younger than she, had married a prosperous farmer of Italian descent not long after Isabelle's own marriage, and they had grown apart.

At the Villa Claudia nothing was required of Isabelle except to await the birth of her child, but even she couldn't ignore the winds of change that had already begun to blow across the former French colony, or her growing realization that her husband was incapable of managing the estate he had inherited. From childhood he had been a mechanical wizard, and he preferred to spend his days tinkering with the big old Citroën that had belonged to his father

137

rather than attending to his workers and his accounts. At night he drove into Tunis, where he drank heavily, smoked hashish and gambled, pretending he was involved in important business negotiations. The violent quarrels that had erupted between him and Isabelle soon after their marriage had stopped, and now they hardly spoke. Their lovemaking, too, had ceased soon after she discovered she was pregnant, when Raoul suddenly became impotent. He blamed his condition on his worries, but Isabelle knew it was caused by his drinking and addiction to hashish, weaknesses that filled her with contempt.

Isabelle's only friend in the household was the Moresque servant, a girl only a few years older than she, who came silently through the door just then, bearing a basin of cold water and a towel over her arm, her djellaba rustling as she walked. She had the habit of speaking under her breath in Arabic in a melodious whisper that Isabelle had found irritating at first, but which she now found soothing. Her small, brown eyes shone from an olive face delicately tattooed above the cheeks, and she wore a bright scarf tied low on her forehead. From the beginning there had been a bond between the Moresque and Raoul's bride, like a strong beast of burden fostering a smaller, weaker one.

'I brought some cold water for madam to cool her forehead in the heat.'

The sixteen-year-old girl about to become a mother looked up at the older girl with empty eyes that had already seen enough of life. In an hour or so the servant would be busy in the house and Isabelle would be left alone again, nauseated, uncomfortable and so bored that death seemed preferable to living. She allowed herself to be led to the big carved bed, trying to ward off a feeling of vertigo, while the servant helped her to lie flat and pulled the coverlet over her swollen abdomen. Isabelle closed her eyes as the Moresque smoothed her mane of golden hair away from her forehead and stroked her long slender arms as if she were a treasured doll. The rustle of her djellaba, the sweet smell she exuded of female sweat and rosewater, her musical whispering, gave Isabelle a pleasant illusion of safety, which made her drowsy. Suddenly she was awakened by a painful churning in her womb. She looked up with

138

eyes full of mute fear as the Moresque wrung the cloth in the basin and laid it gently on her forehead.

'You have a fever and you're shaking. You need the doctor. Should I call *madame*?'

'No, please don't. Tell me a story. That will make me sleep. Then the fever will go away.' Isabelle gripped her stomach as a pang like a knife drove through her insides. Her fear of what it could mean was dulled by a strange resignation that death was preferable to pain. 'Please, a story,' she whispered. The face of the Moresque hovered over her, featureless and distant as the moon in the sky.

A story had come to mean talk of anything to distract Isabelle when she was bored or ill, and the servant had an unlimited fund. Isabelle felt herself drifting away as she listened to the Moresque describing the birth of her first son in the *gourbi*, where she was attended by women. The baby had refused to come out, she said with a chuckle, so the women began to chant and shout while forcing her to jump up and down until the infant was expelled into a pair of hands waiting beneath her. Hearing that, Isabelle fell into unconsciousness.

She awoke not knowing where she was or what time it was, only vaguely aware of a face hovering over her. As her vision cleared, she saw it was not the Moresque but a middle-aged man wearing glasses, who seemed familiar. Her throat was parched with thirst and she felt weightless.

'*Bonjour*, Isabelle. You've had a close call,' he said. 'You've lost a lot of blood, but you're all right now.'

'Is this the hospital?' she murmured, realizing the man was the doctor whom she had consulted in Tunis when she discovered she was pregnant.

'No. There wasn't time for that.'

The morning light pouring through the double doors of the bedroom hurt her eyes and the chirping of birds and the whisper of the fountain seemed louder than normal.

'What day is it?'

When he told her, she realized that more than twenty-four hours had passed. It was hot in the room and he had rolled up his shirtsleeves, revealing strong arms that had helped to bring hundreds of children into the world, a thought that had comforted her when she first went to see him, frightened at the prospect of giving birth. He had calmed her fears, though he had shaken his head when she told him her age.

'The baby?'

He shook his head. 'Try to relax, and don't think about it now.'

'What happened? Tell me, I want to know,' she said anxiously.

'You've had a miscarriage. There was nothing that could be done. You're lucky to be alive.' He pulled up a chair and looked at her sympathetically. 'I want to talk to you.' He seemed to be weighing his words as he took off his glasses and polished them. 'My dear, I'm afraid I must tell you that there is a serious reason for losing your baby. It's because of a condition called gonorrhoea. Do you know what that is?'

For a moment Isabelle couldn't answer, she was so shocked. Then she nodded, feeling a sickening sense of shame at the word, which for her had connotations of filth and degradation.

'This is quite a common venereal disease, and it is easily cured,' the doctor continued, 'but you must have immediate treatment. Unfortunately, it has proved fatal for your unborn child. Of course, it's my duty to tell your husband, because he must seek treatment as well. I'll discuss the matter with him.'

Isabelle could no longer meet his eyes. She felt defiled.

'Now, please try not to hold it against your husband, my dear. Most young men are too impatient to wait for marriage and they are careless. He's not entirely to blame.'

'What you're saying is that he became infected in a brothel,' she retorted savagely, forgetting her shame.

The doctor looked surprised, as if a convent girl shouldn't know about brothels. Then he tactfully changed the subject.

'Didn't your father used to run a fabric shop off the Avenue Jules Ferry?' He called it by the old French name, though it had been changed since the country had become independent.

'My father died six years ago, and my mother runs the shop now.'

'Ah yes, I remember. I didn't realize you were her daughter when you came into my surgery.'

140

His eyes were full of understanding. He had the doctor's access into the intimate lives of human beings and nothing was a secret from him, even the squalid struggles that had shaped her existence. She wondered if he knew her shrewd, beautiful mother, whose only interest was her business, who had pushed both her daughters into early marriages. Isabelle was aware that the doctor probably knew all about her husband's family and its humiliating decline. She resisted his pity, knowing it might pry loose the despair that she was now determined to conquer.

The doctor thought for a minute, as if he were choosing his words carefully. 'Are you – all right here?'

She shook her head and tears came to her eyes, but she bit her lip to keep them back. 'They despise me, and I despise them. It would have been better if I had died.'

He shook his head. 'You're much too young and lovely to have such negative feelings.' He addressed her as '*tu*' as if she were a child, yet he was talking to her like an adult. 'I know how difficult it must be for you. But soon most of us will be going back to France. Don't look so surprised. We're not wanted here. Oh yes, the people may like us, sometimes even love us: people like your Moresque, who tends you like a mother. She saved your life. But the French won't stay on much longer, any of us, and you should remember that when you feel there's nothing to live for. You have all of life ahead of you. Imagine, some day you'll be living in France, and you'll start all over again. I can read in your face that you have an interesting destiny ahead of you.'

'Do you really think so?' she asked, wondering if he was merely being kind. Yet this echoed her own view of herself as a person set apart from others, a conviction that had begun to slip away in the last months.

The twinkling eyes behind the doctor's glasses became serious. 'There's something more I must tell you, something you ought to know, though it might upset you at first. I think it's possible that you may never be able to have children after what has happened. Of course, a miracle might occur, but in case it doesn't, you must learn to build your life around other things. Being without children doesn't have to mean you will be unhappy.'

141

He talked for a while about the treatment of her illness, then left, promising to come again soon. When he had gone, the thought that she would probably never have a child aroused no feeling whatsoever in her. If anything, she saw it as a kind of release. Later, the Moresque brought her lunch on a tray, a variety of tempting little dishes of olives and figs and some fresh bread, but Isabelle didn't feel hungry. The doctor's words about destiny had opened a door in her mind. When she awoke in the morning, her head was filled with thoughts of escape to a new life far away. Now that she had found something to live for, life and strength began to flow back into her.

When no one but the Moresque came to her room, Isabelle realized the family must have learned that she was barren, and found in this another excuse to despise her. It wasn't until mid-afternoon that Raoul burst angrily through the door. She was still in her nightdress on the bed, and clutched the blanket protectively around herself when she saw him. He was unshaven and obviously had been drinking.

'You stupid bitch! What did you tell the doctor?' he shouted, his eyes blazing with rage.

'I didn't tell him anything. He knows the truth about you, and now so do I. There was no way to keep it from him, Raoul. It killed the baby.'

He rushed to the bed and started to beat her with his clenched fists. She struggled but refused to cry out, which enraged him further. Then, as suddenly as his anger erupted, it left him, and he sank down by the bed, sobbing uncontrollably.

'Forgive me, oh God, Isabelle, why this, why now? Help me,' he begged.

She looked at his collapsed figure and saw that nothing was left of the suave young blood who had caught her attention in a café in Tunis. Raoul was only twenty-two, but his sharp, handsome features had already taken on the unhealthy pallor that alcohol and hashish bestow. All the laughter and sensuality that had aroused her passion had vanished and it seemed impossible that he had ever possessed the courage to overrule his mother's objections to their marriage. As he lay crying pathetically at her feet, clinging to her

142

nightdress, Isabelle didn't care whether Raoul was crying for her or the baby, or himself. She hated him then more than she had ever loved him.

'Please, Isabelle, help me,' he implored in a quivering voice, raising his tear-stained face. 'Let me hold you. It can be like it was between us. It's not too late.'

'Get away from me, you filthy pig. You disgust me.' Leaping from the bed, Isabelle ran to the bathroom and locked herself in. She didn't emerge until she heard the bedroom door slam.

It was the last time Isabelle saw him. A week passed and he didn't come to see her. She guessed he was ashamed of breaking down in front of her and had probably sunk even more deeply in debt in the gambling dens of Tunis. His mother and sisters appeared briefly, talking distractedly about nothing, and it seemed to her there was something strange about all of them, as if they were losing their reason along with their fortune, although she began to suspect they had always been like that. She stoically faced the fact that the Loval family were themselves facing imminent ruin, though it terrified her. She had nowhere to go; her mother had already washed her hands of her and wouldn't welcome her back to the cramped apartment above the shop in Tunis.

When the Moresque told her that a number of servants had staged an angry protest at not being paid, Isabelle didn't waste any more time. Still weak, but gathering strength, she managed to pack a suitcase of belongings and hide it under the bed. The day that she was waiting for arrived, a sunny day after a week of unsettled weather, when she was alone in the house except for the servants.

Everything had gone quiet, except for the sound of the gardener dragging a broom across the gravel in the courtyard. Isabelle got out of bed and crept down the tiled corridor, scattered with rugs and lined with old chests, to her mother-in-law's bedroom, which was always kept locked. She had long since discovered where the key was kept. She slipped on a pair of gloves and ran her fingers along the ridge beneath a chest outside the door, looking cautiously up and down the hall. She felt weak with relief as her hand touched a piece of cool metal.

The shuttered room was heavy with stale scent and crammed

143

with gilt furniture upholstered in red velvet. Every corner was taken up with chairs, commodes and tables bearing crystal lamps with deep-fringed shades, and there was a big, high bed smothered in lace. Isabelle went across to the imposing gilt-and-white Empire dressing table crowned with a triptych of mirrors. Catching sight of her own pale image, Isabelle thought that illness had given her the ethereal countenance of an angel. She looked into her pale brown eyes, which seemed to reflect the deep gold of her hair, seeing her own beauty with a sudden objectivity. Her face, her body, would be her passport to the destiny the doctor had spoken of. But before destiny could work, it needed a push. On the dressing table was a big rosewood jewel box inlaid with an enamel miniature of Marie Antoinette. Lifting the lid, Isabelle was dazzled by the sparkling gems nestling in little compartments, the jewellery her mother-in-law had accumulated over a lifetime.

Isabelle selected the best pieces with a sharp eye she had inherited from her mother, stuffing the heavy gold chains, the emerald solitaire and a diamond pin into a special bag she had made. For good measure, at the last moment she took the velvet box containing the garnets set in heavy gold. This was an act of spite; Isabelle had always thought the garnets were hideous but she knew that they were her mother-in-law's wedding gift from her father and that she treasured them more than all the rest. Before leaving the room, Isabelle opened the door to the courtyard so it would look as though the thief had entered there. Returning to her own room, she hid her booty where no one would find it, suspended from a pipe inside the panel of the bath.

That night she was lying in bed when chaos broke out. The family hadn't been at home long, and she heard shouting and screaming coming down the hallway. Raoul, it seemed, had dropped off his mother and sisters and returned to Tunis. Soon the three women burst into her room, raving hysterically that there had been a theft and demanding to know what she had been doing. Isabelle pretended to be horrified, saying she had been asleep most of the time, and when they accused her of stealing the jewels herself, she sank back on the pillows looking incredulous and tearful. Her mother-in-law's thickly powdered face set in disgust and she

144

unleashed her pent-up resentment about the marriage between her only son and a penniless, barren girl, a girl who was so stupid that she hadn't even known there were thieves in the house.

When the police came to question her the next day, Isabelle was propped up in bed looking frailly beautiful. She hadn't slept in the night, not from fear but from excitement. The theft had triggered off a demonic energy inside her, giving her all the courage and will-power she needed to battle on the inside, while appearing outwardly demure. The inspector investigating the theft was kind and gentle with her, and his probing questions revealed her empty existence. Giving the impression that she was deeply grateful for someone to talk to, Isabelle mentioned the miscarriage that had kept her bed-ridden. She confessed that, though they had tried to protect her, she knew the family had money troubles. Breaking down, she sobbed that her own husband could easily have taken the jewels himself to pay his gambling debts, adding that the real thief might have been the Moresque who, though gentle and sweet, was light-fingered.

A few weeks later Isabelle escaped from the Villa Claudia. On a morning when everyone was again absent she arranged a ride in the back of a truck full of vegetables, bribing the driver lavishly to keep her flight secret, and slipping some money to the tearful Moresque, who was terrified that she might be arrested for the theft of the jewels. Isabelle left the Villa Claudia with nothing but a small suitcase, bought for her honeymoon, and all the jewellery she had stolen sewn carefully into the folds of her dress.

That night she sailed out of the Bay of Tunis, bound for Marseille on a steamboat called the *Marguerite*, just as the light turned a deep violet above the jagged hills that rose beyond the twin-peaked Bou Kornine. The giant moon hung like a gaping hole in a universe filled with leaping stars, and the city lay above the black bay like a funnel of light pouring into the water. Isabelle stood regally on deck, face to the wind, hair flying back as she watched the shore slip away. She fantasized that all the people and places she left behind were being swallowed up in some terrible disaster and she was the only person to be saved. Looking down into the glistening water, she mentally tossed away the past, imagin-ing it like a suitcase full of rubbish sinking to the bottom of the

145

bay. She stared at the dark northern horizon, shuddering with delight at all the wonderful things that were waiting there. When she sensed a man leaning on the railing staring at her, she turned her head.

'*Bonjour*,' he said with an inviting smile.

One glance at his cheap wristwatch and his rumpled suit told Isabelle that, though the man was attractive, he was not worth her notice. She left the deck abruptly before he could say another word to her, resolving never to look too deeply into the eyes of a man until he had redeemed her beauty with the most extravagant promises that she would be sure he could keep.

The man she was waiting for did come along, but not for three years, when she had almost given up hope. She had established herself in Paris, landing a job in an exclusive *parfumerie* near the Place Madeleine, and living in a tiny, primitive rooftop studio in the eighth *arrondissement*. Her tastes had become consummately Parisienne in so far as her budget allowed, and she had learned to groom herself to perfection. During those three often lonely years, during which she had made few friends, Isabelle had realized the necessity of broadening her education if she was going to enter the right circles. She began by tackling novels by Gide and a book by a man called Sartre, as well as volumes of Baudelaire and Rimbaud, unheard of at the convent school in Tunis. She also bought books on etiquette and comportment. More important, she devoured newspapers to the point where she could now interpret world events and stock-market figures. She had even joined an English class, thinking she might meet a rich Englishman or American, and was pleased to discover she had a gift for languages. Soon she extended her interest to the arts, and made a point of keeping up with the latest exhibitions, memorizing the names of the artists showing their work in galleries of the seventh and eighth *arrondissements*. She longed to be part of the smart crowd invited to *vernissages*, and always felt the pang of exclusion when she saw noisy, glamorous parties in progress on her way home from work. The Louvre and the Jeu de Paume were her places of study on Sundays, when she needed to escape the stifling heat of her studio in summer, or the cold in the winter.

146

Then one day all that came to an end. The man who came through the chrome-and-glass doors of the *parfumerie* was of a type she had encountered nearly every day. It was November, and he was wrapped in a superb cashmere coat, with a white silk scarf knotted at his throat. Tall and ascetic looking, with world-weary eyes, he seemed English, rather than French because of his homburg hat and clipped moustache. From his thinning grey hair and lined, sun-tanned face, she judged him to be in his mid-fifties. His clothes, combined with the way he carried himself, told her he was a rich aristocrat. There were two other girls at the counter, a redhead and a brunette, but it was Isabelle he approached. She was wearing her favourite dress, a deep Prussian-blue sheath with a wide belt that was demurely elegant, but showed her figure to advantage. The one piece of jewellery she had hung on to besides the garnets – she had become morbidly superstitious about selling those – was a diamond pin, which she wore on her lapel. It was a mark of distinction, a badge of status that suggested the women she was descended from hadn't always worked for a living. Had she met Gilles de Montjoi much later, Isabelle would have realized how slight were her chances of attracting such a rich sophisticate. But her instinct told her to treat him exactly as she would treat a desirable young man on the make, with a combination of reserve and charm.

She took a great deal of trouble, helping him choose a very expensive bottle of perfume as a present. She had wrapped it and given him his change, when he surprised her by asking her to deliver it to the bar at the Hôtel Crillon, five minutes' walk away, when she had finished work. He explained that he couldn't carry such a large package with him to a meeting, after which he would go directly to a party, and that the perfume was for his hostess. When he left her holding the perfume and walked out the door, the other shop assistants argued that she shouldn't keep the appointment and that the *patron*, who was strict about socializing with customers, might fire her if she discovered what had happened. Isabelle went to the Hôtel Crillon at six that evening.

It wasn't until after they were married a year later that Isabelle discovered this was all a ruse, that Gilles de Montjoi, a

147

fifty-eight-year-old confirmed bachelor, the wayward, somewhat eccentric brother of a marquis, had fallen in love with her through the shop window one day when he passed, and had devised an amusing way to meet her. In September Isabelle Catherine Brunet married Gilles Sebastian de Montjoi at the *mairie* in Paris. The wedding was followed by a reception for a hundred people, excluding most of the groom's family, at a suite in the Hôtel George V, before the honeymoon in Martinique.

The only thing that marred Isabelle's happiness was the reminder of Raoul Loval, her legal husband, whom she was almost certain must have come to France when the very last of the old French colonists had been driven out of Tunisia. His existence, which she had conveniently ignored, would have altered her husband's image of her as the pure young woman who had adamantly refused to become his mistress when he had asked her. But when she woke up in a sumptuous hotel suite after her wedding night, having lost her virginity a second time, Isabelle decided it would be foolish to let worry destroy her happiness. She reasoned that her life had changed for good and that nothing could ever harm her again.

Isabelle's journey into the past ended when a door slammed somewhere in the depths of Terre Blanche, the shock of which made her heart pound violently. Time seemed to be moving forward again, though slowly. But the gates guarding her past strained at the weight of the secret pinned behind them.

*

'Where are we going, Daddy?'

'We're just taking a drive,' said Alain.

'It's a wilderness out here, isn't it?'

Alain smiled absently. 'Yes, it's a wilderness, like in the movies.'

Oliver peered down the dirt track lined with fields, seen through a shimmering haze of heat. The hot sun reflected brilliantly on the white interior of the open car and glanced off Alain's dark glasses. Turning off the stereo, he listened to the unremitting rasp of cicadas, the sound of summer in Gascony he thought he had all but forgotten.

148

When he slowed down to ease the car over a baked ridge of white mud, Oliver exclaimed, 'This is fun. It's like a safari to the middle of nowhere.'

Oliver's small voice was swallowed up by the silence that now enveloped them. There were no birds, and even the cicadas had fallen silent. Alain's eyes, hidden behind sunglasses, were trained on the end of the track. Even after all these years he knew exactly how far it was to the end, though he had never driven over it in a car. He braked before a ruined farm guarded by twisted dead elm trees overgrown with ivy.

'This is a ruin, isn't it?' said Oliver, hopping out of the car.

'Yes, it's a ruin. It used to be a farm a long time ago.'

'Why did you want to come here, Dad?'

He shrugged. 'No special reason. Somebody I used to know lived here. I wanted to see what it looked like.'

'Who lived here?'

'Oh, a friend of mine at school.'

'What was his name?'

'His name? It was – Pierre.'

They walked along the hard clay road towards the farm, where lizards darted across the bleached stones. Oliver jumped at a scuttling sound in the long grass.

'What was that?'

'A rabbit or a fieldmouse.'

Alain walked up to the only standing wall of the ruin. Oliver followed in his footsteps, trying to hoist himself up to peer in through the empty windowframe. Alain lifted him for a moment so he could have a look, then set him down.

'It's all tumbledown. This farm must be really old. Really, really old.'

Alain didn't reply, and registered no expression as he studied the rubble of the fallen roof that now covered the floor of the cottage.

'This place is really creepy,' Oliver whispered. 'Do you think it's haunted?'

Alain smiled. 'No, it's not haunted. The ghosts must have moved out years ago. There's nothing here, not even for ghosts.'

'Tell me about your friend Pierre who lived here. You never talked about him before. What was he like?'

149

'His father was a poor farmer, and his mother died when he was small, before he could remember. He had three older brothers, but by the time Pierre was your age they had all moved away and he was left with his father to work on the farm. He had to get up very early and feed the pigs that lived in sheds behind the house before he went to school. Sometimes he spilled the feed on his trousers or his boots got dirty, so when he went to school, he felt embarrassed and the other kids teased him.'

'But weren't all the other kids the same? I mean, like you and everybody, if their dads were farmers too?'

'Pierre was different. He didn't want to stay the way he was. All he ever wanted was to leave here, to go away, and that's what he did.'

'You don't know where he went?'

Alain shook his head. 'Do you know, it was so cold sometimes in the winter when he got up that he had to break the ice in a tin basin to wash. He didn't warm up until he stood in front of the big fireplace, where his father had built a fire. For breakfast he had hot milk and a piece of dry bread with goose fat instead of butter. After feeding the pigs he had to walk to school in the village.'

'You mean Roquelaire? That's a long way.'

'Yes, it was. But he didn't have a bicycle like a lot of the other children.'

'He was lucky to have a friend like you, Dad. You must have helped him a lot. Did you ever get in a fight over him when the other kids teased him?' Without waiting for an answer, Oliver said passionately, 'If anybody said anything about my friend Toby, I'd punch them on the nose.'

Alain ruffled his son's hair. 'I know you would, and you'd be right, too.'

They walked around the side of the house, where a small brick outhouse had outlasted all the other buildings. Its door hung on one hinge.

'What's that little house?'

'That's the bathroom.'

'The bathroom!' Oliver said incredulously. 'You mean they had to go there all the time, even at night? Wasn't he scared? I mean,

150

there could be wild animals around here at night, that might eat people.' He looked around uneasily.

'No, I don't think he was scared. He was used to it.'

'He was brave, wasn't he? I'd be as brave as he was if I had to be, don't you think so?'

'I think you would.'

On the way back to the car Oliver gazed into the distance, towards Brissac. 'What's that big castle on the hill?'

'That's the Château Brissac. It's nearly seven hundred years old.' Alain was tempted to say more, but knew there would be time enough for that.

'Maybe King Arthur lived there.'

'No, I don't think so. But King Edward of England stayed there during a war between England and France that lasted a hundred years. He was called the Black Prince because his armour was black.'

'Like a devil. How can a war last a hundred years? Wasn't everybody dead by then?'

'When they died, the next generation took over.'

'England and France must have hated each other.'

Alain opened the car door. 'History lesson over. Time to go.'

Oliver looked back at the ruin. 'Dad, what do you think happened to Pierre?'

Alain paused. 'I don't know. He just dropped out of my life. I don't know where he is.'

'That's too bad,' said Oliver, climbing into the car beside him. 'Now, can we go and see your house?'

'No, that's not possible. Other people live in it.'

'Can't we just drive past so I can see what it's like?'

'No, we can't do that. You know, when you move away from a place, you can't go back just like that. It doesn't belong to you anymore.'

'You sound like you don't want to go back.'

'Come on, let's go,' said Alain. His son's innocent questions, thrown like pebbles into a still pond, had sent out disturbing ripples.

Alain turned his back on the farm, thinking that one day he would tell Oliver the truth. By that time, it wouldn't matter.

# Chapter 8

'Go on, I say, go on with you!' cried Roch. Rising up in his stirrups, he glared impatiently at the huntsman, who was running clumsily across the field. Feeling the peregrine falcon attached to his wrist become restive, Roch steadied his gloved hand and whispered softly to it. The bird's golden eyes never left the lure held aloft by the huntsman while Roch loosened its jesses. Just as the huntsman was about to begin swinging the lure, he tripped and went sprawling on his face.

'You wretched idiot!' cried Roch, leaping in his saddle without regard to the falcon. She strained dangerously at the jesses, causing the bells on her talons to ring. Roch swore under his breath, then struggled to calm the excited bird before she could do herself harm. Dropping the reins of his charger, he fumbled with the flagon at his waist as he tenderly whispered the falcon's special call. He quickly rinsed out his mouth, then took in some water and sprayed it on the bird's head, which seemed to calm her at once. He glared angrily in the direction of the red-faced huntsman, who was running back towards him.

'Forgive me, my lord, but this ground is not as smooth as it seems. The straw hides potholes as big as a man's head.' Rubbing his knees, he gestured to the wide clearing bordered by trees.

'That's no excuse, dammit. Go at it again, and this time watch your feet, not the lure, you dolt.'

'Yes, my lord,' the man replied, his chest heaving with exertion. He hastily rearranged the lure, a pair of heron's wings tied to the corpse of a hare, then held it up to the falcon to reacquaint her with the scent. When the bird had inspected it and given a shiver of recognition, he took a few shreds of meat from the pocket of his jerkin and fed the falcon from his hand.

Roch looked impatiently across the field streaked with morning shadows, but there was no sign of Roxonde. He had expected her to join him by now. He poised himself in readiness as the huntsman bolted forward with the line. This time all went smoothly and the man didn't stumble as he ran to his place a good distance from his master. As the man swung the lure in huge circles above his head, Roch released the creance, which held the bird's jesses to the line. The falcon lifted her powerful wings and flew towards the lure with no hesitation.

Roch made the huntsman repeat the exercise several times, each time allowing the bird to feed on a little meat before continuing. At last Roch signalled he had had enough and the bedraggled huntsman returned, wheezing with exhaustion. His master was slipping the hood over the falcon's head.

'She's got the hang of it, my lord. I've never seen a falcon learn as fast as this one. Many think it's size that counts, but speed is what makes the kill, every time.'

'I'm beginning to think you're right,' Roch agreed, 'though at first I was sorry I didn't choose a more powerful specimen. But there was something about the look in her eye, the sharpness of it, that drew me to her. She's turned into a beauty, hasn't she?' Surveying the magnificent bird, he smiled as he watched her preen after her fine performance. 'I'm going to change her name to Diana, goddess of the hunt. That will give her something to live up to.'

'A good name, my lord. So good that you may decide to keep her.'

'It's a tempting thought, but one I can't consider. Diana is bound for Roxonde's uncle, and he already knows it. Let us hope he will value her as much as I. You've done well with her, Selwyn.' He spoke in fluent English to the huntsman, whom he had brought back from Wales and whose race was renowned for falconry. 'I'm thinking that if a heron appears, we ought to put her to the test.'

The huntsman frowned. 'She's too unseasoned, my lord. I advise you to wait a while yet, at least a week or more, to break her in.'

'She's as ready as she'll ever be to fly free and, by God, if I see a

153

heron, I'll let her go. Think what a boast that would be when I present her.'

Excited by this thought, Roch turned at the pounding of hooves in the distance to see Roxonde and her lady-in-waiting cantering towards him across the sun-drenched field. He manoeuvred his charger so he could better enjoy the sight of the two women on grey palfreys as they approached. Roxonde's deep-green gown billowed around her legs, exposing a fetching pair of red boots. As she spurred her horse faster, sensing his eyes were on her, her own mane of tawny hair loosened itself from its ribbons and bindings, like pennants of gold around her face. She looked every inch a goddess in the rich morning light, with the towers of Brissac jutting above the dark forest at her back. Wreathed in smiles, her face flushed from the ride, Roxonde brought her horse to a halt by his side so abruptly that she made the falcon stir in its jesses again. Roch clucked his tongue and softly crooned the bird's special call.

'I think he loves that bird better than me, don't you, Mathilde?' Roxonde remarked to her lady-in-waiting, a slight, pale woman, who was white with fear after following her intrepid mistress at a gallop across the rough field.

'Nay, that could never be. No man could love a bird as much as a woman,' the lady-in-waiting replied prosaically.

Roch conveyed his opinion on the matter with a private smile meant for Roxonde. The world fell away for an instant as unconsummated desire flickered between them.

'And how goes it?' asked Roxonde, leaning forward in her saddle. 'Did she please you this morning?'

'Not nearly as much as I would have liked,' Roch said pointedly.

Roxonde blushed when she understood his meaning. He had stolen into her tent at dawn, entreating her to give herself to him, in what had become a ritual that inflamed him close to the limits of his endurance, and had taught Roxonde the true meaning of carnal desire, though she had already been twice married.

The two of them led their horses away while the huntsman readjusted the slipping saddle on the lady-in-waiting's mount.

154

'And what of the Sire Montferrand? How is he this morning?' Roch inquired bitterly.

'Failing, it seems. But then I thought as much yesterday.' Roxonde turned to look at the outline of the castle. 'It's all I can do to keep a pleasant expression in his sickroom. I can't even see for the pall of smoke that hangs over him from the herbs they burn, and his sores are caked with some unguents brought by the barber that make my stomach turn.' She shivered. 'Better to die from a devil's curse, quickly and without agony, than by such slow torture.'

'What do you think? Will it be today?'

She sighed impatiently and brushed her hair from her face. 'Who knows? I don't intend to camp here until the first frost, of that you may be sure. When the fires are lit in the hall this autumn, I intend that you and I should be warming ourselves there, not his rag-bag of retainers. The nuns particularly are a trial, especially the old one named Clothilde. She's often at his side, praying and reading from a psalter, as if he could understand.' Roxonde bit her lip impatiently.

She was now in her mid-twenties, and past her prime, but her freckled complexion had the beauty of ivory sprinkled with gold dust, and the full bosom nearly bursting from her bodice had a womanly ripeness that had fanned Roch's lust the moment he saw her. Ethereal damsels with no hips or breasts, idolized by the troubadours in the past, had never appealed to him. Nor was his dream of femininity shaped by the stark images of women saints in churches. Roch's ideal of womanhood conformed to the full-blooded Greek and Roman goddesses described by storytellers, heavenly women like ripe fruit to a man's touch, who often had to be carried from their pedestals by force before they would yield up their secret treasures.

'It would be a kindness to put a pillow over Montferrand's face and have done with it,' he said casually. He looked at her surreptitiously to gauge her reaction to the idea. 'He might thank you for it.'

Her eyes widened. 'No, that would be much too dangerous. And anyway, killing is a mortal sin.'

'An indulgence is easy enough to come by. And you remember that the bishop said in church that killing wasn't as bad as sodomy.

But I speak in jest,' said Roch with a laugh. 'What does it matter if the old dog lingers on a while. We shall enjoy our days here as much as is humanly possible and let nothing dilute our pleasure.'

'Yes, let us.' She lowered her eyes coquettishly, remembering his hot kisses at daybreak. She had awakened on her couch to find him kneeling by her bed in only his chemise, leaving nothing about his manly anatomy to her imagination. Roch's ardour, and the power it gave her over him, pleased Roxonde almost as much as the delicious prospect of capitulation. Beneath her well-filled bodice was a heart that had long resisted siege but was now perilously close to yielding what belonged only to marriage.

'And what are you thinking?' he asked when he saw the look on her face.

'In truth, I was thinking forbidden thoughts.'

'Forbidden, but all the sweeter for that, I'll wager.'

'If you are half as tenacious in war as in love, I pity your opponent.'

He threw back his head and laughed. 'Any woman conquered by me has yet to complain.'

They crossed the field back to their camp, with Roch riding between the two ladies, and the huntsman trailing behind. The hooded falcon now seemed completely used to travelling on horseback, and had latched her talons tightly round her master's gloved wrist to steady herself. Roch conversed with the women, but his eye kept returning proudly to the bird, whose ticked plumage gleamed in the morning sun. Leaving the clearing, they halted on a crest overlooking a pond. Roch saw the unmistakeable outline of a heron at the waterside, standing motionless among the reeds when it sensed their presence. He raised his fingers to his lips, then carefully removed the hood from the falcon's head, all the while keeping his eye unflinchingly on the immobile heron. With a stealthy hand, Roch detached the jesses from the strap that secured the bird to his wrist. He felt her little shudder of recognition that she was now free.

The movement of the huntsman as he caught up with the party was enough to startle the heron into flight. As Roch lifted his wrist, he revelled in that rare moment of ecstasy unique to the

156

chase, that suspenseful instant that precedes the kill. The falcon launched herself powerfully into the air, swooping towards the airborne heron. In spite of its size, the heron seemed a poor match for the agile falcon, which had climbed above it with incredible swiftness, then dived steeply towards it, so quickly that Roch and his party of bystanders could hardly follow her movements.

Roch whispered in encouragement and his heart leapt at the grace and speed with which the falcon launched its talons towards the heron's arched neck. But for some reason the attack was awkward and the falcon missed her prey. The beak of the heron now came down, and all the spectators could see was the clash of wings. The birds flew apart, then, stunned but victorious, the heron took slow flight as the falcon fell to the ground.

Roch watched in horrified silence as his beloved bird fell from the sky like a flag dropped from a tower. He spurred his horse and set off towards the pond with a cry of alarm. The huntsman had already started to run pell mell down the slope. Roch galloped to his side and found him cradling the dead falcon in his hands, its head drooped to one side, exposing a breast bright with blood. The huntsman looked up at him wordlessly, tears staining his dusty face.

'Put it in your pouch. Don't leave it here,' commanded Roch angrily.

'What should I do with her?'

'Do with it what you will,' Roch retorted. He drew himself up in his saddle, hiding the grief that filled him. His throat was full of unshed tears as he glared at the devastated huntsman, who was wiping his tear-stained face with a dirty sleeve.

Roxonde had followed Roch and reined in her horse by his side. She gasped when she saw the huntsman stuffing the corpse of the falcon into his bag.

Roch had already mastered the sudden and violent grief that had overtaken him, and showed no sign of how deeply it had shaken him. He observed the horror on Roxonde's face, realizing when she crossed herself that she interpreted the bird's untimely death as a bad omen.

*

157

The sun was going down when a servant called Roch to supper just as he was finishing a letter.

'The Lady Roxonde awaits you, sir,' came a muffled voice from outside the tent.

'Tell her I'll be there shortly.' Roch rose from the chair in front of the writing table, which was nothing more than a piece of oak, polished from use, laid on two trestles. Along with chests, carpets and other equipment that had accompanied him on his numerous journeys across France to England, and back, these were his accoutrements for travel. The journeys had begun simply enough, when he was armed with little but his courage and a charger *en route* to England to offer his services to the king in his campaign to win back Aquitaine. Now, ten years later, his camp was elaborate enough to suit a noble. He had a few grey hairs in his beard, there were lines at the corners of his eyes, and he had property and a title granted by royal favour. The summit at which he now stood was far above what he had ever dreamed of the day he left a peasant's hovel to begin life as a postulant in an abbey through the grace of an influential abbot.

Folding the parchment, he lit a taper and melted some black sealing wax on to the join, which he then stamped with the seal that carried the coat of arms King Edward III had entitled him to bear, which depicted a scallop shell beneath two crossed swords. The shell he had chosen, not for pilgrim's piety, but because it stood for a wandering existence like his own, and he had chosen the sword mindful that it was what had won him his noble status in the first place. The days when he composed a letter, though they were rare, he thanked providence that he had been taught to read and write by the Church when he was studying to take holy orders. These were weapons as powerful as his sword.

Roch opened the tent flap and called to a messenger, who had been waiting outside. Handing him the missive, he said, 'Leave at once for Moirax. Give this to the abbot there and wait for a reply. I expect you to return here not more than five days hence. Besides the letter from the abbot, you will bring back with you a boy named Thomas, on the horse that will be given you for the return journey.'

158

'Yes, seigneur.'

'And mind you take care, for the boy is not just any boy, but one I value above all others.' Roch said no more on this point, but everyone in camp already knew that his son by a previous union was hidden at Moirax. After instructing the messenger carefully on the boy's care, Roch gave him a generous purse for his expenses, then dismissed him.

Roch went back into the tent, where his body servant was pouring water from the ewer into the basin. He stood as the man stripped him to the waist, restraining the peasant impulse to undress himself, and enjoyed the refreshment of cool water on his hot chest and back before being rubbed down with a towel. The servant then patted his skin with Spanish orange-flower water and gave him anise seeds to chew, habits that gentlemen employed to please ladies, which Roch had picked up on his travels.

As a fresh linen shirt was pulled over his head, Roch caught the aroma of meat being roasted over the fire, which aroused his appetite, and chased away the gloom hanging over him since the death of the falcon that morning. He had been to confession in the chapel at Brissac in the afternoon and had repented of all wicked thoughts and intentions, and had said fervent prayers for much that he hadn't yet accomplished, so that now he could safely say his soul was in a state of grace. It was a pleasant enough state to be in, but one that he didn't expect to last. As the servant helped him into a bright yellow tunic over his pale blue hose, and secured it round his waist with a silver girdle, Roch turned his thoughts to the pleasures of the evening: eating, drinking and, he hoped, fornication.

His servant took several pairs of fine shoes from a chest and Roch chose one in crushed purple velvet, so fine that the slightest drizzle would ruin them. But it was a dry evening, and he was in the mood to flaunt himself. He waited impatiently while the servant secured the long curving tips of the shoes with fine chains round his ankles, restricting his usual stride to the leisurely stroll of a gentleman of leisure.

Roch left the tent in his finery and walked across the camp towards Roxonde's tent, which had been erected in the shadiest,

159

most pleasant spot at a discreet distance from his own. The round tent had been crafted of the finest white canvas and scalloped in blue, and a standard bearing the Montferrand coat of arms had been pegged to the centre pole. The few drab tents erected on the edge of the clearing, occupied by the higher-caste retainers of the party, were much more modest affairs, without any scalloping or trimmings to adorn them. Further along, the servants had pitched camp by the baggage wagons, horses and pack mules. There they tended the cages of fowl and rabbits they had brought with them, as well as sheep for slaughter.

Roxonde had insisted on the privacy of her own camp, where she and Roch could speak and move freely as they waited for the old seigneur's demise. They had left a small hamlet she owned in deepest Gascony the previous month, and planned to decamp from Brissac as soon as the old man died, in order to be married on Roch's own property. Roch thought of how their ranks would swell with visiting nobles on the Feast of the Assumption, when they would be invited to celebrate both their forthcoming marriage and Roxonde's acquisition of Brissac. He couldn't help feeling vexed at the prospect of old Montferrand hanging on to life until then, spoiling their pleasure.

Roxonde was seated on her travelling chair, which had been placed on a carpet in front of her tent. As she embroidered a handkerchief, the silky little dog that usually travelled in her sleeve played with a ball at her feet. She wore a gown of silk the colour of faded roses sewn with pomegranates and leaves. The low, tight bodice barely satisfied modesty, exhibiting the cleft of her breasts through a piece of gauze, a style French noblewomen had been quick to copy from the fashion-conscious Italians. It was they who started the rage for the long sleeves Roxonde wore, trailing almost to her knees. A thick coil of pale-blue velvet wound with gold and seed pearls crowned her gleaming hair, which had been plaited with flowers. To complete her toilette she wore large cabochon sapphires in her ears and a garnet carbuncle on one finger. Roxonde had come from an austere, miserly family, and had vowed to enjoy every luxury, including the costly attar of roses she had splashed on her bosom. When her dog began to gnaw her slipper, she gave

160

it a tap, while she listened to a story read by her lady-in-waiting from a book of French romances. The tales, written long ago, proved that the human heart had not changed since the first Crusade, and Roxonde preferred such entertainment by far to the dreary lives of saints and martyrs.

When she saw Roch coming across the clearing, Roxonde did not cast her eyes down, as a lady should, but took pleasure at the sight of his strong legs and broad shoulders beneath the short tunic, comparing his manly strut to the proud walk of a fine stallion. Every detail of his person pleased her, from his cropped dark hair, his bushy beard and bright blue eyes to his love of finery that was akin to her own. At such moments she always found herself thinking of her two former husbands with amazement, wondering how she could have tolerated them in her bed. One had been deranged, the other diseased, but at last she had met a man who pleased her beyond measure. She had first set eyes on Roch as he jousted at a tournament in Burgundy, and she had known at once that he would henceforth be the champion of her heart. Gauging his mood to be somewhat solemn that evening, she mused that later she would lift his spirits with a gift he would not be expecting.

A welcome cool had descended on the valley and Roch and Roxonde walked a few paces from the camp to a clearing under some great oak trees, where a carpet had been spread and the table was richly laid for a supper for four. A few paces behind them came the lady-in-waiting and a Gascon knight that Roxonde had already picked to be her steward at Brissac. A liveried servant passed a ewer of water and a towel for the company to wash their hands. When the goblets had been filled with wine cooled in the stream, Roxonde's minstrel appeared and bowed with a flourish.

'Felix – there you are. You're late,' she said, pretending to be vexed. 'Lords and ladies expect to be serenaded to the table when they have their supper.'

He bowed again. 'Forgive me, my lady. I was composing a song for the occasion. I was so entranced by my own music that I didn't see the sun sinking.'

'Then sing it,' ordered Roch. He disliked the handsome minstrel, known as the Cat, who Roxonde had persuaded to join her household for the summer after hearing his music at a village fair, but he had to admit that the music the man coaxed from an instrument known as the viele was one of the sweetest sounds he had ever heard. When the minstrel started to sing, Roch guessed he was only improvising and had pretended to be composing when he was idling.

As the minstrel played, course after course was brought to the table, including joints of meat, fowl, sorrel and eggs, a paste of larks' tongues, and some little cheeses sprinkled with herbs and served on vine leaves.

Roch sat back and surveyed the scene with a sense of unparalleled satisfaction. The elegance of the table, the linen, the silver plate and goblets were a far cry from the crude boards that he had known as a child. Long ago he had made a vow that candles would always light his darkness after dusk, that he would eat white bread, not black, and have furs to warm him in winter and servants to see to his wants. And now, after ten years of using his sword and his wiles, he was what he had always wanted to be: a knight with his own domaines, the future bridegroom of a woman from a prestigious noble house who was about to inherit one of the choicest properties in Gascony. Roch reflected that when his son was at his side, and when he and Roxonde were installed in Brissac, he would be a perfectly contented man. To complement his bliss he would beget more heirs, acquire more property and fight wars to his heart's content.

Roxonde was dipping a wafer into honeycomb when a servant came forward bearing a pyramid of fruit arranged on a bed of leaves.

'Peaches!' exclaimed the steward in an awed whisper. 'This is indeed a feast.'

'Their rosy faces remind me of a maiden's blush,' enthused the lady-in-waiting. Throughout the meal she had become more and more animated under the admiring glances of the new steward, who made sure that her goblet was never empty. Sinking his teeth into the soft fruit, he looked deeply into her eyes, leaving no doubt as to what his intentions were.

'The walled orchard of Brissac is laden with unblemished fruit,' Roxonde said casually, as if she didn't know that peaches weren't almost as prized as rubies. She took a pearl-handled knife from the little purse at her waist, and when the peaches were put in front of her, she selected one and began to peel it delicately.

'The orchard is like the Garden of Eden, with apricots, cherries, pears and quinces,' said Roch proudly, already feeling a sense of proprietorship.

'Poor Montferrand has no appetite now his hour is at hand, but it took a good deal of persuasion to get his steward to hand over the key. He watches over the orchard like a hawk,' remarked Roxonde, nibbling at her peach.

'It will be my great pleasure to serve you, my lady, when you are installed there, and not to deprive you of the key,' said the ferret-faced steward, laughing at his own impertinence.

The others joined him, but Roxonde's mind had moved on to the day when she would at last be chatelaine of Brissac. She had amassed two fortunes from her dead husbands. Now she was her own mistress she planned to live the life that was depicted in romances, a life of pleasure and ease, which would allow her to indulge her every whim. She imagined noble lords and ladies flocking to the castle, elegant and discriminating beings whose conversation was clever, who appreciated music, poetry and fashion, and pleasure in every form. These would be her companions, not men at arms who talked of nothing but war, not the priests and prelates, not the sisters whose eyes were lifted to heaven and whose hands were held out perpetually for charity, not the squabbling horde of family leeches, who had poisoned her existence. She and Roch, who would be the guardian of her fortune, were birds of the same nest. They had shed a previous, more humble existence and were poised to slake their worldly ambitions.

Roch watched Roxonde, enthralled, feeling the heat start to rise in him as she licked the last shreds of the peach from its stone. He could already taste her ripe lips devouring his as they consumed one another.

After supper had ended, they walked back to the tent and sat in

163

a semi-circle under the stars, talking of the conjunction of the planets that seers were saying had caused the pestilence. For a few moments the spectre of death that lurked beyond the tranquil domaine of Brissac ruffled their contentment. Disliking the turn of conversation, Roxonde dismissed the minstrel, whose singing had begun to tire her. He gave a courtly bow and walked off, stifling a yawn, not caring much that he had displeased his mistress, because he had pleased himself so much that day.

'His music didn't seem half as fine as usual,' Roxonde said petulantly.

'Perhaps he has been playing another of his instruments elsewhere,' suggested the steward. He and Roch guffawed at the suggestion, while the lady-in-waiting pretended to blush.

'Tomorrow I'll send him packing and tell him he can go where he likes,' said Roch. 'Minstrels are two a penny.'

'No!' Roxonde cried. 'There's no one like him in the whole land. Be patient. Tomorrow he'll be himself again.' She thought a moment, then clapped her hands excitedly. 'If we can't have music, we'll have laughter. Bring on the fool! Where are you, fool?' she shouted.

There was a scuffling of feet as a stunted little man with bulging eyes came stumbling into the firelight. His dazed expression as he wiped the grease from his mouth made them all begin to laugh. He had been curled up with some left-overs from their dinner, thinking he would be left in peace while the minstrel sang, but seeing that he was required, made comic use of the situation by turning himself into a gluttonous bishop with a few gestures of mime. His grimaces and contortions made everyone shriek with mirth, Roxonde most of all. When she had recovered, she declared wickedly that as soon as they were installed at Brissac, she would invite all the local clergy to witness the same performance.

When the torches had been extinguished, when the embers of the flares and campfires had burnt low, Roch, who had been stretched out on the cot in his tent in only his chemise and loose breeches, opened the flap and went outside. A great orange full moon had risen behind the trees, and now gilded Roxonde's tent in the distance, beckoning him. The light of one bright star, the planet Venus, seemed to be directing its beam at the white shape that sheltered Roxonde, and Roch took this as a favourable omen and crept stealthily across the camp. Passing the tent of the lady-in-waiting, the rhythmic creaking of her cot told him that Roxonde's prim companion and the weasel-faced steward were already engaged in amorous combat, and he laughed in the dark at the sighs and groans that signalled the conquest was nearly complete. Bursting with impatient ardour, he arrived at Roxonde's tent.

Inside, Roch was met by the heady scent of rosemary and lavender being crushed beneath his feet. The back of the tent had been opened to admit the cool air, and he could see Roxonde's sleeping silhouette on the pile of rich cushions that was her bed. The contours of her body, veiled by a white nightshift, recalled the splendour of a citadel he had once breached and plundered, a thought that fanned his lust. Bent on victory now, Roch slipped from his breeches and chemise without making a sound, then stretched out on the cushions beside Roxonde, taking the precaution of putting his hand to her mouth so her cries of surprise wouldn't awake any of the courtiers. Roxonde seemed so sound asleep that his sudden embrace hardly stirred her. It was she who surprised him by her laughter.

'You've been awake all the time, you little vixen,' he whispered, charmed by her ruse. Where before he was almost ready to conquer her by force if necessary, he was now ready to beg for her favours, he was so consumed with desire.

'No, you have awakened me,' she whispered, 'awakened all my senses.' She opened the muslin shift that loosely covered her nakedness and wound her legs round his torso. As he felt her soft eager lips on his and the swell of her naked body in his arms, Roch thought he would go mad with excitement. Stunned by this sudden capitulation after so many previous refusals, he realized she was now waiting eagerly to be taken. The citadel fell before him as his battering ram pierced the entry gate in one well-delivered movement.

165

# *Chapter 9*

Alain drained the last drops of coffee from his cup as Fernande came on to the terrace to clear breakfast from the table. When she had gone, Isabelle laid out a set of architect's drawings and the accompanying specifications in front of them. She leaned forward with the air of rapt attention that she always gave to anything concerning the hotel.

Fernande returned a moment later to inquire, 'What about *monsieur* in the *pigeonnier*? Will he want breakfast?'

Isabelle glanced at Alain over the top of her gold-rimmed, tinted spectacles and then frowned as she looked at her watch. 'It's nearly nine-thirty and we have to be in Roquelaire by ten. It's too late for breakfast, but you'd better go over and see if he's awake,' she said to the housekeeper.

When Fernande had gone Alain said, 'I wonder why he's sleeping so late. You don't suppose anything is wrong, do you?'

'He probably has a hangover. I heard the car drive away very early this morning, before dawn, then come back again. I was so groggy I thought it was the gardener, but then I looked at the clock the second time and it was only five-thirty. It wasn't even light yet.'

'I wonder where he went at that hour?' mused Alain. Rising from his chair, he went to the edge of the terrace and leaned over to look at the swimming pool, where Oliver was playing with Lucien.

'Some conquest or other, I imagine.'

'In Roquelaire?' scoffed Alain. 'That's unlikely.'

'Every village has a few pretty girls. Perhaps she's a tourist. Pity her, whoever she is, getting mixed up with him. In business he's superb, but in private . . .' she grimaced, then regarded Alain with concern. 'You're looking worried again, Alain. What is it?'

'All this waiting is beginning to wear me down. There's Oliver

166

to think of. I've got to prepare him for the idea that he won't be going back to Sonoma to school, and that he'll be here with you while I'm there tying up everything. He's not going to like it, you know.'

'He'll get used to it. It will give him and me time to get to know each other,' Isabelle said matter-of-factly. 'It isn't as if he hasn't been given everything he wants – a pony, a bicycle, toys, a room of his own. What more could a child wish for? Why, when I was a child . . .' She stopped abruptly and turned her mind back to the specifications.

Alain thought about what she had said. 'You're so strong, Isabelle, sometimes it disturbs me.'

'Me? Strong?' she laughed. 'No, Alain, you're much stronger than I am. That's the first thing I noticed about you.'

'What makes you say that?'

'You're strong because you've always been yourself.' It was as close as she had ever come to telling him the truth about her past, but she didn't elaborate. He knew that she had grown up in Tunisia, a *'pied-noir'*, that she had a middle-class upbringing and had fled to France when she was very young, but that was all.

He moved behind her and grabbed her round the waist.

'Not now, *mon amour*. How can I concentrate if you do that?'

'It will give you something to think about. I wanted you so badly when I woke up this morning.'

'Did you?'

'But you had already got up and you were exercising in the bathroom when I came into your room.'

'Couldn't you have waited a minute? But I forget – you had to get back to your own room in case Olivier came in. I don't see why you simply don't forbid him to enter your room. That would solve the problem of pretending we don't sleep in the same bed. I really hate this charade.'

'We've been through all that. Rachel is still here, so we've got to be careful. I'm going to have to see her or talk to her today because we don't want her coming out here again.'

At the mention of Rachel, Isabelle's face darkened.

'Alain, you can't allow her to stay in the village. It's going to be very awkward if she does. Tell her now that you'll be back in September while Oliver stays here with me, and that you want custody.'

'I don't know. I just don't know,' he muttered. 'I was dumbfounded when she left a message saying she had rented a house.'

Tossing the pencil aside, Isabelle took out her diary and began sifting through the pages. 'I really haven't got time to worry about this now. There are too many other things that come first.' Seeing the look of resentment this remark aroused, she added in a soft voice, '*Chéri*, we can't afford to start arguing about Oliver and your wife, don't you see? Everything is at stake. We must save our energies.'

'Isabelle, anything to do with Oliver is sacred with me, you know that. I have to work this out in my own way.'

The tension between them broke when they saw Julian sauntering towards the house from the *pigeonnier*, putting an end to what threatened to turn into an argument. He mounted the stairs, then glumly sank into a chair, observing them from behind his sunglasses.

'Morning,' he said in a hoarse whisper. 'It's going to be a scorcher today, isn't it?' He pretended to study the hard, blue sky. 'I'm in dire need of some coffee.'

Isabelle looked at Alain, then said coolly, 'I don't really think there is time for coffee. We're supposed to meet the architect at ten. I sent Fernande to wake you up when you didn't appear for breakfast.' She spoke in English for Julian's benefit.

With an engaging smile he said, 'You'll have to give me some coffee first. I can't possibly function without it.'

Isabelle's lips set in a red line as she rose abruptly from her chair.

'I'll go,' said Alain, moving from the table. 'Then I'll go down and tell Oliver we'll be back before lunch.'

When he had gone, Julian said, 'What time are we supposed to be there? Ten, did you say?'

'That's right. Unless you want to cancel.'

'In that case, we have plenty of time.' Julian stared at her, his fingers knit together. Suddenly he saw her like a prism. He perceived her as a startling arrangement of colours against the backdrop of the cream stone house. The line of cocaine he had taken before leaving his room was taking effect.

'Aren't we putting the cart before the horse? I haven't had a chance to talk to you properly since you came back from Paris.'

'So?' she said with an indifferent shrug. 'You're here; you know exactly what's going on.'

'When are you going to approach the old lady about the château?'

'I believe the whole thing will be resolved very soon. In the meantime I have two bits of good news.' She reached into a cream leather folder and took out a letter. 'This is the letter from the Department of Health, more or less giving us the go ahead about the spa. The final approval from the inspectors will be in our hands well before the builders start.'

Julian took it from her and looked at it. 'I wish my French wasn't so appalling. Read it to me, will you?' When she had translated it, he said, 'That was bloody quick. How did you manage it?'

'I have some influential friends,' Isabelle replied, pleased at his reaction. 'This isn't the actual permission, of course. We can't get that until we have the title to the house. But it's just as good as the real thing. Show it to your investors. And that's not all.' Reaching into the leather case again, she handed him a glossy white folder stamped with a gold shell logo.

Julian opened the folder. 'This is very slick. Who did it for you?'

'I thought you'd like it. A friend of mine from Paris did all the graphics and artwork. He's only seen the château once, in March – that was when I had access to it. The drawings of the completed main rooms of the hotel and the courtyard were done from the few sketches he made on the spot. I think he's done a marvellous job. The shell makes the connection of the Romans and Venus, and the pilgrims to St Jacques de Compostelle.'

'Very impressive,' said Julian. 'I like the design of the logo and the copy line: "a crossroads where saints, soldiers and goddesses meet,"' he read out with a chuckle.

169

'The logo is going on everything – towels, matchboxes and china. I had a rubbing taken from a monument known as the Pilgrim's Stone below the château – you know, the place I showed you where the pilgrims stop.'

'This is bloody marvellous. They're going to be impressed with this. You still have to have the sale on the way, even if it's not actually concluded, before I meet with the board on the fourteenth. But this, this will go a long way to illustrate the details.'

She smiled contentedly as she watched him turn the pages of the proposal.

'I have to hand it to you, Isabelle. It's superb. It will really whet their appetites.'

'I'm so glad you like it,' she said with a modest smile.

'The artist's conception of the courtyard is splendid. I wish to hell I'd seen the interior. It's an absurd situation, when you think about it. Here I am, about to recommend the investment of several million pounds, and I can't even get into the place.'

'There's time for that. I was thinking that you simply ought to go there some day. The gate is always open, and you could pretend to be a tourist wandering around if anyone challenged you, which they probably won't.'

'That's not much use. What I really want to do is have a look round inside. What about the pool in the courtyard? Refresh my memory.'

'The present one doesn't look anything like what we want. We're going to enlarge it and improve it. The statue of Diana in the picture isn't there either, of course. I think I've located quite a good Roman statue in Italy. The decorator is in the process of negotiating for it. Basically, the château has to reflect the fourteenth century, when it was built, but there's no harm in drawing on its Roman past. In the brochure we strongly emphasize the Roman connection, particularly as the Romans were renowned for their love of water. This will appeal to your investors and, of course, to the hotel's clients. But we'll touch on the aspect of the pilgrims too; it has a certain cachet.'

'It's brilliant,' pronounced Julian, brightening visibly as he saw Fernande approaching with a silver pot of coffee.

Following the housekeeper on to the terrace, Alain said, 'I've told Oliver that we'll be back for lunch. I gave him permission to go down to the pond with Lucien and go fishing, just in case Rachel decides to come over here. I told Fernande to see that the gardener keeps the gates closed after we drive out.'

'Having marital troubles, old boy?' asked Julian, pouring himself a cup of steaming coffee.

'What do you mean by that?'

'Everybody is talking about your wife arriving. That's really bad luck, her following you here.'

'What do you mean "everybody"?' asked Alain indignantly, looking from Julian to Isabelle, who shrugged and shook her head.

'You can't keep any secrets in a small town. Bob Cooper heard she asked for you at the hotel. The priest met her, apparently, and when there wasn't room in the hotel he put her in touch with Bob. I was there on Monday night when she arrived.'

'People should mind their own business. How do you know this Cooper, anyway?' asked Alain.

'A friend of a friend in Paris. The same friend who introduced Isabelle and me.'

'The world is so small. I used to think it was so big . . .' said Isabelle. She was about to add 'when I was young', but stopped herself.

'It certainly is small,' said Alain irritably. 'My private life is none of anybody's damn business. They can all go to hell in the village.'

'They'll forget about it in no time,' said Isabelle breezily, jotting down a note.

'Bob told me yesterday that some Englishman who has a house in the village has befriended your wife. They've apparently been seen at the café together.'

'Why are you telling me all this?'

'Thought you might like to know, that's all. I mean, if my wife was tracking me down – mercifully I don't have one, of course – I'd want to know her every movement. Sorry if I offended you.'

'You didn't offend me,' Alain said coldly. 'Hadn't we better get going?' he said to Isabelle.

'You can't keep any secrets in Roquelaire,' said Julian with a shake of his head. He was thinking about making love with Rosamund the night before, wondering if he would call her again.

Alain stared at him. 'I don't give a shit what people say.'

'Did anyone ever tell you that you speak English like a native? I wish I knew how to say "I don't give a shit" in French.'

'*Je m'en merde*,' Alain growled.

Isabelle said solemnly, 'The only way to keep a secret is not to tell anyone − anyone at all.' Her own words recalled the previous afternoon; the memories that had come back, unbidden, still persisted. She picked up her briefcase with a determined gesture. Following her, Alain paused, looking over the balcony at Oliver who was playing football with Lucien in the tree-filled garden.

'It's a paradise for children here, isn't it?' said Isabelle with pride.

'It is. I want my son to be always in that paradise, to feel he's a little god in his own kingdom. That's what I've striven for all my life.'

Julian shifted into low gear as he drove his red Porsche into the centre of Roquelaire and looked for a parking place in the crowded square. The market was in progress. His attention was caught by the flash of a mane of thick platinum blonde hair swinging down the back of a girl crossing the street just ahead of him. His eyes fastened on her and he quickly assessed the lines of the beautifully proportioned figure beneath her dark green linen sundress. Julian muttered appreciatively to himself, and when she paused to hoist her bag over her shoulder, he reacted by pressing down on the accelerator. At the distinctive growl of the Porsche, the girl glanced back in his direction, revealing a stunningly pretty heart-shaped face with a high-bridged, rather noble nose, and very blue eyes. Julian smiled broadly at her, but she returned his curiosity with an insolent look, tossed her head and walked on, a defiant gesture that set his blood racing. Everything about the girl suggested she was a tourist from northern Europe just passing through, not a native of Roquelaire. A car behind him began to honk its horn and he pressed down hard on the accelerator again. The resulting roar of the engine filled the square.

When he had found a parking place, Julian walked through the market and saw Isabelle motion to him impatiently from a corner on the far side of the square, where she and Alain were waiting for him. He walked towards them, noting with a backward glance that the girl he had just seen had joined another girl at the café, who was wheeling a baby in a pram. Julian wondered impatiently how long the meeting with the architect would take and whether the girl would still be there when he got back.

Rosamund walked through the square and up the Rue St Jacques, reading the numbers on the houses as she passed. Not far from the end of the street she found the narrow stone house she was looking for, its white shutters flung open. Seeing Rachel inside, she shouted enthusiastically, 'Yoo-hoo, it's me!'

'Rosamund, hi, come in,' said Rachel, seeing her face at the window. She went to open the door. 'How nice to see you,' she said, genuinely pleased.

'How are you?' Rosamund asked brightly, kissing Rachel's cheek. She removed her sunhat and set it on the coffee table. 'This isn't bad at all, is it? A bit sparse, but perfectly comfortable.'

'Come and sit down. Can I get you a cup of coffee?'

'Yes, lovely. You *are* organized. I can see you're much better off here than staying at Bob's. I was surprised to hear you had moved out so suddenly. When I saw your room was empty, I thought maybe you had gone back home, but then Bob told me you were here.'

Rachel hesitated only a minute before deciding to be open with Rosamund. 'Just let me get the coffee and I'll tell you everything,' she said, disappearing into the kitchen.

Rachel returned with the coffee and sat down across from Rosamund. She had gathered by the breathlessness in her voice and the look on her face that something was different about Rosamund since the last time they had been together.

'Have you got a morning off from your watercolours?'

'No, it's not that,' Rosamund said with a mysterious smile. 'No, the thing is, I just couldn't work this morning, and so I told Bob I

173

was going out for a walk. But first I want to hear about you. How did you find this house?'

'There's an English journalist, Michael Lowry, who lives a few doors down. We met at the café and he arranged it all. It was very lucky. The house belongs to some English people who come here in the spring and autumn.'

'Michael Lowry. Yes, I remember him from last summer. He's charming.'

'I suppose he is. I didn't really notice,' said Rachel, knowing it wasn't true. 'But he's been very helpful.'

'I'm glad you've got someone next door. I was worried about you being all alone. That's one of the reasons I came by.'

'I knew you'd probably be wondering what happened after I left, but since I last saw you my whole life has been turned upside down.'

Rosamund bit her lip. 'As bad as that?'

'I'm afraid it's worse than I thought. Alain is leaving me. He wants a divorce.'

'Oh, how awful for you,' exclaimed Rosamund.

Rachel was surprised at the way her own words had come out, without a trace of self–pity. Now, only one day after her world had shattered, her emotions had seeped underground, trapped until they could dissipate into a private grief that wouldn't destroy her.

When Rachel had recounted what had happened, Rosamund shook her head sympathetically. 'So they're really true, all those rumours?'

'Yes, I'm afraid so. Though Alain denies he's leaving me for Isabelle de Montjoi. He says they're only partners.'

'And do you believe him?'

'I've had moments when I wanted to. But how can I?'

'It might interest you to hear that people are saying Agnès Grimal will never sell the château to a Ribard.'

'Really?' said Rachel, surprised.

'Someone said that to Bob. Apparently the Ribard name has aroused some old grievances, something to do with the war.'

'Something to do with the war?'

'You mean you don't know?'

174

'I'm in the dark about nearly everything, remember. To my knowledge Alain isn't even aware of it.' Rachel looked puzzled.

'I don't think it was anything to do with his immediate family. Something to do with his grandfather, who was thought to be a German collaborator. Some terrible atrocities were committed in a village near here and the whole family was ostracized for years. Feelings about the war still run deep in this part of France.'

'Oh my God. He never told me.' Rachel fell silent as she thought about it, blotting out Rosamund's voice for a moment. She had a quick flash of her visit to the abandoned farm. The revelation seemed to explain the profound misery that lingered in the place where Alain had grown up.

Rosamund was saying, '. . . so they're saying that the whole project hasn't got a chance. I don't know whether it's anything to do with this collaborator business or what. Of course, everyone is dying to know what the old woman will do with the château, but no one has the nerve to ask her.'

If the sale was definitely off, Rachel wondered what Alain would do.

Rosamund guessed what she was thinking. 'Do you suppose that this turn of events will change your husband's plans? And if so, would you take him back?'

Rachel found herself hesitating. 'Yes, of course I want him back. I want everything to be the way it was. It's as simple as that. I've had time to do a lot of soul-searching in the last twenty-four hours.'

'For your sake, I hope it will happen, I really do. But are you sure it's possible to turn the clock back?' Rosamund's blue eyes were full of doubt.

'I have to believe it now. I've been thinking so much, and I've decided I can never be happy again unless I give my marriage every chance. That means swallowing my pride and fighting for Alain – not just for our own happiness, but for Oliver's.'

'I suppose that equation depends on how much a person is willing to forgive or ignore.'

'There's only one answer to that – everything.' Rachel hadn't known how desperate she was to cling to that conviction until she voiced it to Rosamund.

175

Rosamund's eyes took on a distant aspect and she smiled ironically. 'I used to think that. My husband has had several affairs, one quite recently. I came here with the idea that I would just put the past behind me and go back to normal in two weeks. Now, I'm not so sure.' She drew in her breath and said in a rush, 'I've started an affair with Julian Paine.'

Rachel looked at her uncomprehendingly, and the alarm bells went off in her mind. She felt a sudden concern for Rosamund, which she was careful to censor.

'You look surprised,' Rosamund said. 'I suppose you're wary of him after what he said about your husband. But he couldn't be nicer. Underneath all his flamboyance and flash there's a tender, vulnerable man who needs to be loved.' Rosamund raised her eyes from her coffee cup. 'You look sceptical, too. You probably think I'm very foolish.'

'Oh no, please don't think that. How could I judge? I don't even know him. I'm just concerned for your sake. I'm glad you told me, Rosamund, because you've been a great help these last few days, and if I can ever return the favour, I'd be very glad to.'

Rosamund's eyes filled with sentiment, a kind of reflected luminosity from the night before. She smiled. 'I had to get away from Bob's and talk to someone. Isn't it lucky that you and I happened to meet? We both needed someone to talk to.' She sighed. 'I have so much to think about. My life seems to have changed from night to day.'

Rachel nodded sympathetically. 'Just remember the advice you gave me – don't do anything hasty.'

'I'm afraid it's too late for that,' Rosamund replied with a smile. 'I've had flirtations before, but for the first time in my life I woke up knowing for certain that I had found something remarkable, something that I'll never find again. He's younger than me and he's no angel; he's mad and he's impetuous, but he's swept me off my feet. He's already talking about meeting in London, asking if I could get away with him at weekends.'

'Oh, Rosamund, be careful,' Rachel couldn't refrain from saying.

But Rosamund wasn't listening. 'He took me to dinner at the Auberge last night, then we went back to where he's staying in a

176

*pigeonnier* made into a guest house on Isabelle de Montjoi's property.' Rosamund looked guiltily at Rachel at the mention of Isabelle before she continued. 'It was utterly idyllic, a warm night with moonlight streaming through the windows, music playing. I must confess I had a bit too much to drink. Of course I told myself it was much too soon, but I capitulated because I wanted to. Suddenly, in one evening the dam burst and I realized what I'd been missing with Charles – that's my husband. There's been no passion, no warmth between us for years. Last night I realized I couldn't live without those things for a moment longer. I'm too young to resign myself to living without love. I had a breakdown last year, quite a serious one. Oh, I'm much better now. In fact, meeting Julian has made me feel whole again for the first time in years . . .'

As she listened to Rosamund, her voice so full of hope and excitement, Rachel thought about her own marriage. Reflecting on the Ribard wartime shame and the spectre of abject poverty that Alain had never fully shared with her, she imagined herself years hence if her marriage survived, pouring her heart out to a friend.

\*

The meeting with the architect in his stuffy little office seemed to be grinding on interminably. Julian, whose mind could work on two levels simultaneously, was listening with one ear, while thinking of the tall, bewitching blonde he had seen in the square.

The architect, a wiry, balding man in his forties, looked sceptically at Isabelle through his tortoiseshell glasses. 'You're being very optimistic.'

'I want your promise that the decorators will be in by the following January, no later. Otherwise, Jacqueline Gadel won't take the commission. In the meantime Alain wants to supervise every detail of the kitchen himself, and he wants it completed by May.'

'We'll try our best, as I said, but in my experience old buildings like this always conceal a lot of surprises. I must allow a time over-run of at least ten per cent to cover it, and a detailed addendum to the specifications as well. I wouldn't be honest with you if I didn't. Right now, I have to tell you that the schedule you suggest is impossible.' He looked at Alain and Julian, who said nothing.

Isabelle smiled, but there was no warmth in her eyes. 'We used your firm because that's what we want, the impossible. Isn't that right?' she said, looking to Julian and Alain for support.

'Then that means we'll have to hire extra labour.'

'That will cost money. Look, Gilbert, I know you can do this, but if you think you can't, you'd better back out now.'

A tired little sigh escaped the architect's lips. 'I'll talk to the mason today, before he leaves on holiday, and try to get his promise. But he's a craftsman and won't do a rush job.'

'We don't want any rush jobs. It's the plumbers and plasterers who are always unpredictable. Make sure they understand their commitment to finish by December of next year. The hotel must be open by the following summer.'

Alain shifted impatiently in his chair as Isabelle and the architect covered the same ground they had been discussing for the last fifteen minutes. His eyes wandered to the long window of the second-storey office that overlooked the square below. He was reminded that later in the day he was supposed to take Oliver to visit a farm he had contracted to supply the restaurant. He had been looking forward to showing Oliver this aspect of Gascon culture and the way of life behind it, which was the basis of the cuisine he was now developing for the Château Brissac. The sight of a market, even Roquelaire's, overflowing with summer produce usually fired him with enthusiasm. Now, however, it was as though his creative dynamo was idle. No ideas, no earth-shaking thoughts sprang to his mind. He felt a strange detachment as he stared out the window. A sharp voice intruded on his thoughts.

'Alain, did you hear me? Do you have anything more to add about the kitchen? Gilbert wants to know.'

'No, not at this stage. I want to study the specifications of the equipment further, but there's time for that before we sign the contract. We want to have the possibility of enlarging the floor space, if we need it, into the area marked as storage.'

'I'll have a look at it,' said the architect, pencilling in a note.

'Well, I think that about wraps it up,' said Julian, rising and looking at his watch.

'Are you in a hurry?' asked Isabelle, gathering up her papers.

'I'm always in a hurry. I have a very important engagement.' He shook hands with the architect, nodded to Isabelle and left.

By the time Alain and Isabelle were standing on the street corner, Julian had disappeared.

'I think the meeting went very well, and that Gilbert has got the message.' Isabelle dug into her bag and substituted big dark glasses for her reading spectacles.

'You gave him a hard time, but he seems very competent to me.'

'Of course he's competent,' Isabelle said with a laugh. 'We're saving a fortune by commissioning a local architect. I'm convinced he's as good as anyone in Paris and, believe me, I went into this thoroughly.'

'I'm aware of that,' Alain answered absently, his eyes combing the crowd milling around the market in the brilliant sunshine.

'And giving him a hard time is part of the job. You must know from experience, Alain, that you've got to crack the whip all the time with these people, make them understand you mean business. He must feel that we know every detail of those specifications. There's no mystique about it. I don't intend to let a single detail out of my grasp. That's my forte. You're the creative genius, I'm the administrator.' Touching his arm, she whispered, '*Chéri*, it's all beginning to happen. I can feel it.' She looked towards the market.

'Alain, look, there's Agnès Grimal in the stall in the corner.'

He followed her eyes, instantly spotting the rabbit-seller in a straw hat standing by her crates. She was chatting to a farmer.

'I've made a point of coming in every Friday since Armand died to see whether she was there, and she hasn't missed a single market. It's typical of the people around here. She's rich now, but she's still selling rabbits as if she needed the money. Pathetic, isn't it?'

He mumbled a reply. A cringing dread overcame him as he looked in Agnès's direction. He countermanded it by saying, 'Perhaps we should both go up and have a few words with her. It might break the ice.'

179

'That would be the worst possible move,' Isabelle replied firmly. 'Listen, I'm going to the pharmacy and the bank, and I'll meet you here in fifteen or twenty minutes.'

When she had gone, Alain stood rigidly on the sidelines of the bustling market, feeling the avenging power of the past breach the wall he had built, a wall of stubborn contempt that had always protected him. Through dark glasses he picked out faces in the crowd that might have been those of people he had once known, but he didn't try to place them. During his trips to the village earlier in the year he had spoken to no one except the mayor, who couldn't have been more cordial and who was highly enthusiastic about the hotel project. He had given no sign of remembering the Ribard shame.

As Alain moved anonymously among the people who had seemed so superior and condescending when he was young, he was both relieved to be incognito and disappointed that no one could see how dramatically his circumstances had changed. But his visit to the farm had left him feeling uneasy, as if he had roused a sleeping demon. All the years he had spent in America – years that had altered his language, his outlook and his status – seemed to dwindle away, leaving him naked and alone. On that sunny August morning nearly twenty years later he reflected with bitter irony that in spite of everything he had achieved, he couldn't kill the spectre of that green and angry young man, whose feet would always be rooted in the soil, who was nothing but a peasant in his bones. He watched the crowd of ordinary people whose ways he had outgrown, resenting deeply that he still cared so much for their opinion. His eyes passed once more to Agnès Grimal, the insignificant little woman who held his fate in her hands. Knowing he was helpless to do anything at the moment, he left the square and walked up the Rue St Jacques.

*

Rachel was saying goodbye to Rosamund at the door of the house.

'Let me know what's happening, won't you?'

'Of course I will. Thanks for letting me unburden myself to you.

Why I needed to, I can't imagine. It's not as if I was going through a crisis like you,' she said sympathetically.

'No, you're happy. Enjoy it.' Rachel stopped short of saying, 'while it lasts'.

'Isn't it marvellous?' said Rosamund, oblivious of the doubt in Rachel's eyes. She put on her hat and glasses. 'I'm going back to Bob's now to do the damnedest watercolour that I've ever done. I can feel it in my bones.'

'Good for you. Say hello to everyone for me.'

'Come by some night for dinner. Bob and Ted would like to see you.'

'I'll do that. Thanks for coming by, Rosamund.'

'I'll keep you posted,' Rosamund called. Just as she began to walk down the street Michael Lowry came out of his house, a market basket on his arm. He paused as she passed and she acknowledged him with a cheery wave.

'*Bonjour. Ça va?*'

'*Ça va*, thanks.' Seeing Rachel still on her doorstep, he called out 'Good morning' as he approached her. 'She's in a fine mood, isn't she?' he said, indicating Rosamund's retreating figure.

'Do you suppose it's catching?' asked Rachel with a smile.

'It must be. That's the first time I think I've seen you smile in twenty-four hours. Any developments?'

'Not yet. I was just debating whether to get in the car and drive out to find Oliver. I've had enough of the waiting game.'

'I wish I could be of some help.'

'You are – you're nearby.'

'If you'd like to come to dinner tonight, I'm just going to the market and I thought, that is if you could stand another bout of my cooking . . .' he broke off, waiting for her to finish.

'Thank you, but isn't it my turn to ask you?'

'You've got other things on your mind. Some other time.'

A current of understanding passed between them that was as warming as the morning sun, wiping away the strangeness that appeared initially whenever they saw each other. Looking at Michael's freshly shaved face brightened by a smile, Rachel felt a wave of affection for him that was as startling as it was unexpected.

181

A light had pierced the darkness of the last days, making her feel confident again. She was about to say how much she would enjoy having dinner with him again when she saw Alain coming up the street. Seeing the change in her expression, Michael followed her eyes.

'It's Alain, my husband.'

'Perhaps I ought to disappear tactfully.'

'No, please stay for a moment. Why shouldn't you?' Alain's sudden appearance threw her into a turmoil. She felt fear and anxiety where moments ago she had felt serene in Michael's presence.

When Alain saw the two of them, he didn't alter his stride. A few feet away, he removed his glasses and looked coldly at Michael.

'Good morning, Rachel,' he said, as if Michael weren't there.

'Alain, this is Michael Lowry. He found this house for me.'

'I only have a few minutes. Can we go inside?' He brushed past Michael without acknowledging him in any way.

The embarrassment Rachel felt at his rudeness cleared her mind. 'I'll see you later, Michael.'

Michael nodded and walked off down the street.

As Rachel led the way into the house Alain said, 'What is this with the Englishman?'

'What is what?' Rachel whirled around. 'Is that why you came here?'

'Forget it,' he said with a tired sigh. 'I've only got a few minutes. We've got to talk things over.'

'Did you get my message?'

'Of course. That's how I knew you were here. What the hell do you mean by this, camping on my doorstep? What are you trying to prove?'

The injustice of his anger hardened Rachel's resolve. 'This isn't getting us anywhere. You'd better sit down and we'll talk it over.'

Her even-tempered manner took Alain by surprise. Lowering himself reluctantly into a chair, he looked at her belligerently. 'All right. What are your intentions – to stay here until I come home with Oliver? You don't really care about the damage you're doing to him, do you?'

182

She ignored this. 'I'm glad you came by because I want to see Oliver right away, today. Please don't try to deny me what is my right, because I won't accept it.'

'No one's denying you anything,' he muttered, seeing the determined look in her eyes. 'All I came here for is to talk reason into you. All right, so what if you do see him? Whatever story you concoct, it would only upset him at this point. Why can't you just leave him alone and let him enjoy his holiday?'

'I'm afraid it's too late for that,' she replied, refusing to rise to the bait. She kept all the bitter rejoinders to herself.

Alain thought for a minute. 'And if I agree, what do you intend to tell him?'

'As little as possible for the moment. Obviously he's going to sense that things aren't right between us, but I hope to prepare him for that little by little.'

'I still don't understand why we can't postpone all this until I come home. I know you're angry, hurt that I want out of the marriage, but it doesn't help to take it out on Oliver. I expected so much more from you, Rachel, so much more than this.'

She gave him a withering look. 'Oh, Alain, stop it. You don't deserve anything better. You deserve nothing, period. You made the decision that it was over between us, and now you're trying to make it sound as if I'm at fault. I want my son. He's all I have now.'

These words seemed to startle him. 'But the business. It's in Oliver's interest . . .'

'The business can go to hell. It's of no concern to me now that you've opted out.'

Her words pierced his defences and he was at a loss for a reply. Rachel looked away, feeling a trace of pity as she recalled Rosamund's sad revelation about Alain's past. But the vibrant, exciting man she had always looked up to was now caught in this labyrinth of his own making and she fought the blind instinct to rescue him. The question of whether she still loved him crept into her mind, but it was clouded by hurt and confusion. Knowing she had to appear stronger than she felt, Rachel stood up to signal their meeting was over.

183

'You can bring Oliver here later today or, if that's not convenient, I'll come out and fetch him.'

'That's impossible without any preparation. I insist on telling him in advance that you're here.'

'All right. Tomorrow, then; I don't want to be unreasonable.'

He hesitated. The look on his face told her he still had not entirely accepted her arguments.

'He has a riding lesson early in the morning, then he goes into the pool to cool off. Why tear him away from the pool in this hot weather? He practically lives in it, playing with the housekeeper's grandson. Is that what you want, to bring him here, to this tiny village house where he'll have nothing, no one to play with?'

His words had the opposite effect to what he intended. It was intolerable to Rachel to imagine her son preoccupied by activities arranged by Isabelle de Montjoi. 'What you say may be true, but I'm his mother and I want him here with me, under my roof for a night.' She was shaking and perilously close to losing her temper.

They looked at each other across a divide, and Rachel realized what was bothering Alain; he was afraid she would disappear, taking Oliver with her. She wondered if that was what he had intended to do himself all along.

'I'll agree to him coming here for the day, but not staying the night. It's too disruptive. Even you ought to agree to that. He's comfortable where he is, in a room next to my room,' he said pointedly.

But Rachel hardly noticed the reference to 'my room'. She wasn't sure any more what the answer was. At last she said, 'For the moment, all right. I agree that he can stay where he is at night.' As she spoke, she regretted giving in. 'But only for a day or two.'

Alain turned to go. 'Is there a telephone here?'

'It's not connected. Just tell me now what time you're coming tomorrow.'

Seeing he was trapped, Alain said, 'As soon as I can manage. It depends on his riding lesson, but it probably won't be until eleven.'

'Fine. You can pick him up before supper. Tell him that I'm here and that I'm not sure how long I'll be staying.' Swallowing her pride, Rachel asked the question that was in her mind. 'Does he miss me? Has he asked to talk on the telephone?'

'I don't know. Ask him when you see him.'

As he walked through the door she said, 'All these years I thought I knew you, but I never suspected you could be so cruel, Alain.'

He departed without looking back. When he had gone, Rachel pressed her cheek against the cool stone wall in the hallway. A flood of hot tears she didn't try to hold back coursed down her cheeks.

When he left the meeting, Julian walked quickly to the café. To his amazement and delight, the girl he had seen earlier was still sitting at one of the tables, but her friend with the baby in the pram was gone. He took the table next to her just as she was gathering up her handbag to go.

'Excuse me, *mademoiselle*, but do you speak English?'

The surprise in her clear eyes aroused the first stirrings of the chase in Julian.

'Yes, I speak English,' she admitted. She was looking back at him with interest, revealing that he had made an instant impression.

Julian beamed, congratulating himself on his luck. A few words more would tell him whether they could communicate.

'I'm so glad to meet someone who speaks English. You see, I'm here on business and it's very frustrating not to be able to have a conversation. I've been here over a week now, and you're the first person I've talked to, almost.'

His confession seemed to unlock her reserve and she smiled sympathetically. 'It must be terrible.'

'It's absurd. It makes one feel so helpless not being able to communicate. When I saw you I had a feeling you might be English.'

'I understand,' she said. 'When I was in England at first sometimes I used to go to places where I knew French people would be, hoping to hear my own language.'

Her friendly manner prompted Julian to move his chair closer to her table. 'I wish I could speak French half as well as you speak English.'

185

'Thank you very much, but I'm afraid I'm losing it. I haven't been back to London for – let me see – three years. I spent two summers there with a family in Hampstead, as an *au pair*. The first summer was awful, but by the second summer I found I could really speak. But now . . .' she shrugged. 'I don't get the chance very often in Bordeaux.'

'You live in Bordeaux?'

'I was born here, but I've been studying accountancy there.'

'You're from Roquelaire?' he asked incredulously.

'You seem surprised. Is that so very strange?'

'No – it's wonderful. It means you must be here for a while, and not visiting, that's all.' His lips parted in a half smile and he studied her so intently that she blushed.

Pascale turned away and pretended to study the passers-by. Seeing someone she knew, she called a greeting. When she turned her head back, Julian was still observing her.

'Excuse me, but why are you looking like that?'

'I'm sorry to stare, but I can't help thinking how beautiful you are.'

Her eyes widened in disbelief for an instant, but, seeing the look of vacant contemplation on his face, she was amused. She registered the details about him that intrigued her: his unconventional ponytail and the fashionable, understated clothes he wore with such elegance.

'It's a remarkable coincidence that I sat down next to you when you must be the only person in Roquelaire who speaks English.'

'I'm not the only one.'

'Yes you are. You're the only one I want to meet,' he replied, making her smile. 'I'm not being a gentleman. Waiter,' he called in English. Pascale began to laugh.

'What's the matter?' Julian asked with a grin.

'You have to say "*monsieur*". He doesn't know what a waiter is.'

'Of course. How stupid of me.'

When the waiter came to their table, Pascale glanced up at him. '*Bonjour*, Claude,' she said, almost shyly.

'*Bonjour*, Pascale. When did you get back?'

Julian caught a critical look in his eye and saw that Pascale was suddenly ill at ease.

'I heard Étienne is coming home this week.'

'That's right,' she said, not looking at Julian. They ordered a drink, a pastis for him, an orange juice for her.

When the waiter had moved away, Julian saw that Pascale's mood had changed; she was restless. 'What was all that about?'

'He's a family friend. He was just asking about me and how I've been.'

'Maybe he doesn't approve of you talking to tourists.'

She gave a self-conscious little laugh.

'Where do you live?'

'Not far. Down that street across the square.'

'I saw you earlier with a girl who had a baby.'

'That was my friend Annie. She was married last summer and this spring she had a little girl.' Pascale saw Julian looking at the third finger of her left hand, which bore her engagement ring, a minute sapphire surrounded by tiny diamonds.

'I'll be honest with you. I saw you before that, when you were crossing the square and I was driving by.'

'Really? I don't remember,' she said, pretending not to have realized that he was the man who had ogled her so blatantly from his red Porsche.

'When I saw you, I thought you were a tourist from northern Europe. It's obvious, isn't it, with hair like that. Swedish, I said to myself.'

'Did you really think that? How funny.' She bolted her orange juice and picked up her handbag.

'Will you have dinner with me tonight?' Julian said as she stood. He enjoyed the way her eyes widened in surprise.

'No, I'm sorry, but I can't. Thank you very much anyway.'

'Well, what about tomorrow? Can you have lunch?'

Pascale hesitated, then shook her head. 'It's very kind, but I can't.'

He leaned forward, concentrating all the intensity of his gaze on her. 'I just realized I don't even know your name. Mine is Julian. Julian Paine.'

'Mine is Pascale Gachpour.'

When she extended her hand in an automatic gesture, he held her fingers for a few seconds longer than necessary.

'Pascale, Mademoiselle Gachpour, I would be flattered if you would have lunch with me any day you name. We could go to the Château Labardens or the Vieille Auberge.'

She stood up abruptly. Looking down into his pleading eyes, she was suddenly lost. It was impossible to resist this glamorous Englishman. She pictured them driving up to the chic restaurant in his Porsche. She said, 'And if I came tomorrow, what time should I meet you?'

Julian concealed his jubilation. 'How about twelve o'clock, here?'

She shook her head. 'No, not here.' She thought quickly. 'Maybe we could meet at the *lavoir* on the edge of town outside the ramparts.' Seeing he didn't understand, she added, 'It's the pool with a roof, where they washed clothes in the old days.'

'Of course, I know where you mean. That's absolutely super. I'll look forward to it.'

'Goodbye, Julian,' she said, formally extending her hand to him.

Julian noticed that she had nearly called him Monsieur, but had caught herself. '*Au revoir*, Mademoiselle Gachpour, *à demain*,' he whispered, fixing her with his gaze.

'But you speak French!' she exclaimed, then started to laugh. 'You said you didn't speak a word.'

He shrugged and gave her an ingenuous smile. The spontaneous laugh that rose in her throat filled Julian with the thrill of conquest, a blinding bright flash that had become rarer once he had passed thirty. Watching her walk across the square, he made a wager with himself that he would have her in his bed within a week.

# Chapter 10

That afternoon a short, plump woman with dyed brown hair walked up the path of Agnès's cottage and knocked at the door, which was ajar.

'Come in,' said Agnès, raising her head. She was seated at the kitchen table, preparing a pile of green beans. The aroma of soup simmering on the stove filled the kitchen, which was illuminated only by the light from the open door and from a small barred window over the sink. She dumped the beans in her apron on to the table as she rose and held out her hand to Armand Bataille's former housekeeper, who wore a red-and-white-spotted dress and smart red shoes that made a splash of colour in the drab cottage.

'*Vous allez bien?*' she said cheerfully, pretending not to notice that Hélène's eyes were moving around the room, passing judgement on everything she saw, including Agnès herself.

'You're preparing such a lot of beans. Not just for one, I imagine?'

'Oh no, Pascale is home for the holidays and we're having her fiancé to lunch at my sister's on Sunday. Beatrice has enough to do with the bakery on weekends, so I try to help.'

'Are Pascale and Étienne getting married soon, then?'

'As soon as he leaves the army at Christmas.' Agnès could not keep the note of pride from her voice as she spoke of it, and she was aware that Hélène Briault couldn't help being impressed that Pascale was going to marry the son of the bank manager.

They avoided discussing the reason for Hélène's visit, touching on the weather and the forthcoming village fête instead. Agnès watched the housekeeper's eyes dart furtively around the kitchen where nothing had changed since the war. She could not conceal her curiosity at the black stove and the big fireplace, where a

189

charred pot was suspended over a neatly laid pile of faggots. Strings of garlic and bunches of recently gathered thyme and bay leaves hung from hooks in the blackened beams, and on the shelves were glass jars of lime leaves and camomile flowers for tea in the winter. The kitchen continued to serve its original purpose, to preserve and prepare the bounty of the garden. It was an outmoded way of life that had all but disappeared.

The two women had had little contact over the years. Hélène had worked at the château after her husband, a postman, had died just a few weeks after Armand had become a widower. Agnès remembered seeing Hélène walking the distance from the village to the château in all seasons, all weathers. She lived in a white cube of a house with brown shutters at the end of the village. The bright red begonias in white pots set uniformly on the fence posts spoke of her orderly, precise nature. It was Hélène who had admitted her to the house the last time she had seen Armand, and Agnès had not forgotten the look of indignant surprise on the housekeeper's face when she saw Agnès standing at the door. In the interim Agnès had heard that Hélène was not happy with the small bequest she had received from her dead employer. She had expected much more of a reward after so many years in Armand Bataille's service in the light of his childless state. Now she could not conceal her anger that Agnès, who was no more than a stranger, had inherited the bulk of his property.

'I spoke with Armand's sisters this morning,' said Hélène, 'and I thought you ought to know that they are coming together by car. Madame Trènta is staying with Madame Duclos in Limoges and they'd like to pass by on Monday, if that's all right with you. As you have no telephone they asked me to pass on the message.'

'Certainly,' said Agnès. She surprised Hélène by saying, 'I wonder if you could do me a great service and pack up Armand's things on your own, Hélène. You know much better than I where everything is that he wanted his sisters to have.'

Hélène looked at her coldly. 'Of course, if that's what you prefer.'

'Just put everything in boxes. I noticed there were some in the cupboard downstairs.'

'I have a copy of the notary's list. All the mementoes are very small ones, such as the photographs, though I'm sure they'll be glad to have them.'

Agnès ignored the reproach in her voice at the mention of what Armand had left his two sisters besides the money she knew they had already received. She suddenly thought of a photograph she had seen on the table in the grand hall when she last visited the château, a photograph that she knew meant more to her than to anyone else.

The housekeeper turned to go. 'I'll need the keys to get in.'

'Of course. You could get Monsieur David's keys, but I have an extra set. Let me get them.' She went to the other room of the cottage, her bedroom, and brought back an enormous pair of rusted old keys attached to a chain. 'I assumed you had your own set,' she said pointedly, knowing it would annoy Hélène.

'Monsieur used to let me in himself; these keys are much too bulky to carry about.'

'Yes, indeed,' said Agnès. Under Hélène's accusing gaze she suddenly regretted asking her to go to the château but it was too late to change her mind. Until then she hadn't realized how much she disliked Hélène.

'I'll go there tomorrow morning and return the keys afterwards.'

'That will be fine,' Agnès replied, glad the housekeeper was about to leave. Just then she saw Pascale appear at the gate.

'But who is this?' Hélène stopped in surprise. 'Not Pascale? My, how lovely she's become, really lovely.'

'*Bonjour,*' Pascale called to Agnès. '*Bonjour, madame,*' she said, taking off her sunglasses and extending her hand to Hélène.

'I haven't seen you for a long time,' Hélène exclaimed, peering at her. 'You're a grown woman now!'

Pascale shrugged noncommittally, a fixed smile on her face. She felt a wave of intense curiosity coming from the woman she knew had been Armand Bataille's housekeeper.

'You're studying in Bordeaux, aren't you?'

'Yes, that's right. I've just finished a course in accountancy.'

'Isn't that nice.' Hélène's tone implied she thought Pascale's knowledge would come in handy following Agnès's remarkable windfall. 'How old are you now?'

'My birthday is in September. I'll be twenty-one.'

'Will you really? How time flies.'

At the mention of Pascale's age Agnès stiffened with apprehension. Since the word had got out about her legacy she was tormented by the idea that someone, particularly someone so close to Armand as Hélène, might put the missing piece in the puzzle that had made her the talk of the village.

Pascale saved the day by asking 'Are those the keys to the château? I haven't seen it yet,' she added brightly, as if she were completely oblivious to all the upheavals this legacy had caused.

'Your aunt has asked me to perform a little errand.' Hélène slipped the keys into her pocket as if she were afraid Pascale would ask for them back. 'I hear you and Étienne are going to be married soon. He's a fine young man. His mother tells me that he wants to go into banking, just like his father.'

'That's right,' Pascale replied breezily.

When at last Hélène had gone, Pascale followed Agnès into the house. 'What a curious old bag that woman is. What did she want, anyway?'

Agnès gave a sigh of relief and sat down in front of the pile of beans. 'She's just packing up a few things that Monsieur Bataille left to his sisters. One of them lives in Limoges and they're both coming down on Monday. I was hoping you'd come for lunch tomorrow so I could take you up to see the place.'

Pascale hesitated at the lie she was forced to tell. 'I'm dying to see the château really, but I promised Annie I'd come for lunch.'

'Tomorrow?'

'Yes, because she's all on her own and we have so much to catch up on. She's going on holiday soon and I may not see much of her . . .' She stopped, aware that the breathless quality of her voice might give her away.

'I see. Well, that doesn't matter. We can do it another time. Perhaps later in the afternoon.'

'Yes, perhaps,' murmured Pascale, wondering when she would be back from lunch with Julian Paine. Saying goodbye to him that morning, she had been glad to escape his penetrating gaze, which implied he knew so much about her, but she had been unable to get him out of her mind. She was ridden with guilt that she had accepted his invitation for lunch the day before her fiancé was supposed to arrive, and now she was confused that the reunion to which she had been looking forward so intensely had taken second place to a date with a total stranger. Watching Agnès busily snipping the ends of the beans, she was aware she had hurt her aunt's feelings by not jumping at the first chance to explore the château, and now she wondered how she could bring up the real reason she had come.

'Perhaps I ought to have gone up to Brissac and packed the things myself,' Agnès said.

'You should have. Mother told me Hélène was upset at the legacy she received. She might take something out of spite.'

'Hélène? Never! She's as honest as the day is long. No, that's not it.'

'Then, why?' Pascale reached for a plum from a bowl on the table.

'To tell you the truth, I've always thought Hélène was sly. She's very capable, I know, and honest, but sly. In fact, she's a thoroughly dislikeable woman.'

'Why did you let her go alone to the château, then?'

Agnès thought a moment. 'Because I didn't want her to think I didn't trust her.'

They both laughed at this reasoning, and Pascale said, 'That's typical of you, *tatie*.'

Agnès's eyes shone as she looked at Pascale. 'You look so pretty today, very smart. I like the new styles this year.'

'I bought this with some of the money you sent me. Thanks again, by the way. If I had to pay for clothes on top of my rent and food, I'd be naked. Mama still thinks dresses cost what they did ten years ago.'

'I know. And she need never know how you can afford to dress so well. It's just between us.'

'Didn't you ever like pretty clothes?' Pascale looked at Agnès's faded blue cotton dress and thick brown shoes.

'Of course I did. But we didn't have any money during the war or after it. There used to be a shop in Roquelaire called La Belle

Parisienne. It had the most beautiful clothes, at least I thought so at the time. I never went past without stopping to look. You think when you're young that you'll buy whatever you want when you grow up, but you don't. I'm exactly like my mother.'

'I'm not at all like Mama. I mean, I love her dearly, but our tastes are completely different.'

'No, you're not like her,' Agnès agreed with a nod. 'Not at all.'

'But really, Aunt Agnès, you should do some shopping for yourself. The shops in Roquelaire are getting some quite nice things. I was surprised.'

'What do *I* need? Very little. But I'm happy.' Agnès stood up and dumped the beans into a colander in the stone sink.

'*Tatie*, what are you going to do with the château? Are you going to sell it?'

Agnès looked at her thoughtfully, having expected to be asked the question once they had a moment alone.

'Your mother and father have been wondering about that. And I'm sure Étienne's parents must be curious too.'

'It's nothing to do with them.'

'But of course it is. I haven't any children, as you know, and I'm an old lady. I'm not going to live for ever.'

Pascale's cheeks reddened and she looked embarrassed. 'That's not what I meant.'

'I know you didn't. But some day you'll benefit from this legacy in some way. At my time of life there's not a lot that I want or need.'

'You could travel, buy another house. Have you thought of that?'

'What for? I was born here. Can you imagine me living in a little box of a house like Hélène's, with no vegetable garden, no place for my rabbits? As for travel, I can't imagine anything worse than getting in a bus and going to Spain with a lot of strangers.'

Pascale smiled to herself. 'I didn't mean anything like that. I meant going to Paris, or Egypt; some place far away.'

'Who would look after my rabbits? No, travel doesn't interest me. Anyway, I don't have any money yet. Just a big house.'

Agnès took the lid from the pot of soup simmering on the stove and gave it a stir as she looked lovingly at Pascale's blonde head. The deep love she felt for her daughter had been disguised over the years to pass as the love of a childless woman for her only niece. A long time ago she had discovered that there was no need to hide her feelings if she gave them a different label. Agnès had been free to take Pascale to her heart, and had come to believe that she understood her daughter far better because she had lived one step removed from her. It was too late to undo what she had done those many years ago, but the pain she had suffered had been healed by the love between them.

'So what are you going to do then?' Pascale persisted.

'I don't know yet.' There was a stubborn edge to her voice.

'Mama was wondering this morning why Madame de Montjoi hasn't approached you yet.'

Agnès frowned. 'I saw her a week or two ago in the market. She said hello to me.'

'That must mean something. What's she like? I haven't seen her for years.'

'Oh, you know, very elegant, sure of herself. She goes out of her way to be charming to people who are useful.'

'Is it true what Mama said, that her lover used to live here and that his name is Ribard?'

'How do I know? There is a lot of talk about Madame de Montjoi because she is rich and glamorous and because she lives in high society.'

'I think it's absolutely fascinating. Apparently his American wife has tracked him down, and they have a son who is living at Terre Blanche with his father.'

'Who told you that?'

'Annie told me. She filled me in on all the news. Everybody is talking about it – and about you, *tatie*, they talk about you, too.' When Agnès turned, Pascale was looking at her with excitement in her clear blue eyes. 'What will you do if she tries to buy it? Everybody is wondering.'

'They can wonder if they like. But I'll tell you the truth, Pascale: I don't know.'

'You really don't know?' Pascale asked incredulously. 'But the taxes, the upkeep. Papa is really worrying about it, but I suppose you know that.'

'He doesn't have to worry on my account,' Agnès said sharply.

Pascale rose from the table and hugged her. 'Don't be cross. It's the biggest thing that's ever happened in this family, but I don't want it to change us.'

'It will change us, Pascale, whether we want it to or not. It already has.'

'It's true,' the younger woman admitted. 'I felt somehow different when I walked into the square today. Different than when I was home two months ago, I suppose, because I'm aware people are talking.'

'What have you heard?' asked Agnès, alarmed.

'I've heard nothing particular, only what I've already told you,' Pascale replied, wondering why Agnès was so touchy.

'You haven't told me what Étienne said to you when he heard the news.'

'He wrote to say he was thrilled. And his parents were too, naturally.'

'Yes, naturally,' said Agnès, stirring the soup. She had a sudden image of Étienne's parents, who lived in a big modern villa set in a large garden on the edge of town.

The old clock above the fireplace showed that it was nearly three o'clock. Pascale looked at it and rose from her chair.

'Are you going home? You can stay and eat with me if you like. I have some nice goat's cheese and some figs, as well as the soup.'

'I really have to go. Aunt Agnès . . .' she hesitated. 'On Sunday, if Mama asks, would you tell her that I was here tomorrow and had some lunch with you?' Pascale's heart was pounding furiously as she said it.

'I don't understand. Why should I tell your mother that you are eating here tomorrow? What's the necessity for that?'

'You know what Mama is like. If I say I'm going to Annie's again, she'll be furious. But if I say I'm coming here, then she won't mind.' Seeing Agnès was unconvinced, she added, 'She doesn't understand that I like to see my friends as much as I can. She'll say I'll have plenty of time later, but I won't really. I'll just tell her I'm here with you and she won't know the difference. It's not a big thing, is it?'

Agnès tried to interpret her daughter's anxious expression. For the first time she could remember, a shadow passed between them: Pascale was not telling her the truth.

'All right, if that's what you want. I don't like it, but I'll do it.'

'Thanks so much, thanks.' Pascale hugged her exuberantly. 'I have to dash off now. Thanks again.'

There was a look of dreamy anticipation of Pascale's face that suggested her mind was already far away. Agnès supposed she must be thinking of Étienne.

'If you want to go in the château on your own, ask Monsieur David for the keys.'

Pascale stopped and turned around. Her smooth complexion was dappled by the shadow of the chestnut tree, her thick, pale hair ruffled by a hot breeze. She looked slightly shy as she said, 'I've been getting up the courage to ask you. There's something I've wondered about ever since I heard the news. Why do you suppose Armand Bataille left you the château?'

Though she had been expecting it, Agnès was caught off guard. Pascale had asked the question she had seen reflected in the faces of everyone in the village, making Agnès wonder for an anxious moment whether Pascale or anyone else could possibly suspect the truth.

'Pascale, this isn't the time to talk about it, perhaps, but something happened during the war when Monsieur Bataille was in the Resistance. I can't tell you what it was. It must remain a secret, but I helped him in a way that was greater than I realized at the time. You mustn't tell anyone, because no one knows a thing about it.'

'The Resistance!' Pascale's voice was full of awe. 'Is that it? Now I understand. Aunt Agnès, it's very moving that he should remember you in this way, and that you can't tell anybody about it. Just imagine! I wouldn't have guessed something like that in a thousand years. But you were still so young in the war, younger than I am now.'

Agnès saw the look of respect and wonder on Pascale's face. 'Not so young. We grew up very fast then.'

197

'Thanks for telling me. I promise to keep it to myself. And thank you for helping me out.' She kissed Agnès's cheek.

Agnès looked down at her daughter's long tapering fingers, thinking how beautiful they were. Everything about Pascale had always seemed perfect to her.

'Tell your mother I'll be there early on Sunday if she needs me.'

Agnès watched her until she had disappeared down the road. She finished her work in the kitchen, put a basket on her arm and departed for Brissac.

Later that afternoon Agnès entered the silent courtyard of the château, slumbering in the afternoon heat. The shimmering dome of blue sky rose above the bleached stone walls, where lizards, sunning themselves, scuttled as she approached. She glanced round the courtyard, her appreciation of its perfect symmetry dulled by her own distraction. She looked up at the sightless windows, then down at the dark oval pool. Its smooth surface was barely disturbed by the water trickling, as it had for centuries, from a mossy stone outlet. Peering over the edge, Agnès saw the outline of her hat and shoulders on the surface, an image that suggested she was nothing more than a shadow. Her body had dissolved to a translucent reflection and looked back at her, as insubstantial as a ghost. As she stared at the opaque pool it seemed to become luminous. From the edges a procession of the ages passed before her eyes. Romans in leather jerkins, kings in armour, nuns' faces staring from their wimples, the cowled heads of monks, the coarse faces of peasants twisted by weather and want. They all passed by, then disappeared. There was a lull as a breeze rippled the water's surface. She saw Armand, his face young, his frame full of vitality, his dark eyes full of hope. Though he seemed to see her, she knew he was beyond a barrier that could never be breached. The suggestion of him so close, yet unreachable, stirred an aching grief that only death could mend. She closed her eyes, not wanting to see more, and when she opened them the pool was opaque again. She stood motionless for a long time, conscious of a wound that would never heal.

Coming back to the present, Agnès found she was in the

courtyard alone. All the people she had imagined had gone, their voices and shadows absorbed by the stones of Brissac's high walls. Soon she would join the cortège of ages. Though she was not really very old, she felt that her life was almost over. Her own image, which had floated on the water, was already in the process of fading away. The keys of the château, so heavy in her pocket, would pass to someone else in time, next week, next year, but soon.

She walked to the door of the château anguished by what she had seen and felt, yet not sure whether it was real or some sort of hallucination. She even wondered if she might be going mad.

She turned the big key in the lock and pushed open the heavy door. She didn't pause in the hallway, which was dimly lit by the light from a barred window above the door, but hurried up the staircase pursued by the echo of her own footsteps. In the main reception room Agnès switched on the heavy brass chandelier. It did little to illuminate the dark corners of the huge room. Old chests, heavily carved *armoires* and big tapestried chairs were little more than gloomy silhouettes among the huge nineteenth-century portraits and landscapes and the collection of guns and lances lining the dark walls. The number of bulbs blazing overhead aroused Agnès's fear of a huge electricity bill and made her hurry. She went across to the photographs standing on a long table against a wall and picked up the one she wanted. It was of Armand, taken the day he received the Légion d'honneur. She stared at it for a moment, then wrapped it in an embroidered velvet square she found on the arm of a chair and put it in the bottom of her basket.

Turning out the lights, Agnès left the hall and walked down the passage to Armand's bedroom. She opened the door and stood for a moment gazing at the dark contour of his canopied bed. A single chink of light, as small and bright as a star, chased the shadows of the shuttered room and outlined familiar objects she had failed to notice when she had come to see Armand for the last time. She sank into the scrolled chair in front of the desk, clasping her hands round the carved arms and thinking of him. She had the poignant illusion that Armand was somewhere in the château and would soon be standing in the room. The grief she had carried inside her since his death, the sadness that overshadowed her entire life because of him, would not be quelled by the stoic denial with which she always faced the past. Now life seemed unable to go forward until she had returned to 1943 and lived that time again.

She recalled how painfully thin she had been at just seventeen and how plain. Her pinched face, graced by a straight nose and pointed chin, was dominated by huge black eyes. Her fine eyebrows, which someone had compared to two brush strokes, arched gracefully to a high forehead. Her light-brown hair was always braided and tied with a ribbon the same faded blue as her patched dress. Her feet were much too big, causing her father to joke they would carry her far in life.

One day stood out among all the other harrowing days of the war. It was summer, and Agnès had cycled to a neighbouring village on an errand for her mother. She pushed her bicycle up the last steep slope towards the Château Brissac, from where she had a sweeping view of the parched hills, and stopped to catch her breath. An unexpected movement near a copse of trees below the château made her freeze with terror. Her knees went limp when she saw a young, dark-haired man she didn't recognize materialize from the shadows.

'Agnès!' he called in a loud whisper as he beckoned her to approach.

Surprised that he knew her name, she hurried towards him, realizing as she got closer that it was Armand Bataille, a young man from an outlying farm, whom no one had seen since the war broke out. She had heard that he had joined the Maquis and the implied danger of meeting him so unexpectedly made her tremble.

He took her bicycle and hid it behind a tree, then he grasped her shoulders with powerful hands. Armand Bataille was the handsomest man she had ever seen, with jet-black hair and thick eyebrows above light blue eyes that had a probing intensity. His face was deeply bronzed by the summer sun and he emitted a superior strength, earned by living at close quarters with death. She stared at him speechlessly, dumbstruck with awe.

'Agnès, listen to me, I need your help. You're only a young girl, but you've got to be brave and strong and promise never to tell anyone what I'm about to reveal to you. Do you understand?'

'Yes, I promise,' she whispered, acutely conscious of his hands still gripping her shoulders. She was so overwhelmed by the aura of strength and purpose radiating from him that at that moment she would have promised anything.

'There's a dead man here. I need you to help me carry his body across the clearing towards those bushes by the château walls. We mustn't leave any marks on the ground.'

He motioned for her to follow him through the trees. The body of a heavy-set, grey-haired man, wearing the blue worksuit of a farmer, was lying face down.

'We must be quick. There's a German patrol that often comes by. I'll take the shoulders and you take the feet.'

He rolled the body over and Agnès gasped when she saw who it was. She stared into the sightless eyes of Paul Ribard, who lived on a farm outside the village.

'Come on,' said Armand gruffly when she hesitated.

She was panting with exertion by the time they dumped the body by the edge of the shrubbery. Armand disappeared without a word into a gap she would never have guessed was there. When he came back, he motioned for her to take the feet again, and they struggled through the thicket to the base of the wall, where an entrance had been made by removing some of the stones. Armand backed inside, tugging the body as Agnès pushed with all her might. When she crawled in after him, she found, to her surprise, that there was enough room for her to stand up. While Armand dragged the body away into the depths of the passage, Agnès stood shivering in the cool, musty air that seemed to come from deep underground, bringing a strange evocative odour she couldn't identify. She realized then that the Maquis must have discovered this ancient hidden chamber beneath the château, though she had always assumed its existence was only a legend. When Armand touched her arm, she gave a start. His eyes glinted softly in the dimness.

'I'm sorry you had to witness this. Now you must put it out of your mind and never think of it again. The war will soon be over and life will begin afresh. All such things will be forgotten.'

The gentleness of his voice comforted her, but her eyes filled with involuntary tears when she thought of the dead man. When she swallowed a sob, Armand seemed to guess her thoughts.

'Paul Ribard was a traitor, Agnès. He had to die. I can tell you no more.'

She nodded.

'Remember, Agnès, if you should ever tell anyone what you saw today, it will almost certainly mean my death.'

'Even if they tortured me, I'd never tell anyone, ever!' she whispered fervently. Her shock that Armand had killed Paul Ribard was blotted out by the revelation that he was entrusting her with his life.

He pulled her towards the gap in the stone, and for a moment they crouched together in the circle of light.

'*Bien*, it's time for you to go home now. I must wait here for a while.' He hugged her tight for a moment and kissed her cheek. '*Au revoir, et bon courage,*' he whispered.

Stunned by the touch of his lips, Agnès gathered the impressions thick and fast, sensing she would for ever cherish her encounter with this *maquisard*, who seemed to embody all the heroic courage of France's wartime struggle.

When she left the passage, she glanced over her shoulder to see Armand still watching her. He touched his finger to his lips in a gesture that seemed to convey both a parting kiss and the need for silence before he abruptly disappeared.

The cry of swifts in Brissac's towers roused Agnès in her chair and the exhilarating sensation of youth pervading her daydream slowly seeped away. It was only after a moment that she fully realized that the girl in the patched blue dress and the handsome young *maquisard* had both gone for ever. Before leaving the room, she paused to touch the frayed velvet counterpane of the bed where Armand's head had once rested, aware there was more of the past still to remember, like a piece of embroidery she must trace and retrace to understand.

*

Rachel closed the door of the Peterson house behind her, leaving it unlocked. An evening cool, heralded by swifts painted on the enamelled sky, was softly invading the shadowy doorways and overhanging eaves. Finding Michael's door ajar, she pushed it and went in. 'Anyone at home?' she called into the house, wondering if her voice would be heard over the jazz coming from the stereo. The evening light suffused the white walls with pink, filling the long, narrow room with a welcoming warmth. Rachel's eyes moved to the clutter of the desk. She saw the chronicle lying open not far from the typewriter, and noticed that the wastepaper basket was full of crumpled paper, as if Michael had discarded one sheet after another in frustration.

'I'm in the kitchen,' called Michael. He emerged, wiping his hands on a towel. 'Come in. I left the door open in case I didn't hear you. The spaghetti sauce needed a stir. I hope you like spaghetti.'

'As long as it's loaded with garlic.'

'Ah, a woman after my own heart. Some people here still rub it on a bit of bread toasted on the fire and consume it with a glass of red wine for breakfast. Delicious.'

'I should try that to fortify me for the day.'

'Do you need fortifying?' When she smiled and shrugged, he continued, 'How are you, anyway?'

'Oh, I'm fine.'

'I want to hear all about what you've been doing today.'

Watching him cross the room to the tape deck, she felt a release from the gnawing sensation that had gripped her stomach since she had seen Alain that morning.

'I don't suppose you like Dizzy Gillespie, do you?'

'I won't say that I never heard of him, but only just.'

'You're too young. I've got a good ten years on you, and in jazz that's a whole millennium. What about Ashkenazy playing Chopin?'

'What could be better?' As he changed the tape, Rachel was soothed by Michael's diffident charm and gladly let the tension slip away for a little while. She watched him, his shock of brown hair speckled with grey falling forward as he riffled through a pile of tapes. Suddenly she yearned for the simpler pleasures of life, which

203

had been crowded out by the pressure of the harried existence she had shared with Alain. It had been years since she and Alain had passed a quiet evening listening to music and talking about something other than business. Always in motion, Alain's titanic energy had ruled out anything as undemanding as sitting passively in a chair. It occurred to Rachel that living with him was like living with the wind at her back, that she was in the habit of hurrying to keep up with him. It was a pleasant change to be in the company of someone who was more like her in temperament.

'I won't be a minute in the kitchen, if you'd like to go out on the terrace. Or perhaps you'd rather sit in here where it's cooler?'

'The terrace, I think. I don't mind the heat.'

He slipped his arm impulsively around her shoulder. 'You can't imagine what a pleasure it is to have you here to supper. I'm bored with cooking just for myself.'

'I was delighted to get out of the house. It's a charming place, but I feel very . . . alone there.'

She was acutely conscious of the pressure of his hand until he released her and went through the archway. Looking at his broad shoulders as he moved away, she yearned to cling to him for a moment, longing for the reassurance of a pair of strong, capable arms around her. Until someone held her close, she would have to live with the grief she had buried so resolutely, grief that could be healed only by human touch. She was still standing in the same place when Michael came out of the kitchen again, and she realized that by some miracle he understood a lot more about her than she ever needed to tell him.

He handed her a glass of *rosé*. 'Let's go and sit outside. How did your husband's visit go?' he asked when they were both seated.

'It was very tense. I stood firm, though, and he agreed to let me have Oliver tomorrow; but I backed down about keeping him overnight, and then I regretted it.'

'What are you going to tell your son when you see him? Have you thought about that?'

'I think I have a plausible excuse worked out about why I'm staying in the village. I can only go by instinct really. I don't want him to have any idea that there is something wrong between me and Alain.'

204

'Children are very perceptive. Don't you think he might sense it?'

'It's a chance I have to take. You see, I still have every hope of saving my marriage. It would simplify things if Oliver never found out what had happened.'

Voicing her conviction to Michael, Rachel realized how desperately unrealistic she must sound. 'Because of Oliver, I have to do everything I can to keep our marriage together. I really have no other choice.'

'That's only natural,' Michael murmured.

Michael had sized Alain up immediately as a proud, unbending type, who was not about to back down on a decision he had made. Without being told, Michael could guess that he was a perfectionist in his work, who demanded the same tireless dedication in others that he gave himself, a man who had often put his wife and son second.

Rachel was saying, 'Of course, time isn't on my side. If he and Isabelle manage to buy the château from Madame Grimal, then it might be too late. Alain would be caught up in events that he couldn't control and he would find it difficult to change tack.'

'You know, Isabelle might get bored with the whole thing and scrap the project,' Michael suggested, trying to sound encouraging.

'He says they're only partners – and friends.' Michael didn't comment, but she saw the doubt on his face.

'Maybe he's telling the truth,' Michael said at last.

'Please don't think I'm asking you to get involved. It's just that I find it such a great relief to talk to you.'

'Look, if the shoe were on the other foot, I'd be confiding in you. You may not realize it, but you seem much calmer than when we first met.'

'Am I really? I guess the worst thing was not knowing the truth. I prefer that to groping in the dark the way I was when I arrived here.'

'I was just thinking that maybe your son will be able to enlighten you about what's really going on between Isabelle and your husband.'

205

She looked confused for a moment. 'Oliver worships his father. I could never do anything to turn him against Alain. Unless he volunteers something, I don't feel I can question him. But even if Alain weren't having an affair with this woman, it amounts to the same thing, doesn't it? He says he wants a divorce and that he's leaving California.'

'You told me you were worried that Alain has your son's passport. Do you think he wants to get custody?'

'I just don't know. But he'd better not try, because I'll never, never consent to that. I'd fight him every step of the way.'

'I wonder if your husband knows what he's up against.'

Rachel's readiness to fight for Oliver bore a powerful resemblance to Margaret Prior's devotion to her son. Michael allowed himself to dream that the seeds of her love for Thomas had lived in the stones of the village, germinating for six hundred years.

Rachel was looking into the distance, where the last colours of the sky were being swept beneath a dark cloud. 'I was thinking I would take Oliver on a picnic tomorrow, but I wonder if it's going to rain.'

'I don't think so. It doesn't have the feel of rain, and the wind is from the east. It doesn't often rain here in the summer, and then usually only at night.'

'Good. I trust you've been here long enough to know all the nuances of the weather.'

'Sometimes I feel as if I've been here for centuries.' He sipped his wine.

There was another silence, then Rachel said, 'I'm such bad company tonight, you ought to order me home.'

Michael smiled, 'What you're implying is that we don't know each other well enough to be silent together.'

He got up, and for a moment she thought she had offended him. She wondered what dark forces ruled the other side of Michael's character. However deep and incomprehensible, she guessed that he was a man who would probably wound himself before he would hurt anyone else. He returned with a candle and set it on the table between them. Watching the flame flicker, she said. 'I feel as if I've really poured out my heart these last few days, like flinging the contents of my handbag on the table. I have no more secrets. And strange to say, in spite of all the turmoil, I'm becoming fond of this village. I ought to hate it, but I don't. Roquelaire gets under your skin.'

Michael's interested expression suggested he was listening politely, while in fact he was coping with a sudden desire to take Rachel to his bed. He imagine that there, through tenderness and loving, they could both forget everything for an hour. Time that he had been squandering with such abandon since his arrival in Roquelaire was precious now he had met Rachel. He was aware that all her energies were focused on the handsome but unscrupulous Frenchman and their son, and that she was blissfully ignorant of what was going on in his mind..

When Rachel asked him to tell her more about himself, Michael talked mechanically about his work, hardly aware of what he was saying.

'What a life you've led,' she remarked.

'It seems to be my fate,' he replied, wondering if it were true.

'Character is destiny, isn't it?' She seemed to have heard his story before, from Alain. Their lives had the same elements of escape, the hallmark of constant searching, but there the similarity ended. Michael was infinitely wiser than Alain.

'Do you ever go back home?' she asked.

'I haven't in years, and now there's no need to. My mother died last year and I have very little in common with my sister, who's married, with three children.'

'Soldiers of fortune don't adapt well to domesticity.'

He smiled. 'That's putting me in a very romantic light. The truth is, I suspect that my wandering days are almost over. I can now sit in a pub and talk about my shrapnel to impressionable youngsters.'

Rachel smiled. Just when she thought he was about to become serious, Michael appeared bent on puncturing her illusions. She could not help thinking again of Alain, whose vanity and pride had filled the room that morning.

When they were having dinner, Rachel brought up the subject of Rosamund, realizing she must be with Julian Paine at that moment.

'I like Rosamund. She seems a lot happier this summer than last,' Michael said.

'Yes, she told me she'd had a breakdown,' said Rachel, realizing that Michael probably knew as much about Rosamund as she did.

'I was only here for a short time last summer, but I met her at Bob and Ted's then. She seemed quite fragile and said she'd just come out of a clinic. I think the course put her back on her feet and helped to restore her confidence.'

'She's seeing Julian Paine, the English property consultant,' said Rachel.

Michael shook his head. 'The last thing she needs, I imagine, is to meet a bastard like him. I can't stand his type.'

'I don't even know the man, but I don't particularly like the look of him either. But I'm probably prejudiced because of what he said about Alain. He seemed arrogant and brash to me.'

'I wonder if Rosamund knows that this morning he was at the café flirting with the baker's daughter.'

Rachel put down her fork. 'Oh no, you're joking!'

'I'm afraid not. Young Pascale has turned into a real beauty. He seemed to be chatting her up.'

'Are you sure?'

'It looked like it. I wonder what he's up to. After all, she is Agnès Grimal's niece and Isabelle must be trying to figure out a way to wrest the château away from Agnès.'

Rachel suddenly recalled the photograph of the beautiful girl she'd seen at Agnès Grimal's cottage. 'Do you mean you think Julian might be trying to influence Madame Grimal through this girl?'

'I wouldn't put it past him. And I suppose his task is a lot more pleasant because she happens to be young and beautiful. If it were Agnès herself, he might have a credibility problem.'

Rachel smiled in spite of herself. 'Can't we do anything?'

'Not a thing, if the look on her face was anything to go by, Pascale was pleased and flattered at the attention. She's engaged to be married, by the way.'

'What a shame. I hope she doesn't mess up her young life with somebody like him. Poor Rosamund, too. I'm not the only one in trouble,' Rachel murmured. 'What's happening in this village, anyway?' The tight little knot of dread inside her returned.

# Chapter 11

Hélène entered the door of the château early on Saturday morning, just as she had done for nearly twenty-two years, until the day Armand Bataille died. Normally she would have headed straight for the pantry off the big, vaulted kitchen to drop her bag and put on her work coat, but this morning she stood in the quiet hallway listening to the echo of the heavy door as she closed it behind her. A shaft of light from the narrow unshuttered window above the door fell on the stone staircase that climbed into the darkness above. She paused for a moment, thinking how uncomfortably dead the château had become in the space of a month. The golden pendulum, whose discreet tick once marked the passage of time, had fallen silent now there was no one to wind it. She ran her hand over the film of dust on a heavily carved medieval coffer, dust that always entered the house when the harvesters cut the wheat and sunflowers in the fields below the château, and that she had always polished off as soon as it had settled. She took a cardboard box from the hall cupboard and then switched on the series of shaded sconces that illuminated the stairs. Armand Bataille's light had dwindled to a mere flicker towards the end, but even then he had seemed to brighten the great house, which was now inert, as if nothing would bring it back to life again. Hélène recalled a remark she had made to someone years ago when she had first begun to work for Armand Bataille, that he was the only man she had ever met who could fill such a vast house alone. By the sheer force of his personality he had rescued, then dominated the historic dwelling, which had been inhabited by nobility and princes of the Church over the centuries.

Hélène laboriously climbed the stairs, disheartened by the long gloomy passage ahead, which seemed to have been closed for years rather than weeks. A musty odour filled her nose when she opened the door of the main reception room, which had seldom been used. She switched on the big brass chandelier and, from habit, plumped up the cushions on a frayed damask sofa before going to the table holding the collection of framed photographs. She began to wrap each one carefully in newspaper and set it in the box she had brought with her. She knew them all by heart: the ivory one etched with flowers containing a photograph of Armand's wife before they were married. There was one of her employer with his wife and son, taken on a yacht in Antibes, with the snowcapped Alpes Maritimes in the background. Madame Bataille wore a brightly patterned bathing suit, espadrilles and a turban; she was tanned and smiling alongside her ten-year-old son, a thin, tall boy with an engaging smile. Armand had been captured in his prime, his powerful arms folded across his broad chest, his dark hair, wet from swimming, combed to one side. There were wedding pictures, baby pictures, pictures of family holidays and special occasions. Hélène had nearly finished packing them when she realized that one picture she had dusted for years, perhaps the most poignant of the entire collection, was missing. In a simple wooden frame was a photograph of Armand Bataille taken on the day, not long before his marriage, when he had been decorated by the local *député* for his heroism in the Resistance. Concerned that it was missing, the housekeeper looked quickly around the room to see if it had been moved, then under the table to see if it had fallen there, but it was not to be found.

Hélène rested on her knees, trying to imagine where the photograph could have gone. Suddenly it occurred to her: Agnès! Agnès had taken it, she thought to herself with a knowing smile. As she stood up, Hélène remembered her last meeting with Agnès, and now she began to think of Pascale, too, with deepening interest. Ever since she had called at Agnès's cottage, a vision of this extraordinary looking girl, so unlike her mother and father, and yet somehow familiar, had been weaving in and out of Hélène's mind. Forgetting the missing photograph of Armand for the moment, Hélène rummaged through the photographs she had just packed until she found the one she was looking for. She sucked in her

211

breath in amazement and stared at the faded sepia photograph, taken nearly a hundred years earlier, of Armand Bataille's Alsatian grandmother, a statuesque blonde beauty with a high-bridged nose and an aloof, challenging expression. Armand's grandmother looked exactly like Pascale Gachpour. The likeness was so remarkable that it was uncanny.

Hélène began to calculate, sensing she was on to something. She remembered that Armand Bataille had spent two nights in seclusion at the château the Christmas after his wife had died. A quick calculation revealed the interesting fact that Pascale had been born nine months later. Looking for a connection, Hélène recalled the surprising coincidence that Agnès had left the village for several months from spring to autumn that same year, ostensibly to visit her sister in Nantes, and long enough, Hélène reckoned, to conceal a pregnancy begun at Christmas and to give birth. The next link fell automatically into place when Hélène remembered Beatrice, Agnès's sister, coming back to Roquelaire to live with her husband and children, including Pascale, whose birth the previous September coincided neatly with Agnès's absence. Hélène smiled triumphantly to herself, realizing that she had stumbled by accident on to a secret she couldn't wait to disclose.

On Saturday morning Rachel got out of bed before seven and watched the sun rise above the rooftops of Roquelaire. She had slept badly, playing out scenes between herself and Alain and Oliver all through the night as the church bell tolled the hours. When she threw back the shutters, swifts were sailing high against the pale pink sky and she was greeted by the crowing of a cock from the depths of the village. She took a deep breath of cool air, fragrant with flowers, old stone and brewing coffee, and gathered her courage to face the day. The thought of seeing Oliver galvanized her into action and filled her with a joy that not even her anxiety for the future could take away.

After a quick breakfast, she dressed in a pair of trousers and a T-shirt and left the house with a basket on her arm. The coolness of the night was beginning to dissipate, replaced by the suggestion of heat descending from a sky now richly blue. The Rue St Jacques

212

was deserted except for a woman sweeping invisible dust into the street from the corridor of a house. As she passed Michael's door, Rachel glanced up at the half-closed shutters, alert for some sign of him. They had parted after midnight, when she had waved a silent goodbye and walked up the street, feeling his eyes follow her until she had opened her own door. Once in bed, she had lain awake for a long time, their conversation running like a smooth thread through all her turmoil.

As Rachel entered the square, she saw that Roquelaire was already bustling with cars, and people were chatting on the street and going in and out of the shops. Some children were playing football in the empty market hall. A tourist bus full of sightseers was pulling up not far from the church, where she met Père Auguste about to enter the main door.

'*Bonjour, madame,*' he said with a smile, raising his hand.

'*Bonjour,*' Rachel responded, pleased he had acknowledged her. He was looking at her in a kindly way and the realization that he knew so much about her and her situation no longer made her feel uncomfortable. As they exchanged polite banalities, Rachel sensed the priest knew a great deal about the realities of the world even though he had lived all his life in Roquelaire. Meeting him again, she was struck by the openness of his expression and the clarity of his eyes.

'Are you still staying in Roquelaire?' he inquired as they stood in the brilliant sunshine.

'I'm staying a little longer than I planned now that Monsieur Lowry has found me a house where I can be a bit more private than I could at Bob Cooper's.' Her French came easily with Père Auguste.

'I hope you're enjoying your stay and that it's not too hot for you.'

'Yes, it's going to be warm today, isn't it?' she said, looking up at the sky. 'Roquelaire is such a pleasant place that I hope to come again some day when I have more time,' she added vaguely.

'Yes, it has an atmosphere that seems to attract a lot of people. It hasn't been this popular for nearly seven hundred years,' he said with a chuckle.

213

Reminded of the Middle Ages, Rachel found it easy to imagine that priest in a monk's rough brown robe, the way he might have dressed centuries ago, instead of his black soutane.

'Thank you again for your help the other evening. I don't know what I would have done if I hadn't met you,' she said.

'I was happy to be of service. We really need more hotels for tourists in the village.'

She wondered if he was thinking how her husband's plans, if they materialized, would change the village irrevocably; almost certainly, as Père Auguste was aware of everything that went on in Roquelaire.

They said goodbye and Rachel walked on to the *charcuterie*, where there was already a queue of people. An appetizing aroma filled the shop, which was festooned with batallions of dry-cured hams, sausages and salamis. Modest looking housewives in espadrilles and flowered summer frocks were ordering giant cuts of pork for roasting, miles of sausages, and slabs of rosy pâté for the ritual Sunday lunch sacred to France. Hearing the woman in front of her recount the details of preparing a roast, Rachel projected herself into a village house where people of all ages gathered around a table as the basket of bread and jug of wine made the rounds. The oldest members of the family would speak in a broad Gascon accent, and the youngest would refuse nothing heaped on his plate. During the unhurried afternoon they would never run out of conversation, but exchange the endless trivia that was the cement of family life. Just thinking of it made her yearn for the kind of communal existence that bound the generations together. Loneliness crept over her as she waited in the queue of smiling people who had never know what it was to feel alien and strange in a faraway country.

When her turn came, Rachel looked over the white mounds of goose fat that smothered the *confit* of goose, the glossy yellow mayonnaise, pigs' trotters dusted with crumbs and the bewildering variety of pâtés. She ordered a few slices of ham, some salami and a salad that she thought Oliver would like. She was waiting for her order when she caught snatches of quiet conversation between a man and a woman behind her.

214

'But what is she going to do? She has to sell it. Imagine what it would cost to keep,' said the woman.

'Possibly, but she's right to take her time. Everybody is advising her. I was saying to my wife only yesterday that maybe it's for the best. We don't need a big hotel in the village. The disadvantages outweigh the benefits, if you ask me.'

'I'm resigned to it. Anyway, my son might move back here if he could get a job. Oh, she'll sell it, you'll see. But I hope she doesn't wait too long. She might regret it . . .'

'*Voilà, madame,*' the butcher said to Rachel, handing her her change. She took the money distractedly and put it in her purse, murmuring, '*Au revoir, messieurs, 'dames.*' Nobody stared at her, but she felt self-conscious as she left the shop, her pulse quickening at the mention of the hotel. The people of Roquelaire were as anxious as she was to know whether Agnès would sell, but their very lives didn't depend on it.

Rachel bought some peaches in the *épicerie*, then went to the bakery. She recognized Agnès Grimal's sister behind the counter, but seeing the brisk movements of the plump, smiling woman with faded, permed hair Rachel again found it hard to imagine that she was the mother of the beautiful girl whose photograph she had admired and whom Michael had noticed with Julian Paine. Madame Gachpour presided over shelves of breads in all shapes and sizes, freshly baked in a wood-fired oven. Rachel waited as the woman in front of her was served. There was no hurry as they chatted.

'Yes, she came home yesterday, and Étienne is coming back late tonight. He's coming for lunch tomorrow. He has leave just for a few days.'

'He's stationed in Berlin, isn't he? A long way to come for so short a time.'

'Yes, but he and Pascale haven't seen each other since early summer and they have to start making serious plans for the wedding if they want to get married in December.'

'It's going to be as soon as that?'

'Yes, not long after he comes out of the army. They don't want to wait. Étienne has an offer of a job in Bordeaux, starting as a trainee with the Crédit Agricole.'

215

'*C'est très bien,*' said the customer. 'He has done well.'

When her turn came, Rachel bought a baguette and leaving the shop she saw by the church clock that it still wasn't even nine o'clock and she had an hour to kill before Alain came with Oliver. On impulse, she crossed the square and walked towards Bob Cooper's house, curious about Rosamund.

Arriving at the house, she found the door ajar and heard Ted's voice in the sitting-room. Setting down her basket in the hall, Rachel saw him coming through the room with a tray of coffee cups.

'Rachel, hi! What a pleasant surprise. I'll be right out,' he said, disappearing into the kitchen with the tray.

She crossed the comfortable, sun-filled room smelling of polish and flowers. In broad daylight it exuded an inviting familiarity and she realized how lucky she had been to stumble upon this refuge when she did.

Emerging from the kitchen, Ted saw her looking at the coffee-table, where a jug of roses had been arranged on a blue chequered cloth. 'That's this afternoon's still life. I thought I'd add a hunk of bread and a peach or two. I'm the unofficial props man.'

'I've never taken up a brush in my life, but just looking at your arrangement gives me the urge,' she said wistfully.

'How are you?' he asked, giving her a searching look.

'I'm fine, thank you. I've settled into the house, though I don't intend to be here very long.'

'Getting things worked out?' His eyes were concerned and deeply curious.

'In a way, yes. Alain and I are probably separating, and this morning I'm seeing my son for the first time. The last few days have been pretty rough, but not as rough as they might have been.'

'We thought you'd be taking your son and going back home. That's what I said to Bob. "I'll bet she'll take him straight back home where he belongs."' Ted reached for a dirty ashtray and gave it a wipe.

'Alain and I have a lot to discuss first.'

'Well, I hope you take him to the cleaners. He deserves it. It's that awful Isabelle de Montjoi. She must be fifty if she's a day.'

216

It amused Rachel the way Ted was getting worked up. 'I can hardly remember what she looks like, to tell you the truth. Maybe I ought to see her again.'

'Now there's an idea. Have a showdown.'

Seeing he wasn't joking, she couldn't help being amused at the thought.

At the sound of footsteps, Rachel turned to see Rosamund at the terrace doors, brush in hand. A big straw hat shaded her face. 'Hello there, Rachel. I though I heard your voice.'

'I've got to get the *morue* out of water, for lunch, so I'll leave you two. If you want coffee, there's some in the thermos in the kitchen.'

'Do you have a minute to talk?' Rachel asked Rosamund.

'Haven't I just. I'm very slow this morning. I just ruined three sheets of my best paper. Why don't you go out in the sun, and I'll bring us a cup of coffee.'

Rachel did as she suggested, gauging Rosamund's mood wasn't as euphoric as when she had last seen her. Rachel sat at the table outdoors and saw that the group had set up their easels in the usual spot, with Bob making the rounds.

Rosamund came on to the terrace carrying two cups of coffee. 'Any excuse to get away from still life. If I botch one more fruit bowl, I think I'm throwing in the towel – and the brush,' she said with a laugh.

'I'm sure whatever you're doing, it's great.'

She sighed. 'Not really. Not today, at any rate.'

Rachel saw her blue eyes were clouded with unhappiness.

Rosamund said quietly, 'Julian hasn't called me since I saw you. I'm feeling very depressed about it. I can't seem to get my mind off him.'

Rachel felt hollow for a moment, as if it had happened to her. She said sympathetically, 'Try not to jump to conclusions. He may be tied up with business or something.'

Rosamund shook her head. 'There's no excuse, really. He must have regretted what happened. That's all I can think of. But at the time he gave absolutely no sign of any problem. I don't understand it.'

Rachel was not truly surprised by Julian Paine's callous behaviour.

'I'm not going to leave it at that. I've got to see him again. If he thinks he can treat me like that and . . .' she broke off. 'There's no point in delivering ultimatums. The truth is, I'm shattered. It's the first time in years that I've felt anything when a man made love to me. If there's a genuine reason why he hasn't called I want to know it. I'm not ready to break it off just like that.'

'Think carefully before you try to see him. You might regret it.' Rachel thought of Julian sitting at the table with the baker's daughter, but decided it would be cruel to disillusion Rosamund by telling her.

'I was thinking. You have a car. This is an imposition, I know, but do you think I might borrow it for a little while later this afternoon, if you don't need it.'

'Of course you may. I don't use it much. It's a ridiculous expense, really, but I need to keep it on.'

'I thought I'd drive out to where Julian is staying and see if he's there. Maybe if I see him, then I can get back to work. I've been so looking forward to coming here and getting away from it all, and now I'm embroiled in this.'

'Don't be too downhearted,' Rachel said. They arranged that Rosamund should borrow the car that afternoon.

'I ought to get back now,' said Rachel, looking at her watch. 'Alain's bringing Oliver over soon. I saw him after you left.' She rose to go.

'Are you nervous?'

'Yes, a bit,' she admitted. 'I've decided to try to keep the divorce from Oliver for the time being. There'll be time enough for the truth.'

'A wise decision. After all, you don't even know which way the axe is going to fall yet. If the hotel falls through, your husband might think again. When you saw him yesterday, did you still feel you wanted him back?'

Rachel hesitated. 'Not in the same way, but of course I do,' she said with more conviction than she felt, resisting the uncertainty that had begun to creep over her.

218

Rosamund bit her lip and looked thoughtful. 'I find the thought of going back to Charles after this holiday devastating. In fact, I'm not sure if I can go back home after what's happened.'

Rachel looked surprised. 'But your husband doesn't need to know what's happened if you don't tell him. Surely that would be for the best.'

'It's not that. It's that I don't know if I could, now, knowing what I've missed all these years.' Tears came into her eyes. 'The truth is, I had my breakdown when I found out about Charles's last affair. I should have been able to handle it – after all it wasn't the first. But then I finally cracked and had to go into a clinic. What's happening now has dredged up all those terrible old emotions . . .'

Rachel found herself comforting Rosamund rather than the other way round, but soon she rose to go. 'I'm sorry, but I have to leave. I wish there was something I could do for you. Come over any time, please, if you need someone to talk to.'

'Thanks,' Rosamund said with a smile. 'It's been such a help to have you to confide in. As if you don't have enough problems of your own.'

'If for any reason I'm not around later on, I'll leave the key to the car in the mailbox outside the door.'

In the Rue St Jacques the sun had moved to Michael's side of the street. Walking by, Rachel noticed the shutters were still half-closed. She imagined him sitting on the back terrace drinking a cup of coffee as he read a newspaper. Or perhaps, she thought, he was sitting unshaven, in his dressing gown, a cigarette in his mouth, as he worked at his typewriter. Musing about Michael Lowry and his chronicle had become a diversion from her own problems.

Half an hour later Rachel was waiting nervously in the little sitting-room with the window open, pretending to read the French newspaper she had bought, but listening for the sound of footsteps coming up the cobbled street. Hearing them approach, she felt a suffocating combination of joy and fear. She put down the paper and stood tensely in front of the window; then, not wanting to appear anxious, disappeared into the kitchen to await the knock at

219

the door. She composed herself and vowed not to let nervousness betray her state of mind to Oliver. Walking to the door when she heard the knock, she felt her knees go weak when she heard Oliver's voice.

'Mom! It's us, are you there?'

She flung the door open with a smile on her face.

'How are you, sweetheart?' she cried, throwing her arms around him. The profound relief she felt at holding him in her arms at last made Rachel tremble. She drank in the sight of him, reassuring herself that nothing about him had changed: his bright blue eyes, his shiny dark hair and smooth brown cheeks. Oliver clung to her, and the bubbling laugh that escaped from his throat told her all she wanted to know: that he had missed her as much as she had missed him.

She stepped back and faced Alain, who was making no attempt to pretend. He looked at her with a blank expression. 'Come in, won't you? Would you like some coffee?' she suggested, hoping her manner made it seem that their arrival at the little house in Roquelaire was nothing out of the ordinary.

'No thanks. I've got things to do. I should get back.' His voice gave away nothing.

'I heard you had a riding lesson this morning,' she said to Oliver, ushering him into the sitting-room.

'I've had lots of lessons, haven't I, Dad? Well, maybe two, anyway.'

'Yes, and you're improving every time.'

'Can I keep doing it when we get home?' he looked from one of them to the other.

Rachel looked at Alain. 'We'll have to see about that. Don't forget, you're just on holiday here. That means you have time to do things you don't do at home.'

'I'd better get going,' said Alain. 'I'll pick you up about five, Oliver. Don't forget that Lucien is coming over to go swimming.'

'Tell me about Lucien,' Rachel said to Oliver, ignoring Alain's obvious impatience to leave. She wasn't willing to let him go until she had gauged the mood between father and son. 'Who is he?'

'He's Fernande's – the housekeeper's – grandson. He's a year older than me, really, but he's kind of a baby in some ways. He doesn't know about video games or movies, things like that. I'm teaching him English and he's teaching me French.'

'You wouldn't believe how much French he's picked up in a week,' said Alain, smiling for the first time.

The remark seemed like a private boast. 'That's wonderful,' Rachel exclaimed. 'Are you sure you don't have time for a cup of coffee, Alain?'

He glanced at his watch. 'No, thanks. I really have to go now. I'll be back at five. See you later, Oliver,' he said, patting him on the head.

When he had gone, Rachel glanced at Oliver, who was slouched in a chair, looking at her thoughtfully. It seemed impossible that he hadn't noticed the strained atmosphere between his parents, but she didn't want to confront it right away. Her only thought was to escape the little house with him so she wouldn't have to answer the questions in his eyes. For the first time she could remember she felt obliged to distract him so that he wouldn't be bored. The riding lessons, the swimming pool, the companions, the bicycle all seemed to overshadow what she could offer, and she wondered if it would be like that from now on.

'I thought we'd go on a picnic,' she said, going into the kitchen with Oliver behind her. 'Did you eat a big breakfast?'

'We just have toast with funny things on it, like chocolate paste and honey. I get hot chocolate or just milk.'

'No cereal?'

'Isabelle keeps saying she'll buy some, but I think she forgot.'

'Come on,' said Rachel, taking her bag with one hand and scooping up his hand with the other. The mention of Isabelle's name had galvanized her. 'Let's take a walk around Roquelaire, then we'll come back and organize our picnic and take a walk outside of town.'

They strolled down the street hand in hand. 'Tell me what you've been doing. It sounds like you've been having a wonderful time.'

'It's been fun – just about the most fun I've ever had, I think,' he said, enthusiastically describing the trip to France.

221

'What happened when you got to Paris?' she asked cautiously.

'Isabelle was there to meet us, but Dad didn't know she was coming and he was surprised. We were supposed to come to Bordeaux, but she had Dad change the tickets and we stayed in her apartment in Paris. The only part I didn't like was when I had to stay with the maid. She was nice and took me to the Luxembourg Gardens, but we couldn't talk very much. Mom, do you know Isabelle?' he asked as they entered the market square.

'I met her once in California last year, so I don't exactly know her. What's she like?'

'She's OK I guess. She's given me lots of presents and does lots of nice things for me. I don't know ...' He stopped in mid-sentence, which was what he did when he wasn't sure of his feelings. 'Does Dad like her a lot or something?'

Rachel paused, trying to interpret what was going on in his mind. 'Well, I don't know. He hasn't told me. What makes you say that?' She waited to hear him confess he had seen or heard something that told him his parents were drifting apart, that Isabelle was taking her place in Alain's life.

'He talks to her in a – I don't know – in a different sort of voice. They seem to spend a lot of time talking, sitting next to each other, and she's always looking at him. Mom, what's going to happen? Are we going to move here so Dad can work here?'

'I don't know yet. What did your father say?'

'But why don't you know, Mom? Didn't he tell you anything?'

The directness of his questions took her by surprise. 'I should know, but I'm afraid I don't. You see, we haven't had much time to talk, and his plans aren't settled yet. His new plans have come up very suddenly. But you mustn't worry about it.'

'I don't think I want to live in France.'

'What makes you say you don't want to live here? Has someone put the idea into your head that you're going to?' She couldn't keep the alarm from her voice. She stopped in front of the church and looked down at him.

'No, nobody said anything, but if Dad is spending a lot of time here, I guess we'll come and visit him sometimes, won't we, or even live here?'

222

'Oliver, I just don't know,' she replied as she struggled to remain calm.

His brow puckered under a fringe of short dark hair. 'I don't understand why you can't stay at Isabelle's with me and Dad. She's got plenty of room. And I don't understand why you didn't just come with us when we left, instead of later. Dad said you'd gone to Tahoe and that's why we couldn't call you.'

Rachel frowned at this lie. Anticipating his confusion at finding her suddenly in the village, she replied, 'I didn't go to Tahoe after all. I changed my mind and came here instead. But I had to go to the wedding first, remember.'

'That's right. I forgot.'

'So, when it was over and I started missing you, I thought it would be a nice surprise if I came over too. The thing is, you were in Paris instead of here, and so I had to find a place to stay. I paid money in advance, and so I may as well stay here. Anyway, it's nice because you and I can do things together when your Dad is busy.' He nodded and looked somewhat satisfied with her explanation. 'Let's go to the bakery, shall we? I bought some bread, but we could buy some tarts for later, if they have some left.'

'Neat,' he said enthusiastically. 'I like the yellow ones with *citron* written in chocolate on top.'

'I can see you're a regular customer of French patisserie,' she said with a laugh, slipping an arm around his shoulder. As they walked across the square it seemed as if they were mother and son on holiday, like any other tourists.

By the time they had returned home to collect the picnic, Rachel had heard all about life at Terre Blanche, including the fact that Isabelle and Alain slept in separate bedrooms. She was unable to decide whether Alain was being considerate for Oliver's sake or merely careful. Then she began to wonder if Alain had been telling the truth after all, knowing it would make a difference, a great difference if he and Isabelle weren't lovers. Perhaps their marriage stood a chance.

When Rachel and Oliver passed Michael's house, they didn't see him standing near the window. He watched them disappear down the street carrying a basket with a baguette sticking out, and he supposed they were going on a picnic. He wondered if they might be heading for somewhere near the Château Brissac.

It was nearly twelve o'clock and he had just come in from buying the morning paper. Instead of drinking his usual beer at the café, he had come back with a baguette and some ham, intending to eat a sandwich at his desk. He had risen at daybreak to take advantage of the quiet, cool hours of early morning to work on the chronicle. But so far he had produced only stilted prose that seemed a far cry from what he intended.

Now he sat down and rearranged his papers, and took out the chronicle yet again. The tiny print blurred before his eyes and he sighed. Sitting back, he began to reconstruct Roquelaire into a town of only a century or two in age, and imagined its church, its houses, its ramparts and stone archway, and its markets. A wealth of detail, collected in his subconscious from all the thinking and reading he had done, began to flow through his head, slowly turning back the clock nearly seven hundred years. He could almost hear the footsteps of the people, sensing their comings and goings in the narrow street outside the windows where babies cried, the sick moaned and pilgrims prayed. Raising his mind's eye above the red tiled rooftops, he could picture smoke rising from the chimneys, hear the distant rumbling of cart wheels across the cobbles, smell the rank odours common to the age. The faces of the people were ruddy and smiling, though everyone looked older than their years because of hardship and disease.

This picture died away and Michael came back to the present, feeling enthused by the burgeoning powers of his own imagination. Ripping a half-finished sheet of paper from the typewriter, he tore it up and put in a fresh one. He began again and as his fingers hit the keys his ideas began to flow.

Pascale walked self-consciously through an arch in the ramparts just after midday, smartly dressed in a white linen suit. Seeing there was no red Porsche parked by the *lavoir*, she felt a crushing sense of disappointment. She halted for a moment, debated whether Julian was merely late or had stood her up, then walked to the *lavoir*, determined to wait. There were no sheltering trees where she could hide and she had to stand in full view of passing cars. She was afraid someone might recognize her shock of blonde hair, unique in the village. She took her sunglasses from the smart new tan bag, which, like her suit, had been bought with the money Agnès had given her.

The minutes ticked by with agonizing slowness. Pascale was about to give up and go home when she saw a red car come roaring towards her. She had only been waiting just over five minutes, but it had seemed an eternity.

'Hi! Been waiting long?' Julian was looking over the top of his sunglasses as he reached over to open the door.

'I just arrived,' she said coolly.

When she was in the car, he smiled and pushed down hard on the accelerator, giving her a taste of its powerful engine. She was alarmed when he took the road that passed Agnès's cottage, but they drove by at such speed she realized Agnès would have no chance of recognizing her, even if she happened to be looking.

'This is the wrong way to Labardens,' she said.

'I know. It's a bit of a roundabout route. Do you mind?'

'No, I don't mind.' Pascale sank back in the luxurious car, content to enjoy the sensation of speed.

'I hope you don't mind driving fast.'

'I love it.'

He gave her an appreciative glance. 'You look absolutely sensational today, gorgeous.'

Her cheeks burned as she looked straight ahead. His compliment, spoken in a deep, sensuous voice, sent disturbing ripples up her spine. As Julian shifted the gears she was acutely conscious of his muscular forearm flecked with golden hair so close to her leg. His ponytail, which would have looked peculiar on any other man, made him seem virile and exotic, as did his khaki trousers and yellow polo shirt. The only jewellery he wore, apart from his watch, was a gold and cornelian signet ring engraved with his family crest – the ultimate cachet in Pascale's eyes, although she hadn't noticed it when they met.

Fifteen minutes later, they drove through the impressive stone gateposts of the château hotel and up a drive lined with cedar and magnolia trees. Pascale's heart leapt at the prospect of the afternoon. This was the sort of life she wanted.

'I've never been here, so I don't know how good it is,' said Julian.

'It's very good,' she replied, not bothering to add that she hadn't been there either.

He parked the car at the end of a line of Mercedes and BMWs in front of the rambling pink-brick château set against a wall of towering trees. They walked up the staircase that rose to the entrance flanked by bay trees in white tubs. Julian guided her forward by the elbow. 'I booked a table on the terrace. Should we go directly there rather than have a drink in the bar first?'

'Yes, why not?' she replied, using one of her favourite English phrases. It already seemed to her that she was often invited to lunch at château hotels by Englishmen in sports cars.

The *patronne* led them through the panelled hall to a wide terrace shaded by massive oak trees and set with tables covered in pink cloths and glittering with crystal and silver.

'We'd like the table near the fountain,' Julian said.

Pascale noticed the *patronne* hesitate, as if it were reserved for someone else. Glancing at Julian, she seemed to decide that he passed muster and could have the table anyway.

Julian flashed Pascale a triumphant smile, which she returned. She knew a single glance at him was enough to make up the *patronne*'s mind, and this filled her with a luxurious sense of superiority.

When they were seated at a table adorned with a bouquet of pink roses, Pascale looked over the huge menu the waiter had brought, not really taking it in as she discreetly glimpsed the chic, sophisticated people lunching at the tables around them. She heard a number of languages being spoken by well-dressed sun-tanned couples. Most of the other diners were Belgian, French and English couples of retirement age, who, she imagined, were staying at the château.

'Does lobster salad with truffles appeal to you?' asked Julian. His smile brought her forcefully back to his presence.

'I don't know. I've never tried it,' she said.

'Well then, it's about time you did.'

He ordered the salad for both of them, with *foie gras* to start. 'We'll have two glasses of champagne right away – no, how about a kir royale? And send the *sommelier*, would you?' he said to the waiter.

Julian leaned forward, locking Pascale's eyes. She hadn't noticed before what an unusual colour his eyes were: golden at the rims and pale green in the middle. He had an impish smile, as if he had some outrageous remark on the tip of his tongue, and his receding hairline ennobled his strong, bronzed face. She liked the laugh lines etched around his mouth, which was generous and cleanly cut. His nose was prominent and distinctly English, and though he wasn't what she considered handsome, he radiated a fierce magnetism that Pascale found irresistable. She decided he was the most attractive man she had ever met.

When the *sommelier* came, Julian took the wine list and said, 'Do you speak English?' The man in the burgundy jacket with a silver *tastevin* around his neck nodded. 'Good. Now, what about a white Burgundy? A Puligny-Montrachet, perhaps?' The critical disdain on the waiter's face evaporated when he realized that Julian knew something about wine. When he had gone, Julian smiled, and leaned toward Pascale again.

'I've been as impatient as hell all morning. I haven't thought of anything else since I met you.' When she gave him a sceptical smile, he added. 'You don't believe me, do you? I suppose you have dozens of boyfriends who all tell you how beautiful you are.'

'Oh no, it's not true.' She was determined not to appear gauche. Something, she was not sure what, seemed to be at stake, as if he were judging her, testing her confidence. He treated her with intense but somewhat detached curiosity, which disturbed and excited her at the same time. When the waiter brought the kirs, Julian clicked his glass to hers and she took a sip, forming a question in her mind.

'You didn't talk about why you came to Roquelaire. Are you on holiday?'

'No, I'm not on holiday, even though I'm not working all the

227

time. I'm in property development. Our group invests in luxury hotels and apartments all over Europe.'

'But what are you doing *here*?'

'Just that. Developing a hotel project with Isabelle de Montjoi and her partner, a chap by the name of Ribard.'

'But . . .' as she spoke it dawned on her. 'You're a friend of Isabelle de Montjoi? So . . .' A warning light went on in her head.

'That's right. I represent the other backers.' He had to explain what a backer was.

'I understand,' she said.

'Anyway, I'm very glad I came down here, because I wouldn't have met you otherwise.'

Pascale hardly heard the compliment. She sipped her kir, the same pale pink as the tablecloth. Her clear blue eyes were troubled. 'So, I think I understand. This hotel, is it the Château Brissac?'

'None other.' He was watching her every movement, gauging how to play the moment. 'Is something wrong? Maybe you're one of the people who are against the idea.'

'I'm not sure,' she said cautiously. The champagne was taking effect and she felt bolder. 'It depends on what happens. My aunt owns the château, you know.' She couldn't keep a note of pride out of her voice. It amazed her even as she said it. She had had little time as yet to get used to the idea.

'Your aunt? Do you mean to say she's the old woman who's inherited the château? What a coincidence.' The look of amazement that crossed his face gave no hint that he had discovered exactly who Pascale was from Bob and Ted moments after she had left the café, and that he regarded their meeting as a miraculous piece of good fortune.

'Yes, so you can see I was surprised by what you said. She owns the château, so . . .' She shrugged and smiled.

'Yes, I've been told there are some problems. I'm just the consultant. I don't know what Isabelle de Montjoi and her partner are planning. I knew there was some hitch over acquiring the property, which she expected would be hers, but I assume they're sorting it out.' He searched for simple words, wondering if Pascale was understanding everything he said. 'You know, I've never been in

228

the château, though I feel as if I have. I've seen a mountain of photographs, studied the architect's drawings, but it's odd that I've never actually been inside.'

She looked thoughtful. 'I've never been there either. I was studying in Bordeaux until last week and I haven't had time to see it since my aunt became the owner.'

'Your whole family must have been bowled over.'

'Yes, it was a big surprise.'

For the moment, he refrained from delving further. 'Perhaps we could go there together. This afternoon, after lunch?'

'I'm not sure . . .'

'It would be absolutely great if you could let me have a private view. After all the time I've spent on this project I would love to see the château just to satisfy my own curiosity. I may never have the chance again if your aunt doesn't sell it.'

Pascale pretended to think this over, though she already knew what she would do. 'I guess it would be all right. Do you mean that Madame de Montjoi and her partner really want to buy the château?' Pascale registered the interesting news she would have to tell the family when she returned home.

'I suppose she does, but it would depend on the price your aunt is asking. I believe Isabelle has begun looking at other places on the market. There are several choices at the moment, and I suspect she might be going off the idea of buying Brissac because it needs so much work done anyway.'

'But if Madame de Montjoi has done so much planning already, why would she look for another property? That doesn't make sense.'

Julian leaned back and laughed, and a slow appreciative smile grew on his face. 'You're very sharp, aren't you? And you're nobody's fool.' When she looked puzzled, he said. 'Never mind the meaning. It's a very attractive quality in a woman as young and beautiful as you are.'

She looked flustered. 'You shouldn't tell me I'm beautiful.'

'Well, I *am* telling you: Pascale, you're very beautiful.'

The waiter swept up to their table bearing two enormous plates, which he placed before them with a flourish. Pascale looked down at the thick slice of pale pink *pâté de foie gras* resting on the gold-rimmed plate, but her mind was elsewhere.

'So, it's true that Madame de Montjoi wants to buy it?' She reopened the conversation.

'Of course she would – at the right price. It has a unique historical significance. Think what it would mean to the village if it were a hotel. But to get back to the main point, people here don't seem to understand the enormous cost of converting property. They see a ruin sold for next to nothing, then, as if by magic, it's resold at ten times the price. They don't realize what it costs to achieve the transformation. You see, it has to be profitable for anyone to want it in the first place. Do you get my point?'

'Yes, of course I understand. I studied accountancy.'

'So you did. Well, if the project went through, I have no doubt that there would be a job for you in the hotel. They'll be hiring local people and you would be perfect. You've got all the credentials.'

As she considered it, the idea took hold. Pascale couldn't deny to herself that working in the glamorous atmosphere of a château hotel like the one where they were lunching was preferable by far to toiling in an office.

'That sounds interesting to me,' she admitted.

'You'd have a golden opportunity right on your doorstep.'

Pascale toyed with her food: she didn't seem to have much appetite. 'We'll go to the château after lunch if you like. I can get the keys from the caretaker.'

'That would be wonderful. It would be the perfect end to the day. Pascale, will you have lunch or dinner with me tomorrow? If you don't say yes, I'll fade away from grief,' he said, taking a forkful of pâté.

She laughed a light, sparkling laugh, then her face became serious. 'No, no, I can't. I'm busy tomorrow. It's Sunday.'

'Of course. I suppose you'll be having lunch with your family. That's what the French all do on Sundays, isn't it? They have these huge family gatherings that go on for hours. What about afterwards? If you could escape, we could go for a drive, have a drink somewhere.'

230

She cast her eyes down. At the thought of Sunday her whole perspective changed. 'There's something I didn't tell you when we met. I wanted to say no when you asked me to lunch – I mean I ought to have . . .'

' "I should have said", that's what you mean.'

'Yes,' she nodded, 'I should have said no. I didn't tell you, but I'm engaged to be married. My fiancé is coming home tomorrow.'

He stared at her as if crestfallen, although he had in fact noticed her engagement ring when they first met and had had the details from Bob.

'So that's why I shouldn't have come today.' All the guilt Pascale had kept at bay now drowned her euphoric mood. She sensed sadly that this was the most exciting moment in her life, lunching with a fascinating man in a glamorous restaurant, enjoying what was perhaps the most carefree afternoon she would ever have.

'So, you're engaged to be married.' Julian looked confused for a moment. 'Just my luck,' he said with a shake of his head. 'But that doesn't mean we can't be friends, does it? Why can't we see each other while I'm here? There's nothing wrong in it, is there? All right, I admit I find you very attractive, but if you're engaged, then that's that. I won't deny that I'm sorry. But I'd still like to see you, enjoy your company. We could be careful that no one saw us together if you like.'

Pascale bit her lip. 'No, it wouldn't be right. I can't see you . . .'

'How long is your fiancé staying in Roquelaire?'

'For a few days. Until Thursday, I think. He's in the army in Germany and he is on leave for a few days.'

'But I won't be here more than ten days.'

Pascale didn't say anything, but the anguished look on her face told him he had won. 'Listen, let's make a vow, a promise, not to talk about this today. Today may be the only day you and I have together in our entire lives. Let's look at it as a gift that we don't have to share with anybody except each other.' He spoke slowly, choosing his words carefully so she would understand, touching his fingertips to hers for emphasis.

'A gift,' she said softly, watching as the waiter filled her glass with wine.

231

*

A stream of water flowed from the pump into the stone basin in the kitchen, rinsing it clean as Agnès worked the handle. When it had drained away, she dusted the crumbs that clung stubbornly in the grooves of the table and then returned her soup bowl and plate, the thick-rimmed glass, the napkin in a ring and the tin cutlery to the carved *armoire* that covered one wall of the kitchen. She had lunched on soup, a piece of cold rabbit, goat's cheese and a salad made from herbs and greens she had picked from the garden that morning, accompanied by half a baguette and red wine from the vineyard nearby that her father had once owned.

Agnès untied her apron while she studied Pascale's photograph on the mantelpiece. Throughout the day Pascale had never been far from her mind, and worry had crept in where before there had been nothing but happiness at the prospect of her daughter's return. Since the hour when she first looked into her daughter's eyes soon after her birth, Agnès had always known when she was anxious or when she was lying. Thinking of her visit on the previous day, Agnès could not imagine what truth was so terrible that Pascale couldn't reveal it.

Agnès hung up her apron and for the first time in years hesitated about what to do next. It was her habit to sit on the porch and doze over a newspaper for a few minutes after lunch, and when it was too hot even to doze, to shell dried beans or perhaps do some mending. She picked up a tablecloth she was making for Pascale's trousseau. Taking it to the porch beneath the vine, she worked on it for a while, crocheting a cream lace edge on the pure white fabric. As her calloused fingers moved methodically, she was lulled by the droning of bees in the garden. Her thoughts were mostly of Pascale, but her mind flitted to the château, specifically to the great hall, and the table crowded with photographs. By now Hélène would have packed them all away.

After a while she put down her crochet hook, deciding it was no use. A restlessness had seized hold of her and she returned the cloth to its basket, then went back into the house to fetch her hat.

232

When she came out, she was also carrying a basket containing a torch and a long metal rod. A last-minute thought prompted her to go to the garden shed and get a sturdy pair of secateurs. Then she set out on the road to the château.

Agnès arrived at Brissac out of breath, with perspiration running down her face. Standing before the eastern approach, she was reminded how easily in her youth she had bicycled up the hill and down again to Roquelaire. She stood in the shade of an oak tree, one of the few that had survived the harsh winter winds on top of the hill, and looked down the eastern slope. The solid rock retaining wall that shored up the foundations of the château was overgrown with brambles and nettles. Agnès knew that when Armand bought the château he had cleared away some of the undergrowth, but she wondered how close he had ventured to the entrance of the tunnel that held Paul Ribard's body. In her heart she didn't believe that Armand would have wanted to return to the spot where they had buried the man he had killed.

It was nearly two o'clock and the sun beat down. A hot little wind churned up the white dust on the chalk road, telling Agnès the heat was building up to a storm. She was tired and no longer had the energy to perform the errand that had brought her there. But, thinking it might rain, she went down the eastern slope, though not before she had looked carefully in every direction to see that she hadn't been observed. Reassured that she was alone, Agnès went to explore the tightly woven bank of bushes beneath the château, where she felt sure the entrance to the tunnel could still be found.

# Chapter 12

Michael pushed his chair back from his desk and took a long, hard look at the last sentence he had just typed and amended. Then he removed the sheet of paper from the typewriter and added it to the pile, enjoying that rare sense of accomplishment that came when he had written something as near perfect as he was able to make it. Switching off the lamp, he got up and stretched, resisting the temptation to reread what he had done. He knew from experience that a freshly written piece of work was like a cake emerging from a hot oven and needed time to cool before he could be certain it was as good as he thought it was.

He stood for a moment, stroking his chin absently, not quite knowing what to do with himself as a thousand details of the plague year sifted through his mind like the aftermath of a blizzard. The drab tranquillity of the sitting-room, shrouded by the half-closed shutters, seemed worlds away from the savage splendour of Roquelaire in 1348. Feeling drained but exhilarated, he decided he needed a break, and went out to fetch his seldom-used bicycle. Moments later he was speeding into the countryside, revived by the sensation of hot sun baking the listlessness from his bones.

The long road that led to Brissac was deserted. As he started the climb, Michael saw the landscape through John Stratton's eyes as it had been long before vast fields of corn and sunflowers had replaced the forests, a world that still belonged to nature and not to man. Beneath the black asphalt, shimmering in the heat, he supposed lay the ancient stone track worn smooth by the passage of pilgrims, merchants and nobles on horseback. As if summoned by his imagination, a band of children with sun-tanned faces appeared on the road in the company of a priest. They carried sticks with scallop shells dangling on the end, and he realized they were retracing the pilgrim's route. The spirit of St James still lived.

Rachel was exactly where he had hoped she would be, in the shade of a huge spreading oak within sight of Brissac. His intuition had told him that she might choose to bring Oliver here for a picnic.

'Who's that man coming up the road, Mom?' asked Oliver when he saw Michael approaching them.

'That's Michael Lowry. He's an Englishman who lives across the street from where I'm staying.' She smiled and brushed her hair from her face in an unconscious gesture as she waved to him.

She and Oliver had passed the afternoon on a blanket she had spread on the bleached grass. He was brimming with things to tell her, and she had listened for clues about what was really happening at Terre Blanche. From Oliver's innocent observations, there could be little doubt about Alain's true relationship with Isabelle de Montjoi. By now Rachel was beginning to feel the strain of hiding her hurt and pretending to Oliver that everything was normal. The sight of Michael's bronzed, smiling face and his strong shoulders as he pushed his bike up the hill towards them, suddenly reassured Rachel that she had made a friend who would be there to see her through the crisis.

'What a nice surprise,' said Rachel as Michael laid down his bike.

'I saw you from the road as I was passing and thought I'd come to say hello.'

'Michael, this is Oliver.'

Oliver stood and offered his hand.

'Hello, Oliver. I'm very glad to meet you.'

Rachel watched her son look up curiously at Michael in the way he always did with strangers, as if he were weighing him up. His instinct for detecting phoniness or insincerity had often surprised her, and she was pleased when she sensed that he accepted Michael without hesitation.

'If you're hungry there's plenty of food,' Rachel offered. 'Salami, ham, some salad. I can't seem to break the habit of going overboard in a French *charcuterie* whenever I walk through the doors.'

'You brought enough for an army, didn't you, Mom? But we ate all the lemon tarts already,' he announced to Michael.

'Now that's what I call rotten luck, because I happen to be particularly fond of lemon tarts,' Michael replied. Sitting down beside Rachel on the blanket, he added, 'Thanks for the offer, but I had a quick sandwich at home. I've been working most of the day and decided I ought to get some air.'

'I thought I heard your typewriter as I passed. How is it going?'

He gave her a disarming smile. 'Do you know something, I think I can say that I'm finally getting somewhere.'

'Michael's a writer, Oliver,' she said.

'What do you write?'

'Well, normally I'm a journalist. I write for newspapers. But at the moment I'm writing a book based on things that happened in this part of the world hundreds of years ago.'

'How many hundreds?' asked Oliver.

'Over six hundred and fifty, to be almost exact.' Michael launched into a description of what life was like in the Middle Ages for Oliver's benefit, and Oliver was clearly fascinated. 'Ever heard of the Black Death?' asked Michael.

'Sure I have. And the Black Prince. He stayed in that château, didn't he?' said Oliver, pointing to the tip of Brissac's towers visible on the brow of the hill.

'Are you sure the two are related?' asked Rachel.

Michael said, 'Your mother's right. The Black Prince became Edward III of England. He came here about fifteen years after the Black Death. So you know about him, do you?'

'I don't know much. I know that they called him the Black Prince because his armour was black.'

'I don't know where he picks it all up. But he's always liked history,' Rachel said proudly.

Oliver looked up at Michael quizzically, cradling his chin in his hands. 'I saw a movie once about the Black Death. It was really gruesome.'

'That's what Oliver likes, don't you? Anything gruesome – preferably with monsters. Those are the current favourites.'

'And treasure,' Oliver reminded her.

'Not to forget treasure,' Rachel concurred.

'Treasure? Well, in that case you might be interested in a legend about this place. There's supposed to be treasure buried somewhere under Brissac.'

'Really?' Oliver jumped up and stared at the château. 'Did the Black Prince put it there?'

'I don't think the Black Prince stayed long enough to hide any treasure,' Michael replied. 'Anyway, he was always running short of cash because he spent all his money on wars. No, this was long before then, in about 1308. The Gascon pope who built the château is supposed to have hidden a fabulous treasure in a secret passage underneath.'

Oliver's eyes grew wide. 'Do you mean gold and silver and jewels, and things like that?'

'That's right. It might only be a legend. At any rate, no one has ever found it.'

'They could use metal detectors. If it was me, I'd get a metal detector.' He began to illustrate.

'Well, I suppose no one has ever thought of doing that,' admitted Michael.

'You were telling me about Tintin looking for treasure. He didn't have a metal detector,' Rachel reminded Oliver.

'No, because he and his friend had a map. Wouldn't it be neat to find the treasure? If I had a shovel, I'd start looking today. Can we go up to the château now, Mom?'

'It's quite a long way up that hill and it's still awfully hot, you know,' she said doubtfully. Her immediate thought was that Oliver would tell Alain that they had been snooping around the property.

'Please, please,' Oliver begged. 'I want to see if we can find the treasure. Can't we just have a look?'

'Looks as if I've started something,' said Michael, amused.

Rachel smiled and said, 'Oliver, I doubt whether the owners would like us to dig for treasure. After all, anything buried on their property belongs to them, don't forget.'

'But if we found the treasure, wouldn't they let us keep some?'

'I suppose they might, but better not get your hopes up,' she replied, gathering up the picnic.

'Let's just go and see if we can see anything. Can't we, oh, please . . .'

237

Seeing his excitement, Rachel exchanged a glance with Michael.

'I can take everything back to the house for you,' he offered. 'Just roll the bag in the blanket and I'll strap it on the bike so you won't have to drag it along.' He grinned at Oliver, who was prancing up and down, his eyes trained on Brissac dominating the horizon.

'I have a better idea. Why don't you come with us.'

'Are you sure? I don't want to be in the way.'

'I'd like you to come. We'd both like it, wouldn't we, Oliver?'

'Yes! Then we can all look for the treasure.'

At bottom of the hill Michael said, 'I'll leave my bicycle in that gully over there and pick it up on the way back.'

'Fine. I'll put the sack and the blanket with it.'

'That's a neat bike,' said Oliver. 'How many gears does it have?'

'I've forgotten, but two dozen or so,' said Michael. To Rachel he added, 'I bought it in a moment of insanity, thinking it would help me get fit. But as you can see it's hardly been used.'

'Can I ride it?' asked Oliver.

'It might be too big for you, but I suppose we could try it with the seat and handlebars down.' Michael made the adjustments and Oliver got on and pedalled the bike a short distance up a slope before coming to a halt.

'Let's just leave it here, Oliver,' called Rachel. But he had already started up the steep hill. 'You might fall off and hurt yourself,' she called after him. When he ignored her, she shook her head and said to Michael, 'The minute you tell him he's not able to do something he'll try to disprove you. What a kid.' Her voice dropped to a whisper. 'Today he could ask for the moon and I think I'd try to get it for him though I've always been careful not to spoil him too much.'

'He seems like an exceptionally nice, bright boy. It's obvious that he's as happy as can be to have you here. Is everything all right?'

'Yes, thanks, things seemed to go a lot better than I expected. The truth is Oliver's having the time of his life here. And why shouldn't he? He doesn't know what's going on. But Alain should never have brought him. He had no right . . .' she broke off. 'Reading between the lines, I can guess what is going on between

238

Alain and Isabelle, though obviously Alain has been very careful to hide it from Oliver.'

'I hope so,' said Michael doubtfully, 'because he strikes me as being a very observant, perceptive little chap.'

Pain flashed across Rachel's face, then she changed the subject. 'Nowadays children seem to be so much more aware of the world around them. I used to worry constantly about what computers and television were doing to his imagination, but not any more.'

'From what I've seen just now he seems consumed with curiosity about all sorts of things.'

'I sometimes worry that it will get him into trouble.' Just then she saw the bicycle wobble and Oliver tumble off, but he picked himself up immediately. 'Are you all right?' she called.

'I'm OK!'

'He'll have a few scratches and bruises to attend to when you get home,' Michael commented.

'That's par for the course. He's absolutely fearless. I've tried so hard not to smother him, to give him the freedom he needs. It's just that today he seems more precious to me than ever. Tell me honestly, Michael, do you think I should leave here right now and take him with me?'

'You're really asking yourself that question aloud, aren't you?'

'Yes, I suppose I am. Something is holding me back, but I don't really know what it is.'

They caught up with Oliver, who was wheeling the bike and panting with exertion.

'Want me to take over?' suggested Michael.

He shook his head vehemently. 'I can do it by myself.'

'We'll wait for you at that monument with the cross just ahead,' said Rachel. 'I should think by that time the grown-ups will need a rest. He hates to be babied,' she added when he was out of earshot. 'What is that cross mounted on a stone, anyway? I noticed it before.'

'Since time immemorial pilgrims have stopped here on the road to Compostela in Spain. In fact, I think they still do.' When they reached the lichen-encrusted monument, Michael continued, 'The base was a Roman shrine to Venus. The Latin inscription has been worn away, but you can still make out the shell.'

239

'Do you suppose a half-naked goddess once reposed on the top?'

Michael laughed. 'I hadn't thought of that, but it's perfectly possible, I suppose. So many pagan shrines were destroyed by the early Christians, but this survived when the pilgrims to Compostela adopted it because of the shell, and added the cross.'

'Of course, because the cockleshell is also the sign of St James. An interesting coincidence.'

'It was the pilgrim custom to lay a wreath or sprig of *Buxus sempervirens* – box – symbol of eternal life. It looks as if the tradition still lives,' he said, picking up a withered branch of box at the base of the monument.

Rachel turned to see that Oliver had nearly caught up with them. 'What indomitable people those pilgrims must have been to have come so far searching for an ideal. I find it very moving to think of all the wishes laid at the feet of this old stone. I'm not in the least bit superstitious but I'm tempted to make a wish myself.'

'Why don't you?'

'*I* will if *you* will.'

Michael watched her close her eyes for a few seconds, and when she opened her eyes he said, 'I hope it comes true, whatever it was.'

'I take it you didn't bother.'

'I'm still thinking about it. Never squander a wish. They're too valuable.' He gave her a thoughtful smile.

'What's this thing?' asked Oliver, coming up to them. 'It sure looks old to me.'

When Michael told him how old it was, he whistled through his teeth and said, 'Did knights on horses make wishes too?'

'Sure they did.'

'I'm afraid Oliver is much more interested in knights in armour than in pilgrims, aren't you?' said Rachel.

'I bet anything that the Black Prince stopped here. What did people do? Did they throw money, like at the wishing well in the park at home?'

'This shrine doesn't accept money as far as I know. Do you see this branch? It's called box. The pilgrims gave that as an offering because it stays green a long time.'

'Hey, I know this stuff. It grows in the garden at Terre Blanche. It smells like cats,' he said, making a face.

Rachel laughed. 'That's exactly what it smells like.'

Oliver moved his lips in a silent wish, then he threw down the branch at the base of the monument.

'No, silly,' said Rachel. 'You've got to pick a branch and make a wreath,' she explained 'Isn't that right, Michael? That's like taking somebody's nickel out of the wishing well and throwing it back in.'

Oliver smiled up at her impishly. 'Hey, look. What's that shell?'

'We'll never get up that hill to find the treasure,' said Rachel laughing. But Oliver wouldn't be budged until Michael had told him all about it.

'Why did the pilgrims wear shells on their hats? What did it mean?' he persisted.

'Now that's a good question . . .'

Hearing the pleasure in Michael's voice as he talked to Oliver, Rachel realized he had a natural gift for turning thousands of years of history into stories an eight-year-old boy could understand.

'. . . and so the legend goes that St James – St Jacques in French – performed a miracle where a young fisherman had drowned. He pulled the man up from the bottom of the sea, covered with shells, after his young bride said a prayer. The fisherman was brought back to life and reunited with his bride, and they lived happily ever after. And ever since then the pilgrims coming to visit the shrine of the patron saint of Spain have always worn shells on their hats.'

Walking up the hill, Rachel said, 'Now he's really hooked. I could see he was enthralled by what you told him.'

'Perhaps you have a budding novelist or historian on your hands. All it takes is a spark, and who knows what he might make of it.'

'A budding daydreamer is more like it. His mind is prone to wandering at school and he gets in trouble for not concentrating.'

'Daydreams quite often come into their own much later in life.'

Michael and Rachel arrived at the summit of the hill just ahead of Oliver, and stood gazing at the sweeping view of the patchwork of cultivated hills and distant hamlets distorted by a haze of heat.

'No wonder Armand Bataille fell in love with this place all those years ago,' remarked Michael. 'Just look at the view.'

'I found myself trying to visualize Armand Bataille when I was here the other day. What a terrible thing to have to leave something like this behind.' Rachel turned to look for Oliver, who wasn't far away. They waited as he came trudging doggedly up the hill wheeling the bicycle, tired but triumphant.

'Good for you,' said Michael. 'You kept on going and didn't give up.'

Oliver beamed. 'I'm no quitter. I never give up, do I, Mom?'

'Absolutely never,' she said, hugging him.

The three of them walked down the chalk road towards the archway.

'Madame Grimal doesn't seem to mind if people go into the courtyard,' said Rachel. In spite of Alain she was anxious to visit the château again. Seeing its clean lines against the blue sky, she realized that it had been looming at the back of her mind.

'Popes, monks, knights on horseback, even a king or two have passed under this arch,' remarked Michael as they walked beneath it.

Oliver craned his neck to see the portcullis, locked into position at the top of the arch. 'Wow! Just think what would happen if it came crashing down,' he cried excitedly.

'Yes, just think,' said Michael. He was staring at the courtyard of golden stone filled with the cry of swifts. 'I never knew it was so beautiful.'

They went to the pool and looked down at the dark water, its surface hardly disturbed by the trickle from the mossy stone outlet. Oliver dragged his hand across the surface, then dashed towards the front steps.

'Look at the nails in this door!' he called, running his hands over the weathered surface. 'This is really old.'

'He's in his element,' said Michael.

'I'm so glad we came. The other day when I was here I wasn't sure what Alain's plans were. I stared into the water for the longest time until the reflections seemed like faces. What you told me about the plague year made a deep impression.'

They stared down at the pool in silence for a moment, absorbing the atmosphere. Michael glanced round at the towering walls

242

pierced by the small transom windows that reflected the sky. 'I've thought so much about Brissac. But until now I seem to have forgotten that it's a real place. What did those people think and feel when they were waiting for the plague to pass them by, I wonder? I'd like to believe that the past isn't really lost to us, that the human imagination can cross the divide back into history. At moments like this what happened here centuries ago seems within reach.'

Rachel murmured, 'How lucky you are to inhabit two worlds – your own and an imaginary one. I wish I could do the same. It must be a wonderful escape.'

'On the contrary, I can't escape it. It seems to have taken hold of me and won't let me go.'

Rachel was about to reply when she became aware that Oliver had disappeared. 'Where's Oliver? He was here only a minute ago and now he's gone.'

They looked round the empty courtyard.

'He probably went back to get the bicycle and ride it on the flat. Perhaps he's had enough history for one day.'

'I'm afraid he might have sneaked off to look for treasure,' she frowned.

When Rachel called him and there was no answer, they went back through the arch and down the road; they found Michael's bicycle lying where he had left it.

'Oliver!' shouted Rachel. 'Where are you? We're leaving now.' When there was no reply, she looked puzzled. 'Where do you suppose he went?'

'I'm sure he must have decided to have a browse on his own but he can't have gone far.'

'I hate it when he does this.' She called several times, and still there was no answer. 'Oliver, dammit, where are you?' she shouted. A sob came to her throat, which she couldn't suppress. 'I know I'm being ridiculous and that he hasn't gone far, but I've had this terrible forboding ever since he left home. I haven't mentioned it to anyone, it seemed so neurotic on top of everything else, but I've been haunted by the idea that something will happen to him.'

'He hasn't gone anywhere, he's just wandered off, that's all. It's

243

perfectly natural for you to feel like you do in the light of what's happening. He'll turn up any minute.' Michael cupped his hands to his lips and shouted Oliver's name.

'I wasn't this sort of mother before. Now I feel panicked if he's out of my sight. Oliver! Oliver!' she cried, her throat tightening with desperation as her eyes searched the landscape in every direction.

'Well, he had to have come out of the courtyard, because there isn't any other exit. Perhaps he decided to go round to the other side by the road at the bottom of the slope,' said Michael, peering into the distance, but there was no sign of Oliver.

'He wouldn't have had time to get that far, would he?'

'No, I suppose not. Look, just to be sure I'll circle the château and you wait here.'

She nodded. 'All right. He'll probably come looking for us at any moment.'

Michael strode down the eastern slope of the château, taking a backward glance at Rachel, who was watching anxiously for her son. He remembered Margaret Prior's search for Thomas, and felt a twinge of uneasiness he told himself was a product of his overactive imagination.

Oliver was hiding behind a rock when he heard Rachel call his name, but he didn't move at the summons. He had gone bounding down the road to fetch the bicycle when a movement near the base of the château had caught his eye. He crept stealthily down the slope towards the thicket hugging the massive stone foundation, arriving just in time to see an old woman in a faded navy dress disappear into what looked like impenetrable undergrowth. The busy snipping of secateurs suggested she was cutting her way deeper inside, which immediately aroused Oliver's curiosity.

'Treasure,' he whispered excitedly to himself, unable to believe his luck.

Oliver held his breath as he listened to what sounded like the clank of metal against stone, imagining that the old lady had started digging. He crouched low and darted closer to the thicket to try to make out what was going on. There was a loud crack as he crushed a branch underfoot. He quickly dived for cover, but his feet were entangled in a creeper and he went sprawling on the ground. At the rustling of shrubbery, he glanced fearfully over his shoulder to see the old woman appear.

'*Qui est tu?*' she demanded.

As she moved closer Oliver became frightened. Her staring eyes, set in a pinched face, and her unkempt grey hair reminded him of a witch.

Oliver swallowed nervously and got to his feet. Rigid with guilt, he met her accusing eyes. He understood her question well enough to mutter, '*Je suis* Oliver Ribard.'

'Ribard,' she mumbled, clapping her hand over her mouth. Connecting the boy before her to the Ribard who had recently come back to Roquelaire, Agnès was deeply shaken. Why had this child suddenly appeared the moment she was examining the tunnel containing Paul Ribard's remains?

'*Je m'excuse, madame,*' Oliver murmured, repeating the phrase he had heard his father use in awkward circumstances, but his apology seemed to have no effect. The old lady was still looking at him so strangely that he turned and bolted across the open ground without looking back.

Agnès watched him in a daze, then retreated back into the copse with her heart beating so violently that she thought it would break through her chest. Perspiration was running down her face from her efforts to gain access to the spot where she had entered the tunnel with Armand almost a lifetime ago. When she had hacked a passage through the shrubbery, she discovered a pair of stone blocks at the base of the wall that had not been mortared like the rest. Now she edged her way back to that spot and pressed herself against the cool stones for a moment to regain her strength. Although disconcerted by the appearance of the Ribard boy, she was too distraught to worry about what he had seen or to think of the implications. Hot and nearly prostrate with exhaustion, Agnès had to finish what she had started.

Taking up the crowbar she had brought, she applied all her strength until at last she dislodged one stone, then another. The resulting hole was no larger than would allow a dog to pass. As

245

Agnès crouched down and thrust her head into the hole and the dank odour of the tunnel, lodged in her memory after all these years, came wafting out of the blackness. She flashed her torch round, then backed out of the hole, suddenly feeling repelled by the thought that she had disturbed a tomb. As she sank defeatedly into the dust, Agnès was seized by a memory of Armand so real, so painful that tears came to her eyes. She seemed to see him standing in the shadows in the full vigour of youth as he poised himself to meet danger. He was looking at her with intense concern, his fingers touching his lips.

She wiped her eyes as she got to her feet, shaken to the core of her being by how recent it seemed. She came out of her daydream utterly drained, and realized that she was too exhausted to do more than push the stones together again and pile up some branches in order to cover the traces. Agnès left the thicket without looking back, wishing she had never come.

When Rachel spotted Oliver appearing as if out of nowhere, she gave a shout, then ran to embrace him.

'Oliver, where have you been? We've been searching all over for you!' She grabbed him and hugged him to her, feeling indescribable relief.

He looked up contritely. 'I was just having a look around, that's all.'

'What made you go off like that without telling me? Didn't you hear us calling you?'

He shrugged. 'I just saw something in the field and I thought maybe it was a wild animal.' He had decided not to tell Rachel about the old woman he had met; what he had seen signified a mystery he was determined to explore on his own.

Rachel was dusting him off, her hands still shaking. 'Oliver, don't do that ever again, please. What was I supposed to think when you disappeared into thin air? Sweetheart, do you realize you've been gone for over ten minutes and I've been frantic with worry?'

'I'm really sorry, Mom. I didn't go very far. Were you really scared?'

'More than you'll ever know, you little monkey.' She looked down at him, trying to smile. He wriggled out from her grasp, but

246

she needed to touch him as if to confirm he was all right. The terror that had taken hold of her, which Rachel knew would haunt her for a long time, was the same nameless dread she had experienced before leaving home.

'Where's Michael?' he asked.

'He's gone to look for you. When you didn't come back after we called, we got really concerned. Just look at you, covered in dust. What were you doing?'

'I was just watching something.'

'Looking for buried treasure, I'll bet.' Hugging him closer, she wondered what he would say to Alain about his adventure, about the visit to Brissac, but it no longer seemed to matter.

Soon they saw Michael walking towards them up the slope.

'So, the vagabond has turned up, has he? That was quite a vanishing act you did,' he said to Oliver, slipping his arm round his shoulder. 'Your mother was quite worried about you, you know.'

'He was apparently stalking something, and he didn't even hear me call. I was really shouting too, at the top of my voice.'

'Rabbits, eh? We thought for sure it was treasure.'

Oliver smiled but didn't reply.

'Did Agnès Grimal come by this way, by any chance?' asked Michael.

'Madame Grimal? No, why?'

'I went round the other side, then came down the road. I felt sure it was her walking ahead of me. I called to her but she didn't stop. Perhaps she's getting a bit deaf.'

'I wouldn't want her to think we were trespassing, but when I saw her the other day she seemed so friendly and I got the impression she wouldn't mind.'

'She couldn't have seen us. Otherwise she would surely have come to say hello. She's probably halfway to the village by now.'

When Oliver started to fidget, Rachel said, 'I suppose we ought to be getting back.'

Michael picked up the bicycle and said, 'It's been nice to meet you, Oliver, and I hope to see you again sometime.'

'Goodbye,' said Oliver. Looking at the bicycle, he added, 'Next year I'll be big enough to ride it.'

'Next year? Are you coming back?'

Oliver gave a bemused smile, looking to Rachel for an answer, but she didn't reply either, and Michael knew that his innocent remark had touched a raw nerve.

'Well, until next year, then. But probably sooner.' He waved goodbye, then sped down the hill.

'Was Michael a friend of yours from before, Mom?'

'No, we just met.' Rachel watched the back of Michael's blue shirt as he disappeared down the black ribbon of road.

Twenty minutes later Rachel and Oliver were walking through the deserted square, where most of the shops were shuttered. A group of old men were playing cards at the café next to a table of sunburnt tourists eating ice-cream and a man was unloading suitcases from a car with an English number plate in front of the Hôtel de France.

'Have you been inside the church yet?'

Oliver shook his head and Rachel led him up the steps, feeling a sudden need for the particular peace and silence it offered. They entered the cool interior and stood at the back for a moment.

'It's beautiful,' whispered Oliver, gazing at the splashes of blue and red light pouring through the stained-glass windows on to the frescoed walls.

The church appeared to be empty except for a woman in the front pew, but when they approached the chapel of St Anne, Rachel saw that a woman was kneeling on a prie-dieu below the reflection of the wavering candles. Realizing with a start that it was Agnès Grimal deep in prayer, she put her finger to her lips and looked down at Oliver, who was staring fixedly at Agnès.

After they had left the church, Oliver asked, 'Who was that old lady in the church, Mom?'

'That was Agnès Grimal. She's the person who owns the château.'

'Honest?' he exclaimed, amazement all over his face.

'Do you know who she is?' Rachel asked, wondering what Oliver might have overheard.

'I've never seen her, ever. I just wondered, that's all,' he murmured.

They walked up the Rue St Jacques and every step of the way Rachel was conscious that she would soon have to give Oliver up for the night. Rebelling inwardly, she imagined the argument that would ensue if she told Alain she was going back on her word and wouldn't let him take Oliver back to Terre Blanche. But Oliver began talking excitedly about Alain's promise to take him to the seaside the following day.

'And then, Dad says a carnival is coming here at the end of the week. You know what? We saw one on the way coming here. There was a merry-go-round in a truck that has thousands of pieces . . .'

'That sounds great,' she said, unable to think that far ahead. 'Well, next time you come to see me, we'll take a drive somewhere.'

'You mean with Dad, the three of us?'

'No, probably just you and me. What do you say? We could explore.'

Rachel could tell by his slouching posture that Oliver didn't want to be without Alain. Keeping her voice even she said, 'Maybe that's not such a good idea.'

Oliver didn't say anything until they reached the door. As she turned the key in the lock she saw there was confusion in his face.

'Mom, aren't we ever going to be together anymore, the three of us?'

She realized then that he knew, that he had already read the signals. Perhaps, she thought, he had known what was happening between her and Alain even before she did herself. Putting her hand on his shoulder, she said, 'Come and sit down before Daddy comes back for you. We have to talk.'

Isabelle picked up the ringing telephone. '*Bonjour*, Hélène. How nice to hear from you. Are you well?' She injected a note of enthusiasm into her voice when she heard who it was, and settled into a chair, realizing by her tone of voice that Hélène had something important to relate.

Isabelle hadn't heard from Armand Bataille's housekeeper since the will had been read. They had speculated a long time behind the closed doors of the study at Terre Blanche, but neither of them had been able to come up with a satisfactory explanation for why

249

Armand had left Agnès such a huge legacy. Isabelle had always cultivated Hélène, remembering to bring her little presents from time to time and suggesting latterly that there would always be a place for her in the château when Isabelle took it over. In spring, when Armand was unwell, the housekeeper used to admit Isabelle quietly into the house with the architect and the surveyor without the old man's knowledge.

Alain walked into the study as Isabelle hung up the telephone.

'Who was that?' he asked suspiciously when he saw the startled look on her face. 'I hope it wasn't Rachel. I'm just about to drive into Roquelaire to pick Oliver up.'

'No, it wasn't Rachel.' An amused smile was playing about her lips. 'Come and sit down for a minute.'

'Bad news?'

'On the contrary. That was Hélène Briault on the phone, Armand's old housekeeper. You wouldn't believe what she just told me.' In a few words Isabelle related Hélène's astonishing discovery.

'You're joking,' said Alain, amazement spreading across his face. 'Do you mean that Armand Bataille had a daughter?'

'There are ways to confirm it, but I believe Hélène is right. The sly old bastard.' Isabelle quickly calculated when it had happened. 'Hélène says that the girl, Pascale, is now twenty-one. That would make it 1970 when Agnès conceived her child. I remember that Gilles and I came to Terre Blanche for Christmas that winter. Armand's wife had died a few months before, and we drove to see him on Christmas Day, but he wasn't home.'

Isabelle didn't see the ironic look Alain cast at her when he realized that she was talking about the moment he had first set eyes on her, wrapped in mink as she leaned against a silver Jaguar. It was a turning point that had changed his life, though it had left no impression whatever on her.

'It wasn't until two years later that we really began to see more of Armand when we were here, because he was travelling constantly. And, of course, it wasn't until after Gilles died in 1980 that Armand and I really got to know each other. There's no way I would have known about him and Agnès unless he chose to tell me or unless I had heard about it through local gossip. It would appear the whole thing was hushed up completely. It's almost too incredible to comprehend. I mean, think of her with him. Can you imagine?'

'But it doesn't make sense. Why did he do it this way? Why would he lead you to think you could take over Brissac all those years, and then change his mind?'

'Don't you see? He didn't know about it himself, that's why. Hélène reminded me that Agnès came to see Armand not long before he died. She had already told me the notary was summoned to his side not long afterwards, but neither of us connected it at the time. It all fits.'

'But even so,' said Alain, shaking his head, 'it seems pretty far-fetched to me.'

'When people are about to die, they sometimes do things that seem out of character. But who knows what really happened? Anyway, let me tell you the rest of the story. Hélène certainly doesn't remember Agnès ever coming to the château when she was there. If they did sleep together, it must have been something that happened out of the blue, because they weren't having an affair. Hélène would have discovered it if they were, I'm sure. In fact, I seem to remember now that Armand was away most of the year after his wife died, and that he didn't come back here for ages. Everybody assumed he couldn't bear to be here with his wife and son gone, which I'm sure is true. You realize, Alain, that this changes everything, don't you?'

'That's just what I was thinking. Even if the child was a bastard, any court would defend her rights.'

'No, that's not what I mean. I've all but given up the legal angle anyway. This girl – Pascale. She's been raised thinking that her mother is her aunt. That's how they managed to get round the awkward fact of her origins. It fits because apparently Agnès's sister and her family weren't living here at the time, but came back the following year. You can be certain that the girl has no idea who her real parents are.'

'But why would Agnès keep the thing to herself? Surely she would have told Armand!'

'She obviously did tell him – but not until he was on his deathbed. Who knows what went on inside her head? The whole thing was probably a bizarre accident in the first place. She was ashamed and frightened, and he had gone away. What was she to do? It makes perfect sense to me. Something tells me that Agnès Grimal would guard her secret with her life.'

'I'm beginning to get your drift, but it could prove a dangerous game. I mean, if she thought you were trying to blackmail her, she might turn on you completely, and then where would we be?'

'Oh, I'm sure that won't be the case. Quite the opposite. This could be the loose stone that makes the wall come down. What a piece of luck!'

When Alain had gone, Isabelle curled up on the sofa and allowed herself to dream for a moment, something she had stopped doing since her troubles over the château began. She revelled in her vision of Brissac after millions had been lavished on it, transforming it from a dour medieval castle into a spa hotel of unrivalled luxury. She could picture the sophisticated clientele driving up to the courtyard in cars with number plates from all over Europe. She would be waiting to greet them at the entrance against a huge arrangement of flowers flown in fresh from Nice every day. Alain would make a discreet appearance, immaculately turned out in his starched white uniform. Just thinking of it sent a charge of energy through Isabelle and brought her old optimism back. Realizing there was no time to lose, she jumped up and rushed to the telephone. A moment later she was speaking to her lawyer in Paris.

'Yes, that's right. I need an investigator who can work fast. I want you to trace where Pascale Gachpour was born and who her real parents are.'

\*

It was after four o'clock by the time Pascale and Julian left the restaurant. As they drove towards Brissac, it seemed to Pascale that the château had never looked so magnificent as it did through the windscreen of the Porsche, its towers set against a hot blue sky. Brissac stood out proudly on the horizon, as it had for nearly seven hundred years, commanding the attention of travellers on the pilgrim's road now as it did then. And it belonged to her Aunt Agnès.

She and Julian had hardly spoken during the drive there. He had speeded recklessly over the narrow country lanes that cut through hills of ripening sunflowers, skilfully playing the gears of the powerful car. Pascale brushed her wind-whipped hair from her face as she watched Julian's strong hands gripping the steering wheel. She was strangely excited by the idea of entering the château alone with him.

'Stop at the road just ahead,' she said. When he had slowed down at the unpaved track that led to the caretaker's cottage behind Brissac, she added, 'I'll go alone to collect the key.' The words seemed an admission of guilt on her part, and her heart thudded against her chest at the thought of what she was about to do.

Julian seemed to sense her nervousness and gave her a searching look. 'Are you sure you want to do this? I wouldn't want you to get into trouble.'

'Of course. We've already decided, haven't we? You can drive through the arch into the courtyard and wait for me there. It's the next road to the left. I'll walk round in a minute.'

'You don't want me to wait?'

'No – please.'

He smiled patiently. 'Whatever you say.'

Pascale hopped out and watched him drive off. The engine growled ferociously and she looked towards the cottage uneasily, half-expecting to see the old caretaker fling open his shutters to see what the commotion was, but all was still except for the hot wind bending the parched grass. Pascale's mouth was dry from nerves, the heat and the wine at lunch, and her head was pounding as she stumbled up the stony path in her elegant shoes. She began to regret her promise to take Julian to the château as she started to think what the entire family, and Étienne, would say if they found out. She argued with herself as she walked, working herself up to a state of stubborn self-righteousness.

'I'm a grown woman. I can do what I like,' she said aloud, and recalled Julian's words about the day being a gift that belonged only to the two of them. She went to the door of the stone cottage and knocked several times before she heard footsteps approaching.

'*Bonjour*, Monsieur David,' she said with a cheerful smile. 'I'd like to borrow the key to the château. My aunt said you keep a spare one here.'

'*Ah, bonjour, mademoiselle.* How nice to see you. *Vous allez bien?* Did you have to knock very long? I'm getting deaf, you know.' He spoke with a friendly smile that revealed tobacco-stained teeth.

He was in a talkative mood and she was forced to waste precious minutes chatting in order not to arouse his suspicions.

'Your aunt is very proud of you. I hear you took a diploma in accountancy.'

'Yes, this summer.'

'I always said to Laurent accountancy would be a fine profession, and he was good with figures, but now look where he is – an antique dealer selling rubbish that nobody wants. But still, he seems to make a living. Have you seen him since you came home?'

'Yes, I saw him in the square and we said hello.' Pascale looked sympathetically at the old man, whose son was thought to be a dreamer and a wastrel. Seeing his anxious face, she forgot her haste for a moment. 'I wouldn't worry, *monsieur*. His shop seems to be doing very well, particularly now so many tourists come to Roquelaire. They'll pay a hundred francs for things like old orange-water bottles.'

When at last he went down the grim passage to fetch the key, Pascale thought how bare and uninviting the old widower's house was, so unlike the welcoming atmosphere of her aunt's cottage, though she too lived alone. After an interminable wait, he returned. Pascale took the key and turned to go.

'I'll be here, but if I'm not, just leave it behind the front shutter there. Will you be long?'

'Not very long. I really don't know,' she said, anxious to get away.

'I can come around and lock up if you want and save you coming back here. As soon as I feed the chickens I'll walk over . . .'

'No, no, it won't be necessary.' Pascale thought quickly. She didn't want him to discover she was there with Julian on any account. 'I'll leave the key as you suggested. Say in an hour or so?'

'Yes, or you could leave it at the château behind the pot by the door. You'll want to have a good look round.'

254

He screwed up his face and looked at her, suggesting that he was as curious as anyone how Agnès had come to inherit the château.

'Goodbye, and thank you,' Pascale said, waving as she went, hoping that he wouldn't come to the château before she had gone.

Her stomach in a knot, she retraced the long way round the eastern slope of the château. The countryside lay under the pall of the afternoon heat, with no sign of movement except an occasional lizard scuttling over the rocks on the side of the road. She hurried towards the arch, propelled by an anticipation that was almost like dread at the thought of Julian waiting for her. He was standing by the pool and turned at the sound of her footsteps. She waved the huge key triumphantly, not letting on how anxious the whole episode had made her.

'Good girl.' When he closed his hand around hers, a current seemed to shoot up her arm. She stared at him, spellbound by the intensity of his gaze and his provocative smile, yet when he released her hand, she felt a sudden urge to escape. As if sensing her reluctance, he took the key from her and sprinted up the steps to the front door, where he slipped it in the lock. He gestured for her to precede him through the door, but she hesitated.

'What's the matter? Why are you so nervous?'

'I'm thinking about my aunt. She wanted to show me the château herself. She'll be disappointed.'

'We're here now. But suit yourself. If you don't feel good about it, let's not do it.' He waited for her to make up her mind.

If he had been pushy or aggressive, she would have felt justified in changing her mind, but the mocking amusement on his face was a challenge.

'Let's go in,' she said. A rush of cool air hit her face as they entered.

'We should leave the door open,' she said.

'Not a good idea. Someone might wander by and steal something if we're upstairs. There are some valuable things here.' He came very close to her and for a moment she thought he was going to kiss her, but he merely smiled and motioned towards the stairs.

They spent the next half hour wandering round the château. Julian seemed to forget all about her. He was obviously making calculations in his head as they roamed from room to room, and he forged ahead of her, opening the doors to every room and cupboard. Pascale followed him with the uncomfortable feeling that they were trespassing; it dampened her initial excitement at the prospect of seeing the château's treasures for the first time and she observed everything with a strange detachment. Now she was there she could not quite take in that Agnès, her quiet, modest aunt, was the owner of this magnificent property.

At the end of the long hallway, furnished with chests and old prints, they entered what had obviously been Armand Bataille's bedroom, overlooking the courtyard. Julian opened the shutters and squares of light illuminated the big tower room.

'It's lovely,' whispered Pascale, though it wasn't at all her idea of what a bedroom should be. She felt a tangible sense of well-being in the room, as she had in no other. The floor of uneven tiles, polished to a deep patina, was strewn with faded Persian rugs. The high ceiling was crossed with dark, frescoed beams, and near the vast fireplace with a stone mantel was a massive old chair with curving arms and spiral legs, its green brocade upholstery frayed from wear. On the desk facing it rested a reading lamp and a stack of books, lending the impression that someone had been sitting there a moment ago. Pascale had a sudden image of Armand Bataille, whom she had seen no more than half a dozen times in her life, and then only from a distance, reading in the chair by the lamp. While Julian walked round the room, Pascale looked at the antique bed, hundreds of years old, hung with heavy, dark fabric.

'This must be where he died,' she said in a low voice, feeling sad even though she had hardly known Armand. Her most vivid memory of him was meeting him once when she was a child, out picking mushrooms with Agnès. He had stopped his big black Citroën and exchanged a few polite words with them. His kind, almost courtly air had made Pascale think well of him ever afterwards. She had forgotten the incident, but it came back to her now how oddly wistful Agnès had looked when he drove away.

She looked round to see Julian thumbing through one of the leatherbound books on the desk. 'St Augustine's *Confessions* – what you'd expect,' he remarked. 'What was the old man like?'

256

'I didn't know him,' said Pascale with a shrug. A sudden fit of gloom oppressed her and made her want to leave the room. She moved impatiently to the door, waiting for Julian to follow her.

'I heard that he was very cultured, a self-made man. Apparently he was a Resistance hero and married some sort of heiress after the war.'

'I think that's true. People say he was an interesting man, though I don't think anyone in the village knew him very well. For some years he hardly came here at all, especially after his wife and child died. It must have been terrible for him,' she said, thinking of the old man living alone in the vast rooms of the château.

'Why did he leave your aunt this château, do you know? You have to admit it's incredible.'

'I don't know. Nobody knows. People do strange things when they're about to die,' she replied, conscious that no one, not even Julian, could induce her to reveal what Agnès had confided in her.

'Was he ever in love with her?'

'Aunt Agnès?' Pascale said incredulously. 'No, that's impossible. That's not the reason.'

'She must have been young and pretty once.'

'Maybe, but they were different people. So many young men from Roquelaire died in the war. There were no husbands. I think that was what kept her away from men. Her life was filled with other things. No,' Pascale said with a shake of her head. 'Absolutely not.'

'My aunt doesn't know why he left her the château,' she added, wanting to change the subject. It seemed a kind of betrayal to talk about Armand Bataille and her aunt in that room where his spirit still lingered.

'Yes, you're right, of course. The two of them would have had nothing in common. They lived in different worlds,' said Julian, visualizing the old rabbit-seller he had seen in the market and Armand Bataille, whose appreciation of beauty and sense of history still seemed to inhabit the château that he had restored with such care. Carefully not looking at Pascale, he announced, 'She's a spinster, so if anything happened to her . . .'

Pascale pretended not to know what he meant.

257

'Let's go downstairs now. I have to go soon.'

'Sure,' he said, taking one last glance at the room, memorizing all the details for future reference. Along the passage she followed Julian into the big hall, where he turned on the chandelier.

'This room was supposed to be the dining-room of the hotel. Imagine it full of tables. You can almost hear the clink of silver and china, the buzz of conversation, can't you? That huge sideboard over there would look magnificent. The furniture in this place must be worth a packet.'

'I think some of it is donated to the museum to pay the death taxes. That, and the paintings and tapestries.' No sooner had she spoken than Pascale regretted it, thinking she should have kept silent on her aunt's private affairs. She looked at Julian imploringly, anxious to go.

'In a way it would be a shame to see all this furniture dispersed. He probably bought it for nothing in the Fifties. It would look very good in the hotel – eventually. My advice to you is to help your aunt make the right decisions. It's my guess that Madame de Montjoi would give her a better price than she could get anywhere else.'

Pascale met his eyes and realized that the hotel project had not died; it was a living reality that he and others were determined to make happen, even over the heads of those who might be against it. The thought made her uneasy, and she swallowed a pang of guilt that she was betraying Agnès by her mere presence there. But then, seeing Julian's face light up with enthusiasm, she found herself imagining the hall as he had described it. She was fascinated by the thought of the vast, dark, shuttered room transformed into a hotel dining-room bustling with waiters in black coats, flowers everywhere and crystal and silver glittering on the tables. People like the ones in the restaurant where they had had lunch would wait in anticipation as the waiters lifted silver domes to reveal culinary masterpieces, while the *sommeliers* hovered with bottles of vintage wine.

Julian read her thoughts. 'Wouldn't it be sensational?'

She nodded. 'Yes it would, if it happens.'

'Perhaps you could help make it happen. Think of that.'

258

The slow, enigmatic smile that she was beginning to know spread across his face. 'Thanks for the tour.' His fingers touched her wrist and his eyes softened. 'I can see you felt uncomfortable, so it was very sweet of you to come here with me. You're a very nice person. Beautiful, yes, but considerate too, and generous.'

She made a move towards the door. 'That's all right. But I think I ought to get home now – really.' Her voice had a nervous tremor that gave her away, and she didn't dare look at him. 'We must go.'

Julian reached out and pulled her into his arms. At the first touch of his lips a wild charge of desire ran through her body. He kissed her softly at first, then powerfully, deeply, until all her resistance had drained away. When he released her, she was weak and trembling.

'I had to kiss you. You know that, don't you? I knew that the moment I saw you.'

She looked at him speechlessly, her chest heaving with the shock at the violent sensation one kiss could arouse. The vast room was filled only with the sound of his breathing and hers. His body seemed to emanate a kind of fire even at a distance. A pulse beat around Pascale, encircling her. She bowed her head, as if to a yoke, momentarily unable to combat the force that held her. Then, raising her eyes, she looked at him defiantly. She threw her head back, fighting the tears and suppressing the helpless rage at what had happened, knowing that she would never be the same again.

Julian, sensitive to her mood, kept his distance, but his eyes caressed her, defying her to deny the explosive chemistry between them.

'I think it's time to go now,' he said quietly.

Pascale nodded and left the room with him following her. She went through the motions of closing the door and turning out the lights only half aware of what she was doing.

They sat in the car in the courtyard for a moment, listening to the swifts chasing each other round the towers. The stones had mellowed in the deepening light, fading Brissac like an old photograph.

Starting up the car at last, Julian said, 'It's been a memorable day. One I'll never forget. I'll always think of it as a gift.' He

259

seemed to be drinking in a last impression of her face as she looked at him helplessly. 'Pascale, I can't bear the thought of never seeing you again, of you walking out of my life and belonging to someone else. Not now, just when I've found you.'

She swallowed hard, struggling to gain control of herself. 'I don't know. I have to think.'

'You're seeing him, your fiancé, tomorrow, aren't you?' She nodded. 'I'll be thinking of you, and about what happened between us in the château. It's something rare and precious. You and I were more alive in that moment when we touched than we have been in our lives, and may ever be again. Think deeply about that — promise me. If you want to see me, I'll be waiting at Terre Blanche.'

She heard the words clearly, but they hardly made sense to her. As they drove through the archway, Pascale glanced back at the elegant symmetry of the courtyard disappearing behind them, at the old stones that had witnessed her momentous awakening, and all she could think of as they drove back to Roquelaire was what she was going to do about it.

Julian drove back to Terre Blanche in a triumphant mood with his foot hard down on the accelerator. The tape of rock music he had put into the stereo reverberated through the car, its erotic lyrics inspiring a host of fantasies. The asphalt road, shimmering with heat, gave rise to sinuous images of Pascale's naked body, taunting his imagination. Though he knew the sweet torment she had brought him would find no release until she surrendered, he was prepared to wait. He speculated that it might take a day or two, or even more, but in the end he knew she was bound to seek him out. Julian was confident that with one kiss he had aroused her desire for a kind of lovemaking she had never known. He imagined making love to her for the first time, slowly and exquisitely. His fantasy faded into thoughts of the château. Seeing it in broad daylight for the first time, uninhabited and waiting for development, had sharpened his ambition to get his hands on it, a goal as powerful as his desire to seduce Pascale. The thought that the two went together amused and delighted him.

260

When he drove the car through the gates of Terre Blanche, arousal still throbbed through him. He brought the car to a screeching halt on the gravel in front of the *pigeonnier*, and was so preoccupied that he didn't notice a small white Renault parked discreetly behind a pillar.

Bolting up the stairs two at a time, he burst into the apartment as he unbuttoned his shirt on his way to the shower.

'Hello,' said a husky voice from the corner of the room.

He wheeled round and saw Rosamund sitting in the shadows. She seemed much older than he remembered her, and her eyes, full of pain, stared accusingly at him.

'What are you doing here?' There was no displeasure in his voice, merely astonishment. He had hardly thought of her since he had driven her back to Roquelaire two days earlier.

She stood up nervously. 'I'm sorry to arrive like this unannounced, but I simply had to see you. I borrowed a car from somebody in the village. The door was open so I walked in. I've been here for about half an hour and was on the brink of leaving. Please don't be angry with me Julian . . .' Her voice broke in a self-deprecating laugh that was almost a sob.

He stood very still for a moment, then dropped into the chair across from her by the window, where a wave of heat came through the slats of the closed shutters. He looked directly at Rosamund with a stricken expression. 'You must be wondering why I haven't called you . . .'

'Yes, I was wondering.' She lit a cigarette to calm her nerves, not caring whether her hand shook. 'I thought to myself: is this the way he does it, makes love to a woman like a god, then swoops back to Mount Olympus?' She looked at him accusingly.

He sighed and ran his hands through his hair, looking contrite. 'It was rotten of me, I know, and I apologize, as weak as I realize that must sound.'

She shrugged, determined not to seem angry or hurt.

He watched her smoking languidly, remembering what had attracted him that night in Bob Cooper's garden. Then, as now, she had radiated an impeccable glamour coupled with a frank sensuality smouldering beneath her ladylike exterior, a combination he had

261

never been able to resist. His irritation at her unexpected arrival subsided at the prospect of the release of the sexual tension that gripped him after spending the afternoon with Pascale.

'Look, I didn't call you because, well, frankly I felt I was a bit out of my depth with you. I started to think about what it would mean, and I realized that if we carried on, it wouldn't just stop here. We'd get back to London and we'd be up to our necks in an affair. You're a married woman, you have children. The complications, the risks, seemed enormous. We'd have to sneak around; I couldn't call you at home. I don't know if I could handle it.'

She smiled. 'You sound as if this has happened to you before.'

'I've been around long enough to know the score.'

In those first few vital moments Rosamund had regained command of herself and now she sensed she was recapturing Julian's interest. The fire in him seemed far feebler than the night he made love to her, but she needed him all the same.

'Getting involved with married women is not something I would do by choice, you know. It can be hell.'

'That's rich. I always thought the shoe was on the other foot.' There was no sarcasm in her voice. Only infinite tolerance. The other Julian, who lived inside the cool self-possessed property developer, had surfaced, revealing a vulnerable, insecure side to his nature that made Rosamund forget his callousness. She gave him an indulgent look that said she had forgiven everything already.

'I'm the one who stands to really lose,' Rosamund remarked, 'but I wouldn't let that deter me from having an affair with you while I'm here. If it doesn't work out back in London, then we'll part friends. But I can't stop thinking about what happened the other night – the chemistry between us. I had to see you to make sure there wasn't something I'd said or done to put you off.' She added, 'And I admit, I was going to give you a piece of my mind.'

He looked at the bed smothered in chintz cushions, where they had made passionate love. Though it had been pleasurable enough, and he had needed a woman, Julian had not thought of the encounter since. He turned to Rosamund. His eyes followed the outline of her full breasts beneath the deep-pink T-shirt and dropped to her generous thighs, encased in tight jeans.

262

Rosamund stabbed out her cigarette in an ashtray on the table. She wanted Julian fiercely and she didn't care about the risks or consequences. She want him to take her there and then, without tenderness, without excuses or promises. She was seized by the need not only to purge the misery of the last two days, but to banish the many loveless years with her husband. Her eyes implored him to make love to her.

Without another word, Julian went to the door and locked it. Flinging back the covers of the bed, he began to undress. Rosamund slipped out of her clothes in a way that amused him, suggesting she was not used to undressing in front of men in broad daylight. When her back was turned, he took a good look at her ripe, firm figure, at the same time taking the phone off the hook and pushing it under the bed. When she turned around, he was naked and proudly exhibiting his virility. Her eyes dipped appreciatively, then she went to him and clasped him to her with a deep sigh for a moment before they slipped into bed.

When they had kissed passionately for a few moments she whispered, 'Tell me how much you adore me. I need so much to hear it.'

'I adore you,' he whispered obediently. 'And now, let me show you how much.'

263

# Chapter 13

Beyond the vineyards on Brissac's southern slope the stubbled fields sloped to a stream bordered by a thick wood that was part of the domaine. At midmorning it rang with the clash of metal on wood and the cries of men felling ash and oak to feed the mighty chimneys of the château during the coming winter. They had discarded their blue smocks, and their muscular backs rippled as they struck their axes against the trunks, some of which were bigger in circumference than half a dozen men.

Florentine, the baker's daughter, could hear the woodcutters, whose noise drowned the calls of larks and thrushes, as she walked down a rough track with a basket of freshly baked loaves over her arm. Her father had risen as the moon set to make the braided loaves of betrothal bread that symbolized her union with Luc, the forester's son.

She longed for refreshment after the hot, dusty walk from the village and, seeing the stream glinting through the trees, she bounded through the undergrowth, grasping her skirt and apron above her knees. Tossing aside her sandals and the straw hat she wore over her kerchief, Florentine waded into the stream, sighing at the blissful sensation of the cool water on her hot, aching feet. She hitched up her skirt and tucked it into her apron, then began to splash herself all over, basking in the moment of unaccustomed idleness. Bending down, she saw her own nakedness reflected in the water. The droning of bees and the soft green light filtering through the trees engulfed Florentine in a powerful wave of sensuality. The wavering image of her white thighs awakened thoughts of her wedding night in a week. When she became Luc's bride, the mysteries of carnal love would be revealed.

264

Conscience-stricken at her impure thoughts, which she knew was the devil's influence, she crossed herself and prayed she wouldn't die before she had a chance to confess to a priest. Florentine glanced warily round the silent forest, aware as never before that woods were enchanted places where demons and fairies dwelled, waiting to lead humans into temptation. She crossed herself again and prayed for the safety of her soul.

Hearing the creaking of cart wheels and the chatter of women's voices in the distance, Florentine came to her senses with a feeling of relief. As she leapt from the water a rustling noise on the opposite bank made her turn with a start. She was shocked to see a man rise up from behind a log and stretch lazily. He was wearing brightly coloured hose, one leg of which was purple, the other yellow, and his gaudily embroidered leather jerkin and raffish face suggested that he was a vagabond or minstrel, but he was so lithe, so handsome, that she wondered for an instant if he could be a devil in the guise of a man. Florentine blushed with shame when she realized he must have been observing her nakedness.

'Your splashing woke me, pretty damsel. I thought it was a water bird or a deer. And then, to my delight, I saw a nymph had appeared from nowhere.'

'Who are you?' she demanded in a quaking voice.

'I am known as the Cat,' Felix replied.

'Is that because you sneak up on people so quietly?'

He returned her indignation with a melodious laugh that sent disturbing ripples through the air. 'If you're worried that I saw your ankles and feet, let me reassure you I was sound asleep. Because if I had chanced to see you entirely as God made you, I would now be blind from beholding such beauties, so dazzling are they. But my sight has not yet left me, alas. Would that it had.'

She glared at him in pretended anger, but in reality was disarmed by the beguiling quickness of his tongue, having never heard such clever words before. She turned haughtily, picked up her hat and sandals and stalked off, fully expecting him to call her back. He didn't, and after a few steps, she was consumed with curiosity.

265

Looking over her shoulder, she discovered that he wasn't even watching her, but was busy peeling a piece of fruit with his knife. Seeing her pause, he waved at her.

'Farewell, beauteous water sprite. You vanish as you came, in the twinkling of an eye. Perhaps we shall meet again.'

'Not likely,' she said angrily. No man had ever spoken so brazenly to her, nor treated her in such an offhand manner. She had been secure in her place as the village beauty from the time she had reached puberty, and was accustomed to adulation and compliments, but not such teasing provocation. She fetched her basket and stormed off to convey her displeasure, pursued by the spectre of the vagabond with the impish grin.

Florentine ran into the clearing where the betrothal celebration would be held just as a cart drawn by two oxen came down the road. The six women riding in the back of the cart, who included Mother Clothilde, Florentine's mother and the forester's wife, were trying to keep themselves upright, and the food they had brought from overturning. They were complaining loudly at the incompetence of the driver, who was hunched over his whip with a long-suffering expression and muttering to his oxen in a private language. Florentine suppressed a laugh at the sight and watched as the cart was brought to a halt near a crude table and benches of split logs, which the woodsmen had made that morning. As soon as the carter leapt down to tether the oxen to a tree, a man dressed in green, Florentine's future father-in-law, went to help the women.

'Good morning, my daughter,' he said cheerfully when he saw Florentine.

'Good morning, Father,' she said happily. It was the first time he had addressed her thus. She looked round for Luc, who hadn't yet appeared.

At the sight of the baskets of food the women handed down from the cart, the men began to down their axes, ignoring the forester, who shouted that they must continue until the meal had been laid. The forester, a dour, spindly man, threw up his hands, as much as admitting that the day of his only son's betrothal was a joyous occasion when he could afford to relax his authority.

266

'Your father is coming with the rest of the loaves straight from the oven,' said Florentine's mother, handing her a basket. 'You could just as well have waited and come with us. You didn't get here much more quickly, I see.'

'Perhaps she wanted to dawdle,' chided one of the women. 'Whatever the reason, it's put roses in her cheeks.'

'Florentine was born with roses in her cheeks, alas. I sometimes wonder if it isn't a curse to be so fair,' said her mother with a shake of her head. She was a plump, florid-faced woman, who bore no resemblance whatsoever to her beautiful daughter. She had also given birth to six sons, of whom only two had survived.

'Better once fair, than never fair,' commented a toothless laundress who had joined the festivities.

A woodsman who had heard the comment about Florentine's beauty began to improvise a bawdy song about cupid's bow and arrow, which made everyone laugh. Aware that she was blushing with shame and embarrassment, Florentine saw Mother Clothilde looking thoughtfully at her as she righted her coarse brown habit and wimple after the rough ride. Florentine helped her from the cart, then genuflected reverently. Happiness, as profound as if it were Florentine's own, shone from the nun's face.

'You have my blessing, child,' she said. 'How I rejoiced when I heard that you will stand in the church next week and make your promise to Luc before God. Your mother and father asked me to join the feast.'

'I'm honoured that you came, Reverend Mother.' The girl cast her eyes down under the venerable gaze of the abbess, whom she had always revered as the wisest and holiest of women.

'This marriage of yours was indeed good news to me after all the sadness of the summer, what with tidings of plagues and calamities all round us, all well as Seigneur Montferrand's grave illness. I was heartened more than I can say to know that you and Luc had decided to pledge yourselves at last.'

'We have been intended ever since we were children, but only between ourselves. If it hadn't been for the help of the seigneur . . .' She searched shyly for the words to express her gratitude, realizing now that the nun must have had something to do with

267

his sudden and unexpected generosity in providing her with a dowry.

'The seigneur is a good man; there was never a better one. Even in sickness, he remembers others.' Love shone in her eyes as she said it, making her look young for a moment. 'But, come, we must do our part to help prepare the table,' she chided to hide the tide of sentiment that filled her at the sight of the angelic Florentine framed in a halo of light streaming through the foliage.

'I don't know where Luc could be,' said Florentine, looking round.

'He'll be along soon. Don't worry. He probably went to wash his hands and face to please his future bride.'

Including the woodcutters, more than twenty people had now gathered for the party. Père Xavier arrived with Florentine's father, who was red-faced and sweating after trudging up the hill with what seemed enough bread for an army. While the women set out hunks of cheese and cold roasted meat and fowl, the hungry men were lining up behind the cart for jars of wine being dispensed from a barrel. They had been in the forest since daybreak with nothing to sustain them except water and dry bread, and now they were full of good humour, inspired by a morning's hard work completed early, combined with the prospect of eating and drinking their fill.

Florentine helped the other women set out the picnic, sparing a thought for the old seigneur of Brissac, to whom they owed the bounty of the day. Her mother had told her that, as he lay dying, he had expressed a wish that her marriage to Luc be celebrated by Père Xavier before Assumption. As well as the dowry, he had provided the food and drink for the betrothal party. Florentine had accepted the miracle of his largesse, supposing that the prospect of death had mellowed the old warrior and caused him to be charitable to his forester.

When the roast meats and fowl had been divided in heaps down the table, when the bread had been cut and laid alongside, the abbess whispered to Florentine that she should let her hair down. Free-flowing tresses were the mark of a maiden, and Florentine took off her kerchief realizing that soon she would forfeit this simple right.

268

'There, now you look like a bride,' said the abbess, arranging the girl's hair about her shoulders. 'Such hair, such rich lovely hair with all the gold of summer in it.'

Florentine imagined the nun's cropped head beneath her wimple and noticed there was a faraway look in her eyes that suggested the old woman had not entirely forgotten her own departed youth.

Mother Clothilde patted her hand and said, 'Before you go, I have something for you.' Turning her back to the table she slipped a leather purse of coins into Florentine's hand. 'Put it somewhere safe, child. And a word of advice: don't tell your husband about it. Keep this as your own in case you should ever need it. Tell no one I gave it to you and don't ask where it came from.'

'Thank you, Reverend Mother,' Florentine murmured, as astonished as she was pleased.

Then, fearing she had somehow revealed her true motive, Mother Clothilde whispered, 'It came to me in a dream that I should give a bride a purse. Since providence inspires all our dreams, I have obeyed.'

Florentine had always set store by dreams, but she suspected that the old woman, like the old seigneur, was inspired by the need to perform whatever charity she could now her life was near its end. For a fleeting moment she thought perhaps life was not as long as it seemed.

'I wish I could give myself to God like you,' Florentine whispered.

Mother Clothilde shook her head. 'No, that's not for you. Your destiny lies elsewhere. Luc is a fine boy, and he'll cherish you. Wife and mother, that's what God made you for.'

Mother Clothilde clasped Florentine's tender young hand in her rough old one, remembering her on the day she was born in secret, in a shepherd's hut outside Roquelaire. No one, not even the baker's wife, to whom Mother Clothilde had given her, knew who her real parents were. Florentine was as pure, as wholesome as any mother could wish for, proving that Clothilde's ceaseless prayers to St Anne had not been in vain. Now, watching Florentine tuck the purse into her sash, the old nun felt sad at what the future held in store for her child. The transience and frailty of mortal existence seemed to Mother Clothilde a terrible secret that was kept from the young, and she was heavy with the knowledge that Florentine's innocence would soon be marked by the loss of virginity and the birth of her first child. For a moment she wished her daughter had taken the veil, which might have protected her from the pain of child-bearing.

She led Florentine to the table, where the guests were impatiently waiting to sit down. The forester gestured to the head of the table, reserved for the bride. Scanning the clearing with a vexed look on his face, he said. 'Where is that son of mine? Is he not here yet?'

'Maybe he's changed his mind and bolted,' suggested one of the woodcutters, making everyone laugh.

'Luc has surely gone to make himself presentable,' retorted Luc's mother. 'Which is more than I can say for the lot of you,' she added, causing more laughter.

A man reached for a roasted fowl, then hastily put it back as Père Xavier prepared to give the benediction.

Sitting down at last, everyone fell on the food with gusto while jugs of the potent red wine of Brissac made their way up and down the table.

Someone crashing through the undergrowth caused everyone to turn their heads. Luc ran into the clearing, his axe over his shoulder and a sheepish grin on his face, and a cheer went up around the table.

Tall and clean-shaven, his coppery hair cropped close around his face in the fashion that the Crusaders were said to have copied from the Romans, Luc acknowledged their welcome. The rough, bearded men with soiled clothes and matted hair, who were his comrades, forgot their food and wine for a moment as they gaped enviously at the strong, handsome youth who was privileged to marry the beautiful Florentine.

As Luc made his way towards the head of the table his comrades slapped his back and shouted coarse remarks about the horrors of wedlock being too much for him. Like his father, Luc was a free man, and as the son of an overseer of the domaines of an important

270

noble, he had a stature greater than their own. Florentine drew herself up proudly at the knowledge that she was to be his bride. The dream that had been born at a village fair several years ago was becoming a reality.

Luc's face was full of adoration as he approached his bride and held her hand aloft, a triumphant gesture that evoked shouts of approval. His father wiped his mouth and stood to make a short speech of welcome and announce the betrothal in a few gruff words, met by more cheers.

'Where have you been all this time?' Florentine whispered.

'I went to gather this posy for you, but wandered so far that I had to run all the way back.' He reached into his tunic and brought out a crushed bouquet, which he pressed into her hand.

'It's lovely,' she murmured, pressing it to her nose. She knew the name and use of each flower by heart: violets for fertility, vervain for purity, tansy for immortality, angelica to ward off evil. As she tucked the nosegay into her bodice the impish smile of the vagabond sprang into her mind for no reason, diluting her joy. The stranger had slyly insinuated himself into her thoughts, as if he meant to cloud her happiness. She was looking at Luc, but it was the vagabond she saw.

'I hope the flowers please you,' whispered Luc.

'Yes, I like them.' She gave a little laugh and put the man who called himself the Cat out of her mind. 'Where did you find them so late in the season?' She was as touched by his gesture as if he had brought her a jewel.

Luc took a long draught from the jar of wine in front of him. 'Wait until you hear. I went all the way to the pond on the other side of the forest, where I knew I could find you a posy. What I saw excited me so much that I couldn't tear myself away and I stayed much too long.'

'Tell me, what did you see?' she asked, sensing some mystery.

'I saw a knight in purple on horseback and his lady, whom I took to be Roxonde de Montferrand. I watched their falcon killed by a heron. It fell to the ground like a handkerchief. I've never seen anything like it.'

'An omen,' she gasped.

271

'Perhaps,' shrugged Luc. 'But it has nothing to do with us.' His belief in portents was not as strong as hers.

Florentine was troubled, believing that anything that affected the fortunes of Brissac, where Luc hoped to follow in his father's footsteps as forester, touched their own lives.

There was no time to hear more. Now that they had begun to eat and drink, the men were becoming more lively. Those who could, sang or recited poems. Although none of them could read or write, or had even seen a book, except a Bible in church, they had a fund of stories, poems and riddles, which they repeated on every occasion. One pulled a pipe from his pocket and began to play, which prompted a few of the guests who were feeling the effects of the wine to leap up and dance round in a circle. To see the stout laundress cavorting about until she lost her kerchief and apron made Florentine and Luc laugh until they cried. The most glorious moment of the afternoon was when a brawny young woodcutter with red hair and legs as thick and strong as beech trees was delegated to come forward with two chaplets woven of ivy, which the men had made for the engaged couple. Placing them on their heads, he declared Luc and Florentine king and queen of the forest for the day, and made a wish that their hearts would always dwell there, where they had been betrothed.

The sun reached its zenith and the piper played a lively jig, trying to rouse his audience, but they were either picking over the carcasses of the fowl, talking or snoring with their heads on the table. In a self-important voice Luc's father was relating the story of how he came into the service of the old seigneur, embellishing it with details of his master's exploits in Edward's campaigns against France. Luc listened respectfully, though Florentine supposed he had heard it hundreds of times. Only Père Xavier looked unusually grave, and seemed to be only half listening to the abbess explaining how to prune fruit trees against a sunny wall. Florentine, basking in contentment, began to dream of how life would be when she and Luc were married. She supposed the new chatelaine of Brissac would keep all the old retainers and thus provide them with lodging, that Luc would pass his days overseeing the forests with his father, and that she would keep the hearth

272

fires burning to warm them and their children. The terror of war, the times of drought and famine that had indelibly marked her childhood, the fears of death and hell that disturbed her thoughts so often, receded into the distance. Even the strange and frightening rumours of the deadly pestilence raging to the east seemed far away from the sylvan glade where she and Luc ruled the day as king and queen.

'Greetings, good people, and salutations. The Cat is here at your disposition.'

The vagabond Florentine had seen at the stream was suddenly standing only a few feet away. He had donned a bright red cap sewn with bells and carried a stringed instrument and bow, suggesting that he was not a vagabond after all, but a minstrel. He glanced in her direction, but gave no sign that he recognized her.

'A *jongleur*! Well, I'll be!' exclaimed the forester, rising from the table.

'No, not a common *jongleur*, good sir. Better than that: a master musician and raconteur.'

'Where have you sprung from, then?' Crossing his powerful arms across his chest, he regarded the interloper.

'Tidings of this happy gatherings have spread far and wide sir, and I ventured near, expecting to hear the wood ringing with music, but I see you have none.'

'Unless you can call that music,' said the forester with a chuckle, nodding at the piper, which caused titters of amusement.

'Then let me have the honour of favouring you with my songs, songs that have made kings rejoice and queens weep. And if that should fail to amuse you, I have a store of fables collected on my travels to the four corners of the earth, all of them astounding and true. If this should not satisfy you, then I'll not ask for as much as a chicken bone.'

The man's precious manner of speech, a type not often heard in Roquelaire, caused the rough woodcutters to howl with derisive laughter.

The forester peered at the minstrel suspiciously. 'You look like a rogue to me, but play if you will. It's been many a long year since I've heard anyone play the viele.' He nodded at the stringed instrument made of highly polished nutwood.

'There are few of us left, sir, who possess the skill to coax forth the unique sound of this instrument, which has been compared to the singing of angels. I was told by the old man who gave it to me that he had bought it himself from a dotard who had reached four score years and had played for Queen Eleanor in England.'

There were gasps of amazement round the table but no one bothered to reflect if such a boast were possible.

The Cat paused dramatically until he had his audience's attention, then lifted his instrument to his chest and plucked the strings to satisfy himself of the tone. The melodious notes produced when he drew the bow across the strings caused a murmur of delight. The minstrel seemed to lose himself in a slow, resounding melody that touched the hearts of every man and woman present.

'This fellow is exceptional,' whispered the forester.

Florentine didn't hear. She was spellbound by the music, which seemed to entwine itself round her very soul. When the last notes of the song had died away, she came out of a trance to find herself gazing into the compelling eyes of the minstrel, eyes that suggested worlds she had never dreamed of. There was a stunned silence, then raucous shouting and applause from the audience, who begged for more. The Cat bowed graciously and obliged them by singing song after song, songs of love to please the ladies, and songs of prowess in war for the men. He ended his performance with the illicit love between a chatelaine and a knight, playing all the parts himself in voices that were remarkably convincing. The twists of the plot, leading to a tragic and violent ending, held the audience in the grip of suspense. When he had finished, the Cat gave a dignified nod, as if to say he was perfectly aware of the spell his performance had cast.

The forester approached him with a satisfied smile. 'Now you shall eat and drink, minstrel. You have entertained us royally.' To show his magnanimity, the forester pressed coins into his hand, which the musician quickly pocketed before the other man could change his mind.

The minstrel sat at the opposite end of the table from Florentine, where the villagers plied him with food, drink and questions. Though he ignored her studiously, Florentine felt acutely aware of

274

his presence, as if the party had disappeared and they were alone in the clearing. A little pulse had started to beat inside her that made her restless. A distant horizon beckoned, spiriting her away from the present and from Luc, whose frank, happy face and boyish laughter she found insupportable all of a sudden. When Florentine's head was turned, the minstrel vanished as mysteriously as he had come, just when the party was breaking up and the men went back to load the wood they had cut on to the cart. She couldn't believe he had gone without a word, and stood up to look round for him. He had vanished. She became aware that Luc was smiling at her, his face flushed with wine and happiness.

'I must go and help the others just for a little while or they will never cease in their jesting. Will you wait for me here?' he asked.

'No, my father expects me at home to help prepare the loaves for tomorrow.'

She could see Luc was disappointed, and when he had gone away with the other men, she was oppressed by the lie that had slipped so easily from her lips. She didn't have to help at home – no one expected it on this day – but she was desperate to be alone to think, not about Luc, but about the minstrel and his songs.

Soon she was trooping up the hill with the rest of the party after the wood-laden cart. It was mid-afternoon now. The women were carrying the nearly empty baskets, chatting and laughing as they went. The air was still and hot, and the sound of cicadas was deafening.

On the road they met a band of dust-caked pilgrims, most of them old and exhausted from their journey. Greeting them, the villagers, who were used to pilgrims, took little notice of their relentless piety, their predictable tales of the pilgrim's road or their diseased, tortured bodies, which spoke of the sacrifice they had made to God. Florentine thought their harrowed faces beneath their broad hats were pitiful as they trudged towards the village, which would provide a haven for the night. She preferred to imagine what it would be like to roam the world at the minstrel's side.

A little way down the road, a crippled old man laid his wreath of box at the foot of the Pilgrim's Stone and renewed his vow. Then, to everyone's surprise, he tore off his cloak and began to

275

scourge his arms and legs with a leather whip until be drew blood. The villagers watched him in perplexed silence. His scrawny ribcage heaving with the effort, and tears streaming down his cheek, the old pilgrim urged them all to do likewise in order to purify themselves before God before it was too late. When the man prostrated himself on the road and pressed his face in the dust, Florentine thought he was dead, and all round her she heard murmurings about the terrible pestilence that was creeping east, which caused people to lose their heads. She heard someone say the pilgrim had gone mad from heat and hunger, but the mention of the pestilence had made everyone uneasy. In the confusion she slipped out of sight and waited for everyone to be gone.

The sight of buzzards circling in the hot, blue sky had reminded Florentine of Luc's tale about the death of the falcon. She darted across a field between the haystacks, as the voices of the villagers disappeared down the road. As she approached the dark line of trees, she wondered if she dared to go alone to the pond where Luc had said the falcon had met its death that morning. The cool, shadowy forest exhaled mystery. Florentine's footsteps through the undergrowth were swallowed up by a thick silence, broken only by an occasional bird. She flinched when a hare broke cover and scampered across the carpet of dead leaves and into the shadows. Although she knew her way as far as the pond, the forest was so vast that she had no idea where it ended, or even in what country. She had been weaned on tales of spirits and demons who preyed on humans in the woods, and touching the wreath of ivy she still wore on her head, Florentine no longer felt like the queen of the forest but a mortal who needed to summon all her courage to go on.

She was relieved to come to a vast clearing, a hunting field forbidden to trespassers, from which the towers of Brissac were visible beyond a bank of trees. Below the slope she recognized the pond, marked by cat's-tails. She hurried towards it, searching the ground for some sign of the battle between the heron and the falcon, but saw only the trail of horses that had passed that way.

At the bottom of the slope she stopped and looked towards the stockade of cat's-tails that encircled the water. A breeze whispered

276

like tiny voices, reminding her that ponds were often inhabited by the souls of dead children, who transformed themselves into twinkling lights at night. Now, she thought, they must be sleeping. A frog leaping into the water startled her as she began to search round the pond for some sign of the dead bird of prey. At last she found what she was looking for. Dangling from a cat's-tail she spied a bloody falcon's feather, which she snatched and pressed to her cheek before tucking it away between her breasts.

Dropping in the grass at the water's edge, she watched the brilliant blue dragonflies with irridescent wings skim the water. That day was perhaps the most memorable of her life, and yet her heart was heavy. She lay back in the grass and let hot tears course down her cheeks, tears caused by a terrible aching in her heart that she could not explain. The minstrel's song filling her head, she closed her eyes and fell into a doze.

Florentine awakened to the sound of music, recognizing it at once as the instrument played by the minstrel. Turning her head cautiously in the grass, she was amazed to see him through a haze of green. He was sitting on a log, singing softly to himself, as if he were unaware of her presence. His music seemed to fill an emptiness inside her, weaving a spell that took away all her will and reason.

'And that is the story of two lovers who lived happily ever after in a kingdom by the sea.' Felix drew out the last quivering note on his instrument, then looked over at her.

'Did you follow me here?' This time there was no indignation in her voice.

'No, it was you who followed me, my beauty. I came in search of water nymphs, like the one I saw this morning. They teach men beautiful songs, songs to enchant hearts and enslave a beloved.' He threw her a smile that made her belly contract with the strange longing she had felt that morning in the stream.

Florentine got up abruptly and dusted herself off while trying to exhibit a presence of mind she did not feel.

'If the forester catches you here, he'll be angry,' she said. 'You may even be put in the dungeon of the château, for he regards anyone he finds here as a poacher.'

277

'And what about you? Will you be imprisoned too?' he asked mockingly.

'No, because . . .' she broke off, not wanting to speak Luc's name in his presence. Snatching the wreath of ivy that had slipped from her head, Florentine took a few steps backward. Instinct told her that if she stayed another moment in this spot, she would be enchanted by the minstrel and nothing and no one could ever rescue her. The minstrel made no move to approach her, yet he held her fast, as if he had thrown a rope over her head. When she commanded her limbs to move, Florentine discovered she was incapable of leaving. She began to shake as she realized that something powerful bound her to the Cat.

'Come hither,' he said. She did as he commanded, sinking to her knees in front of the log where he sat, her breast heaving violently, as if a wild bird were caged inside her. She was too frightened to look at him.

The Cat sank down beside her in the grass, took her hands delicately in his and began to kiss them. His soft lips seemed to scorch her palms, making it seem that the devil himself had hold of her. The violent need his nearness aroused sapped her of strength, like a draught of wine taken too quickly. She didn't resist when he untied her kerchief and eased her back on the grass, then began to undo her bodice, freeing her breasts. Discovering the blood-soaked feather nestled between them, he placed her precious talisman in his palm and blew it away before she could protest. She saw a flash of red at the corner of her eye as the minstrel's mouth came down on hers. The sound of him unbuckling his belt jarred her for a moment, but when he slipped his hand beneath her skirt, she drew her thighs together tightly and held it there, not wanting him to stop. She heard herself whisper to the Cat to take her in a voice that did not sound like her own. In the soft bower Florentine lost her maidenhood to the minstrel, surrendering to a burst of sweet pain that made her cry out.

The Cat caressed the sigh from her lips and cradled her in his arms. He did not spend his passion entirely, but gave her only a faint taste of real rapture. All the while he primed her with kisses on

278

her lips and eyes, and whispered sweet words of love she had never heard before. Then, feeling her excitement rekindle, he drew away, knowing from experience that with virgins the fruit is best when ripened without hurry, and that nothing breeds regret so much as satiety or excess. He looked again at her ravishing nakedness sprawled against the grass and his own desire quickened at the prospect of the rich rewards he would reap for his heroic self-denial. He fancied the prospect of whiling away what was left of the summer with the ravishing baker's daughter acting the part of the exquisite instrument to his ardent bow.

When the Cat crossed the stubbled field, the long shadows made by the haystacks told him it was after four o'clock. He walked jauntily along, his viele strung over his shoulder. Never had it brought him a sweeter harvest than the maidenhead he had conquered that afternoon. He had extracted a promise from Florentine that she would meet him in the same place as soon as she could break free tomorrow. When they parted, her cheeks were flushed with ardour and her eyes filled with the adoration of the conquered maiden who could see and hear nothing but her beloved. Whistling cheerfully, the Cat rounded a haystack and was taken by surprise to find a woman slumped there disconsolately.

'Goodday, fair lady,' he said, courteously, doffing his cap.

She looked up at him piteously. She was sprawled at the base of the haystack, rubbing her bare ankle, a bag of plants by her side.

'Perhaps you can help me get back to the village, sir. I twisted my ankle while harvesting some herbs. I've managed to hobble this far and was just thinking I'd have to wait until the threshers returned to gather the haystacks before I would be saved. My name is Susan Wyndgate.'

'My homages, dear lady. Allow me to present myself. I am known as the Cat.' He bowed low. Raising his eyes, he got a good look at her. She was English and long past her prime, but she was handsome and well-built, and with the fair hair he admired peeking from beneath her kerchief. She was looking up at him as coquettishily as a young girl.

'I'll gladly help if I can. What's the trouble?' As he bent to examine her ankle he got a good look at her plump white legs, which he found pleasing even though they were many years older than Florentine's perfect limbs. His mind began to turn on the possibilities of the situation; though he was prepared to play the waiting game in pursuit of a virgin, he knew better in the case of a matron such as the one before him.

'You're a minstrel, are you?' she asked with an appraising glance, liking what she saw.

'Yes, I am indeed, my lady.'

He began to massage her ankle, saying he was a barber as well as a musician and skilled in such matters, and she didn't push his hand away. Then he rubbed the soles of her aching feet, which was the the best way he knew to kindle fires in such women.

'Does it feel any better?'

'I think it does.' She blushed, looking up at the slim-hipped minstrel, his shapely legs sheathed in yellow and purple tights and his leather tunic so short it barely covered his manhood. She judged he was a good ten years younger than she. He looked down on her with kindness and concern, which she interpreted as admiration, a look she hadn't seen in a man's face for a long time. Smoothing her hair from her forehead, she smiled self-consciously.

'I suppose you wonder what this is,' she gestured to her pack. 'I've been collecting plants to make paints and dyes. I have a small trade in psalters in the village and I sell them to pilgrims.'

'A craftswoman. Now that *is* something I truly admire. Are you convent-trained?'

Susan was pleasantly taken by the minstrel's cultivated conversation, and found his worldliness a refreshing contrast to untutored pilgrims and villagers. In her youth she had been privileged to glimpse the sophistication of the king's court, and she had always hankered after refinement. The intriguing minstrel had travelled far and wide and had a smattering of knowledge on many subjects, including astrology, alchemy and literature, and they became deeply engrossed in conversation. Soon they were laughing like two old friends and he spread out the food he had tucked in his satchel at the betrothal party. He had Susan in fits of giggles as he regaled her with ribald stories he had not dared tell that afternoon in front of the priest and the abbess.

280

'And I thought I had travelled! You seem to know the world,' she sighed.

'Yes, I've been to Flanders, Italy, and Spain, but I prefer England to all other countries,' he lied glibly. He hated the climate and the uncouth ways of the English, who were barbarians compared to the French. Even those of noble status often had no table manners, could seldom read or write, wore coarse woollens instead of silk, and had little or no appreciation of poetry or music.

'You've made me long for home,' said Susan. Her round face flushed with pleasure, she had grown more attractive to the minstrel by the minute. The desire he had so manfully restrained an hour before was now coursing through him violently. He watched the voluptuously plump Englishwoman sigh contentedly as she lay back against the haystack and picked her teeth.

They finished their meal with a draught of very strong wine that the Cat kept in a flask for liniment or gargling. The shadows were lengthening, but Susan, replete and slightly drunk, had lost all track of the time and was no longer concerned with getting back to the hostel. The impromptu repast with the handsome, attentive minstrel had unlocked a gaiety that she thought had passed from her life with her first flush of youth. The last year seemed one long litany of prayer and work, without a single pleasurable event to enliven it until now.

Watching her, the Cat played his instrument and sang of love until tears ran down Susan's face and she collapsed with a quivering sigh, her eyes full of what he knew was concupiscence.

'You have a voice of angelic sweetness,' she murmured. But piety was not what sprang to both their minds as he laid down his bow and asked if he shouldn't see to her ankle once more.

'I can't help noticing that your flesh is as white as the fabled city of Jerusalem. Would that I could knock at its gate,' he whispered, grasping her foot in his hand. The softness in her eyes evoked by his flattery told him if he slipped his hand further, he would meet no resistance.

Susan couldn't remember afterwards how it happened, but in an instant she and the minstrel were linked passionately together in

281

the haystack. Her squeals of enjoyment rang out across the field, disturbing the deep evening silence that had settled on the land. The Cat and Susan were so engrossed in their pleasure that they didn't see a shepherd pass at a distance with a flock of sheep.

'Father, what's that over there?' asked the small boy at his side. Tugging at his father's smock, the boy pointed over the sheep's backs to a haystack that seemed to be moving.

The shepherd grinned when he saw the tangle of arms, legs and buttocks protruding from the hay. 'That, my son,' he remarked, 'is what is known as the beast with two backs.'

Mother Clothilde could hear the chapel bell. She was torn by the call to prayer and her desire to keep her vigil by the bed where Guirard de Montferrand lay at the portals of death. A glimpse of his ashen face in the dim light spoke of untold suffering, which she could not let him bear alone. Deciding to postpone her departure, she felt sure that God would not wish otherwise.

A maidservant came through the door with a bundle of fresh herbs, which she began to toss on the fire, causing a puff of acrid smoke to billow from the vast chimney into the room.

'Leave it be,' commanded the nun.

'But the barber said . . .'

'Never mind what the barber said,' Clothilde replied firmly. 'Remove them at once.'

The girl hastily took the offending herbs from the fire and departed. Mother Clothilde pressed her hands to her temples and opened the window of the tower room to admit the balmy evening air to chase the smoke away. Invoking the aid of charlatans such as barbers and healers seemed a blasphemous interference with God's will, but she had assented in hopes it would do some good. None of their concoctions had improved Guirard's condition, which she knew in her heart was incurable.

A few swifts were still circling in the twilight that had overtaken the valley in the distance, giving it a fairyland remoteness. The flares and tapers being lit in distant Roquelaire reminded Mother Clothilde of the glimmer of fireflies she had seen, years ago, the summer she had fallen in love with Guirard de Montferrand.

Seeing him now, so small and insignificant against the velvet counterpane, Mother Clothilde found herself remembering the words of a sad old idyll that had once made her dream, words that seemed to be waiting in her heart until this moment. She whispered them, knowing that he couldn't hear her.

'"Neither herb nor root nor potion can ever cure the wound within your flesh: For that there is no healing. The only balm to close that sore must be brought by a woman who for her love will suffer such pain and sorrow as no woman in the world has endured before. And you, knight, you shall do and suffer great things for her that not a lover beneath the sun, or lovers who are dead, or lovers who yet shall be born, but shall marvel at the tale . . ."' Her throat closed with tears. She tensed as she saw Guirard stir, as if aroused by the potent memory they shared: a knight, wounded and widowed, broken, and a young novice whose love had brought him back to life in the very bed in which he now lay dying.

Mother Clothilde took his hand in hers, not shrinking from his oozing sores. To her amazement, he opened his eyes for the first time in days and seemed to recognize her. She dipped a cloth in water and dabbed it to his parched, peeling lips.

'Clothilde −' came his quavering voice. The pain she knew it cost him to speak became her own.

'I'm here, Guirard. I shan't leave you.'

'Do you promise?'

'Fear not, Guirard. I'll stay with you − always.'

His glazed eyes travelled around the room, as if he were familiarizing himself afresh after a long absence. The sight of swifts circling the violet sky in the distance seemed to revive him as neither prayer nor the healing arts had done. His eyes glowed and he muttered something Clothilde couldn't understand as he struggled to sit up. Helping him, she didn't dare to hope that his sudden lucidity meant that her prayers had evoked a miracle. His stubborn refusal to succumb to death was proof not only of his endurance, but also of his reluctance to be called to God right away no matter what it cost him in suffering. Now the closing of day had acted as a tonic, giving him a precious glimpse of the world he thought he would never see again.

Looking up at her, his lips moved slowly. 'Has the deed been done, then?'

'Yes, she was betrothed today. I returned from the party in the wood not long ago. It was a glad occasion. Florentine sends her thanks for all you've done.' An old fear was banished as she spoke, a mother's concern for her child's future, which was now secure.

She was almost certain that he had guessed the secret she had deemed it wise to keep for all these years. The look that passed between them then was the only acknowledgement she would ever have that he knew her unholy scheming to obtain a dowry for a young village girl, who supposedly meant nothing to her, hid an ulterior motive. They would never speak of it, just as they had never spoken of the passionate night they had spent as one flesh. Her love for Guirard, doomed by the difference in their stations in life, was the sole prize of Mother Clothilde's youth that she still clung to. She had repented of the sin they committed, and she had suffered and done her penance, but sweetness had remained in her cup of anguish. Had she been free to follow her heart, and Guirard his, Clothilde would never have remained in the convent to take her vow, never have given her daughter to the care of the baker and his wife. Instead, they had travelled through life like two pilgrims on the same road, always keeping each other in sight but never again side by side. Now that Guirard's days were numbered, like the last stitches on a tapestry, Mother Clothilde's one wish was to see her time out in the convent, but it was rumoured that Roxonde de Montferrand had her own body of sisters whom she intended to install in the quarters, and there would be no room for the cluster of Benedictines who had lived there for nearly two decades under Guirard's protection. Clothilde knew that nothing short of a royal order could alter the law of succession, but while there was breath in the old man's body, the nun resolved to keep any suggestion of intrigue from him.

Guirard had slipped back into a doze, his sudden awareness fading as quickly as it had come. His face hardened into a mask, his mouth a grim line and his eyes, dark hollows. But as she looked down at him, Mother Clothilde saw only the young, virile warrior whose head once lay beside hers on the pillows of the velvet-hung bed. When, an hour later, vespers rang, she rose and smoothed his forehead, wondering if this would be their final parting.

# Chapter 14

Agnès pushed the plate of pâté towards Étienne, who was seated next to her in the Gachpour dining-room, a small room off the bakery nearly filled by a table and sideboard. The faces around the table were cast in shadow by the half-closed shutters.

'You must have the last slice, Étienne. It's only right,' Beatrice insisted. Her eyes glowed with undisguised pleasure at the sight of him sitting next to Pascale, whose fairness was in such striking contrast to his dark good looks.

Étienne shook his head. 'Really, I couldn't eat another bite.'

'Not for me, either,' said Pascale when Agnès looked at her. 'But it was really excellent.'

'You'd better do what she says, Étienne,' said Bernard. 'You won't get much *foie gras* when you're back in Germany.' He extended a brawny forearm and filled Étienne's glass with wine. Bald, broad-faced and stockily built, Bernard had the baker's pallor from rising in the middle of the night to attend to his ovens.

'Well, if you're really sure no one else wants any more, then I'll have it,' said Étienne, spearing the last slice of pâté with his fork. 'It's a real treat.'

'It's how Aunt Gertrude used to make it,' said Pascale. 'There's some secret that Agnès won't tell anyone.'

Agnès laughed. 'It's no secret. You just have to put in lots of freshly ground black pepper.'

Half-listening to the conversation around the table, Agnès's eyes kept straying to Pascale. In the last few days, whenever she had looked at her daughter, she found herself searching for a resemblance to Armand, a comparison she had unconsciously resisted for the last twenty years.

Agnès heard Étienne answer Bernard's questions about army

286

life, observing how the months in the army had changed him. The moment he had entered the room she had been impressed by how lean, sun-tanned and handsome he looked. His thick dark hair, shorn in regulation army style, made him seem years older than when he had left the village. If Pascale had noticed the change in him, she showed no sign. She was unusually quiet, which Agnès attributed to an inevitable awkwardness after the months of separation. When Étienne spoke in the authoritative, confident voice of a young man who had seen the world beyond the confines of Roquelaire, Pascale seemed to listen thoughtfully, as if weighing up everything he said. There was no trace of the starry-eyed adoration on her face that Agnès remembered so well on the day they had gathered around the table with Étienne's family to celebrate their engagement.

'It's a shame that you can't stay a bit longer – until after the fête,' Bernard was saying.

'I was incredibly lucky to get even these few days,' Étienne replied with a smile, reaching for another piece of bread.

'Never mind. Your time will be up before you know it,' said Beatrice with a look of satisfaction on her face that said how much she approved of her future son-in-law.

Bernard was about to pour the last of the wine into Pascale's glass, but she shook her head.

'No, thank you, Papa. I don't want any more.'

'What? Lost your taste for Sauternes?'

'It's too hot, Papa,' she said with a shake of her head. She gave him a grateful smile. The heat, the wine and the strong emotions of the day before had left her exhausted.

Emptying the rest of the wine into his own glass, Bernard began to reminisce about his army days in Indo-China. Pascale's eyes glazed over as her father launched into a story she had heard many times. Making patterns on the tablecloth with her knife, she seemed unaware that Étienne was constantly gazing at her.

As Agnès sliced another baguette she glanced at Pascale again, thinking how beautiful she looked with her pale blonde hair swept away from her face. The simple white blouse she was wearing gave her a freshness, an innocence that made her look much younger than her years. She was listening to the conversation and toying with the small diamond and sapphire engagement ring Étienne had given her at Christmas. Her distracted air made Agnès wonder what she was thinking.

'Thank you, *tatie*,' Pascale said, taking the bread. Their eyes met and Agnès saw an expression of helpless bewilderment in her daughter's face.

In the kitchen Agnès silently stirred the fried potatoes and plump mushrooms laced with garlic.

'Agnès? Did you hear what I said? Slip my apron over my head. I don't want to get anything on this dress. It's the first time I've worn it and it has to be dry-cleaned.'

'Excuse me,' Agnès apologized, quickly doing as her sister asked.

Beatrice glanced irritably at Agnès while she struggled to remove the huge roast beef from the oven. 'What's wrong with you, anyway? You seem to be in another world.'

'I was thinking of Pascale. She seems so quiet today.'

'I haven't noticed. She's probably overjoyed to see Étienne, that's all. Oh, she can be moody, as we all know. Hasn't Étienne filled out, though? He's even better looking than before. There's an awful lot to him. I always feel we don't appreciate him because he's so reserved; but I suppose that's what attracted Pascale. It's a good thing, too, with her temperament.'

'I hope they're sure about each other. The knot stays tied a very long time,' Agnès muttered.

'Sure? Why, of course they're sure. They've had years to decide. The young now don't behave the way we used to,' Beatrice remarked, repeating a favourite theory of hers as she put the beans in a bowl. 'They know friendship is more important than romance, an intelligent attitude if you ask me. Having your head in the clouds doesn't get you anywhere. That's why I like Étienne. He's so level-headed, so mature.'

Agnès didn't reply. Any words of wisdom from her on the subject of romance would seem odd to her sister.

Beatrice was humming a tune as she dressed the salad, and Agnès guessed that her sister was already planning what she would wear to the December wedding, as well as the menu for the reception.

Agnès bent down to bring the hot plates out of the oven. When

288

she straightened up, she was overcome by giddiness. The room rocked for a moment, then righted itself, but she caught herself from dropping the plates just in time. Since her trip to the château the previous afternoon she had been deeply fatigued. By the time she had returned to her cottage she was hot and exhausted, and she had lain on her bed in the semi-darkness for a long time, thinking of the past. Of Pascale. Of Armand. Of what might have been.

When dessert was served, Agnès noted that Pascale ate only a small piece of her favourite cake and didn't remark on the bottle of good champagne that Bernard poured into the flutes on a tray.

When everyone had a glass, Bernard said, 'Let's toast your reunion: Pascale and Étienne.'

After they had all taken a sip of wine, Étienne proposed, 'And now a toast to Agnès. Here's to her wonderful good fortune.' He raised his glass.

'Yes, here's to Aunt Agnès,' echoed Pascale, beaming happily for the first time that day. 'She deserves the good things of life more than anyone I know.'

Embarrassed, Agnès looked down, but said nothing. So far that afternoon the family had talked of rising bread prices, events in Eastern Europe and the Middle East among other things, but no one had mentioned the château. A conspiracy of silence had surrounded the issue since the first few euphoric days, when Beatrice and Bernard had bombarded her with advice until they realized that she was not about to be influenced, and that the more they talked, the more stubborn she became. As everyone's eyes went to Agnès, she sensed that all of them, including Pascale, were expecting her to make some kind of announcement.

Étienne filled the silence. 'My father asked me to tell you that if you needed any help or advice, he would be more than glad to give it. He says that your legacy could become a terrible burden, and he'd like to help in any way he can.'

'Please thank your father, but for the moment I don't think I need any advice.'

Beatrice gave a little cough and exchanged a look with Bernard as Étienne continued, blithely unaware of the hornets' nest he was stirring up.

'I'm sure Étienne would love to see the château while he's here,' interjected Beatrice. 'And I wouldn't mind going there again.'

'Any time you wish,' said Agnès. 'Pascale, you've been home for three days and you haven't found time to go near it, which surprised me a little. I thought you'd rush up there first thing.'

Pascale avoided her eyes by reaching for another piece of cake that she didn't really want. The lie she was forced to tell made her stomach contract. 'I've been so busy, *tatie*. I've been helping Annie with her baby every day.'

Étienne leaned back in his chair and said thoughtfully, 'It's not really my business, but do you know what you plan to do with the château? My father says that the inheritance taxes could be sixty per cent.'

Unperturbed, Agnès looked at the circle of attentive faces. 'I've been looking into all that. There's no hurry to decide anything at the moment.'

'Looking into what?' asked Bernard with a frown.

'I went to see the *notaire* again the other day.'

'At least you could have told us,' he grumbled.

Pascale came to her defence. 'She's right, you know. It's not the end of the fiscal year yet. She has plenty of time,' she blurted out. Seeing Agnès under attack, she instinctively came to her rescue.

Bernard gave a snort of disapproval. 'Plenty of time? You'll see how soon the taxes fall due. You might as well slice the château in two and give half to the state.'

Now that it was out in the open the air was full of tension. Old grievances had sprung up like weeds after rain. This sudden tide of fortune had stripped bare all the resentment and misunderstanding that had sprung up between three people who had lived a lie for more than twenty years. Emotions they had buried for what had seemed the best of reasons seemed palpably present at the table and clamoured for release. For the first time Agnès felt an unspoken resentment in her sister and brother-in-law that they had had to shoulder the burden of a child that wasn't theirs. The look on their faces made it clear that they expected to have a full say in how she managed her windfall.

Beatrice said in a tight little voice, 'We all expected you to have

290

made up your mind about the château by now. What are you waiting for?'

There was an unmistakable flash of animosity in her eyes that Agnès hadn't seen since childhood. Carefully choosing her words, she answered. 'I haven't had time to think this matter over fully yet. I'm aware Madame de Montjoi is very keen to turn the château into a hotel. But when I decide how I'm going to proceed, I'll let you all know.' There was an unpleasant silence, which she broke by saying, 'Would anyone like another slice of cake?'

'Not for me, thanks,' said Étienne with a shake of his head. 'Monsieur Gachpour, I still say you make the best gâteaux I've ever tasted. Much better than anything I've had in Germany.' He shifted uneasily, realizing that he had opened up a delicate subject.

Bernard wasn't listening. His face flushed with wine, he was glaring at Agnès.

'I'm surprised at your attitude, you know. We've all been patient with you, letting you take your time. But the matter of the château concerns us all.'

Agnès met his eyes, aware as never before of the debt she owed her brother-in-law. But for the first time she realized that what she had always suspected was true – that he had been an indifferent surrogate father to Pascale, preferring his own sons, just as her sister had been a dutiful but unloving replacement for herself. She was determined never to make another decision in haste again.

'Yes, Bernard, it concerns you all, but the decision is mine.'

'If that's how you feel, fine. Then I might as well say it now we've brought up the subject. I don't like the fact that there's a Ribard behind this hotel project.'

'Ribard?' asked Étienne. 'I don't understand.'

'Let's not talk about it now,' said Beatrice with a sigh as she rose to fetch the coffee. 'We're celebrating Étienne's home-coming. This is a family matter we can discuss later. Let's talk about the wedding, which is much more to the point. We haven't even set a date yet. We ought to book the church and a place for the reception if you want to be married around Christmas, otherwise it will be too late.'

'Not now, Maman,' said Pascale sharply.

'Not now? But when? Étienne's going back in a few days.'

'We want to go for a walk first. Can we be excused after coffee?'

Bernard continued bitterly, 'Paul Ribard was a German collaborator during the war, Étienne. There aren't any Ribards left. They all moved away. The farm they used to own is in ruins on the other side of Brissac.'

'Oh yes, I remember now.'

Unable to bear the turn the conversation was taking, Agnès got up to help Beatrice with the coffee. When she came back to the table Bernard was saying, 'I'm not the only one who has not forgotten what they did. My father would be alive today if it weren't for them. Before he disappeared, Paul Ribard gave away the names of thirteen men who were helping the Resistance. They were hanged by the Germans in Blugnac. My father was one of them.'

Agnès avoided all their eyes. The Ribards had hardly ever been mentioned until now. They were either dead or dispersed for good; now one had returned to the village, while another was a haunting memory.

There was a painful silence, broken by Étienne. 'I can understand how you must feel.'

'This chef – the grandson – left here when he was young and now he's trying to push his way back in here in this hotel venture with Madame de Montjoi.'

Pascale, who had been only half listening, suddenly came to life. 'But, Papa, this Ribard has nothing to do with the war. He wasn't even born then.'

'He's a Ribard, and that's enough. There are people in this village who would take great exception if he were to come back. What business do you have defending him, anyway? You don't even know him.'

'Maybe I don't, but I think it's completely unfair to blame him for something that happened before he was born. Why can't people just forget the past? This is a new era, a new Europe.' Pascale's cheeks were flushed and her eyes were blazing. Talk of the château had rekindled her thoughts of Julian and their clandestine visit there. She had resisted thinking of him that afternoon, but now, looking at Étienne, a rebellion coursed through her.

292

Bernard looked at her in disgust. 'You're too young to understand. As for Madame de Montjoi, nobody has a very high opinion of her either, but that's another story.'

'And why not?' said Pascale, warming to the subject. 'Is it because she's beautiful, glamorous, rich? I think people like you are jealous, that's all.'

'Pascale!' said Beatrice sharply.

Bernard looked at her coldly. 'You're too young to be a judge of character.' Turning to Agnès, he continued. 'There are plenty of people who would buy the château. You don't have to sell it to the offspring of a *collabo*, Agnès. That doesn't mean, of course, that you ought to wait around. The sooner you put it on the market, the better.'

'No one ever proved anything about the Ribards, Bernard,' said Beatrice, handing him a cup brimming with coffee. 'More important, don't forget that buyers don't grow on trees. Montjoi money – even Ribard money – is as good as anyone's.'

'That's your opinion,' he muttered, scowling. 'For all we know he got his start trafficking in war booty. Where did this young Ribard get his money, anyway?'

'That's absurd,' scoffed Beatrice. 'His father died bankrupt and no one knows what became of the other boys. The one who has come back was just as poor as the rest when he went away.'

'Still, he left here with a knapsack, and now he's rich and the lover of the Montjoi woman.'

'What do you think about all this, Étienne?' asked Pascale. There was a challenge in her voice.

Étienne knitted his brow and shrugged. 'You mean about the Ribard business? I can't say I really have an opinion. I suppose if it's going to cause a problem, it would be better if they didn't make a hotel out of the château, with all respect, *tatie*,' he said to Agnès.

'But think of the employment. Think what it would do for the village,' Pascale insisted.

A stubborn look crossed Étienne's face. 'My father says too much development will only cause housing prices to jump up and bring in too many foreigners. He's against putting up a hotel like that here. He says it would be much better if it were a museum or a cultural centre, or even a private home.'

293

'I see – you have no opinion of your own. Only your father's.'

'Pascale, how dare you? Apologize to Étienne,' Beatrice protested vehemently.

All this time Agnès sat quietly, her eyes fastened on the table, impervious to the angry voices swirling around her, thinking of the afternoon before, when she had breached Paul Ribard's tomb. Only she knew the real truth, and that truth must remain her secret always. At that moment she found herself almost regretting Armand's legacy.

Pascale put down her napkin and stood up abruptly. A cauldron of emotion was boiling over inside her.

'I think it's wrong to blame a person for what their grandparents, or even their parents, did. I mean, people don't get any credit for their parents' achievements, so why should they be blamed for their faults? This man is really a stranger. What do we know about him?'

Agnès felt her heart leap violently. She wondered if somehow Pascale suspected the truth about her origins and went numb at the thought of what would happen if Pascale were to discover who her real parents were. She could imagine those blue eyes blazing with the same passion and outrage as now, demanding an answer.

'Please excuse me,' Pascale murmured. 'I'm going out for a walk.' Pushing back her chair, she walked from the room.

'Pascale, come back here,' Beatrice called after her in exasperation.

Étienne gave an embarrassed smile and got up from the table to follow her.

Bernard said, unperturbed, 'Take my advice, and let her go, Étienne. You know by now that Pascale is stubborn and headstrong. You've got a long life ahead of you, so you'd better learn to live with it.'

Étienne tried to laugh it off, but Agnès found herself willing him to go after Pascale and to overlook her impetuous outburst. He disappointed her by sitting down and accepting a cup of coffee from Beatrice.

'We shouldn't talk about these things over lunch,' Beatrice sighed. 'Politics and money, they always cause arguments. I'm sorry about this, Étienne.'

'I guess we have to get used to each other all over again. Don't worry. I won't let it upset me.'

'Good,' said Beatrice, pursing her lips. 'She's probably already regretting it.'

'I'll bet she's on her way to Annie's,' he said.

'Oh, Annie has plenty of problems of her own now she has a baby.'

After a moment Bernard returned to the subject of Alain Ribard, his voice full of condemnation. 'That young Ribard looks like a cocky swine, whatever anyone says. He came into the shop to buy something the other day, swaggering through the door, acting like a millionaire. When you think he left here with just the clothes on his back, and now he thinks he's going to start a luxury hotel. He deserves to be taught a lesson.'

'Well, maybe he just has the knack of cultivating the right people. That's one way of getting what you want out of life,' Beatrice said with a touch of envy.

Agnès was looking at Étienne, who was talking to Bernard as if nothing had happened. Such a lack of emotion baffled her. Finally, to her relief, he finished his coffee and stood up with a good-humoured grin.

'I think, if you don't mind, I'll go out and look for Pascale. Thank you very much for a wonderful lunch. Mother says she hopes you can all come by for an aperitif before I leave.'

When he had gone, Beatrice said, 'I'm so fond of Étienne. He's polite, so sensible. We didn't talk about the wedding, but I suppose there's plenty of time.' She started to gather the coffee cups as Étienne's motorbike could be heard driving off.

No one asked Agnès what she thought, and she got up from the table before Bernard could raise the subject of the château again.

Étienne rode into the empty square. The only sign of life was at the café, where people were gathered in the shade of the umbrellas. He cruised slowly by, but could see no sign of Pascale. A tall, good-looking man in his late twenties hailed him as he passed.

'Étienne, how goes it?'

'Hey, Laurent. How are you?'

'Fine. I thought you were in Germany.'

'I'm still stationed there, but I'm home on leave until Friday.'

'Drop by and see me.' Laurent nodded in the direction of a *brocante* shop in a narrow street off the square. His habitual brooding expression had changed to pleasure at the sight of Étienne.

'Sure, I'll do that,' replied Étienne, still searching the square for Pascale. 'How's business?'

'Not bad. But getting peasants to part with their heirlooms isn't easy. And I used to think my father was tight-fisted! Anyway, I'm surviving.'

'I'm glad to hear it. You seem to have found your calling. Still writing poetry?'

'Not much; no time.'

Laurent's eyes no longer burned with the conviction Étienne remembered when they had argued passionately over philosophy and politics late into the night, though he still radiated the same reckless romanticism.

'You haven't seen Pascale, have you?'

'Yes, she walked through the arch a little while ago.' He nodded in the direction she had gone. 'She seemed to be in a hurry. She didn't even stop to say hello.'

Étienne looked uncomfortable for a moment, not wanting to endure Laurent's amusement once he realized Pascale was angry with him.

'I guess I'd better be going,' he said impatiently, revving the engine of his bike.

'Problems with Pascale, right?'

Étienne shrugged and smiled.

'When's the wedding?'

'December.'

'Congratulations.' Laurent flashed him a crooked, disparaging smile that suggested he thought Étienne was a fool to tie himself down.

'I'll be seeing you,' Étienne said.

Étienne finally found Pascale walking up the hill towards the Château de Brissac. She didn't turn around until he was alongside of her.

'Want a lift?' he said lightly, hoping to provoke a smile.

She stopped, removed her sunglasses and looked at him sullenly. Her forehead was damp from the heat and her chest was heaving from the effort of climbing the hill. Without a word, she hopped on the back of the bike and put her arms around him. Saying nothing, he turned up the chalk road to the château and drove through the arch. When he stopped in the courtyard, she dismounted.

'I remember coming here once with my father, years ago, for some reason. It looked even bigger then than it does now,' he said.

Pascale didn't reply, but looked round the enclosed courtyard, remembering so recently standing here with Julian. Ignoring Étienne, she walked to the pool and gazed into the water, studying the wavering image of herself against the reflection of the blue sky. The memory of Julian's kisses filled her, leaving room for nothing else.

'Look, I don't know what I did or said to annoy you, but you're in a very peculiar mood. What's the matter with you?'

'Nothing's the matter with me,' she replied, coming painfully back to the present.

A look of exasperation crossed his face. 'Well, something must be. Why don't you want to tell me?'

After a moment she said, 'If you don't know why I'm angry, then that's serious.'

He gave an incredulous laugh. 'Come on, Pascale. I just don't get it. We haven't seen each other for six months. Why did you behave that way at lunch? Your mother was upset, your father and aunt too.'

His patient tone of voice only exasperated her more. 'I don't want to talk about it,' she said with a toss of her head.

'OK, let's talk about the wedding, then.'

She paused, feeling her heart beat against her chest and her mouth go dry. 'No, we have to talk about you – about us.'

She said it so quietly he might not have heard, for he only looked round and said thoughtfully, 'Just think, some day all this, or the capital from it, might be yours. You'll be rich, Pascale.'

He seemed indifferent to the effect such a legacy might have on their lives, and his good-natured detachment made her hesitant to

297

express what had been building up inside her since she had seen him standing at her door that morning.

Étienne gave an exasperated sigh. Thrusting his hands into his pockets, he paced round the pool, staring blindly into the water.

Looking at him, Pascale was filled with dread. There seemed only one solution to end the turmoil that had ruled her since she had met Julian: to free herself from an old dream and pursue the new. A moment of courage was all it would take.

Étienne seemed completely unaware of her mood. He was looking at her with eyes full of desire. 'Pascale, why don't we get the key to the château while I'm here? We could come back, maybe tomorrow, to be alone – even later today. You could get it from the caretaker.' His voice dropped to a whisper.

She looked up uncomfortably.

'At least we'd have a real bed. We could even lock the door, and if anyone knocks, we'll pretend we're not here.'

She shook her head, feeling sick, as if she were about to push him into a chasm when he wasn't looking. The times they had made love in the back seat of a car, before and after their engagement, had been rushed, pleasurable but unsatisfying. The passion Pascale had felt then for Étienne had nothing whatever to do with the response Julian had aroused in her the day before. The Englishman's bold, provocative charm evoked a new kind of longing, which was so powerful it almost frightened her. It was what she had always imagined love should be.

'Well, what do you think about the idea?' Étienne asked when she didn't answer.

Pascale searched the face she knew so well, overwhelmed with guilt. 'I don't think anything.' In a rush she added, 'Étienne, this is the hardest thing I've ever had to do.' She swallowed. 'We're not compatible, you and I.'

He stared at her, not quite taking in what she said.

'Recently I've begun to have doubts about us, about getting married, about everything. I think I want . . . I know that . . .' She stopped, finding the look of confusion and misery on his face unendurable. 'I don't think I want to get married in December. Maybe not at all.'

He stared at her. 'What are you saying?'

'Please don't make it difficult. I'm sorry, with all my heart, believe me, but I just can't help it. Try to understand.'

'Understand? How can I? How could you, without any warning, from one day to the next . . .' He broke off and hung his head for a moment. 'Pascale, what's happened to you, to us?' He took a step forward, but the look in her eyes warned him off.

'I'm sorry, but that's the way it is, Étienne. I need time on my own. I want to travel, to grow, to see things, to explore. I can't face getting married right away, staying in the same job for years and years.' She saw the endless petty promotions that had once seemed so attractive stretching ahead like mileposts in a desert. 'Do you have any idea what I'm talking about?'

'No, I'm afraid I don't. I don't remember that ever bothering you before.'

'Well, it does now. This last year in Bordeaux, living on my own, has made me realize what I really want out of life. You and I don't want the same things. I must have known it for a long time really, but suddenly, this afternoon, things became clear.' Pascale was trembling, but now she had spoken she felt purged of any lingering doubts.

'It's your aunt's legacy that's changed your mind, isn't it?'

'Of course not. That's not true.' Pascale's face became hot at the suggestion.

'Yes it is. It's since you've come back here. Your letters were full of things, plans, excitement about the future. How could you write all those things if you were in doubt. I just can't believe it, not from you . . .' He broke off, trying to gain control of himself. When he spoke again, his voice was full of bitterness. 'This château, it's turned your head. You think you're somebody because you'll inherit money one day. I'm not good enough for you any more.' He waited for her to answer him, struggling to hide the pain he was too proud to show.

'You can't believe that it's got anything to do with the château. It's a terrible thing to say!' she cried, unnerved that she still cared very deeply what he thought of her. 'Anyway, my aunt will live till she's ninety and she's only in her sixties now, so I can't see how you can imagine that has anything to do with it.'

'I don't know what to think.' Without another word he whirled round, crossed the courtyard, mounted his motorcycle and started the engine.

She was stunned when he drove straight through the arch and out of the courtyard before she could utter a word of protest. She had expected him to argue with her, lose his temper, to show some sign of how distressed he was.

'Étienne!' she called after him, running to the arch just as he disappeared in a cloud of white dust. Tears were running down her cheeks as she began the hot, dusty walk home.

Michael glanced at Rachel, who was sitting beside him as they drove through mile after mile of vineyards.

'It's been a fabulous day,' said Rachel, enjoying the play of sunlight on the undulating sea of vines heavy with grapes.

Michael smiled. 'I'm glad you enjoyed it. You know, I must admit there have been times when I've been tempted to forget journalism and get involved in the wine trade.'

'I think it's a wonderful idea. You seemed in your element today.'

'The truth is, if I don't do it now, I never will.'

'Why?'

'Well, I've been spinning out this convalescence for all it's worth. Sooner or later my editor is going to get wise to me – in fact, he already has. He's humouring me, but come September I'm due for a new posting. Probably Washington, but who knows – it might be San Francisco.'

'That's a long way from France.'

Michael didn't say anything, but he would have been pleased if she had said how much she would like it if he were posted to San Francisco. When he turned to look at her, she merely smiled.

'What a lot of territory we've covered,' she said. 'Romanesque churches, three vineyards, lunch – all in just a few hours. You could open a shop with what you bought.' She turned to look at the cases of wine filling the back seat.

He laughed. 'I know. I got a little carried away, but at those prices it was irresistible. I think your being there had something to do with it.'

She laughed. 'So I've been a bad influence, have I?'

'Just the opposite. I'll lay them down and in five years they'll be ambrosia. You've got to promise me that you'll come back and try some when the time comes.' He saw that she was looking pensive. 'Are you all right?'

Her face softened in a smile. 'What you said made me think. Oliver will be thirteen in five years – a teenager. I wonder what the future holds for him, for me, for you. I'll be going home with a very mixed bag of memories. I'll never forget today, that I do know.'

'I hope it took your mind off things for a while.'

'It certainly helped. I think I'd have gone completely stir-crazy otherwise. I'm very lucky to have met you, you know. You've made this whole situation a lot easier for me.'

'I could say the same. I'm beginning to wonder what I was doing with myself all those idle months before I met you.'

'You were recuperating.'

'Feeling sorry for myself is more like it.'

'But not any more?'

'Not any more,' he said. There was an easy silence between them as they drove along, past the constantly changing landscape of fields and vineyards. Michael was the first to speak.

'I imagine that's what you'll do when this is all over – recuperate, I mean. You'll need lots of time to put things in perspective, lots of time. Don't forget that.'

'Sometimes I think we overrate time. It's not always as valuable as people make out. Sometimes it's an excuse for not taking action. Do you realize that a week ago I hadn't even arrived here? It seems like an eternity.'

'It doesn't to me. Time seems to have moved too quickly.'

She smiled at his comment. That day more than any other day they had spent together she was acutely aware of so many attractive things about Michael: his expressive voice, his strong gesturing hands, the laugh lines around his disquietingly clear eyes. She knew she was going to miss him. A feeling of closeness had sprung up between them that was as natural and reassuring as an old friendship.

301

'So you've definitely decided to leave with Oliver on Tuesday, then?' he asked as they joined the motorway for the last lap home.

'There's no point in my staying on now that he knows everything.'

'You were right to tell him. He was bound to find out sooner or later.'

'He took it so much better than I expected.'

She found it painful to remember Oliver's stoic, tearless expression when she broke the news just before Alain had come for him on Saturday. It tore her apart to see how bravely he had taken it, and she nearly lost her precarious self-control when, in his clear child's voice, he had asked his father to confirm it the moment he arrived.

'I'm glad you called your family last night. That must be a relief.'

'I don't know why we keep things bottled up from those closest to us. In my case it was pride, I guess. I couldn't admit to my parents that Alain had failed me.'

'And yet you said at lunch that you were still hoping it's not too late. You're tenacious, Rachel. Wonderfully stubborn.'

Michael thought of the chronicle, but he felt more than ever that he should keep his thoughts to himself. To compare Rachel with Margaret to her face would seem like a crude sort of fortune telling, but during the last few days he found himself repeatedly comparing the destinies of those two women, born centuries apart.

Rachel was looking thoughtfully out of the window as they left the vineyards behind. 'I can't shake the feeling that something might happen to change Alain's mind.'

'That's a brave thing to say in the face of what happened.' He was beginning to dislike Alain intensely. 'And the unfortunate thing is that your husband doesn't even know how lucky he is.'

There was a thoughtful silence in the car as they moved along the wide, empty highway. Rachel wondered if Michael was troubled by the idea that he had missed his chance at happy family life and was trying to come to terms with it now he was at a turning point.

'Has it occurred to you that Alain might refuse to let you take Oliver home?'

'Of course, but I really can't believe he would be that stupid.

302

Not now, after what he's done. And if he does cause trouble, well then, I'll cross that bridge when I come to it. Dad gave me the name of an American lawyer in Paris just in case. But nothing and no one is going to keep me from Oliver. As soon as they come back tomorrow night I'm going to pick him up, I'm not wasting another minute. I've got to get back home with Oliver, and back to normal.'

It was early evening by the time they approached Roquelaire. Long shadows streaked the stubbled fields, which unfolded like a coarsely woven tapestry around the town lying at the bottom of the valley. The sun gilded the old stones of the houses above the ramparts, setting the windows afire and tinting the rooftops a rich red. Then, suddenly, Rachel saw Brissac rearing powerfully on the horizon.

Michael spotted a figure walking along the road some distance in front of them. 'That's Pascale Gachpour. I wonder what she's doing walking alone out here.'

'Maybe she's been to visit the château.'

He shifted the gears, slowing to a crawl as they caught up with her. 'Hello,' he said with a friendly smile.

Pascale turned her head with a stricken expression, obviously wishing they hadn't stopped. Her hair was windblown, her cheeks flushed from the heat and it was clear she had been weeping.

'Hello, Monsieur Lowry.' She touched her fingers to her dishevelled hair self-consciously.

'I thought I recognized you. This is Madame Ribard. She's staying at the Peterson house across the street from me.'

'Ribard?' Pascale repeated, surprised. 'Oh, hello. I'm pleased to meet you.'

'Can we give you a lift back to the village? It's still quite a way in this heat and we can squeeze you in if you would like.'

'Oh, thanks very much. But I'd rather walk – really.'

But Michael wouldn't take no for an answer. He had already leapt out of the car and was shifting the wine on the back seat to make room for Pascale.

When they reached the square, Michael parked the car and they

303

all got out. Pascale thanked him and wished them a hurried goodbye before disappearing up the street.

'The poor girl looks miserable,' said Rachel. 'Didn't you think so?'

'Yes, something has upset her. I wonder what it could be? I didn't want to ask about her fiancé, or the château or her family, but something is definitely very wrong.'

'Maybe it's Julian Paine.'

'Young Étienne is worth ten of him any day.'

'Yes, but when you're her age your head is easily turned by all sorts of things. He's so sophisticated, and she's at the age when you can't tell her anything.' She smiled ruefully. 'If she's anything like I was, that is.'

Michael chuckled. 'Yes, I imagine she's quite a headstrong young lady. My goodness, what are we going to do with all this wisdom we've accumulated, you and I?' he laughed again.

As they neared Michael's house Rachel said, 'One thing is for certain: nobody will want our advice. Young Pascale will have to find out for herself what Julian Paine is really like.' She lingered for a moment, not wanting to say goodbye, now she was on the brink of really leaving. 'Would you like me to help you cart the wine home?'

'No thanks. I'm going to drive it to the garage below the terrace and unload it there. But don't forget that there will be a case or two with your name on it maturing in my cellar.'

'I won't forget, Michael. And if you do ever get posted to San Francisco, I hope you'll come up to Napa. We have some pretty spectacular vineyards there too.'

For the first time since they had met they ran out of words.

'Well, perhaps I'll see you tomorrow. If not, I'll drop the key and a cheque for the house rent through your door before I leave.'

'Oh, we'll bump into each other before then.'

'Yes, I'm sure.'

'Listen, I wish you the best of luck tomorrow. I hope everything goes well.'

Rachel waited for him to suggest that they get together again, but he didn't. Nor did he move to shake her hand or kiss her cheek as she expected. Though she had made up her mind to go, this seemed an unsatisfactory end to their brief but intense friendship.

She left him at his door and walked up the street feeling an emptiness, and yet a relief at the prospect of being alone that evening. Evenings in Roquelaire were something she associated with Michael Lowry. Perhaps, she thought to herself, the last thing she would remember him by was the sound of his front door closing as she walked away.

When Pascale left Michael and Rachel, she walked halfway home before returning to the square, where she watched them disappear up the Rue St Jacques. She crossed the empty covered market towards the post office with a coin ready in her hand, glancing round the square before entering the phone box to reassure herself that no one was watching. Hugging the phone to her ear, she dialled the number scribbled on the card in her handbag.

'Julian?' she whispered, feeling a wave of excitement at the sound of his voice.

'Pascale, is it really you? Where are you?'

They were on the phone for only a moment, long enough to fix a date for the following day. When she left the call-box, Pascale was so distracted that she didn't notice Laurent locking up his shop. He watched her hurry along the street towards home.

# Chapter 15

Laurent was reading a book in the fading light by an open window of his house in the narrowest, darkest street of the village. Hearing footsteps, he looked down from the upper storey and saw Étienne standing below.

'Come on up. The door is open.'

Étienne pushed open the ancient door, scoured grey by the elements and set with a rusty hand of Fatima clutching a ball. He entered the dismal ground floor, which was even more depressing than he remembered. It consisted of a single room dominated by a huge, blackened fireplace, in front of which was a long wooden table and several straw-bottomed chairs. In the corner was a stained enamel sink and, beside it, a small grime-encrusted gas cooker, on which sat the remains of what Étienne imagined had been his friend's Sunday lunch. The shabby little house perfectly reflected Laurent's pretended indifference to material things, as well as his eccentric ways. Étienne climbed the narrow little staircase to the upper storey feeling utterly down-hearted. Laurent was lounging in a tattered leather armchair by the window.

Étienne tried to smile. 'I thought I'd drop by and say hello. Are you busy?'

'Oh, I think I can spare a minute or two.' Laurent closed his book and looked at Étienne, seeing he was deeply troubled. He motioned to a chair on the other side of the window. 'Sit down.'

Étienne did as he was told and Laurent got up wordlessly and went downstairs. He returned with a bottle of pastis, two glasses and a jug of water.

While Laurent poured them each a drink Étienne remarked, 'Things must be going well with you. You usually drink red.'

Laurent handed him a glass. 'This is different. You need something stronger.'

Étienne tried to laugh, but it sounded more like a sob.

'Chin-chin.' Laurent's eyes were grave as he studied Étienne. Dropping back into his chair, he said, 'Now, tell me what's happened. It's Pascale, isn't it? You've had a fight.'

'How did you guess?'

'It isn't difficult. You look like a man who's had his leg amputated without anaesthetic.'

Étienne met his eyes. 'She's broken off our engagement.'

Laurent's breath came out in a whistle. 'As bad as that.' He shook his head as if to say that Étienne should have known better than to get engaged in the first place.

'Funny, I remember you always said that beautiful girls bring nothing but trouble. And you ought to know. You've had plenty.'

'There's always been something unpredictable about Pascale,' Laurent mused. 'Those big blue eyes of hers make me uneasy. She looks straight through you. Behind that friendly exterior she's a block of ice. I've always found her incredibly patronizing, as if Roquelaire wasn't good enough for her. The truth is, Pascale is just your typical uptight *petite bourgeoise* . . .' Seeing Étienne bristle, he smiled. 'But you're still in love with her, so that's not what you came to hear.'

'I didn't come to hear anything,' Étienne replied, not really affected by Laurent's opinion of Pascale. 'I just had to talk to somebody, that's all. I can't bear to tell my father. He's going to throw it in my face. He's been trying to talk me out of marrying Pascale for ages, and it was only when he saw that I had made up my mind he agreed. If anybody is a snob, it's my father, not Pascale.'

'Does she know that?'

'Of course not. I wouldn't want to hurt her.'

'So what's the story? Tell me,' Laurent said with a bored air, but his eyes flickered with curiosity.

After Étienne had related what happened in detail, Laurent thought for a moment, knitting his fingers together.

'Doesn't this whole thing seem a bit strange to you?'

'Strange? It's bizarre! Maybe she's right; maybe it's good we

307

found out we were incompatible before we got married,' he added miserably.

'You're not going to leave it like that, are you?' replied Laurent in a shocked tone. He gazed into Étienne's unhappy face. 'Because you're a fool if you do. You'll have to live with it the rest of your life. You'll always think you made a mistake.'

'But what can I do? Go crawling on my knees to her, beg her to come back?' He hung his head. 'I guess I might if I thought it would do any good.'

'Has it occurred to you that you might have competition?'

Étienne stared at him. 'Competition? What's that supposed to mean?'

Laurent leaned forward with the reluctant air of someone about to break bad news. 'I hate to tell you, but I think there's another man. A rival.' He emphasized the last word with relish.

Étienne didn't react for a moment. 'Are you joking?'

'No, I'm perfectly serious. Admittedly, the proof I have to go on is pretty slender, but now, in the light of what's happened, I've put two and two together and I'm sure I'm right.'

'I don't believe you. There isn't anybody else. There never has been. She was only sixteen when we first started going together. What are you talking about?' He sat up suddenly. 'Do you know something? Is there someone in Bordeaux? Tell me,' Étienne implored.

Laurent shook his head. 'You know, now I come to think of it, this was bound to happen. I told you years ago you were boxing yourself in and that you ought to play the field a bit more. But knowing you, I'm sure you haven't even sampled any *Frauleins* since you've been in Germany.'

'Of course I haven't. Pascale and I were engaged.'

Laurent gave an exasperated shrug.

'For God's sake, tell me who this other guy is, will you?'

Then Laurent explained that he had seen Pascale with an Englishman in the square.

'That doesn't mean anything. He might just have been sitting next to her and tried to pick her up.'

'True. But that's not all. She took him to the château yesterday.'

308

Étienne looked at him in disbelief. 'That can't be. If it were, it would mean she lied today. Her aunt said she hasn't even had time to see the château yet, and she didn't deny it. How do you know this?' he asked suspiciously.

'Look, don't get angry with me. Stay cool. Deny it if you like, but my father told me when I saw him last night that Pascale picked up the key yesterday afternoon. A while after she left he started worrying – you know my father – and went up to the château to see if she had closed the door and put the key where she said she would. He said it was a good hour later. He arrived there just in time to see her coming out of the door with the Englishman. His red Porsche was parked in the courtyard. Father ducked and went round the other side of the château because he didn't want her to think he was being nosy. Then he saw them drive away together in the Porsche. He was surprised, because when she picked up the key she didn't give any indication that she was with somebody else. And that isn't all.' Laurent then told Étienne about Pascale using the telephone in the square earlier on. 'Why would she use the public phone instead of phoning from home?'

Étienne's chest was heaving with emotion. 'Who is this Englishman? Do you know him?'

'I heard he was staying at Terre Blanche. He's been around for a while. You can't miss him because he wears a ponytail – he's very flash. And, of course, the Porsche makes him pretty obvious.'

'Oh God!' Étienne went to the window and looked down on the narrow little street that had scarcely changed for six hundred years or more. 'I wish I was leaving tomorrow instead of at the end of the week. I feel sick.'

Laurent poured them each another drink and turned on a lamp, illuminating Étienne's stricken face.

'You realize that if you don't do something now, you'll never be able to live with yourself. You have your honour to think of.'

'Well, I'm not crawling back, even if I wanted to, which I don't.'

Laurent's dark eyes were staring at him intently, reflecting pinpoints of light. The power in his voice was compelling. 'I'm not talking about crawling back. That's not what I mean. I'm talking about vengeance.'

Agnès was sitting outside her cottage watching the sky deepen to a midnight blue in the distance behind the dark towers of Brissac. A loamy smell rose from the freshly watered vegetable garden, and the only sounds were the subdued chirping of crickets hidden in the grass, and the thump of rabbits still feeding in their cages. Tomorrow she would pick the last roses, which were now drooping in the August heat, and place them at the feet of St Anne in the chapel. Every day she went there to pray for guidance.

Agnès's thoughts were broken by the sound of the gate creaking open at the bottom of the garden. She knew at once who her visitor was, because even in the fading light her hair was incandescent.

'Pascale, it's you,' she said, rising to her feet. At the sight of her, Agnès's tiredness vanished and a smile came to her face. She watched her daughter appear out of the dimness. 'This is a nice surprise. What are you doing here at this time of night? Has Étienne gone home?'

When they had hugged and exchanged kisses, Agnès saw that Pascale had been crying.

'What's the matter?' she asked gently.

Pascale said in a whisper, 'I've broken off my engagement.'

Agnès sank into her chair, unable to speak for a moment. 'Are you sure it's what you want?'

'Yes. I'm sure.'

'But it's so sudden.' Agnès looked at her numbly. She had supposed the crisis at lunchtime would pass as quickly as a summer shower.

Pascale sat on a chair beside her, the light from the doorway illuminating her profile. Glancing at her stricken face, Agnès reached for her hand and patted it comfortingly as her daughter cried softly. When she had gained control of herself, Pascale blew her nose and sighed. 'We're so different, really. I don't know why it's taken all this time to discover it. I should have known.'

'Do your parents know?'

'Yes, I told them at dinner. You can imagine how they reacted.'

310

Agnès nodded. 'Yes, I can imagine.'

'Father started shouting at me, and then mother pitched in. Then she began to tell me what a disgrace I was to the family. I got the impression that their biggest concern was what Étienne's parents would say. Anyway, I went to my room for a long time to think. They both came in and tried to talk me out of my decision, but I said I couldn't back down. That's when I said I was going out, and came here to you. I knew you wouldn't shout at me or be angry. I knew you would understand. You're not angry, are you?'

'No, Pascale, I'm not angry. But that's not to say I understand. What's happened to cause this? When did you begin to feel that way? There must be some reason. You and Étienne have been together for so long.'

'Five years, to be exact. If you count right from the beginning, though we weren't even grown up then. Today, as soon as I saw him, I knew something was wrong. I felt cold, unresponsive when he kissed me. It just happened suddenly, with no warning.'

'Has anything . . . has anything else happened in the last few days to make you feel like this?' Agnès began to sift through her impressions of Pascale since her return.

'No, nothing's happened.' Stricken by guilt, she couldn't bring herself to look at Agnès. 'I must have known for a while, but not realized it until today. When we were having lunch, it struck me how unemotional, how totally predictable Étienne is. He seems to lack strong convictions. He doesn't have any real opinions of his own. I want someone who has strong feelings like me, who knows what they think. But the most important thing is that I've discovered I need a man who is ambitious, who wants the same things from life as I want.'

Agnès sat stunned, not knowing what to say. Pascale had freed herself with unexpected suddenness from a bond that Agnès had begun to worry might bring her unhappiness, and yet, now it had happened, Agnès began to wonder if her daughter had made the right decision.

'It's such a pity that you didn't realize all this before.'

'I know. I wish I had, believe me. Oh, I wish . . .'

'*Le pauvre garçon*,' Agnès muttered, imagining his misery at that

311

moment. Earlier in the afternoon she had found herself disapproving of Étienne, being overly critical, but now all she felt was profound pity.

'Where is he now, do you know?'

'At home, I suppose.'

They sat without speaking for a moment, then Agnès said, 'I just hope you're sure, Pascale, because you seem so miserable.'

'I'm all right. I'm just upset, that's all. And don't worry about Étienne, because he'll get over it.'

Agnès ignored Pascale's apparent callousness, realizing that it was only her way of keeping guilt at bay.

'Well, all I can say is that you should make sure that this is not just some passing mood. Because you can't go back on it once it's done.'

'It's not a mood,' Pascale responded quickly. She tried to picture Étienne, but all she could see was Julian's face. His rich English voice was still echoing in her ears. 'I hated hurting him. But what could I do?'

'Nothing, nothing,' Agnès whispered, shaking her head.

For a moment they sat in silence, then Pascale rose to her feet.

'Goodnight, *tatie*. I'd better get back home now. They'll wonder where I am. I dread the next few days. The house is going to be like a funeral home.'

Agnès put out her hand. 'This is going to be a very difficult time for you. Étienne will be in the village until Friday, and you're bound to bump into each other. It will soon get around about the engagement. Maybe you ought to go away. Weren't you and Annie planning to go to the sea for a few days, until her husband can get away to join her?'

'I told her I probably wouldn't. She's so wrapped up in her baby that it wouldn't be much fun.'

'Then what will you do? It won't be pleasant for you at home.'

'I'm not sure yet.'

Disquieted by Pascale's apparent calm, Agnès did not know what to say or do next. It was too soon to ask Pascale what her plans were now that she wasn't getting married. Agnès reflected on the long, hot days of August in Roquelaire, which often ended in

312

storms. She was suddenly anxious for Pascale to go away. 'I could give you some money. You could go for a little trip, go and visit that friend of yours in Paris.'

'No, *tatie*, I'll just stay here, but thank you anyway. Please don't worry. I can feel you worrying in the dark. Oh, another thing. I didn't tell you, *tatie*, but I went to the château on Saturday. Monsieur David will probably mention it. I was out for a walk and went past. I hope you don't mind that I went alone, without you.'

'Not at all. But you didn't mention it today at lunch. I was under the impression . . .'

'Yes, I know. I didn't want to start talking about it in front of Étienne. My mind was elsewhere.'

'Well, we can go there together this week if you have time. Not tomorrow, Hélène's going with Armand's sisters.'

'Yes, some time soon. I'm sorry I'm so busy, but there are lots of people I want to see that I haven't seen for ages.'

'Of course, I understand,' she replied, thinking Pascale was being evasive, even secretive. She didn't have much to say about the château, which struck Agnès as odd.

They said goodnight, and as Agnès watched her go down the path she longed to tuck Pascale in the old oak bed in the spare room with the low beamed ceiling. It had been years since Pascale and she had spent a night under the same roof. Now, long after she had ceased to imagine her daughter there, sleeping peacefully through the night, the desire to watch over her, to protect her, came back like an ache in her heart. Agnès listened to Pascale's footsteps die away in the dark, feeling a sudden anguish that she might never hear them again.

At the sound of footsteps coming up the stairs, Bernard called from the bedroom door, 'Is that you, Pascale?'

'Yes, it's me. Goodnight, Papa.' Her voice was wary.

He closed the door without replying and turned to Beatrice, who was lying on the bed staring at the ceiling. Her face was swollen from crying and she turned to look at him beseechingly as he took off his trousers.

'What are we going to do?'

'Nothing. What can we do? Maybe she'll change her mind.'

'No, I know her. She won't. And if she did, do you think he'd have her back? Right now his parents are probably celebrating. They never thought Pascale was good enough for their only son.'

'Let's forget about it for tonight, shall we? What's done is done.'

'We did everything for her, loved her like our own daughter, and this is how she repays us. The risks we ran, the shame if it had all come out. All those years of worry.'

'What does that have to do with it? If she doesn't love him, then it's better this way, Beatrice. Don't torture yourself.' He folded his trousers over a chair, then began to bolt the shutters.

'We have to suffer in silence, but she'll never know the sacrifices we made, you and I, taking her in as our own.'

'And Agnès? She made a sacrifice too.'

'*She* hasn't made any sacrifices. What sacrifices has she made?'

Bernard sighed tiredly. 'Surely you can't think it was easy for her to pretend all these years that her daughter was only her niece. I've seen the look in her eyes sometimes, holding back when she wanted to speak her mind. But she kept her promise not to interfere. Imagine if it had been one of our boys and the shoe was on the other foot.'

'But we loved Pascale as our own. I think of her as ours. Of course I do. How could it be otherwise? Even now I don't stop to make the distinction. And Pascale wasn't just an ordinary girl. She was always exceptional. So beautiful and bright, that I admit.'

'Then just because she has disappointed you now, you shouldn't hold it against her. She ought to know her own mind.'

'But Agnès – now she has her chance, you'd think at least she'd be anxious to make amends to us with money from the sale of the château, but she hasn't even mentioned such an idea.'

'That may be, and I'm as put out as you, but don't forget that she has always contributed to Pascale's upbringing. And I know she gives her money all the time without telling us. Let's be fair.'

'No – *she* should be fair. She should sell the château right away and give us money to modernize the bakery. The rest she should put away for Pascale. She doesn't want anything for herself. She never did.' Beatrice couldn't keep the resentment from her voice.

'You would think she'd want to do that to show her gratitude, wouldn't you? But then, I never could understand Agnès. If a young girl gets pregnant today, it's very different. People don't bother to get married any more, and having a baby without a ring on your finger is no crime.'

'In my bitter moments I've often wondered what would have happened if you and I hadn't been living in Nantes at the time. If it had been later, if you'd already bought the bakery, then everyone in Roquelaire would have known that Pascale couldn't be ours. Agnès would have had to raise her as her own and live with the shame. Even now I sometimes wonder if people don't suspect something. She doesn't look a thing like any of us. The nights I used to worry that somebody from Nantes would turn up here and the truth would come out. Think of the humiliation.'

'Well, it didn't happen, Beatrice, so let's not go over all that again. We're the only people that know and it will always stay that way. Whatever you say, it was better for everyone. Think of it — you would have refused to come back here if Agnès had been living with a baby out of wedlock. You'd have been too ashamed.'

'I suppose,' she admitted.

'And we would never have had the chance to buy the bakery for practically nothing, and I'd probably be working for someone instead of being my own boss with a thriving business.'

They were silent for a moment as they both realized how different life would have been all these years without Pascale in the house.

Beatrice said, 'There's no doubt in my mind now who Pascale's father was. When the will was read, I knew it was Armand Bataille. He was the last person in the world I would have thought of. And what could he have possibly seen in Agnès?'

'We're still not sure of that. And there's no point in asking either. She wouldn't tell us over twenty-one years ago, so she certainly isn't going to tell us now.'

'Of course it was Armand Bataille. Who else? There is no other possible explanation, otherwise why would he leave her the château? People in the village must be thinking she was carrying on in secret with him all those years she was a confirmed spinster. I hate the

315

feeling they're talking behind our backs, insinuating things. It makes us look so shabby.'

'Nobody thinks that, Beatrice. I don't agree with you. It seems to me if Armand Bataille thought Pascale was his, he would have recognized her in some way, made her his heir while he was still alive. It just doesn't fit.'

'Yes, that's the difficult part to explain. But still, I keep going back to the idea . . .'

'It occurred to me once that Agnès might have had some connection with Bataille during the war, that she helped him in some important way and that this was his way of paying her back. Maybe they got involved then. Maybe something happened that drew them together later in life. After all, when you think of it, Pascale was conceived the year Armand's wife died.'

'What an idea!' Beatrice laughed derisively. 'Agnès was a spindly, scatterbrained teenager during the war. She was never what you'd call attractive. I never saw Armand even speak to her.'

'In that case, I can't imagine how you think that Pascale was conceived. Agnès has become a bit strange these last few years, and very religious, which worries me. God knows what she might do with her legacy. Something foolish, impulsive.'

Beatrice thought a minute. 'We've got to convince her to sell the château before anything happens. Before it's too late.' Too late, too late – the words seemed to circle in the room, until Beatrice fell into a restless doze.

A motorbike roaring down a neighbouring street momentarily disturbed the deep peace that was beginning to descend on Roquelaire.

*

A chink of reflected light danced on the darkened ceiling above Agnès's bed as she lay there, unable to sleep. She had performed her bedtime ritual of ablutions and prayers, of folding the covers down and closing the shutters, with a sense that the room she had inhabited all her life was different somehow. Turning her head on the pillow, she looked towards the mantelpiece. There, among a

316

jumble of familiar objects she had not moved for many years, was Armand's photograph, glimmering in the shadows. She had placed it so she could see it from her bed, not expecting the feelings it aroused to unsettle her. The suggestion of his face, imprisoned in the little square, lured her further back in memory than she wished to go. She struggled against the power of the past, but then her will bent beneath the weight she had carried for so many years like a heavy suitcase whose contents she had never wanted to examine. Her lips forming Armand's name, Agnès let a lifetime of self-denial dwindle away. Defenceless now, she plummeted into moments of remembered richness that even all the drab years could not smother.

She turned her mind back to Christmas Eve of 1969. She had filed with the crowd down the nave of the village church to the uplifting strains of Bach played on the organ, and turned for one last look at the tall gold candlesticks gleaming above the tiers of poinsettias and Christmas roses, a ravishing display of colour, the like of which she knew she wouldn't see for another twelve months. When it was her turn to shake Père Auguste's hand, she smiled up at him, dazzled by his heavily embroidered gold and red cope, which he wore only at Christmas. She shook his strong hand, feeling the power and protection of the Church radiating from him.

'Thank you for your thoughtful words on love and charity. I was especially moved by what you said about the gifts of the heart, Père Auguste.'

'Thank you, Agnès. It means a great deal to hear you say that. This night, of all nights, should be a celebration for us. It's a time to be thankful for God's gifts. He has given us such riches. May God bless you.'

Agnès left the church feeling whole and cleansed, though she had come to mass feeling friendless and very much alone that year. Her mother had died in February, and her sister lived in Nantes with her family, leaving Agnès to spend Christmas on her own. She pulled up the collar of her coat and unfurled her umbrella against the drizzle, conscious of footsteps disappearing down the side streets off the square. The Christmas lights on the lampposts and the beams of the market made festive ribbons of light in the road, and

317

laughter and conversation seeped out from behind the closed shutters of the houses, where people were enjoying their *réveillon* feast as Agnès began the walk home.

It wasn't until she saw the little light she had left on in her cottage burning forlornly in the distance that her optimism began to leave her. On impulse she ignored the path to the cottage and turned up the black road towards Brissac. The cross of the Pilgrim's Stone loomed ahead, and the silvery glow of the moon from behind the clouds seemed to bring it closer. Stopping there to catch her breath, Agnès felt an almost pagan sense of awe, which she immediately condemned, at the same time suppressing the almost overwhelming desire to make a wish.

When eventually she reached the top of the hill and the château was in sight, she saw that lights were burning in the eastern tower, suggesting that Armand was still awake. From her cottage, Agnès could sometimes see the light in the tower, which told her when the Batailles were in residence. She never put it into words, never told anyone of her feelings, but it always gave Agnès comfort when she knew Armand was there. When the light was extinguished, it was as if a corner of her own dwelling was closed and uninhabited. In the last year, since his wife had died, the light in the tower had hardly ever shone, but now it sparkled like a jewel. The rain had stopped and a cold wind had come up that suggested there would be snow before the night was out. Agnès shivered, aware that she couldn't continue to stand on the windswept hilltop, and would have to make up her mind whether to keep walking or return home. She stared at the light in the tower, knowing that, like herself, Armand Bataille was alone that Christmas night.

Earlier in the day she had seen his big black Citroën pass in the distance when she was walking to the village. In the brightly lit *confiserie*, where the shelves were lined with trays of chocolates, marrons glacés and colourful marzipan fruits, Agnès had waited patiently in the queue. When it was nearly her turn, Armand Bataille's housekeeper had entered the shop. They had greeted each other cordially, but then Hélène had turned to talk to the woman behind her in a reverent whisper.

'Yes, *Monsieur* is here for Christmas, but only briefly. He's going to Savoy the day after tomorrow to spend a week with friends; then after the New Year he'll be going to the Far East for several months. I don't expect to see him until June, if then. The poor man is spending Christmas all alone. He told me he didn't want to be disturbed, which is understandable. He's still prostrate with grief.'

As Agnès stood on the cold hill racked by doubt, it seemed to her that the light in the tower symbolized Armand Bataille's isolation and pain. Père Auguste's moving words about the gifts of the heart – compassion, charity, kindness – came to her mind, giving her courage. Clutching her arms to her chest, she hurried up the chalk road to the château.

Passing through the arch into the courtyard, she saw the black Citroën parked in front of the steps. The lamp above the door cast a suffused light on the cobbles. She had never been in the courtyard, and entered it with trepidation. Looking up at the shadowy stone pierced by small, darkened windows, she was conscious only of the man who was suffering alone behind the imposing façade. She picked her way across the slippery cobbles, her eyes trained on the bell set in a circle of brass beside the door. She darted up the steps and pressed it quickly, afraid she might lose her nerve. She was ready to turn away, glad at the thought of escaping, when she heard footsteps behind the door, which opened cautiously. Armand's face appeared in a beam of light. He was wearing a thick dressing gown and a scarf was knotted at his throat. The look of surprise on his face softened the unmistakeable sadness of his expression.

'Who is it?'

'It's Agnès Grimal, *monsieur*.'

'Agnès?' He opened the door wide, staring at her incredulously. 'Come in. It's raining. You must be drenched.'

She entered the hall, lit by a big lamp like a cage made of iron and glass, suspended from the high ceiling. When he closed the door behind her, she took her first good look at him in many years. The once slender, athletic young man had thickened at the waist and his hair was receding and almost completely grey. But even though his sympathetic face was fleshy and lined, he still appeared

319

handsome and vigorous. What struck her most was that Armand's unforgettable blue eyes, so full of courage that day they had concealed Paul Ribard's body in the tunnel, had taken on a haunting emptiness. Stunned by this change, she forgot her own gaucheness.

'Agnès . . .', his hand went to her shoulder, 'your coat is wet. Let me take it.'

Wordlessly slipping out of her coat and hat, she handed them to him. He hung them up and pulled a woollen shawl from a hook on the door. 'Here, put this round your shoulders,' he said.

She did as she was told, acutely aware of how shabbily dressed she was. Her hand went self-consciously to her wispy hair, which had been crushed by her hat, and brushed the collar of her brown wool dress, shapeless from wear. She glanced at her reflection in the mirror, and her bright, dark eyes made her think of a bedraggled bird blown in by a storm. She thought of Armand's beautiful, aristocratic wife, Alycia, who had always radiated glamour, even from a distance, and who had looked much younger than her late forties when she had died. Agnès felt ashamed that she was plain and looked older than her years. It lasted only a moment, for she told herself it didn't matter; Armand was not interested in the way she looked.

'Well, well, what a nice surprise,' he said with a warm smile that suggested he was making an effort for her benefit.

She had rehearsed what she would say to explain her unannounced visit on Christmas Eve, but her mind was blank. Yet his manner put her at ease, making her feel she had been right to come.

'Come upstairs where there's a fire, won't you?' he said.

She followed him up the wide stone staircase, hardly conscious of the faded tapestries and big paintings lining the walls. For years, after the château had been restored, she had imagined Armand there, like a king inhabiting a sumptuous palace. Seeing it in reality, she discovered it had been decorated with dignified simplicity rather than grand ostentation.

He walked ahead of her down a long, narrow corridor, switching on the lights as he went. The doors to all the rooms were shut, except the one at the end, where a light was burning – the light in the tower.

320

'The rest of the house is closed at the moment. These days I find I live in only one room.'

Following him across the threshold, Agnès was surprised to find herself in what obviously served as his bedroom and study combined. An ancient bed of dark, carved wood, canopied in dark-green velvet, stood opposite a massive stone fireplace wide enough to sit in. Placed in front of the fire were two Henri IV chairs upholstered in frayed tapestry. A table was piled with books under a lamp that cast a soft golden light and a big chart desk stood near the window. The scrolled armchair in front of it was pulled back, indicating that he had been working and that she had interrupted him.

Her footsteps sounded on the blood-red tiles, uneven with age and partly obscured by several faded Persian rugs. A tapestry of a hunting scene in autumnal colours covered one wall. Lifting her eyes, she admired the frescoed beams that contrasted vividly with the stark simplicity of the room that had once been the retreat of Gascon noblemen.

'Please sit down,' said Armand, motioning to one of the chairs in front of the fire. He took a big log from the pile and placed it in the grate.

Agnès sat down, the warmth dispelling the curious sensation of weightlessness that had overtaken her. Watching Armand cross the room to a cupboard, she was daunted by the idea of filling the silence with conversation. Until then she hadn't fully understood what different worlds they lived in. The château was a kingdom of itself, as remote as Egypt, and she perceived that the life Armand led here revolved around pursuits of the mind – books, letters, business – involving matters far removed from Roquelaire.

'Will you have an Armagnac?'

He was standing before her, holding two goblets of amber liquid, which caught the reflection of the fire.

'Thank you.' She accepted the Armagnac, though she had not tasted it for years.

He raised his glass in a wordless toast and she sipped the fiery alcohol, chasing away the cold penetrating her bones.

'You said "thank you" just now. But it is I who should thank you. For walking through the rain on Christmas Eve, of all nights, because you must have known I needed someone to talk to.'

She was transfixed by the genuine affection radiating from his face as he settled into the armchair across from her.

'Thank you for remembering me,' he said courteously.

Her voice came in a whisper. 'I think of you often.'

'Do you, Agnès?'

As he spoke, she saw there were tears in his eyes, which she found terrible to behold, a discovery that dissolved all formality between them.

He said thoughtfully, 'That day, all those years ago. To think we've never spoken of it since.'

'It was better that way.'

'We have shared a terrible secret all this time.'

She nodded, looking at her hands, calloused and stained from an autumn of gardening and jam-making. 'I never told a soul.'

'It never occurred to me you would. I knew I could trust you.'

'Yet we didn't even really know each other. I had only seen you at a distance.'

'There are things one knows instinctively. Though you looked younger than seventeen you always appeared to me to be such a serious young girl, one who would be courageous if the circumstances required. It was lucky for me that you came that day. I probably wouldn't be here now otherwise. I thought often in the years after the war that if it hadn't been for you, they'd have caught me and I'd have been killed. Somehow there never seemed to be an appropriate moment to say so before.'

'You were very busy,' Agnès replied, remembering how quickly after he was decorated he seemed to be catapulted so far beyond her reach. His wife was from a very rich Bordeaux family and his marriage took him light years away from the farm where he had grown up.

'In those days I found it easy to put things behind me. At first I thought to myself: this is real life, as it should be. At last it's beginning. I'm a man, I have a career, a family, a purpose in life. But you know, Agnès, nothing that followed ever seemed as vivid to me as those war years, nothing ... And now ...' He faltered, as

322

if trying to cope with the torrent of feeling that welled up in him. 'Now I've begun to think of all my sins and omissions: things I should have done, the people I neglected.'

She looked at him with a startled expression, realizing that he was referring to her. It had never occurred to her that a man who had partaken so freely of all life had to offer could feel cheated of anything. And yet at that moment his eventful past, full of achievements, seemed to have dwindled to nothing in his eyes. He had taken refuge in a single room in the vast château with the defeated air of an old lion who had crept away to die.

'It may surprise you to know how much I envy you in the simplicity, the honesty of your life here in Roquelaire.'

She gave a mute shrug of embarrassment, confused by the discovery that fame and fortune had made so little difference to Armand's happiness. He was looking at her with undisguised envy, she who had never travelled, or dined with nobility or made speeches, who lived the same uncomplicated life tied to the seasons, the rituals of the church and the village as her parents and grandparents.

He was staring into the fire, deep in thought. Then he smiled, chasing the years from his face. 'So you see, it's an unexpected gift to be able to thank you in person tonight for saving my life.'

Agnès blushed to the roots of her hair, not knowing what to reply. The word 'gift' struck a chord already vibrating within her, the gifts of the heart. The precious minutes in Armand's company were ticking by and she was aware that this time she was collecting them to remember later.

'You are a brave, courageous and honest woman.'

'Anyone would have done the same.'

'Anyone? You could say the same about me, even though they gave me medals.'

'No, that's different,' she protested. 'You were a *maquisard*.'

His smile flashed, reminding her of the old Armand. 'Now let's not argue about who is more noble, shall we?'

Her eyes widened in surprise, then her sudden laughter filled the room. This relaxed, intimate conversation was not at all what she had expected. A warmth enveloped her, a strange, wonderful feeling that Armand and she understood one another.

323

He got up, put another log on the fire and went to fetch the bottle of Armagnac. When he offered her some more, she didn't refuse. He eased back into his chair and his face became serious.

'So many things have come out since the war,' he said reflectively, 'things that should have remained secret.'

'Some things will always remain secret,' Agnès remarked quietly, conveying with a look that she would never betray him.

'I know that, Agnès.'

'But even if it had come out about Paul Ribard, would it have mattered that much? Oh, I know it's much better that it didn't, but . . .'

'It would have mattered to me, yes. You see, Agnès . . .'

She sensed a dark struggle going on behind his eyes.

'Agnès, Agnès, the look of innocence in your eyes haunts me. Please, we should say no more.'

'Why should you harbour guilt for doing your duty? Please don't torment yourself.' Try as she would, she could not address him by his Christian name. She checked the impulse to rise to her feet and lay a reassuring hand on his shoulder.

For a long moment he hung his head. When he raised his eyes, he murmured, 'I'm silent because I'm arguing with myself whether to tell you the truth, whether I have the right to unburden myself to you.'

'To unburden what?' She was suddenly alert. The room was quiet except for the crackling of the fire.

'Agnès, I murdered Paul Ribard.'

She stared at him, not understanding. 'But it wasn't murder, it was the war. He was a traitor. You mustn't say such things.'

'Paul Ribard was not a German collaborator, Agnès. Oh yes, it's true he was trafficking in war booty. So did many others. But the real traitor was my own father.'

The words thundered in her ears, reverberating until she understood the significance. She gasped and closed her eyes, clasping her hands to her face. When she opened her eyes, she saw tears running down Armand's cheeks. She looked at him beseechingly, hoping she hadn't heard correctly.

'Paul Ribard was about to divulge who the real traitor was. One other *maquisard* who died, and I knew this. I killed Paul Ribard to protect my father, and now you are the only other person who knows the truth.'

Agnès hung her head and started to tremble all over. Repulsion overwhelmed her, making her feel nauseated.

'So you see, it wasn't an act of war,' Armand continued. 'It was murder. You saved the life of a murderer, Agnès. It might have been better if you hadn't, because if the Germans had discovered me that day dragging Paul's body to the tunnel, they would have shot me on the spot, not a hundred yards below where we are sitting now. Then justice of a sort would have been done.'

There was a long silence. Devastated, Agnès could hardly bring herself to look at Armand. She whispered hoarsely, 'Your father – why?'

'Initially, for money. He became involved in some very lucrative transactions, helping the Third Reich transport money and valuables and to keep them in hiding until they could be sent back to Germany. They were generous with him. But one day they came to call in the debt. He was asked to name the members of the Resistance in the village nearby. He had already deeply compromised himself. No one suspected my father, but the Maquis put the pressure on Paul Ribard to find out the truth. Then, as I said, I, too, found out. I knew that Ribard walked from a plot of land he was leasing to his farm at about the same time every day. I went to Brissac and waited for him. It happened much further from the entrance to the tunnel than I had anticipated and I was caught out. I saw you and called you over to help. And then ... and then, later, it was easy to spread the rumour that Paul Ribard had been the traitor, not my own father. That one act negated every good thing I might have done in the war, and in my entire life.'

Agnès stared numbly into the fire. An urge to run away and hide from this sordid truth came over her, but she was unable to move. She sat there, her eyes cast down, glancing up every now and then at the man she had long thought of as the living embodiment of everything she admired. He was slumped in the chair, staring into the fire as if seeing his past in the moving flames. At last he broke the silence in a dead voice.

325

'So that's the story of my life, the real story. The end is sad. My father killed himself after the war, though it was passed off as a hunting accident. I married well and I prospered. I became a rich man, I bought this château and restored it. I became a friend of influential people. I travelled and saw the world. I had a son. Then it came time for me to pay my account, just as my father had had to pay his. My son, as you know, died tragically young. And then Alycia, my wife, died too. From a disease, yes, but really from a broken heart because of Thierry. I'm only fifty-two years old, but I have lost every reason for living. I can't forget Paul Ribard. I wasn't sent to prison, but I have been punished in another way. My conscience is my prison until the day I die.'

Agnès struggled against the weight of this stark confession, wondering whether she should leave. But as the shock of what she had just heard subsided, she began to understand that she had been drawn there that night, to a man she had met so briefly long ago, for a reason. The horror she felt turned to pity. The bond between them, forged in an intense moment filled with danger, had somehow endured all these years, and now once more he needed her help. A virile young *maquisard* had once made an indelible impression on a young girl and she could not abandon him now. Agnès rose and went to his chair, placing her hand tentatively on his shoulder. Without saying anything, he took her hand and placed it on his unshaven cheek. The first contact with his flesh came as a shock. She stood stiffly for a few seconds, aware of a sensation moving up her arm, as if she had become a channel for his grief. He began to cry softly, his tears running through her fingertips.

'Forgive me, forgive me,' he whispered, his head fallen forward on his chest.

She sank to her knees before him and levelled her eyes with his. 'There is nothing for me to forgive. It's up to God. It's his forgiveness you must seek.'

He reached out and drew her to him, tenderly kissing her forehead and murmuring what sounded like a prayer, his touch rekindling the ashes of the years. Her hands moved instinctively to his arms, feeling them young and strong beneath his thick dressing-gown. She was not thinking of what he had done, but what he

326

meant to her, acknowledging that she needed him as much as he needed her. He looked down into her face, where compassion and gentleness shone from her eyes. Cupping her chin in his hand, he saw that the woman who looked back at him was still the girl who had answered his summons twenty-six years ago, the fresh-faced girl on a bicycle with the wind blowing in her hair. But tonight there was no terror in her heart, and there was no danger. His lips brushed hers, tentatively at first. And then she kissed him back, unleashing a tremor of feeling that destroyed all the real and imagined obstacles between them.

He released her gently, and they both stood, their hands entwined. Armand's face was ravaged with doubt, but a long look into her dark eyes seemed to reassure him. The shawl fell from her shoulders as he slipped his arms around her waist and drew her to him again. Faint with joy at being held so securely in his arms, she felt him tremble, as she was trembling. Her arms slowly embraced him so that he could not fail to know that she needed him too.

He turned off the lamp. The room was lit only by the fire, which sent long shadows up to the beams. Taking her hand, he led her to the bed, where he flung back the heavy quilt to reveal the white linen sheets. He began to unbutton her dress with an infinite delicacy, as if he were a child again and had to think of each movement. His eyes glinted in the dark as he uncovered her thin shoulders under the wool vest. The blush of shame and vulnerability at her nakedness died when she felt the sureness of his strong hands close round her arms. Then he kissed her, almost chastely. She lowered her eyes, knowing that never again would she have to love Armand Bataille at a distance, that whatever happened, she would always have this moment.

He took off his dressing-gown, the outline of his body etched by the firelight, and she sank back on to the pillows, waiting for him with her eyes averted. When he had slipped in beside her and pulled the covers over them, he placed his hand on the curve of her hip and laid his head next to hers on the pillow, as if waiting for her to adjust to the strangeness of it all. In a gesture that stirred her very being, he gathered her rough chapped hands and tenderly kissed them. As he moved closer she rejoiced at the sensation of his warm body pressed against hers.

327

Smoothing her hair from her forehead, he whispered, 'I don't know by what miracle you came here tonight. Just as I don't know what miracle brought you to me that day. But I need your strength, your honesty, your kindness. Your purity.' His words ended in a sob, releasing the pool of grief in the depths of his soul. She lay immobile next to him, letting it unleash itself against her. She felt an infinite compassion, and as sobs racked Armand's body, quiet tears slipped down her own cheeks, falling in the hollow of her throat, tears that expressed the accumulated sadness of her own life.

When his sorrow ebbed and he fell into a light sleep, Agnès lay holding him, watching the patterns made by the dying fire on the beamed ceiling and not thinking of anything at all. The future and the past were barred from her mind as she moulded her body protectively to his. When he awoke, he found her next to him, warm and giving.

'Agnès,' he whispered.

He caressed her tenderly and she reached shyly to touch him. The discovery of his maleness both frightened and awed her, but her body responded in spite of her fear. When Armand guided himself to her, stars of pain burst deep inside her. She gasped, trying not to cry out, as he moved within her. The pain was over in a moment, followed by a wave of joy at the voluptuous fullness his love gave her. His passion spent itself with unexpected gentleness, and as Armand whispered her name it seemed to Agnès the sweetest sound she had ever heard. When he withdrew, he cradled her to him, kissing her cheeks and eyelids. The scent of him, a warm, living fragrance as evocative as freshly tilled earth, imprinted itself on her for ever. She lay very still, conscious of her body throbbing and burning as though she had passed through a furnace. Thoughts of the mortal sin she had just committed beat down on her like rain on a tightly closed window, unable to touch what she had just experienced.

An hour or more later Agnès awoke from a light sleep to hear Armand's deep breathing beside her. The fire had dwindled to glowing embers and the tiles were icy under her feet as she slipped out of the bed. Wrapping herself in a blanket folded at the foot of the bed, she walked to the window and looked out at the blue valley lost in the deep peace of Christmas morning. Reluctantly, she turned to gather her clothes, to dress and depart, as quietly and unobtrusively as she had come.

That morning Agnès woke up later than usual. A crack in the shutters revealed a slit of sky that seemed brighter than usual, and she rushed to the window to behold a sight that she had seen only a handful of times in her life. The snow that had been falling lightly as she left Brissac had continued through the night and blanketed the garden with white. She stood there for a moment, looking in wonder at the contours of the fence, the garden chairs and the pump buried beneath the snow. In the blank white light reflecting from the sky there were no colours, no shadows, no familiar shapes to mar the perfection of this newly created world. Thinking of the night before, this transformation of the landscape seemed to celebrate the change in herself. Agnès turned from the window, not quite knowing how to begin a day so utterly unlike any other of her life.

When she had melted the ice in the sink, built a fire, done her household chores and fed the rabbits and chickens, she walked to the village to church. By the time she returned the snow was starting to melt into a grey slush on the road. When she saw tyre marks in front of the gate where a car had stopped, Agnès's heart began to pound; she realized it might have been Armand. Pushing open her door, she almost stepped on an envelope lying on the floor. It had her name written on it in bold black ink.

Agnès put the envelope on the table while she took off her coat and hat, hesitant to open it, fearing what it contained. Since she had woken up that morning she had thought of nothing but Armand, but had not dared to wonder when or how they would meet again. When she had built up the fire, she pulled up a chair and reached for the envelope.

Dearest Agnès,
I drove by, hoping to find you at home this morning, but perhaps it is better this way. I have decided to leave immediately for Savoy.

I awoke this morning feeling for the first time in perhaps years that I am really alive. I can truly say that I almost felt happy, all because of you. What you gave me last night was the most precious gift you had to give – yourself, a gift we both know I am unworthy of. The compassion, the humanity that inspired the gift of your love is beyond my own aspiration, and I thank you from the bottom of my heart. That you could feel this way after my confession that I had murdered a man in cold blood touches me infinitely.

My first thought when I found you had gone was that you might regret what happened between us, though I pray you don't. And I hope you will not be angry that I have left without seeing you again. Our lives have crossed twice now and may well do so again. In the meantime, we must go our separate ways, fulfil our separate destinies. I think that you must realize this as well as I. The common bond we share is buried beneath the complexities of our separate lives, but nothing can ever take it away. Please know that I regard you as a true and miraculous friend, perhaps the only one I will ever have. You have my deepest admiration and respect. It would be better, perhaps, to destroy this letter after you have read it. I could not go away without expressing all it contains.

My deepest sentiments,

Armand

Stirring in her bed, Agnès found her face was wet with tears. The chiming of the kitchen clock had summoned her back from her reverie just when she had been on the brink of reliving all the fear and pain of bearing a child in secret. She recalled how long she had sat thinking in the darkened kitchen that day with Armand's letter in her hand, coming to the conclusion that she could never destroy the only tangible memento she had of him. From that day on she was conscious of a void inside her where hope had never been allowed to grow. But in the years that followed, those hours with Armand had always remained a shining microcosm of life as she would have liked to have lived it. Now, as she turned her head to take a last look at Armand's photograph, it seemed as if a light had gone out for ever.

# Chapter 16

Isabelle stood up restlessly and paced behind the sofa, thinking of Rachel's call moments earlier. 'You realize she intends to come here to deliver some sort of ultimatum. That's why she was so vague on the phone.'

'I really don't know,' said Alain, an exasperated note in his voice.

'Well, it's certainly not a social call.'

'She's probably curious. After all, wouldn't you be?'

'I don't understand why you didn't simply put her off by saying we were going out or that you just don't want her to come here.'

'I wanted to appear perfectly normal. If I had forbidden her to come here, it would have put me on the defensive. Things are strained enough between us as it is. She seemed calm on Saturday, reasonable even. I really thought we had turned a corner and that she was beginning to see there was no sense in hanging around here any longer. For a start, she must be bored out of her mind in that claustrophobic little house.'

'Don't you see, that's just it. She's been stewing away there on her own and she's bound to do something rash. I'm telling you, she'll never return home without Oliver.'

'In that case she can stay here until hell freezes over. From now on she only sees him if I'm around. Even though I've got Oliver's passport, I'm not taking any chances.'

'Maybe we should just leave, close up the house and come back in September. She would clear out, and you could serve her with divorce papers and say you intend to take custody.'

He looked perturbed. 'Go away? We have to resolve the matter of the château before we can do anything. We're stuck here, whether we like it or not.'

'Then I warn you, *chéri*, when your wife arrives here this evening, you must be prepared to have a showdown. You must tell her that Oliver is not going back to the United States – ever.'

'If it comes to that.'

'It will, believe me.' Isabelle slung a large, white leather bag over her shoulder. 'How I loathe this interview with the priest. It's a difficult day for both of us,' she said, trying to smile.

'Are you sure it's the right thing to do – talk to the priest?'

'Yes, I'm sure. Pressure is always best applied indirectly first. Then if that doesn't work, you hit the target straight in the middle.'

'All right. When will that be?'

'I'll give him a day or two to contact the Grimal woman. I don't think Père August can choose to ignore what I'm going to tell him.'

'I think I'll unwind by the pool with Oliver. I've got a mountain of work, but I spend too little time with him. Every day there's some crisis, and frankly it's wearing me down. The phone hasn't stopped ringing all morning. First the lawyer, then the architect, then Rachel.'

'This is what it means to have a full life, *chéri* – lots of things going on. Ups and downs, highs and lows. You'd better get used to it.'

'I don't need you to point that out. I was a big boy long before I met you. You'd better get moving or you'll be late.'

'Don't pout. I won't be long.' She leaned to kiss him.

'Don't patronize me, Isabelle.'

'I'm not patronizing you,' she said, pulling back in surprise.

He looked contrite for a moment, then said, 'You're looking very prim and proper today. Almost like a schoolmistress.'

'I tried to look the part,' she said, catching her own reflection in the mirror above the fireplace. From her wardrobe she had unearthed a plain pleated skirt and a simple blouse. The only jewellery she wore was the glittering solitaire that had been her engagement ring and a gold watch. She slapped Alain's hand playfully as he gripped her naked thigh under her skirt.

'If you keep on like that, I'll miss my appointment with the good father.'

'It might give him a thrill if you told him why you were late. How do these poor buggers live without it?' Alain asked with a sigh.

'How do they? How do I?'

'What do you mean?' he said, nuzzling her thigh. 'Are you complaining?'

'Not exactly. But don't you think it's time you came permanently to my bed?'

'Wait a bit. Oliver's still upset from yesterday. He'll probably want to continue sleeping in my bed for a while. I have to be there in case he wakes up. Sometimes he has nightmares.'

'What if I have a nightmare?'

'You're a big girl. You can take care of yourself.'

She found it hard to smile at his remark. It wasn't what she wanted to hear. Before going out of the door she said, 'If I see Julian on the way out, I thought I'd tell him to bring Pascale Gachpour for lunch.'

'Good idea. I have a feeling she could prove to be the key to the whole deal. What a stroke of luck that she fell for Julian. His womanizing has paid off.'

'The biggest stroke of luck is what the lawyer discovered, thanks to Hélène. I'm going to tell the priest that we know the truth, beyond any doubt.'

'Be very careful how you bring it up with him. It could backfire.'

'Do you want to handle this?'

'I wouldn't dream of it.'

She kissed the top of his head. 'Relax, save all your energy for the meeting with your wife this afternoon. I was thinking, perhaps to be on the safe side, we should send Fernande on an errand somewhere and have her take Oliver and Lucien with her until you can get rid of Rachel. It would be dangerous having Oliver around. There could be a scene.' When Alain shrugged, she said, '*Chéri*, don't be mistaken: your wife coming here means total war. This time you'd better be ready for her.'

After Isabelle had left, Alain stood and looked gloomily out at the park, dreading the prospect of Rachel coming to Terre Blanche. He turned as the housekeeper came in.

333

'Fernande, I want you to take Oliver and Lucien for a drive this afternoon at four o'clock. Take them to ride the donkey at old Branger's place or to the trout farm, wherever you like, but don't come back here until at least six o'clock, do you understand?'

Isabelle came out of the house and nodded to the gardener, who was watering the pots on the terrace. Descending the flight of steps to her car, she saw it had just been washed, and was sparkling in the sunshine. '*Merci bien*, Jean-Marie,' she called to the gardener, injecting a pleasant note into her voice, though she was preoccupied with the hurdles lying ahead. One of her greatest joys in the country was the sense that everyone in her well-ordered household was going about his or her daily routine in her service. Consulting with the housekeeper and gardener was a long-established ritual that affirmed her sense of being mistress of Terre Blanche. She paused a moment to look at the cream stone mansion set in the park suffused with morning light, drawing pleasure from the sight. Everything in this little kingdom, protected by high walls and an iron gate, was as perfect as she could make it, and she was secure in the knowledge that nothing could ever take it away from her.

Driving past the *pigeonnier*, Isabelle noticed that the shutters were closed, indicating that Julian was still asleep. Now that he was bringing Pascale Gachpour to them Isabelle was ready to forgive his self-indulgent habits.

On her way down the drive she slowed the car as she saw Oliver riding his bicycle. With exaggerated cheerfulness she called, '*Au revoir*, Oliver. I'm going into the village. I'll stop at the bakery for some lemon tarts.'

'OK, thanks,' he mumbled.

'But wait – I forgot! How stupid. Today is Monday. The bakery is closed,' she said with mock horror. 'I'll find you some other treat. Bye-bye,' she called as he stared after her. Accelerating down the drive, her face hardened to a frown. She thought of Sunday, when she and Alain had taken Oliver to a picturesque village in the Pyrenees, where there was a restaurant Alain wanted to visit. Oliver's sulkiness had tried her patience, even though she knew the reason. She suspected that now he was aware of his parents' separation, he was beginning to hate her. Isabelle thought how convenient it would be if Rachel were to take the boy home to California, if only she could be sure Alain would not follow him.

Isabelle drove past a field of sunflowers, a sea of brown faces fringed in gold, basking in the sun. The sight of them reminded her how passionately attached she was to this corner of Gascony, how much she wanted to own Brissac. Seeing the château on the crest of the hill as she approached the village filled her with a sense of impotence. After all these years of waiting, it still wasn't hers.

She parked the car in the sunny square, and walked towards the street where the *presbytère* was located. Realizing she was a few minutes early, she walked to the antique shop, where she had once bought a few pieces from the insolent young man who owned it. It was closed, but peering through the window at a pair of gilt candlesticks, her eyes lit on a poster advertising the village fête, which, Isabelle realized with a start, was only four days away. The word *carnaval* printed in bold black letters made her heart stop. She was suddenly engulfed by the same terror she had felt the previous week at the motorway stop, when she had locked eyes with the strange man travelling with the convoy of gypsies. The events of the past few days had all but crowded the incident from her mind, but now it came violently home to her with all its shattering implications. She stared at the poster, her palms sweating, trying to convince herself that she was imagining things. But there was no way she could be sure whether or not the man she had seen there was the person in the photographs locked away in the safe, or even whether it was the same carnival that was coming to Roquelaire. She hurried across the square, driven by a panic that did not abate for several moments.

Isabelle was breathless when she reached Père Auguste's house, which was the last in a row of plain stone dwellings huddled together in a cul-de-sac. The grey shutters of the old *presbytère* needed painting and the garden was bordered by a high stone wall smothered by rampant ivy and rambling pink roses. The doorbell gave a quaint metallic ring, suggesting it had announced callers to generations of priests.

A white-haired old woman wearing a blue work smock and carpet slippers opened the door and peered suspiciously at Isabelle.

'*Bonjour, madame.* I have an appointment with Père Auguste.'

With a curt nod, the old woman led Isabelle through the sterile hallway, paved in ugly modern tiles and smelling of disinfectant, to a small sitting-room. At a glance Isabelle took in the crucifix hanging over the black marble fireplace, the predictably threadbare carpet, the disparate collection of gloomy, uncomfortable furniture and the religious periodicals on the table.

In a moment Père Auguste came through the door. '*Bonjour, madame,*' he said. When they had shaken hands he motioned to a chair. 'Won't you sit down?'

'Thank you, father.'

'Very hot weather we're having, isn't it? I hope we get some rain, but not so much that it will spoil the fête.'

At this reminder of the fête she gave him a startled look. The priest settled in the chair across from her and knitted his hands together, waiting for her to speak.

Isabelle had met Père Auguste on numerous occasions over the years, but had never felt comfortable in his presence. She knew he was from the Aveyron, a wild, remote part of France that produced shrewd, rugged people who were not easily flattered or persuaded. A halo of close-cropped white hair surrounded his severe but intelligent face. She guessed that when he was young he must have been quite good looking in a coarse sort of way. The steely look in his eyes reminded her more of a lawyer or policeman than a priest. She swept everything else from her mind, focusing all her attention on this decisive meeting.

'Father,' she began. 'Perhaps you can guess why I've come to see you.'

'No, *madame.* Please tell me.'

'It concerns Madame Grimal, the woman to whom Armand Bataille left the Château Brissac. I need your help.'

'*My* help? In what way?'

Isabelle looked at him thoughtfully, adopting a helpless expression designed to arouse his sympathy. 'I understand she is a devoted member of your flock . . .'

He smiled at her quaint way of putting it. 'Yes, Agnès is a very ardent Catholic.'

336

'I'm sure you must know that when she inherited the château, it came as a shock to me.'

'No, *madame*. I didn't know. But I won't deny I have heard that it was not what you expected. It must have been a shock to Madame Grimal too,' he said with a humorous glint in his eye.

Isabelle did not smile. 'This unexpected reversal threw me into complete confusion, as Monsieur Bataille had always led me to believe that he wished me to take over his property. He had no children, and I was a member of his late wife's family by marriage. I was his closest confidante, I believe, and gradually we came up with a plan to ensure a continuity for Brissac after his death. He was very relieved, enthusiastic, as the idea gained momentum. I had no doubt at any time that he felt it was a fitting way to preserve what he had built. And I think he saw the idea of a hotel and restaurant, with a spa, as a bequest to the entire village, because it would provide jobs and increase business in the local shops. Under the terms we discussed and, I thought, agreed, I would lease the property. So you see, it wasn't an outright gift. I never expected that. His sisters and their families were the benefactors.'

'Was the lease a large sum?'

'Perhaps not by today's standards. We came to the arrangement some time ago and I never questioned it. After all, it was *en famille*. The leasing arrangement took into account the huge investment required to convert the château to a hotel, costs that will be enormous in today's world, as you can imagine, requiring very substantial backers. But that's not the point. No one was more taken aback than I to hear that he had willed his property to this Grimal woman, who is no relation. I'm quite surprised that his sisters and their children haven't chosen to contest it. The change was made very late, almost just before he died. From what I have been able to piece together, it was after Agnès Grimal came to see him – two days before his death. Before you gave him absolution.'

'You seem to be very well informed on the matter,' Père Auguste replied, raising an eyebrow.

Ignoring the irony in his voice, she retorted, 'Of course, one can't help hearing about these things. They always come out. You may be aware that the notary approached Madame Grimal on my behalf about a possible sale of the property immediately after the will was read. She turned us down and refused even to discuss money. She said she needed time to think. Well, she's had time to think, nearly a month. I'm willing to pay a fair price, more than the lease would have cost. I've been waiting for her to contact me with her answer, but so far I've heard nothing. I'm beginning to wonder if perhaps she enjoys playing along. After all, she's not used to all this attention.'

Père Auguste smiled and shook his head. 'Madame, I think you're imagining things. Madame Grimal is the soul of kindness. Perhaps for her time moves at a different rate than for you. You must remember that she has lived a quiet life away from all the pressures and complexities of the world. Perhaps a little more time is a good idea. I don't really know what she intends to do with her legacy. Of course, I can't advise you. I'm merely suggesting . . .'

'Father, this project will mean new prosperity for the village – jobs, prestige, increased tourism. I can't put it off indefinitely. The investors need an answer very soon or they'll drop the whole thing.'

'Not everyone in Roquelaire is as enthusiastic about this scheme as you seem to think they are, *madame*.'

'And you, what do you think?' Isabelle asked.

'It seems to me that it could be positive if handled properly,' the priest replied evasively.

'My partner in the enterprise is Monsieur Alain Ribard, who was born near this village, as I'm sure you know.'

'Ah, yes,' he said noncommittally.

'He's become very well known as a chef in America, his adopted country, where he is at the top of his profession. He will lend his immense prestige and a great deal of creative energy to the project. He has the dynamism, the outlook to give Brissac an international reputation and he's a local man,' Isabelle began to warm to her sales pitch, unaware the priest's eyes had glazed over with boredom.

Père Auguste looked at her wearily, seeing the hand on the clock over the mantel had moved to nearly eleven. 'I don't know what to suggest, I'm afraid.'

'Can't you reason with her, talk to her? Surely she would listen to you.'

338

'You don't seem to understand that it's not my place. I can only stand by and advise if asked, and even then I must be objective.'

Isabelle, who was perched tensely on the edge of her chair, felt herself changing gear. She was ready for his neutral response. 'When this terrible reversal happened a few weeks ago, and when Madame Grimal refused to negotiate for the château, naturally I had my lawyer make inquiries.'

'Inquiries?'

'I was curious to know how it had come about that Armand Bataille had left his property to a stranger. That's how I discovered the truth.' She waited a moment, enjoying the surprise that animated his face. 'Père Auguste, this will probably come as a shock to you, but I've discovered that Pascale Gachpour, whom everyone thinks to be Madame's niece, is really her natural child by Armand Bataille.' As his jaw dropped in astonishment, Isabelle repeated, 'Yes, *un enfant naturelle.*'

Well before five o'clock Rachel was dressed and ready to drive to Terre Blanche. Since she had telephoned Alain the time had gone by with agonizing slowness. Her suitcase was packed and her clothes laid out for the morning departure to Bordeaux airport, where she and Oliver would catch the early flight to Paris. Envelopes lay on the table with money for the house rent, and for the caretaker, who would tidy up the house when she was gone. When she came down the stairs with her bag over her shoulder, the echo of her own footsteps seemed to follow her. The little house, which had become her refuge, was beginning to get on her nerves. She was tempted to leave Roquelaire that evening, as soon as she had picked up Oliver, and go to a hotel somewhere on the way to the airport but had decided to see the ordeal through to the end in an unhurried manner to reassure Oliver.

She left the house and walked down the street, hearing the rattle of Michael's typewriter as she passed his house. She hesitated for a moment, then suppressed the impulse to knock on the door. She hoped there would be time to say goodbye when she returned with Oliver, although she would have welcomed a few reassuring words with him now. 'Pull yourself together. You're on your own now,' she told herself.

339

Her car was parked in the sun at the edge of the covered market in the deserted square. The cooing of doves perched on the beams overhead broke the deep silence. She put the key in the car door and paused for a moment's private leave-taking, realizing this might be her last unhurried glimpse of the square. As she scanned the timbered houses, her eyes were drawn to the entrance of the church, as the bell chimed sonorously, fifteen minutes before the hour. Her eyes swept past the café, where the inevitable tourists sat under the red and white umbrellas, and to the narrow entrance of the Rue Cazat, reminding her of the painting group. She had gone to say goodbye just before noon, feeling as if she were leaving old friends behind. Rosamund's eyes had filled with tears when they exchanged a kiss and promised to write. Rachel felt helpless to console her when she announced matter-of-factly that Julian had failed to call since Saturday. She had left Rosamund with a heavy heart, disturbed by the look of anguish on her face.

Rachel drove away from the square, feeling as if she knew Roquelaire as intimately as if she had lived there for years. She wondered if she would ever come back, or whether she would want to after what had happened. The only reason she could think of was to see Michael, and she sensed that he was already passing out of her life. She imagined that he would meet someone new as soon as he got back to London, concluding to herself that such an attractive, interesting man was unlikely to remain alone for long.

Until she turned down the private road leading to Terre Blanche, Rachel had felt sure of what she was doing, but when she saw the formidable gates to the property ahead, she felt a violent fluttering in her stomach that tore her confidence to shreds. Turning up the white chalk drive that had given Isabelle's estate its name, she was full of foreboding. On Saturday, when Alain had left with Oliver, she felt for the first time since coming to Roquelaire that he was as concerned for Oliver's happiness as she was. When Oliver demanded to know if they were separating, Alain's patient, gentle way of answering convinced her that he was starting to feel guilty about what he had done. Because of that, she had relinquished Oliver for the night as she had promised. Now, forty-eight hours later, she realized she had made a terrible mistake, that she should

340

have bolted with Oliver when she had had the chance. She had been too trusting, she told herself, too scared, too uncertain. This flood of self-recrimination unnerved her once again. Cruising down the avenue of dark cedar trees, whose branches sweeping the ground seemed to menace her approach, she wondered what she would do if Alain refused to let her take Oliver away. But as the house came in sight she reminded herself what was at stake.

'I've got to stay calm,' she whispered, taking charge of her frayed emotions. She thought of what life would be like without Oliver, how her every waking moment would be centred on trying to imagine what he was doing in this place. Little by little, as much as he loved and needed her, if he stayed in France with Alain, he would slip away from her. Imagining such a future filled her with all the determination she needed.

Getting out of the car, she searched the garden for some sign of Oliver, expecting to hear his voice in the quiet garden now filled with the sound of birds. The only sign of movement came from the gardener, who was watering the roses beyond the house. The idea that Oliver might not be nearby simply hadn't occurred to her. She walked up the steps, feeling that the big, old house was even more formidable than she remembered it.

She rang the bell and was surprised when Alain answered it. 'Hi, come on in,' he said, his face unsmiling. Rachel followed him down the long, cool, black-and-white-tiled passage into the sitting-room, where the shutters were half closed. He motioned her to the sofa and she sat down, feeling vaguely conscious of the cluttered formality of the room. Alain sat on a chair across the coffee table and looked at her without speaking. He seemed a handsome, hostile stranger.

'Now, what did you want to see me about?' he said after several seconds had passed. His unwavering voice told her he was in control.

'Where is Oliver?' She looked around, thinking she might hear his voice coming from the swimming pool, which she knew was at the back of the house.

'Oh, he's gone somewhere with his friend Lucien, I think.'

'You think? Don't you know?'

341

'What do you want, Rachel? Out with it.'

'I told you I was coming at five. I want to see Oliver. You've had him for the weekend, and now I want him.'

He folded his arms belligerently across his chest. 'He's not here. And even if he was, I wouldn't agree to your taking him off like this. We've been through this before, Rachel. Oliver stays here with me.'

Her mind worked fast, noting that this time he made no mention of their coming home together. 'Does this mean that you're refusing to let me have my son?'

'If that's the way you want to interpret it.'

She stared at him, hardly able to speak. 'And what are your plans?'

'My plans? I don't know at this moment. But when I do, I'll let you know. You may as well go back home, Rachel. This whole thing will have to go through the normal legal channels.'

She stood, unable to bear it a moment longer. It was all she could do to keep herself from rushing to the window and calling Oliver's name.

'This is what you had in mind all along, isn't it? To leave California and take him with you. But I upset your plans by following you here.' She heard her own voice on the edge of hysteria and dug her nails into her palms to keep herself in check.

'Think what you like. Quite honestly, Rachel, considering the state you're in, I think it best if we communicate through our lawyers from now on. When I'm back in California, we'll work things out, but not before. You're wasting your time here; in fact, you're only making things worse.'

For a moment she veered between rage and tears. She was on the verge of arguing with him, but something held her back. A curtain dropped in her mind, smothering all her grief and rage, allowing her to think clearly for a few vital seconds. Alain was clever, intuitive, and he knew her better than anyone, but she had to outwit him. She appeared to crumble.

In a quavering voice she said, 'In that case, you leave me no choice. I'm not going to make a scene, Alain. You laid your plans very carefully. You took advantage of me in every way. As you pointed out, I'm wasting my time here. I thought I could appeal to you as the mother of our child, but I see now that I was a fool. I should have gone back home on Tuesday and started divorce proceedings. I'll get custody of Oliver whatever happens, Alain. The only thing you respect is force, and believe me, the law is on my side. The word for what you're doing is kidnapping, but you won't get away with it. I'll make you pay, in every way.'

'You can try,' he said, seemingly unperturbed. 'But I think you'll find it's too late for that. I'm not that stupid, if it's money you're referring to. As for Oliver, he's my son too. And we're in France, you seem to forget.'

'You'll be hearing from me before the week is out, and from my lawyers.' When she got up and abruptly left the room she saw a flash of blond hair as a woman hurried down the passage and into the room next door. She knew it was Isabelle, and that she had heard every word. Rachel raced down the hall after her, her shoes resounding on the tiles.

'Just a minute – that's the wrong way, Rachel. The front door is at this end,' Alain called after her.

But Rachel was already on the threshold of the office, facing Isabelle, who was looking back at her with a startled expression. The glamorous image Rachel had of her, which had loomed so large in her mind, evaporated completely.

Rachel said quietly, '*Madame*, I don't know why you felt you had to eavesdrop. I would have been glad for you to hear what I had to say to my husband. You're obviously supporting him in his bid to take my child away, but it won't work. Your lives are going to be hell from now on.'

'Rachel!' Alain shouted behind her.

When he grabbed her arm, Rachel pushed his hand away angrily. 'No – now I'm here, let me say what I think of a woman who steals another woman's husband and breaks up a family. You're trying to build your life at the expense of my and my son's happiness. You're a conniving and selfish woman, and I don't want Oliver to have anything to do with you.' Whirling around, she looked contemptuously at Alain. 'The two of you deserve each other.'

With that, Rachel brushed past Alain and walked down the hallway as quickly as she could.

'How dare she!' Isabelle shrieked, and then came an outburst of French too rapid for Rachel to understand.

At the front door, Rachel put Alain and Isabelle out of her mind as she looked around frantically for some sign of Oliver, knowing it was hopeless. Alain had guessed what she planned; she had been a fool to let him know she was coming.

She got into the car and fumbled with the keys. She glanced up at the doorway once more, but there was still no sign of either Isabelle or Alain. Tears of rage and humiliation streamed down her face as she steered the car down the drive. When she reached the entrance, she stopped, unable to see. Suppressing her sobs, she looked bleakly out at the carpet of sunflowers spread over the slope ahead. The vibrant yellow and green had a primitive beauty that made her ache inside. For a moment she didn't know where to go or what to do. Restarting the car, she began the drive to Roquelaire and her only refuge – Michael.

The drive back to Roquelaire took only ten minutes, but it seemed like hours. Parking the car in the square, she got out shakily and walked back to the house, her eyes downcast. Standing before Michael's door, she felt delirious with grief, as though she had a fever. He immediately answered her frantic tap at the door.

'Rachel!' He was transfixed by her tear-streaked face. Without another word he led her inside, then, closing the door, gathered her in his arms and let her cry until her tears were exhausted.

Approaching the blue cottage, Père Auguste could distinguish Agnès beyond the hedge by her straw hat bobbing up and down as she passed along a row of beans with a watering can. Setting down his fishing pole and basket, which provided the only convenient pretext for passing that way, he opened the rusting iron gate. Its squeaking hinges alerted Agnès, who stood erect and gazed down the path, her face in the shadow cast by her hat. She put down her watering can and walked to greet him, wiping her hands on her dark blue apron.

'Are you going fishing? And where's your faithful companion?'

'Sisi is at home today. She has a sore paw. I thought I'd drop by and say hello.'

344

'How nice. Isn't it hot? My poor lettuces are exhausted, but they'll revive with a little water.'

'You're lucky they get shade the greater part of the afternoon,' he said amiably. Looking at the pump outside the house, he added, 'And there's nothing like well water.'

'If we don't soon have rain, I'm worried it might run dry. As far as I know, that hasn't happened since my father was a boy. There were four summers in a row with hardly a drop of rain and they had to bring water here by mule cart.'

'That was a long time ago. Let's hope it doesn't come to that again.'

'Not so long ago as it used to seem when my father talked about it. Time shrinks when you're old.' Agnès sighed, motioning to a pair of green wicker chairs round the table under the thick foliage of the fig tree. 'Lately, not a day goes by that I don't think of my father and mother.'

Père Auguste sat down, still thinking of Agnès's reference to her parents. In all the years he had known her, she had never mentioned them. 'Do you find yourself thinking of the past, Agnès?' he asked with concern. It seemed utterly out of character for her.

'I think of the past more and more. Perhaps because the future is now so short. I've had a very uneventful life, but still, I find a lot to reflect upon.'

'But you're still young yet,' he protested. Père Auguste looked into Agnès's vibrant black eyes, which seemed to belong to a much younger woman. It was only the weathered face that gave her away, the hands gnarled from gardening and tending to her animals. It seemed to him that flickering in those dark eyes was an untold mystery.

'Thinking about the past excessively isn't a good idea,' he reminded her.

'No, but it's a way of keeping people, things, events alive, even after they're dead and gone.'

'Yes, I suppose so,' the priest agreed, wondering if she was thinking of anyone in particular.

'Perhaps I'm sounding morbid,' she said. Not waiting for the priest to comment, she added, 'The terrible thing about death is that it always seems to come at the wrong moment. It interrupts us in the middle of things that we wanted to complete.'

'That is for God to decide. And after all, what might be so important to us may not be to him.' He looked at her closely, surprised to hear her talk in this way.

'I let my imagination run away with me sometimes. I hope that maybe he gives us another chance to finish things, to right wrongs if we didn't get it right the first time round. Maybe we have the chance to come back again.'

Père Auguste looked at her to see if she meant what she said, then remarked, 'The best thing, I think, is to get things done the first time, not to leave them uncompleted. That relieves the worry.' Père Auguste thought he could see the way her mind was working, which was exactly the direction in which he wanted to lead the conversation. He guessed she was thinking about the château, but then she seemed to change direction.

'It may be heresy, but I'd like to believe there are second chances for our spirit. It might take a generation, it might be several. I'm thinking of Brissac.'

'Ah, yes. I see what you mean.'

She smiled, suggesting he did not see what she meant at all. If she were to mention that she sometimes had the odd impression she had lived before, it would bring the conversation to a halt. 'You see, I think Brissac should belong to everybody.'

'I'm glad you brought up the subject,' he said, relieved she had beaten him to it.

'Yes, it ought to be open to the public, in a manner of speaking.'

He was just thinking she had unknowingly averted a crisis with Isabelle de Montjoi when she said, 'When I say open to the public, I don't mean just anyone. But those who have a need for it.'

'A hotel of that type would necessarily be exclusive.'

'Oh, not that.' She smiled. 'Père Auguste, I suppose the days are gone when people give châteaux to convents.'

'I'm afraid so,' he replied with a bemused expression. 'I don't quite understand.'

'I think you should be the first to know I've decided to give the château to the Church.'

'The Church?' He was too surprised to say anything more.

'For a hostel, and a museum for the pilgrims of St Jacques.

346

They have no place to stay when they come here. And more and more are coming on foot from all over France, all over Europe. People say a new age of faith is dawning. I don't have the details worked out in my mind, but I think it could be done, don't you?'

He thought for a moment. 'I don't see why not. But, Agnès, are you sure?'

'I've been thinking about it for a long time. Perhaps longer than I realized.' She remembered the day she had stared into the pool in the courtyard and seen all the faces.

'Well, what a surprise,' he uttered, thinking of Isabelle, of Alain Ribard, of the many people whose lives seemed to revolve around the château.

'You see, I don't want to sell it. I don't need the money. I've come to the conclusion that it wouldn't do any of us any good to have the money.'

'Even Pascale?' he couldn't refrain from saying.

'Especially Pascale.' Agnès told the priest about Pascale's broken engagement. 'Not that the château has anything to do with it. But I can't be sure. I'm very worried about Pascale. But that's another matter entirely.'

'I heard what happened from Étienne's mother. Apparently he's so heartbroken he's decided to go back to Germany earlier than he planned.'

While they talked Père Auguste could not stop thinking about what Isabelle de Montjoi had told him. Even now he could not believe it was true. After a few moments he got up to go.

'This is surprising news. The council will be unprepared for it, but I hope they'll like the idea. It seems a good compromise. Yes, the more I consider it, the more I think it's an amazing, wonderful idea. Something I never thought of. But it won't make everyone happy.' More than that, he couldn't bring himself to say.

'I'm aware of that. I doubt if my sister and her husband will ever speak to me again.'

'Well, that's something you have to consider. I'd like to think Armand Bataille would have approved. Though he wasn't a church-goer, he had a lifelong fascination with the history of St Jacques de Compostelle.'

347

'Is that so?' she said wistfully. 'I didn't know. But, then, how would I?' After a pause, she continued thoughtfully, 'Monsieur Bataille had mellowed towards the end of his life. But I think he was too tired to see far ahead.'

'He thought far enough ahead to will the château to you, Agnès.' It was as close as he had ever come to asking her why she thought Armand had bequeathed her this munificent legacy. He watched her face closely as he spoke, for some sign that would give her away. He saw in her faraway look a wistfulness that made Agnès seem young for an instant. This confirmed to him that she had loved Armand.

Agnès walked him to the gate, where he collected his fishing rod. She seemed calmer, as if telling him of her decision had lifted a burden from her shoulders.

The sun had sunk behind the hills by the time they said goodbye. The priest walked down the road, his steps in time with the crickets beginning to chirp in the tall grass. His amazement at Agnès's decision was quickly followed by an awful premonition of the consequences. Knowing Isabelle's determination to have Brissac, he thought that if she were thwarted, she would probably seek revenge. Her veiled attempt at blackmail could end with Pascale being confronted with a shattering accusation about her origins, one which even now Père Auguste couldn't believe was true. Later, as he cast his line into the rippling pool, pink with the sky's reflection, the priest prayed silently that it wouldn't turn out that way.

*

When Rachel came down the stairs of Michael's house shortly before nine o'clock, she found him in the kitchen chopping onions. Hearing her footsteps, he turned with an uncertain expression.

'You always seem to be there with a brandy when I need it. I fell into a deep sleep. I couldn't believe what time it was when I woke up.'

He smiled. 'Shock does that. The body can go into a dormant state while the mind repairs itself. You look a lot better than when you arrived. How do you feel?'

'Not bad. As well as can be expected.' She came into the small kitchen and sat at the table, watching him as he stirred some garlic frying in a pan. 'I woke up completely disorientated, not knowing the time of day or where I was. Do you know what brought me back to reality?'

'No, what?'

'The cry of swifts and the colour of the sky. That's how I'll always remember Roquelaire. That – and you. I don't know what I would have done if you hadn't been here.'

'I'm glad I was,' he said gently. '*Rosé?*'

She nodded. 'Please.'

Michael went to the fridge and fetched the bottle, acutely aware of Rachel's presence in the kitchen. Earlier in the day he had suddenly become aware of the emptiness of the house. Now it was alive once again. He handed her a glass, then picked up his own. Raising it in a silent toast, he acknowledged to himself that now he had held Rachel close as she sobbed into his arms, shadowy possibilities of their affinity of mind and body had emerged into the light.

Later, after supper, they remained seated at the table, where a candle sputtered in the lantern.

'I've come to a decision,' said Rachel, leaning her elbows on the table. Her eyes had cleared, like the sea after a storm. She seemed to be steeling herself, as if knowing there was worse to come.

'Are you sure you ought to be making decisions tonight?'

'There's no alternative in this case. Thinking won't change things. I've done enough of that. Michael, I need your help. I've got to kidnap my son.'

Just before eleven the next morning Rachel was sitting on the terrace of Michael's house. Hearing the door open, she got up and saw him come in with a basket of shopping.

'I was beginning to think you'd decided to make a getaway,' she said with a smile.

He laughed and went into the kitchen. 'The shops are full of queues of starving Frenchmen on Tuesdays. I made a point of mentioning to a couple of people that you had gone home. They

349

expressed polite interest, and no doubt it will soon be common knowledge that you're no longer here,' he said, putting a baguette on the counter.

'I'm sure Alain will check up to make sure I'm gone. I wouldn't be surprised if he hasn't already walked past the Petersons' house. The thing is, he wouldn't give me any credit for being devious. Even now, he doesn't seem to understand what he's done to me.'

'I wouldn't worry. No one will ever know you're in hiding here. As I was filling the basket in the *épicerie* I began to wonder if people might suspect I was buying more than usual. I felt myself being cautious, as if someone were looking over my shoulder. Silly, isn't it?'

'I confess I woke up this morning feeling completely paranoid, too. I was sure the neighbours must have heard us bring my suitcase in last night and that the whole village saw you bring my car round to the garage and exchange it with yours.'

'It was so late there wasn't a soul around. Luckily, the garage is below the terrace, which is a good excuse for why I don't always go to the trouble of parking there. No, I wouldn't worry about that.'

'I hope not,' she said. Just talking about the elaborate precautions they were taking tightened the knot of tension between her shoulders. It had been there for so long now she was learning to live with it. 'I phoned the embassy in Paris, and my father, too. I don't think there will be any problem about getting Oliver a passport.'

'Good. I knew there was a way. Wait till you hear this. I had a stroke of luck in the village. I ran into a fellow called Carlo, who's on the fête committee. He asked me if I wanted to buy a lottery ticket, which I did. Guess where he was this morning?'

'Not . . .?'

'Yes. Oliver was there with Alain and Isabelle and his riding tutor, having a lesson, and Carlo spoke to Oliver.'

Relief coursed through Rachel. 'That means he's still here, that they haven't hidden him away somewhere.'

'At least you can be at rest on that score. There didn't seem to be any reason why they should.'

'What did this man say?'

350

'Carlo was impressed that an American boy could speak French. Anyway, they bought some lottery tickets, and they are definitely coming to the fête. I was able to gather that much, at least.' He recounted word for word what Carlo had said.

'I tossed and turned all night, afraid they wouldn't come. What a piece of luck.'

'They'll be there all right. Apparently Oliver has been looking forward to it enormously because he's never been to one.'

'Of course. It would have been out of character for Alain not to keep his promise. Now all we have to think of is how we're going to get Oliver when the time comes.'

'I've been mulling over a few ideas. I'll explain what I have in mind while I fix us some food.'

Over lunch on the terrace Rachel said, 'Friday seems such a long way off. I wish there was a way to do it sooner.'

'Be patient if you can. What we have planned has a much better chance of coming off in a crowd. I realize it's going to be hard for you being cooped up here, relying on me to be the messenger from the outside world.'

'Michael, I just hope all this isn't going to get you into trouble. I'd feel terrible if it did. It's asking so much of you.'

'It wouldn't matter if it did.'

She looked at him for a moment, feeling a gratitude she couldn't put into words. It had only dawned on her that morning how confident, how safe she felt in his company. She said. 'I thought that since I have so much time here, it would be a good chance to read the chronicle.' Rachel had thought of it all morning since she had seen the faded blue folder lying on Michael's desk.

'If you find it as absorbing as I did, it will make the time pass quicker. You can have a look at the rough draft of my book if you like. I finished it early this morning.'

Rachel thought of the villagers imprisoned in the courtyard at Brissac, and an unexpected kinship with the people who had waited, full of hope, for the dark angel to pass them by. And now she wanted to read their story.

351

# Chapter 17

In the shade of a spreading oak tree Margaret ate a stolen plum as she watched pilgrims straggling along the road to Roquelaire. They hung on to their billowing cloaks and wide-brimmed hats when a sudden gust of wind swept down the slope, lifting straw from the haystacks in the field below. Clouds shrouded the sun and the heat seemed to have left the land. Though it was only the middle of August, the weather was already changing. Margaret watched the birds gathering to fly south, trying to interpret what their early departure could mean. In the last year seers had noted strange phenomena in nature, occurrences that were out of rhythm with the usual seasons. Earthquakes had been recorded, as well as drought, plagues of locusts and floods, giving rise to famine in Christendom for the first time in living memory. These things, the seers said, were a warning of worse to come.

When another gust of wind shook the fruit from the trees of the orchard, Margaret could not help thinking that, like the unripe fruit, she might be shaken from the tree of life before her time. She clutched her arms around herself, feeling strangely vulnerable and exposed in the thin dress and apron that she had bought from a woman in the baths that morning. She had emerged from a tub of hot water refreshed and free of vermin, and had passed a strange and lonely afternoon waiting anxiously for John Stratton to return from a visit near Roxonde's camp to see what he could discover. Trying to curb her restlessness, Margaret opened a worn, leather-bound psalter and began to read the Twenty-third Psalm to calm her nerves, but her mind soon turned to other matters.

Margaret had been surprised to see Susan Wyndgate limping into the baths that morning, and shocked at Susan's offhand confession that she had fallen into lechery again. Although she had heaved a contented sigh as she joined Margaret in the steaming tub, Margaret had detected a sorrow in her eyes that hadn't been there when they had met before.

'Perhaps I'll get to Compostela yet to repent for my sins,' Susan had remarked. 'I ask you, why did God make sin so pleasurable?'

'For that very reason – to tempt us.'

'And we fall every time. I agreed to meet him again,' Susan had confessed.

'Do you think that's wise?'

'Of course not, but what could I do? Perhaps I should marry again after all.'

'Perhaps you should. Marry the one who set your heart beating yesterday, whoever he is.'

'Him?' Susan had giggled. 'You might as well keep a bird on a leash as marry *him*. And you, do you ever intend to marry again?'

'No, never,' Margaret had replied firmly. 'It brought me only pain before. I'll probably end my days in a convent.'

'Perhaps I'll join you there. Let me know your whereabouts, and if there's a place for me, I'll come. They could use me there, making psalters. But make sure there's no monastery next door, will you?', she had added with a twinkle in her eye.

Margaret couldn't help being amused at Susan's unbridled earthiness. When Margaret had told her that she had approached John Stratton, Susan had responded in a conspiratorial whisper, 'I'm glad he's a help to you. Don't worry, I won't tell a soul. Didn't I tell you? He's a fine-looking specimen of a man – so virile and with that powerful look in his eye that I always admire.' Susan had sunk deeper into the tub, with a look on her face that told Margaret she was reliving her moment of sin with almost as much pleasure as it had given her the first time round.

Margaret thought of Susan's descriptive words again when she saw John trudging up the hill, silently agreeing that he was indeed a fine-looking man. Just the sight of his greying head, his strong shoulders and manly stride instilled confidence in her. His serious expression was broken by a smile when he saw her, suggesting that he had come bearing good news.

353

'I thought you might have given me up for lost,' he called.

'Not at all,' she replied brightly, as if she were unconcerned that her life depended on the news he brought. She didn't want him to see her always racked by worry, and since she had replaced the androgynous pilgrim's gear with light, summer clothes she felt like a woman again. She tossed away the plum she had been eating. 'I found some fruit and I bought a piece of cheese from a shepherd who passed. It's a long time since I idled away the afternoon in such a fashion.'

He nodded appreciatively. 'I wouldn't have recognized you. Where is your cloak and staff?'

She told him how she had come by the dress.

'To tell you the truth, I wasn't sure it was you. I thought it might be someone else.'

She laughed. 'Oh, but it's good to be free, to feel the wind and the sun again.'

'And now, prepare yourself, for I have news.'

Her heart came to her throat as they sat down under the tree.

'Just outside the camp, by chance, I met a huntsman, a Welshman by the name of Selwyn. I was surprised to discover that he is now attached as huntsman and falconer to your husband.'

'You know him?' she asked, amazed.

'Incredible as it seems, yes. He was equally surprised to see me, I assure you. I crossed him at a bridge spanning the river in the forest below Brissac and we hailed each other like long-lost kinsmen. He was a bowman at Crécy, attached to the company I fought with. He's a good, brave soldier, and I remember him well.'

She shook her head. 'His name means nothing to me.'

'Your husband took him into service not quite a year ago. You don't seem surprised.'

'I was merely thinking that for all his preoccupation with divorce and child-snatching Roch wasn't too busy to look after his pleasures,' she said, unable to disguise her contempt.

'My lady, steady yourself, for you haven't heard the best of what I have to say: your son, Thomas, will almost certainly be in Roquelaire at the end of the week for the festival of Assumption, when Roxonde de Montferrand and your husband will host a banquet for the local nobles.'

Margaret stared at him in disbelief. 'Is this really true?'

He nodded, warmed by the joyous incredulity on her face. 'This is what Selwyn told me.'

'Thomas, here, in Roquelaire ... it would seem my prayers have been answered. But how does the huntsman know all this?'

'Servants talk freely among themselves, as you know. Selwyn said the messenger who was bidden to fetch your son bragged to all the others of the lavish purse he was given to pay his expenses on the way from Moirax.'

'Moirax.' She shook her head in amazement. 'That was where Roch began as a postulant before he turned his back on the Church. I was not more than a short journey from there a week ago, yet I never thought to go there.'

'I doubt if the abbot would have told you of your son's whereabouts. He was probably paid to keep silent.'

'How can I thank you for what you've done, sir? You've given me back a reason to live.' Margaret bit her lip to hold back the tears. For the first time in months she felt free of torment.

'It pleases me greatly to be the agent of your happiness, my lady,' he said quietly.

'You have my deepest thanks and prayers for what you've done, truly.'

He swept away her seriousness with a self-deprecating smile. 'It's been a long time since prayers have been offered on my behalf by a pious lady. I'm sure the angels have forgotten me. Curses sent down below are more what I'm used to.'

A joyful mischievousness welled up inside her. Eyes dancing she said, 'How indeed could you be called wicked?'

'I am very wicked, believe me,' he assured her, dazzled by the happiness in her eyes, the sudden colour in her cheeks. For the first time he became aware of her unblemished neck and throat, her proud head, and shoulders that suggested to him that the rest of her was equally well-made. Polished by the elements and burnished by hope, this beauty he beheld was but a shell for a spirit that had captured his admiration after a single day of

355

knowing her. Yet John felt himself falling from the lofty pinnacle of virtuous intention into flaming carnal awareness caused by the hint of her breasts held snugly by a high sash, the swell of her hips and thighs through the coarse linen. He was transported far from the blustery, hot hill in plain view of the road to a shady nook he had passed in the woodland. There he imagined them becoming lovers, by a stream, the image of their entwined bodies painted on the moving water, their whispers accompanied by the song of nightingales. At the sound of her voice, John came back to the present, where such a thing could never happen.

'Moirax,' she was repeating. 'To think I was not more than a few leagues away only days ago, with no idea that Thomas was there. I ought to have known.'

She frowned as if vexed, and he reminded her, 'A mother is not a vixen who can find her cub in the forest.'

'Had I known Thomas was in Moirax, I would never have come so far south, and then I would not have made your acquaintance. That would have been sad, sir, but had I not intruded, you would have remained undisturbed in your writing.'

'Whatever the cost in time and effort I'm at your service, my lady.'

His polite declaration masked a palpable warmth, which she knew she must ignore. John Stratton exactly fitted Margaret's image of the tenderhearted warriors who worshipped maidens from afar in the stories she had loved as a girl. In such a tale she would have given him her colours to wear in tournaments and he would have sworn his eternal fidelity, and after years of intense wooing, she might have given herself to him without the knowledge of her husband. But now there was no such code to govern the attraction she had felt almost from the first moment she had set eyes on John Stratton. They were a man and a woman alone, whose only restraint was conscience. Never, since Roch, had Margaret been drawn to a man with such force. The night before, when he had shown her to the stable, both of them full of the pleasure of each other's company, she had sensed that one gesture from her and they would have tumbled into the soft straw together. When morning came, she wondered if she would have

356

regretted such an impulse. She had been a virgin at her marriage and a faithful wife thereafter, but the holiness of pilgrim shrines and churches she had seen in abundance now seemed no protection from yearnings she thought she had put away forever. Yet a voice whispered that her life was not her own, that all pleasure and happiness must be postponed or even forbidden.

Margaret's eyes moved to the distant towers of Brissac, where the armorial pennants of Guirard de Monferrand hung limp in the stillness of afternoon. The thought that Roch was camped not far away with his mistress filled Margaret with an anger she might once have called jealousy, but no longer.

Seeing the preoccupied look on her face, John said, 'You seem to be searching for something. May I know what it is?'

'I was thinking what a vain fool Roch was to give a lavish purse to a servant. Without that, I might never have known he was here. He may well live to regret it.'

Beneath her contempt for her husband John detected a taste for vengeance.

'If I were a man, I could go to his camp now and challenge him. But we women have to be content with other weapons. At one time I even thought of poisoning him.'

This made John smile. 'Your greatest weapons are silence and stealth. What do you plan to do?'

'Wait my chance, then strike. I want Thomas back even if I have to take him by force.'

'You must take care. If your husband has taken the trouble to hide his son away, then it is because he doesn't plan to part with him.'

'He'll have to see me dead first.'

'That would be a great pity.'

Margaret's eyes blazed. 'Only if it were in vain, because I would think it worth my life if it would save Thomas. If I can get him safely back to England, to my brothers, they'll protect him from Roch if I am taken.'

John told her that the Welshman would come to the house early on the morning of Assumption to report whether Thomas had arrived. 'You had best wait in hiding until then. Will you be coming back to stay the night again?'

357

'Yes, I will stay tonight,' Margaret agreed, wondering if it was wise.

'Very well, then. I'll expect you at sundown.' John's gruff reply didn't reveal his happiness at her decision.

Walking down the hill, she said, 'There may come a time when I need to hide my son away from my husband before we can make our escape. Would you be willing to help? If not, I shall understand, but I need to know.'

'You have my word on it.' John heard himself assenting to what was madness with the blithe disregard of an adolescent. But his appetite for danger was whetted by the prospect of defending a lady from a man John supposed would be violent and unscrupulous if his wrath were aroused. He and Margaret began to hatch a plan to spirit Thomas away.

'Selwyn seems certain that Roch, Roxonde and their guests will come to Roquelaire for mass on the festival of Assumption. That would be the moment to steal your son away in the confusion.'

'But if we could escape, where would we hide? Roch would ransack the village for us, including your stable, I should think.'

John stroked his stubbled chin as he thought. 'The best place for concealment would be under his very nose. I'm thinking of the convent in Brissac. Mother Clothilde might help you. I doubt she has much love for Roxonde, who will surely replace the Benedictines with sisters of her own, widows and orphans of the nobility.'

'But then what do I do, where do I go?'

'Spain would be the best place. From there you could get a passage back to England. Why not continue from here as you came, as a pilgrim, with your son following you disguised as a servant?'

'Yes, that's it, that's the answer,' Margaret replied with enthusiasm.

The light was fading and they made their way to the road, where they were overtaken by pilgrims and merchants hurrying towards the village before the close of day. They agreed to walk apart when the ramparts came in sight so that no one would see them together, but before they could take their leave they were

358

distracted by a clamour behind them. Turning, they were astonished to see a band of people, nearly a dozen in all, who looked like half-naked savages coming down the road. Their blood-curdling wails pierced the air, and as they approached Margaret and John saw they were scourging themselves with nailed whips that drew copious streams of blood.

'What in God's name . . .?' whispered John, mystified by their wild, emaciated appearance.

Margaret clutched his hand. A chill went through her at the wailing voices, which seemed hardly human.

'Repent! Repent! The end of the world is near, the second coming is nigh. Repent to Christ before it is too late. A pestilence is on us, and death is at hand.'

Peasants returning from the fields and women taking their washing from the *lavoir* stopped in their tracks to see what the noise was. Some people fled, struggling under their loads. Children started to cry and hid behind their mothers' skirts. The skeletal penitents, caked in filth and wearing only loincloths that barely covered their genitals, formed a circle and began to chant, whipping themselves in a frenzy until their backs ran red with blood. There were cries of horror as a filthy, wraith-like woman flailed her breasts with a whip of nails until they were a bleeding pulp. A wild-eyed man with a trailing white beard besieged bystanders, exhorting them to repent with terrifying descriptions of what purgatory held in store on Judgement Day. One by one the villagers sank to their knees sobbing and praying for forgiveness before they entered the circle of the penitents, some of them tearing at their clothes and beating themselves as if they were possessed.

For several moments Margaret and John watched what was happening in stunned silence, united by an unspoken conviction that these raving madmen, who foamed at the mouth and talked incoherently, were possessed by devils rather than by the Holy Spirit. The August sun had disappeared, a roll of thunder sounded across the hills and drops of rain started to fall. The green valley was in the grip of unseen forces.

John touched Margaret's sleeve, motioning to her that they should slip away from the hysterical crowd.

359

Looking over her shoulder, she muttered, 'I don't understand what it means. Do you think that this is what God wants from us?'

John shook his head disapprovingly. 'No, not God. Some strange power has overtaken these people; their souls are eaten by fear.'

The terror the penitents had aroused in the villagers dug deep into his mind. In one moment the good people of Roquelaire had become a mob of incoherent madmen. Terror had seeped through the thin membrane that protected the integrity and sanity of the town. In his bones John knew that the terrible pestilence was creeping closer. He observed the mob dancing against the bruised sky, feeling its nearness as never before.

'John' – it was the first time she had ever called him by name – 'I'm so afraid suddenly. Tell me, do you think this means the end of the world?'

He looked down at her gently, wishing he could quell the uneasiness in her eyes. 'No, of course it isn't the end of the world . . .' His voice was all but drowned by shrieks from the crowd behind them.

Two day later, at daybreak on the Feast of Assumption, the penitents moved on, leaving a wake of uneasiness behind them. The villagers were glad to get rid of them, as their ceaseless exhortation to repent day and night had begun to pall. Yet, the atmosphere in the town had changed imperceptibly.

John rose earlier than usual and entered the courtyard that led to the stable, where Margaret was still sleeping. He filled his lungs with cool air, feeling a rush of gratitude at being alive as he listened to the sparrows chirping in the eaves and the doves burbling from the rooftops. In the quiet of morning he could almost believe that life had returned to normal. But streams of travellers on their way north had been passing through the village with disturbing tales of the pestilence, which was reported to have reached well beyond Marseille and almost to Toulouse. A few people had fled the village, but most went on about their daily routine with a false cheerfulness. He and Margaret had spent the

360

last two evenings in companionable seclusion, dining, playing chess and conversing about all manner of things. All night he had thought of the moment when she would leave him. Now, as the day dawned, he was tempted to go with her.

He tapped on the stable door and heard Margaret's sleepy voice answer. Opening the door a crack, he saw her nestled in the hay, her auburn hair uncoiled, her sash undone. A gladness filled his heart at the sight of her.

'Is something wrong?' she whispered when she saw him.

'No, nothing is wrong. But I expect the huntsman will probably come as soon as the gates are open. I thought I ought to wake you in case you slept too long.' It was a lame excuse, but he knew he would cherish this intimate glimpse of her after she had gone.

Margaret self-consciously slipped on her sandals and tied her kerchief under his scrutiny. She had been dreaming of him, and seeing him brought back that sense of heightened awareness that dreams bestow. However, there was no explaining why, after only a few days in his company, she should feel as close to him as if she had known him all her life. She looked up at him with questioning eyes, weighted by the knowledge that her life had already flown into his, and that there was nothing she could do to alter the future. But neither smiles nor tears could change the fact that at nightfall she would be sheltering in the convent with her son, perhaps never to see John Stratton again.

He crouched down in the hay beside her, struck by the bitter-sweet sensation that her nearness aroused. Nothing would have been easier than to close the door of the stable and take her in his arms. Shutting the world away, he imagined, they could love passionately, completely, using their bodies and hearts for what they were intended and thus conquer the pain of an uncertain future, if only for a little while.

John got up and walked out of the stable door, battling with an aching need for Margaret that no village harlot would ever satisfy. 'I'll be in the house,' he said over his shoulder. 'Cassius is making some porridge and it will be ready soon.'

Margaret got up from the hay and the searching look she gave him as she passed him in the doorway weakened his stoic self-denial. He wondered then if he was a fool not to speak his mind while he had the chance, but it was too late. The church bell was ringing insistently, and the sounds of the square coming to life beyond the gate – the clatter of a bucket, the clucking of chickens in the courtyard – thrust him towards the abyss of solitude that would be his lot when Margaret had gone.

After breakfast Margaret returned to the stable, where she was mending her satchel and cape in preparation for the journey, when she heard John running across the cobbled courtyard. She looked up expectantly as he pushed in.

'The huntsman has come and gone. The entire party from Brissac will leave camp after nine o'clock. Thomas is with them – he and the messenger arrived yesterday evening. I'm saddling a horse to ride to the convent to make sure Mother Clothilde is ready for you and that nothing can go wrong.'

'Is there nothing I can do?'

'You'd best stay here and wait. I'll be back as soon as I can.'

Margaret's mind raced ahead to the moment she and Thomas would leave the village hidden in a cart going to Brissac carrying reliquaries and vestments that had been borrowed for the procession.

'I'll see you here before I go, surely,' she said.

'Perhaps. But only briefly. It's much better that we are not seen together. I'll be watching over you from a distance. And if anything goes wrong, be assured that I'll defend you. Have faith that all will go well.'

She began to gather her cloak and pouch resting in the straw, 'Perhaps someday I'll pass this way as a true and honest pilgrim to give thanks to God for granting an impostor's wish.' She knew as she said it that life would never prove long enough to climb the same mountain.

'Should you come back, my lady, try looking for me here, in the same place.' John's eyes were full of false brightness.

'If I return, do you suppose I'll find you at your desk, still writing your chronicle?'

'By then it will be either long since completed or abandoned. But I'll find some other work to occupy me.'

362

'Farewell, John. I hope we meet again.' She couldn't bring herself to address him as 'sir' any longer. 'If you come to England, you'll send word, I hope, so we can receive you in Chepstow.'

'It is my greatest wish.'

There seemed nothing more to say. John bowed courteously and went to fetch his horse. A moment later Margaret heard the clatter of hooves on the cobbles, but she didn't look up. Her tears fell on to the satchel she was mending, which contained clothes for Thomas to wear when they escaped.

Florentine ducked through the low door of the bakery bearing a basket full of bread, with her mother in close pursuit.

'You've left it much too late, my girl. You're going to miss mass as well as the procession. And anyway, the abbess and the nuns will all be in church, and there will be no one in the convent kitchen to take the bread. What's wrong with you? Since you've been betrothed you're behaving like the village idiot.'

Before her mother could stop her, Florentine escaped down the street with the basket of loaves. Her face was flushed from the heat of the brick oven that filled the house and was lit well before dawn every morning, winter or summer. She broke off the end of a loaf and chewed it, not tasting what she ate as she hurried through the town pretending to be in too much of a hurry to speak to the people who greeted her. People were already crowding into the square, where a fair-like atmosphere prevailed, to get a good place. There were mimes and musicians, the usual itinerant confessors and pardoners, and vendors selling buns in the shapes of crosses. Banners had been hung, and the streets had been washed clean and laid with fresh straw for the holy day, when the bishop would parade through the streets with the church relic, a gold casket containing a fragment of St Anne's shroud.

Florentine jostled her way through the crowd and down the street through the arch, her clogs clattering loudly. People turned to stare at the beautiful baker's daughter, a basket of bread over her arm, her cheeks flushed, her hair escaping her kerchief.

The sky glowed an angry red after a storm in the night and Florentine realized how wet the ground at the pond would be, but

363

she didn't care. Thinking of the Cat waiting impatiently for her there, she fled up the hill as if on wings, past a stream of people heading for the village. She slipped from the road to avoid two nuns from Brissac hobbling down the hill in distinctive brown habits and white wimples. Exhilarated by her escape, Florentine broke into a run across a rain-drenched field that sparkled in the sun. She was entering a magical kingdom where nothing could harm her.

It wasn't until the pond came in sight that she stopped to catch her breath. The sight of the Cat's dark head rising from the thicket made her giddy with relief. She dropped her basket where she stood, not caring that the loaves fell out, and, hiking her skirts to her knees, she ran through the long, damp grass into his arms. As their mouths met in a voracious kiss fire leapt between them.

'I couldn't sleep all night for thinking of you,' Florentine whispered. 'I ran as fast as I could, afraid you might leave.'

'Leave? And where would I go? Where else would I find such beauty?' A triumphant smile played on his lips. Love in the morning was one of his favourite pastimes. Without further ado, he released her hair in a cascade down her back, while whispering suggestive endearments to rouse her ardour. He compared her lips to a golden cup as he kissed them again and again, her eyes to sapphires, her body to a mysterious island that he longed to explore.

As they tumbled down on the soft, dry bower of love he had made with his cape she gave herself up to that insistent pulse that had ruled her since they had parted, that painful gnawing in her loins, which had deprived her of sleep and killed her appetite. The Cat, more provocatively handsome than she remembered, moved in unhurried counterpoint to her impatience. He stroked her thoughtfully while he undressed her, fondling and kissing each of her charms until she was as naked as the day she was born.

'You are truly fair, my adored one,' he whispered, his eyes dilating with pleasure at the elegant sweep of her pure body against the red lining of his cloak. A sound night's sleep and a leg of mutton washed down by wine for breakfast had completely restored his vigour after pleasuring Susan again in a haystack the previous afternoon and now he was ready to enjoy the real prize.

Florentine dreamily watched him unbutton his bright tunic against the wall of rain-washed blue sky. She had no thoughts whatever, but waited in silence just as the strings of the viele awaited the bow to elicit a melody. A proud smile spread across the Cat's face at Florentine's shy amazement on seeing his anatomy. He stretched out beside her, taking her hand and pressing it to his groin. The discovery of his virility thrilled and awed her. Slowly she conquered her shyness, smiling up at him as he caressed her. And then he gathered her to him and began to do what she had dreamed of. Her eyes flew open at the sound of undergrowth being trampled. She saw an irridescent streak, like a kingfisher threading through the greenery. A face that looked familiar flashed into view, and a hand wielding a knife. Seeing the glint of the blade, she screamed, but it was too late. Everything went dark for a moment as the Cat's lifeless weight pinned her down. Florentine struggled to get free, but could not. It took her a moment to realize that Luc was standing over her wielding a blue-handled dagger, its tip red with blood.

'Get up,' he cried, dragging the Cat away from her.

Whimpering from shock, Florentine stared in horror at the naked buttocks of the Cat below his blood-soaked chemise as he lay face down in the grass.

'Get up, I said,' Luc barked tremulously.

Florentine struggled to her feet and began to dress, her hands shaking so hard she could not control them. Then Luc made her march ahead of him towards the village, leaving the Cat for dead.

When the pond was out of sight, she began to tremble so hard that she couldn't continue.

'Come on, move,' Luc cried in a gruff voice she didn't recognize.

'No!' She turned away defiantly, and when he grabbed her hand, she said, 'My basket – I must go back and get it.'

He looked at her contemptuously. 'Hurry up then and don't think you'll get away, because I'll come after you, you whore, you strumpet . . .'

Blinded by tears, Florentine ran back to the pond for her basket, but really because she knew her life would be worth nothing if she

365

left the Cat lying there. He was gone. There was no sign of his clothes or the pack in which he kept his instrument, only a patch of crushed, bloodstained grass where the struggle had taken place. She bit her knuckle until it bled, looking round for him, mystified. Remembering how badly he had been bleeding, all she could think was that he had crawled into the undergrowth to die. Luc's shouts made her dart for her basket. Running to him across the field, she fell on her knees and began to cry. Her only conscious thought was that her life was now over.

'What is your intention?' she sobbed.

Luc glared at her, unnerved by the sight of her bowed blond head. 'I've done what I came to do. And now I'm taking you home.'

'You've killed a man,' she cried, thinking that the Cat was dying somewhere.

'I've killed an animal, not a man. And when they find him, they'll say that wolves have savaged him, because his body will be torn to bits before morning – the body you found so pleasing.'

She shuddered and watched him fondle the blue-handled dagger, which she knew belonged to his father. When he suddenly pointed it towards his heart, Florentine realized that he had it in his mind to kill himself too.

'No, Luc, whatever you do, please I beg you,' she cried, prostrating herself. 'Kill me first. Take your vengeance out on me.' She fell to her knees and swept her hair over her head, exposing her neck.

The sight of her lying before him seemed to break his resolve and the dagger shook in his hand. The consequences of what he had done began to dawn on him. 'Florentine, I did what any man would have done to avenge his honour.'

She raised her eyes. 'Any man? Only the vilest man on earth would stab another thus. It was a cowardly thing to do.' She said it coldly, hating Luc as much as she hated herself. Years seemed to have passed since she ran to the pond to meet the Cat, driven by an enchantment that even now held her in its thrall. Florentine rose heavily to her feet, feeling sick. The sight of a heron coming to land near the pond reminded her how this wretched moment

366

had its roots in the day of her betrothal. She thought of the omen of the blood-stained feather, and of her lost maidenhead, shuddering at the power of the emotion that had driven her into the Cat's arms: it had been madness.

They didn't say another word on the way to the road, where there were still people walking towards the village. Luc looked down at her tear-stained face, her dishevelled clothes and hair, his rage reduced to a feeling of emptiness.

'Where are you going?' Luc asked when Florentine started to walk, not in the direction of Roquelaire, but towards Brissac.

'To the convent. It's the only place I can go now. My only hope is they won't refuse me because I have nothing to give them but a basket of bread.'

She walked on resolutely, her shoulders hunched forward, her head hanging low. She came to a halt and whirled round at the sound of a horn from the village blowing the ceaseless urgent call that meant siege or war.

'Did you hear that?' cried Luc, running after her. 'What do you suppose it can mean?'

They stared at each other, their minds wiped clean of the Cat's spilled blood. Florentine was gripped by a fear that had darkened her childhood, the fear of rape and pillage. At the wail of the horn she could hear the death shrieks that accompanied a siege, she could see the bloodstained, mutilated bodies lying on the cobbles, images that always inhabited her unconscious mind.

'Come, let's go back to the village, quickly, before it's too late,' Luc urged her.

She nodded and together they ran towards Roquelaire.

The mounted company of nobles cantered gracefully down the hill from Brissac, with Roch and Roxonde in the lead. From a distance they formed a ribbon of colour, the ladies in shimmering silk gowns, their trailing sleeves like pennants in the breeze; the men in embroidered coats worn with hose of every colour of the rainbow. Their palfreys and chargers had been brushed and combed to a deep gloss beneath their gaily coloured caparisons, silver bridles and richly worked saddles. The party numbered over two dozen nobles, not including their mounted retainers. They had come from neighbouring fortresses for the celebration of the Assumption, which would be followed by festivities to celebrate the forthcoming marriage of Roch and Roxonde. Peasants streaming down the road to get to the church in time for the procession stopped at the sound of so many horses overtaking them. At the sight of the dazzling company, led by the man who would henceforth be their lord, they dropped to their knees and doffed their caps to pay homage.

'Long live the king and queen,' shouted a simpleton, pressing his nose in the dust kicked up by the horses' hooves.

'Did you hear that?' said Roch, with an amused smile, to Roxonde, who rode at his side.

She cast the simpleton a disdainful look, but her chin rose a little higher. Richly dressed in a gown of pale blue silk and mounted on a grey palfrey caparisoned in scarlet, she seemed every inch a queen. Her elaborately braided hair shone like gold through the gossamer wimple held under her chin by a golden chain. Cabochon sapphires, chosen particularly for their size so they could be admired at a distance, adorned her fingers and ears, and her jewelled purse contained a handful of gold sovereigns intended as a gift to impress the bishop.

Not to be outdone by his future bride, Roch dazzled the bystanders, who beheld their future lord for the first time, arrayed in a startling costume worn by nobles of fashion in Italy, consisting of yellow hose and a scalloped coat in gold and black cut well above the knee. A cape embroidered with gold filigree and seed pearls, which had belonged to Roxonde's late husband, was draped over his shoulder, and his hat of coiled black velvet was worked with gold. Oblivious to the discomfort of the hot, heavy gear, Roch had never felt more pleased with himself or the world than on that fine morning. He viewed the ragtag of pilgrims and peasants gaping up at him with a sense of unparalleled satisfaction that only one swaddled in coarse homespun at birth could know.

'I expect that the bishop and priests will be waiting to greet us at the door as if you were already chatelaine,' he remarked, wishing that they were already married so he could fully share the honour.

He had been awakened just after daybreak by Brissac's chapel bell. Thinking it was the death knell that signalled the old seigneur's demise, Roch had made an undignified exit from Roxonde's tent, leaping into his leggings and chemise, then bounding barefoot through the trees back to his own tent before anyone could see him, though by now the nightly reverberations of their lovemaking had not gone unnoticed in the camp. On returning to his tent he had been bitterly disappointed to discover that the old seigneur hadn't died after all, and that the bell had been heralding the day of the Assumption. He had proceeded to Thomas's tent to ensure that the boy would be properly attired for the procession, even though he would be riding ignominiously in the rear in the guise of a page. His heart had swelled with happiness upon the arrival of his beloved son, and not even the old seigneur's failure to die as predicted could spoil his ebullient mood.

By the time the procession of nobles had reached the ramparts a crowd had gathered to witness the arrival of the future chatelaine of Brissac and her husband-to-be. Even the pomp and glitter of the priests assembling in front of the church in their gold-encrusted copes and chasubles could not compete with the magnificence of handsome lords and beautiful ladies on horseback. Such an array of splendour, never seen before in Roquelaire, rolled back the gloom that had recently settled over the village and seemed to herald a new and prosperous era.

One insignificant pilgrim, whose face was in the shadow of her wide-brimmed hat, had placed herself in front to get a view of the procession. Margaret stared up at Roch's arrogant, bearded face as it passed before her. She was terror-struck for an instant when he glanced in her direction, but his eyes swept over her unseeing. It came to Margaret that Roch's pompous vanity blinded him to everything and everyone but himself, as if he were walking with a mirror in his hand. Seeing Roxonde for the first time, Margaret felt none of the emotion she had expected – not anger nor jealousy that the Gascon noblewoman had usurped her place – but only a dawning recognition that they were as different from each other as a unicorn and a dragon. That Roxonde was beautiful was undeniable, and the haughtiness of her expression matched Roch's own, suggesting how much they were alike.

Knowing that Thomas would be in the rearguard, and hoping against hope that he hadn't been made to stay behind for some reason, Margaret watched the other lords and ladies pass before her in a blur of colour, accompanied by exclamations of wonder from the crowd, akin to the lowing of cattle. Then, suddenly, Thomas came into view mounted on a small black mare. Margaret looked upon him with disbelief that after so many months he was not more than a few feet away. His sombre grey suit was enlivened by red piping, a red hat and shoes to match, so that she could not help feeling proud of him. He seemed so much more grown up than she remembered. His chubby face was puckered above his stiff collar and his hair had been allowed to grow well below his chin. It moved her to see the tension with which he held the reins in his child's hands, suggesting how nervous he was in this grand procession. Margaret tried to guess what he might be thinking as his eyes, so like her own, darted right and left. A groom rode at his side, ready to guide him if need be and tell him what to do but Margaret knew Thomas must be feeling the ambiguity of his own position. It had never occurred to her that he might have forgotten her, but she wondered now, accepting that a year was so much longer in his life than hers.

Margaret was swept along with the crowd as it followed the procession through the gate of the ramparts and up the narrow street. When the square was in sight, she pushed her way forward as strongly as she dared, not wanting to draw attention to herself. She strained to catch a glimpse of John, but was kept down by the crush of bodies, which gave off a suffocating, rank odour. John had paid a man to slip Margaret's silver crucifix into Thomas's hand at the last minute, before he entered the church with the rest, an object she was sure he would remember instantly because he had cut his first tooth on it. The plan was that she would be waiting a few feet away, where Thomas could see her, but Margaret began to panic at the possibility that she might miss the crucial moment when it came.

'Let me by, I beg, let me by,' she shouted, trying to force her way with her staff. Her cries were drowned by the noisy mob, and people she touched shouted for her to wait her turn. 'Please let me by. I must go forward,' she pleaded, her voice trailing to a sob of desperation.

Suddenly, the narrow street erupted in chaos at the clatter of hooves coming up behind the crowd. Margaret felt herself jostled in every direction as she heard urgent cries from the unseen horsemen to give away. Amidst hysterical shrieking, people hurled themselves against the houses and into doorways to avoid being crushed by the galloping horses. 'The horsemen of the Apocalypse,' a woman screamed, yet no one jeered at this preposterous suggestion. Margaret's staff tumbled to the ground as someone shoved her violently aside. She looked up to see hooves pounding inches from her face and the thought went through her mind that an attack was being mounted. Struggling to her feet, she saw the troop of horsemen thunder into the square, followed by excited villagers and pilgrims. From their surcoats and swords, she identified the men on the horses as knights, although they were without armour.

The knights stopped in front of the church and the crowd surged forward to see what was happening. Pressed on all sides, Margaret couldn't move and writhed in frustration that her carefully laid plan was being ruined by this untoward event. Tears flowed down her cheeks as she tried to get closer to the party of nobles, who had already dismounted. In the crush it seemed she would never be able to get near Thomas, much less signal to him. Waves of confused murmuring surrounded her.

'What is happening?' she cried, but no one knew any more than she.

After what seemed like an eternity Margaret heard the plaintive wail of the horn from the ramparts, not the call to close the village gates at sunset, but a warning. She was buffeted to and fro as the crowd reacted in panic, scattering to see to their ungathered crops, to animals left untended. The voice of a priest calling for calm was drowned out by a terrified wailing, and chill went down Margaret's back at the awful presentiment that the world was about to end – her world, Thomas's world, John Stratton's world.

'Margaret!' A hand latched painfully on to her wrist and tugged her violently forward. John had forced his way through to her. 'Come with me.'

371

He pushed people out of the way and helped her get to the church, where people had dropped to their knees to pray. She was too dazed to ask John if he knew what was happening, but followed him mutely to the street that skirted the church and into a cul-de-sac, at the end of which was a barn. At the sight of a young boy in a grey suit trimmed in red she broke into a run. Thomas was standing by the hunchback she had met on the pilgrim road, holding her crucifix.

'Mother!' he cried as soon as he saw her.

Margaret clasped him blindly to her, enfolding him in her cloak like wings.

'Thomas, Thomas, my child, my boy,' she repeated over and over. There followed a moment of pure undiluted joy, during which she neither heard nor saw anything but him. The way his arms held her told Margaret how unhappy he had been and how much he needed her, expunging the last desperate year from her memory before the present could take hold again.

Then she remembered the hunchback and gave him a grateful smile, grasping his gnarled hand. 'It's you who brought him to me . . .'

'Glad to repay your kindness, my lady, which I have not forgotten. I've been delayed in Roquelaire for a few days, and I happened to meet our fellow countryman here.'

'This is my son,' she said, her hands proudly on Thomas's shoulders.

'Why are you dressed like a pilgrim, Mother?' whispered Thomas, his hand resting in hers.

'I'll explain everything to you in time, but not now,' she said, patting his cheek.

'Margaret –,' came John's voice.

'Yes, we must go quickly,' she replied, coming to her senses. She opened her satchel to take the suit of clothes she had brought Thomas for their escape. 'Change into these at once, Thomas.'

'Margaret, wait. It's too late.' John put a restraining hand on hers.

'Too late? Why is it too late?' She looked at him uncomprehendingly. She had been so preoccupied that she had failed to notice the gravity in his eyes.

'The horsemen who rode into the square . . .'

Remembering the horn sounding the warning, she realized what he was thinking. 'There must be some mistake. It can't be war. France is in tatters. The English at Blaye will come to our aid.'

'It's worse than that, Margaret. The pestilence is at our doorstep, not more than a few leagues away. This black death that kills everyone in its wake.'

Even then she could not quite take it in. 'Pestilence? Are we to die from such a thing after coming this far? Dear God . . .'

Thomas was looking up at her for an explanation, but she hadn't the heart to tell him that the end of the world was indeed at hand.

# Chapter 18

A whispering movement followed by a faint tapping intruded upon Rachel's sleep. She stirred, resisting whatever was nudging her towards consciousness. Through half-closed eyes she saw a light in the doorway, which now took the shape of a cloaked figure. Then, Rachel saw a woman's sun-browned face emerging. She had a high, smooth forehead and a straight nose that gave her face a serious cast, yet there seemed to be laugh lines round her deep-set eyes. Tendrils of auburn hair had escaped from the thick braid tumbling over her shoulder, as if she had been braving the elements only moments before. In one hand she clutched a pilgrim's staff that seemed too big for her, and in the other she carried what seemed to be a breviary. Telling herself she was dreaming, Rachel closed her eyes only to open them again at the strange sounds that had awakened her. It came to her that what she had heard was the swish of a cloak followed by the tap of the pilgrim's staff, and that the woman was Margaret Prior.

Rachel sat up wide awake and stared at the doorway, her heart pounding, but there was no one there. As she fumbled for the light, her hand brushed Michael's manuscript on the bedside table. Falling back on her pillow, she realized that reading this moving story must have given rise to an illusion.

Certain she wouldn't fall asleep again, Rachel slipped into her dressing gown and went downstairs. In the darkened sitting-room, full of unfamiliar shadows, she found she was attentive to any sound or movement that could suggest Margaret was somewhere nearby. She wanted to believe that she had seen, and not merely imagined, the figure of her dreams, but a rush of cool air and the sound of crickets greeted her when she opened the terrace doors, dissolving the illusion. Outside, Rachel sat down and watched the heat lightning flickering on the horizon, her mind still on Margaret Prior, who had come to life so vividly in Michael's book.

The minutes ticked by and Rachel came out of her reverie with the numbing realization that on Friday she would be making her escape from the village with Oliver, just as Margaret had planned to spirit Thomas away all those centuries ago. At the sound of bare feet on the tiles she turned and saw Michael's silhouette in the doorway.

'Rachel?'

'Yes, it's only me. I hope I didn't wake you, but I couldn't get to sleep, so I came downstairs for a breath of air.'

'No, you didn't wake me. I think I was having some sort of nightmare. Suddenly I was wide awake.'

'Were you? I was dreaming too.'

He sat down next to her. 'It's not surprising. You probably won't sleep a wink until you're safely back in California with Oliver.'

'Yes, I've been thinking about it, but that's not what woke me up.'

'I should have given you some tablets before you went to bed. I couldn't do without them last spring, but now I usually sleep like a baby.'

'I don't know where that expression came from. Babies don't sleep all that well. They usually wake up and cry in the night until their mothers come.'

She heard him chuckle softly and a warm feeling crept over her, knowing he was there beside her. 'What was your nightmare about?'

'I'm not sure,' he answered untruthfully. Part of his mind was still in the confused, disturbing dream, where he had been searching for someone. Even now he was troubled by what had seemed to be the cry of a child coming from an impenetrable blackness. He had woken in a cold sweat, his heart pounding with dread. It was too distressing to tell Rachel. 'And what were you dreaming? Do you remember?'

'It didn't seem like a dream, but of course it was. I dreamt I saw Margaret Prior standing in the doorway in her pilgrim's cloak.'

'Margaret?'

'Yes, isn't it odd? It was so real. Her face had a sweetness, a strength that seemed not of this world. It was hard to believe I was dreaming. I've been sitting here in the dark thinking about her.'

'As far as I know there are no ghosts in the house. But even if there were, I don't suppose either of us would believe in them, would we?'

She sighed. 'No, we'd have to find a much more rational explanation – like your book. Of course, that's why I was dreaming about Margaret. I finished it before dropping off to sleep.'

'I've had a few sleepless nights over it myself. I hope it didn't bore you.'

'Bore me?' she said with an incredulous laugh. 'Anything but.'

'It's good to hear you laugh. You haven't laughed since you arrived on Monday.'

Her impulse was to reach out and touch his hand in a kind of acknowledgement. As if reading her thoughts, we took her hand in his for a moment, making her feel unsure of herself all of a sudden. His touch in the dark seemed as intimate as a kiss. Her hand slipped from his and she felt the silence between them was palpable.

'I didn't want to say what I thought of your manuscript until I finished it, but I can tell you now.'

'I'm aware of that. The suspense is killing me.'

'I'm no judge.'

'I can't thing of a better one.'

After a pause she said, 'If you really want to know my opinion, I think it's pure genius.'

Only part of Michael was listening. The joining of their hands had ignited the dry tinder inside him. Now Rachel's words both elated and humbled him. 'Genius is a big word to use. I don't know if I deserve that sort of accolade.'

'Well, maybe I'm prejudiced, but for what it's worth, I was spellbound. You've succeeded in bringing to life a great, a wonderful story with such beauty and sensitivity that I was in tears at the end. It rivals anything I've ever read for pure emotion.'

Michael didn't say anything for a moment, he was so unexpectedly moved by her reaction. 'That's very encouraging,' he murmured. He had held himself correctly at a distance since she had arrived on his doorstep in tears, reverting once more to adviser and confidant. Now Rachel's words of praise broke the thin membrane of his reserve, drawing them close together.

'I know what you're thinking: that in my frame of mind I'd cry at the drop of a hat.'

'No, I wasn't thinking that. It's not so much your critical opinion that matters. What's important is that it obviously meant something to you, that it moved you. Now you've read it, I think I should tell you, if you haven't already guessed, that the character of Margaret is based on you.'

'Me?' Rachel turned to stare at him in the darkness. 'You based Margaret on me? But I've only been here a week.'

'Everything you've read was written since you came to Roquelaire. I was at it day and night once the idea struck me. I'd been casting around trying to breathe life into the characters when I met you. You triggered off something in my mind as surely as if a key had turned in a lock. Without that, who knows? Turning it into a book might have just remained a good idea that came to nothing. And I still have a long way to go.'

She gave a little laugh. 'Of all the things that have happened since I've been here, this is perhaps the most remarkable and, apart from meeting you, the nicest.'

'I debated whether to tell you. And now I'm glad I did.'

'It's a great compliment, because you've brought her so fully to life. When you're famous, I'll cherish the thought that it had something to do with me.'

'There's a long way to go before that happens. Instant best-sellers only happen in movies and novels, not in real life.'

'Tell me how it happened: Whatever was there about me that gave you such an idea? Can you remember?'

'Well, when we met at the café, the truth is I had already seen you in the church, standing in front of the statue of St Anne, the way John first saw Margaret. What could have been more obvious? And then, when I heard your reasons for being here – a search so similar to hers – it all fell into place.'

377

'I hope the similarity ends there.'

'I'm not trying to draw a parallel between your life and hers. I wouldn't want you to think that.'

'But just imagine if destiny, fate if you like, was amusing itself with a giant replay of those intense few weeks in Roquelaire, hundreds of years later. I wouldn't know whether to laugh or cry.'

'As far as I know, history doesn't dovetail so neatly, except in dreams and fantasies, so I don't think you need worry,' he reassured her gently. 'When we met, I recall I made some allusions to the idea, but I didn't seriously believe it for a minute.'

'Honestly?'

'Honestly.'

When she didn't speak again, he said, 'Such a thing might influence your thinking, God forbid. And that would be on my conscience.' He stopped, knowing he had said enough. It suddenly mattered deeply that she didn't even flirt with the idea of parallel lives that had so intrigued him. Yet prophecies seemed to be fulfilling themselves as he spoke.

Rachel was still turning the idea round in her mind. 'You once compared me to a pilgrim; I remember now. This afternoon when I began reading your manuscript I found myself thinking about Margaret – this woman who went through exactly what I'm going through, over six hundred years ago. I kept reading to the end, as if the story would tell me what lies in my own future, but if that were so, there wouldn't be much hope, would there?'

Michael avoided an answer by saying, 'Of course, we don't really know what happened in the end. The chronicle stops as the plague breaks out at Brissac.'

'I know. It's awful not to know what happened to everyone. The idea will always haunt me. What do you suppose became of all the people of Roquelaire, of John, Margaret, Mother Clothilde?'

'I'd like to think that they all survived and lived happily ever after, but it's unlikely. I always arrive at the same conclusion when I think about it, that they all died together at Brissac.'

'If that's true, where do you think they were buried?'

'Nobody knows. No records exist to tell us. But then, all over Europe, entire villages disappeared without trace.'

378

'Without trace,' she repeated. 'It's almost impossible to imagine.' She was silent for a moment. 'And now, what happens next? When are you going to send your manuscript to a publisher?' she asked.

'It needs a lot of work first, and I'm afraid there won't be enough time to do it before I leave.'

'What a shame it all came about so late in the day.'

'You should have come to Roquelaire sooner,' he said, making her smile. 'There's this matter of earning a living. It always seems to get in the way. Oh, I know on Sunday I was all carried away with ideas of going into the wine business, but you know as well as I do that it was just a pipe dream.'

'But it seems like such a good idea. Are you sure?'

'Of course it's a good idea. Things like that always are until you start translating them into concrete terms. The problem is that it takes so much time, time I haven't got at this moment. I've toyed with the idea of wangling a few more weeks from my editor, but the truth is, Rachel, I feel my time in Roquelaire is up.' There was a finality in his voice.

'What do you mean?'

'I'm thinking of putting the house up for sale.'

'For sale?' She stared at him in amazement. She realized then that she had been counting on the fact that Michael Lowry would be waiting in Roquelaire if she ever wanted to come back. A little dream that some day, when her life was in order again, she would return to France, that they would find themselves once more on his terrace, wrapped in conversation, the way they were now, faded.

'It's a good time to sell the house,' he was saying. 'The market conditions are right and Roquelaire seems to be on the map, as they say. Even though it's late in the summer, there will be buyers around until the weather turns cool.'

'You never mentioned it until now,' she said. 'I remember only the other day, Sunday, you were talking of laying down wine in the cellar. You said you'd save some for me. So I'm just surprised, that's all. I guess I've been so wrapped up in myself that I didn't think what was going on in your mind.'

'How can I say this without sounding as if I'm beating my

379

breast? But this summer has been the end of an era for me, a turning point. I don't think the role of lone wolf in Roquelaire suits me any more.'

'You've been telling me not to do anything hasty. Now it's my turn to say the same thing to you. You might regret selling this house. You're part of Roquelaire, and it's part of you, as trite as it sounds. What can I say to make you think again?'

'Everything you say is true, but I've more or less made up my mind. Listen, I'd better let you get to bed. You can't go on living on your nerves until Friday. You need to save your energy.'

She was acutely disappointed when he got up from his chair.

'Please don't rush off to bed because of me. I still feel wide awake.'

'It gets cold out here at daybreak.'

Rachel saw herself sitting on the terrace until sunrise, thinking not just of her flight with Oliver, but of Michael. Time was passing too quickly for her to examine what she was feeling and why. All she knew was that the vital spark between them might die if she didn't breathe life into it.

'It seems the conversation always revolves around me,' she said. 'From the moment I came here. Never about you and what you might want.'

Michael didn't reply, but she could feel him thinking. Her mouth went dry and a little drum of anticipation began to beat inside her.

'Your enthusiasm about the book is wonderful,' he said at last, 'and I thank you for it. It means a great deal to me. You're generous, kind – you're many, many things . . .'

'What about you, Michael. You're all those things,' she said, swallowing the lump in her throat. The halting sincerity in his voice had caught her unawares.

The horizon was convulsed with light for a moment, followed by the rattle of distant thunder, which vibrated round the terrace. With it came a little breeze that brought the smell of rain-drenched earth. Rachel waited for Michael to fill the potent silence.

He followed her eyes to the sky brimming with stars. The sight of the unfathomable dark scattered with pinpoints of light so distant and unreachable made him hungry to live the present moment to its fullest. When he looked down at Rachel, he was aware that the silence was charged with possibility.

She said, 'At this time of the night life takes on a strange perspective, doesn't it?'

'Maybe that's why I'm hesitant to say something to you that perhaps I ought not to say.'

'There is nothing you can't say to me.' Rachel was surprised at the sound of her own voice, unwavering and full of conviction.

He smiled. 'Did Margaret say that to John, I wonder? A moment ago I was thinking about the two of them in the tower at Brissac towards the end.'

'It was the most moving part of the story.'

'I can't resist comparing the two of us to them. Here we are, shut away from the outside world, just the way they were. There's a paragraph at the end of the chronicle, between the passage about war and death: "And thus I came close to telling this lady what was in my heart, but there came a knock on the door and later, when the world was in chaos and seemed about to end, I regretted that I hadn't told the caller to wait a moment, for then it was too late. From that day on I was bound in chains of memory, knowing that I had not done what I meant to do, said what I intended to say." I don't know why I'm talking in riddles, because I'm trying to find the courage to tell the truth.'

She rose to her feet. 'Then say it. Say what you want to say, Michael.'

He gathered her hands in his. 'Can't you guess?'

'I need to hear it.' Her voice dropped to a whisper.

'I've fallen in love with you.' Not waiting for a reply, he added, 'I've fought with myself since you came back, knowing I have no right to add any further burdens to your life. I care too much for you to give you pain. But I was afraid that if I didn't tell you, I'd be bound, like John Stratton, by chains of memory, that you'd go away and we'd lose each other. I didn't want to live with that. I don't expect an answer now, or ever, but I had to tell you how I feel,' he whispered.

The wounds Alain had made were still fresh, and Rachel wavered at the thought of a new beginning within her grasp. She couldn't make promises, but suddenly she was conscious of the seconds passing and the future stretching ahead. She took a deep breath.

'This week I thought my heart would break. And now I'm locked in a battle for Oliver. But there's more to life than that. At least I hope there will be some day. I'm deeply attracted to you, Michael. You must have sensed it. I don't care how it's happened, or why, but it makes me feel alive again, knowing that you love me.'

They drew together and as he kissed her, gently at first, then deeply and with a passion she returned, Rachel felt herself becoming weightless in his arms. When he let her go, they were both trembling.

He whispered urgently, 'It may be too soon, but I want you. I want to take you to bed. I want to love you.'

'No, it's not too soon. It's the right time.' Tears she couldn't hold back were coursing down her cheeks. She gripped his hand and they went upstairs together.

Oliver awoke, rubbed his eyes and made his way to the bathroom, guided by the nightlight on the table. On the way back to bed he quietly opened the door to the connecting bedroom to reassure himself that his father was still there. The sound of his even breathing and the outline of his body beneath the covers confirmed that Alain was sleeping peacefully not far away.

Oliver climbed back in bed and fumbled for the torch and comic book under his pillow. Moving the circle of light across the page, he pored over the pictures, his lips forming the words in French, which he was beginning to understand. This was his favourite book, which he had reread countless times, and he became completely absorbed in the adventures of Tintin and Captain Haddock as they searched for buried treasure.

Half an hour later Oliver closed the book, went to the window and looked out, resting his elbows on the sill. He pretended the tangled old trees were giants with tiny stars caught in their hair, standing in pools of moonlight. The mysterious night landscape made him feel uncomfortably conscious that he was in a strange place, far from home, without his mother. He thought of her in Sonoma and wondered what she was doing.

Gradually, as he stood absolutely still, feeling the damp night air

382

touch his face like a veil, he forgot his homesickness. He became aware of the chirping of crickets, and the elusive quality of their music drew his imagination beyond the confines of the house and into the unknown. Leaning out of the window, he looked down at the gravel path around the house, reckoning it was too far to jump. Oliver decided that if he tied two sheets together and secured them to the shutter latch, he could make a secret escape to the moon-drenched park. He saw himself bounding barefoot round the house to the shed where his new bicycle was kept. Mounting it in one leap, he would race swiftly and silently down the white drive towards the gates of the property, where at last he would be free. He could almost feel the wind in his hair as he envisioned himself speeding down the empty road past fields of sunflowers bleached by moonlight, like a sea of silent beings watching him, hurtling tirelessly through the night, until at last he reached Brissac, the dark citadel whose secret only he knew. With only his torch to guide him, he would retrace his way through the undergrowth to where he had seen the old lady disappear. Under the cover of darkness he would surpass the adventures of the boy in the comic book by discovering the treasure that lay buried there. A wave of excitement went through him as he imagined the flabbergasted faces of his parents when they saw his picture in the newspaper and on the television newsflash, hailing him as the discoverer of the treasure of Brissac. In the resulting euphoria his parents would call off their divorce and the three of them would return triumphantly to California, and Isabelle de Montjoi would disappear.

Oliver dived back under the covers and curled up into a ball as he thought about what he would do with all the money from the jewels and gold he would find. He got as far as choosing a jet plane and a racehorse for himself, an expensive car for each of his parents, and a trip to Disneyland for all of them. Then his eyes closed in sleep.

\*

In the bedroom at the end of the hall Isabelle stirred through the haze of sleep as she touched the space next to her, hoping to find

Alain by her side. The crunch of shoes on the gravel beneath her window brought her violently awake. Her eyes flew open and she listened intently, but the only thing she could hear was the steady song of crickets. Slipping from bed, she went to the window and stared down at the empty yard. She stood there listening and watching for some sign of movement as the heat lightning on the horizon sent dull patterns of light through the lace curtains.

Finally she turned back to the bed, trying to calm her jangled nerves, telling herself she had only been dreaming. But the clear memory of footsteps below the window sent renewed terror through her. She opened the drawer of the night table, feeling for the small revolver she always kept there, then remembered that she had left it in the study. When her hand touched the bottle of sleeping tablets, Isabelle hesitated. If she were to take some, her reflexes might be too dull to react in a crisis. It never occurred to her to expect anyone, including Alain, to come to her rescue. She knew if the worst happened, she would be facing it alone.

She sat down on the edge of the bed, her eyes turned towards the moonlight pouring through the window, half expecting a man to appear, the man she had seen at the motorway stop. She was unable to shake off the feeling that he was coming closer, even as she lay in the peace and security of her own bed. Trembling all over, she reached for the bottle and shook out enough tablets to ensure that she would sink into oblivion for a few hours at least. Then she lay there rigid with anxiety until she felt the drug pumping through her body and bringing release. Her last thought as sleep overcame her was of a frightened young girl, herself when young.

Alain awoke at the sound of the bedroom door closing softly and sat up in bed. Realizing it must have been Oliver, he called his name, but there was no answer and he fell back on to the pillows wondering if he had only been dreaming. Not a sound interrupted the measured chirping of crickets that filled the night beyond the windows.

All his life Alain had slept profoundly and easily, but during the

384

past week he had been tormented by sleeplessness in the dead hours between midnight and early morning, the time when he always felt most vulnerable to his hidden fears. As he lay staring at the moulded ceiling, he tried to resist the black tunnel of despair that was certain to hold him prisoner until daylight. His mind teemed with painful images of the past few days: Oliver's face when he asked about the divorce; Rachel's haggard, pained expression when they last parted.

Sitting up in the darkness, his heart heavy, Alain stared at the dark shapes of the *armoires* and chests in the room, feeling a mixture of gloom and strangeness. He couldn't stop himself from wishing that the present was only a bad dream, that he would awake in the morning to find that everything was as it had been the year before. A powerful longing took him to his sunlit bedroom in California, ready to start another day at Chez Alain. The illusion was so strong that when it faded he felt sickened by a kind of emptiness. Filled with contempt for his own weakness, Alain struggled to concentrate on the image of Brissac. Whatever happened, he would have his dream at any cost. His self-respect, his pride, his future depended on it. He thought of Agnès Grimal's brown, cheerful face, wondering just how far he would go to get what he wanted.

Julian pulled Pascale closer to him, letting the lyrics to the music that filled the *pigeonnier* speak for him; ' "Baby I want to make love to you," ' he sang softly in her ear. All the windows of the room were open to the moonlit night. The bedside lamp cast a giant circular shadow on the beamed ceiling, enveloping them in a soft glow. The coke he had snorted was making him restless and the long, slow song was getting on his nerves. Cradling Pascale's hips in his hands, he rocked her back and forth in time to the music on the square of parquet in front of the bed. When the song was over, Julian held her tight until the last notes of the music had died away. The impatient desire coursing through his body passed into her like a current, neutralizing her resistance. Pascale gave a little sigh and opened her eyes to see him smiling down at her. His dilated pupils glowed with an incandescence that penetrated her very thoughts.

385

'Let me look at you,' he whispered, his eyes roaming over her flushed face. His hands sketched the outline of her body a millimetre from her skin, as if he didn't dare to actually touch her. 'God, you're beautiful,' he whispered. His eyes were drowsy with enchantment as they swept from the tousled mane of gold spun hair that framed her flushed face to her long-legged, curvaceous figure poured into a tight black mini-skirt. He reached for two flutes of champagne resting on a table and handed her one.

Pascale, the rush of cool bubbles in her throat, refused to meet Julian's eyes, which were now staring at her with disturbing intensity. She straightened her shoulders and put down her glass, determined to seem in control though she was shaking with the arousal that had overtaken her the moment they had begun to dance. Throughout their long romantic dinner that evening Pascale had felt she was safe, but here in the *pigeonnier*, alone with Julian, was different. Stepping back, she tried to smile.

'Julian, I mustn't stay any longer. My parents will be so angry if I do. They might not let me come out again.'

'Look, they don't know you're out with me. Why are you worrying?'

'Yes, but already they're asking why I keep coming home so late every night. I can't keep telling them I'm with Annie. Anyway, she's leaving on holiday tomorrow.'

'Hey, you're almost twenty-one years old. You're a grown-up girl. You should assert yourself. Everybody has to grow up, break away for their parents.'

'No, you don't understand. They're still angry about . . . about my fiancé.' She couldn't bring herself to say Étienne's name. Just the sound of it evoked a terrible misery she didn't want to examine.

'All right, all right.' Julian took her hands in his and began to toy with her fingers, twisting the small silver and jade rings she wore. 'You're driving me mad, do you know that? When I wake up every morning, do you have any idea what I'm going through?' His voice was a husky monotone.

She blushed, but her desire quickened at his words.

'I'll tell you what it's like. I've got a tight ache in me, from my knees to my gut.'

386

His fingers glided to her nipples, but she didn't push him away. She was looking at him, transfixed, her lips parted.

He pulled her towards him and began to explore her ear with his tongue as he whispered, 'Do you know what it's like to live in constant pain? Day and night to live with it? The only thing I can think of is you, every part of you.' He looked at her pleadingly. His eyes dropped to her half-parted lips and he began to trace them with trembling fingers. 'Pascale, beautiful Pascale.'

She backed away and shook her head, her breath coming in quick little spasms. Feeling her body slacken, he gathered her to him and kissed her hard again and again until they were both breathless. Flicking her hair away from her face, Pascale looked around numbly for her handbag.

'I have to go now – *please*,' she begged.

Julian shook his head and sighed. 'All right, if that's what you want, but you realize that sooner or later we're going to give in to this thing.' His voice dropped to a whisper.

Pascale moved away nervously. 'I have to go now, really I must.'

He drained his glass in a gulp, then smiled impishly at her.

She was taking a last look round the sumptuous *pigeonnier*, as if trying to memorize every detail. The guest quarters at Terre Blanche evoked a world of luxury where anything was possible, a world that had been closed to her until now.

'What about tomorrow night?' Julian asked. 'We could have dinner again at the Auberge, or go back to Labardens . . .'

'I told you, I can't, because my brothers are arriving for their holidays. I have to be there the first night at least.'

'All right, Thursday then, and Friday. Saturday too. We could go somewhere for a few days. Think about it.' He took her hands and pressed them gently.

She hung her head. 'It's not that I don't want to, it's just . . .'

'What about Annie? Couldn't you figure out a way to make your parents think you're with her?' When she bit her lip doubtfully, he persisted. 'You know you can if you really want to. If you seriously intend to break free, to come to London, to the Seychelles with me in September, then you have to start somewhere.'

Pascale looked up at him feeling like a stupid, tongue-tied child. The intensity in his eyes unlocked a wild desire to break every convention, every inhibition that had ever held her back. When he turned with a sigh and picked up the car keys, she felt a sharp sense of disappointment that told her how close she had been to giving in.

'Thursday I'll pick you up at twelve, the same place.' When she didn't reply, he added, 'You are coming, I hope. Isabelle and Alain are expecting you for lunch.'

'Yes, I'm coming,' she replied, not bothering to add that she wouldn't have turned down the chance to see what Terre Blanche was like for anything.

As they walked towards the door Julian smiled to himself in amusement when he saw Pascale cast a backward glance at the big canopied bed. Catching her hand in his, he tugged her laughingly after him down the stairs. When they were at the bottom, where the car was parked, Julian crushed her to a pillar under the porchlight and kissed her until she was out of breath, his body hard against hers.

'No matter where we are, no matter what time of day it is, I'll want you. Whether it's broad daylight and there are other people around makes no difference. I'll be wanting you all through lunch tomorrow, and as I go to sleep tonight and tomorrow when I wake up, that ache will still be inside me, here.'

She didn't protest when he placed her hand between them, against his trousers.

From the cover of a massive cedar tree in the park, Étienne watched Julian and Pascale passionately entwined. He clenched his jaw until it hurt, stifling a cry of rage and pain. As the shock bore down on him, Étienne was filled with a savage impulse to destroy something. He banged his fist into the tree, oblivious to the pain as he stared at Pascale locked in the Englishman's embrace. Seconds later, he watched the Porsche drive into the darkness. The rich purr of the powerful engine reverberated in his chest and pounded in his ears.

Étienne remained slumped against the tree for a long time, incapable of moving. Eventually he made his way through the

388

moonlit park, back to where he had climbed over the wall earlier in the evening. He found his motorcycle still carefully concealed in the bushes. He froze at a rustle in the undergrowth somewhere behind him, and crouched low as the dark shadow of a man emerged. At first he thought someone, a guard or caretaker, had spotted him and was following him, but the man, whoever he was, hurried away in the opposite direction. Étienne pointed his bike towards Roquelaire and quickly started the motor. As he drove off he heard a van start up. Moments later he pulled to the side of the road to let it pass, wondering who the driver was. Too distracted to care, he drove as fast as he could back to the village, paying no attention to the sharp corners along the way. Parking his bike in the still street where Laurent lived, he entered his house.

'Well?' said Laurent when Étienne came into the sitting-room, ashen-faced.

Étienne dropped into the chair opposite him. 'They were there.'

'What did I tell you?' Laurent smiled triumphantly over the top of his book.

Étienne couldn't bring himself to speak for a moment. 'I saw everything. I had a perfect view into the guesthouse from behind a tree. All the windows were open.' His voice broke and he looked down at his dusty, stained hands.

'Did they go to bed?'

Étienne shook his head. 'The lights were on all the time.'

Laurent laughed. 'So what? That doesn't mean anything.'

'They didn't go to bed, I tell you. They were just dancing and laughing.'

'The guy is a professional seducer. He knows just how to prime a woman, and he'd be too smart to rush things with a straight girl like Pascale. But if he's leaving in a week, like the architect told me, then he's got to make his move soon.'

'I can't understand it. You wouldn't believe the way she was kissing him, Laurent, as if she had gone crazy. She's changed into a completely different person.' Étienne felt too ashamed to meet Laurent's mocking eyes, ashamed for Pascale, as if he were betraying her.

'Sexual pyrotechnics, pure and simple.'

'She was never like that with me. I mean, not to that extent. He must have some incredible power over her. What the hell has he done to her to make her act like this? It was awful. ' He closed his eyes, still seeing the picture of the two of them together.

'At the risk of destroying your ego, you're no match for the likes of him. He's had a lifetime of experience. He knows exactly which buttons to push. She's putty in his hands, as the old cliché goes. And the Porsche probably has something to do with it.'

'That's not true. Pascale isn't like that. Whatever she's done, money's got nothing to do with it, that I know.'

'Look, you can't have it both ways. She's betrayed you in the cruellest way a woman can, with a rich stud she's only just met. It couldn't be any worse.'

'I blame myself. I failed her somehow,' Étienne mumbled, struggling to swallow his pride.

'You still put her on a pedestal, don't you, you poor fool? All right, blame it entirely on that bastard for corrupting her if it makes you feel better.'

'What do you mean? Are you saying that he's not in love with her?'

Laurent threw back his head and laughed. 'Are you joking? He'll get her into bed for a while, as long as it's convenient, then he'll drop her.'

'How could she do this to me, how? She must hate my guts.'

Laurent threw down his book. 'Never mind how. She did it, the bitch.'

Étienne's eyes flashed angrily, but he didn't say anything.

'Well, make up your mind. Are you or are you not going to get on that train back to Germany without doing anything about it?'

Étienne stared at his friend, feeling as if his mind had stepped out of his body. A blind rage was coursing through him, hardening his resolve.

'I'm staying.'

'Good. You can be back in camp by Saturday if you take the night train.'

'I'll be gone long before then. But what do I do in the meantime?' He glanced round the shabbily furnished little sitting-room.

'You can lie low here. The time will pass much quicker than you think. You know, I think I'm going to enjoy abetting a *crime passionnel*,' he said cheerfully.

Étienne frowned. 'I wish you wouldn't joke about it. Anyway, it's not a crime to beat up a man who is seducing your fianceé.'

'Of course not. There's nothing the Englishman can do about it.'

'He might report it to the gendarmes; it would be assault.'

'I doubt if even he is that much of a coward.'

'I don't really give a shit if he does.'

'That's the spirit. You're bigger than he is, younger and a lot angrier, don't forget.'

'Maybe I should have cornered him tonight. Maybe I should have waited for him to come back.'

'No, it would be better to wait until they are actually in bed. Catch them by surprise. Then you'd teach her a lesson at the same time.'

Étienne looked at Laurent, horror-stricken. 'I don't know . . . it might be better to get him alone. The problem is getting up to the window. He probably keeps the door locked.'

'We'll think of a way around that. But what you have to do is catch them in the act. I'll bet you anything Pascale is waiting until she knows you're out of town, and then she can breathe easy. The two of them are bound to be exactly where you saw them some night this week for the seduction scene. I'd bank on it.'

Étienne wouldn't allow himself to think of Pascale lying naked with the Englishman. 'How am I going to kill the time all day, waiting to catch them at night?' He leapt up and began to pace.

'It's only a day or two. Nobody will even suspect you're here, except Madame Gachpour, who'll wonder why I'm buying so much bread,' he said with a smirk.

'I've got to be back in Germany by Saturday at four o'clock in the afternoon at the latest. If I'm not, I'll be court-martialled. And somehow I've got to make my parents believe that I'm really leaving. My mother will want to see me off, you know.'

'Pick a time when she's busy. When she's having her hair done or something. Just say you have to go then.'

'She has it done on Thursday morning.'

'Good, there's your answer. You say I'm taking you to the train. I'll pick you up, drop you off outside the village, and you sneak back here later. Then you wait your chance on Thursday night, or Friday if necessary, and come back here on the bike and I'll take you to the train.'

Étienne nodded, trying to turn his jumbled thoughts into a plan. He got as far as imagining himself climbing through the window of the *pigeonnier* when the image of his father's bone-handled hunting knife flashed into his mind. It hung there stubbornly, refusing to go away. It eased his pain, somehow, to think of it.

\*

At first light Rachel and Michael awoke in the pine bed in Michael's room and turned towards each other. Their waking moment was filled with the cooing and fluttering of doves in the eaves outside the window and the muffled sounds of day beginning in Roquelaire. The look that passed between them over a heap of tangled bedclothes turned into a shared smile.

'Good morning,' she said.

'Good morning.'

Nestling her head in the pillow, Rachel looked at Michael, finding a deep enjoyment in the sight of his tousled head next to hers. He looked younger, happier than yesterday. His blue eyes were soft and clear like the light on that summer's morning.

'What are you thinking?'

'How rested you look.'

'And I was thinking how beautiful you are.' He read her eyes, searching for regrets or a latent embarrassment, but found only peace. Her hand reached out to him, and as he kissed it he was filled with the remembered beauty of the night before.

Rachel drew closer and cradled his face in her hands. 'Last night was a miracle,' she whispered.

'I feel as if I'm still there, living it.' He brushed her hair tenderly from her forehead.

She pressed close to him, feeling the touchpoints of their bodies meet in warmth and harmony, as if it had always been so. Contact rekindled passion's fire, enveloping them in the warmth and caring that had charged their lovemaking with such power and meaning. Hours later their hearts still seemed to be beating with the rhythm their bodies had shared.

'Words can never say what I feel,' said Rachel. 'But one thing I do know: that now I can conquer anything that comes because of what's happened between us.'

Her words sent a fresh wave of desire surging through Michael's body. Gently he gathered her to him again, rediscovering the sweet ecstasy of her love.

# Chapter 19

The church bells rang ceaselessly to alert Roquelaire to the crisis. Some people fell to their knees and began to pray, others rushed home to lock themselves in or to collect a few belongings and flee, but most huddled in bewilderment in the square among the gaunt-faced pilgrims, merchants and travellers, who had no idea where to go or what to do.

Margaret and John had returned to the square with Thomas. The horsemen who had started the commotion were already on their way to the next village, but the news they had brought had changed Margaret's life in an instant, blocking her escape to Spain. Though she took comfort that Thomas was now by her side, part of her wished that he was still at Moirax to the north, where, she guessed, he might have been safer than in the heart of plague-ridden Gascony.

A babble of excited voices had risen near the church as the clergy and nobles argued what to do. Père Xavier climbed on to a barrel and appealed for calm when he perceived that the nobles and high clergy showed no more presence of mind in the face of catastrophe than the ordinary folk.

The nobles began whispering among themselves and started to move towards their horses.

Père Xavier called after them. 'Why are you leaving us, lords and ladies? Our plight concerns you. Roquelaire is fief of Brissac, is it not?'

His stentorian voice made some of the men blush in embarrassment at their haste to get away.

'There's nothing we can do here,' said Roch coldly nodding to Roxonde to mount her horse.

Thomas looked up at Margaret at the sound of his father's

voice. She realized Roch was so agitated that he had not even noticed his son's disappearance.

Père Xavier said, 'I believe that our only hope is for all of us, every man, woman and child in Roquelaire, to retire to Brissac and draw up the bridge. There is ample water there, flowing from sources so deep that there can be no fear of poisoning. The water in the courtyard has never dried up, not even in times of drought. By evening the people can bring what they have harvested and put it in the stores of the fortress. The harvest has been good, and will keep us all until spring comes, when surely we will be able to return to our homes.'

Roxonde, who was about to put her foot in a stirrup steadied by her page, scowled at the priest.

'The chatelaine of Brissac has not been consulted about this plan. By what right do you open my house to everyone?'

Père Xavier fixed her with an unwavering stare. 'My lady, you are not chatelaine yet, not until the seigneur is dead, and, as far as I know, he still lives. Were he conscious, there is no doubt that he would wish to help his people.'

Her eyes glared at his insolence. 'The old seigneur has not spoken for days and I act in his stead. What's more, every knight in Gascony would come to my aid if you defied my wishes.'

'Is that to say, were you chatelaine of Brissac, you would refuse to give shelter to your people? Roquelaire is your fiefdom, for good or ill, my lady. Charity is surely your first duty.'

'Charity? By what law must I take these people in? And how can we protect anyone from what is surely God's will? The villagers, and all the rest of them, must stay where they are, come what may.' In a defiant gesture she gathered her train and nodded for her page to assist her to mount her horse. When she had taken the reins, Roch followed suit.

There was an ominous murmur as the crowd closed round the party of nobles, who had followed Roxonde's lead and mounted their horses, which began to shy nervously. A silent resolution united the villagers and they formed a solid wall to prevent the nobles from moving. Seeing they were outnumbered, they glared at the peasants and merchants, and the men placed their hands ready on the hilts of their swords.

'Lock them in the church!' came a voice. Others began to shout, and the crowd pressed forward.

Such a breakdown of order had never happened before, and confusion threatened to become chaos until Père Xavier called desperately for the people to listen to him.

'We must not lock them in the church. It is not a prison, but God's house and must remain undefiled. I invite you to dismount, lords and ladies.'

Seeing they had no choice, they reluctantly did so.

'The Pope and the King shall hear of this. You are now the enemy,' said Roch angrily to Père Xavier.

'No – the enemy is the pestilence. And a noble's first duty, after God and his King,' the priest reminded him, 'is to defend his people, not to save himself from danger.'

As he had no rejoinder to this, Roch had to content himself with a rancorous glare.

At dusk Margaret stood with Thomas on the battlements at Brissac, watching the last carts loaded with sacks of grain and oats thunder over the drawbridge. She could hear the rumble of the heavy chain as it unwound to let down the portcullis. Some people had to scramble beneath it when it was almost to the ground, having risked their lives to make one last trip to collect more of their possessions. All Margaret owned was in the satchel at her feet. She took out some bread and cheese she had packed for the journey to Spain and gave it to Thomas, who ate it hungrily. He had turned his back on the view of Roquelaire and was watching the villagers settling in the courtyard. An almost congenial atmosphere filled the fortress now the population was safely gathered inside and the gate was sealed. People were bustling about, gossiping, lighting fires to cook, and making themselves comfortable in the barns and stables leading off the courtyard.

Margaret leaned over the battlements, emptying her mind of all thoughts as she took in the rare, magpie's view of the world from such a height. To the west, the sky blazed with colour, which seemed to her a cruelly beautiful spectacle. To the south, she could make out the jagged purple line of the Pyrenees, capped with snow, beckoning like a forbidden city that would always elude her.

At the sound of someone approaching she turned, expecting to see John. She found herself face to face with Roch, who was regarding her with eyes blazing with fury. Thomas, who was also taken by surprise, shrank back, as if he feared his father's retribution for being with his mother.

Margaret had almost forgotten what it was like to be the object of her husband's wrath, but the hard months that had passed since she had seen him taught her that he wielded no power over her any longer. His elaborate yellow and black costume, like the plummage of some preening bird, suddenly made him a figure of absurdity. She wondered how she could ever have loved him.

'Margaret Prior,' he said, his arms across his chest. 'And what brings you so far south?' His voice was full of irony.

'I'm a pilgrim, as you can see, my lord,' she answered calmly.

'You, a pilgrim?' He gave a contemptuous snort. 'You lie. You were searching for Thomas.'

'Fate played me a happy turn. I chanced upon my son on the pilgrim's road when I was least expecting it.'

'As soon as this siege has ended, you will have to continue south, pilgrim, alone. Your plan to vex me has failed.'

'It wasn't to vex you, Roch. Unlike you, I wish for nothing that is not mine already.'

This remark so enraged him that she was sure he was about to strike her, when the sound of footsteps coming up the stairs made him whirl round. John Stratton stepped on to the parapet. Roch made no move to salute him, as one knight to another, but sneered. 'Now our group is complete. You're the Englishman who has been spying on me to help her. Don't deny it.'

'I deny nothing,' John replied unperturbed.

Margaret looked from one to the other, certain that in other circumstances they would have drawn swords, and though John had suffered nearly mortal wounds in battle, which had weakened his fighting strength over the years, she didn't doubt for a moment that he would win any duel with Roch.

397

'You look surprised, Englishman, that I know so much about you. You're a friend of the huntsman Selwyn, are you not?' When John didn't reply, Roch continued, 'He paid heavily for his disloyalty to me. He was hanged this morning before we set out for Roquelaire. Before he died he was forced to reveal how you had used him.'

John paled. 'It's you who deserves hanging, Roch Arnaud, for all your crimes.' He looked at Margaret, who was struck with horror.

'Watch what you say and remember where you are, as I will soon be master here. During these troubles there will be a truce, but it will end as soon as the gates open. And I always repay treachery.'

Roch motioned to Thomas to follow him, but Margaret stepped between the two of them. All her hatred for Roch and the suffering she had borne because of him was contained in the defiant courage with which she faced him now.

'You will have to put your sword through me, here and now, Roch. You took Thomas from me once, but not again.'

As Roch's hand touched his sword, Margaret sensed she could easily die, but she stood firm. Seeing John make a move to intervene, she cried, 'Keep back, please. This is between me and my husband. No one else should suffer.'

'You're a raving madwoman. Thank God I'm rid of you,' muttered Roch, dropping his hand. 'Lucky for you I have enough trouble on my hands not to rise to your bait. You think to defy me, to avenge yourself against me, but that can never be, never. You have a reprieve, but only for a while.'

When he had stormed away Margaret started to shake. Thomas was ashen, but she knew that to comfort him would be to weaken him now that he was only a few years shy of manhood. What he had witnessed was a harsh lesson in the way of the world.

'Thomas, go below and fetch some water,' she said, handing the flask to him as if nothing had happened.

Thomas nodded mutely, then ran off, leaving her and John alone.

John looked at Margaret, homage shining in his eyes.

398

'Thomas will attach himself to whom he wishes in his heart. That's all that matters, isn't it?' she said.

'You strengthened your son a moment ago more than if you wove him a suit of mail with your own hands, because he will never forget your courage – and neither will I.'

She hung her head, feeling unworthy of his praise. Suddenly she was tired deep in her bones. She and John stood silently on the parapet. The fortress was like a ship sailing into night on uncharted seas, and they were two passengers looking up at Orion's belt and the Great Bear studded in the sky. They exchanged a look of complicity and together gazed down at the people tending their fires, making beds with straw and drawing water from the pool. As the villagers bent down to the water, they caught the silhouettes of their own faces set against the pale reflection of the oncoming night.

Mother Clothilde watched Florentine disappear down the white corridor of the convent, wondering if she had done the right thing. It was late and most of the villagers had already settled down to an uneasy sleep under the stars in the courtyard. After compline she had been overjoyed to find her daughter waiting outside the little chapel, but she saw that something had happened to change Florentine since the day of her betrothal. Clothilde supposed at first that the girl was terrified at the news of the approaching pestilence, but when they faced each other in her cell, furnished only with a cot and a crucifix, Florentine's lacklustre eyes and torn clothes pointed to something more. Mother Clothilde had listened in disbelief to the tearful confession of what had happened that day. In her conscience-stricken state, Florentine had begged to take the veil, but Mother Clothilde had stubbornly resisted the temptation to shelter her daughter safely under her wing.

'No,' she had said firmly. 'You're not ready yet to leave the world. Your life will knit itself together in time, though you find it hard to believe while you are so unhappy.'

Florentine had begun to cry, having set her heart on a clean escape from all her problems, but Mother Clothilde had held firm.

The two of them had knelt before the crucifix and prayed. Mother Clothilde could only hope that the doom that hung over them all would mend the broken vows and shattered hearts of Luc and Florentine.

Before she retired to bed, she opened the small shuttered window of her cell and looked out into the night, feeling as never before that she was resting in God's outstretched palm. Now that the villagers had been gathered under Brissac's roof there would be more work to do than ever. Guirard, who never left her thoughts, was unconscious and might never recover, but, observing the stars, Mother Clothilde believed that his stubborn will to survive had served a purpose, for had he not lived, the unfeeling Roxonde de Montferrand might have condemned the villagers to certain death. Catching the rich scent of summer's last roses coming from the small patch of garden outside, she closed the shutter with a vow that she would soon gather all there were to offer to the patron saint of mothers in Roquelaire, one last time.

John set down his quill when he heard shouting. Sticking his head out the tiny window of the tower room tucked away beneath the eaves, he saw the sentry on the keep was shouting to travellers at the gate, who were begging to be admitted to the fortress.

He went back to his writing table with an uneasy feeling. During the three days he had been incarcerated with all the others, Brissac had been besieged by droves of people fleeing the advance of the pestilence and seeking sanctuary, but they had all been turned away: men, women, children, nobles and clerics, beggars, scholars, travelling merchants and entertainers, even prostitutes. Feeling in the fortress was already running so high there had been talk of pouring boiling pitch or oil on the head of anyone who tried to scale the walls or loitered too long before the gates because the people so feared contamination, even at a distance. Daily they watched the clear blue sky for any sign of a miasma bringing death, though what it looked like no one knew.

John took up his quill again and continued his writing. In the sure rhythm that had possessed him for the last days he recorded all his thoughts. What he wrote was not the history of Edward's war to win back Aquitaine from France, but the chronicle of the people of Roquelaire before they came under the threat of an invisible but deadly enemy. What significance it had he didn't know, but he was compelled to harvest a sheaf of impressions he had been gathering long before they had heard the calamitous news in the square. As he wrote, he disregarded all the conventions he had been taught, treating the life of Roquelaire as a human saga richly populated with diverse characters, who each had a story to tell. The result defied any classification he could think of, and pleased him far more than any of his writings about war and the glory of kings. He worked feverishly, admitting in his darker moments that this might be his only bid for immortality.

Later, after supper, when Thomas had gone to sleep on a pile of straw in the stairwell, John and Margaret played chess by the moonlight pouring through the window. Like the others, they had already begun to establish a routine to help the time to pass, seeking each other out as much as possible without ever discussing the need that drove them together.

John leaned on his elbow and studied the bone and ebony pieces he had prudently brought with him, whose life-like shapes threw sharp shadows across the board.

Moving a pawn forward, Margaret said, 'What will we do when the moon wanes, I wonder?'

'Play like blindmen,' John replied, taking her bishop. When she exclaimed in surprise he laughed. 'Should I light a taper?'

'A taper? Oh no! Let us save our precious tapers for darker days without the moon, and for reading if we tire of chess.'

'I'm tired of it now,' he said. Pushing back his stool he went to a satchel and took out a taper, which he managed to light after striking a tinder repeatedly. As light filled the room the pleasure on Margaret's face prompted him to pick up one of half a dozen books he had hastily gathered from home. Life as a soldier had taught him that books, writing materials and light would prove as valuable as clothes or food if their incarceration in Brissac lasted the winter.

'What should I read you, the lay of Equitan, of Yonic, of Graelent?' he asked, thumbing through the pages.

401

'None of those, if you please.'

He turned to the story of Tristan and Ysolde, which he knew Margaret was especially fond of. Both he and she were soon absorbed by the immortal tale of tragic love. As the taper began to burn low John came to a passage that always moved him. Conscious of Margaret's spellbound expression, he read it slowly, finding that the words had taken on an even deeper meaning that night: '"But one day, friend, we shall go together to a fortunate land from which none returns. There rises a castle of white marble; at each of its thousand windows burns a lighted candle; at each a minstrel plays and sings a melody without end."'

On the fourth morning of their confinement Mother Clothilde rose with the first crow of the cock and opened the shutter of her cell. After she had returned from laudes in the chapel with the other sisters, she retired as usual for an hour's private devotion, then went into the convent garden. There, under the fading morning stars, she cut all the roses that remained and wrapped them in ferns growing by the wall. Returning to the empty chapel, where a feeble lamp still burned beneath the crucifix in the nave, she looked round warily before disappearing into the confessional. From behind a niche Clothilde took an oil lamp she kept there and lit it, then moved the seat, revealing a spiral staircase. Descending the narrow stairs to a locked grille, she balanced the lamps and the roses in one hand, fished a key from her habit with the other. She let herself through the barrier then locked it scrupulously behind her, ever fearing that someone else might discover the secret passage that Guirard had shown her long ago.

In a few moments she emerged from a bank of shrubbery along the retaining wall beneath the fortress. Taking great care not to be seen or heard, Clothilde darted across an open space to a long line of trees and stayed behind them for some distance until she was safely out of sight of the château.

A while later she passed through the gates of Roquelaire, open now there was no one left to guard them. An eerie silence reigned in the narrow street that led to the square, which was empty except for a few stray dogs. As she hurried towards the church,

402

the sound of a crowing cock that had been left behind startled her, but there was no other sign of life in the houses, which stood with their doors and windows ajar, as if their occupants would return at any moment. People had fled in such haste that they had dumped anything too cumbersome to carry. Clothilde picked her way over cooking pots, rugs, a chair or two and a mewing cat. By the time she was at the church steps, she had begun to regret her wish to pay one last visit to the shrine of St Anne, where she had worshipped daily since Florentine was born.

The abandoned church, on the dawn of this terrible, strange day, had never seemed more like God's house than now, with pale light streaming through the high coloured windows. The doves burbled beneath the eaves, breaking the monotony of Mother Clothilde's sandals resounding on the stone. She approached the statue of St Anne, anguished that the little saint, for whom she had always harboured a fanatical devotion, would be condemned to perpetual solitude in her niche. There would be no one to care for her and love her the way she was accustomed to.

Mother Clothilde set to work putting the shrine in order, sweeping aside burned tapers and wilted flowers. Laying the pile of roses at the hem of the figure's blue gown, she knelt to pray. She lost all track of the time while she begged God to spare the village from the pestilence. When at last she opened her eyes, the light in the church told her that an hour or more must have gone by. Crossing herself, she bid a silent farewell to the statue, knowing that the future was so uncertain she might never look on her face again. She left the church as the sky turned pink above the rooftops, pursued by the sound of her own footsteps. Hurrying down the street towards the arch, she was so preoccupied that she didn't see a shadowy figure appear in a doorway as she passed.

The Cat wiped the grease from his mouth and set aside the leg of mutton he had found in a pot when he entered the empty house the evening before. His hair was matted from sleep, and his once-fine clothes were torn, blood-stained and caked with dust from the road. Seeing the abbess scurrying away, he thought it might be prudent to follow her and see where she was going. He grabbed the satchel containing his instrument and dashed after her in

403

stealthy silence, frightened by the idea that his life might depend on it.

Nearing Brissac, Mother Clothilde moved behind the trees in order to hide herself, and the Cat did the same. His fear mounted when she abruptly disappeared from sight until he realized she had only stumbled. It surprised him that she seemed to be making for Brissac, for he had already heard the grim news, from travellers he had met, who had been turned away, that the drawbridge was tightly closed and that no one could gain admittance, not even the Pope himself. Now he was confounded to see Mother Clothilde avoiding the approach to the fortress, choosing the road that passed below it, suggesting that Brissac wasn't her goal after all. Then, as she cautiously kept near the cover of trees or shrubbery, her eyes trained on the towers, the Cat dared to hope that she was leading him to a secret entrance. It would be the only way in, for the lack of watchmen on the keep above told him that the good citizens of Roquelaire were confident that their sanctuary could be breached by no one.

The sickness, which travelled faster than the fastest horse, seemed to be nipping at his heels as he bounded after Mother Clothilde, who vanished into a thicket at the base of the fortress. He waited for a moment, not wanting to alert her by the rustling of shrubbery. When he had fought his way through the thicket, he discovered a gap in the wall that he could pass through only on his hands and knees. He heard the echo of Mother Clothilde's footsteps, and saw the feeble glimmer of the light she carried disappearing down a passage. The Cat was left in darkness pondering a dilemma: whether to risk the dangers of facing Florentine's betrothed within or to return to the plague-stricken world. The memory of the putrefying bodies he had seen on the road south of Roquelaire the day before summoned up the threat of a fate far worse than yet another dagger wound from a jealous lover. He inched his way forward in the blackness, inventing a plausible excuse for his sudden appearance.

At the end of the passage the Cat entered what he sensed was some sort of entrance chamber. He moved round it slowly and carefully until at last he saw a grille and a steep narrow staircase behind it spiralling up towards a chink of light. The grille was locked! A wave of despair that he was so near and yet so far from sanctuary swept over him. Cold sweat trickled down his neck at the thought of going back to Roquelaire or travelling north, where the pestilence might have preceded him. In the hush he caught a sound of something rolling on the stone floor followed by a clatter. Deciding he had no choice but to risk all in one toss, he called out, hoping whoever was making the noise might hear him. The noise ceased at once and the Cat called again. After repeating his call, louder each time, he saw a small boy come hesitantly down the stairs.

'Don't be afraid. I'm not an angel or a devil,' the minstrel whispered, peering up at him. 'Who are you, boy?'

'Thomas Arnaud,' came the whispered reply.

This was Roch Arnaud's son, the boy who had been hidden at Moirax. The Cat explained who he was.

'You're the minstrel? I've heard of you. My father and the lady Roxonde were wondering where you'd gone. But how did you get down there?'

'I sneaked down here this morning to see if there was any way I could escape, and then someone locked the door.'

'It was the abbess. When I saw her enter the chapel, I hid myself behind the altar. She went into the confessional and disappeared.'

'Did she?' He felt like laughing for joy. 'Be a good boy and go find me a nail or something like that, as quick as you can.'

Eventually Thomas returned with a hook he had found. He watched the minstrel straighten it and begin to pick the lock on the grille. Turning locks without keys had been one of the earliest skills in the minstrel's armoury to circumvent jealous husbands. He expelled a sigh of relief as the gate swung open, then closed it behind him and followed Thomas up the stairs and into the chapel.

'So this is . . .' He stopped himself. A few more words would have revealed that he had never stood on that spot in his life. When Thomas stooped to pick up a wooden ball and pins he had been playing with, the Cat said with a chuckle, 'So that's the noise I heard.'

'This is the best place to play. The tiles are flat and smooth. I used to play in the chapel at Moirax sometimes when the monks weren't there.' Suddenly he looked doubtful. 'You won't tell anyone, will you? Because they might not like it.'

The Cat smiled. 'Now we both have a secret about each other that we'll never tell. I won't tell anyone that I saw you here, if you promise the same.'

An hour later, after making himself as presentable as he could, the Cat appeared casually in the courtyard with his viele tucked under his arm. People looked at him curiously and stepped back to let him pass, as if they were trying to remember if the minstrel had been among the mob who poured into the fortress before it was sealed.

'Where did you come from? I don't remember seeing you before,' a burly blacksmith challenged him. He was repairing a hinge and held his hammer up menacingly, ready to strike if he wasn't satisfied with the answer.

The minstrel shrank inwardly, but adopted a confident air, knowing he was a hair's-breadth away from death if the truth were known.

A shriek pierced the air and everyone turned to look in the direction of Susan Wyndgate, who had fallen to the ground, overcome by the sight of him. He smiled broadly, supposing she was still sick with love for him and cheered by the prospect that he might renew their pleasurable coupling to help the time pass. The courtyard became silent and, feeling eyes on him, the Cat sauntered to the oval pool and sat on its edge. Pretending he hadn't a care in the world, he began to play a sweet tune on his viele, which sent a murmur of surprise through the crowd.

'It's the minstrel from the betrothal,' exclaimed Luc's father, who had been supervising the stacking of wood in the courtyard.

By now everyone knew that Luc and Florentine had become estranged. Their faces were gloomy, and they hardly ever spoke or held hands as lovers do. No one knew what had happened or what part the minstrel had played in disrupting their lives.

When the Cat had finished playing, he sensed that all was not well, and that the silence that had fallen over the people was not a hush of anticipation, but of suspicion. He was poised, waiting for the inevitable question posed by the surly blacksmith, who could easily have bent him in two.

'Where did I come from?' he repeated. 'I'm in the service of Roxonde de Montferrand.'

Luc's father regarded him closely. 'If so, where have you been since the gates were closed? No one has seen you here, have they?' he said, turning to the crowd.

'Where? I've been hiding behind the altar in the chapel. And truth to tell, I'm starving because all I could find to eat there was the host and I couldn't touch those, could I?'

Nervous titters broke out, but the blacksmith was still glaring at him. 'But why were you hiding, minstrel?'

Just then the Cat spotted Luc and Florentine, who had heard the music and were standing, ashen-faced, at the edge of the crowd. He said with a nod, in their direction. 'Ask them if you will.'

Florentine was stunned by the appearance of the Cat, and for a moment she believed he must have returned from the dead or was even the devil himself come back to torment her. When she realized it was really the minstrel in the flesh, she was filled with the bitter-sweet memory of his embrace, tainted by the fear of what was going to happen now he had reappeared. It was the suffering on Luc's face that brought her to her senses, a suffering so acute that she was ashamed at her own selfishness.

Luc was trying to rekindle the hatred he had felt for his rival only days ago, when he saw the cat had set down his viele and was approaching him with a friendly smile.

'It was a deep wound you inflicted on me and it has not quite healed yet, but even though it pains me when I play, I still live. Why not just agree we were all bewitched that day, and say no more?'

'What's going on here? Where the devil have you been?' It was Roch, who had heard the commotion from the window of the hall that he and Roxonde had taken for their quarters. The crowd parted as he came across the courtyard in an obvious rage.

'My lord,' said the Cat, bowing with a flourish. He apologized for his absence, explaining that he had been hiding in the chapel for fear of his life.

'And why is that?' asked Roch incredulously.

'My music steals hearts,' he replied with a shrug towards Luc and Florentine.

Roch looked from the minstrel to Luc and guessed what had happened. It didn't concern him. The only thing that mattered was that Roxonde had been bored to distraction and had been pining for music and gaiety since their incarceration in the fortress.

'If any man dares to touch a hair on the head of this minstrel, I'll put my sword through him. Is that understood?'

'Yes, seigneur,' whispered Luc.

'Come with me, minstrel, to the gallery above, where you can entertain the lords and ladies with your songs. Break hearts . . .' he laughed contemptuously. 'If that is so, you must teach me how to play the viele, now, this very morning.'

'I'll be delighted to, my lord.' The minstrel grabbed his instrument and scampered after Roch.

The next morning Margaret stole on to the parapet, expecting at any moment that a sentry would chase her away. Rumours of the deadly miasma travelling towards them and of the pestilence being contracted by the mere sight of an infected person, even at a distance, obsessed the people, whose thoughts had had time to turn in on themselves. She filled her lungs with cool fragrant air, determined to enjoy a few moments of tranquillity on such a fine summer morning. She found herself gazing at the distant silhouette of the oak tree where she had waited for John to return to her that day, thinking how black her mood had been and how she had compared herself to a fruit falling from the tree before its time. Now, within the space of a few days, she felt strong enough to defy the bleak reality around her, armed with the knowledge that Thomas was with her, and by the joyful realization that she was in love with John Stratton, and he with her. Though neither of them had alluded to their feelings, Margaret dared hope that the day the drawbridge went down at Brissac they would be free to tell each other what was in their hearts. Every passing day had brought them closer and promised a future where she had thought there was none. Her introspective moment was interrupted by a band of travellers toiling up the road past the fortress. They looked towards it, but hurried on, giving the impression that all the world was now aware that Brissac was sealed until the dark angel had passed.

Margaret turned at the sound of someone on the stairs and saw John appear on the parapet. The day had only just begun but his face was drawn, she supposed from spending his time locked in his hot little garret with pen in hand.

'I thought you were the sentry come to chase me away,' she said with a smile. 'I shouldn't be here, I know. Some people went by just now in great haste. The poor souls, they have nowhere to go.'

He stood beside her and looked towards the ramparts of Roquelaire, just visible beyond a bank of trees at the bottom of the valley. After a moment he said, 'This sweeping view disturbs me because it wants life. It is as if we are already dead and gone and the world is empty.'

'You're troubled. Why?' she asked in surprise. She had never heard him speak like this.

'Margaret . . .' It was the first time he had ever called her by her first name. He was about to take her hand, and then thought better of it. 'How to tell you . . .'

'How to tell me what? Is it Thomas?' She went cold.

'No, not Thomas. Margaret – the minstrel, the one attached to Roch, who appeared two days ago – he's dead.'

'Dead? How? Did the young Luc kill him?' she asked, having heard gossip about him and the baker's daughter.

'Would to God that it were so. No, much worse than that. Père Xavier came to me just now as I was writing. The minstrel's body was found in the corridor outside the chamber where Roch sleeps. The putrescence of his black sores and the foul effluvia emitted from his every orifice leaves no doubt how he died: it is the pestilence.'

They looked helplessly at each other; neither of them could bring themselves to speak for a moment.

'The horsemen were too late in bringing their warning,' she whispered. 'Thomas – I have to find him.'

John put a restraining hand on her arm. 'I saw him not long ago playing with some other boys. Don't call him from his play. The truth will be known soon enough.'

'To think that I have brought him to this. John, tell me, what are we to do?'

'Wait. We must wait and pray.'

A week later there was no more hope left in John as he slouched over his desk just after first light, his hand exhausted from writing through the night. A hundred people had already died within the fortress walls. John had helped to place the bodies in the secret passage revealed by Mother Clothilde in the hope that by quickly disposing of the dead in their midst those remaining could save themselves. Even now John could not take in the swiftness with which the pestilence had spread. He had been struggling blindly to make sense of it and to record what had happened, though he had little heart for writing.

'The very pure in heart have perished as swiftly as the evil doers,' he wrote. Tears, which had remained unshed since Margaret had died, began to roll down his cheeks. 'Why? Why?' he whispered to himself, refusing to pray any longer to a God who was so bent on destruction. He was now alone in his tower, alone as he had once expected to be, but without the comfort of her light somewhere else in the world.

He wiped his tears on his sleeve, knowing that to give in to grief would lead to madness. His faith in God had been shaken to the foundation when he reflected that even the greatest goodness and piety seemed unable to protect men and women from the most degrading form of death he had ever witnessed, a death that reduced the body to a blackened, stinking hulk within hours of its visitation.

Mother Clothilde had been among the first, passing away hours before the old seigneur. Initially, those who took charge had kept the truth of what was happening a secret among themselves, as they feared someone would break out of the fortress and spread even more contagion in the countryside. Whereas before they had shut the pestilence out, now they had to shut it in. Père Xavier had not survived long either because he had given last rites to the dying when other churchmen had locked themselves in their rooms, refusing to come out for anything. Young Florentine and Luc had died next to each other, as had Roch and Roxonde. It was only Margaret's death that touched John personally, and with a cruelty that gnawed at his heart. He had seen her in good health in the evening and, then, never again. With her passing, his taste for life had gone. All that was left was to give young Thomas what comfort he could.

Taking up his pen again, John began to write his memorial to Margaret, feeling somehow these would be his final words.

'. . . and thus I came close to telling this lady what was in my heart, but there came a knock on the door and later, when the world was in chaos and about to end, I regretted that I hadn't told the caller to wait a moment. From that day on I was bound in chains of memory, knowing that I had not done what I meant to do, nor said what I intended to say.' With that he buried his head in his arms, his body shaking with sobs.

When John awoke, he was surprised to see the sunlight, having said what he thought would be his last prayers before going to bed. Hearing him stir, Thomas popped his head round the door, looking at the knight mutely with haunted eyes that were so like his mother's. He had spent the night curled up on a pallet in a niche outside the door.

'Come in, Thomas,' John said. Pulling on his boots, he came to a sudden decision. With the boy looking on, he prepared a pack of food, money, and anything else he could think of that would be useful for a journey. Then he picked up his quill and wrote a letter in both Anglo-Norman and in English that began: 'To any kind stranger who can help an orphan return safely to his homeland . . .'

Without a word of explanation, he motioned for the boy to follow him down the stairs before he could change his mind.

'Where are we going?'

'You'll see in a moment. Just follow me.'

They entered the courtyard, which was now nearly empty. Those who had survived the night crept furtively through the shadows,

411

seeking a dark, safe corner to hide from death in the fortress that now belonged to no one. There was no weeping or groaning, only silence, broken by the chirping of sparrows in the eaves, and the constant cry of the swifts. The intolerable stench of death penetrated everything.

John led Thomas to the chapel, where the two remaining nuns kept a vigil round the clock. Lost in prayer, they didn't look up as he helped himself to a lamp, then led Thomas into the confessional.

'The secret passage!' exclaimed Thomas. It was the first time he had shown interest in anything since his mother had been taken.

'How do you know?' asked John, sure that its existence was still a secret between himself and a dwindling number of others.

Shyly, Thomas told him how he had discovered the minstrel behind the locked grille.

'And you opened it? How?'

'He did it himself, with a hook I found.'

John hung his head for a moment, sick with horror as it dawned on him that it was almost certainly the minstrel who had brought the pestilence into their midst through the innocence of a child, though how he had come to discover the whereabouts of the passage John didn't dare to guess. A sense of tragic futility overtook him when he contemplated how Margaret and the others might still be living if it hadn't been for a cruel accident. He was filled with a bitterness that made him wish to demand an answer from God. Swallowing his blasphemous anger, he gave Thomas a rag soaked in vinegar to hold to his nose against the stench, and motioned for him to follow down the spiral staircase and into the pit of hell.

'Don't look right or left, Thomas, I command you.'

John retched at the stink, forcing himself not to look as he pulled Thomas past the piles of putrid, blackened corpses, tormented by the knowledge that somewhere among them was all that was left of his beloved Margaret. He felt Thomas's shoulders tremble beneath his guiding hand, but the boy proved himself to be brave beyond his years, saying nothing and following John dutifully through the burial chamber and passage.

412

'Be careful. Don't fall into the pit,' whispered John, shepherding Thomas away from the cistern.

At the exit John made Thomas crawl through the hole, then followed him into the daylight and led him from the thicket. Resting his hand on Thomas's shoulder, John surveyed the hill to the road below. Nothing moved. An uncanny silence gripped the landscape.

'Follow the pilgrim's road, Thomas, north, back to England and your uncles if you can. Give the letter to anyone you might find who can help you, but be careful whom you trust.' He handed the boy the bundle he had prepared and slipped a purse round his neck.

Thomas gazed up at him, perplexed. 'Aren't you coming too?'

'No, I must stay here.'

There was still time to change his mind, but John wondered if he was right to send a child from the plague-ridden château back into the world. Yet his burnt-out spirit nursed a wild hope, perhaps because of the love he bore Margaret, that Thomas would not succumb to plague, that he would reach England safely and live.

'Go on, boy. What are you waiting for?' When Thomas shrank back, John gave him a shove of encouragement with his hand. 'Don't let your courage falter for a minute. Think of your mother. It's what she would have wanted.'

As Thomas looked down at the dew-soaked hill shimmering in the sun John was reminded of the first man confronting a newly created world.

'Go on, run,' he said. This time Thomas did as he was told and set off, looking back doubtfully over his shoulder several times. Before he was out of earshot, John called once more. 'Before you go, stop at the Pilgrim's Stone. You'll see it on the pilgrim's road. Make a wish there and pray that you will see the journey through. Don't forget.'

He watched the boy run down the hill. Thomas stopped and raised his hand in farewell when he got to the road. John didn't return to the darkness until the boy was out of sight.

413

# Chapter 20

On Thursday afternoon Alain, Isabelle, Pascale, Julian and Oliver were grouped around the dining-room table at Terre Blanche. Bars of light coming through the slatted shutters, closed as usual against the heat, fell in a random pattern on the white tablecloth. The large, airy room, panelled in pale glazed wood, was an oasis in the intense August heat. The high ceiling frescoed with clouds, the pale blue and cream oriental carpet, the painted chairs and the old, dark landscapes on the walls suggested the cool, verdant glades of northern France, far beyond the sun-baked hills of Gascony.

'Would anyone like more coffee?' Isabelle asked. 'What about you, Julian?' Seeing him stifle a yawn, she smiled and raised an eyebrow. She had heard him drive away to take Pascale home in the early hours of the morning and she wondered if they had become lovers yet. 'Would you like some, Pascale?'

'No, thank you,' Pascale answered, shaking her head. She had noticed Oliver's tantalized stare directed at a silver basket of chocolates on the table and, giving him a conspiratorial smile, she nudged it towards him. His hand darted out; then he remembered to glance at Alain.

'Go ahead, but only one more. You've already had three.'

'*J'adore les truffes au chocolat*,' he exclaimed, popping one into his mouth.

'Your French is so fluent,' Pascale said. 'Soon it will be better than my English. It's true,' she added, looking at Alain, who had put her at her ease immediately when they had met that afternoon. Beneath his veneer of acquired sophistication she perceived a Gascon earthiness, which expressed itself in the strong, loving bond apparent between father and son.

'Just one more, please,' begged Oliver.

'No, that's enough or you'll be sick,' Alain said firmly.

Pascale's expression suggested to Oliver that she knew what he was thinking: he would like to pocket the rest of the chocolates and run off into the garden. Oliver had been dazzled by her cloud of pale blonde hair and her clear blue eyes, which reminded him of a fairy princess, and had hardly taken his eyes off her. He had asked to sit next to her at the table, liking the way she spoke to him as an equal, in a lilting accent peppered with errors. The mystery of who she was and why she had been invited to lunch deepened when he noticed that Julian was looking at her with an intensity that excluded the rest of them.

Alain said, 'I think I'll change my mind and have another cup of coffee, Isabelle. I promised to take Oliver into the village later and this heat is making me drowsy.'

'*C'est la canicule,*' said Isabelle, pronouncing the word crisply.

'What's that?' asked Oliver.

'It means a heatwave.'

'*Canicule.*' The word rolled off his tongue. 'Are we going to watch them put up the carousel in the square, Dad?'

'That's the plan.'

The saucer moved in Isabelle's hand, causing her to spill a few drops of coffee on the tablecloth. She dabbed at them irritably with her napkin. A sleepless night had made her edgy.

'I can't really say I'm in the mood to go into Roquelaire in this heat,' said Alain. 'We ought to have a nap until it cools off a bit.'

'Dad, you never take naps in California, but you always seem to want one here,' Oliver said.

Julian threw back his head and laughed. 'Out of the mouths of babes.'

'That's true, but this is supposed to be a vacation,' Alain replied with an amused shake of his head.

'And you sure seem to work a lot for a vacation,' Oliver continued, making Alain smile.

Isabelle began to reminisce about heatwaves in the past. Half listening, and distracted by the looks Julian kept giving her, Pascale studied Isabelle closely, admiring her elegantly simple white T-shirt and skirt. Her wrists were clamped with thick silver and turquoise bracelets, worn with the casual chic that, to Pascale, was the hallmark of a Parisienne. Isabelle was much warmer and friendlier than she had expected, but her impeccable glamour made Pascale feel gauche and provincial by comparison.

'I remember years ago when we had a drought,' Isabelle was saying. 'We drained the swimming pool to water the roses we had just planted. I told my husband afterwards that was why they grew to be as big as water lilies.' She gestured at the huge bowl of roses in the centre of the table.

Pascale's eyes roamed the room, lighting on the precious china in cupboards lined with turquoise silk, the embroidered organdie cloth on the table, the vermeil and blue enamel teaspoons resting on the paper-thin Limoges coffee saucers stamped with the Montjoi coat of arms. Even the Louis Philippe chairs were obviously genuine. Every precious object spoke of unassailable wealth and social standing, passed down from generation to generation.

'Could I please leave the table now?' Oliver asked, squirming restlessly in his chair.

'All right, *vas-y*,' Alain said. As Oliver dashed from the room, he called after him, 'Hadn't you better say goodbye to Pascale? You might not see her again.'

Oliver came to a halt and trotted back. 'Goodbye, Pascale,' he said, extending his hand to her. 'It was very nice to meet you. I hope we see each other again soon,' he added.

'And it was nice to meet you, Oliver. I hope to see you again too – *a bientôt, j'éspère*.' Leaning down, she kissed him on both cheeks. Taken by surprise, Oliver responded with a dazed smile, then ran from the room.

Pascale shook her head and laughed.

'You've made a friend for life,' said Alain, beaming at her. 'I can tell you that Oliver has already developed a crush on you.'

'What's a crush?'

'It means he's in love with you,' said Julian, adding under his breath, 'and he's not the only one.'

Pascale shot him an embarrassed look, thinking the others had overheard.

Alain rose from his chair and looked at Isabelle. 'Would you

416

excuse us for a moment? There's something I want Julian to look at in the study.'

'Pascale and I will wait in the sitting-room,' she replied. Laying down her napkin, she rang a silver bell to summon the housekeeper.

From the doorway Julian blew Pascale a kiss and called, 'Don't worry, I haven't forgotten that you have to be back at the bakery by three.'

The mention of the bakery was an unwelcome reminder to Pascale that in half an hour she would be in the dark, closed little shop doling out baguettes, a world away from Terre Blanche. She followed Isabelle into the sitting-room, where Isabelle gestured for her to sit down beside her on the sofa.

'Do you really have to leave so soon? I thought you and Julian might like to spend the rest of the afternoon by the pool. You're more than welcome to stay.'

'I wish I could, but I always help out in the shop in the afternoons when I'm here. My mother doesn't like the heat. They stay open in August so they can go away in September when the weather is cooler.'

'It's not much of a holiday for you, I imagine, working in the bakery,' said Isabelle sympathetically.

'I don't really mind. I get to see a lot of people I'd never see otherwise while I'm at home.' Pride welled up in her, not allowing her to admit how tedious it could be sometimes.

'Tell me, does your aunt ever help out?'

'Aunt Agnès? Never. She has her own life, her chickens and rabbits, her garden.'

'I've only spoken to her once or twice, I'm sorry to say.'

Pascale was suddenly aware of the watchful, cat-like quality in Isabelle's manner.

'You wouldn't see my aunt very often, even though Roquelaire is small. The two of you live in such different worlds.'

'That's true, of course. But there's something fundamental that we have in common now. I'm sure you know what that is.'

'You mean the château?'

Pascale sensed that Isabelle had been waiting to bring up the

417

subject, and her heart started to thump. The unsettling thought surfaced at the back of her mind that this was why she had been invited to lunch at Terre Blanche.

'I'm glad to have a minute alone to talk with you, Pascale, because I hope that you might be able to help me.'

'Me?' she replied, on her guard.

'I don't need to fill you in about the château and what a surprise it was to all the family when the contents of Armand's will were revealed, because I'm sure you've heard all the details at home.'

'I only arrived last week, and I was away when it happened,' Pascale said quickly.

'Even so, this unexpected legacy of your aunt's must have already affected your family profoundly.'

'Well, yes, of course. I mean, it was a surprise, a wonderful surprise, but it means a lot of problems and responsibilities. Anyway, it's really nothing to do with me. It belongs to my aunt.' Pascale forced a smile, hating the uneasiness that any mention of the château aroused in her.

'Armand's last-minute decision about his property was a big shock to me. I don't mind telling you that. But such is life, and I am determined to deal with it as best I can. It's very forward of me to ask this, but do you know why he did such a thing? After all, as a member of his family, I feel very hurt by it.'

'I'm sorry, but I have no idea. My aunt doesn't know either.' As she said it, Pascale thought of Armand and Agnès, and the Resistance. She looked up nervously, hoping Isabelle couldn't detect that she might be hiding something.

'It's just remarkable that such a thing could happen. Pascale – can I be frank with you?'

Pascale nodded, dreading what was coming.

'When we made an offer to your aunt to buy the château after the will was read, her answer came back so quickly that I simply couldn't believe she had had time to think. I concluded that she needed a bit more time, so I left the matter there.'

'You made an offer?'

'You didn't know about it?'

'No – no, I didn't. But . . .'

'Yes, I made a very generous offer on behalf of Alain and myself and the others. We're partners in the venture with a very prestigious development group, represented by Julian, as I'm sure he's told you. We tried to buy the château back at a generous price, but she turned it down without even considering it.'

'I didn't know. Maybe she was confused at the time. You know, it was all such a surprise.' Pascale gestured helplessly.

'Your aunt must be aware that we're waiting for her to contact us. When Julian told us he'd met you and what a lovely, intelligent girl you were, I wanted to meet you too. And now you're here I know you are the right person to talk to. Your aunt is a charming, sweet woman, but after all, what does she know of business? She's led a very quiet life away from the cares of the world. Tell me, is it simply a question of money?'

'She hasn't said anything to me.'

'You have a business head on your shoulders, Pascale. Perhaps you can explain the situation to your aunt, make her realize she must make up her mind soon, that I can't wait for ever. Because in my heart I can't believe she intends to keep the château. She would have to possess a fortune of her own to do so.'

'Of course,' Pascale murmured, aware that Isabelle's point of view neatly echoed what her own parents had been saying.

'Would you talk to your aunt, prepare the way so that perhaps we could have a meeting, say, tomorrow? I feel somehow that if you talked with her, we could come to an agreement that would suit everyone.'

'I could try, but I don't know. My aunt is very independent.'

Isabelle waved this aside. 'I'm sure, but if you could arrange a meeting between the two of us on Friday, say, at ten, I could send the gardener to fetch her in a car.'

'Oh no, I'm sure she'd rather you didn't.'

'I'll leave that to you, then.'

Pascale nodded with a sinking heart, knowing she was trapped. 'I could go there this evening and ask, then call you if you like.'

'Marvellous. You know, I was thinking at lunch, if things work out, there would be a very good position for you at the hotel, should you be interested. You're just the sort of girl I'd be looking for to work as an assistant manager. While the hotel is being built I know the group would be happy to train you in Switzerland for several months, if the idea appeals to you. It would be a great opportunity.'

Pascale looked at her in amazement. 'That would be wonderful – if it happens.'

'It can happen. I believe in being optimistic. Optimism has always been the driving force of my life. If I wanted something, I've always applied myself to achieving it.'

Pascale forgot her misgivings as she gazed at Isabelle in a state of captive enchantment, imagining her life as an exotic fable spun out against a backdrop of fabulous wealth and social position. Suddenly she could see no reason why the same thing might not happen to her. She was fired by the idea that there was nothing really mysterious at all about destiny. It was no more than malleable clay, which could be shaped to the heart's desire.

'Do you know,' Isabelle's words broke into her thoughts, 'I can tell that you and I are going to be such good friends. We hardly know each other, yet I sense that you would be very good in business and can deal with people. Whom do you take after, your father or your mother?'

'I'm not really anything like either of my parents, or my brothers.'

'Really? How interesting. You're some kind of phenomenon,' Isabelle said with a little laugh.

Isabelle was looking at her with such scrutiny that Pascale was relieved when she heard Alain and Julian coming down the hall.

Isabelle's hand touched hers. 'Will you call me this evening and let me know how everything went with your aunt?'

'Yes, of course. I promise.'

'I don't even need to mention this, of course, but it would be better if you didn't tell her about our conversation. She might misinterpret my interference, and that would spoil everything, wouldn't it?'

*

420

Rachel was curled up in a chair in Michael's sitting-room, trying to read a book on the Middle Ages she had taken from the shelf, all the while listening for the sound of his footsteps. The minute the door handle turned she rose tensely. Her face lit up when she saw Michael appear.

He set the shopping down on the table. 'It's just me.'

She smiled. 'Who else?'

'The look on your face – it was if you expected a demon to walk through the door.' He took her in his arms and hugged her reassuringly. 'You still don't feel safe here, do you?'

'I can't shake off the feeling that someone might discover where I am. Stupid, isn't it?'

'Not a bit. I don't blame you. I saw Alain and Oliver in the square.'

'What? Just now? How very odd. It's as if I felt it. Did they come this way?' she asked anxiously.

'I don't think so. They were watching the carousel being erected for the fête. When I saw them, I went up and said hello. Oliver seemed pleased to see me, but Alain gave me the silent treatment.'

The fleeting annoyance Rachel felt at Alain's rudeness was chased away by the upsetting realization that Oliver had been so close to her without her knowing it.

'I asked Oliver if he was coming to ride the carousel tomorrow, you know, casually, as if I was making conversation.'

'And?'

'He said he was.'

Rachel could hardly believe her ears. 'That was very quick thinking on your part. Now at least we know for certain that they'll be there. What a godsend. Do you think Alain suspected anything?'

'No, not at all. He was just glad to get rid of me. I don't really know what was going on in his mind. Perhaps he was embarrassed because he thinks I know so much about his private life. After I left them I went to the bakery and asked Pascale if she could drop by when it closes, and she agreed. I made the excuse that I had a book I thought she'd like to read.'

'I keep wondering if it's fair to ask her to help us. And whether we can trust her.'

'There's no choice. It's too risky otherwise, and probably doomed to failure. You haven't changed your mind?'

She shook her head, feeling the churning nausea start in her stomach at the thought of tomorrow.

'Let's try to live through this one minute at a time, all right?' Michael held her shoulders and looked squarely at her, imparting his own strength.

'I'm like a blind person on a precipice. I need your reassurance every step of the way,' she whispered, embracing him.

'You have that, and so much more, Rachel. You know that, don't you?'

Her troubled eyes expressed a mute gratitude. There was so much she wanted to say, but she held back, as if she were clinging to her emotions like precious reserves she couldn't afford to squander. The gentleness in his eyes conveyed he understood exactly what she was thinking.

'I bought some éclairs at the bakery. How about a cup of tea while we read the papers? Does that appeal to you? That's what the English always do in a crisis – make a cup of tea,' he said, causing her to laugh.

She followed him into the kitchen. 'That would be wonderful. Suddenly I have a raging appetite.'

'Nerves. You hardly ate anything at lunch.'

Rachel watched him set out the teacups, noting the line of his shoulders beneath his denim shirt, the way his hair fell on his collar. Every waking moment since morning that she wasn't thinking of Oliver, she had thought of Michael. The memory of their lovemaking came back to her with irresistible force. As he walked away from her, Rachel felt the first sharp reminder of what it would be like to say goodbye.

Rachel held her crossed fingers up for luck as Michael went to answer the knock at the door. Hearing Pascale's voice, she could hardly breathe for suspense. Pascale looked surprised to see her there, but her sweet unassuming manner gave Rachel hope.

Motioning to a chair, Michael said, 'Pascale, I asked you to come here for an important reason. The book was only an excuse. We have a favour to ask of you.'

422

'A favour? Of course. What is it?'

'Have you met Mrs Ribard's husband?'

'Monsieur Ribard?' Pascale paused, looking from one to the other of them. 'Yes, I met him today for the first time. I was invited to lunch at Isabelle de Montjoi's by a friend of hers.'

'Was it Julian Paine?' asked Rachel. The thought of him made her furious.

'Yes – yes, I went there with Julian. But it's a secret, because my parents don't know I'm seeing him.'

'We won't say anything,' said Michael. 'On the subject of secrets, though, no one in the village knows Mrs Ribard is here. Please don't mention it to anyone.'

'My husband thinks I've gone back to California, Pascale. We're going to get a divorce.'

'I didn't know. He didn't mention you at all.'

'Did you see my son, Oliver, at lunch?'

'Yes, I saw him. He's a very nice little boy – adorable.'

Rachel smiled at the compliment, but the sound of his name and the fact that Pascale had seen him only hours ago aroused the familiar emptiness of not knowing how he passed the time.

'Pascale, Mr Lowry asked you to come here today because I desperately need your help.'

A while later Michael closed the door behind Pascale and looked confidently at Rachel.

'Do you know, I think she's going to do it.'

'I hope you're right.' Rachel wiped the tears from the corners of her eyes. She couldn't stop crying now they were alone.

'You mustn't worry,' he said, holding her tight. 'If anything goes wrong, she'll simply say she agreed to help you see Oliver for a few minutes alone. And what could Alain say to that? He wouldn't get much sympathy from anyone. After all, you're Oliver's mother.'

'I know. That's what I keep telling myself. I feel as if I'm about to set out on a tightrope in a high wind. Have you ever felt that your entire life depended on one particular moment?' Rachel smiled ironically at herself. 'Of course you have. You've been living like that for years.'

'Perhaps, but never so much as now. Because, Rachel, I feel as if my life depends on tomorrow too. We've become part of each other, and I couldn't bear to see you fail.'

She nodded, swallowing her tears. A shaft of late afternoon light had penetrated a crack in the shutters, reminding her of John and Margaret in the tower at Brissac, where the late summer sun would have poured through narrow windows, filling their prison with light.

Michael said, 'Later, when it's dark, I'll go down and start the car and check that everything is in running order. It might be a good idea to put your luggage in the boot tonight, too. That way you'll be ready to make a dash for it tomorrow before anyone discovers what has happened.'

Rachel nodded, her mind leaping ahead to the crucial hour.

Pascale decided to go straight to Agnès's after leaving Rachel and Michael. She walked through the square, where the shops were beginning to close and the men from the carnival were putting the finishing touches to the carousel and other amusements for the fête. She held her head high, refusing to be cowed by the cat-calls from the raffish-looking men on the carousel, who stared after her with undisguised lust. She was so preoccupied that she nearly collided with Laurent, who was just locking up his shop.

'Hey, Pascale – *ça va?*'

She gave a flustered half-smile, feeling repelled, as she always was, by his curious, weasel-like face. She guessed, without having to be told, that Étienne had confided the intimate details of their break-up to him.

'I can't stop now. I have to hurry.'

'Sorry to hear about you and Étienne,' he called after her.

She stopped, unable to keep herself from staring back at Laurent with indignant coldness, which, to her fury, seemed to amuse him.

'I saw him off this morning. He was pretty broken up about the whole thing, but he'll survive, I suppose.'

Pascale glared at him, immobilized by anger and embarrassment, but unwilling to let him have the last word.

'It's really nobody's business but ours.'

'That's wishful thinking in a village like this. You'll probably be

424

glad to get back to the anonymity of the big city.' Under his breath, just loud enough for her to hear, Laurent added, 'You bitch.'

Pascale gasped, then hurried on, feeling as if the breath had been knocked out of her. The mellow colours of the square warmed by the evening sun blurred as tears smarted in her eyes. Alone on the road that led to Agnès's house Pascale could still hear Laurent's devastating epithet ringing in her ears. She was pursued by the painful image of Étienne on a train hurtling towards Germany.

Approaching the blue cottage she stopped, not wanting to face Agnès. But it was too late. Agnès, scything the long grass by the ditch for her rabbits, had already seen her and waved.

She called, 'I'll send some tomatoes back with you for supper, and I'll pick you some beans as well.'

'I'll help you,' said Pascale, relieved to postpone her reason for coming.

They went into the garden and walked through a row of well-tended tomato plants. Pascale held the basket as Agnès rummaged through the fragrant leaves, exposing clusters of ripe tomatoes. Watching her aunt, it struck Pascale how gnarled her fingers were, with their yellow, misshapen nails; how pinched her face was becoming, how frail and bent she looked, things she had failed to notice before. It was as if Agnès had aged overnight. Observing her with fresh eyes, Pascale felt an odd mixture of shame and pride at her aunt's eccentricity and her shabbiness, which she had accepted unthinkingly all her life.

When Agnès looked up with her usual good-natured expression, Pascale wiped the quizzical look off her face, hoping her aunt hadn't guessed what she was thinking. They walked back through the garden, picking beans and talking about the bakery and the weather. At last they went to the porch and sat down at the garden table to pick the ends off the beans.

During a lull in the conversation Pascale said casually, 'I had lunch at Terre Blanche today.'

Agnès looked up. 'What brought that about?'

'I was invited by a friend of Madame de Montjoi's whom I met at the café, an Englishman.'

'He's not the one who drives around in that red sports car, is he?'

'Yes. How did you know?' Pascale's stomach contracted.

'Oh, I've seen him somewhere. He doesn't look French. Is he nice?'

'Very. He's a property developer.'

'Ah, so that's the connection. He's quite a lot older than you, isn't he?'

'A bit. I suppose that's what I like about him. He's so mature. He's unlike anybody I've ever met in my life.'

'What's he doing here?'

Pascale swallowed nervously. 'You'll never guess – he came here to work on the plans for making the château into a hotel, but then you surprised everybody by inheriting it,' she laughed, deciding to make light of it.

'I'm sure I did,' Agnès said, unperturbed.

Pascale took a deep breath. 'Are you going to sell it at some point? I think they're anxious to talk to you.'

'Did they say that?'

'Not exactly,' Pascale replied, feeling her lie was transparent.

'They shouldn't have approached you. That isn't right.'

'The subject just came up . . .'

'Because they brought it up, I'm sure.'

'Won't you talk to them?'

'Yes, if you like.'

'Would you really?'

Pascale looked at her, feeling a sense of anticlimax. 'I'm so glad, because I think you ought to hear what Madame Montjoi and Monsieur Ribard have to say. They're very nice.'

'But I've already made up my mind. I just haven't felt ready to talk about it, that's all.'

'You have?'

'Yes, but as it seems to mean so much to you, I'll go and see Madame Montjoi.'

They agreed that Agnès would go to Terre Blanche the following day. Pascale stared at her in astonishment, as if she had won a personal victory, but something about Agnès's sudden openness

426

made her uneasy and the only question she dared to ask concerned a time for the meeting.

'Yes, ten o'clock will be fine.'

'I'll borrow the car and drive you there.'

'That won't be necessary. I'll go by bicycle.'

When the last bean had been done, Agnès said, 'It may be none of my business, but are you infatuated with this Englishman?'

'Yes,' Pascale admitted, realizing that with Agnès she could never keep anything hidden for long. 'I know what you're thinking – that it's very soon after Étienne. On the rebound.'

'If that's what they call it.'

Pascale didn't look up. She scooped the beans into a bag, bearing the weight of the silent accusation in Agnès's eyes. As close as they had always been, Agnès couldn't possibly understand what she was going through, and Pascale reflected how infinitely sad it was that her aunt had never known what it was like to be in love.

# Chapter 21

On Friday morning Agnès bicycled into the village square, which had been completely transformed by the carnival. The market had been moved to an *allée* of chestnut trees beneath the ramparts and a carousel, a shooting gallery and a platform of little cars stood in its place. For the first time she could remember, Agnès would not be setting up her stall as usual. That morning she had been indifferent to the basket of eggs she had gathered, the harvest of tomatoes and beans, the rabbits in their cages; she felt detached from everything to do with Roquelaire.

She greeted a neighbour, who touched his beret. '*Trop chaud pour les lapins?*' he asked with a broad smile.

'*Mais, non,*' she replied. She chatted with him for a moment then went on her way, passing the team of brawny young men making final adjustments to the ornate carousel, which almost reached the rafters of the market. Although it was an old one, it had been carefully maintained, and Agnès stopped to admire the dappled horses, decked with plumes and bright saddles, fixed to the shiny brass poles. Every inch of the carousel itself was covered in a riot of cherubs, gilded mirrors and panels painted with scenes of Arcadia. Agnès smiled to herself, remembering that she and Beatrice had ridden on a similar carousel in the square only days before war was declared. The recollection of going round and round to the music with her laughing sister while her smiling parents watched was a bright chip of happiness embedded in the dark days that followed.

Agnès parked her bicycle and, lifting an armful of fragrant roses from the basket, mounted the steps and entered the cool church. The familiar smells of polish and burning candles banished the bitter-sweet nostalgia of a few moments before. When she had arranged the flowers in front of the statue of St Anne, she knelt to pray. Agnès's eyes followed the folds of the statue's blue gown, glinting with gold stars, to her serene countenance, streaked by wavering candlelight. She didn't see Père Auguste watching her from the shadows. He had come silently through the door from the office and noted her bent figure, as predictable as sunrise, arranging her usual summer offering of roses from her garden. He had intended to speak to her, but she had hurried from the church with a preoccupied air.

Outside in the sunshine, Agnès went directly to the notary's office, from which she emerged a quarter of an hour later, shaking hands with a young man in a gaudy sports shirt and tortoiseshell glasses, whose father and grandfather before him had handled her family's affairs.

'I'm putting you to a lot of trouble. I'm sure you have so much to do if you're leaving on holiday on Sunday.'

'It's no bother, but it's a good thing you caught me in time. Just come in after nine on Monday morning and Marianne will have the amendment to your will ready to sign. You have until then to change your mind.' He still registered surprise at her decision.

'And it won't be final until then, you say? I could still change my mind?'

He nodded. 'Think about it over the weekend. That's always best.'

'I'll do that.' For some reason Agnès was relieved that her decision to dispose of the château wasn't final yet.

Deafening rock music began pouring from loudspeakers in the square. The coloured lights of the carousel had been turned on, and men were lifting the canvas flaps of the shooting gallery and other concessions. The delicious smell of burnt sugar, so redolent of carnival, scented the air. Seeing by the clock over the *mairie* that it was nearly nine-thirty, Agnès mounted her bicycle and set out for Terre Blanche with a sense of resolution.

She could already feel the heat rising from the earth as she pedalled up and down the gentle hills, where the sunflowers had begun to wither and giant wheels of straw cast shadows on the bleached stubble. Perspiration collecting on her forehead evaporated

429

as quickly as it formed in the breeze churned up by her swift, steady progress. Turning through the open gates twenty minutes later, she felt uplifted by the sight of the tree-filled park suffused with morning light. But when the house which she had seen before only in a photograph came into view, she felt resentment at being lured there by its owner.

As she climbed the steps Agnès saw Isabelle de Montjoi was already waiting for her in the doorway with a man she realized must be Alain Ribard standing beside her. She was relieved there was no sign of his son, who had seen her exploring the entrance to the tunnel.

'Madame Grimal, *bonjour!*' Isabelle said warmly. 'How kind of you to come all this way. I hope it wasn't too exhausting for you. I would have been happy to come and fetch you in the car.'

'*Bonjour, madame.* Thank you, but I preferred to come on my own,' she said with a restrained smile.

'May I present Monsieur Ribard.'

'*Bonjour, madame,*' Alain responded warmly. 'I'm very pleased to see you again.'

As their hands met Agnès felt herself go cold. She was staring into Paul Ribard's dark-fringed blue eyes set in the face of a stranger.

'I don't know if you remember me. My father was Claud Ribard,' he said matter-of-factly.

'Of course I remember you, even though it was a long time ago.' She was still reeling from the memory of Paul Ribard, but the name Claud evoked the picture of Alain's father, a pathetic, broken man, who always smelled of alcohol and who had died alone on his rundown farm.

While they talked about the weather with polite formality Agnès noted that although Alain Ribard still spoke his native tongue with a marked local accent, he had none of the easy-going familiarity that characterized the people among whom he had been born. The alien soil of California seemed to have changed him into a sort of hybrid, toning down his Frenchness to an almost unrecognizable degree, so that he might have been an American who had settled in France rather than vice versa. Thinking of his charming wife and

430

young son, Agnès felt a wave of disapproval when she looked at the glamorous Isabelle, whose charm she was set to resist.

They walked down the long black-and-white tiled passage past a gilt commode and a huge mirror, dark *armoires* and tables polished to a deep sheen. Agnès looked indifferently at the luxury of Terre Blanche; it seemed more like a museum than a home to her.

When they were seated in the drawing-room, Isabelle said, 'Would you care for some coffee, or perhaps a cool drink after your ride?'

'No, thank you.'

Isabelle glanced at Alain, her pleasant smile fixed to her face. 'In that case, I suppose we shouldn't waste your time, but get directly to the point.'

Agnès sat perfectly straight, not letting her back touch the sofa. She listened disinterestedly to Isabelle's reminiscences about Armand, which seemed so insincere. All the while she was acutely conscious of Alain Ribard's presence; his strong resemblance to the man Armand had murdered affected her more than Isabelle's words ever could. One glance had told her of the success he had made of himself. His sleek, immaculately groomed exterior, impenetrable as a disguise, induced her grudging respect when she thought of the simplicity of his background. Her conscience was pricked by the stigma he had had to bear because of Armand's self-serving actions, making her lose track of what Isabelle was saying.

'It seemed to us it was time to invite you here in person to discuss the matter. We're willing to be very generous, to take Brissac off your hands for a very fair price, far more than we can really afford. Please understand that this is the final offer. We can go no higher,' she added pointedly.

Isabelle named a figure, and Agnès pretended to consider it, though she hardly counted the number of zeros. Seeing the suspense in Alain's face made her hesitate, but only for a second.

'*Madame, monsieur*, I regret, but I cannot accept the offer.'

Isabelle's mouth set in a hard line and Alain's dark eyebrows shot up in surprise.

'Madame Grimal, I really wonder whether you have fully considered what our project would mean to the village. Of course I

431

want to buy the château for my own reasons, but that's only one aspect. Isabelle and I are builders, dreamers. We want to pour our lives into Brissac and transform it into what it deserves to be. It's much too large for a private house, so what other use can there be for it? Turning it into a hotel is the only way to save it from decline. And there's no one who could do it better than we could.' Alain focused the full force of his terrible eyes on her.

'I'm sure that's true. I'm sorry, truly sorry that you are so disappointed, but I've made up my mind.'

'So you've made up your mind,' he repeated, weighing up the situation. He felt an unexpected sympathy for the dowdy old woman. She embodied the uncompromising values of another era, a way of life that was almost gone, a way of life he had despised when he left Roquelaire behind. Agnès Grimal had a trusting, naïve quality that called for tact and consideration. But her simplicity, which had survived the influences of a complicated world, was embedded in a core of native shrewdness that he knew he understood far better than Isabelle did. He believed he could make her change her mind.

'I wonder if you have any idea what Brissac means to me,' he continued. 'But, then, how could you? We hardly know each other, you and I. Since I was a boy and saw the château outlined against the horizon from the farm where I was born it has been a symbol to me of everything worth having in life – not that I ever thought it would belong to me. In my wildest dreams I never expected that you and I, who used to pass in the square, would be haggling like two peasants over a goose.' He stopped, as if surprised at his own outburst, and smiled at her.

Agnès smiled back, finding his passionate sincerity hard to resist. It almost seemed as if some unseen hand were trying to work a sort of reckoning, to compensate for what he had suffered long ago.

'*Monsieur*, you have been honest with me, and now I'll be honest with you. You deserve a more reasoned response to your offer. It isn't a question of money. And I'm not opposed to the idea of a spa or hotel in the village either. But I hope Brissac will become a refuge, not for rich tourists but for pilgrims on the road to St Jacques de Compostelle. This is my answer, that is my plan, if you want to know. I want the Church to take it over.'

432

Isabelle was so dumbfounded she could hardly speak. 'A hostel for pilgrims? Brissac, with all its tradition and the beauty that Armand coaxed back to life with such love and care? You can't be serious, *madame*.'

'Yes. I'm afraid I am.'

'But Armand – think of him. Surely you can't imagine that's what he would have wanted. Why, he had nothing to do with the Church. And as for pilgrims, most of the people who come to Roquelaire are really only tourists with rucksacks and sandals. They aren't on a religious quest.'

'Who is to say whether Armand Bataille would have approved of my idea? I like to think he would.' Agnès stood up to go. She felt weary now. 'I'm glad we've had this chance to talk in person and to clear up what has been an obvious misunderstanding. If I had known, I would have come sooner. And may I say, *madame*, that you're wrong: pilgrims do still exist, as they have for hundreds of years. Goodbye, *monsieur*, *madame*.'

'No – wait,' Isabelle said tersely. 'Alain, would you leave us for a moment? There is something I have to say to Madame Grimal, and I think it would be better if we were alone.'

Agnès was taken aback at the sudden imperiousness in Isabelle's manner.

When Alain had gone, Isabelle said, 'Would you sit down just for a moment longer. We haven't finished our conversation.' She stared at Agnès intently, and she was no longer smiling. 'There's one thing I find very strange about this whole affair, and that is why you would deny your own daughter her rightful inheritance.'

Her words had a startling impact. Agnès held her breath, unable to believe what she had heard. In a shocked whisper, she said, 'You've made a mistake. I don't know what you mean. I have no daughter.'

'I'm surprised that everyone else in Roquelaire hasn't already guessed who Pascale's parents are. Does Pascale know? Because if she did, I'm sure she would feel betrayed at what you're planning to do with the legacy her father left her indirectly through her mother.'

Agnès seemed to shrink under her gaze. 'What are you suggesting, *madame*?'

'Come now, don't try to hide it, Madame Grimal. You seem to forget how close I was to Armand all these years.'

'That's a lie. He didn't tell you anything. He wouldn't have, even if . . .' Choked with emotion, she hadn't the strength to fight the whirlwind that seemed to have sprung from nowhere.

'As a member of Armand's family, I would feel it my duty to act if you decided to throw your windfall away on this scheme of yours and disinherit Armand's *enfant naturelle*. That would be wrong, don't you see? Armand never would have allowed it. He trusted you to act for your daughter,' Isabelle went on remorselessly.

Agnès's hands, resting in her lap, felt as if they were made of stone, and her breath came in short gasps. Her secret suddenly seemed a helpless living thing that had been brutally wrenched from the darkness and flung at her feet. 'So that's how it is,' she whispered, her lips pursed.

'I'm afraid so. I hope, therefore, that you'll reconsider our offer.' Isabelle's voice was sweet once more, but firm. 'I need to know by Sunday evening at six o'clock, and not a moment later. If you decide against me, on Monday I will have to take steps to ensure that Armand's *fille naturelle* has her rights restored. Do you understand?'

'I don't know. I can't think.' Agnès pressed her hands to her temples. 'Even if such a thing were true, there's no way anyone can prove . . .' She shook her head, her eyes shut tight at the thought.

'Unfortunately one can never cover up all the traces of these things. They leave tidemarks in the form of documents somewhere.'

Agnès got to her feet. When the room swayed, she groped for the back of the sofa.

'Think if you must. But not for long, I hope. You are shocked, upset, I'm sure. But consider my position as a member of the family. You have no right whatever to Brissac. I have to do my duty.'

Agnès followed Isabelle out of the room and into the passage. She hurried blindly down the dazzling black and white tiles towards the door.

Alain and Isabelle watched her wheeling her bicycle down the drive until she had disappeared from sight.

434

'You told her?'

'Yes, of course. But she still insists she needs time to think, the old fool. Pilgrims! She must be out of her mind.'

'She looks a bit unsteady on her feet. Perhaps I ought to offer to drive her home. It might be a nice gesture,' said Alain.

'There's no need for gestures. You know these people – they're as stubborn as bulls and just as tough.'

'Well, what happened when you told her?'

'What could she say, confronted with the truth? She tried to deny it, of course, but soon realized it was useless. She'll fight with her life to keep it a secret. I told her I'd have to know by Sunday at six o'clock. Only a couple more days to wait, *chéri*. What a relief it will be.'

Alain hardly heard. He was unable to take his mind off Agnès's stooped figure as she had trundled down the drive with her bicycle.

'What's the matter with you? You don't seem very pleased.' When he didn't reply, Isabelle said, 'Alain, if you're feeling sentimental, guard yourself against it.'

'Don't be absurd. She's probably shrewder than you and I put together. I wonder what really happened between her and Armand Bataille.'

'That's something I'll never understand. It's inconceivable to me that those two ever got into bed together. By the way, that was an inspired speech you made about how much Brissac meant to you. For a moment I thought it was going to tip the scales.'

He turned to stare at her. 'It wasn't a speech. It's how I feel,' he said, already regretting his outburst. He didn't respond when Isabelle kissed him on the cheek, but murmured, 'If anything happens to her before we strike a deal, it would be a hell of a setback.' Agnès's disarming innocence, of a kind he had encountered only in children, seemed to linger reproachfully in his mind.

'Stop worrying, will you? You'll feel just fine, believe me, when she telephones to accept our offer.'

Far from Terre Blanche Agnès came to a halt on a hilltop and stared unseeingly at fields of sunflowers bowing their heads in the heat. For a long time she slumped over the handlebars of her

435

bicycle while she considered the consequences of her meeting with Isabelle. The whoosh of a passing car broke through her thoughts, and when the dust it kicked up had settled, she saw the towers of Brissac rising through an ethereal white haze in the distance, making her wish Armand had never left her a legacy that had brought nothing but trouble and heartache. She felt defenceless in the face of Isabelle's threats and in her mind she already saw the château not as a hostel for the pilgrims of St Jacques, but as a glamorous spa hotel. Trying to imagine how Isabelle had discovered her secret, she drew a blank, but Agnès was still smarting from her accusation that Armand had known about Pascale.

In June, when she had heard rumours in the village that Armand was dying, Agnès had been thrown into a quandary about what to do. Finally, driven by her conscience, she set out one afternoon for Brissac, unhappy at the prospect of seeing Armand pitifully eking out his last days in a twilight of painkillers. She remembered how surprised she had been to find him propped up in bed with a pile of documents by his side, his glasses on the end of his nose. His face lit up when he saw her, confirming she had been right to come. Closer up, his gauntness and pallor revealed how gravely ill he was, but she was full of wonderment at the vitality he still projected. When he took her hands in his, conveying a warmth she hadn't expected, she felt the same old awkwardness she had experienced so many years ago.

Her nervousness abated when it became obvious Armand had no intention of bringing up the past. That familiar sense of well-being in his company came back again, so much so that it was easy to forget what had brought her there. But she had come to the château armed against the emotions aroused by his condition that might tempt her to tell him about Pascale. Any doubts she had ever had about keeping her secret had long since faded and been replaced by a prickly self-righteousness.

'And your family? Are they well?'

'Yes, they're all very well, thank you,' she assured him. She talked about Beatrice, her husband and the boys, but avoided any mention of Pascale.

After a moment Armand asked, 'And what about your niece? How old is she now?'

436

'She'll be twenty-one this autumn. She's going to be married at Christmas, you know.' Avoiding his eyes, Agnès talked about Pascale in a matter-of-fact way, though inwardly she was apprehensive. Then, without warning, she seemed to dry up in mid-sentence, and was unable to bring herself to utter another word about Pascale. Something she had been fleeing all these years seemed to catch up with her, leaving her vulnerable. The room was silent except for the screams of swifts circling the tower.

Not knowing where to look, Agnès turned towards the window above Armand's desk, only to be reminded how she had stood in the same spot wrapped in a blanket on the Christmas Pascale had been conceived. The season had changed, the light was brighter now, but she recalled how happy she had been as she gazed down at the snow-covered valley at daybreak. Agnès turned back to Armand, her chin quivering, but not supposing for a moment he could interpret her silence.

'Pascale,' he whispered, his eyes ablaze with sudden feeling. 'Twenty-one is a fine age to be with all the world in front of you. Everything seems possible and indeed it is when you are beautiful, intelligent, so full of life and hope. She's a lovely girl. A girl any parent would be proud of. I know, I've seen her.'

This time the silence was deafening. Finally Agnès heard herself say in a hoarse little voice how much Pascale resembled her parents, as absurd as it was. Desperate to get away, she stood up. 'I'm sorry Armand, but I really must be going. I hope my visit hasn't tired you too much. But I'll come again if you like,' she added.

To her dismay Armand slumped back and closed his eyes. When she saw tears streaming down his cheeks she shrank from the idea it might have something to do with her. Her cheeks were burning with what she later knew was shame.

'Forgive me, if you can,' he whispered.

'It was all so long ago. The war is over. Please don't keep torturing yourself.'

He shook his head in what seemed like exasperation and brushed his tears away. 'No, not that, dear Agnès. That's not what I meant. So many times I've asked myself why, I . . . but I don't have an answer.'

437

She bowed her head, afraid to utter another word that might open the floodgates and destroy her tightly closed existence.

When he had gained control of himself, Armand said in a whisper, 'Long ago I remember saying to you I thought there were things we shouldn't speak of . . .'

The candour she read in his eyes was like an invitation to confess, but she stubbornly refused to understand. She waited in terror for him to finish, then, mysteriously, he appeared to change his mind.

'Perhaps there are things better left unsaid after all,' he remarked.

These were nearly his last words to her, and from that day on it had been easy to suppose she had only been imagining things. When Armand was dead and his surprising testament made public, Agnès had let his troubling mention of Pascale slip from her mind, explaining her remarkable legacy as a gift of atonement for other matters. But now, three months later, on a dry hilltop overlooking Brissac, she stopped fighting the notion that Armand had never guessed her secret.

Agnès came to her senses, wondering how long she had been standing there. She mounted her bicycle and began to coast downhill, a cleansing wind bathing her face. She entered the shadowed valley serene in the knowledge that Armand had died happy because he had known Pascale belonged to him.

Oliver rounded the corner of the house just as Agnès was leaving. He scurried out of sight the second he recognized her as the old woman he had met emerging from the shrubbery at Brissac. Throughout lunch he pecked at his food with no appetite, keeping an eye on Alain's face to determine whether the old woman had come to Terre Blanche to warn him that his son was up to something, but his father didn't even mention her visit.

Afterwards, sent to his room for a rest, Oliver lay on the bed thinking of Agnès, wondering if she was really a witch and whether she possessed the power to mind-read.

Oliver waited until the house was quiet, then slipped out of his room and down the stairs, past the ticking clock to the big white-

438

and-yellow tiled kitchen. Seeing the blackboard by the door, he considered leaving a note to say he'd be back soon, but changed his mind, cheering himself up with the thought that if he were late and his father discovered he had left the grounds without permission, it would all be forgotten when he returned with the treasure.

He went out of the kitchen door into the heat and looked round the park, resounding with the deafening whir of cicadas. Pausing to glance up cautiously at the rank of closed shutters at the back of the house, then towards the glimmering swimming pool, he shrank back when he saw Julian lying on a sunbed. Realizing he was fast asleep, Oliver darted past him to the shed.

Moments later he was wheeling his bicycle through the trees in the park, away from the exposed driveway, in case anyone was looking. Once he was through the gates he pedalled furiously down the shady road, tasting the sweet exhilaration of escape.

He arrived on the outskirts of Roquelaire tired but triumphant after fighting his way up hills that had seemed so insignificant in the car. People were beginning to come in from the countryside for the carnival and were parking their cars below the ramparts, but no one paid any attention to him. Catching the sound of the music drifting from the square, Oliver thought of going back, but reminded himself that he would never have another chance to look for the treasure of Brissac.

By the time he saw the château rising against the sky his enthusiasm had dimmed and his sweat-soaked shirt clung to his back. The parched landscape, combed by a hot, whispering wind, created an eerie aura of isolation that cut him down to size. Knowing how his father despised cowards and quitters, he kept going. His spirits revived somewhat at the sight of the Pilgrim's Stone, the only landmark on the little-travelled road. He laid down his bicycle and went up to it, peering at the letters defaced by time. He took a crude box wreath he had made that morning from his pocket and made a wish, not for treasure, but for a blessing, as he imagined a knight travelling with the Black Prince would have done. It made him feel older, taller and better armed against the unknown when he laid his offering at the base of the stone.

When he finally stood on the hilltop dominated by the château,

Oliver felt elated, and told himself that the hardest part of his adventure was over. He coasted beneath the château to a copse of trees off the road, where he hid his bicycle in a gully, enjoying a sense of drama as he covered it with leaves. He had come armed with a plastic bag of tools he had taken from the shed, not knowing what he would find. He crouched at the edge of the copse for a moment, listening and watching to be sure he was unobserved, then made his way to the tangle of shrubbery where he had seen Agnès Grimal, on the day he had gone to the château with his mother and Michael Lowry.

The undergrowth was far thicker than he had supposed, but he eventually found a way that had been cleared. He reached the stone wall beneath the fortress out of breath and covered in scratches. His heart seemed ready to burst from his chest with excitement when he saw that two stones were loosely wedged in a gap at the foot of what seemed an impenetrable wall, proving his hunch that the old woman had been looking for treasure. The stream of cool, musty air that hit his face as he crouched down confirmed the existence of a passage there, but it took a long time and all his strength to pry away the stones, using a chisel he had brought with him.

Oliver stared in awe at the gap he had made. In a moment he had wriggled through to a dark, cool underworld, whose ancient odour both intrigued and repelled him. He paused, sniffing the complex blend of mould, earth and stone, laced with the faint hint of decay. The sound of his own breathing was magnified in the silence, striking the first note of fear in him, real fear, which had not been a feature of his dreams. He lit a match and discovered that the brick-lined passage was much higher and deeper than he had imagined. He dared himself to explore, but his feet wouldn't move.

Images of his comic book heroes fearlessly entering caves, tombs and mysterious chambers ran through his mind, making him feel like a coward. Taking a deep breath, Oliver moved forward. Keeping his eyes on the square of daylight at his feet for reassurance, he lit a candle. As it flared he expected to see the flash of gold and jewels that had been left in a careless heap centuries ago, but the light glancing all round him revealed nothing but bricks and stones,

440

and the shadows made him think of ghosts. Before the idea could get a grip on him, Oliver spotted something in the dimness that looked like a row of stones. He edged towards it cautiously and discovered the stones formed a rim around a pit, the sort of pit that could easily be a treasure cache.

He peered down into the blackness, which the light from his candle couldn't penetrate. The thought that he was staring into a bottomless well made Oliver sick with dread and he stooped to feel for a stone, which he tossed into the void. The thud it made told him the pit was dry and not too deep, but it still seemed horribly sinister. As he turned away the candle caught the gleam of a familiar shape not far from the pit. It wasn't the gleam of gold or jewels, but of something white and smooth. A skull! Oliver was transfixed with terror. The hollow eyes stared at him above the leering jaw, its teeth still in place. A noise somewhere outside made him jump and the candle flew from his hand. Oliver gasped and whirled round to get his bearings from the light behind him, but as he moved, his shoe struck the edge of the pit, sending him out over the edge.

'Where have you been?' Isabelle called to Alain, who was striding towards where she lay by the pool. She sat up when she saw something was wrong.

'I've been looking for Oliver. Have you seen him?'

'Not a sign. Have you been looking for him all this time?'

'You were still sleeping when I got up. I took a shower and got dressed, then knocked on his door, but he didn't answer. When I saw he wasn't in his room, I came down to look for him.' His face was grave. 'That was nearly an hour ago.'

'Well, he couldn't have gone very far,' Isabelle said with a frown. 'I wouldn't worry. He's around somewhere.'

'That's just it. I've been all round the domaine. I went to the gardener's cottage, and even to ask Julian, but he hadn't seen him. His bicycle isn't in the shed.'

'*Chéri*, he was probably just bored. I wouldn't be surprised if he's playing a trick on you. He'll soon come out if you pay no attention.' She reached for his hand and squeezed it, sending a

441

potent reminder of their lovemaking that afternoon, which had restored the harmony between them. 'Did Julian say if he's coming to supper after we get back from the carnival?'

'He's got other plans apparently.' Taking off his sunglasses, Alain searched the distance and shouted Oliver's name.

'Maybe Fernande has seen him. She's just gone to get something cold to drink.'

In a moment they saw the housekeeper crossing the lawn with a tray. Alain strode impatiently towards her, then followed her back to the table, looking as grave as ever.

'No, Fernande hasn't seen him either.'

'*Madame*, I have already told *monsieur* that I've seen no sign of him at all.' She set down the tray, her face betraying her own concern, and returned to the house.

Alain looked at the lemonade and cookies she had brought for Oliver. 'I'm at my wits' end. It's after five, and he knows we're going to the carnival at six. It's not like him.'

'You know children have no sense of time, Alain. Still, he is a naughty boy to run off like this without telling you. Do you suppose he went for a ride down the road?'

'He knows that it's absolutely forbidden. I've made that clear.'

'Little boys often do things they're not supposed to.'

'Well, I'm going out in the car to look for him. If he comes back while I'm gone, tell him he'd better stay put and that he's in real trouble.'

'Fernande will be here, *chéri*. I'm going upstairs to have a shower and get ready.'

*

As the hall clock chimed the quarter hour, Isabelle came down the long staircase and entered the kitchen, where the housekeeper was preparing vegetables for supper. She looked worried when she saw Isabelle.

'You still haven't seen him? What a nuisance,' Isabelle muttered. 'If we should go out, Fernande, stay close to the telephone. If Madame Grimal calls, be sure to tell her I will return her call the minute I come back.'

'I doubt she even has a telephone in that shack of hers.'

'Do you know, I hadn't thought of that,' said Isabelle. 'But just in case. Oh, and in case there is news of the boy, of course.'

Isabelle was just coming from the office, where she had confirmed to herself that Agnès indeed had no telephone, when she heard the sound of a car coming to a halt on the forecourt. Going out to the terrace, she saw Alain getting out of the car, alone.

'Still no sign?' she said as he mounted the stairs.

'Nothing. Not a trace.'

'Do you suppose he went into the village? Maybe he was so excited to see the carnival that he decided to go in on his own without us.'

'It's so out of character for him to do something like that.'

'Well, we have to think of every possibility.'

Alain stroked his chin thoughtfully. 'Rachel!' he hissed under his breath. 'Rachel's gone off with him.'

'How could that be? She's gone back to California.'

'How do I know that? I haven't called her. She hasn't called me. My God . . .' He clenched his fists. 'I was a fool not to think of it before. She didn't go home at all. She's been hiding in the village, waiting to abduct him. I'd be willing to bet anything that's where he is.'

'Alain, get hold of yourself. How could she get in touch with him? Surely you don't suppose she climbed the wall of the park and waited there. It doesn't make any sense.'

'How can I be sure? Maybe she got a message to him somehow and asked him to meet her.'

'You would have sensed something was on his mind, surely. He couldn't have kept something like that a secret from you.'

'I don't know what to think,' he muttered. 'Come on, let's go into the village.'

Rachel reached up to kiss Michael's cheek as they stood in the hallway.

'I'll be thinking of you every single minute.'

He hugged her tightly. 'It's going to be hell for you just waiting. If I'm gone longer than you expect, it will mean that they haven't come yet, that's all. So don't give up.'

443

'Of course I won't. And don't worry about me. I'll be fine.'

'We haven't talked about what will happen to us. You'll be gone soon and we won't see each other again until God knows when. Rachel, I'm going to miss you terribly.'

'Oh, Michael, it's hard to let you go after all we've been through. Even though I'll have got Ollie back, part of me will be here with you, believe me.'

'Don't think of me now. You shouldn't think of anything but getting back home safely. I won't rest until you do. Will you be sure and phone me tonight?'

'Of course I will. By the way, I booked our hotel room in the name of Margaret Prior,' she said with a wry smile.

Michael hugged her. 'Then I'll know who to ask for if I ring first.'

They kissed once more and he left. Closing the door behind him, Rachel pressed herself against the warm wood, listening to his footsteps receding down the street. She felt bereft. To ease her tension she began to pace the room methodically, punctuating her steps with a prayer that Michael's plan would reunite her with Oliver within the hour. Once she had him back, Rachel vowed they would never be parted again.

Michael entered the noisy, crowded square and walked around for a few moments. He could see no sign of Alain or Isabelle, and went over to the café to wait for Pascale. Soon he saw her striding alone in his direction as if she hadn't a care in the world. For a moment he almost felt guilty about involving her in the affair.

'*Bonjour,*' she called with a smile.

'*Bonjour*, Pascale. *Ça va?*' he replied. He could tell at once by her pretended surprise at seeing him that she had decided to throw herself wholeheartedly into the scheme.

'I'm not late, am I?'

'No, not at all. Right on time.'

'Are they here yet?' Her eyes darted over the crowd.

'No sign of them. But it's only just after six. How long can you wait?'

'I have plenty of time. I have a rendezvous but not until seven-thirty.'

444

Her rich perfume and the immaculate care with which she had dressed told him that she was meeting Julian.

'You feel all right about this, don't you? You're not nervous?'

'No, no. Not at all, really,' she insisted. She looked around cautiously. Without knowing why, she felt as if Étienne's eyes had been following her everywhere since she left the house, even though she knew he had left for Germany the day before.

'Do you want to go through it again?'

'Sure. When I see them, I walk up and say hello. Then I ask Oliver if he would like to come to the bakery because I want to give him a special treat. And I should say to his father that we'll be back soon.'

'That's right. And remember, afterwards, when I've taken over and the two of us have disappeared, just pretend you have no idea why I wanted Oliver to come with me. It won't be easy, Pascale, because Alain is going to be angry when he finds out his wife is still here and that she used false pretences to get her son back. He might try to blame you, but just pretend you don't know what he's talking about.'

'No problem. I'll do it.' she shook her head. 'Parents shouldn't fight over their children. It's very sad.'

'Yes, it's sad. But I hope it will have a happy ending.'

'They're here,' she whispered. 'I see Isabelle.'

Michael followed her gaze across the square. Isabelle's height and colouring, and her mannequin-like perfection, distinguished her even from a distance. Alain was at her side, conspicuous in white jeans and a pink-striped shirt.

'I don't see Oliver. Perhaps he's on the carousel. They seem to be looking at it.'

'Should I go now?'

'Yes, now. When he gets off the carousel, that would be a good time.'

Michael peered over the heads moving in front of him as Pascale walked towards the carousel, poised to move the moment she returned with Oliver. This would be his cue to whisk the boy back to Rachel and then to her car, which was packed and waiting in his garage. It would be over in minutes, and Rachel and Oliver would

445

be out of Roquelaire before anyone realized what had happened. His thoughts had gone no further when Pascale returned abruptly – without Oliver.

'What's wrong?' he asked, seeing the confusion in her face.

'Monsieur Lowry, Oliver has disappeared. He left Terre Blanche on his bicycle after lunch and no one has seen him since. Monsieur Ribard is very worried. They came to the village to look for him.'

Rachel was waiting, aware of every small sound, when she heard Michael running up the street alone. She was already at the door when he came barging through. He stopped and looked at her wordlessly. Then he reached out and took her by the shoulders.

'Rachel, Alain and Isabelle are in the square. Oliver has been missing from Terre Blanche since after lunch and they're here looking for him.'

While he recounted what had happened, Rachel's mind seemed to empty of all coherent thought. She looked up at Michael uncomprehendingly.

'Very likely he'll turn up at any moment, wondering what all the fuss is about. They might even have found him already. Just try, if you can, not to jump to conclusions.'

'What should we do?' she asked in a small whisper, her eyes dilated with fear.

'The thing is, when they find him, they'll probably go straight home, so our plan is out the window.'

'If . . . he doesn't turn up?' She looked at him blankly.

'Just for the moment let's think what we'll do when he does.'

'I'm completely off balance. He's never done this, never.' She fought the panic that was starting to overtake her. Her body seemed hollow, her will gone.

'Look, one thing is certain. Alain is just as upset as you are at the moment. Whatever harm he's done, you can be sure he'll do everything possible to find Oliver.'

'What should I do?'

'We could wait and see. But in the meantime that leaves your hands tied. You won't be able to leave this house to go and look for him. Would you be able to bear that?'

446

'No, I'll have to tell Alain I'm here. There's no alternative.'

A knock at the door silenced them. Rachel ducked through the archway, and Michael opened the door to find Alain standing there.

'Michael Lowry?'

'Yes.'

'I'm Rachel Ribard's husband.'

'Yes, I know. We met before,' he said, feeling the wave of hostility emanating from Alain. 'How can I help you?'

'I'm here because I want to know if you're hiding my wife and son.'

Michael stared at him speechlessly. He was wondering how to answer, when Rachel came up behind him.

'Yes, Alain, I'm here. I've been here all along.'

'I knew it,' Alain muttered.

'But Oliver's not here. We only just heard from Pascale Gachpour that he's gone missing.'

'Do you expect me to believe that? Oliver! Oliver!' he cried over their heads. He tried to push past, but Michael barred his way.

'Just a minute! This is my house, and you're not barging in here unless you're invited.'

'Get out of my way. If you're hiding my son, you're in big trouble.'

Rachel grabbed Alain's arms. 'Would you be quiet for a minute and listen. Oliver isn't here, I swear it. I wish to God he was.' The tears streaming down her cheeks had an immediate impact.

'Then what the hell is going on?' Alain whispered.

'Did you really think I would go home just like that? What kind of mother would I be if I gave up my only child so easily? But none of that matters now, for God's sake. All that matters is to find Oliver.'

Alain hung his head. 'I've looked everywhere already.'

'Come in a moment while we decide what to do,' Michael murmured.

As Alain and Rachel looked at each other in tormented silence their heated conflict of the last week dwindled to insignificance. Michael felt that he was superfluous and went into the kitchen.

447

When he came back Rachel was saying, 'He might have run away because of us, the divorce. It would make sense.'

'No, I can't believe that. He sulked for a day or two after we told him, but since then he's seemed to accept it.'

'That's what you say, but how can you be sure?' Rachel said heatedly. 'Alain, I think we should go to the gendarmerie.'

'Do you want me to come?' Michael asked.

'Would you mind staying here?' Rachel said. 'It might be better if there was somebody near a telephone just in case.'

'Of course. Whatever you think.'

He wanted to reach out and comfort her, but she had stepped behind an invisible barrier now that she and Alain were united in their anxiety.

'Thank you for your help, Michael,' she said with a brave little smile that none the less seemed to put him at a distance.

Alain gave him a civil nod, but Michael guessed that conflicting emotions were already beginning to move within him. He was no longer so cocksure, his arrogance had vanished and he seemed to be leaning on Rachel in the crisis. Michael watched them go, feeling strangely ambivalent, even jealous.

Rachel glanced back at Michael as she went through the door, but her eyes weren't really seeing him. There was only one thing that mattered to her now. In the space of minutes old loyalties that preceded the days they had shared had come between them.

Rachel hurried down the street at Alain's side without looking back. 'We'll take my car to the gendarmerie,' Alain said. 'It's too far to walk. Isabelle can either come with us or wait for us here.'

'Wouldn't it be better if she waited here, in case he turns up? You don't believe anything has happened to him, do you, Alain?' Her voice had lost its force and was just a whisper.

'No, of course not. He's just got lost somewhere, that's all. We mustn't jump to conclusions. He probably went for a ride and had a flat tyre or something. I've checked all the roads, but maybe I didn't go far enough.'

'Of course. That must be what happened. He'll be so contrite, so tired when we find him, poor little mite.'

They stopped at the end of the street, when Alain's repressed

448

anger erupted. 'Before we go any further, you'd better tell me why you lied and said you were going back home. This has completely thrown me.'

She looked at him squarely. 'If you've learned anything at all about me all these years, you ought to know Oliver is the centre of my life. You can't cut him out of it, so don't even try. When this is all over we're going to have to sort things out between us. It won't be one-sided, the way it's been up to now. You didn't think about me at all.'

He considered what she had said. 'What about you and the Englishman? What has his role been in all this?'

'I have nothing to say about that. I've been very lucky to find a friend like Michael. Otherwise I would have had to go through this ordeal alone. But let's deal with one thing at a time, shall we? I can't think any further than having Oliver back safely. As far as I'm concerned the past and the future don't matter until then.'

The square was a blur of colour and movement against the pale evening sky. So many people had come to the carnival that it was difficult to move.

At the café Alain gave an exasperated sigh. 'Where did Isabelle go? I told her I'd meet her here. Maybe she found Oliver – but surely she'd have waited in that case. Listen, maybe I ought to call Terre Blanche to see if he's come home before we do anything.'

Rachel waited while Alain went to the call-box. Although numb with shock, she recognized that she was letting Alain dictate what should happen next, just as she had in their married life, and realized she had to act independently from now on. Her stomach contracted when she saw him coming back looking distressed and shaking his head.

'Look,' she said, 'we're not accomplishing anything. The car I rented is parked in Michael's garage. I'm going to go and get it and drive to the gendarmerie. Are you coming or not?'

'Yes, I'll come. Isabelle can find her own way.'

\*

449

Isabelle raced as fast as she could to her car parked outside the ramparts, her high-heeled sandals slipping on the gravel, her keys ready in her hand. Out of breath, she leapt into the driving seat and fumbled for the door. She started the engine with a roar and began to reverse, but slammed on the brakes when she saw a Deux-cheveaux behind her blocking her way. Flying into a rage, she pressed on the horn again and again, which seemed to make the driver move even more slowly. Seeing his broad, florid face beneath a beret, she screamed out of the window, 'Idiot! Fool! Peasant! Get out of my way!'

At last the way was clear and Isabelle sped recklessly down the road, forcing her way around other cars. She didn't take her foot off the accelerator until she passed the walled cemetery overshadowed by tall cypresses, where she skidded round a tight corner and crawled to a stop on the verge. Turning off the ignition, she slumped forward on the steering wheel, tasting dust in her mouth as she gasped for breath. She knew Alain would be searching for her, but nothing could induce her to return to the square. Her mind reeled backwards, reconstructing what had happened from the moment Alain had charged off to Michael Lowry's house to look for Rachel and Oliver, leaving her in front of the carousel.

She had stood there impatiently for a few moments, searching amongst the moving horses for Oliver, her ears ringing with the music blaring from the speakers. Her eyes were roaming over the riot of painted garlands and cupids to the centre column, which hid the workings of the machinery, when a door opened and a man stepped out. Leaping on to the revolving platform, he walked against the movement of the carousel like a swimmer fighting a powerful current. Children held out their tickets as he passed, but he ignored them. His smouldering dark eyes were fixed on Isabelle, who watched in disbelief as he came ever closer. His mocking smile was obviously directed at her. Panicked by the memories it evoked, she turned and fled from the man she had seen last week at the motorway stop.

After Michael left her near the café, Pascale continued to search the square for Oliver. It was nearly seven-thirty when she gave up.

It was time to meet Julian, and she was hardly conscious of anything else. Threading her way through the crowd with a distracted air, she came face to face with Laurent.

'*Bonjour*, Pascale. *Ça va?*' She tried to brush past him, but he blocked her way. 'Can't you say hello?'

'Not to you.'

'Look, I'm sorry if I offended you the other day, but you have to admit, you can be pretty cold-blooded when you want to.'

'I have nothing to say to you.'

'I still think you're the prettiest girl in Roquelaire and that poor Étienne is a damn fool to have lost you. I hope you both find somebody else. In fact, it seems you already have.'

His sarcastic laugh followed her as she darted past him and was swallowed up by the crowd. Her face was burning with indignation, but she didn't give him the satisfaction of turning round and he began to follow her at a discreet distance without her noticing. Losing himself in the crowd passing through the arch, Laurent stationed himself near the *allée* of chestnut trees, from where he could see Pascale walking down the road to the *lavoir*. She stopped, as if waiting for someone.

Bob Cooper looked at his watch yet again. 'You know, getting this group together is like trying to collect a gaggle of geese. Where is everybody anyway?'

They were standing in the garden by a table set with drinks. Glancing at her watch, Rosamund saw it was nearly time to leave for the *mairie*, where the mayor was going to inaugurate an exhibition featuring the work of Bob's pupils and a number of local artists.

'Maybe this isn't such a good idea,' Ted said, pushing a bottle of champagne back into the ice. 'After all, there will be drinks at the *mairie*.'

'Gnat's piss,' said Bob, winking at Rosamund. 'All those sickly sweet aperitifs and ersatz Pernod. There's nothing like a good kir royale to kick off the evening. And we always end the course with the popping of corks. It's a tradition. Your glass is empty – here, let me fill it.'

'I've already had two,' said Rosamund, stubbing out her cigarette.

'Nervous?' asked Bob.

'Do I seem as if I am?'

'You've had a lot of heartache this year, my dear Rosamund. If it's any consolation, I want you to know that I think it's given your work a depth, a dimension that no amount of technique ever could. You're my star pupil. I mean that. Here's to you, long may you flourish,' Bob said, raising his glass.

'Thank you. You've been a sweetheart to nurse me through it all.'

'We let him know he wasn't welcome here any more. Not after what he did to you, didn't we, Ted?' said Bob.

'He's a real shit,' echoed Ted.

'That's very loyal of you, but it isn't necessary to disown him. He's a friend of yours.'

'Not any more. Julian's a shallow son of a bitch,' Bob said, warming to the subject. 'And next time I see him, I'm damned well telling him so.'

'I wouldn't bother.'

'No, seriously, why don't you give him hell yourself? It would serve him right and it might make you feel better.'

'I wouldn't give him the satisfaction. Anyway, it was my own fault. Listen, I've already resigned myself. He won't call again. It's over, and it probably never meant anything to him anyway.'

'Don't keep it bottled up. If you need to let it out, let it all out. Don't let it fester, whatever you do.' Bob put his hand on Rosamund's shoulder, noticing that her eyes had taken on an indelible cast of sadness.

'I can't stand people who moan on about unhappy love affairs and I don't intend to be one of them. I'm just sorry it took up so much of my time here,' she said.

'Well, it wasn't wasted. Emotion is never wasted. Look how you've profited from it.'

Rosamund slipped her arm affectionately through his. 'You're just being kind, but don't think I'm not grateful for it.'

'You see if I'm not right. I'll bet you'll have a sell-out at the exhibition.'

'Now that's going too far.' She smiled weakly.

Rosamund wandered off by herself to the edge of the garden and looked out over the ramparts at the silhouette of Brissac against billowing pink clouds. The usual birdsong had been replaced by the sound of traffic as people from the surrounding countryside converged on Roquelaire for the fête. Leaning on her elbows, she watched families with excited children walking below, and lovers strolling arm in arm. As the chain of street lights came on, her attention was caught by a lone figure standing at the *lavoir*. It was too far away to see clearly without her glasses, but the unmistakable blond hair and long legs filled her with aching sadness. Rosamund knew who it was and guessed who she was waiting for. Bob called to her from the terrace.

'We're about to make the farewell toast, Rosamund. Come and join us.'

'I'm coming,' she called back. The familiar growl of a Porsche engine made her knees go weak. As she pressed against a lilac bush to hide herself, a sharp pod pierced her cheek and drew blood, which she wiped off with her finger. The instant of pain seemed like a warning of what was to follow.

She couldn't see Julian's face when the car stopped in front of the *lavoir*. All she could see was his white shirt and the outline of his shoulders as he moved to open the door for Pascale, who strode up to the car as gracefully as a young colt. When the roar of the engine was swallowed up by the distance, it left an unbearable emptiness in its wake.

'Rosamund, dear girl, we're all thirsty as hell,' called the colonel.

'I'm coming,' she said with a bright, vapid smile, and went to join them.

453

# Chapter 22

Rachel looked up as Alain walked through the door of the stuffy little room at the gendarmerie, furnished with a desk, hard chairs and a clock on the wall, whose hands she had watched advance for the last hour as darkness fell outside the gauze-curtained window. The bleak expression on his face told her he had nothing to report.

He shook his head and sighed. 'The captain says we can wait here as long as we like. All night if we want.'

'What are they going to do now?' She raised her tormented eyes to him. Her body was stiff and wooden from sitting motionless in the chair waiting for Alain to come back. Every half hour or so, when they could bear it no longer, he went to check with the gendarmes.

Alain sank down into a chair beside her. 'Look, we've covered every single road within a radius of twenty kilometres. They've had an announcement going out every half-hour on the public-address system at the carnival, and there's an alert out all over the *département*. And now they're proceeding one step at a time to try to eliminate all the possibilities. There are two men in the village still making inquiries. Apparently they went to Terre Blanche while you and I were out in the car, but that didn't uncover anything we don't already know. I don't know. I just don't know,' he muttered.

'But what about the dogs? Didn't you insist that they put dogs out? And a search party! Why don't they get out there with lights and dogs, and a big group of people – all of us, everybody who is willing and able – to look for him? Why can't they do that?' She looked at him beseechingly, with tears that she had kept in check for the last four hours streaming down her cheeks.

'Look, Rachel, he could be anywhere. They have to come up with some kind of idea where to start before sending out search parties. He could be miles away.'

'No! He's not miles away. I know it, I feel it. He's somewhere close, and he can't get back. He's either lying unconscious, or he's . . .' She broke off, swallowing the word she refused to say, even to herself. When Alain took her hands, she clutched his fingers tightly to ward off a wave of panic that threatened to engulf her.

She whispered, 'I just feel they aren't doing enough. We can't just sit here and let the precious hours tick by. We must try to do something to come up with an answer. Little boys don't just vanish into nowhere.'

'Just now the captain mentioned the possibility of kidnapping, but he said it would be premature before they had contacted more possible witnesses.'

Rachel looked at him, horrified. 'Kidnapping?'

'Yes, it happens in France, as well as everywhere else. Children get abducted by strangers.'

The devastating implications of this possibility drained the life from Rachel's body.

'What they do in that case is to put out a national alert through Interpol. But it's much too soon for that yet. The trouble is that now it's dark, and any clues they might find – most important of all, his bicycle or an item of clothing – won't be visible until it's light again. We have no choice but to wait until dawn and start again, from the beginning. Look, there's no point in staying here all night in this hot, uncomfortable little room.'

'There's nowhere else to go.' Then she remembered Michael. She hadn't contacted him since they had parted four hours ago.

'The captain said he wants to go back to Terre Blanche again and have another look around, talk to the neighbours within a few kilometres of there, who will probably be home by now. I said I'd go with him. It would be better if one of us stays in the village in case there's some news. You could wait at Michael Lowry's, where there's a telephone. I'll tell the captain where you are.'

Rachel was torn, preferring the uncomfortable cell at the gendarmerie to a familiar place. There at least she could eke out the hours feeling close to what was happening.

'If anything should happen, the officer on duty will contact you immediately,' Alain urged gently.

'Maybe it's better.' She stood up. 'Have you spoken to . . . your friend?' She couldn't bring herself to speak Isabelle's name.

'When I telephoned her she explained she had fallen ill suddenly at the carnival and that's why she wasn't waiting for me in the square.'

'I don't really give a damn if she's ill,' Rachel retorted, not caring how bitter she sounded.

Alain seemed more embarrassed than angry at her remark, which made her angrier still.

'None of this would have happened if it weren't for her.' Rachel broke off. She was too proud to lash out, but something as close to hatred as she had ever felt raged within her.

'I know what you're thinking, Rachel, but it's not Isabelle's fault. If anyone is to blame, then I am.'

At this admission of regret, Rachel regarded him in thoughtful silence, sadness stirring deep inside her. Going out the door, Alain put his hand on her shoulder, but this familiar gesture no longer had the power to comfort her. She felt an infinite grief that they had forfeited the right to be close at a time when they needed each other more than ever before. Yet when their eyes met in the fathomless pain that no one else could share, Rachel wondered if a force greater than they was already moving to breach the distance that had grown between them.

Feeling as if days had passed instead of hours, Rachel drove back to the village. A long queue of traffic blocked the road approaching the ramparts, forcing her to crawl along with unbearable slowness. She came close to abandoning the car on the roadside, tortured by the thought that she might miss an all-important phone call from the gendarmerie. Whenever the headlights picked out a boy, any boy, of Oliver's age and height, she couldn't keep herself from staring in hopes that it might be him.

She parked the car in Michael's garage and climbed the narrow stairs that led to the terrace. Loud music from the square echoed over the darkened houses, their roofs clearly outlined against the sky, flushed pink from the coloured lights.

As her feet touched the gravel a burst of fireworks overhead lit up the night. With a bottomless despair, she watched the cascade of blue and green sparks disappear into the blackness.

456

'Is that you, Rachel?' came Michael's voice from the terrace.

Rachel saw him outlined in the doorway. 'Yes, it's me. Did I startle you?'

'I thought I heard your car. Any news?' he asked anxiously, coming to greet her.

'No, nothing. There's no sign of him.' She bit her lip to keep back the tears.

'Dear lord', he whispered, touching her shoulder. 'Where could he be?'

They stood at the corner of the terrace while Rachel told him what had happened. Even the deep compassion in his eyes could not penetrate the numbness that had taken hold of her. Her devotion to Oliver seemed to stand between them now, and she could tell Michael sensed it. Facing Michael, she felt a sudden awkwardness, followed by guilt, as if the forces that had taken Oliver away were determined to punish her for giving in to her own desires.

'I should have called you before to let you know what was happening. I apologize for that. You've been stuck here, waiting, haven't you?'

'Of course not. I understood that your mind was elsewhere. Anyway, I wasn't going anywhere. I was so hoping you'd come back tonight.'

Michael's warm response at her return unsettled her conscience.

'Come and sit down here on the terrace,' he continued. 'The doors are open, so we can hear the telephone. I haven't moved since you left, but the neighbours told me they heard the announcement about Oliver at the carnival.'

The thought of a public appeal brought back all the horror. She imagined a disc jockey's voice announcing the disappearance of a little boy, her little boy, between a popular song and the reading of lottery winners.

'The gendarmes are now considering the possibility of kidnapping,' she whispered, dropping into a chair.

'It's just routine. They have to do that.'

Rachel buried her face in her hands and cried for a moment. Then she wiped her eyes and looked up at Michael.

'Rachel, the one thing you mustn't do at this point is to give up

457

hope. That would be fatal. Nothing is conclusive yet. They've barely started the search. My feeling is that Oliver could easily turn up safe and unharmed. Now I know that it's your instinct to prepare yourself for the worst, that's only human nature, but please try to hang on for just a bit longer if you can. I understand how hard it must be, but please try.'

She took a deep breath. 'All right. I'll try.'

'Building your hopes and conserving your strength is the best way to get through these hours of darkness before it gets light and they start the search again. Don't burn yourself up in grief, not yet. For Oliver's sake.'

His words had a powerful, bracing effect, and she took them to heart. 'Do you really think that Oliver is all right?'

'Yes, yes, I do. And I think you should believe it too at this point. It will help you to endure the waiting.'

She let out a quivering sigh and wiped her eyes. 'That's what I needed to hear more than kind words. Words of hope.' She smiled at him, the fluttering in her stomach subsiding somewhat.

'I had the lady who takes care of the Petersons' house make the beds because I thought you might want to go back there. I mean, it seemed to me that now that everyone knows you're here, you might prefer that. I don't know if I did the right thing.'

'That's very thoughtful of you.' She looked at him gratefully. His tactful gesture moved her deeply and made her conscious that she was repaying him with an indifference he didn't deserve. Michael's sensitivity was what had drawn her to him from the very beginning.

'I'm here by the phone in case the gendarmes have any news. And if Alain calls or comes back, I'll tell him where you are.'

She thought about it and realized it might be a relief to be alone for a while. 'If you're sure you don't mind.'

'Not at all. I won't leave the phone for a minute and if you fall asleep, I've got the key. I'll come and wake you.'

She went upstairs to collect her bag. When she came down Michael was waiting for her by the door.

'Got everything?'

'I think so. Toothbrush and slippers,' she said with an uncertain smile. A reminder of what they had left unspoken welled up between them. She deliberately resisted the memory of Michael making love to her, their conversation, their laughter. He had awakened powerful emotions and now that her life had gone dark so suddenly she felt confused. She looked around, knowing she was leaving this safe haven with a burden entirely different from the one she had brought with her, and she could tell by the look in Michael's eyes that he understood.

'Goodbye,' she said abruptly, needing to escape the implications of their parting. He surprised her by leaning forward to kiss her. As their lips met, Rachel had a presentiment of finality, as if it were for the last time.

Michael said, 'You can come here for breakfast as early as you want, if I don't see you before then.'

'Thank you, but I'd better leave it open if you don't mind.'

She walked up the street, where the usual night calm had been invaded by the din of the carnival. When she slipped the key in the door she turned to wave to Michael just as she had in the past, knowing he was watching her from the doorway. Entering the house she had never expected to return to, she took her bag upstairs to her old room, opened the shutters and stared at the glowing pink sky. The sound of an accordion accompanied by raucous singing reverberated through the night. Turning off the light, Rachel sat by the open window to begin her vigil, summoning up all her best, her happiest memories of Oliver.

When Rachel had gone, Michael automatically went to put on some music to fill the quiet in the room, a habit he had acquired that summer. But this time Rachel's departure left a vacuum too great to fill. He poured himself a generous whisky and went on to the terrace, letting thoughts wash over him. Even the lone cricket in the garden had stopped chirping, heightening his sense of isolation. To distract himself, he thought of John Stratton, wondering if that knight's moods were similar to his own as he brooded alone in the tower at Brissac during his last days. His mind flipped back to Oliver and he racked his brain for where the boy might have gone, thoughts that led him to Rachel and Alain. The near-certainty that the severed bond between them was already in the process of reknitting itself in the face of crisis, taking Rachel from him, filled Michael with a gnawing helplessness. Earlier that day he had been full of plans for the future, pondering how he and Rachel would work out the practical side of their lives now they had found each other. A knock at the front door startled him and he sprinted into the sitting-room wondering if it might be Rachel. He tried to hide his disappointment when he opened the door and saw Père Auguste standing there.

'Père Auguste, come in.'

'I hope I'm not disturbing you.'

'Not at all. I was just sitting on the terrace.'

'I knew you'd probably be at home, not at the carnival.'

'Normally I'd take a wander through the square, but not tonight.'

The priest looked towards the chessboard sitting in a pool of lamplight exactly as they had left it.

'Don't worry. I have no intention of taking up the challenge at this hour. When I heard the upsetting news about the Ribard boy I thought I'd call by and offer a word of encouragement to Madame Ribard, and see if I could help in any way. The Petersons' caretaker said she thought she might be here.'

'She's gone to get some rest, I hope, and I'm standing by in case there's any news. Her husband is out with the gendarmes.'

'I saw an officer in the square and he told me what had happened. I've been thinking it over and I'm mystified at what could become of an eight-year-old boy who simply went out for a ride on his bicycle. It sounds sinister, doesn't it?'

'Yes, but I think we shouldn't lose hope at this point. At daybreak they can begin a proper search for him.'

'How are the parents holding up?'

'As well as anyone would in the circumstances, but you can imagine what they're going through.'

Père Auguste accepted an Armagnac, his first in a long time.

'Won't you come to the terrace, where it's a bit cooler?'

'Thank you. Carnival is one night of the year when I accept that I must sacrifice my sleep. The music is so loud, even in our remote

460

little street, that it would wake the dead. I don't want to sound uncharitable, but I'm grateful that I was born before the age of amplifiers and am not intimidated by silence,' the priest said with a rueful smile. Making himself comfortable in one of the chairs on the terrace, he continued, 'I wonder where that boy could have gone. Do you suppose he ran away because of his parents' separation?'

'No one seems to think so. If he was disturbed about it, he didn't let on. He's an adventurous little kid with a vivid imagination, so maybe he did something foolish like hitchhike to Bordeaux or take a train somewhere. Who knows? Madame Ribard mentioned that the gendarmes haven't ruled out abduction.'

'Here? In Roquelaire? One hears of these shocking child crimes, but it seems unthinkable on our doorstep. Still, I know that the carnival brings some strange characters into the town and I confess that it's the only time I ever lock my door at night.'

They talked for while and Michael confided all the events of the last few days to the priest, feeling he ought to know. 'So you see, the situation is much more complicated than meets the eye. The father tried to keep the boy away from his mother in an underhand way, and she was merely trying to get him back. I agreed to help her.'

'She was lucky to find a friend in you. I had no idea that all this was going on.'

'We had to keep quiet about it. That's why I put off our chess game the other day with the excuse that I was hard at work. Rachel was staying here with me, but Oliver went missing only hours before she planned to get him back.'

'Do you know, it's my guess that whatever happens, this incident is bound to bring the Ribards together again. In my experience that nearly always happens if there's a crisis involving a much-loved child.'

Michael shrugged, but didn't reply. He looked up at the stars, which seemed much smaller in the reflected brightness from the square. Finally he said, 'Do you remember the other day when we discussed the chronicle and I mentioned the parallels between the plague year and now?'

461

'Of course I remember. I compared you to John Stratton or some such nonsense.'

'Yes, it's nonsense. But events seem to keep cropping up that bear so much resemblance to what happened then. Or, at least, if one twists the glass to distort it, it might seem so.'

'Such as?'

'John Stratton has met Margaret Prior.'

'I'm not quite sure what you mean. The story is a bit fuzzy in my mind.'

'Nothing changes, does it, Father? It all fits beautifully. Madame Ribard was searching for her son and she met me, just the way Margaret met John. There's hardly any difference between us.'

'You certainly have acted the part of the chivalrous knight in helping Madame Ribard, haven't you?'

'Not so chivalrous. I think now that I've only complicated things for the lady.'

'Did you dream yourself into this, do you suppose?' asked Père Auguste when he understood Michael's meaning.

'That I'll never know.'

A moment later Père Auguste said, 'What happened to Lady Margaret's child in the chronicle? You keep bringing up parallels between the past and present. Who knows, maybe it will give us a clue.'

'Wouldn't that be a neat solution? Unfortunately, the chronicle ends without saying what happened to Thomas. If I thought for a moment that the past and present were really intertwined, that they were patterned along the same lines, then I'd move heaven and earth to find a clue, even if it meant making a fool of myself.'

'It was only a silly idea. About as sensible as palm-reading or star-gazing, I'm afraid. There's even a woman in the region who claims to help find missing people by vibrations. I hope they aren't thinking of consulting her.'

'If people are desperate, they'll try anything. But this is now a matter for the police, I'm afraid.'

Père Auguste rose to go. 'I'm sorry about what's happened to Madame Ribard. Please give her my best wishes. She's a charming woman and doesn't deserve all the trouble she's had. It's an

462

unhappy end to a turbulent summer, a summer full of false hopes and changes for many people here, all related in some way to Brissac. Its ancient sense of tragedy seems to have touched almost everybody connected with it.'

They said goodnight. Michael went back to the sitting-room and turned on the lamp on his desk. Though he knew it was probably useless, he couldn't resist trying to find some hidden meaning, some metaphor lying undeciphered in the tale. He sat down and started reading the chronicle from the beginning, hoping to discover what, if anything, it had in common with the present that would suggest the whereabouts of Oliver Ribard.

'I think we've done all we can here for the moment,' the gendarme said to Alain. They were standing in the doorway of Terre Blanche. Two other officers were waiting inside the blue Renault parked near a floodlight that illuminated the park.

'Thank you, Captain, for all your help. I feel almost certain that my son isn't on the property or anywhere near it, or we would have found some indication.'

'The only person we haven't talked to is the gardener, but as he wasn't here at the time, I suppose he won't be much help.'

Alain's eyes went to the park, where any number of shadows could be mistaken for the figure of a small boy. He started forward, thinking he saw a movement in the trees beyond the *pigeonnier*, but then realized it must have been his imagination.

'If we come with the dogs tomorrow, it will be before seven,' said the officer, adjusting his kepi. 'But as your boy went by bicycle somewhere, I'm not confident about that. It's very unlikely they could pick up his traces. Let's hope it doesn't rain, because that would prove an added handicap. Goodnight, *monsieur*. Try and get some sleep.'

Alain watched the gendarmes drive away, then turned and walked slowly down the hallway as Fernande came down the stairs with a tray in her hand.

'*Madame* has gone back to bed,' the housekeeper said in a worried whisper. 'I took her some tea to calm her nerves, but, *monsieur*, I'm concerned. I've been in this house since she first

463

came here and I can't remember her having a day's sickness, except an occasional cold. She won't hear of calling a doctor.'

'She's had a lot on her mind lately and is a bit tired, so I wouldn't worry.' He climbed the stairs and entered the bedroom. Isabelle was stretched out on the bed, where he had found her on his return an hour before.

'Have they gone?'

'Yes, but they might be back early tomorrow morning with the dogs.'

'Oh God,' she moaned, taking a sip of the tea by her bedside. Her face was drawn, her hair crushed against the pillow. 'Did you suggest they leave a man here?'

'I said that you had requested it, but the captain didn't think it was necessary.'

'I should have talked to him. He knew my husband, I could have persuaded him.'

'Isabelle, you're on the wrong track. There's no need to leave a man on the premises. What good would it do?'

'What good does it do to tear the place apart with dogs?'

He sighed in exasperation. 'That's not worth answering.'

She bit her lip. '*Chéri*, I didn't mean it like it sounded. I just meant that perhaps they could put valuable time to better use.' She turned her head towards the nightstand where she kept her sleeping tablets, tempted to take a dose but knowing she mustn't. 'I'm still convinced that your wife got a message through to Oliver, and that something happened when he was looking for her. She wouldn't admit it if she had.'

'Even if that were true, what could have happened? And would you stop bringing Rachel up?'

Isabelle lay motionless, her eyes closed, listening for the footsteps of the man at the carnival, whose image she could not put out of her mind.

Seeing the haggard look on her face, Alain said, 'Hadn't you better call a doctor if you're ill?'

'No, I don't want a doctor. I just need to rest. I told you, it's something I ate and I'll be all right. Alain, be sure and see the gate is closed, will you? You may have to walk down and do it yourself. I told Fernande to make sure it was locked before she went to bed, but you'd better check just in case. She doesn't like doing it.'

'It should stay open.'

'Does this mean I have to get up and do it myself?'

'Julian isn't back yet.'

'He has a key.'

'Fine. But it ought to be open just in case . . . in case Oliver should find his way back.'

'Alain, get hold of yourself. He's not going to simply wander back in the middle of the night.' There was an edge in her voice. 'It isn't safe to leave the gate open, not with . . . with the carnival.'

'If you wish, I'll close it after me when I go.' He walked towards the bathroom, knowing he wouldn't do as she asked.

'Where are you going?'

'Back to Roquelaire.'

'But why? What can you possibly do there at this time of night?' Isabelle sat up and stared after him.

Returning with his shaving kit in hand, Alain said, 'I have to be with Rachel now, Isabelle. That's where my place is tonight. She's at the Englishman's house.'

'You're going to spend the night with Rachel?'

'For God's sake, Isabelle, that ought to be obvious.'

'It isn't obvious. Your place is here, with me. Surely you can wait to hear any news here as well as in town. I'm upset and I need you by my side. I particularly don't want to be alone tonight. We need to console each other at a time like this, don't we?'

Alain, struck by the hunted expression in her eyes, found it baffling. He was overtaken by a desperate urge to get as far away from her as he could. He said, 'I realize you must be feeling vulnerable because you're not well. That's why you should call the doctor. You have to understand, Isabelle, that my only child, my son, is missing and I can't rest until I find out where he is. Rachel is his mother, and she and I have to get through this nightmare together. Surely I don't have to explain that to you.' He kissed her cheek, feeling oddly indifferent to the tormented look on her face.

'Don't go, Alain, please.' There were tears in her eyes. He walked on without looking back. Leaping from the bed, she leaned over the balustrade as he was walking down the curving staircase.

'Alain, if you leave me alone tonight, you'll regret it from this day on. You can't do this to me.' Her voice was shaky, her eyes wild.

'What is this, an ultimatum? Or have you gone crazy?' The sight of her hanging over the staircase made him obdurate.

'Alain, I'm afraid to be alone,' she cried as he turned to go. 'I heard noises earlier on. I'm sure somebody's been trying to break into the house. That's the real reason why I wanted to have a gendarme here. I don't feel safe. For God's sake, Alain, come back!'

'That was Alain in Isabelle's car,' Julian said to Pascale as they approached Terre Blanche. The Golf had just passed them at a tremendous speed and left a trail of white dust mushrooming before the headlights of the Porsche. 'I wonder where he was going so late? Actually it's not that late. It's only a quarter to twelve.' He hummed softly to the music playing on the stereo.

'Maybe he and Isabelle had a fight.'

'Now that wouldn't surprise me. They're two very volatile people.' He explained what volatile meant. 'They've both been on edge because of the château. What do you think will happen? Is your aunt going to sell?'

'I think she will,' answered Pascale, more concerned with her own future. Her stomach went into a knot as she thought how the evening might end in the romantic guest house at Terre Blanche. During dinner at a country *auberge* the sexual tension between them had reached breaking point. A sudden thought roused her from her day-dream with a gasp.

'Julian, what about Oliver Ribard? Maybe they haven't found him yet.'

Trying to allay her concern, Julian squeezed her hand. 'I'm sure he must have turned up. Where would a little boy go around here?' he said soothingly. Sensing that she was still worrying, he added urgently, 'Hey, Pascale, come on – everything is going to be all

466

right. They'll find him. He was probably mad at everybody and ran away, then couldn't get back before nightfall. I ran away from home when I was about his age.'

'You ran away? What happened?' Oliver slipped from her mind.

Julian chuckled as he remembered. 'I had planned to go to Tuscany, where a charming and indulgent aunt of mine lived, but I didn't get very far. The head gardener found me in a tree near the gate eating a sandwich that cook had made me to take on my momentous journey. I had packed a suitcase that weighed a ton and I was so exhausted by the time I got to the end of the drive, I couldn't go a step further.'

'Was it a long walk?'

'A very long walk, to a little boy at least. Today, of course, I can walk it in five minutes.'

Pascale compared the drive of Julian's family estate with Terre Blanche, realizing then how big it must be, and how rich his family was.

'I'll take you there when you come to England,' he said as he swung the car under the floodlit arcade of the *pigeonnier*.

'I want to see the tree where you ran away.'

'Alas, it fell down in a storm,' he said, kissing her cheek.

He got out, and irritably turned off the bright porch light, then opened Pascale's door and helped her from the car. She kicked off her high-heeled shoes and tugged him on to the dew-soaked grass. Together they looked up at the steep tiled roof of the guest house, topped with a weather vane silvered by the moon. Beneath the curling eaves a window cut in the white stone shone with amber light. Pascale caught a glimpse of the pleated canopy of the bed and the flowered wallpaper, the edge of a lace curtain ruffling in a soft breeze. 'It's magic,' she whispered, repeating the word she had heard Julian use.

He looked down at her face blurred by moonlight. 'Let this be our night of nights. When you are one with me, that's what I promise you – beauty and magic.' She was waiting, her lips parted, for his kiss. His muscles tensed against her soft, giving body, a sign of the passion waiting to unleash itself. 'Come on, let's go upstairs,' he said, his voice gruff with desire.

467

They walked hand in hand over the soft grass in their bare feet and climbed the stairs. Inside the room, Julian locked the door and went to close the window.

'No, please leave it open. I want to see the stars.'

'Then stars you shall have, my lady, my love.'

There was a spray of roses on the writing table, and the bed had been turned down to expose the snowy linen sheets trimmed with lace. Pascale took in every detail of the sumptuous, romantic room, determined never to forget a single detail. Julian put a tape on the stereo and turned the full power of his eyes on her as a ripple of guitar music saturated the air with a haunting melody. He went to the fridge in the alcove and brought out a bottle of champagne. When he started to pour her a glass, she shook her head.

'Not for me, thank you. I really don't want any more.'

'All right. In that case I have something much better.'

'What's that?'

'You'll see.' He kissed her tenderly and led her to the bathroom. 'There's a dressing-gown behind the door. I'll be waiting.'

As the door closed, Pascale blinked at the speed with which it had happened, then stared at the reflection of her own flushed face in the mirror, thrilled by Julian's boldness. With a beating heart, she did as she was told, taking off her clothes until her perfect naked body reflected back at her from the wall of glass over the basin. The sight of her upturned breasts tipped in pink and her flat abdomen ending in a shock of downy hair sent the first stirrings of arousal through her. Gazing into her own pupils, she drowned in their blackness, seeing there the unfathomability of desire governing her body, desire so strong that she was helpless against it. Not a single thought about tomorrow marred her voluptuous anticipation of what was about to unfold.

She slipped on the lace and silk dressing-gown hanging behind the door and, as it coolly caressed her skin, was vaguely aware that it smelled of some exotic fragrance.

Turning off the light, she entered the dark room, where she could see Julian stretched out naked on the bed. At the sight of his virility clearly outlined in the moonlight Pascale was filled with nerve-tingling expectation. Her shyness, all her decorum, was

468

crushed by a passion so absolute that it swamped her other senses. She was an instrument of love ruled by a pounding heart. In a whispering walk she approached the bed, looking down at Julian's finely made body etched on the white sheets. All the images of what that moment would be like, images that had filled her mind night and day since they met, were eclipsed by this tempestuous reality. His eyes glimmered in the darkness as she allowed the dressing-gown to fall in a pool at her feet. She stood poised for a moment, glorying in the consciousness that she was the object of his rampant desire. When Julian could bear it no longer, he locked his hand on her wrist and drew her down to the bed. Instead of embracing her as she expected, he sat up and offered her something in his hand.

'You didn't want any champagne, so have this.'

Looking down, she saw two small white pills resting in his palm. 'What is it?'

'Ecstasy.' Julian popped one in his mouth, then stroked her lips with his fingertip. 'It will take your spirit and your body further than you ever imagined. Every sensation you feel tonight will stay in your mind for all time if you just have the courage to try it.'

Pascale's lips parted and she felt him place the pill on her tongue. She swallowed it and he kissed her.

They stretched out on the bed in the moonlight. Julian didn't touch her for a moment but hovered over her, tracing the lines of her body, making her tingle with arousal. He dipped his head to kiss her, gently at first, then more passionately, as the drug began to take effect. The sensation of liquid fire burning inside her frightened Pascale at first and she struggled against it, but soon it seemed part of her, dazzling her with the illusion that her body emitted sparks each time his lips grazed her skin. She felt herself being dragged into a dark, hot tunnel by the weight of her own desire, as Julian plunged his mouth on hers in a series of raw kisses. Through half-closed eyes Pascale delighted in the moon-bronzed swell of strong shoulders as he dipped his tongue to her breasts, then between her thighs. When Julian moved astride her, she wrapped her legs round him, responding eagerly as he nudged hotly against her again and again. Her cry of surrender was a

469

shuddering sigh, answering his rich murmurs in her ear. Pascale's senses were filled with the heady ripeness of male and female mixed together as she watched Julian rear above her in the darkness. Too dazzled to speak or move, she awaited the sublime moment. Heat seemed to pass from his body to hers as he began the long, measured strokes that caused her to buck ecstatically against him.

As he drove himself home, the sight of her lover's face transfixed with pleasure was replaced by the terrifying image of a demon. Horrified, Pascale saw a flash of silver in the darkness and the outline of a knife hovered not far from her face. In the moonlight she saw a pair of hands come down above Julian's shoulder blades, and felt the shock of his weight collapsing against her, pinning her down. A bubbling gasp that seemed hardly human filled her ears as she struggled violently to lift Julian's body, which threatened to suffocate her. She heaved herself out from under him, her gasps of panic turning to hysterical screams as she stumbled in the darkness to escape the shadowy figure at the window.

# *Chapter 23*

'Isn't it sweet?' whispered Rosamund to no one in particular. She reached for the little china model of the ramparts of Roquelaire resting before her on the garden table.

'Yes, it is remarkable,' said the colonel with an absent smile.

'It's really quite well executed,' his wife joined in. 'Apparently the potter who makes them can't turn them out fast enough. Reggie, did you see the mayor's face when he handed it to her? You'd think he was awarding a silver loving-cup from Asprey's.' She gave a hearty laugh.

'I've never won a prize before. Never in all my life,' said Rosamund. 'Of course it's not much of a prize, but I was thrilled.'

'You did jolly well. First place,' said the colonel with a touch of envy.

The students had returned to the garden for a late supper after the exhibition, and now some of them had wandered off to bed. Ted was gathering up glasses, and Bob was talking to the two schoolteachers while the young bank clerk stood by.

'Look at those two,' whispered the colonel's wife. 'Vying to outlast each other so neither of them will get any time alone with Nigel. I think Barry and Melissa have slipped upstairs together.' Her eyes lingered amorously on her husband.

Rosamund wasn't listening. She was still fondling the little model of the village. 'It's very life-like, isn't it? I mean, it's not in the best of taste, but it's so detailed. Look, there are even tiny geraniums in the window-boxes. That's how I'll always remember Roquelaire – eternal summer, full of flowers.' Tears came to her eyes, blurring the spotlights in the garden.

'How are we doing here?' asked Ted with a grin.

'We could use another bottle of *rosé*,' Rosamund suggested.

471

'Sure,' said Ted, exchanging a glance with Bob, who had wandered over to the table. 'I'll go and fetch one.'

'It's up early tomorrow, don't forget,' Bob said tactfully. 'The bus will be leaving for the airport at nine and it's breakfast at eight.'

'I hate to be reminded,' said the colonel sadly. 'One more nightcap and it's off to bed. I suppose most of the villagers are still up searching for that little boy. I heard someone talking about it at the exhibition.'

The conversation turned to Oliver.

'Oh God, oh no,' Rosamund exclaimed when it dawned on her who they were talking about. 'Do you mean that Rachel is still here, in Roquelaire? I didn't hear anything about it. The poor thing, she must have been trying to get him back. Oh no . . .'

'I heard the announcement just as we left the *mairie*,' Bob said, 'but I didn't connect it with Rachel at first. I was shocked when I heard the name. I hope to God they find him.'

'I heard someone say they suspect abduction because he's been gone for hours,' said Ted, arriving with the wine.

'What's this town coming to, anyway?' demanded the colonel. 'Things like this didn't used to happen in the French countryside. When they catch the bugger, they should string him up.'

Tears were quietly streaming down Rosamund's face, tears of sympathy for Rachel, and tears for herself, which did nothing to relieve her deep misery.

'Come on, Rosamund, they'll probably find him.' Bob put his arm around her and gave her a hug. 'He couldn't have gone very far.'

'I wonder if he was running away,' she said, dabbing at her eyes.

Bob raised his glass. 'I think we should have one last special toast to Rosamund's sell-out at the exhibition. It's never happened to any of my students before.'

'Hear, hear,' said the colonel.

'Thank you very much,' Rosamund said, trying to smile. 'I can't really think why anybody wanted to buy my watercolours or why I got the prize.'

'Because you're damn good, that's why, and because you've got a brilliant instructor.'

But the lost boy was on everyone's mind and they couldn't recapture their pleasant mood. Soon Rosamund climbed the stairs, the sight of the empty room across the hall reminding her again of Rachel and her son. Letting herself into her own tiny room, she closed the door and slumped heavily on the bed as if she could carry the weight of herself no longer. She stared at the bottle of pills on the nightstand, her mind going back to the moment she had caught sight of Julian picking up the beautiful girl at the *lavoir*. She reached for the bottle and swallowed the tablets one after the other, washing them down with a glass of tepid water. As she sank back on the bed waiting for darkness to come, she heard the muffled sound of a woman's laughter followed by the creaking of a bed somewhere in the depths of the house.

Rachel was curled up on the bed, counting the seconds, when there was a knock on the bedroom door.

'Who is it?' she cried, jumping up and fumbling for the light. 'Alain,' she murmured when she saw him standing there.

Her heart thudded violently against her chest as he walked through the door, then sank as she interpreted the look on his face.

'There's nothing new, Rachel. The Englishman told me you were here.'

She sighed and ran her fingers through her hair, seeing by her watch that it was only just after midnight. 'I wasn't asleep. I was having a sort of waking dream.'

'Are you all right?'

'One minute at a time is about all I can manage.'

'If you don't mind, perhaps I could stay here. I brought my shaving kit.'

Rachel nodded. 'Another room has been made up next door.'

When Alain came back into her room she was sitting on the bed, staring out of the window. 'In the last hour I've been trying to get through this by thinking only good thoughts, happy thoughts. Not gloomy ones. It seemed like the right thing to do.' Rachel looked up at him, feeling herself precariously balanced on the edge of an abyss that might soon claim her, although she was still resisting with all her might.

473

He sat down opposite her by the window, his face ravaged. 'All the way back into town I've been going over every minute of this trip with Oliver, trying to find some reason, some clue, but I could think of nothing. If I thought he had disappeared because of something I did or said, something that happened, I just don't think I could live with myself.'

'But we don't know the reason yet, so what's the point?'

'I don't know what else to think. The idea that somebody has taken him is even more terrible.'

There was a long silence before Rachel said, 'What's happening about your plans for developing the château?'

'My plans?' He shrugged. 'I don't have any plans now.'

'No, I suppose not. Not until this is over. I just wondered, that's all.' She could feel nothing, not even anger any more.

'Rachel –'

The look of a bewildered small boy on his face pierced her to her very heart.

'Is it too late now, after what's happened? I have no right to ask you at this time, but if I thought there was a chance, a chance that maybe we could try again, or at least talk about it, then it would help me now.'

Rachel didn't reply for a moment, feeling none of the happiness she would have experienced a week ago at his astonishing change of heart. She assumed it was because she could think about nothing except Oliver at present. 'I don't know what to say. We've both strayed a long way from each other in the last week, haven't we? You deliberately, it seems, and me by chance, with someone I just met.'

The shock registered on his face when he understood what she meant, though she hadn't mentioned Michael's name.

'*Je n'ai pas le droit* . . . I don't have the right . . .,' he murmured. '*Ça m'angoisse* . . .' For a moment he couldn't look at her.

'I didn't do it to hurt you. That wasn't the reason. It went far beyond that.'

'Far beyond? What does that mean?'

She shrugged. The hurt that she had never had time to examine or forget was still there, but so was the joy she had felt with

474

Michael. Looking at Alain, his pride in tatters, Rachel felt pity take the place of a love that was once unshakeable. 'We can't talk about this now. You don't know your own mind, and neither do I.'

'I know. So much has happened, so much. He is our child, yours and mine . . .' Alain's control broke and he started to cry.

Rachel had never seen him in tears, and instinctively put her arms around him. His body shook against hers as he sobbed in despair. The one thing he loved most in the world – his son – had gone, leaving him hollow. Silently, she grieved with him, but even this intense suffering seemed unable to unite them.

When Alain had regained control of himself, Rachel whispered, 'We'll get through this somehow.'

He left the room without another word and she returned to the window to await the dawn.

Michael had been awake for a long time when dawn began to light the sky. He stirred from the sofa, where he had fallen into a shallow sleep for a few hours, the telephone at his elbow, and opened the front door, letting in the cool morning air. Stars still shone faintly overhead, and there was no light coming from the windows of the Peterson house, suggesting that Rachel and Alain were asleep. Michael avoided looking too closely at the shutters that would have told him whether one bedroom was occupied or two, and went to the kitchen to make himself a cup of coffee. Crossing over to his desk, he stared down at the chronicle, turning over in his mind an idea that had come to him during a long, confused dream he had had about Brissac. Half an hour later, having quickly shaved and dressed, Michael pinned a note on his door for Rachel and was walking down the street as the church clock chimed seven o'clock.

It was a perfect day, with the pallor of dawn deepening to a rich blue overhead. The gaudy carnival concessions in the square were draped in canvas and all the shops were tightly closed. The only sign of movement was the fluttering of pigeons on the eaves of the houses. Turning a corner, Michael was surprised to see a blue gendarmerie car surrounded by officers in familiar blue shirts and

475

kepis. One of them was talking to two men from the carnival, who looked as if they had just woken up. Dishevelled and smoking, they peered sullenly at the gendarme who was asking them questions. Walking by, Michael saluted the others.

'*Bonjour*, Monsieur Lowry,' said one he recognized.

'*Salut*, Émile. I suppose there's no news about the Ribard boy, is there? His parents spent the night at the Petersons' house.'

The gendarme shook his head. 'We're short of men at the moment. As if this wasn't enough, we had another incident last night. An Englishman by the name of Paine is in the hospital. Is he a friend of yours by any chance?'

'No, but I know who he is. What happened?'

'It's not related to the Ribard case as far as we know.' He nodded in the direction of the two men being questioned. 'The Englishman was stabbed last night and is in a critical condition. That's all I can tell you.' As Michael started to walk away, he heard one of the gendarmes say, 'I'm going back to Laurent David's house again. This time I'll keep pounding until he answers the door. I'm certain he's there.'

Michael glanced at the *brocante* shop at the edge of the square, wondering what the owner had to do with Julian Paine. Julian didn't mix with any of the local people – except Pascale! Could there be a connection? The bakery was, unusually, still closed and Michael crossed the square to read a sign posted in the window. It informed customers the bakery would be closed until further notice, offering no explanation. Unable to answer his own questions and deciding it was important for Alain to know what had happened Michael returned home and scribbled a postscript about Julian on his note to Rachel. This time he pushed the message through the Petersons' letterbox, noting that there was still no sign of movement in the house, then walked quickly back down the street with a sense of mounting urgency. A few moments later he had picked up his car and was driving towards the château.

There were no tourists or pilgrims at the Pilgrim's Stone, but Michael stopped the car, unable to believe his eyes when he saw a fresh box wreath had been laid at the base. He picked it up and examined it, struck by how clumsily it was made. As his mind flew back to the walk he had taken with Rachel and Oliver, Michael vividly remembered telling the boy about the ancient pilgrim custom of laying *Buxus sempervivens* at the base of the shrine. He walked back to the car with the wreath in his hand, a collection of disparate images beginning to converge.

He stopped the car below the approach road and looked up at the fortress. In the early morning light the cream stone had deepened to pink, and the windows caught fire as a suggestion of molten sun appeared above the dark line of the hills. Michael stood for a moment in the silence, detecting a murmur in the air that sounded almost like voices. The wind that always moved across the hilltop brushed his face like a soft veil. Seeing the château like this strengthened Michael's conviction that all those who had died at Brissac during the plague were buried somewhere within or below its walls. At that moment it seemed less like a castle and fortress than a monument to the dead, as enigmatic and mysterious as the pyramids. He considered the idea that had seemed so promising an hour ago, realizing that it would take far more than the fragment of a dream to crack the puzzle it presented. Yet, an inexplicable certainty had seized him that lying somewhere beneath Brissac were catacombs containing the bones of the plague victims, John and Margaret among them. And he had begun to wonder if not far from here there might be an unconscious, injured, lost little boy. He refused to believe that Oliver could be dead.

Not sure how he should begin his search, he first walked down the chalk road towards the arch. He had an eerie sensation that he was being observed from the windows in the tower, but the movement he saw was only a trick of light on the old, irregular glass. When he came to the spot where he and Rachel had stood the day Oliver had disappeared, Michael stopped and tried to recall every detail about their visit, hoping that he might remember something significant. Oliver's wide-eyed interest in buried treasure suggested he had a strong imagination, and his sudden disappearance the day before seemed proof that he was capable of pursuing adventure on his own.

Half an hour later Michael returned to his car. He had explored the entire area around the château and found nothing. Bitterly disappointed, he drove back towards Roquelaire on the road that passed Agnès's blue cottage. On impulse he decided to stop for a moment. He could see the front door was ajar, but there was no sign of Agnès pottering in the garden or feeding rabbits as he would have expected at that time of morning. Unlatching the gate, he felt as if he were entering a private retreat that offered the simplest of earthly delights, and the most desirable: the shade of a spreading chestnut tree, a vine heavy with grapes, a fig tree laden with purple fruit ripening in the morning sun. His eyes swept past the porch, where the light fell like confetti on the tiles. A fragrant coolness came from the direction of the vegetable patch, carrying with it the peppery smell of ripening tomatoes and a suggestion of freshly watered earth. A chicken was drinking from a stone basin beneath the pump, and a wine bottle lay in a basket outside the door as if waiting to be filled. Nothing seemed to be lacking and nothing was superfluous in Agnès's tiny kingdom.

'*Il y a quelqu'un?*' he called.

Agnès came through the door. Michael was taken aback to see that instead of the smile he expected her face was ravaged by sadness. When she looked at him mutely with red-rimmed eyes, his instinct was to pretend that he hadn't noticed.

'*Bonjour, madame.* I hope I'm not disturbing you.'

'*Bonjour, monsieur. Ça va?*' she said.

Michael was conscious of her preoccupied air, and now he was sure that some crisis had occurred that involved Pascale. His reserve and a respect for Agnès's privacy kept him from prying.

'Won't you sit down?' Agnès motioned to a frayed wicker chair.

Normally nothing would have given him greater pleasure than chatting with her for a while, something he had always meant to do, but he shook his head. 'Thank you, but I can only stay a minute. I came here to ask you something about Brissac. Have you heard that the Ribard boy has gone missing?'

'Yes, my sister mentioned it this morning when I saw her. I was shocked. People are saying it has something to do with the carnival.' She shook her head sadly. 'His parents must be sick with worry.'

'They are. I came here now from Brissac, where the boy's

478

mother and I and young Oliver went walking last week. It's only an idea, but it occurred to me that it's a place he's familiar with and that he might have gone back there for some reason. He disappeared for a bit while we were there.' When Michael told her about Oliver's interest in buried treasure, Agnès nodded, but he wasn't sure she had taken it in. Michael said, 'This may sound like an odd question, but do you know if there is any kind of underground passage beneath the château?'

The effect of his words were not what he might have expected. Instead of looking puzzled at the question or pausing to consider it, she turned and looked at him warily.

'Why do you ask me this?'

'Because I told Oliver about the legend of the papal treasure and he was fascinated by it. I hope you don't mind, but I had a walk around the château this morning to see if I could pick up any trace of him. It even crossed my mind that you might have seen him somewhere there yourself that day. I'm almost sure I saw you walking on the lower road.'

'I don't remember,' she said flatly. 'Perhaps I went to see Monsieur David, the caretaker.'

'Can you think of any place where the boy might have gone – a well, a pit, an enclosure of some kind where he could be trapped? It's too long to go into now, but I have my own theory about Brissac and what might be underneath it, after reading some manuscripts Père Auguste gave me. If you can think of any place where a small boy might be lost, it could prove important.'

'No,' Agnès said emphatically, 'it's impossible.'

He was surprised at her use of the word, but sensed that she was stubbornly uncooperative on the subject of the property that was now hers. Michael was used to the eccentricities of rural people, knowing they could be secretive almost to the point of obsession, and he put it down to that – that and Agnès's disturbed state of mind. Seeing it was pointless to insist, he reluctantly bid her goodbye. He walked to the gate, gathering one last impression of her bent figure against the blue of the house.

When Michael had gone, Agnès went into the house and picked up the yellowed envelope lying on the table. Just before Michael had arrived she had taken Armand Bataille's letter from its hiding place to read again, though she knew every word by heart. In the past, reading the words he had written to her so many years ago had always had a calming effect on her nerves. With the letter was Pascale's birth certificate, which Agnès had never been able to bring herself to destroy, and the only picture she possessed of her daughter as a tiny baby. She lowered herself slowly on to the chair and was greeted by a black and white cat, who rubbed his cheek against hers. Absently stroking him, she looked at the clock. It was well past eight, but it would be noon before Pascale came out of her sedative-induced sleep.

Agnès couldn't get the graphic picture of the stabbing at Terre Blanche out of her mind. Beatrice had described it to her in the blunt, factual words of the gendarmes who had brought Pascale home in bloodstained clothing. The degradation and the horror of it hurt Agnès so deeply that she felt herself drowning in a wave of grief. Pascale, whom she loved more than life, had seemed like a stranger and Agnès had begun to blame herself for committing some undefinable wrong that had led to such senseless tragedy. Now Étienne was in gaol while Pascale's English lover lay close to death in hospital. A terrible swirl of vertigo swept over her and she sought to relieve it by putting her head on her knees and taking several deep breaths.

As her head cleared, Agnès thought about Michael Lowry's visit. She had lied to him because the Ribard tragedy seemed to have nothing to do with her and her only concern was to protect Armand's secret from prying strangers. But then she remembered the day he mentioned, when she had encountered the Ribard boy, an incident submerged by so many other preoccupations it seemed insignificant until now. She recalled the child's quizzical little face watching her from a distance, and how shocked she had been to learn that his name was Ribard. She had been so distracted that it had not occurred to her until this very minute that the boy might be curious about where she had been and try to investigate for himself.

Agnès got to her feet, deeply fatigued, yet relieved she had a task to fill the morning. A walk to Brissac and back to satisfy her doubts about the little boy would occupy some of the time that was lying so heavily on her hands until Pascale was awake. She fetched her hat and a basket, into which she put a pair of heavy gloves, the secateurs and, in case she needed them, a torch, a crowbar and a chisel. She was closing the gate behind her when she realized that in her haste she had left Armand's letter on the table. The door was locked, but an old superstition that decreed that the letter, the photograph and Pascale's birth certificate should always be safely hidden made her pause.

Agnès had her hand on the latch and was about to go back into the house when all the light went out of the morning. The green of the vegetable patch turned to sepia, like an old photograph. A gushing torrent filled her head, accompanied by a searing pain that travelled up her arm to her chest. Agnès was thrown into a black tunnel ending in a circle of light, where Armand was waiting for her. On the edge of the darkness time ceased to matter, and they walked out together into an eternal summer's day.

The three candles Rachel had lit flickered by themselves on the highest point of the candelabra near the statue of St Anne. The church was empty at this hour and utterly silent. As she knelt on the cold marble step beneath the altar, her eyes travelled up the spotless altar cloth past a bouquet of roses that touched the saint's gown. It was a moment before Rachel had the courage to look the statue in the face, and then she spoke the only prayer she could think of, the Lord's Prayer, hardly moving her lips. She couldn't bring herself to beg for Oliver's safe return, feeling the saint would not be fooled by unbelievers who came to petition her as a last resort.

'"For thine is the kingdom, the power and the glory for ever and ever. Amen."'

Rachel stood up and paused for one last look at the statue, knowing St Anne's face would live in her memory for the rest of her days. She walked down the aisle promising herself that, whatever happened, she would come back to say a private farewell to the little saint before leaving Roquelaire. Lingering at the back of the church, she compared the muted light of early morning seeping through the windows to her first visit to the chapel, when it had been ablaze with colour.

481

The village was beginning to come to life, with shops opening and men attending to the carnival machines. Rachel was anxious to stay near a telephone, yet gripped by a compulsion to make the rounds of the square, asking everyone she met whether they had seen Oliver. Just then, Michael appeared. He was walking towards her, head down, his hands in his pockets. For a moment her only thought was how glad she was to see him.

'I found I couldn't sleep when it got light so I thought I'd look around.'

'That's what happened to me. I thought there was no use lying there.'

While they spoke her eyes darted round the square, as if she hoped to see Oliver appear at any moment.

'In case you're worried that there was no one to tend the telephone, I told an officer I met where you were. I take it there's no news. Did you get my note?'

'Yes, thank you. As far as I know nothing has happened yet. Alain has gone off to the gendarmarie and I've been in the church for a quiet moment by myself. At times like this one needs special help.'

'I've always envied people who could pray.'

'So have I, and I wish I was one of them, like the people in the chronicle. Think of how much time Margaret and John must have spent in the church. To them praying was no different from breathing.'

'Margaret and John have been on my mind too, now that you mention it.'

'They never leave you for long, do they?'

'So much so that I'll probably miss their company when I get back to normal life.'

'Normal life,' Rachel repeated. 'I never knew what it meant until now.'

They paused in the shadow of a wall, and he sought her eyes, full of unshed tears. Michael couldn't bring himself to mention his futile trip to Brissac, thinking it would only make matters worse. He had hoped to bring Oliver back to her, and was conscious of a painful sense of helplessness that he had come back empty-handed.

Seeing her by chance brought home how deeply he cared – and the necessity of keeping his feelings to himself.

'Did you get any sleep?' he asked as they started up the street.

'Not much. I tried to follow your advice about being positive, and I'm struggling to keep my hopes up. It's hard, though.' Feeling the tears come back, she tried to smile. 'There were times when the night seemed very long. Basically, I got through it by pretending that I would wake up this morning and find Oliver had spent the night somewhere, and had come back safely.'

'That could still happen. I hope it will. I'll do anything I can to help you keep your hopes up. Come back to the house and have some breakfast. A cup of coffee would do you good.'

'I couldn't, really. Maybe in a little while. Do you think I ought to make the rounds this morning asking people if they have seen him? Maybe if they see me it might jog their memories because I was in the village with him one day and they might have seen us.'

'No, no, Rachel. That won't help. There's nothing you can do that the gendarmes can't.' He opened his front door.

Hovering indecisively on the threshold, she said, 'It's this waiting, Michael. I seem to have done nothing but wait for two weeks. What really upsets me is that if you and I had managed to get to him hours sooner, this wouldn't be happening now.'

The telephone started to ring and Michael sprinted into the house, with Rachel following. When he had answered it he handed it to her.

'It's Alain calling from the gendarmerie.'

Rachel became even paler, her hands shaking with mixed hope and dread as she took the receiver. Hearing what Alain had to say, her body slackened. She hung up, murmuring, 'He just wanted to tell me that they're doing a systematic search of houses around Terre Blanche and that he's going with them.'

They were condemned to pass the morning in suspense, noting every hour's passing by the dull ringing of the church bell. Rachel sat on the terrace in the sun, pretending to read or look at a magazine, but Michael could see she was listening for the telephone. As time went by with no word of any kind, he watched Rachel's painful struggle to hold her emotions in check. He forced her to eat a sandwich, and later they sat under the trellis together, waiting.

'I can't imagine why Alain hasn't called again. Maybe he's run into people he used to know who could help him.'

'It must seem strange for him, seeing people from his past under these circumstances.'

'Quite honestly, I don't think Alain knows whether he's alive or dead at the moment, Michael. No matter what he's done, it's clear to me that he loves Oliver more than anything.'

There was a knock at the door. Michael got up and a moment later ushered Père Auguste into the sitting-room.

'*Bonjour, madame,*' the priest said to Rachel, as she came in from the terrace.

'*Bonjour*, Père Auguste,' she responded, taking his extended hand. She felt sympathy pass from him to her as he clasped her hand in both of his.

'I thought I'd look in and see how you are.'

'Waiting. Holding on.'

'I've been praying for you.'

'Thank you. It means a great deal to know – that I'm not alone.'

'You're not alone, believe me. Everyone in the village is aware of what has happened and they're very concerned. Several people I met this morning asked me to convey that their thoughts were with you.'

'That is very kind, Father. Please thank them.'

Michael said, 'Would you come out to the terrace, Père Auguste? A cup of coffee, perhaps?'

'No coffee, thank you, I'll only stay a minute. Saturday is such a busy day, especially today.'

'Of course. You have all those confessions to hear. Roquelaire is steeped in sin,' Michael said mischievously, and Rachel saw he was trying to keep her spirits up.

'He's a real heretic, isn't he?' Père Auguste said with a chuckle.

'They used to burn people like me at the stake.'

Out on the terrace, the priest became serious again. 'I'm afraid I have several items of sad news to deliver. Nothing to do with your son,' he added quickly, looking at Rachel. 'Where to begin?' he muttered. 'You, Madame Ribard, would probably be shocked to hear that Rosamund Morton, from the painting class, tried to commit suicide last night.'

'Rosamund!' Rachel had a sudden picture of Rosamund's tortured face when they last met.

'She's in the clinic and will recover, but she is lucky to be alive. She took an overdose of barbiturates.'

Rachel sat in devastated silence. 'I knew that she'd had a breakdown last year, and she was feeling depressed because of . . . emotional problems. If I had realized how serious it was, I might have done something.' For a moment she forgot everything but Rosamund's brave gaiety, which had obviously masked total despair.

'Apparently she won first prize at the art exhibition last night. I don't know what distressed her,' said the priest.

Michael and Rachel exchanged a meaningful look. They were both thinking of Julian.

'*And* there was an incident last night at Terre Blanche. Perhaps you've already heard?'

'No, what now?' Rachel became more tense at the mention of Isabelle's house.

'It appears that young Pascale Gachpour's former fiancé, Étienne Dufour, stabbed the Englishman whom she was, uh, spending the evening with.'

'So that's what it was,' muttered Michael.

Rachel gave a fleeting thought to Pascale, on whom she had pinned her hopes to bring Oliver back to her yesterday.

Michael shook his head. 'The idea of Étienne stabbing anyone, even Julian, is inconceivable. Violence seems utterly out of character for him.'

'Apparently Pascale broke off their engagement quite suddenly. No one realized how badly Étienne took it. But his troubles have just begun. If the Englishman survives, then there is the army to contend with. Otherwise, I hate to think of the consequences. I think the circumstances in which the stabbing occurred in the guest house at Terre Blanche were not very, how should I say? edifying,' the priest reported.

'How awful for Pascale,' Michael remarked, remembering her radiant face as they waited at the café the previous evening, only hours before it happened.

'I wonder what will happen now,' said Rachel. It was too much to take in – all her energy was concentrated on Oliver. An invisible spring inside her coiled even tighter.

'It's strange, isn't it, Michael,' Père Auguste was saying. 'We were talking the other day about history repeating itself. And this morning on my way here I was reflecting on what you said about the chronicle. The events of the last twenty-four hours have an uncanny familiarity.'

At the mention of the chronicle Rachel looked anxiously at Michael. The combined force of fate and coincidence, which had once seemed so romantic, now frightened her, as if Oliver had fallen victim to some malign riddle to which they would never know the answer. She fought her rising panic when she remembered how Michael had compared the past and present.

Brushing aside Père Auguste's comment, Michael remarked, 'I should think Madame de Montjoi is distraught about the stabbing. The Englishman is the lynchpin of her hotel project.'

Rachel thought of Alain, supposing Isabelle would be distraught about his absence too.

'Ah well, that brings me to the last bit of news, and the saddest of all. News that I haven't quite taken in myself. This morning, around nine o'clock, the postman found Agnès Grimal outside her garden gate. She was dead, I'm afraid.'

Rachel sat in numbed silence and Michael shook his head sadly at the priest's latest revelation. This catalogue of tragedies seemed never-ending.

Père Auguste rose to go, and Michael walked with him to the door.

'If there's anything I can do, let me know. I don't like descending on you with such bad news, especially in the circumstances, but I thought you ought to know. I'm going to offer a special prayer at six o'clock mass tonight for all those who are suffering, Madame Ribard included, and of course, Agnès. A light in the church has been extinguished. There's really no one to replace her.'

'I can't believe it. I didn't say so in front of Rachel, but I was possibly the last person to see Agnès.' Michael explained about his visit to Brissac and to Agnès, and she had looked as if she had been crying. 'I realize now it was because of Pascale. I asked Agnès if there were any passages under Brissac, and when it came to nothing, I thought it was better not to mention it to Rachel. If Agnès knew anything, she wasn't telling. Now it's gone with her.'

'It appears she died instantly. A heart attack. No one will ever know if it was brought on by strain, or sadness perhaps. The postman said he found her lying near the door, her hat nearby, as if she was on her way somewhere. She had been carrying a basket containing, for some reason, a pair of heavy gloves, some tools and a torch. Odd. Oh yes, and she seemed to be carrying a heavy crowbar too. Now what would she be doing with that, do you think?'

When he had closed the door, Michael returned to the terrace, where Rachel was wiping tears from her eyes.

'She was a lovely person. She was so nice to me. I felt as if I had known her all my life from the moment I met her. I can't believe she's dead. And Rosamund – trying to kill herself. What a mess, Michael.'

Michael had no reply. The account of the last days of Brissac loomed over him and he reflected that he and Rachel seemed to be dwelling in a dark tower. He was reminded of the dream he had had a few days before of a child's terrified cry in the darkness. His mind began to turn stubbornly on Agnès. He asked himself if his visit had upset her, trying to imagine what she had meant to do with the tools in her basket.

Minutes later Michael was driving urgently towards Brissac, having promised Rachel he'd be back within the hour. A wild idea had come into his head, and with it a desperate hope pinned on the contents of Agnès's basket. Before going to the car he had rummaged through a cupboard and filled a bag with his own tools to take with him.

The heat of mid-afternoon was stifling by the time he got as far as the Pilgrim's Stone. He automatically slowed down as he passed it, thinking of the wreath he had found, the wreath that now took on a real significance. It was the hottest part of the day, too hot even for walkers and pilgrims to be about, and the road was deserted.

He parked the car on a farm track below the chalk approach road to the château and walked back to where he had found Rachel and Oliver that day. Looking down at the parched, rocky ground near the retaining wall of the fortress, his eyes quickly found a spot that was so obvious that he couldn't imagine why he hadn't noticed it before. A thicket of shrubs clung around the stones here, but a few branches were lying on the ground nearby, as if they had been cut away.

He ran to the wall and began to search in earnest. The undergrowth was impenetrable – almost. He found that the branches had been cut, but it had been done neatly, with secateurs, so it would not be noticeable at a distance. Some dead branches had been stuffed back in place, as if to hide the gap, and their wilted leaves told him they hadn't been cut that long ago. Tearing them aside impatiently, Michael uncovered a space big enough for a small person, a woman or a child, to creep through on their hands and knees, a passage he began to enlarge with his own secateurs. Ignoring the scratches from the thorns, he kept cutting his way through furiously until he was deep within the foliage.

Towards the middle, the dense thicket thinned out, but the leaves overhead wove a thick canopy that cut out the light. Suddenly the wall was visible again where nothing grew by the closely packed stones, cut and placed to fit like marquetry. He found himself in a dim hollow, with dry, bald ground under his feet. At first Michael couldn't believe it when he spotted a small cavity in the base of the wall, made by the removal of several stones. He gave a shout, thinking that he had found the legendary passage that had lain in his imagination for so long. He pulled out the torch and fell on his knees with hope and fear churning inside him. A cool rush of dark air hit his face as he peered inside the dark hole. Straining to hear, Michael could detect no sound at all. Drawing in his breath and saying a prayer at the same time, he shouted Oliver's name. He waited for a moment, but there was no reply, only the whisper of the wind. He bellowed into the hole, 'Oliver, are you there? It's Michael Lowry. If you're there anywhere, shout back as loud as you can.'

After a tense moment Michael heard a distinct whimper echoing from the depths of the passage, followed by sobbing.

'Oliver!' he shouted into the gap, rejoicing at the feeble signal that told him the boy was there. Oliver's helpless whimper was the most welcome sound that Michael had ever heard. It was followed by an inarticulate wail, which encapsulated the horror of Oliver's long ordeal and tore into Michael's heart. Michael tried desperately to pry more stones loose with his chisel so that he could wriggle inside the passage, but he soon realized it was futile. He put his face to the gap.

'Oliver, listen. I'm going for help because I can't get inside to rescue you. I won't be long, I promise. Just hang on a little while more and we'll be coming in to get you. Can you do that?'

All he got in return was another wrenching sob. Michael realized how traumatized Oliver must be. Twenty-four hours of terror had deprived him of speech. All sorts of horrors went through Michael's mind, including whether Oliver might be seriously injured.

He got to his feet, shaking and stunned at what had happened. Realizing that he was wasting precious moments, Michael fought his way out of the thicket, using his arms to protect his eyes as the thorns tore at him. He drove back to Roquelaire as fast as he could, hardly noticing his arms and hands were covered in blood from hundreds of scratches and cuts. He brought the car to a halt outside the ramparts, where people were starting to arrive for the carnival. They turned to stare as he ran through the arch into the square.

He burst into his sitting-room. Rachel had been on the terrace, curled up in a chair in a corner of shade. Hearing the door open, she leapt up and ran into the sitting-room. When she saw him, she gasped.

'Michael, what on earth has happened? Look at the blood . . .'

'I found him! I found Oliver! He's all right, I think, though I don't know yet if he's injured. He's there, Rachel, do you understand? He crawled into a passage at the base of Brissac and he can't get out.'

Her hands flew to her mouth. 'What?'

He clasped her to him with more energy than he thought he had left in his body and felt her collapse against him sobbing. When she looked up at him, tears were flooding down his own cheeks.

'What do we do? How do we get at him?'

He explained the situation. 'I don't honestly know if he's injured or not, but I imagine the worst of it is that he's just frightened.'

'Let's go. Please, right this minute,' she pleaded, but she was shaking so badly she could hardly stand.

'We must get help from the gendarmes, and the fire brigade, because the entrance to the passage isn't big enough for anyone but a child to pass through. I tried to force a passage, but I couldn't manage it.'

'He must be injured badly or he would have come out. My poor baby,' she whispered, a fresh wave of fear taking hold of her. 'Tell me how he sounded.'

'Just frightened, that's all. I have to call the rescue service and then we'll go straight to Brissac ourselves. What Oliver needs more than anything is to hear your voice.'

As she waited for Michael, Rachel felt sick with impatience, which was now running counter to her anxiety. All her joy and relief were held in check by the fear of what they might find when they got to the tunnel.

'It's ringing. Do you want to talk to the gendarmes?'

'No, you do it, please. I don't think I could get a sentence together.'

She waited tensely while Michael spoke with the gendarmes, then the fire brigade. It seemed to take for ever. She was frantic to get to Oliver.

Finally Michael hung up. 'Because it's August, the chief of the brigade said it might take a bit longer than usual to round up the men, as some of them are on holiday. They'll try to contact Alain, though they don't know where he is. Let's go.'

Passing the church, they met Père Auguste going up the steps, dressed in a white soutane for mass, and stopped just long enough to tell him the news.

'Brissac? How remarkable.' His eyes were round with the significance. 'God speed. I'll pray for his quick rescue and return.'

They raced along the road to Brissac, Rachel sitting with her hands clenched together in her lap. As the Pilgrim's Stone came in sight Michael told Rachel about the wreath.

490

'I still don't know if it was Oliver who put it there, but my guess is that he did.'

In a hoarse whisper Rachel said, 'When we were here the other day the wish I made was for Oliver – that he would come safely through this crisis.'

'Isn't that strange? After seeing the Pilgrim's Stone with you and Oliver, the business about the wreath struck a chord in my mind. It's one of many things, not the only one.'

'You mean you had some kind of hunch, something to do with the chronicle?' Rachel asked.

'Yes, but at first I couldn't quite take myself seriously.'

Michael's mind seemed to be open and free, like a dark room suddenly – full of light. A weight had gone from him now that the chronicle had vindicated all his stubborn instincts. Everything fell into place as he thought about the conundrum it represented. The characters and events from six centuries ago took on a compelling new significance: they had saved the life of a small, lost boy. Seeing the honey-coloured battlements outlined on the horizon, he felt more deeply moved than he could ever remember.

He stopped the car on the lower road, in view of the wall.

'That's where the tunnel is,' he said, pointing.

'What on earth made him come here in the first place?' asked Rachel, leaping out of the car. The adrenalin was coursing through her at the sight of the dense thicket hugging the wall, where no one would ever have thought to look. The realization that Oliver would have remained trapped there for ever made her sick.

She eagerly followed Michael up the slope towards the wall, which was now in shadow. They were panting with exertion when they reached the spot where Michael had dropped his tools outside the break in the shrubbery.

'Follow me, but take care. There are some nasty thorns and sharp branches barring the way.'

He took Rachel by the hand and together they inched their way forward into the dark thicket.

'Oliver! I'm here, Oliver!'

'He can't hear you yet, but we're nearly there.' Michael stood aside and let Rachel pass in front of him when the gap in the base

491

of the wall came in sight. 'There, there's the entrance. Here's the torch, although you can't see much.'

Rachel dropped to the ground and put her face to the hole. 'Oliver, Oliver! It's Mom. Can you hear me?' She gave Michael a look of desperation when there was no immediate reply, then called again. 'Oliver, answer me if you can hear me,' she cried.

An agonizing moment of silence passed, until at last they heard a muffled sobbing.

Recognizing Oliver's voice, Rachel shrank back for a second, too emotional to speak.

'Ollie, sweetheart, listen to me. The police and firemen are on their way here to rescue you this minute, because the hole is too small for us to get inside and reach you. Hold on tight, darling. Can you do that?'

'Yes,' came the small, uncertain voice.

'Michael, he answered. Thank God,' she cried. 'Oliver, are you hurt? Can you move?'

'I can't move.' He began sobbing again.

Rachel wedged herself in the narrow space as best she could and talked to Oliver for a few minutes in a soothing voice and was able to get monosyllabic replies to her questions. She lay in the dust, every muscle tensed as she tried to coax him out of the terror he had lived through in the last twenty-four hours. All the time Michael worked stubbornly to loosen some of the other stones, but without much success.

After what seemed like an interminable time, they heard the sound of voices beyond the thicket.

'It's the rescue team – they're here!' cried Rachel. Pressing her face to the hole, she shouted the news to Oliver.

She followed Michael out of the undergrowth, where half a dozen rescuers in blue suits were running up the slope. They had been followed to Brissac by a car of gendarmes and an ambulance. It was only then that Rachel became aware of numbing exhaustion, which she knew she mustn't give in to until Oliver was safely asleep in a warm bed.

Michael took charge of the volunteers, showing them the way into the thicket. All Rachel could do was stand by as the men swarmed over the little slope, going back and forth to get equipment, and began to clear a path through the shrubbery. She spoke to one of the gendarmes, who told her that Alain would be arriving soon. He then hurried to the road below, where Rachel was surprised to see that several cars of curious onlookers had stopped. Somehow the word had gone out that Oliver was there in the tunnel. In her heart Rachel believed the people had gathered not from idle curiosity, but to share her and Alain's trouble.

Only a quarter of an hour had passed since the rescuers had arrived, but it seemed far longer as Rachel waited for word that a way into the tunnel had been cleared. She stood with her arms folded rigidly across her chest, listening and waiting for any sign from the thicket that the ordeal was over. She was beginning to worry about the nightmares that were going to torment Oliver when it was over when she saw a familiar white car streak past and come to a screeching halt on the road below. Alain jumped out and charged up the rocky slope in the late afternoon sun. His sudden appearance set off a chain of conflicting emotions in Rachel. From a distance he seemed like the husband she had loved so dearly. Then, as his handsome, bearded face came closer and she saw the familiar outline of his strong shoulders and forearms, he appeared to her like someone she used to know and hadn't seen for a long time.

He ran towards her shouting breathlessly, 'Is he all right?'

She made the victory sign and waved her hand above her head.

'I came as soon as I heard,' he exclaimed, reaching her side.

'They've been at it for half an hour, but they still haven't broken through the wall,' she said, explaining what had happened.

'When the gendarmes passed on the message, I couldn't believe it. Of all places that he could be! My God, Rachel,' he embraced her. 'The relief, Rachel, the overwhelming relief when I heard that he was all right. Tell me, how did his voice sound when you spoke to him?'

He put his arm comfortingly round her shoulder as she told him. 'The things that have been going through my mind this last twenty-four hours. I don't need to tell you. And now it's almost over.'

493

'It was all Michael's doing. He had some kind of hunch, and eventually he tracked Oliver down here. We'd never have found him otherwise.'

'I can't begin to even think what the little guy has been going through. Can you imagine, being stuck in a place like that? The fact that he had the courage to even go in there shows what guts he has.'

Rachel smiled at this. 'I could do with less guts and more caution,' she said, feeling numb satisfaction that Alain was at her side to share the last tense moments of the vigil.

They stood silently together watching the men at work in the thicket and sharing the unspoken horror of what might have happened. Rachel couldn't help wondering whether the awesome power that Brissac had wielded over Alain's destiny had chastened him. As he looked up, the sight of the château seemed to trouble him, and the thought struck her that his plans had begun to go wrong from the start, as if he wasn't meant to possess something so grand and so fine. It had managed to elude him, and now it had come close to depriving him of the boy he cherished more than anything in life.

'Brissac – of all places. But why did he want to come here? I want you to know that I never brought him here,' Alain muttered.

Rachel mentioned their walk together and the story Michael told him about the treasure. 'But how he found the passage is a mystery.'

'A passage. So it's really true. People used to talk about it, but no one believed it.' Alain turned to scan the curious faces trained on them.

'Word travels fast in a small town. And this is a very small town,' Rachel reminded him.

The tension mounted as they waited with growing impatience. Finally, Alain stopped a passing rescue-worker.

'Can you tell us what's happening? We're desperate to know.'

'He's about five metres or so inside the passage at the bottom of a shallow, dry cistern. The doctor is just going in to supervise the sling we'll use to lift him up in case anything is broken. It shouldn't take long. He'll be all right. We even got him to smile.'

494

'But don't you think it would help him if we were there, close by?' Rachel asked, her eyes pleading.

'No, *madame*. It's really much better if you wait here.'

'We'll only be in the way,' Alain agreed. 'It can't be long now.'

The doctor went into the thicket with the rescuers, and the medics placed themselves nearby with the stretcher, making Rachel's heart contract. As she and Alain waited in tense anticipation, Rachel said, 'He'll almost certainly have to stay in the hospital for observation or whatever. I'll stay with him tonight.' Her voice was emphatic. 'I suppose you'll want to go back to Terre Blanche.'

'I don't know yet what I'm going to do.'

'It's entirely up to you. I'm sure he'll want you to be nearby, but he won't be able to travel for several days at least. I wouldn't want to take him on a long trip until he's completely fit again.'

Rachel looked at Alain with unswerving directness, conveying her intention to take Oliver home. Before he could reply, shouts came from the thicket, followed by an excited babble of voices. Rachel and Alain pressed forward anxiously to see what was happening. Michael appeared first, flashing a victorious smile in their direction. He was followed by three rescuers, the last of whom carried Oliver in his arms.

Rachel was shocked when she saw him. He was covered with dust and there was a dark bruise on his forehead. His eyes, which he rubbed in the sudden brightness, were almost swollen shut, perhaps from crying.

It took Oliver a moment to realize that Alain and Rachel were there. He looked from one to the other of them in confusion for a second, then reached out unhesitatingly for Rachel, who took him in her arms.

'That's what he needs,' the doctor said with a smile, 'to be comforted by his mother. It's as important as anything that I can do for him now.'

Oliver buried his head in Rachel's shoulder. Gathering his frail, trembling little body to her, she was dazed by a happiness that almost eclipsed the day he was born when he had held him for the very first time. She kissed his dusty head, her arms wrapped around her precious burden. He didn't cry or utter a word, but pressed himself like an infant deep into the safety of her shoulder. Rocking him back and forth, she whispered a private prayer of gratitude. He and she were lost in their own little world, oblivious of all the excitement that had broken out around them. Alain stood nearby, resting a protective hand on Oliver's shoulders, as if he, too, were claiming part of him. When Oliver smiled up at him at last, Rachel realized that Alain was bound to be hurt that it was her Oliver had instinctively reached for, and not him.

'Madame Ribard,' said a voice.

She looked up to see the young doctor, his stethoscope round his neck, waiting to take Oliver from her. The air was filled with excited conversation, so many voices chattering at once that Rachel couldn't understand where they came from until she saw a crowd of several dozen or so bystanders, many of whom she recognized by sight, had formed round them. The gendarmes were half-heartedly trying to keep the villagers back, but they seemed as happy as she was that Oliver had been found. Rachel smiled at them over Oliver's head, glad that they were there.

The doctor drew her to one side, where the stretcher was waiting. It took a great deal of coaxing to get Oliver to loosen his grip, but finally he allowed himself to be laid out and examined. She knelt beside the stretcher, holding his hand and whispering words of encouragement.

Looking round for Alain, she saw him talking to a stout, red-faced farmer wearing a beret. Several villagers were greeting him with smiles and handshakes, as if he were an old friend whose trouble they had come to share. She was amazed to see him responding with uncharacteristic shyness, suggesting that he was unprepared for such an outpouring of concern. He was no longer a stranger, but one of them, and they seemed to be welcoming him back. The vignette encapsulated something Rachel had always known, how much Alain wanted to be liked by those he pretended to despise.

'We'll X-ray his head first thing to make sure there's no concussion,' the doctor said when he had finished examining Oliver. 'There are some other bruises, but they're only minor.'

'What about his mental state? How badly do you think this has

496

affected him?' she whispered in French, as the men picked up the stretcher.

'It's hard to say at this moment. But it might take a while for him to forget what happened.'

It wasn't until Rachel was in the ambulance that she realized she had completely forgotten to thank Michael, who had disappeared in the crush. She looked back as the ambulance drove down the road, Alain following in the white car, but there was no sign of Michael.

# Chapter 24

Watching the ambulance drive off, followed by Alain in the white Golf, Michael came to the harsh conclusion that there was no room for him in the Ribard family circle now it had closed tightly in on itself. He had been standing on the sidelines when he saw Rachel accompany the stretcher down the hill without a backward glance. He struggled to justify her thoughtlessness, telling himself that it was only natural that all her attention was focused on her injured son, but after all they had been through together, he felt slighted none the less. His elation at finding Oliver had been replaced by a sinking resignation.

Detaching himself from the crowd that had gathered, he looked up at the towering façade of Brissac, now bathed in the amber light of evening. Swifts lazily circled the western tower, breaking through the sound of human voices with their cries and inviting him to dream. Michael deliberately turned away, aware that the fortress had lost its hold over him. He was weary of the chronicle and tired of Roquelaire and the interminable summer. The exhilarating fantasy of the Middle Ages that had overflowed into his own life receded in importance now it had served the purpose of rescuing a lost child, though he thought he might never fully understand how or why it had all come about. The familiar emptiness of one episode in his life closing before another was in sight had already made him restless and moody. All he wanted now was a hot bath, a beer and to sit on his terrace and watch the sun going down over the horizon.

Just then he saw Père Auguste, still wearing his white soutane, hailing him from the middle of the slope. Michael was about to tell him the good news, when the priest said, 'I've already heard the glorious tidings from six different people and came as soon as I could. I was as curious as the rest of them to know the outcome.'

Michael reconstructed the events that led to Oliver's rescue while the priest looked at him in reverent astonishment. 'It was the chronicle that saved him, as sure as day,' said Père Auguste. 'It verges on the miraculous.'

'Yes, it does, doesn't it?' agreed Michael. 'It's quite uncanny how everything fell into place. The chronicle was the catalyst, but you may be interested to know that the Pilgrim's Stone played a part too.' Père Auguste listened, spellbound, as Michael recounted how he had found the box wreath at the monument's base and how the tools Agnès was carrying when she died had triggered off his deductions. 'Of course, it's only conjecture that Agnès was heading for Brissac after I called by, but I'm convinced she was on her way here after what I'd said. The tools were a crucial give-away,' Michael concluded.

Père Auguste nodded and smiled, his arms folded across his chest. 'You pieced the whole thing together brilliantly, Michael, and you alone did it. You had the courage to act on your hunch, as far-fetched as it must have seemed to you at the time. Well, congratulations. This is a happy outcome to what could have been another terrible tragedy.'

'No one is happier than I am, believe me,' Michael said, wiping the sweat from his brow.

'You were looking a bit sombre when I saw you just now. I imagine you must be pleasantly exhausted after the excitement of today.'

'What I really feel is a sense of anticlimax, to tell the truth. When you came up the hill just now I couldn't help thinking to myself that John has lost Margaret yet again.' Michael gave no sign of how shattered he felt, or how foolish, and saw that the priest hadn't understood his meaning.

Père Auguste put a sympathetic hand on his shoulder. 'Your friendship with Madame Ribard was crucial in tying events together. Just think, if you hadn't met her, you would certainly never have found Oliver.'

'Or he might never have got lost at all. But let's not stand here talking,' said Michael, not wanting to think about it any more. 'The rescuers discovered something besides a little lost boy inside the passage, something that will intrigue you.'

499

They joined the gendarmes and rescuers at the gap in the shrubbery, where they were conversing avidly.

'We're going to have to mount a guard tonight until the hole can be blocked up satisfactorily. It's too late to do anything about it now,' the captain was saying.

'No one should disturb the body until a coroner can be called in,' said another officer.

'Body?' said Père Auguste, looking at Michael.

Michael said, 'The lights they set up revealed what might have frightened Oliver, and even have sent him hurtling into the pit. There are the remains of a body in the tunnel not far away from the cistern he fell into.'

'A body?' repeated Père Auguste, at once concerned. 'Who was it?'

'It would have been difficult to tell, given the amount of time it's been there,' said the captain of the gendarmes. 'By a bit of luck we identified him just now from the identity card in his pocket. His name was Paul Ribard. Perhaps you remember him, Father. One of the men reminded me that he was a collabo who disappeared in '44 or thereabouts.'

'You found his body in there?' The priest stared at them in open-mouthed astonishment. 'This whole affair is getting harder and harder to comprehend.'

'We found some other documents on him as well that might prove interesting.'

'I wonder what he meant by that,' Père Auguste said, following Michael through the cleared undergrowth. He paused and poked his head through the entrance the rescuers had made in the wall.

'This is very interesting indeed,' said Père Auguste, looking around. 'They certainly knew how to build things to last in those days. Some parts of this ceiling look as if they could have been built yesterday.'

'Come inside,' said Michael, stepping back. As they passed into the tunnel, illuminated by an arc-light the rescuers had set up, the stifling smell of centuries-old air hit them, along with the lingering odour of decay. They paused at the cistern, which was several metres deep. Michael illuminated it with a torch.

500

'There's a well through the gap you see at the bottom of the cistern. It's probably very deep and apparently still has water in it.' Michael's voice echoed in the depths of the passage.

'It's an ancient safety device and it saved the Ribard boy. Just imagine his terror being trapped down there for so long. It would have tested the endurance of a grown man,' the priest remarked, his voice resounding in the pit as he peered over the edge.

'And there's the body,' said Michael, beaming his torch beyond the well and illuminating a human skull. The blue worksuit Paul Ribard had been wearing was dusty but clearly identifiable and the bones of his hands protruded out of the sleeves.

Père Auguste stared at it for several moments as he thought back. 'Well, well,' he said at last. 'Everyone supposed when the old man was never seen again that he had been eliminated by the Maquis. But who put him here? And how did Agnès know about this tunnel, I wonder – if indeed your assumption is correct. Armand Bataille must have told her about it. Do you suppose Armand was the *maquisard* assigned to do the job?'

They speculated for a few moments and Michael said, 'My guess is that Agnès helped Armand out in some way, if, as you suggest Armand was responsible for Paul Ribard's death. It seems almost certain to me that if Armand had simply discovered this passage when he renovated the château, he would have told the police about the body. But, if he had committed the deed himself, he would probably have preferred to keep it a secret. Who knows? Maybe that was why he bought the château in the first place.'

'I think there was more to it than that, Michael. You didn't know him, but this house became his life.'

'Probably, but something tells me that he was covering up, whatever the reasons. Otherwise, as I said, he would have reported finding Paul Ribard's body to the police. And if Agnès had helped Armand, it would certainly explain how she knew about this tunnel and also why he left Brissac to her,' said Michael, thinking of his last conversation with her, which seemed much longer ago than that morning. 'The way she recoiled when I asked whether there might be a passage here makes me think that she knew about it all along and was on her way to make sure Oliver wasn't trapped in it.

501

Perhaps Oliver saw her come out of the thicket the day we walked here, because I'm sure I saw her near here then. That's the only way I can figure out how he would have known about it.'

'We'll find out soon enough, when he's able to talk about his experience. But just now you mentioned that Agnès was protecting Armand when she refused to talk to you; that doesn't make sense. He was in the Maquis and it was the war. Paul Ribard was a collaborator, or said to be, so Armand would only have been doing his duty.'

'No, you're right. It doesn't quite fit, does it? I was just thinking of Alain Ribard. This discovery is going to be very unpleasant for him. After all, it was his grandfather.'

'Yes, but perhaps it will matter less to him now than it might have in the past.'

'Maybe now Agnès is dead, he'll be buying Brissac.' As he said it, Michael envisioned the emotional tangle that was going to ensue between Isabelle and Alain and Rachel.

'That remains to be seen,' said Père Auguste, remembering Agnès's plans for the château.

'I'm going deeper into the tunnel,' Michael said, 'Do you want to come? It will probably be our only chance, because they're bound to close it off, and it will be swarming with officials, who won't let anyone in.'

'If you're looking for the legendary papal treasure, my guess is that they used all their gold to finance wars in those days.'

'I'm more interested in finding an answer to what happened to plague victims of Brissac, including John and Margaret.'

They penetrated deeper into the dark tunnel, guided by the light of Michael's torch.

'I reckon we're beneath the château by now,' Michael's voice resounded in the darkness. Beaming the light ahead, he whispered, 'Look, it opens up into a chamber. We're almost at the end.'

He directed the light at the floor and both he and Père Auguste stopped in their tracks. Skeletons, seemingly dozens upon dozens of them, were scattered on the earthen floor. Skulls, lying among the bones, leered grimly at them in the darkness.

'Oh, là là,' muttered Père Auguste, 'Oh, là là.'

Though he had been half-expecting to find the place where the plague victims were buried, Michael was stunned by the discovery of the mass grave. The careless way the bodies had been piled together bore tragic witness to the helplessness of the people of Roquelaire. He had seen the catacombs in Rome, the bones of saints, even the remains of war victims long after they had ceased to be men, and though they held a morbid fascination for him, Michael usually felt a certain detachment, as if such inanimate fragments had nothing to do with human life. The tragic reality of Brissac's last days there at his feet brought the chronicle to life in a way that John Stratton's words never could. When his shock had receded, Michael was moved beyond words to be standing in the final resting place of the people who had become so real to him. Probing beyond the macabre anonymity of the bones of the plague victims, he remembered the villagers whose faces were immortalized on the capitals in the church, individuals whose words and deeds had been recorded in the chronicles. Michael stared like an intruder into their eternity.

'Look at this,' said Père Auguste. He bent down and picked up what looked like the remains of a tooled leather gauntlet and handed it to Michael.

Michael touched it, wondering if it could have belonged to the knight chronicler he had come to know so intimately. Seeing a white fragment at his feet, he picked it up and saw, to his amazement, that it was a cockleshell. Of all the things that he might have found, the sign of St James was the most moving.

'Here's something interesting, the badge of the pilgrim,' he said, showing it to Père Auguste.

'So it is.'

Michael slipped it in his pocket as a memento.

Père Auguste made the sign of the cross and murmured a prayer. Then he said, 'This is where they ended their journey, all those pilgrims, lords and ladies, abbots and sisters, the saints and sinners of Roquelaire.'

Isabelle was deeply engrossed in composing a letter when she heard a car coming to a halt in the drive. She dropped her pen at the clamorous ring of the old-fashioned doorbell, and listened to the click of Fernande's shoes on the tiles as she went to answer it. At the echo of Alain's voice in the hall she stood up expectantly and rushed towards him when he entered the room.

'Alain, *chéri*! I was hoping it was you.' She threw her arms around his neck, failing to notice that he didn't respond to her touch. '*Chéri*, I'm so glad to see you.' She let out a great sigh of relief and stepped back to look at him with a radiant smile on her face. 'You and I have such a lot to catch up on. It's unbelievable what has occurred in a matter of hours. The first thing is Oliver – I want to hear everything that's happened. You sounded in such a hurry on the phone that I didn't want to keep you. What a blessed relief that you've found him! You must be dying for a drink.'

He nodded and she picked up a decanter and poured two glasses of whisky while he slumped on the sofa with a sigh and began to relate what had happened since he had left the house the previous evening.

'But he's basically all right?' she asked when he had told her about the rescue.

'He's pretty bruised, and his shoulder is sprained, but there's no concussion, thank God. It's the psychological scars that will take more time to heal than anything. He seems perfectly normal now he's safe, but you can imagine the trauma it was for him. He seems to have a complete blank how he got there and exactly what happened. The doctor said that happens sometimes. When I think how close it was! We might never have found him.' He shook his head, still unable to get the deep pit out of his mind.

'So there was a chamber under Brissac after all. How fascinating. Do you suppose Armand was aware of it? But tell me exactly how it all came about? I simply don't understand.'

Alain told her, mentioning the role Michael Lowry had played and the connection with Agnès.

'Agnès? What could she have had to do with it?'

They speculated a moment and when Alain drained his glass, Isabelle took it and went to fill it up again. Over her shoulder, she said, 'I don't suppose we'll ever know the absolute truth about Armand and Agnès and what brought them together. It must have had something to do with the Maquis and the war. Anybody who remembers what happened won't be telling. And now Agnès is dead too. I was dumbfounded when Hélène called me this afternoon to tell me. You realize what this means, don't you?'

'Quite frankly, Isabelle, the only thing on my mind is Oliver. It's after midnight and we've been at the hospital since just after seven.'

'Of course, you're exhausted. We don't have to go into everything tonight. But I can't help being deeply relieved at the way things have turned out. Not that I would have wished harm to anyone, even Agnès. I don't think we should approach the Gachpours for a week or so. It wouldn't go down well if we seemed over-eager, because they'll be in mourning. The whole thing with Julian and Pascale is really unfortunate, but that shouldn't make any difference, really.'

He looked solemnly at her without replying.

She studied him sympathetically, trying to read his troubled expression. 'You've been through a terrible ordeal, *chéri*. You need time to get your enthusiasm for work back again. I was thinking, after September, maybe we could get away for a week or two, perhaps to Martinique, or even the Seychelles.' Before he could reply, she said, 'But please go on. I'm anxious to know what's going to happen now.'

'Oliver has to stay in the hospital for several days. Rachel's there with him tonight. He wouldn't let her out of his sight. And then . . . we've decided that he should go home.'

'Oh, Alain, I'm so relieved to hear you say that, so very relieved. That's the best solution at the moment, though I know it must be hard for you. He needs to be with his mother, the poor child. Listen, about the other night – I mean, last night – it seems ages ago, doesn't it? I wasn't myself when you came back. I was in such a nervous state,' she said, toying with the diamond heart around her neck as she gauged Alain's reaction to every word she said. 'From what you said on the phone, you heard the details of what happened to Julian.'

'I didn't hear about it until this morning, and, quite frankly, I was too preoccupied to think about it.'

'Well, when you left you know what a state I was in. It must have been telepathic, because an hour later, or even less, Pascale was pounding at the door in a state of shock, with a blanket wrapped round her and nothing on underneath. She was sobbing and talking incoherently, blood on her hands, on her face. I could hardly make sense of what she was saying, she blurted out that some maniac had attacked Julian. Imagine! It gave me an awful fright, I can tell you, because I was sure I had sensed someone lurking in the park – remember, I mentioned it?'

'Yes, I remember. How could I forget?' he murmured.

'So you see, I wasn't imagining things. There was someone outside. It turned out to be Pascale's former fiancé, who, it appears, went off his head after they broke up. By the time the police came with an ambulance my nerves were shot, I can tell you. Luckily, Fernande knows a bit about first aid, but my God, Alain, the blood! The whole room will have to be redone. It was a nightmare. I saw Julian being put in the ambulance and he was as white as the sheet they put over him. The poor man – I really thought he wouldn't make it. It was simply terrible,' she said, tears coming to her eyes. 'Did you hear about him at the hospital? I thought maybe you'd have had a chance to speak to the doctor.'

He shook his head. 'As I said, I'm afraid Rachel and I had our own troubles.'

'Of course you did. Well, I was so exhausted this morning that I slept until noon, but I feel fine now. And Pascale – I felt so sorry for her. The gendarmes questioned her and then took her home. When I called the hospital this afternoon, they said Julian was still in intensive care. It seems unlikely that he'll be in any shape to meet with the backers in two weeks. I hope to God he pulls through. But a delay will give us the time we need to negotiate the purchase of Brissac. Another drink? Or something to eat, perhaps? I could bring you something on a tray if you feel hungry, *chéri*.'

He shook his head. 'Julian was a fool to get involved with Pascale, knowing she was engaged. Frankly, I can't have too much sympathy for him.'

A silence fell between them. When Alain looked at his watch, she said tenderly. 'You're probably exhausted and want to go to

506

bed. Before you came I was just dashing off a few letters, one to the ministry about the plans for the spa, another to the bank about a mortgage, because I want the loan to be in place to bridge the gap before you get sorted out. Things are going to go full steam ahead now, I have a feeling, and . . .'

'Isabelle,' he interrupted her.

The harshness in his voice made her wary, and he was staring at her with disconcerting gravity. Isabelle gave him a querulous little smile, ignoring the pulse that was beating at her throat. 'We won't talk about it any more tonight . . .'

'It's no good. You realize that, don't you?'

'I don't understand. What's no good?'

'Us, the hotel venture. I can't go through with it.'

She stared at him incredulously, then whispered, 'You can't mean it.'

'I'm afraid I do. I want out. There's no way I could go back to the way things were after what's happened. I was hoping you might understand that.'

She gave a nervous little laugh. 'Alain, you don't know what you're saying. Your mind is in an exhausted state after what's happened with Oliver. Tomorrow, next week, you'll see what a turmoil you've been in. I can't even take what you just said seriously. Why, we're halfway there.'

He paused to weigh his words. 'It's not just what happened to Oliver. Not in the way you think, though it's true that the prospect of losing him for ever has made me take a long, hard look at my priorities. On the contrary, my thinking has never been more lucid. To be honest, I suppose I began to have doubts about us, about the project, even before he disappeared. I know now what I care most about. This is going to hurt you deeply, and I'm very sorry, but there's no point in pretending. I want to go back to being the way I was before us. I can never come back here for good. I know that now.'

'Are you saying that you're going back to your wife? That's what you're really saying, isn't it?'

'I'm going to do everything in my power to put my marriage back together again, yes, and to continue to build the business in

California. This whole episode has brought me and Rachel closer together than we've been in a long time. We talked about it tonight for a few moments at the hospital. Try to imagine what we've been through. She's been absolutely marvellous throughout. You're looking at me as if I've gone mad, but Rachel has been my wife for over ten years, for God's sake. It might be very hard for you to understand, but both of us feel that we have something much more precious than our own lives to preserve – we have a son who has been through a terrible ordeal. We have a duty to him to try to save our marriage.'

Calmly, Isabelle rose to her feet and looked out at the floodlit park through the window. 'Do you know, Alain, you're talking such bullshit. That's what they'd call it in America. Sanctimonious bullshit. All this self-sacrifice business is totally out of character for you. How do I know? Because we're alike, the two of us. This sudden guilt you're feeling, this outpouring of sentiment, it's just a passing mood, the aftermath of the worry about Oliver. We're survivors, reachers, doers, you and I, not martyrs. In ten years Oliver will be in college. And then what will you do? It will be too late to make your life all over again. Do you really think that rocky marriage of yours is going to stand another ten years in order to raise a child who won't be needing you any more? Then, when it's too late, you'll discover there aren't any more châteaux going begging, that now was the time to invest, to return to the country where you were born and that formed your character. You'll be homesick then, Alain. You'll begin to hate America and the way of life there, which is alien to you. And you'll wish you hadn't thrown away the chance to make something big, something worthwhile. Because you could be at the top, where you belong, Alain, here, with me. But not where you are.'

Her eyes blazed with passionate intensity as she looked down at him, conveying the confidence and vitality to do the impossible. The years, the cares vanished from her face. Isabelle had never seemed more formidable, or more desirable. Alain was hypnotized for a moment as he thought about what she had said.

'No, it's no good,' he said at last, shaking his head. He got up from the sofa with the uncomfortable feeling that he had no place to go but a bleak hotel room that had become vacant in the village. 'I meant what I said. I wish to God that you and I had never started this whole thing. But you know, I have a feeling you can find someone to replace me. You've got the backing, you've got the ideas, the contacts, everything you need to get the project going yourself. I'm expendable.'

'Is that how I make you feel?' she asked incredulously. 'Because it's not true. I love you, Alain, and I need you. Without you, I'm helpless.'

He hardened himself against the vulnerability written on her face. 'You're not helpless, Isabelle. Of the two of us, you're much the stronger. If you love me, as you say you do, then you can just as easily hate me now I've disappointed you.'

With that, Alain walked through the door, leaving a cherished dream in the gilded lamplight of Terre Blanche.

A little while later, when Fernande had gone to bed and the house had fallen quiet, Isabelle was at her desk, poring over letters and documents. After Alain had left, she collapsed on the sofa and cried for a while. Then she dried her tears and forced herself to attack the work she had been putting off for too long. Immersing herself in facts and figures, she managed to put Alain's visit out of her mind.

When the ormolu clock on the fireplace struck two, she put down her pen and rubbed her eyes, an act that brought back images of the last thirty-odd hours she preferred to forget: the man at the carnival, who now seemed like some terrifying figment of her imagination; Pascale covered in blood; Julian on a stretcher; Alain walking out the door. Cradling her chin in her hands, she began to think back over her past, sifting through the countless times that she had faced ruin or despair. Tomorrow, she reminded herself, could easily bring about a change of circumstances more to her liking. She was consoled by the thought of Alain slipping into bed with his wife sometime soon and finding an unresponsive stranger, not the loving helpmeet he used to know. The ghosts of the past weeks would henceforth divide them; she knew that as surely as she knew anything. Tomorrow, next week, next month, Isabelle predicted, Alain would come back when he found out the truth for himself. Having reassured herself that this setback was only temporary, Isabelle pushed back her chair, satisfied that she had done enough for the day.

She had just put away her papers and was about to get up to close the office window for the night when she heard a scuffling sound in the hall, the sort of noise someone might make trying to creep across the floor.

'Who's there?' she called, on her guard.

When there was no answer, she quickly unlocked the side drawer of her desk. As her hand touched the revolver she kept there, a shadowy figure appeared in the doorway. She slammed the drawer shut and opened her mouth to scream, but, as it dawned on her who the intruder was, the only sound that escaped her throat was a dry rasp. Standing on the threshold was the man at the carnival, her estranged husband, Raoul Loval. He was dressed like a tramp in a faded T-shirt and a grimy pair of jeans. His dark, greasy hair tumbled over his eyes as he fixed her with a twisted smile.

'Who are you and how did you get in here?' she demanded shrilly, rising to her feet.

'Isabelle, Isabelle, *la belle* Isabelle.' His accusing whisper dissolved into a chant. 'You're staring at me like I'm a stranger, as if you've never seen me before. Now, I find that funny, really funny. Have I changed as much as that?' His distinct sing-song accent triggered off a host of memories, all of them unpleasant, which had lain like a residue in her mind for thirty years. She stared at the face that had become a grotesque caricature of the young husband she remembered. The destroying power of the years had reduced his arrogant good looks to ruins haunted by the spectre of poverty and broken pride. Without having to be told, she knew how he had passed the time, sinking to the bottom of the heap wherever he happened to be. In his bloodshot eyes, lined with darkened pouches, seethed a terrifying hatred that was now directed at her.

'Why don't you answer me?' he demanded angrily. 'And what are you staring at? This is the man you made, the man you thought you left to rot like a piece of garbage.' He jabbed at his chest with tobacco-stained fingers. 'You caused my downfall, you caused my ruin. Don't look at me like I was dirt, because I don't like that.'

510

Inwardly she was quaking so hard she found it difficult to think. Instinct told her that she must maintain her outward calm, because her very life might be at stake. Sensing Raoul's fury was nothing to toy with, she said in a placating voice, 'All right, Raoul. I recognize you, I acknowledge you. Is that what you came here for? Surely you can't imagine that I'm glad to see you after all this time, especially as you didn't even bother to knock.'

'I came in as if it were my own house. It should be mine, everything –' He gave a sweeping gesture. 'I could have had something like this, but you ruined me. If it weren't for you, I would be a rich man today, not working in a carnival.'

'You ruined yourself. How could I have ruined you?' She couldn't hide her contempt at his stupidity.

'You made a fool of me and that was enough. I lost respect everywhere, the man whose wife ran away. Everybody despised me after that. That was the beginning of all the troubles. And as if that wasn't enough, you robbed my mother of her jewellery, the jewellery that could have saved the domaine and paid off all my debts.'

'I took nothing. I left empty-handed, just the way I came.'

He scowled. 'Denying it won't do you any good, Isabelle. You're a whore and a thief. I want half a million francs for the jewels, and I want it now. I've been looking for you for a long time to collect. Give me the money now. It will be enough for a start.' He lunged forward and banged his fist on the desk.

Seeing his bloodshot eyes at close range, Isabelle realized he still had his taste for hashish, a discovery that terrified her, knowing how unpredictable it could make him.

'I didn't take the jewels, Raoul. Your mother certainly lied to you, because she always hated me. And even if I had, they wouldn't be worth half a million francs.'

'I want money, and I want it now, tonight. Half a million francs.'

'And if I haven't got it?'

'You have money, all right. I don't have to kill you to get what's mine, though it would give me great pleasure. Once I tracked you down, I made it my business to find out where you got all this,' he gestured, 'but we're still legally married, you and I. You're not the

511

widow of Monsieur de Montjoi, and you were never his bride. I have all the proof I need.' He patted his pocket.

She thought fast, wondering if he was merely bluffing. 'Raoul, you really take me for an idiot, don't you? We're no longer married, you and I. Do you really think that I would take such a risk? Our marriage was annulled on the grounds of desertion and cruelty. You're completely unaware of the law, I see. All that was done years ago by the man who married me.' She delivered the lie with a scathing smile.

'That's not true. I know it's not true. And if it is, I want to see the papers.'

'I don't have to show you anything. Get out of here now or I'll call the gendarmes. You're trying to blackmail me, but it won't work.'

When she picked up the telephone, he produced a knife from his pocket and flicked it open in front of her face.

She gasped and put the receiver down.

'Don't try anything else, do you understand? You've got plenty of money and I want some of it. I'm not leaving here until I get it.'

'All right! I'll give you as much money as I have, but only because you force me. Don't think you can walk in and take me by surprise a second time.' She opened the desk drawer and slipped her hand inside, keeping her eyes glued to his. When she found the gun, she took a careful grip before pulling it out as adroitly as she could and aiming it at his heart. She pulled the trigger before he could react. A deafening retort echoed through the room. Raoul froze for a second with a look of open-mouthed incomprehension, then buckled forward, hit his forehead on the desk and fell to the floor with a thud.

Isabelle dropped the gun. Shaking with terror she waited for some sound of movement behind the desk, then edged round it, her breath coming in short little gasps. Raoul was sprawled on the floor with his mouth and eyes open. Blood was pouring through his T-shirt and had already blackened the carpet. Isabelle's initial revulsion turned to superstition. In death Raoul's repulsive face suggested a slaughtered demon who had the power to come to life again and do her irreparable harm. The thought that he might be

512

able to prove their marriage was never dissolved sent shockwaves through her, and she forced herself to rifle through his pockets. When she found nothing but a few franc notes, panic engulfed her.

When Fernande rushed into the room in her slippers and nightdress she found Isabelle standing rigidly by the body on the floor as if she could neither see nor hear. Isabelle was moaning incoherently, like a wounded animal, and was oblivious to the housekeeper's hysterical screams.

# Chapter 25

Rachel put her head around the corner of the hospital room and found Rosamund propped up against the pillows, looking drawn and pale.

'It's just me. May I come in?'

'Rachel, what a nice surprise.' Rosamund's smile said she was genuinely glad to see her. 'I heard from Bob and Ted that you were still here. They told me all about Oliver and what's happened.'

'I've been wanting to come since I heard. I brought you something to cheer you up.'

Rachel walked to the bedside bearing a bouquet of flowers she had found growing by the roadside on her way to the clinic.

'What a kind thought, cornflowers. I've always loved their pure cerulean blue,' murmured Rosamund. 'I've tried several times to paint them but they're almost too simple.'

The sight of them seemed to bring the colour back to her cheeks. 'There's a glass on the basin over there if you want to put them in water.'

When Rachel sat down she felt a wave of understanding cross the divide of the separate crises that had filled their days since they last met.

'I want to know how you really are,' she said, reaching out for Rosamund's hand, which looked so white against the sheet.

'All right, I suppose. They've put me in here for a week to rest and so the psychiatrist can observe me.' She gave a self-deprecating smile.

Rosamund's clear blue eyes seemed to have lost their sparkle. Her face, empty, yet strangely serene, was like the portrait of a saint Rachel had seen somewhere in her travels who had wrestled with the devil and won, but only just.

'I had a little walk today and I'm eating again. I feel a bit like a newborn baby discovering the world for the first time. I'm very lucky to be alive.'

Rachel was touched by her openness and her lingering fragility, and by the determination surfacing from beneath her fatigue. 'Yes, you are very lucky. I don't know if you realize how many friends you have here, including me, who care about you very deeply.'

Rosamund smiled gratefully and reached for Rachel's hand. 'No, I suppose I didn't, but it's beginning to come home to me. And it matters more than I can say. The colonel and his wife wired that enormous bouquet of flowers over there from London with the kindest note. That's the sort of thing you wouldn't expect, really. When I think that sometime I used to mimic him behind his back.'

There was a pause, then Rachel said, 'When I heard about what had happened I felt as if I might have been more of a help to you if I hadn't been so wrapped up in my own problems.'

'You mustn't feel that way. It was just a foolish, impulsive act of despair, despair that would have passed if I had given it a chance. And when I heard yesterday about what happened to Julian, I felt very odd. First, better, triumphant. I cheered that divine retribution had been done without my lifting a finger. But now I just feel sad and wasted. He wasn't the reason I did it, really. He was the tip of the iceberg, and I was a fool to ever get involved with him. The terrible thing is that the feeling of being such a fool lasts and lasts, doesn't it? You see yourself in a kind of movie in your head doing stupid things.'

'Rosamund, there are worse things than being a fool, believe me. It only seems that way now.'

'Yes, I suppose even fools have hearts that break and mend. Mine will. I think the process has already begun.'

'Good. You'll soon start to be your old self again. And this seems like a good place to be.' Rachel glanced at the window, which gave a view of treetops filled with singing birds.

'Yes, it's lovely. If it wasn't for the reason I'm here, I might imagine I had prolonged my holiday. My husband is on his way down from London. In fact, I wouldn't be surprised if he arrived at any minute.'

515

'In that case, I won't stay long.'

'No, please don't rush off. It's so good to have someone to talk to. And I'm dreading seeing Charles, not because I'm afraid of breaking down or anything, but because he's bound to make things worse with an outpouring of guilt and self-recrimination. That's what he did last time I went to pieces, and then he persuaded me to start all over again. But the truth is, all those loveless years have finally caught up with me.'

She was smiling wistfully as she said it, and Rachel realized, to her relief, that Rosamund wasn't at all full of self-pity. She was fighting her way courageously out of the dark pit, a pit as deep and dangerous as the one Oliver had fallen into.

'Ted and Bob came by yesterday,' Rosamund continued, 'but they were trying so hard to be jolly and comforting at the same time that I couldn't wait to get rid of them. I think they blamed it on themselves, which makes me feel worse. It was Ted who found me. I'd left my prize from the exhibition on the table and he brought it to my room. I'd passed out leaving the light on, and didn't respond to his knock, so that's an ironic little twist. If I hadn't won that prize, maybe . . .' she broke off with a helpless gesture. 'Ted and Bob asked about you, and hoped you'd drop in to say goodbye before you left. Now, what about you? When I heard what had happened I couldn't believe it. I thought you'd long gone. What agony you must have been through, you poor dear.'

They talked about the events of the last few days, and Rachel said, 'I'm taking Oliver back to America, either tomorrow or the day after. And Alain is coming too.'

'You've patched it up?'

'We're trying. Only . . . ,' she hung her head, 'the truth is, I've got to piece things back together for Oliver's sake. That's all that counts. It's not going to be easy, but I've accepted that.'

'Of course. That's how you feel now, and it's only natural. But are you sure it's right? So much has happened in the short time you've been here. Once you're back in California you're going to start to think.'

'I know. Michael Lowry and I became . . . involved while I was hiding out in his house.'

516

'That doesn't surprise me at all. You were already halfway there when I last saw you.'

Rachel looked surprised. 'Was it that obvious?'

Rosamund nodded. 'I knew the minute I saw you together that he was madly attracted to you, and you to him.'

'I don't know what I would have done without Michael during those dark days.'

'Are you sorry it happened?'

'No, I'm not sorry. He's kind, sensitive, he makes me laugh – a lot of things. I have such enormous respect for him. That's the hard part, living with the fact that I've been so unfair to him. I think I'll always regret that we didn't get to know each other better.'

'My theory is that you discover all there is to know about somebody in the first five seconds of eye contact.'

Rachel nodded, remembering the day when she and Michael had met at the café. Michael had been on her conscience since she had left Brissac with Oliver. Speaking of him now made her yearn to see him, a thing she had decided was wiser not to do until just before her departure. She said, 'I don't know if you've heard, but Isabelle de Montjoi has been accused of manslaughter.'

'Has she really? Bob told me she had shot somebody dead, a prowler or something.'

'He wasn't a prowler, but her estranged husband, from whom she was never divorced.'

'What? Now that takes some beating. Who would have ever imagined that a woman like her had such a skeleton in her closet.'

Rosamund's eyes took on their old sparkle at the news, and Rachel knew they were both thinking the same thing – that Isabelle had got what she deserved – but neither of them wanted to say it.

'It seems the police found the documents in his caravan, which prove she had a powerful motive to kill him. It's going to be a national scandal when the papers get hold of it. Beautiful, rich widow, married young into a noble family, shoots estranged first husband. I'm relieved we won't be here. We'd be beating off reporters from *Paris Match* and I don't think either of us could take it. Alain is pretty upset about it. He didn't know she had been married twice.'

517

'She killed him just in time, when you think of it, though it sounds awful. Because if she hadn't . . .'

'I know what you're thinking, but Alain pulled out of the hotel venture and broke off the relationship with Isabelle before it happened.'

'Good, because otherwise, you'd always wonder, wouldn't you?'

Rachel didn't reply, thinking to herself that in the circumstances she could forgive Rosamund's trenchant honesty; it was as if her brush with death had brought her against raw truths that she was compelled to share. But her remark stayed in Rachel's mind.

They talked for a while about Agnès, Pascale, Julian, all the people whose lives had been laid bare by mishap or tragedy in the last few days. Finally, when Rachel rose to go, Rosamund said, 'This may sound strange to you, but I've decided to book in for another two-week course next year, that is, if they'll have me.' When Rachel looked at her in amazement, she added, 'Apparently some gallery owner saw my pictures at the *mairie* and wants to talk to me about an exhibition in London.'

'That's wonderful news, Rosamund.'

'The upshot is that I've decided to start working seriously when I get home. But I want to come back here next summer. Heaven knows why. That's assuming I can afford it when I'm separated, because I've decided to leave Charles. I'm going to tell him today. I've thought about it and, quite honestly, there lies the root of all my troubles. If I stay with him, it will be a slow, painful death instead of the quick one I thought I preferred, but it boils down to the same thing, dying by degrees with every affair he has. I've got to learn to stand on my own two feet.'

'You've come out of your ordeal with so many positive things, haven't you?' said Rachel, full of admiration. She contrasted Rosamund's battling optimism with her own uneasiness about the future. 'I wish I could say the same about myself.' Realizing how it sounded, she added, 'I didn't mean that. The only thing I ever wanted was to get Oliver back.'

'I know what you meant,' said Rosamund. 'Remember what I told you once, to look before you leap. The old cliché still applies. I never met your husband, but I feel I know quite a lot about him.

518

He's chastened and you've forgiven him. And the man who came to your rescue, Michael Lowry, is an unknown quantity. I wonder if the doubts that you're feeling now have something to do with that. Because, though I hardly know Michael, he seems to be worth his weight, as they say, here.' Rosamund tapped a vague spot below her shoulder to indicate the heart.

This observation, a glimmer of light brought back from the darkness that had nearly taken her, profoundly unsettled Rachel. She leaned down to kiss Rosamund's cheek, aware of a richness in her friendship and a sadness that they had to part. 'It's done me so much good talking to you. You've been the one to lift my spirits, not the other way round. I was thinking on my way here that it seems like we've known each other for years, as different as our lives are.'

'I know. I feel that way too. We've both lived through something extraordinary in this little village, and neither of us will ever be the same again. What is it about this place, I wonder?'

They had never talked about the chronicle together, but Rachel was reminded of it again. It hadn't crossed her mind before, but Rosamund corresponded precisely with her picture of Susan Wyndgate, the artist pilgrim whose colourful psalters she imagined might have been buried with her under Brissac. She could imagine Susan and Margaret Prior talking together in the same way Rosamund and she were talking now.

'Goodbye, and don't forget to stay in touch. Here,' Rosamund said, retrieving a card from the drawer on the bedside table, 'who knows, maybe we'll meet again next year, back where it all started. Though I suppose you'll probably be glad to see the back of this place after all you've been through.'

'Not at all. Does that surprise you? I'd genuinely like to come back to Roquelaire, though in my case it seems unlikely.' She had a sudden unbearable image of Michael on his own, the way she had found him.

Rachel left the room and walked briskly down the corridor far happier than when she had come. She had expected Rosamund to be a depressed suicide case, muddled with tranquillizers, but her wry view of herself and the kindness and wisdom she doled out acted like a tonic on Rachel. Buried in their conversation was a truth that Rachel could feel herself reaching for and rejecting at the same time. She stood for a moment looking at the courtyard, where patients in their dressing-gowns were sitting in the dappled shade of the lush garden. She almost felt a pang of envy when she saw a woman in a wheelchair reading a book in silence and solitude. For the first time she could remember she was filled with the desire to escape the pressures of life back home, which weighed on her even from a distance. Her thoughts were interrupted by a man approaching her across the light-filled reception hall.

'Excuse me, but are you the woman who has just been in to see my wife, Rosamund Morton?'

'Yes, I am.'

'The nurse told me Rosamund had a visitor. I'm Charles. How do you do?'

Charles Morton conformed exactly to Rachel's idea of a suave, upper-middle-class Englishman. He was tall and thin, with pale, receding hair that seemed the same colour as his eyes. His lined, sun-tanned face was decidedly attractive, and he was regarding her with frank interest, in the manner of a man who had spent his life charming women and seducing them.

'I arrived by taxi from the airport only a moment ago. How is she?' he asked, his brow furrowing in concern. 'I was simply devastated when I got the news. I came down as soon as I could. Lord, it's so tragic. You're a friend, are you? From the painting course?'

'No, we just happened to meet.'

'It's a consolation to me at any rate to realize she hasn't been entirely alone until I got here.'

Rachel didn't stop to wonder whether he was really suffering; she could only assume he was, but she could feel no pity for him. Firmly on Rosamund's side, she smiled and said, 'I wouldn't worry. I think she is going to be just fine. You know, I came here to cheer her up, but it turned out it was the other way round. She's a remarkable woman, your wife. She's wise, kind, funny. She's been an invaluable friend to me during the last two weeks. In fact, I think just about everyone who knows Rosamund loves her. She's got that quality of brightening a room when she enters it.'

520

He looked at her in amazement, as if they were talking about different people. 'Yes, she is remarkable, really, but so much more vulnerable than we all realized. You see, she had a sort of breakdown last year and we really thought she'd come through it. If I had only seen the warning signs. But I suppose the sad truth is, one had drifted apart.'

This last phrase annoyed Rachel for some reason, making her want to shake him. Instead she said abruptly, 'I'm sorry, but I have to rush off. I hope you have a pleasant stay in Roquelaire.'

A startled look crossed his face at her brusque departure, and Rachel couldn't help wondering how he would react in a few moments when Rosamund told him she was leaving him.

*

'So, you've come to see Étienne Dufour?' said the gendarme. 'Your name please?'

The pale, slim blonde wearing faded blue jeans and a T-shirt, her eyes shielded by large sunglasses, replied softly, 'Pascale Gachpour.'

'Pascale Gachpour. Are you a relative?'

'I am – I should say, I was his fiancée.'

'Fiancée?' He exchanged glances with another gendarme behind a desk.

'It's all right. I know who she is.' He nodded to Pascale.

'*Bonjour,*' she said, trying to summon up a smile.

When the gendarme stood up from his desk and peered at her, she took off her sunglasses. He sometimes came into the bakery, but at the gendarmerie he seemed like a different person in the regulation light-blue shirt with dark epaulettes.

'It's lucky you came today because he's being moved to the prefecture to be charged.'

'Oh –,' she whispered.

The man returned to his desk, but not before he had given Pascale a look of pity laced with curiosity that made her uncomfortable. Knowing that the gendarmes would be aware of events at the guest-house at Terre Blanche, her cheeks burned with humiliation.

She followed his colleague down a corridor, through a security door and past rooms that didn't look like a gaol at all, but like a starkly furnished dormitory, though there were bars on the high, small windows. Most of the cells, Pascale noticed, were unoccupied.

The gendarme stopped at one of the doors and peered through the glass window at the top.

'You're in luck, he's in.'

She smiled thinly at this feeble attempt at a joke, as her stomach began to churn.

When he saw her, Étienne leapt from the chair in front of a table where he had been sitting and stood rigidly to attention, as if he were on parade. After the gendarme had gone out and closed the door they looked at each other silently.

Pascale was immeasurably wounded by the intense suffering in Étienne's expressive dark eyes, eyes whose every mood and nuance she thought she knew. Hot tears began to roll down her cheeks before she could stop them. Trying to compose herself, she felt more awkward than ever, for Étienne was staring sullenly at the floor as though he couldn't bear the sight of her. Had the door of the cell been unlocked Pascale would have fled without saying a word. It was clear that she had made a mistake in coming to see him, but she had been driven here by the knowledge that until she faced him, her conscience wouldn't let her rest.

Pascale's days had been haunted by what had happened in the guest-house, and the aftermath. When the intruder had escaped through the window, she had turned on the light to discover her body was smeared with the blood that came from the gaping wound between Julian's shoulders. How long she had stood naked and trembling in the middle of the room she couldn't remember, but the realization that he was bleeding to death cut through her terror. She hadn't known until afterwards, when the police told her that he had given himself up, that Étienne had been the attacker. What she found hardest to bear was the knowledge that he had witnessed her betraying him with another man.

'I'm sorry,' she whispered, her head bowed.

He didn't reply, but appeared to be wrestling inwardly with her

522

apology. Then he turned his back to her, burying his head in his arms against the wall.

Pascale was preparing herself for an outpouring of contempt, of hatred that would act as an antidote to her misery when Étienne surprised her by whirling round to face her, his eyes full of gentleness.

'I heard about your aunt. Mother told me when she was here. I'm sorry, really sorry. I know how much you loved her.'

Pascale gave him a startled nod as she swallowed tears that threatened to fall again. 'It's just awful. There's such an emptiness without her. On top of everything else,' she gestured helplessly, 'I keep thinking she must have died ashamed of me, and unhappy. Or that I was the cause . . .' She couldn't go on.

'The funeral is today, isn't it?'

Pascale nodded.

'I'm sorry I can't attend, but as you can see . . .'

Wicked humour flickered in his eyes for just a second, then he tumbled back into gloom.

'In case you don't know, Étienne, Julian Paine is out of danger now.'

The fury in his eyes made her momentarily apprehensive. Holding himself carefully in check, he muttered, 'I was a complete idiot to do what I did. A complete and total imbecile. But you hurt me, Pascale. So deeply that I went out of my mind. I let myself be persuaded by Laurent that revenge was the only answer. But he's an idiot too. Now look at the mess I'm in. And what good did it do, anyway?'

'It's all my fault. Just say it if it will help.'

He hung his head. 'Of course it's not your fault. You were right when you said I was weak, that I didn't have any opinions of my own, that I always listened to my father. Well, I proved it, didn't I, by letting somebody like Laurent talk me into committing a crime, not that I can put the blame on him either. If the Englishman had died, I'd spend my whole life in prison, or most of it, which is probably where I'll end up anyway.'

'You're not weak, Étienne. What you did was wrong, but it also took such a lot of courage. Misguided courage, but it was still courage. I'm the one who is really weak. I let my head get turned

523

by such worthless, superficial things, by a man who . . .' She broke off, haunted by a picture of Julian lying unconscious in the guesthouse. Though the thought of him now disgusted her, she couldn't bring herself to utter a word against him. Looking steadily at Étienne, she continued. 'I know now, after what's happened to me, to him and to you that I allowed myself to fall into a total fantasy. It was a mistake that I'll regret for the rest of my life. You see, I've learned a lot about myself and I don't like it very much.' Pascale stopped, surprised at her own outburst. She hadn't known until she articulated it how she really felt. Confiding her deepest thoughts to Étienne released some of her pent-up anguish, just as it had always done from the time they were children.

Étienne shook his head resignedly. 'I've ruined your life, Pascale. And mine. I'll be discharged from the army dishonourably and I'll have a prison record. It would take a lifetime to live all that down.'

'We could live it down together,' she heard herself say in a trembling voice.

He looked at her for a long, painful moment, as if he wanted to believe her, but couldn't. 'No, I don't think it's possible. The past would always come between us. You and I have to go our separate ways, Pascale.'

They were interrupted by the sound of the key turning in the lock.

'Sorry, *mademoiselle*, but lunch is about to be served and visitors have to go,' said the gendarme.

'Well, goodbye,' she said, extending her hand formally under the eyes of the gendarme, who hovered politely beyond the door for a moment.

When Pascale's hand touched Étienne's she had a quick, terrible vision of the knife it had wielded, which had come so close to killing a man. And then, as suddenly as the memory had come back, it dwindled to insignificance, chased away by the realization of how much Étienne must have loved her once, and the knowledge that she loved him still. Slipping her arms around his neck, she kissed his lips almost chastely, telling herself it would be the last time. He seemed stunned by the gesture and stood rigidly, his eyes cast down as he waited for her to release him.

'*Au revoir,*' she whispered, and rushed through the door feeling her heart would break.

*

At three o'clock the church bell began to ring, summoning the mourners to Agnès Grimal's funeral. A single clear note resounded over the rooftops until it died away, when another note was struck, conforming to the ritual cadence reserved for death.

Rachel stood on the edge of the crowd, filled with wonder at how many people had gathered in the shadow cast by the church, hundreds of them. It was a hot, listless afternoon without a breeze stirring to cool the red, perspiring faces of farmers and their wives, many of whom, she realized, must have known Agnès since she was a girl. The church doors were flung open. Below the altar, decked with flowers, she could see Père Auguste in a white surplice standing behind the tall black candlesticks and massive vases of laurel that flanked the bier where the casket would be laid.

Rachel looked for Michael Lowry, surprised that he wasn't there. Trying not to appear too obvious, she turned her head and searched the crowd around her, but there was no sign of him. An intolerable restlessness came over her, which made her feel ashamed. She argued inwardly with herself, knowing full well that as soon as the funeral was over, she would be unable to resist walking up the Rue St Jacques past his house to see if he was there. She was anguished at the thought that he might have slipped quietly back to London without telling anyone.

Soon she saw the black hearse making its way through the arch and into the square, followed by a car that contained the Gachpours, who had followed the body from the mortuary, as custom dictated. They got out of the car, and Rachel recognized Agnès's sister, Beatrice, overcome by grief, supported by her husband and Pascale, while two young men she took to be the Gachpour sons followed behind. Their stricken, tear-stained faces testified how much they had all loved Agnès.

Organ music drifted into the square from the church as the casket was unloaded and carried inside by the six pallbearers, stocky, brawny men, their faces etched with genuine sadness. She noticed a van parked nearby completely filled with floral tributes, her own among them, that would be delivered to the walled cemetery outside the village.

When the signal came, the crowd filed into the church. Rachel watched the mourners dip their fingers in the stone font at the door and cross themselves. Inside the church, light was pouring through the southern windows, casting rainbows that penetrated as far as St Anne's chapel. The casket had been draped in a black cloth bordered in white. The tall candles in black holders and the vases of laurel and box gave the ceremony a dignity that befitted royalty, Rachel thought. Seeing the altar banked with yet more flowers, Rachel wondered if they might have been picked that morning in Agnès's own garden. Her memory of the blue cottage and her first sight of Agnès peeking out from under her hat, carrying a rabbit by the ears, made her start to cry.

After the service Rachel stood in front of the church until nearly everyone had left the square for the cemetery. She looked at her watch, thinking that Alain would be waiting for her to relieve him at Oliver's bedside. When she looked up she hardly dared believe that Michael was actually there, standing in front of her. Neither of them was able to speak for a moment, during which Rachel was torn by conflicting emotions.

'I saw you in the church,' he said, glancing round the square as if to confirm she was alone. He had read the confusion of Rachel's face, and was hesitant. 'Normally I try to avoid funerals, I've always thought they're rather pointless, but I guess that's only a pose. When I heard the bell tolling, I felt drawn here after all.'

'"For whom the bell tolls,"' she quoted. 'Do you know, I thought Hemingway wrote that until I was in college.'

He smiled ironically. 'I'd never even heard of Hemingway until I went to college,' he said, making her smile too. His face became serious. 'The truth is, Agnès's funeral has been a revelation for me. I couldn't help thinking what a rare thing it is to die loved and deeply mourned in the place where you were born.'

The observation, so characteristic of Michael, went straight to Rachel's heart. It reaffirmed how much he loved Roquelaire and

526

how well he understood its people. She became aware that even though the temperature was in the nineties in the shade she was shivering, and then she was painfully conscious that the events of the past few days had not killed her fierce attraction to him, but had deepened it. Michael was looking at her with the veiled expression of someone who had taken a cautious step backwards, away from a painful dilemma, and who would think twice before being so impetuous again. Rachel was wounded by the admission that she had hurt him in her desperate attempt to put her life back in order. And now it seemed too late to do anything about it.

Michael surprised her by saying, 'Do you have time for a drink in the café?'

'I'll make time,' she replied, overjoyed to spend just a few more moments with him. As they walked towards the café she said, 'Did you get the envelope with the rent money that I slipped under your door?' He nodded. 'I've been meaning to drop in, but I've been so tied down with Oliver in the hospital.' She hated the lame uncertainty of her own voice.

'It was more than necessary, because you didn't finish the week.'

'Oh, that's all right,' she replied, sure he must be aware that she was staying at the hotel in the square with Alain.

He led her to an empty table and ordered drinks from a passing waiter.

'How is Oliver?'

'He seems much better. He's starting to talk about home. He's at the stage now where he can't wait to tell all his friends about his exploits. He still can't remember everything that happened while he was in the pit, or even quite how he got there, which is nature's way of healing the mind, I guess. We're leaving here tomorrow morning, by the way.'

Michael didn't react to this. 'I was hoping very much to see him again, but maybe it's better if I don't under the circumstances.'

Her cheeks burning with embarrassment, Rachel supposed that by 'circumstances' Michael meant Alain. She could only assume that the time she had let elapse without contacting him was evidence enough that she was trying to put her marriage back together, especially now it was common knowledge that the hotel project would never go through. They talked of Isabelle, of Agnès, Pascale and Julian, and Rosamund, dredging up people and incidents that had filled the last two weeks, though they pointedly avoided mentioning Brissac, John Stratton, Margaret Prior or themselves.

When there was a pause, Rachel glanced round the tables filled with tanned, smiling people on holiday. 'Now that I think of it, this is where it all began.'

As she spoke she regretted what sounded like a flippant remark, but Michael had not interpreted it that way. His face wore the same appealing, interested expression as the day they had met, even though they had been lovers, and even though he had shared some of the most passionate, heart-rending days of her life.

'I suppose you've heard what the police discovered about Paul Ribard,' Rachel said, feeling the painful necessity of opening the subject. 'Thanks to you.'

'Yes, I heard. It must have come as quite a shock to your husband.'

'A shock, but a relief. All those years he assumed that his grandfather was some kind of villain.'

'You know, it's a blessing that Agnès Grimal didn't live to know the outcome of all this. I have a feeling that it would have been a terrible blow for her. Of course, whether Armand knew the truth about his father, and whether he had anything to do with Paul Ribard's death we'll never know. But in light of what's come out in the last few days it would seem he almost certainly did. I'm glad for your husband's sake, and your son's, that the Ribard name has been cleared.'

'It means more to Alain than I think he even realizes yet.'

'In that case, I'm glad justice was done.'

'All those wasted emotions, the years he lived under a cloud without telling me . . .' Rachel cut herself off, fighting the urge to confide in Michael all over again, because she believed she had forfeited the right.

She kept up the conversation as long as she could, aware that she ought to be going, but feeling herself sinking under the weight of a forbidden subject, the only one that really mattered. It was time to go. She picked up her handbag and took out the car keys.

'I suppose you're going back to the hospital now.'

'Yes, Oliver will be expecting me. I didn't tell him I was coming to Agnès's funeral. I thought it might upset him.'

'Say hello to him for me, will you? I had a book on the Hundred Years War I thought he might like. He's a bit young now, but someday he might like to bone up on the Black Prince.'

'That's a very kind thought, one that will mean a lot to him, I know,' she murmured.

'I'll leave it at the reception desk of the hotel.'

Rachel opened her bag and fished out her sunglasses to hide her disappointment that he hadn't suggested she come to the house or, at the very least, asked for her address in California.

'Michael, I've left the most important thing until the very last. I must thank you from the bottom of my heart for saving Oliver's life. There aren't adequate words to express my gratitude, and Alain's.'

'Well, what can I say, but that it was my pleasure? Père Auguste calls it a miracle.'

'Yes, it seems so, but calling it a miracle doesn't do justice to the part you played.'

He stood abruptly and extended his hand. 'Goodbye, Rachel. I hope you have a pleasant trip back and that Oliver doesn't entirely lose his taste for adventure after what's happened. Because that would be a pity.'

Thinking ironically that the same thing might be said of herself, she shook his hand with unbearable sadness.

*

That evening Rachel and Alain were sitting on the vine-covered terrace at the back of the hotel, where guests who had dined in the restaurant were gathered at little tables set on the gravelled courtyard.

'I think I'll turn in early tonight,' said Alain. 'I'm tired for some reason.'

'It's not surprising, is it? You've been at the hospital nearly all day. It's not easy keeping Oliver confined to bed.'

'Teaching him to play chess was a brilliant idea of yours. Otherwise he would have been miserable.'

'I hope he keeps it up. He seems to have taken to it amazingly quickly.'

'I'll make sure he and I play as often as we can. He's got a mind that sometimes scares me it's so sharp.' Alain's face softened as he thought of his son. 'I asked him what he wanted to be today, and you wouldn't believe what he said – first, an explorer, and second, a chef.'

'He'll probably end up not being either.'

There was a pause while Alain drained his Armagnac.

Rachel hesitated to say what was on her mind. 'Are you sure you don't want to see Isabelle? You might regret it when you get back, and we have plenty of time to get to the airport.'

'That's very open-minded of you, Rachel, and I appreciate it, but I think it's best to leave things the way they are. And anyway, I have nothing to say to her. The whole sordid mess makes me sick. She'll end up with nothing, which is tragic for someone so addicted to luxury. Even now I find it hard to believe that a woman of Isabelle's experience got herself into a situation like that. It makes me wonder about her judgement. It only confirms that I had a very close call. I'm a lucky man that I got out of it. If it hadn't been for you coming here, things might have turned out differently. You've stood by me, Rachel, and I can't help wondering if I deserve it.'

He gave her a searching look, leaving no doubt of his sincerity. In a soft voice he added, 'And I hope that when this confused time is all over, we will both look forward from now on. I know it's going to take time, but I'm willing to do *anything* to make you happy. You know that, don't you?'

She looked away uncomfortably, unable to withstand the stirring intensity of his vivid blue eyes, which had always had the power to neutralize her will. It was the first time they had talked about Isabelle. The mention of her name still made Rachel angry, but it disturbed her that Alain didn't want even to say goodbye now that Isabelle was in trouble. She unclenched her hands in her lap, realizing that they had been rigid with tension. It was a habit she had unconsciously acquired in the last few days.

530

'Do you know,' Alain said thoughtfully. 'Some day I wouldn't mind buying a farmhouse somewhere near Roquelaire. Houses are still comparatively cheap here. It might be fun to renovate a ruin, and then we could visit from time to time. It probably surprises you to hear me say that, but when Oliver was lost I began to appreciate how warm, how friendly the people are here, what a marvellous environment it has, especially for him. The truth coming out about my grandfather has changed my point of view.'

Rachel didn't meet his eyes, not wanting to reply. They had yet to talk in depth about the clearing of the Ribard name. Alain seemed to find it awkward to discuss his past, and he had kept it from her all these years, but she was sure the discovery of the document hidden in Paul Ribard's pocket linking Armand Bataille's father to the betrayal of the Resistance had altered Alain's image of himself.

'You know,' he continued, 'in many ways, I think you and I and especially Oliver might enjoy getting to know France again. What do you think?'

'I don't know,' she replied, wondering if he were making the suggestion just for her benefit. 'I like Roquelaire very much. You know that. But at the moment I can't imagine ever coming back.'

'It's just an idea, really. When we get back to Sonoma life will take over again. There won't be time for holidays or trips abroad very often.' He rose from his chair and looked down at her. 'Are you coming upstairs?'

'If you don't mind, I think I'll just sit here a minute since it's our last night. You go ahead.'

He was about to walk through the door when she called, 'Alain?'

He turned and looked at her, and Rachel felt a crumbling sensation, as if the physical world had been violently altered by the mood gripping her. 'Would you come and sit down for a minute? I have something to say. There doesn't seem any point in putting it off until tomorrow.'

Puzzled, Alain returned to the chair next to her. Rachel wondered whether he hadn't already guessed what was going on in her mind.

During the moment she paused to collect her thoughts Rachel realized how often in the last few days she must have been

531

unconsciously rehearsing what she was about to say. Though she had left it far too late, courage to speak flowed into her as she embraced the strength of her own convictions.

'Alain, I've come to a decision that as far as I'm concerned everything is over between us. I don't want to go back home under false pretences, because I think that would do harm to us all, especially Oliver. I could never live a lie. Not even for a little while.'

Alain stared at her, his face a mask of hurt and surprise. But after a moment Rachel felt his will assert itself like a tangible force, trying to undermine her quiet resolve. She curbed her urge to end the conversation quickly, neatly, knowing she must hear him out.

'I'm baffled,' he said at last, gesturing aimlessly. 'Why now, all of a sudden? The last two days we've spent together I've felt closer to you than I have for years. And I thought you felt that too. Tonight we've been talking together about so many things, just like we used to. What happened to Oliver will be the making of our relationship if you only let it. It has the power to heal all the misunderstandings we've ever had, and to make us realize what we mean to each other. Think about it: can you really live with your yourself from now on, Rachel, knowing you didn't give our marriage every chance?'

He was looking at her with irresistable sincerity, subtly wooing her all over again.

After a moment she said thoughtfully, 'What you said about the events of the last few days bringing us closer – I can see how you might interpret it like that. But it's a closeness not built on anything real or lasting. It was built on desperation – yours and mine – and a kind of gratitude that we got Oliver back safely. We're not really closer than we were before, and now there are things neither of us can forgive or forget. It seems to me, too, there are lots of things we've avoided talking about entirely, and probably always will, just like in the past.'

'But you haven't given it enough time. How can you expect to iron out everything so quickly? Be fair.'

'I've tried to be fair, but I can't turn the clock back, even if I wanted to, Alain.'

'Wait until we get home, please. You haven't had time to think yet,' he interrupted with a pleading note to his voice.

'That's just it: I've had so much time; more than I've had in years. I think I know my mind better than you knew yours a while back when you were so ready to make a complete break with the past.' She was trembling now, as if afraid with every word they uttered she would lose the ground she had gained at so great a cost.

'I know what's at the bottom of this sudden doubt you feel. It's because I told you the truth about me and Isabelle. But I realized we could never remake the future if I wasn't completely open with you. Don't hold that against me.'

Rachel looked at him pityingly, realizing he expected the same forgiveness and consideration she had always given him. She brushed this aside, eager now to say what she had avoided so scrupulously.

'You've told me about Isabelle, but I haven't told you about Michael.'

He shrugged. 'All right then, tell me now. I assumed you'd talk about it when you were ready.'

'Michael Lowry opened my eyes to so many things in such a short time. The fact is, I can't forget him, and I don't want to. The reason is simple: I'm in love with him.'

Her heart was pounding not with anxiety, but relief that she had expressed her feelings there and then, before her judgement became clouded by all the obligations waiting at home. She and Alain stared at each other across the unbreachable gap she had created with those few words.

After a long, painful silence Alain stood up. 'I don't think we should talk about this any more tonight. Because, Rachel, I just can't believe you really know how you feel. You met this guy under abnormal circumstances and you hardly know him. He was around when you needed someone to talk to, sure, but let's face it, he seems to have disappeared completely now the dust has settled. Anyway, just what makes you think he feels the same way about you?'

The unfairness of the accusation touched a raw nerve, and Rachel was tempted to exhibit her anger at his arrogance, but knew she no longer wanted, or needed, to waste her emotion in this way. Alain had not really changed, but she had. In place of the submissive wife willing to stay in the background and let her husband dictate her life was a stronger, independent woman, who had fought the toughest battle of her life, and won. She shrugged and said, 'At this point I don't know anything except how I feel. There's really nothing more to add now.'

Alain was about to reply and then thought better of it, but she could see he was undefeated.

'I'm going upstairs. Let's not say any more about it tonight, Rachel. There's far too much at stake.'

'Yes, there is a great deal at stake,' she agreed, but not for the reason he supposed. He gave her an abrupt nod and strode from the terrace as if he expected she would change her mind.

When the waiter passed by the table, Rachel ordered a glass of wine, wanting to eke out the last few moments that she would have to herself for the foreseeable future. Glancing up at the back of the hotel, she saw the light in Alain's room go on and his shadow as he closed the curtains. The stubborn darkness of the neighbouring room – her room – symbolized for her the end of their life together.

The waiter set the glass of *rosé* in front of her. She looked into the wine and saw so many happy memories reflected in its shimmering depths. It was the colour of the sunset from Michael Lowry's terrace, and it was the wine with which he had filled her glass on the evenings they had passed together. Rachel sipped the wine, leaving half of it, then walked to the reception desk.

'Did anyone leave a book for me this afternoon?'

'No, *madame*. Not that I know of.'

'I see. Thank you.'

Instead of climbing the stairs, Rachel walked out the door of the hotel and towards the Rue St Jacques. A moment later she lifted the hand of Fatima and the door opened on her future.

The blue cottage dreamed in the deep shade of chestnut trees, its closed shutters like the eyes of a sleeping face. The vine over the door was still heavy with grapes and tomatoes had dropped from their stalks in ungathered ripeness. There were no rabbits thumping in their cages, or chickens clucking round the basin beneath the pump, and no cat lay curled up on a chair; they had all been moved to a neighbouring farm.

The gentle whisper of cicadas filled the air. They sang ceaselessly from the parched grass, as if afraid that the sweetness of summer would give way to autumn before they had finished their song. Pascale paused at the gate and drank in all that was familiar. Her firm resolution to keep her emotions under control could not dispel the image of Agnès in her navy blue dress and straw hat, who would never be there to welcome her again.

Neither her father nor her mother had wanted to enter the cottage since the funeral, and she had offered to have a look round to make sure that nothing had been disturbed. Pascale walked up the path, her eyes falling on the copper watering can that Agnès's father had made more than seventy years ago. Steeling herself against a wave of potent nostalgia, she hurried to turn the big key in the door so she could be done with her painful visit.

The kitchen was completely dark. Like all old country people, Agnès had the habit of locking everything up tight even if she was going to be absent only a moment or two. What had once seemed unnecessary to Pascale, she now found infinitely touching. She opened the shutter over the sink, and went through the house to the bedroom, where the high, ancient bed was neatly covered with a faded Persian shawl, an uncharacteristic luxury bequeathed by some relation long ago. The chamberpot could be seen peeking from beneath the bed near a velvet stool on which Agnès knelt to say her prayers within sight of the ebony crucifix on the wall. Pascale stopped to look at the yellowed photographs of her grandparents on the mantelpiece, placed beside an ivory brush and comb. Their strange, squinting faces stared at her across an impossible gulf of time. She touched a bottle of perfume decades old, called *Soirée des Lilas*, which had never been opened. Its treasure had remained sealed with a violet ribbon that Agnès had never cared to break in order to discover what was meant by a lilac evening. Another photograph, in a simple wood frame, caught Pascale's attention, one she couldn't remember seeing before, of a young man being decorated with a medal. She had no idea who he was. Yet when she studied his face in the gloom, he looked familiar. Pascale was moved by the possibility that Agnès had been secretly in love a long time ago.

Her heart heavy with memories, Pascale returned to the kitchen, where everything was neat and tidy. Beside the old black clock that had wound down on the chimney was her own photograph gazing down at her with the arrogance of a stranger; it seemed to have been taken so long ago. She was about to walk out the door when she saw an envelope that had fallen under the table. Picking it up, she saw Agnès's name was written on the front in faded ink. Outside, where the light was better, Pascale sat down on the wicker chair by the door and emptied the contents of the envelope on the table: a letter, a birth certificate and a faded photograph of a middle-aged woman holding a baby. When she realized the woman was Agnès, Pascale was both intrigued and perplexed. But it was the birth certificate that threw her into utter confusion. The child's name had been recorded as 'Pascale', and Agnès' name was that of the mother. In the space for the father's name was the word '*inconnu*'. She gasped and dropped the certificate, recoiling from the revelation staring her in the face: it could not be true. Pascale's heart was racing and her hands shook as she unfolded the letter. It was embossed with the coat of arms of Château Brissac. Her eyes leapt to the bottom of the page to the signature.

'Armand, Armand Bataille,' she whispered. The date at the top confirmed the letter had been written on Christmas Day the year before she was born.

> 'Dearest Agnes,
> I drove by, hoping to find you at home this morning, but perhaps it is better this way . . .

Pascale combed over the words several times, then sat back and let its significance wash over her. She tried to remember Armand Bataille's face, but couldn't. Then she recalled the photograph of the stranger in the bedroom. Darting into the house, she brought the photograph into the sunlight. Her hands shook as she looked at the face of her real father for the first time. She sat beneath the vine quietly for a long time, trying to come to terms with this momentous discovery. The astonishing news, which she had heard only days before, that she was to inherit Brissac took on a new significance: the château belonged to her by right. But it did not really matter. What was important, Pascale realized with a terrible sadness after the initial shock had passed, was that her real parents were lost to her for ever. She walked in a daze to the kitchen. There she set flame to the contents of the envelope and placed them on the grate, where she watched them burn until they had turned to ashes.

A while later she went through the gate carrying a bouquet of all the flowers remaining in the garden. Taking one last look at the blue cottage, Pascale walked back to the village to lay the flowers at the chapel of St Anne in memory of her mother.